Other Books by Robyn Williams

A Twist of Fate
Preconceived Notions

A Twist of Fate

by

Robyn Williams

Lushena Books, Inc.
1804 West Irving Park Road
Chicago, IL 60613
(773) 975-9945
E-mail: Lushena@aol.com

This is a work of fiction. The events portrayed are imaginary.

Printed in the United States of America.

ISBN: 1-930097-02-6

Retail: $23.95 in the United States

Library of Congress Catalog Card Number: 99-076596

A Twist of Fate First Printing: 2000

Dedication

This book is lovingly dedicated to the One who makes all dreams come true.

Special thanks are extended to my sister, Valerie Jefferies-McClodden, for her strength, tenacity, faith, and love; to Chanette D. Beasley, my lifelong best friend, for being the testing ground for all of my material; to Patricia A. Toney, masterful wordsmith and angel in disguise, for being a beacon of light throughout my many days of darkness; to Robin Frazier-Teele, my New York buddy who doubles as my sounding board and technical consultant; to Sheila Downer, design wizard and my ace-coon-boon, for helping me pull this project together at the ninth hour; to Alicia Thomas, my reliable girl-Friday; and to the ever wonderful Monnie E. Morris, my spiritual sister who keeps me grounded and always brings sunshine into my life. Thank you, Monnie, for never failing to have an encouraging word.

Lastly, to the many bookstore owners and fans who encouraged me to continue writing despite my publishing woes: *This one is for you!*

Acknowledgement

I am deeply indebted to Tony Gray, president of Gray Communications, and Terrance Harrington, publisher of Entertainment Source Guide. Their vast knowledge of virtually every aspect of the music industry proved invaluable to the completion of this novel.

Also, a huge note of gratitude goes to my editor, Ronald E. Childs, who has the wonderful knack of tearing apart my work piece by piece. I'm always amazed at how he manages to put the pieces back together again in a most magnificent way.

Finally, a thank you in advance to Janet Jackson, singer, dancer, actress extraordinaire, whom I believe in my heart will someday play the character "Ashela Jordan" in the movie, A Twist of Fate. (Who knows? Maybe even alongside Denzel.)

A Twist of Fate

Prologue

New York City

uccess. Ashela Jordan whispered the word, unaware that it slipped from her lips, sounding almost like a curse. She'd craved it and fought all of her life for it, doing some things in the process that even now she wasn't proud of. She'd excused many of her actions by telling herself the end always justified the means. *But what did it profit her to gain the entire world, only to lose her soul?*

The stage was set for her to silence all of her adversaries and critics. Inside her dressing room at Radio City Music Hall, away from all of the chaos that reigned just outside her door, Ashela leaned back into a soft, black, classic leather chair. Within the hour, she would be on stage performing with the legendary Grover Washington, Jr. Nearly five years had passed since the two of them appeared together in concert. Their reunion tonight at the American Music Awards was eagerly anticipated by nearly anyone who had an ear for music. Many of the gossip mongers questioned whether their duet would rekindle a long-rumored romance.

There was much at stake for her with the evening's performance. While it would feel good to see and match moves with her one-time mentor, Ashela knew it would feel even better to prove to him that he'd been wrong to write her off. But not just Grover. Everyone who'd doubted her ability to make a comeback in this tough, dog-eat-dog music industry would know they'd woefully misjudged her. Tonight she would prove that she was a force to be reckoned with. For on this night, the attention was hers alone. The headlines were hers. The adoration was hers. Wasn't this what she'd always wanted? A self-satisfied glow stole over Ashela. It was a coveted honor to be a part of the American Music Awards' entertainment line-up. As one of the chosen few, she knew that her return to the stage would signal to everyone that she was back on top.

All of her hard efforts culminated with this moment. At thirty-four years old, Ashela had reached the pinnacle of her success as a singer, songwriter and jazz musician. She was dubbed by her critics as a musical genius, the ultimate female Grover Washington-Babyface counterpart. To her credit, she'd headlined with the likes of Richard Elliott, Gerald Albright, Najee, Wynton Marsalis, Al Jarreau, David Sandborn and a host of others.

A gift inherited from her mother, composing came easily to Ashela. For years, she'd spent much of her time writing songs for some of the most famous singers in the business: Singing sensations such as Luther, Whitney, Janet, and Vanessa. Ashela's lyrics sometimes sold for millions, and they were sought after by the best of the best. Music fulfilled her, and creating it was all that Ashela knew. As a youngster, it helped her find her way through the oft confusing and tangled webs of life, and as an adult, her music sustained her through a rocky period when she'd lost the will to live. Music inspired her, made her heart soar, and through it she could now understand where much of her mother's own inspiration had come from.

Every track on Ashela's latest CD, *Giving It My All*, had been produced in London, England, where she'd lived for the past three years. The album was released in the United States some months ago, and it was the hottest label release of the year. Already, it had sold well over eight million copies and had reached multi-platinum status. Ashela had racked up an impressive ten nominations for her solo album including, Album of the Year, Record of the Year, and Song of the Year. Her ten nominations were just two shy of the single-year record set by Michael Jackson and Kenny "Babyface" Edmonds. The album's title cut, a duet with Rachelle Farrell, was number one on the jazz charts, another release was number one on the R&B charts, and nearly all of the other tracks were among the Hot 100s. Four of the songs had been made into music videos and each was a hit with both MTV and VH-1.

It felt incredibly good to know that many in the audience, as well as many out there in TV land, would be watching the awards ceremony solely because of her.

While on the one hand Ashela was exultant—she was proud of herself because of the way she'd outsmarted the competition—but on the other hand, she couldn't rid herself of the disquiet that presently engulfed her. An inner turmoil which she knew wouldn't subside until certain issues were faced and dealt with, gnawed at her. On this night, Ashela struggled with her own host of demons. As tumultuous memories of the past resurfaced, some of those demons raged full throttle.

Yes, she was back on top after being in exile for what seemed like an eternity. Now that her star had risen again, she couldn't afford to make the same mistakes. This time around, Ashela would do things differently. In other words, she'd do them the right way. Her time away from the U.S. had mellowed her and given her a new outlook on life. While her demeanor could still be as hard as nails, she wasn't nearly as cold-hearted and calculating as she'd once been. For starters, she'd learned that she couldn't always control everything and everyone around her. She was more level-headed, less prone to fiery temper tantrums where everything in her path invariably wound up being destroyed. And despite ample opportunity to do just the opposite, she no longer thirsted for revenge.

Maybe that's what motherhood did to an individual: Caused one to take into consideration other people's feelings. Such a concept had been foreign to her for many, many years.

The path Ashela had taken en route to her success was certainly not without mishap. She'd done what she had to do to get where she was. If she'd crossed some people and burned bridges in the process, it was all a part of "making it." *To the victor goes the spoils*. Like a soldier crawling through enemy territory, her personal journey was fraught with casualties of war. Memories of bitter recriminations, severed friendships, and images of broken hearts surrounded her like lifeless bodies left littering a battlefield. These talisman were her daily reminders that success came with its own price-tag. She'd found that fame and fortune could be had by anyone so long as they were willing to pay the asking price. Had she paid too much?

In her opinion, money and power, if not used wisely, did corrupt. Without proper stewardship, the more of either one attained, the more one wanted. One of the harshest lessons Ashela was forced to learn was that no amount of either could protect her from the treachery and deceptiveness that accompanies betrayal.

A restlessness stirred deep within her. She rose from the chair and walked to the sofa where her instrument lay. Ashela knew the reason behind her familiar pangs of unease. An indelible yearning infiltrated her system, causing her pulse to race in a way that had nothing to do with her upcoming duet.

Sam. His name hummed through her mind in much the same way his body once hovered over her own. A sudden chill swept over her and she clasped her arms around herself to keep from trembling.

Samuel Ross. Unconsciously, she shook her head. Somehow, Ashela knew deep down in her spirit that the man was somewhere inside the building. Even after so many years, *she could feel his presence.*

If time was supposed to remedy a wounded heart, why hadn't it healed hers? Truth was, there was no magic elixir to soothe the flash of pain that clutched at her heart. Anger, remorse, and, yes, even the one admission she was loathe to confess gripped her as she stood gazing down at her horn.

Sam Ross. How she'd hated and despised him these past several years because of what he'd done to her.

And yet, fool that she was, Ashela acknowledged that she still loved him. How could she not? After all they'd been through, after all they'd shared . . . was this the way things were really meant to end between them?

As long as she was being totally honest about the past, Ashela recognized that it was in part her own stubbornness that had caused the demise of their relationship. She wondered if Sam thought about her a tenth as much as she'd thought of him. She'd be content to know that he experienced a minuscule of the heartache that she'd gone through. The nights were worse for her—endless hours when she'd miss his nakedness next to hers. If she saw him tonight, would he even acknowledge her? Or would he treat her merely as a business acquaintance?

Dear Heavenly Father, if only she could turn back the hands of time! If she wasn't beset with so much damnable pride she could go to him, tell him she'd made a huge mistake, ask if they could start over. But that wasn't how she operated. A part of her wanted to come clean, but the other part would rather go to her grave than grovel for a second chance with a man who probably hadn't thought twice about her since the day he'd made it obvious that he was writing her off.

Ashela steeled herself and decided that maintaining her pride was worth more to her than trying to reconstruct a relationship that in all likelihood would only be one-

3

sided. Her only recourse was to try once more to forget about Sam Ross. Somehow, rather than risk rejection, she'd will her heart to go on. She wasn't the first person to experience such heart-wrenching pain, neither would she be the last. She recognized that every person in life encountered some love and some pain at some time.

There was but one matter that she resolved within herself to disclose to him. Could she find the courage to do it?

A knock at her door startled her. It was the stage manager giving her the nod that she was up next to perform. Ashela picked up her instrument and headed for the stage.

As she and Grover walked into the spotlight from separate entrances, they met center stage. Grover was already blowing his sax, as if serenading her. Ashela stood close to him and was all smiles as she glanced out at the sea of people. She lifted her arm to her forehead as if she were about to faint from being in such close proximity to the legendary performer. She clasped her instrument to her heart adoringly. Her swooning theatrics brought forth laughter from the audience. When Grover reached a lull in his song, Ashela lifted her own sax and chimed in, passionately serenading him. Immediately, Washington dropped to one knee to indicate his love-struck capitulation and the crowd went crazy. The moment he stood, the two of them started blowing their horns in unison, creating a melody of their own, all to the feverish applause of the audience.

***

The cords of Sam Ross' stomach muscles tightened the moment Ashela Jordan appeared on stage. He knew her better than anyone else in the building, and he also knew her on-stage dramatics were just part of what was to be her crowning achievement. He was a mere spectator in her midst as she accepted the thunderous applause. It was her night to shine, Sam thought, and to spend playing to an entirely new audience. He sensed, however, several undercurrents behind her performance. Predominantly, a message that seemed to say, "I didn't need any of you to make it to where I am."

Sam's body had tensed the moment the announcement was made that hers was the next act—even the audience's expectation level had seemed to shoot through the roof. And now that she was on stage, Sam's hungry gaze was riveted. She was sensational to watch. Every note played reminded him of times when she had played only for him. Even though he'd not seen her in years, she looked the same as he remembered her—only more beautiful.

Skin the color of caramel. Hair cropped close around the sides and nape of her neck. Thick, asymmetrical curls topped her head. A square jawline, thick eye-brows, full pouty lips, and dimples for days. Dressed in a Valentino original, the long-sleeved gold lamé gown molded her every curve as her hips swayed invitingly.

An image of her riding him as they laid upon silken sheets flashed through his mind. Beads of sweat shown on her body as Sam reached up to grasp her full breasts. With her back arched and head tilted to the side, he remembered her in the obvious throes of passion. Lips parted in a silent gasp. Nails engraving his thighs. His hands sliding down to grip and pull her hips even closer as she twisted atop him. She was his sensual dream. The vision faded as his hands gripped the arms of his chair. He had a strong desire to possess Ashela in ways that he had on so many other occasions. The urge to reacquaint himself with her womanly ways was overpowering, and he willed his emotions back under control. He couldn't afford to give in to salacious memories of her. Such remembrances were what led to his being stung by her before.

Well over six feet in height, Sam, himself, was a deep, dark, chocolatey, gorgeous, "make-yo'-toes-curl" type of man. Suave *and* smooth, his muscled physique was hidden beneath a dark blue, double-breasted, Gianni Versace suit. He was in his late forties and possessed an animal magnetism that could sneak up on a woman and enthrall her before she even recognized what was happening.

The fact that Sam had much money, and was rumored to be the most powerful man in the music industry, put him on a level far above the likes of a Quincy Jones. Women flocked after him in droves.

Sam's gaze became reflective. He couldn't help but admire Ashela and he knew that a part of him still craved her. Although several years had passed since he'd last seen her, memories of her remained fresh in his mind. Sam still couldn't figure out what it was about her that made it impossible for him to forget her. Maybe it was her craziness and unpredictability, or her "still-waters-run-deep" attitude. Or perhaps it was her fieriness as a lover. No one else came close in comparison.

To be totally honest, Sam couldn't recall all that had transpired to cause them to part as such bitter enemies. But he remembered a time when they'd been able to settle all of their differences through communication and lovemaking. Somehow, unfortunate circumstances forced him to make hard decisions and afterwards, he never had an opportunity to explain himself. They had been too angry with one another. Before he knew it, she'd packed her things and left. Sam shook his head. Now that he thought about it, even convicted felons got the chance to tell their side of the story. Ashela had left without giving him warning. No opportunity to express what he'd felt. No chance for a rebuttal. No chance to change her mind.

***

Like everyone else, Sam thought that Ashela's duet with Grover was incredible. A kaleidoscope of musical genius. Teacher being impressed by the student. He'd sensed from the creative tension in the air that their performance would be a dynamic one. He knew also that the millions of television viewers would be eating it up as much as the people in attendance.

As he watched the two of them harmonize, many emotions welled inside Sam. He wasn't caught up in all the speculative talk about Ashela and Grover. He knew Grover Washington personally and could vouch for the man's faithfulness to his wife. He also knew Ashela. Sam's stomach muscles wrenched as a familiar sadness washed over him. It was unfortunate that the two of them had parted the way they did. His pride had been wounded when she'd left. And as much as he hated to admit it, she'd taken a piece of his heart when she disappeared.

He couldn't comprehend her ability to just walk away from something as powerful as they'd once shared. Sam guessed that this was the callous side of Ashela that he hadn't wanted to see. Not that he, himself, was innocent. He'd done some things out of anger and jealousy, so he could understand her bitterness toward him. Still, regardless of the hostilities that existed between them, he felt there remained some unfinished business.

Sam realized that life's levels, from glorious comfort all the way down to anonymous misery, were unavoidable. He also knew all too well how swiftly a man or woman's fortunes could change: One could be master of the universe one second—and destitute the next. Ashela had persevered and made it back to the top, proving her tenacity. He admired her for that. After what he'd done, she had a right to hate him. But Sam knew also that she had once loved him.

Persistence was the key to unlocking any closed door. And so, too, Sam knew it could be the key with re-conquering Ashela.

Suddenly, a feeling of elation coursed through him. He didn't know how he was going to get Ashela Jordan back. But, just as with everything else in his life, the game wasn't over until he'd won. Somehow, he'd formulate a plan of action, devise a strategy that couldn't miss. Regardless of the stakes—no matter what it took—Sam wouldn't be satisfied until Ashela Jordan was his once again.

Part One

Beginnings

"So sad, so strange, the days that are no more."
— Alfred, Lord Tennyson

"...And life for me ain't been no crystal stair."
— Langston Hughes

Chapter One

dults could be so incredibly rude, thought eight-year old Ashela Jordan. They never thought of anyone else's feelings but their own. Every one of them gathered inside the apartment, right down to Tanya, had conveniently forgotten she existed. Not one of them noticed her dejected posture as she sat in the corner watching them parade through the room. Certainly, no one seemed to take into consideration that it was *her* mother that had been laid to rest hours earlier. And now that she no longer had a mother, who would care for her? Charla had been her world—she'd meant more to her than she had to any of these people who were acting as if they'd already forgotten her.

Yet, each one had appeared so somber while at the Unity Funeral Home on 125th Street in Harlem. Ashela had sat on the front row next to Tanya, her mother's friend and business manager. Tanya hugged her reassuringly each time someone emitted a loud wail. The one person closest to her mother, Tanya had handled Charla's singing career and would double as babysitter whenever Charla went on the road for weeks at a time.

Prettily clad in a black velvet dress with white lace socks and black patent leather shoes, Ashela had watched as the mourners filed past her mother's casket, looking down upon the figure which lay inside like sleeping beauty. Some looked sad, others withdrawn as they turned away to offer condolences to Tanya, and pat Ashela on her head before proceeding back to their seats.

Charla had been an up-and-coming recording artist, and most of the people in attendance at her funeral were somehow involved with the music industry. Those who came to pay their respects were songwriters, producers, agents, back-up singers, and a few well-known stars, while most others were merely groupies and hangers-on.

Afterwards, they all filed out of the funeral parlor and drove to the Ridgeland Cemetery in Queens. Inside the limousine, Ashela sat listlessly with her head resting against the leather interior. Normally, her face would have been pressed to the window so she could view all of the other cars as they raced by. New York City, when seen through the eyes of a child, was a multitude of things: Big, noisy, and full of people. But Ashela didn't take notice of her surroundings on this day. Her heart ached too heavily.

After her mother's burial, the mourners headed to her apartment for the repast.

Several hours later, with all of the laughter and mingling going on between the guests, one would have thought it was a festive occasion. It just didn't seem right to Ashela as she sighed heavily. Grown-ups were just too difficult to understand. As she surveyed the guests, she wondered if any of them had truly cared about her mother. Certainly, none of them seemed to act like it. To her, they appeared more interested in each other and with the food that was being served.

Ashela took a seat in the living room, half hidden by a large palm plant which protruded from an oversized urn. More than one couple strolled by her with arms locked, their drinks in hand. But for music, the occasion could have been a party.

During the funeral, everyone was quick to pat her on the head or on the cheek. But now, no one seemed to care that she was afraid and feeling confused about her future. Even her mother's men friends, the same one's who'd tweaked her braids playfully and told her how special she was while in Charla's presence, didn't seem to care what happened to her.

Ashela thought about drawing attention to herself just to get some of them to talk to her. She could if she wanted to. Whenever she sang loudly, someone always took notice of her. Everyone told her that she had a lovely voice that would one day sound just like her mother's. More often than not, people who heard her would come to investigate the child who could carry such a melodic tune.

Only Ashela didn't feel like singing tonight. Instead, she felt as if she were carrying the weight of the world upon her young shoulders. She rose from her seat and walked through the double doors which led to the terrace.

Outside, the chill in the September air seemed to hint of bitterly cold winter days to come. She walked to the end of the balcony and took a seat on the patio chair, pulling her knees to her chest. With no coat to shield her from the cold, the wind whipped through her velvet dress.

From her vantage point on the third floor, she could hear the traffic rushing to and fro down below, but the familiar din of all of the city noises wasn't enough to drown out the many sorrows and fears that filtered through her mind. She hadn't been able to cry earlier, at least not in front of all of those phony people who lingered inside. Now that she was alone to herself, she couldn't stop the salty tears from pouring forth.

Everyone kept telling Ashela that God needed another angel in heaven and that's why He had taken Charla. But of all the people in the world, why did God have to take *her* mother? It was so unfair, Ashela thought as tears streamed down her face.

Foremost in her mind was the question of what would become of her. Surely none of her mother's many men friends would care for her. And Tanya had already warned her that she might not be able to stay with her because of "that woman in North Carolina."

Suddenly, shivers gripped Ashela's thin body that had nothing to do with the cold. Living on the streets with the homeless people she saw every day might prove a better alternative than going to live in North Carolina. Maybe the only choice left for her *was* to run away and fend for herself.

Ashela had never met her grandmother, Julia. But from all of the stories her mother had recounted, she knew the woman was a wicked old witch. She was so mean that she had driven Charla away from home many, many years ago. Ever since Ashela's early childhood, the mere mention of Julia's name had struck fear in her heart. Every time she was disciplined, her punishment always ended with the warning, "If you ever do that again, I'm sending you to live with Julia." It was enough to cause her bones to quake.

From the few pictures she had seen of Julia, Ashela was surprised her grandmother didn't have horns. She didn't *look* evil. But because Charla had told her of numerous times when Julia had beaten her black and blue, Ashela knew otherwise. Charla never missed an opportunity to remind Ashela of how lucky she was. She would say to Ashela constantly, "When I was your age, Julia never allowed me to do the things that you manage to get away with."

Only Ashela didn't think she "got away" with anything. If she appeared mature beyond her eight years, it was only because she spent more time around adults than she did with children her own age.

Though she knew many of the children at Ethical Culture, the magnate grammar school she attended, she wasn't allowed to socialize with them outside of school. Thus, her dolls became her playmates and the piano her form of entertainment. She considered her friends to be her mother's suitors whom Charla insisted she address as Mr. Kenneth, Mr. James, Mr. Bill, or Mr. Frank, etc. Whatever their first name, it was always preceded by "Mister." Ashela never knew their surnames.

Of all Charla's men friends, and there were quite a few, Ashela liked Mr. Otho best of all. Mr. Otho spent more time talking and playing with her than any of the others. He also gave her shiny quarters every time he came.

As far back as Ashela could remember, she loved singing and playing the piano. Her favorite times with Charla were when they would sing and play or when they would sit together in front of the radio listening to timeless legends such as Dizzy Gillespie, Charlie "Yardbird" Parker, Julian "Cannonball" Adderley, Ella Fitzgerald, Sarah Vaughn, and the brilliant pianist, Bill Evans. Even Charla, who worried about everything, seemed happier at those times.

It was when her mother drank too heavily that she was frightening to be around. Her actions during her drunken bouts left a trail of destruction. Once, Ashela had suffered a cracked rib in the wake of Charla's anger; on another occasion, it was a broken arm and a busted lip. So Ashela learned to weather her mother's storms by steering clear of her when she was into one of her "fits."

Her mother would be happy one moment and down in the dumps the next. If Ashela wasn't sensitive enough to discern Charla's mood, she would easily wind up with several good smacks to the face. After which, she'd be subjected to a shrill lecture of how Charla's circumstances were all "her fault."

No matter how well Charla's career was going, she was never satisfied. She'd recorded several hit singles with Marvin Gaye and Smokey Robinson and had signed a major record deal of her own with Motown. Before the ink could dry on her contract, the demands on her time multiplied exponentially. Soon, Charla was always traveling because of her music. She seemed to be away from home more than she was there. Ashela remembered crying each time her mother left, and monitoring the time carefully until she returned. She would beg to be taken with her, but was told it was not possible.

In Ashela's child-like world, she imagined that someday her mother would take her to meet her father. The two of them would love her and she would love them. She imagined them tucking her in at night and singing her to sleep.

But the only thing waiting to greet Ashela each morning was reality. She knew that she was a constant reminder to her mother of the one person Charla had ever loved, and cruelly, could never have. As a result, she was never her mother's first priority.

Nothing was as important to Charla as her musical career. Definitely not a child who hadn't been planned for or expected. Charla felt babysitters could be paid to keep and help raise Ashela until she returned from the road.

Always an inquisitive child, Ashela would ask endless questions about her father, what Charla did when she was away from home, and why couldn't she come with her. Before long, her pointed, prying questions would annoy Charla and she'd threaten to "beat the devil out of her" if she didn't quiet down.

Charla didn't understand Ashela. Sometimes she seemed child-like. Other times, she seemed too wise for her age. Charla made sure Ashela didn't want for anything. She had more toys and clothes than she knew what to do with—certainly more than many other children. But these things didn't quench Ashela's insatiable curiosity about her father.

When Ashela was seven, Charla brought her a picture of a man in an army uniform and told Ashela that the man was her father, but that he'd been killed overseas. Ashela sat pouring over the man's image, memorizing every detail. Later that night, she got up out of her bed to ask her mother more questions about him. Charla wasn't in her bedroom so Ashela, with the picture clutched to her chest, went in search of her.

She found Charla and Tanya in the kitchen arguing about Charla's excessive drinking, and about the picture. Tanya said the man in the picture was not Ashela's father and if Charla couldn't tell her daughter the truth, she shouldn't be filling the child's head with a pack of lies.

Ashela stood outside the kitchen door and heard her mother utter the crushing words: "What difference does it make whose picture I give her, so long as she quits asking those stupid questions about her 'daddy.' After all, it wouldn't do for her to discover that her father is a holy roller, now would it? I should take Ashela and march into his church right in the middle of his sermon. The self-righteous bastard! Obviously, Ashela's daddy hadn't wanted her and neither did I. I should never have allowed her to be born."

Ashela heard a loud slap followed by muffled sobs that could only belong to her mother. She never forgot the hurt that clutched at her heart that night. She remembered walking back to her bedroom on wooden legs with tears streaming down her face. Never again would she ask about her father. The picture she'd held so close to her heart was long since forgotten, left by the kitchen door.

Later that night, Tanya found the picture frame on the floor and, fearing the worst, she picked it up and looked in on Ashela to see if the child was awake. The lights were out and Ashela didn't answer when Tanya softly called her name.

Ashela couldn't answer her. Tears of pain and sorrow dampened her pillow. She was too busy wishing that she were dead.

As is typical of most abused children, no matter how severely Charla hurt her daughter, physically or emotionally, Ashela loved her just the same. She ignored all of her mother's flaws. About the only thing Ashela couldn't overlook was Charla's drinking. She never could understand why her mother drank so much liquor. Only bad things occurred afterwards with her and Tanya always winding up arguing and spewing hurtful words.

Whenever her mother got drunk, she let Ashela know that if she hadn't been born, she would be a major, big-time superstar. She'd be able to travel more often, have more time to devote to her career and she wouldn't have to work so damned hard just to keep a roof over their heads. The tuition to the private school, the clothes, the toys, they all added up. Charla would explain, as if talking to an adult, that she *had* to sleep with her men friends in order to make ends meet. Besides, she'd tell Ashela, music industry insiders knew sexual reciprocity was a necessary evil that many singers had to endure to get their careers started.

Whenever Charla dressed for a date, Ashela would sit on the bed and listen while her mother instructed her to always follow her heart, but to make sure her heart pointed her only in the direction of men with money. Charla proudly boasted that each of *her* dates had enough money to "burn up a wet elephant."

Whenever Tanya was around, Charla was always more gentle with Ashela. It was almost as if Charla needed Tanya's approval. But the two of them seemed to argue a lot lately. Ashela thought it had something to do with Charla's many men friends. Ever since Charla signed her recording contract with Motown, Tanya seemed to think that her priorities were mixed up. Tanya was angry with Charla because she saw more of Ashela than she did of her. She felt Charla's new circle of friends were running her in the ground. She told her, "If you don't change your ways, Charla, you won't *have* a singing career to worry about."

Only Tanya didn't know how prophetic her words would turn out to be. Two weeks later, Charla Jordan was dead of an overdose.

Ashela dried her tears. Hadn't Charla always said that tears were for babies anyway? All she knew was that soon the only place she'd known as home would no longer be her residence. Somehow, she had the feeling that her life would never again be the same.

Inside the apartment, the man was impatient to leave. He'd been there long enough. He hated funerals. *Let the dead bury their dead.* He hadn't known the deceased personally, having been dragged to the funeral and repast by someone who had. Just when he and the promoter he'd come with were about to leave, his partner had found someone to hit on. The intended target was a hot number and the short length of her skirt seemed to signal her availability. Under a different set of circumstances, he might have approached the woman himself.

Irritated because he couldn't leave without the promoter, he spotted a set of double doors and decided to step outside for a cigarette and a breath of fresh air.

Outside on the balcony, he pulled one from the nearly empty pack. He turned with his back against the rail and cupped his hands to his mouth to light it. Only then did he notice the sleeping figure huddled in a chair in the balcony's corner. *What the hell was a child doing sleeping outside in the cold?* he wondered.

Stubbing out his cigarette, he walked over and lifted the little girl into his arms. She was trembling as he carried her inside. Without thinking about it, he proceeded into a bedroom and laid her on the bed. After removing her shoes, he turned down the covers and slipped the child beneath them.

He remembered seeing the little girl earlier at the funeral home. If the deceased woman had been the child's mother, he wondered if she had relatives or whether there would be others to care for her. If tonight was any indication, it certainly didn't bode well. Had he not come along when he had, she might have suffered from exposure.

Her eyes fluttered open and he started speaking softly to her, assuring her that everything would be all right. Hopefully, she had relatives somewhere who could afford to adopt her. From his experience, it was doubtful that her mother had much money saved up. A Brownstone apartment on New York's Irving Place did not come cheap. In the nine years that he had been in the music business, nearly every person he'd met, from fledgling star to superstar, lived only for the moment with no thought as to the next. None of them stopped to think about what would happen when the hits and the money ceased to flow. They all seemed to think that the good times would last forever. They never did.

He noticed the child's shivers had subsided and that her eyes were becoming heavy again. He ran his hand over her head. She was such a pretty little thing. Surely, there would be someone to care for her.

As he rose from the bed to leave her, he heard the little girl murmur softly, "What's your name, sir?"

"Sam Ross," he told her.

As he exited the bedroom, he could hear her whispering something over and over. She was calling him "Mr. Sam."

Chapter Two

shela was slowly adjusting to life in Durham, North Carolina. Nevertheless, each day she awoke hoping it would be the day that Tanya would come and take her back to New York. After several months passed with no word from her, she resigned herself to having to stay.

The house on Green Street where Ashela lived wasn't as large as her mother's apartment had been, and it wasn't nearly as nicely decorated. Whereas everything in New York had been marble or lacquer, everything in her grandmother's home was wood. Here, there wasn't even a piano. Ashela wondered if her grandmother fell into the category of what Charla had called "dirt poor."

She didn't yet know what to make of her grandmother. Tall and regal with silver-gray hair, she was a formidable woman who wasn't given to much affection or conversation. During the ride from the train station, every time Ashela had stolen a glance at her, she appeared to be deep in concentration and her facial expression remained serious.

Silence reigned during the cab ride to her grandmother's house. Ashela stared out the window because she didn't want her to know that she was trying to keep from crying. When the taxi pulled up in front of a blue and white wood-framed house, the driver got out to retrieve Ashela's things from the trunk.

As the door was thrown open for her exit, a sense of foreboding settled over her. The one-storied home was surrounded by neatly cut grass and a white picket fence. But as she trudged up the walkway leading to the steps of the porch, it seemed the longest journey of her life.

Grandma Julia proved to be a stern figure. It was obvious she wasn't thrilled about having to raise a small child. She had gone through so much turmoil with Charla that she'd eventually washed her hands of her. She wasn't about to re-live any of those experiences with Ashela. Ominously, she set the ground rules for her the first day of her arrival. She would not tolerate any nonsense, for she was certain Charla had raised her to do as she pleased.

So much did Ashela resemble her mother that it was impossible for Julia not to transfer her resentment and unresolved feelings toward Charla onto Ashela. It wasn't something Julia purposefully set out to do. Many of her actions, such as the way she avoided contact with Ashela and the way she constantly criticized her, were all subconscious.

Grandma Julia worked as a housekeeper and was out of the house by 6:00 a.m. every weekday morning. Ashela was expected to dress herself, comb her hair, fix herself breakfast and be at school by 9:00 a.m.

Ashela liked having the house to herself in the mornings after Grandma Julia left. She could sing as loud as she wanted with no fear of her grandmother frowning at her in a way that meant for her to be quiet. In the still of the morning, Ashela didn't feel as if she had to walk on eggshells.

In school, she didn't seem to be having any success at making new friends. She was the "new girl" and it seemed to Ashela that all the other children did was laugh at her because she spoke funny to them. Her east coast accent was much different from their thick southern drawls, so they teased her relentlessly. Self conscious, Ashela did her work quietly and responded only when she was spoken to. To avoid the ribbing of the other children, she played by herself. Her only friends became the imaginary ones she created in her mind.

One day, Ashela was walking to school at the same time as four other little girls who lived on the same street as did she. She quickened her step to try to join in with them, but as she drew abreast of them, one of the girls abruptly shouted, "Here comes 'crater-face!' Everybody run!" As the four girls scampered away, Ashela stood rooted to the spot in shame. She knew they were referring to her deep-set dimples. She had never before been aware of her looks, but from that moment on, she felt the other children disliked her because she was ugly.

As she battled her newly developing complexes, Ashela became even more lonely, unhappy, and withdrawn. With no one to talk to about her feelings, she'd lie in bed at night and pretend that Charla sat next to her talking to her about all the things Ashela longed to discuss.

A sense of sadness and a longing for something she couldn't define enveloped her. During the day, she'd find herself gazing out the school window longing for the time when Tanya would surprise her by showing up to take her back to New York.

It was obvious to Ashela that she was a burden to her grandmother. She thought that by asking if she could go and live with Tanya she'd be doing herself and Grandma Julia a favor. But when Ashela broached the subject one night over dinner, her grandmother thought she was being both ungrateful and unappreciative.

"Child, I'm working five days a week to provide for you—and it looks like I may have to start working Saturdays as well. That's an extra day I'll have to work when I was getting along quite well before you came. You think I don't know how badly you want to go back to that god-forsaken city you came from? Grandma knows, baby. But you need to stop believing that that Tanya woman wants you. If she really wanted you, Ashela, she would have kept you. I'm not the one keeping you in North Carolina, she called me and begged me to take you. I didn't want to, but how could I turn down my own flesh and blood?"

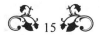

Julia noted the sickening look on her granddaughter's face and felt a note of sympathy for her. "She doesn't even call you, baby. It's time you faced the fact that she has a life of her own. A life that you don't fit into. It's time you got used to the idea that this is going to be your home from now on. I may not be able to give you all the things you're used to, but at least you've got a roof over your head, clothes on your back, and food on the table."

Ashela left her dinner untouched that night. She couldn't believe that Tanya didn't want her. She was sure that Grandma Julia had it all wrong.

In truth, Ashela couldn't afford to let go of her dream that someday she would go back to live in New York—it was all she had.

Sunday was the best day of the week for Ashela. Every morning before they left for church, the smell of Julia's homemade waffles would waft throughout the entire house. Even more importantly, Ashela got to wear the dresses that were bought for her back in New York. They were frilly and made of bright colored lace. Grandma Julia considered the dresses too fancy and felt they should only be worn to church or on special occasions.

Come the Sabbath, even Julia forsook her austere garments and dawned her Sunday's best. Ashela liked watching her dress for church. It seemed nearly the only time she ever saw her grandmother smile.

After breakfast, the two of them would walk hand-in-hand to the corner of Green Street and wait for the Sunday School bus to pick them up.

It seemed to Ashela that Durham was a small town because everyone seemed to know everyone else by name. It certainly wasn't filled with as many people as New York was. But at least the adults were friendlier toward one another, Ashela thought—unlike the children, many of whom appeared mean-spirited. She didn't understand why, even in church, all of the children her age seemed to dislike her. She figured the way they openly ignored her was how they treated all of the "new" children.

When Ashela commented that even the adults in church seemed to stare at her, Julia told her to pay them no mind. She said that if people stared at her, at least she knew that they noticed her.

One Sunday during children's church, Ashela slipped out of the room and sneaked into the recital hall several doors down. She knew that the grown-ups practiced there, and just wanted to see the big piano she'd heard them playing several Sundays ago.

She slid inside the room and quietly approached the piano, knowing that she shouldn't be there, but was unable to resist it's silent lure. As she slid onto the bench, Ashela felt like she was greeting an old friend. The piano wasn't nearly as large as her mother's baby grand, but the ivory keys felt just as smooth to her touch.

Hesitant, Ashela began playing a song that the choir sang regularly, "Amazing Grace." Humming the notes as she searched for the right keys, Ashela sang the words sweetly. Solemnly.

***

A tiny office was connected to the recital hall. Ms. Phelps, the youth choir director, had returned to retrieve several items. When she heard music in the adjoining room, she thought it odd that the church organist would rehearse in her area, especially since it was so close to the start of service. She opened the door and stepped inside the room, completely amazed by what she saw.

Little Ashela Jordan was sitting at the piano singing and playing as expertly as any adult. So crisp was the music that at first, Ms. Phelps thought that the piano keys were moving by themselves. She stood watching the child in awe before realizing that Ashela's eyes were closed.

Hearing her sing, Ms. Phelps marveled at how strong and clear the child's voice was. She wondered where she could have learned to sing and play the piano so fluently. But just as quickly, Ms. Phelps answered her own question: Apples never fell far from the tree.

Ms. Phelps had grown up with Ashela's mother, Charla, and knew exactly why some of the other children, as well as some of the adults, shunned Ashela. It was all so unfortunate. She was such a pretty child, the spitting image of her mother.

Regardless of what happened in the past, Ms. Phelps felt it was wrong to hold the little girl accountable for things that had happened before she was born. Ms. Phelps doubted that Ashela even knew who her real father was. She couldn't envision anyone wanting to tell the child the truth.

When Ashela finished the song, Ms. Phelps started clapping. She was touched by the emotions that this sad and otherwise emotion*less* little girl had exhibited. She walked toward the piano, intending to take a seat on the bench next to her.

Ashela nearly jumped out of her skin when she heard someone begin to clap. She swung around to see Ms. Phelps walking toward her. Surmising that she was in serious trouble, she looked like she'd just been caught with a hand in the cookie jar. With eyes rounded, she became speechless as Ms. Phelps sat down next to her.

"Where on earth did you learn to play the piano with such expertise?" Ms. Phelps asked in astonishment.

Ashela remained quiet. She wanted to answer, but fear had stricken her mute. In her mind all she could envision was Grandma Julia flying into a fit of rage similar to the ones Charla had often thrown.

"Ashela Jordan, I asked you a question. Who taught you how to play?" Ms. Phelps suddenly noticed that Ashela was afraid. Her posture bore no resemblance to the child who'd sung so beautifully only moments before. In fact, it appeared to Ms. Phelps that Ashela had braced herself almost as if she expected to be struck.

A smile lit Ms. Phelps face. She wanted to draw Ashela out of the shell that she had so quickly retreated into. She turned to the piano and started playing.

"When I was your age, I didn't know anything about playing a piano. I didn't learn how to play until I was a teenager." Ms. Phelps spoke while she played and noticed that Ashela seemed to hang on to her every word.

It was the first time since she'd left New York that anyone had sat down and talked to her in such a friendly manner. With her hands clasped on her lap, Ashela listened intently.

What started out with tension segued into a beautiful, shared moment between them. But unexpectedly, an overwhelming sense of sadness overcame Ashela. She suddenly grieved for her mother's friends back in New York. She missed Tanya even though it appeared that Tanya had betrayed her, and, oh God, how she missed Charla. Words the preacher recited at her mother's funeral came rushing back to her remembrance. That when people died, *they never really left you*. Still, Ashela didn't understand. If God truly needed another angel in heaven, why would He take a child's mother?

Didn't God realize that she needed Charla too? Ashela hunched over and gave way to an avalanche of tears. In light of Ms. Phelps' soothing voice, she could no longer contain the loneliness and emptiness that engulfed her.

For one so young, hers was a heavy burden. Stripped of all that was familiar to her, and placed in surroundings where no one showed her love or warmth, Ashela came face-to-face with the stark reality that no one cared about, or loved her. In her small world, she wasn't able to recognize that simply because she wasn't loved, didn't mean that she was *un*worthy of *being* loved.

Sensing some, but certainly not all, of what Ashela was experiencing, Ms. Phelps wrapped her arm around the child's shoulder and pulled her wracking body to hers. She smoothed the hair on Ashela's head and whispered softly to her until her sobs began to quiet. A short while later, when all Ashela had left were sniffles, Ms. Phelps stood up and led her inside the tiny office. She sat her in a chair and began to wipe her tear-stained face.

"Do you know that your mother and I once played tag inside the very next room?"

Through reddened eyes, Ashela looked at Ms. Phelps curiously. She didn't know why but she felt so much lighter now that she'd released all of those tears. "You knew my mother?" she whispered hoarsely.

"Oh, definitely. We were friends."

Feeling closer to her, Ashela began to pepper Ms. Phelps with questions about Charla. *How was it that she'd known her mother? What was her mother like as a child? How old were they when they played together? Did her mother have many friends?* Ashela listened to all the answers intently. And when Ms. Phelps prompted Ashela to talk, she did so by telling her that she'd feel better if she talked about what was troubling her. It was all the coaxing Ashela needed. The words came easily to her as she shared her innermost feelings.

Ashela found herself revealing how lonely she was without her mother. She missed Tanya and even Mr. Otho. She didn't know why the other children disliked her so. She'd never done a thing to any of them. She wanted to go back to her real home. She wasn't fond of Durham because she knew that she wasn't wanted here. Not even by Grandma Julia. She was sure that Tanya would let her live with her if only she could get back to New York.

Ms. Phelps sat listening, taking it all in. She marveled at the inner strength this child possessed unawares. It just didn't seem right for a child her age to be saddled with so many worries. Worries about her past, her present and her future. It seemed to Ms. Phelps that the children of her day had it a lot simpler when they were coming up. These children today, well, they just seemed to be cut from a different cloth, Ms. Phelps thought. They dealt with issues that had never crossed her path when she was a youngster.

The two of them sat talking a while longer until it was time for them both to leave. Ms. Phelps wanted to take Ashela under her wing and cultivate a relationship with her. An idea of how she could do so came to her, and she talked Ashela into letting her ask permission of her grandmother for her to join the youth choir. Ms. Phelps knew that she would take some flak for her decision because only youth twelve years of age and older were allowed to join the choir. But she would do it anyway. There was something that drew her to little Ashela Jordan. In some small way, Ms. Phelps wanted to extend friendship to a child who so desperately needed it.

Chapter Three

ulia wasn't happy at all about having to work on Saturdays. She couldn't afford to hire someone to look after Ashela while she worked, so she had little choice but to take Ashela along with her. On Saturdays, Julia worked from eight until two in the afternoon at the Reeds' residence. During the bus ride there, she repeatedly emphasized that Ashela was to be on her best behavior.

After what seemed an interminably long time to Ashela, they finally reached the Forest Hills section of Durham and had to take a taxi the rest of the way. They arrived at a magnificent estate that was lined with tall, neatly-trimmed cypress hedges. Minutes later, the taxi pulled through pearly gates with huge white lettering that read "Grand Oaks."

The home was more majestic than anything Ashela had ever seen in her life. Golden sunlight beamed down on the tall, white, marble columns gracing its entranceway. A large renaissance fountain added elegance to the carefully manicured lawns. The estate itself was surrounded by woodlands of ancient oak trees and huge, sprawling weeping willows.

As the taxi chauffeured them around to the back of the house, Ashela gasped at the beauty of the grounds. Beautiful flowers in a multitude of colors gave the scenic gardens a relaxed charm, while an array of trees lent it an overall lush, tropical effect.

The rear door to the home was opened and they were let inside the kitchen by a huge, buxom woman whom Ashela would come to know as Billie, the cook. Ashela was given a seat in the corner of the kitchen where she could color and draw while her grandmother made her rounds throughout the house.

She was coloring and softly humming to herself when a young girl came running into the kitchen.

"Billie! Parris has a snake and he's trying to put it on me! Make him stop!" The little girl squealed frantically as she wedged herself between Billie and the stove, clasping her arms around the cook's huge waist. She peered out from behind her.

Seconds later, a boy came waltzing into the kitchen vehemently denying that he'd done anything to make his sister run screeching throughout the house.

Billie paid neither of them any attention as her eyes locked onto the huge, tan-colored Great Dane that came bounding behind the little boy.

"Lawd, haven't I told you two that that dog is not to be in my kitchen?" Everyone froze at hearing the anger in Billie's voice. Neither of them answered her as she wiped her hands on her apron. "I just put that dang dog outside." Billie turned to the little boy with her hands on her hips. "Did you let Mac back inside this house, Parris Reed?"

"No, ma'am," Parris issued meekly with a serious expression on his face. "It was Kyliah who let him in." At Billie's look of consternation, Ashela doubted if the little boy would have admitted it even if he were the culprit.

"No, I didn't!" Kyliah shouted as she stepped out from behind Billie, her fear of the snake obviously forgotten as she sought to vindicate herself. "*You* let him in when you went to get that snake!"

"Sweet Jesus, if the two of you don't give me a heart attack, I don't know what will!" Billie marched toward the dog, who looked as though he knew what was to happen next, grabbed him and drug him to the back door, fussing all the way.

Ashela continued staring in amazement at the animal they called Mac. He was the biggest dog she had ever seen in her life. She wondered if he were part horse.

Ashela's eyes were riveted to the dog as he slid on his hind quarters across the floor. She didn't notice that Parris was standing in front of her.

"Can we have some cookies, Billie?" his sister asked as she, too, came over to where Ashela was sitting.

"Both of you, come here and wash your hands. Probably had them all over that dumb animal. Parris, get rid of that snake." Already Billie was drying her hands and removing a tin of freshly-baked cookies from the counter top. Obviously, the children felt that her bark was much worse than her bite. "And don't go blabbing the fact that I let you eat my cookies this early in the morning."

Still fussing as she poured them each a glass of milk, Billie said, "Don't y'all make a big mess for me to have to clean up, either."

As the three of them sat eating cookies and drinking milk, the beginnings of a friendship was formed. Where Ashela tentatively introduced herself, Parris and Kyliah talked non-stop, often speaking over one another to get their point across. Kyliah was nine, a year older than Ashela. Parris was ten. They'd just finished eating when Parris suggested that they go outside to play.

Ashela shook her head. "My Grandma said I have to sit here at the table. But you all go ahead. I can watch you through the screen door."

"Aw, that's no fun. Billie, can she come outside in the back yard with us? We'll stay in front of the porch where you can see us. Please, Billie? Please?" Parris knew that Billie couldn't resist him or Kyliah.

It was one thing to give them all a treat, but Billie didn't know if she should encourage the children to play together. The Reeds were wealthy and she didn't know anything about the other little girl. Still, she appeared mannerable enough so the cook finally relented as the children knew she would. The three of them scampered through the door.

They ran through the yard chasing one another, playing "Red-Light-Green-Light" and "Simon Says." When the girls retired to the porch to jump rope, Parris threw frisbees while Mac ran and jumped like a frog trying to catch them. She and Kyliah were sitting on the steps playing jacks when the screen door opened and out stepped a tall man with a shock of blond hair.

"Daddy!" Kyliah jumped up and ran into the man's outstretched arms. He lifted her high in the air and she squealed delightedly. Hearing her squeals, Parris came running up the porch's steps so that the man could lift him as well.

Ashela was not in the least taken aback that their father was a white man. Having lived in New York, she was no stranger to mixed couples. Some of her own mother's suitors had been of a different race.

Proudly, Kyliah introduced her father to Ashela. "Daddy, this is Ashela, my new friend."

They greeted one another and Ashela giggled when Mr. Reed charmingly took her hand in his. And then he was off "to do paperwork." Regardless of his skin color, Ashela envied them for having a father that they could call their own.

She and Kyliah were rocking back and forth in a wicker swing when a taxicab pulled up. Grandma Julia stepped outside with her purse, indicating it was time for them to leave. The girls couldn't believe how fast the time had flown. They told each other they couldn't wait until next Saturday when Ashela would visit again.

Not since she'd come to Durham had she had such a wonderful time, or been as happy. She was elated about both of her new friends.

Kyliah, too, felt that she had found a special friend. Not once had Ashela questioned her about her appearance, why her hair was so light-colored or why her eyes were gray. Best of all, when Ashela had met her father, she didn't question why her daddy was white. The same things that the children at school teased her about endlessly, didn't seem to make a difference to Ashela Jordan.

Whereas Sunday used to be Ashela's favorite day, Saturday now preempted it. Each time Julia went to Grand Oaks, Ashela came with her. Every Saturday the girls would squeal in excitement as Ashela exited the taxicab with her grandmother. They would clasp arms and run off as though they hadn't seen one another in years.

They shared everything and because Kyliah had so much, she gave many of her possessions to Ashela. At first, Julia hadn't wanted to let Ashela accept the toys, books, and clothes, but Fredonia, Kyliah's mother, talked her into it.

To Ashela, Kyliah didn't realize how lucky she was. Though she envied her friend, Ashela never begrudged her a thing. There was so much that she admired about Kyliah: Her outspokenness, her fearlessness, and the way she seemed to make friends with everyone so easily. In the short period of time that they had known one another, Ashela began to see Kyliah as the sister she never had. As their friendship deepened, Ashela found herself talking less and less to her "imaginary friends." Her real-life playmate now filled the void of loneliness they had once helped to fill. And, as time passed, each of her "imaginary pals" soon faded from her memory.

***

True to her word, Ms. Phelps interceded on Ashela's behalf and she was allowed to join the youth choir. But her membership opened up a different can of worms. The other children perceived her as Ms. Phelps' pet and to a degree, she was. However, the last thing Ashela wanted to do was give the other children further cause to dislike her.

One Sunday, the youth choir was scheduled to sing prior to the start of service. While they were to sing several songs as a group, only Ashela had the privilege of performing a solo. When the choir finished their trio of songs, they sang back-up for her as she played the piano and sang her rendition of "Amazing Grace." As Ms.

Phelps knew they would be, the congregation was captivated by the little girl who possessed such strong vocal abilities.

The next day, Ashela was eager to get home from school. She was still soaring from what everyone in church was hailing as an incredible solo. She was shy at first, but as she continued to sing, it happened just like Ms. Phelps said it would. The adrenaline pumped through her veins and her lungs felt like they opened up, allowing her to perform at a new level.

Ashela was skipping as she left school, her long braids flopped behind her. She had just exited school property and turned the corner when three girls accosted her, blocking her path. Each one was taller and bigger than she, but when Ashela looked up and saw Tracy Evers, fear gripped her entire body. Of all the girls at school who openly disliked her, Tracy Evers was the meanest of them all.

"Well, if it isn't 'crater face.' Where are you going? Back to the zoo where you came from?" Tracy asked maliciously. The other girls snickered callously.

Frightened, Ashela clutched her book bag tighter and tried to walk around them. But when she moved to the right, they blocked her path.

"Don't walk away from us when we're talking to you."

"Yeah. What's the matter, the cat got your tongue?" One of the other girls became emboldened as well.

"Or, do you think you're too good for us since you sang that dumb song? Amaaaaazinnnng Graeeeeecccce." Tracy started singing in a sheep-like voice, causing her two friends to cackle with laughter.

Why are they doing this to me? Ashela wondered. Even stronger than the fear she felt, was the knowledge that had she been Kyliah, she wouldn't be frightened at all. In fact, Kyliah would kick all three of their butts. But she wasn't Kyliah, and she didn't like to fight—much less even know how. So Ashela just stood looking down at the ground, feeling thoroughly humiliated.

"Hey, 'crater face,' we heard your mother was a whore and a drug-addict queen. Guess that's why you came to live with your old ass grandmother." Tracy spoke in a venomous voice.

With tears streaming down her face, Ashela ran as fast as she could. But the three girls chased her until they caught her. Tracy was the one who pushed her viciously to the ground. Ashela fell hard, skinning both of her knees. She didn't know which one was the culprit, but one of the girls picked up a handful of dirt and threw it in her face.

Ashela knelt crying long after they had run away, leaving her on the ground. When she finally picked herself up, her self-esteem was shattered. She brushed the dirt and leaves from her hair and trudged the rest of the way home. She felt degraded and depressed. But the worst of the entire ordeal was what Tracy had said about her mother.

She skipped dinner that night. She didn't want to face Julia. She feared her grandmother would take one look at her face and know that she was a coward. *If only she had fought back. If only she had defended her mother.* To release her bottled-up emotions, Ashela wrote down all of the feelings that she was experiencing. At times she cried, but after writing for hours, she felt some of the anguish inside her diminish.

During the next several months, the scenario played itself out over and over. Everyday after school, Tracy and her cohorts would be waiting for her. Sometimes Ashela managed to outrun them, other times they'd catch her and pull on her braids before pushing her to the ground. The hurtful things they would say about her mother, and their cruel laughter was what hurt Ashela the most.

The school week became a nightmare for Ashela to endure until Saturday, when she could spend time with Kyliah and Parris. Ashela became thankful that in little over a month's time, school would recess for summer vacation.

Saturday dawned and Ashela and Kyliah were sitting under the tutelage of the piano instructor. Ashela chose not to play because her wrist hurt badly from where Tracy had kicked her the previous day. When asked what had happened to it, she told the instructor that she had accidentally fallen. Ashela knelt on the floor and watched Kyliah as she suffered through the piano lesson.

Even after weeks of lessons, Kyliah still hadn't taken to playing the piano. In fact, she hated it. She would much rather be outside climbing trees, swimming in the pond, or wrestling with Parris. Normally, the instructor focused his attention on Ashela, as she was the one who showed the most promise. Without Ashela to serve as a buffer, Kyliah's frustrations were beginning to erupt.

Sensing her temperament, the instructor sighed and suggested they bring the session to a close.

Kyliah whooped with delight. Springing to her feet, she said, "I'll race you outside, Ash!" and was gone in the blink of an eye.

Ashela ambled after her, content to feel welcomed into Kyliah's circle of affection. The two of them were sitting in the gazebo when Kyliah said, "So tell me how you *really* hurt your wrist."

Ashela should have known that she couldn't fool Kyliah. She curled her knees to her chest and wrapped her arms around them. Shrugging her shoulder, Ashela lowered her chin and rested it on top of her knees.

"Since you seem to have forgotten, code one of our friendship says there's to be no secrets." Kyliah lowered herself to sit in front of Ashela. "What happened?"

"I don't want to talk about it, Kye," Ashela snapped at her. Seconds later, a feeling of guilt settled within her. *Why couldn't she snap at Tracy like that?*

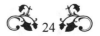

"Okay, suit yourself." Kyliah jumped up and leapt down the stairs and onto the ground, preparing to take off into the wind.

"Kye, wait."

When Kyliah came back to the gazebo and sat down, Ashela muttered, "I, I want to tell you what happened, but I'm afraid you'll laugh at me." Ashela continued to stare downward as she spoke.

Recognizing this was serious, Kyliah said, "Code two says there's nothing we can't talk about with each other, remember?"

Needing no further prodding, Ashela told Kyliah about how Tracy Evers and her gang accosted her every day after school. Ashela had no clue as to why they picked on her of all people, but it must be because they perceived her as a coward. Tracy was by far the cruelest of them all, and lately she seemed to have gotten worse. Ashela was afraid to tell any of the grown-ups because they might tell Grandma Julia. She was enough of a burden as it was, without giving her grandmother something extra to worry about. It was to the point where she didn't want to go to school any longer.

Finally, Ashela said in little more than a whisper, "I hate myself because I don't even have the courage to fight back."

Kyliah sat steaming with anger as she listened to the pain and hurt in her friend's voice. She'd have given anything to be able to whip Tracy Evers' ass. Ashela was just a tiny thing and for anybody bigger than her to gang up on her with several other people . . . why the very thought of it made Kyliah's blood boil.

"Ashela, something happened to me two years ago that made me want to learn how to fight. My mom and dad came up to school for parents'-teachers' day. I was so proud to have both of them by my side that I never paid any attention to the weird looks many of the people were throwing our way. But the very next day, several boys started calling me a zebra and they called my dad a nigger lover. That was the first time I came to recognize the difference between my parents. To me they were just mom and dad. At first, I was hurt by the things that they said, and then something snapped inside of me. All I wanted to do was hurt them the same way they had hurt me.

"I remember throwing one of the boys to the ground and beating the crap out of him. After I finally let him go, I tried to catch the others but they were long gone. My parents had to come up to the school behind that, but I didn't care. I just wanted to lash out. Even now, I know the other kids still whisper about me and Parris behind our backs." Kyliah shrugged both shoulders. "But, my mom says it doesn't matter what the other kids think about us, it's more important what we think about ourselves. I guess that's why I don't have many friends, except for you." Kyliah turned to Ashela with a determined look in her eye.

"What you have to do, Ash, is confront this Tracy person so she knows that she doesn't frighten you any more. She may be bigger than you, but that's okay. The next time she tries to jump you, you pick up a rock and bust that bitch's head."

Ashela gasped at the venom that seeped from Kyliah's voice. It was okay for Kyliah to do something like that. After all, *she* was a fighter. But not me, Ashela thought. I wouldn't know the first thing to do.

Kyliah scoffed when Ashela told her so. "You're too nice, Ash. I know Fredonia's always telling us we have to be lady-like, but you've got to put that aside and learn how to fight back. My dad always says, 'either you're the victim or you're the victor.' So take your choice, Ash. I know it seems frightful because this girl is bigger than you, but trust me. You get a rock or a stick in your hand and you'll both be the same size. Wait a minute, I want to show you something."

As Kyliah scampered off, Ashela's nerves tingled at the very thought of fighting Tracy back. Admittedly, adrenaline flowed through her veins and her heart was pounding, but Ashela suspected it was out of fear.

Minutes later, Kyliah was back with a pair of sticks attached to a chain. "These are Nanchakus. But we call them Chinese sticks. Let me show you how they work."

Ashela watched in fascination as Kyliah began to flip and twirl the sticks with an expertise worthy of aplomb. Before Ashela knew it, she was laughing hysterically because Kyliah started making Chinese-sounding noises, imitating Bruce Lee. It was even more humorous because Kyliah was serious as a heart attack.

Breathing hard, Kyliah came to a halt and dangled the sticks idly at her side. "Just as Parris taught me, I'm going to teach you." When she saw Ashela's eyes widen, Kyliah asked aggressively, "Are you a punk, Ashela?"

"A punk?" Ashela inquired in a hushed tone.

"Yeah, you know—a scaredy-cat." When Ashela slowly shook her head, Kyliah said, "I didn't think so. You're no wimp, Ashela, and you're nobody's coward. That's why you're going to learn how to fight. Come on down here and let's get started."

With a mental toughness that Ashela would never forget, Kyliah worked her over until her fear dissipated and was replaced by a budding confidence in her new ability to defend herself from even the toughest of school-yard bullies.

Chapter Four

he next week in school, Ashela was filled with self confidence. She didn't have to seek Tracy out. Being the bully that she was, Tracy was waiting for her after school. Only this time Ashela didn't try to avoid her. She continued along oblivious to Tracy's

taunts. When the three girls blocked her path, Ashela did something out of the ordinary. Instead of staring at the ground in fear, Ashela sat her book bag down between her legs. She balled her fists at her side and stared Tracy directly in the eye. Ashela's look signaled that she was prepared to fight and that she would not allow herself to be subjected to their usual ribbing.

Tracy and her accomplices were taken aback by Ashela's confrontational stance. Caught off guard, Tracy was the first to back down. "Come on, y'all. We've got better things to do than to be bothered with this heifer." Led by Tracy, the three girls ran off laughing.

Ashela's heart thumped in her chest. She couldn't believe that none of the girls had even pushed her. All she'd done was look them in the eye. Maybe that was what she should have done all along. Ashela was exhilarated when she reached her home. But to be on the safe side, she did exactly as Kyliah had instructed. She practiced with the pair of Chinese sticks Kyliah had given her.

The next afternoon, Tracy and her cohorts caught up with her after school again. But this time Tracy appeared to be spoiling for a fight. Angered by the way Ashela had made her look like a chump in front of her buddies, Tracy was determined to strike back.

There were four of them this time as they encircled her to block her exit. Tracy picked up a handful of dirt, preparing to throw it in Ashela's face. But Ashela was prepared, too. Calmly, she unzipped her school bag and yanked out the pair of Chinese sticks.

She dangled them at her side just as Kyliah had instructed her to. It gave Ashela the opportunity to catch the changing expressions on each of the girl's faces. In the next instant, like a professional, Ashela started swinging the sticks, letting them wrap around her left and right side. Each girl's mouth dropped open in surprise. None of them had expected her to put up much of a fight. Every one of them backed away, including Tracy, who allowed the dirt she held in her hand to trickle to the ground. But the damage was already done. Ashela fully intended to finish the fight which they, namely Tracy, had started. Not knowing what the outcome would be, or where the sticks would land, in one swoop Ashela lashed the pair of sticks outward, whacking Tracy upon the head.

When Tracy Evers dropped to the ground like a sack of potatoes, gasps of shock were emitted from the crowd of girls.

***

Julia Jordan was not a happy camper as she sat in the principal's office. On Wednesday, Ashela had come home with a note saying that she would be expelled from school if a parent or relative failed to show up for a meeting scheduled with Principal Jackson on Thursday morning.

Angry about having to lose a day's wages, Julia had not spoken a word to Ashela, nor had she hit her. When Ashela tried to explain her actions, she silenced

her abruptly. She didn't want to hear her granddaughter's side of the story. *Fighting with the pastor's daughter, no less.* To Julia it was blasphemous—and definitely something Charla would have done. Julia was fully prepared to beat the living daylights out of Ashela in full view of all parties concerned.

Ashela sat quietly in the principal's office. Even though her grandmother wouldn't speak to her, she was determined that Principal Jackson would hear what she had to say. Across from Ashela sat Tracy's mother and father, Bishop & Mrs. Clay Evers. With her hands folded in her lap, Tracy sat meekly with a lump on her head the size of an orange.

It was the humblest Ashela had ever seen Tracy act.

When Principal Jackson asked what happened, Tracy told her version of events first, saying that Ashela had maliciously attacked her when she, Tracy, had only been trying to befriend her. Tracy looked at the floor all while she spoke. To the Evers, Ashela appeared to be a vicious monster who'd stalked and attacked their sweet, innocent and defenseless daughter. When she finished, Tracy couldn't help glancing at Ashela with a triumphant gleam in her eye.

Undaunted, Ashela spoke not a word in her own defense until it was her turn to speak. When she did so, she stared Principal Jackson dead in the eye and told him the true turn of events.

"Principal Jackson, from the moment I arrived at this school, none of the other children have liked me, especially Tracy. They laughed at the way I talk and called me 'crater face' because of my dimples. So I stopped trying to befriend them and started keeping to myself.

"When Ms. Phelps, a woman at church, asked me to join the youth choir, I did so only because I like her. But after she asked me to sing a solo was when everything started. The next day after school, Tracy and two of her friends followed me home. Tracy pushed me to the ground and someone else threw dirt in my face. The worst part, Principal Jackson, was when Tracy started calling my mother a whore and a drug addict." Pain clouded Ashela's voice.

She threw Tracy a glaring look, speaking to her for the first time. "You don't even know my mother! How could you say such things?" Ashela stared at Tracy in frustration. "I didn't fight you or any of the other girls back because I was afraid. Plus, you're all bigger than me." Ashela angrily turned back to the principal. She pulled out her diary to show him how she'd written down names and dates and how she felt after each unwarranted attack.

"For the last seven months Tracy and her friends have been following me home every day, pushing me down, throwing dirt in my face, and saying nasty things about my mother." Ashela looked to Bishop Evers, who never seemed to have a kind word for her like he did for all the other children. She had just one question for him to answer. "How can anybody who really believes in God do what Tracy and her friends did to me every day?" Ashela's tone bore no disrespect, but it demanded a simple answer

When he failed to respond, she turned back to Principal Jackson. "Last week, I finally had enough. I asked my friend, Kyliah, to teach me how to fight just so I could stop Tracy and her friends from ganging up on me every day."

Silence stained the room as Principal Jackson continued to flip through the pages of Ashela's diary. He was amazed at the brutal honesty she exhibited in her writing, but also at the raw pain her words portrayed. Principal Jackson's lips tightened. Pastor or not, he felt an indignant outrage toward Bishop Evers and his wife as they sat before him. It was obvious they weren't willing to believe anything other than the cockamamie story their daughter had conveniently concocted.

The principal believed every word Ashela Jordan had spoken. Though Tracy was a pastor's daughter, he had witnessed how malicious she could be. Everything about her signaled to him that she was a child whose parents spent little time with her. He knew that while many of her vile actions were enacted to draw attention to herself, they were also a plaintive cry for help.

Principal Jackson leaned forward in his seat and asked, "Ashela, why didn't you tell your grandmother or one of the teachers what was happening to you?"

"Because I didn't want people to think I was a coward. I know my grandmother can't afford to take care of me, nor does she want to, so I didn't want to cause her more trouble than I already have. Plus, Tracy is Bishop Evers' daughter. I knew no one would take my word over hers. I thought that if I just ignored Tracy and her friends, eventually they would get tired and leave me alone."

By this time, Bishop and Mrs. Evers recognized that Ashela was speaking the truth. Though they wanted to make excuses for their daughter, they couldn't. Even Julia was ashamed that she had not given her granddaughter the opportunity to talk about what had happened. All Julia had been willing to see were the many times she'd run back and forth to the same school because of Charla. Embarrassed, she felt she owed Ashela an apology.

When Ashela got home from school that afternoon, Julia was seated at the dining room table. She called Ashela and beckoned her to sit down. For the first time since her arrival in Durham, Julia wanted to talk about Charla.

***

"I won't lie to you, Ashela. Bad blood existed between your mother and me. It's sad that such bitterness and animosity lingered between us. Ever since childhood, Charla was headstrong. Regardless of how often I whipped or disciplined her, she remained as obstinate as ever." Julia stared straight ahead of her, almost as if she were talking to herself. "Your mother was different from other children. She was a leader, never a follower. And despite her small size, she would fight anyone at the drop of a hat. I lost count of the many times that I was summoned by the school because of something that girl had done. Her antics nearly drove me insane.

"Granted, I wasn't much of a mother to her. I never had time. Too busy running here or going there. Naturally, Charla got left behind. The rift between us grew, and by the time she entered high school, we were barely on speaking terms; there was nothing I could do with her. About the only person she cared anything about was Clay Evers, and he was the only one who could talk sense into her.

"She and Clay met as children in church. The two of them took a liking to one another and quickly became inseparable. So much so that by the time they were in high school, the presbytery determined that it was no longer appropriate for them to spend so much time alone. I guess the elders wanted to head things off between the two of them before it was too late." Julia shook her head regretfully.

"Right after high school, Clay made it obvious that he wanted to marry Charla. But his parents tried to convince him he was too young to be talking about marriage. Truth was, they just didn't want him marrying Charla.

"After high school, Clay continued on with seminary school right here in Durham, while Charla made other plans. I knew she loved Clay. She just couldn't stay in Durham—it wasn't big enough to hold her. She wanted to get away from me and everything this city had to offer.

"Charla never was any good when it came to hitting the books. But where she wasn't able to grasp the fundamentals of geometry, she flowed fluently when it came to music. Music was the only thing that kept that girl in school. Things here at home had deteriorated—we couldn't even speak to one another without bickering spitefully. The older Charla got, the more we squabbled. It seemed we were destined to be at odds, arguing over the least important things.

"Matters came to a head after graduation when Charla told me that she was leaving to go to New York to pursue a career in music. Someone had told her that if she was serious about singing, she needed to move to Nashville, California, or New York. Of the three, New York had the most appeal to her.

"I told her that she'd never make it in the music industry. I couldn't believe she was willing to give up Clay Evers, who obviously wanted to marry her, just so she could *sing*? It was silly and typical of her. I told her that if she was so determined to throw her life away, that she'd better not count on my support. She'd better find the means to support herself." Julia's voice was tinged with anger before a note of grudging respect crept into her tone.

"And she did, too. Oh, it was rough in the beginning, but Charla always managed to find work by singing background vocals for somebody's group. As talented as she was, and even with the wide range of her voice, it still took her a number of years to forge a career on her name alone. It was only after she felt as though she had made it that she came waltzing back to Durham.

"I admit I was angry. So what that the rest of the Durham natives perceived her as a 'star.' To me, she was still someone who had wasted a golden opportunity." Julia closed her eyes and shook her head at the thought of what could have been.

***

One summer, Charla paid a visit to Durham. She didn't attend church during her brief stay, but she ran into Clay Evers anyway. Despite what she told herself, she was glad to see him. He hadn't changed much to her, he just looked more masculine, and she couldn't deny that she still loved him.

Disregarding everything he knew, Clay convinced her to see him again. He realized how much he missed her and how much of a void she left in his life when she'd left Durham. And now that she was back, she was a famous singer. Clay was so proud of her, and happy for her, too. He always knew that she would make it. Clay figured that there must be legions of men fighting for her affections.

Charla told him the truth. She was far from innocent, but she hadn't found anyone she cared about who could remove him from her heart. In the back of her mind, she still saw herself married to him.

Hearing her words, Clay saddened visibly. He was married now and well on his way to becoming a Bishop of the Apostolic faith. But, if only he had heard from her, if only he'd known, he would surely have waited. Though their circumstances were bittersweet, Charla was realistic. She loved him and she was happy for him, but she was also honest enough to admit that things would never have worked between them. Charla could never be content living in Durham. Even though they weren't together, at least Clay was happy—that was all that mattered to her.

It was inevitable that they'd run into each other, and that they'd fall in love all over again. Unable to fight his attraction for Charla, Clay told his wife that he had a business conference and that he'd be gone for several days. He and Charla escaped to Charleston, South Carolina where for three days and three nights they made love passionately. It was the best love making either of them had ever experienced. When they parted, there were tears on her part and much sadness and regret on his. Clay held her in his arms, comforting her, raining light kisses on her forehead until the warmth flowed through both of them and his male hardness signaled his desire for her all over again. With an air of urgency, Clay laid her on the bed and with gentle insistence guided himself into her. Her soft moans and hisses were sweet music to his ears. The demanding feel of her legs clamped about his waist held him captive and made him give her everything he had to give.

Months later, when Charla discovered her pregnancy, she thought of having the seed aborted. She would never knowingly do anything to hurt or jeopardize Clay's reputation. But a small part of her secretly welcomed the knowledge that she would always have a part of Clay with her. There was just one problem: Charla didn't have time to raise a child *and* pursue her singing career.

So, she decided to go to Julia and ask if she would raise the child for her. With her career taking off as it was, she would certainly be able to provide the finances. Unfortunately, her meeting with Julia didn't turn out like she planned.

Julia looked upon Charla with loathing. In her mind, Charla possessed an inordinate amount of gall to parade into her home like she was *allowing* Julia to partake of her stardom. Julia didn't care if Charla's name was strung in lights from here to Timbuktu. The chasm between them was too wide and deep for her to take any pride in Charla's accomplishments. As far as she was concerned, Charla would never be worth anything.

Enraged, Julia promptly threw Charla out of her home. She held the door open and waited for her to leave.

Charla paused in front of Julia and said, "You never could understand me, could you, Julia? Even though I've managed to become successful, you'll never forgive me for not marrying Clay Evers." Charla's eyes narrowed. "I wonder if it has anything to do with the fact that my father never married you. My refusing Clay's marriage proposal always has been a thorn in your side. What I never understood, though, was how my marrying Clay would have made you feel respectable. You, who crave respectability. When will you realize that the folks in this town will always whisper about you behind your back because you bore me out of wedlock? Times have changed, Julia. But you can't see that. You were more concerned about what other people thought of you than what I thought. Since you weren't capable of being a mother to me, how could I have been crazy enough to ask you to care for my child?" Charla walked haughtily out the door, but Julia's words stopped her.

"As usual Charla, instead of being woman enough to point the finger at yourself, you want to push your problems on to someone else. You're stupid if you expect me to believe your pregnancy was an accident. Did you really think that would cause Clay Evers to leave his wife for *you*? The man's a respectable preacher for God's sake. You blew your chance with him. You should have married him when he first asked you. But no, you had to pursue your ridiculous singing career. You could have made something of yourself. But instead, you chose to be nothing but an embarrassment to both me and to yourself."

She's missing the whole point, Charla thought. *She won't believe that I wasn't trying to trap Clay. Neither can she accept the fact that I never wanted to be Mrs. Clay Evers.*

Seeing the despair-filled expression on Charla's face, Julia continued without remorse, "I'll not raise a child for you. Deal with your own mistake. But then, your entire life has been one big, huge mistake, Charla. You've caused me nothing but trouble and grief since the day you were born. I don't care whether you get an abortion or not. Just don't bother coming here again."

Julia watched as Charla slid into the limousine with slumped shoulders. As she stood in the doorway watching it pull off, Julia wondered why she suddenly felt hollow inside.

***

Julia cupped her face in her hands. It was painful for her to relive the past. "After you were born, Ashela, you favored Charla in every way except for the one damnable feature—your deep-set dimples are an exact replica of Clay's.

"To my knowledge, your mother never made any attempts to see your father after their brief interlude, and she never told him that you were his child. But she didn't need to. It's apparent to all. Though you're a Jordan through and through, Ashela, it's clear that you are also an Evers. I'm sorry to say that Bishop Clay Evers is embarrassed by your presence in this town—so he ignores you. He's not willing to risk his reputation by openly acknowledging you. He can pretend all he wants that you don't exist. The fact of the matter is, every time he looks at you, he's forced to acknowledge the truth within himself."

After that day when Grandma Julia revealed to her who her real father was, Ashela never enjoyed going to church. She noticed it before, but now she knew why everyone glanced at her so slyly. Ashela even withdrew from the youth choir despite Ms. Phelps' protests.

Each Sunday after church, all the little children seemed to crowd around Clay Evers. As pastor of their flock, they loved him and he, in turn, was affectionate towards all of them. All except Ashela, that is, whom he didn't know how to receive. Ashela never approached him as the other children did.

Though Bishop Clay Evers ignored her, he didn't really have to: Ashela made it a point to ignore him.

Although Julia didn't talk about Charla, she did think of her often. She wondered where she'd gone wrong in rearing her daughter. More importantly, Julia thought of how vicious cycles repeated themselves. Julia, too, had hated her own mother—Charla's grandmother, and then Charla had hated her. Somehow, Julia wondered if the destructive cycle would be broken with Ashela. She wondered if there were some guaranteed way that the generational curse of maternal hatred, which ran in their family, could be severed and destroyed.

***

Tracy Evers sat looking malevolently out of her bedroom window. Two squirrels frolicked playfully in the yard below, chasing their tails, as if taunting her with their freedom. All indications were that it was a beautiful day outside. But she wouldn't know it, seeing how she was resigned to her bedroom for the entire week. All because of Ashela Jordan.

Tracy's mouth tightened and her eyes squinted into narrowed slits. How she hated Ashela Jordan! Everything was her fault. Ever since she arrived in Durham, she had caused nothing but dissent and upheaval in her family. It wasn't until *her* arrival that Tracy heard her mother and father arguing at night. Tracy's mother harbored the wild notion that Ashela was her father's daughter. It couldn't be, Tracy thought angrily. Ashela Jordan couldn't be *her* half-sister. That would be too cruel a twist of fate. Everybody *knew* it wasn't possible. Now, Tracy's mother cried heavily at night. All because of Ashela Jordan, Tracy's mother no longer believed her husband loved her like he said.

Before Ashela Jordan came to Durham, Tracy knew beyond a doubt her parents had loved one another. They had even loved her too. Now they barely spoke to each other and acted like Tracy didn't exist. Her parents busied themselves so to avoid each other by doing the work of the church, it was impossible for her not to feel neglected.

To make matters worse, Tracy overheard some of the women at church gossiping about how much Ashela Jordan favored Bishop Evers, with her deep-set dimples and all. Snidely, they pointed out that even Tracy didn't have dimples like the good Bishop's. But what did those old biddies know anyway? Tracy thought. Anybody could have dimples.

All Tracy knew was that she hated Ashela Jordan with a passion. In her mind, she even wished Ashela was dead. Tracy was glad she had beat her up all those times before Ashela learned how to fight back. But the next time, Tracy would be ready for her. Only there would be no fighting involved. She'd think of another way to get even with Ashela Jordan.

Chapter Five

shela held the olive-tinted skirt set to her chest so Kyliah could look it over. "Kye, you should buy this one because it enhances your skin color. Don't you like it?" The two of them were at North Gate Mall shopping for a new wardrobe for Kyliah's freshman year at college. She was leaving for Atlanta in several weeks to attend Spelman College.

On one hand, Ashela was happy for Kyliah. But on the other, she was extremely sad to see her friend go. The two of them had grown closer than sisters and Kyliah had become a major part of Ashela's world.

At sixteen, Ashela still had her senior year of high school left to complete. The thought of facing it without Kyliah as her sounding board was daunting. In so many ways, Ashela had come to rely upon her friend. The thought of not having her as a confidant whenever she needed her, was like having a part of herself torn away.

They browsed through the Mall on a Sunday afternoon. The weekends were when they got to spend the most time together as Ashela held a steady, part-time job working during the week at McDonald's. On Saturday, after Ashela had finished her music lessons, which Fredonia so generously continued to pay for, the two of them would be off and running.

The meager earnings Ashela brought home accounted for not just her personal spending money, but also went to help Grandma Julia pay the gas and light bills. In her mid-sixties now, Julia had trouble with arthritis and worked only three days per week. Julia's plan was to work two more years before retiring to draw her Social Security benefits. But sometimes she ached so badly that Ashela doubted if she'd be able to continue working until then.

Over the years, neither of them had ever grown comfortable with openly displaying affection, but they were respectful of one another. Ashela handled herself in a manner that would never be considered disrespectful to Julia. She honored her curfew on the weekends (except when she spent it over at Kyliah's) and never brought boys to her grandmother's home.

Grandma Julia gave her a certain amount of privacy in return. Respecting her ability to make certain decisions for herself, she didn't contest Ashela's decision to attend church only twice per month. Her grandmother had even given her permission to attend the Reed family's church. She understood the unspoken reasons behind Ashela's refusal to attend a place of worship with which she had so many unresolved issues.

In all the years Ashela lived in Durham, she had not spoken so much as a complete sentence to Bishop Clay Evers. She found it discomforting when Durham natives looked at her as if they recognized or knew her from somewhere only to glance away when they suddenly recalled whose daughter she was. It was also completely embarrassing when people mistook her for Tracy Evers. But the fact remained that Ashela favored Clay Evers even more so than Tracy.

Even though they were teenagers, Tracy's venomous attitude towards Ashela had not waned. Whenever their paths crossed, Ashela could feel the girl's hatred of her. After eight years, it still troubled Ashela that someone whom she'd never given reason to could have such ill will towards her. Regardless of Tracy's feelings about her, the die was cast between them. Whether it was outwardly acknowledged or not, nothing could alter the fact that Ashela was Tracy's half-sister.

The city of Durham had not grown on Ashela. She eagerly looked forward to finishing high school and joining Kyliah at Spelman. What *had* grown on her, though, were her new feelings for Parris Reed. Somewhere between the seventh and eighth grade, Ashela's feelings toward Parris had shifted. He had grown into an extremely handsome young man, as was evidenced by the crowd of young girls who vied for his attention. When Ashela shared her thoughts with Kyliah, she rolled her eyes upward and pointed her finger inside her mouth as if she were about to gag.

It wasn't until Ashela became a sophomore in high school that Parris finally noticed her in the way she wanted. Parris was heading into his senior year at Mount Carmel High, but already his plans were set to attend North Carolina State after graduation. Parris wanted to become a lawyer. Standing six feet, he had broad shoulders and an athletic physique. He wore his wavy hair cropped close to his head and his facial features were strong and keen. He possessed a charming charisma that enhanced his looks many times over.

One afternoon, he and three of his high school buddies were outside in his backyard playing soccer. When the game drew to an end, Parris headed into the house to get sodas for all of them. Kyliah and Ashela were closing the screen door behind them when Parris reached the top of the stairs. He blew by them as he had countless other times. But by the time Parris returned with the drinks, all three of his friends had joined the girls on the porch. They were laughing at a joke someone had told.

Two of the boys, Tevin and Craig, were Black while his third friend, Josh, was white. Josh and Kyliah were engaged in conversation while Tevin and Craig were clearly vying for Ashela's attention.

For the first time since he'd known Ashela, Parris saw her as something other than Kyliah's "play sister." As often as the three of them had traipsed throughout the Grand Oaks estate, Parris never noticed Ashela in any way except as a special friend to both he and his sister.

He had stopped hanging out with them after he entered high school. He'd made new friends, developed other interests and gradually separated himself from their circle. It wasn't done purposely, the split occurred naturally.

Parris glanced casually at Kyliah and shook his head. His sister had grown up without him noticing. Tall and lean, Kyliah was dressed in a red tank top with a short denim skirt. Her long shapely legs were nicely tanned. She didn't have much in the breast department but with her long neck and sandy-colored hair that fell past her shoulders, one hardly noticed. She reminded him of a golden goddess. Always one to call the shots, Kyliah's personality still dictated that she be the one in charge.

Parris stared long and hard at Ashela, who stood in stark contrast to his sister. She was all of five feet four inches and was dressed in a pair of navy blue shorts with a white halter top. Her breasts were nicely rounded and Parris was sure his hands could easily span her waist. She had well-rounded hips and shapely thighs and calves. Her square face was accentuated by her long hair and deeply-set dimples. Ashela had become a tiny bombshell. As Parris gazed at her, he wondered in amazement how he had missed her development.

Parris had never known her to possess anything other than a sweet, gentle disposition. He saw her as the shy, introverted person that he and his family had come to adore. Even his mom, Fredonia, had grown to love Ashela. Since she'd first started coming to their home years ago, Fredonia continued to pay for Ashela to have music lessons. Those lessons continued, even though Kyliah refused to join her, and had been extended to include singing lessons as well.

Like his mother, Parris recognized that she was exceptionally talented when it came to music. He remembered her starting with the piano, but now her musical abilities included playing the saxophone and clarinet.

Suddenly, Parris felt a sense of possessiveness towards Ashela. It was a new feeling for him. All he knew was that he didn't like the way Tevin and Craig hovered so close to her. On impulse, Parris stood and suggested that he and his friends take a ride in his Mustang convertible. The girls wanted to go along as well, but there wasn't enough room. Parris' ulterior motive was to avert his friends' attention from Ashela. He wondered why she never paid near as much attention to him.

Parris and Ashela became an item shortly thereafter. The one required to make the biggest adjustment to their relationship was Kyliah. She was the one who needed acclimation to the idea that her best buddy and her brother had eyes only for each other.

By the end of Parris' senior year of high school, they were together constantly. Although they were linked romantically, the two of them had never engaged in anything beyond heavy petting. Despite Parris' urgings, Ashela wasn't ready to "go all the way." What remained unspoken between them was that one day in the near future, she would.

After Parris' graduation, he went to NC State in Charlotte, North Carolina. As the distance between the two cities was just several hours, they still managed to see one another every weekend.

Several months into her senior year of high school, cataclysmic developments altered Ashela's life. Kyliah was off to Spelman when Parris, who was now a sophomore in college, began to limit his trips to see her to every other weekend. Shortly thereafter, his visits became even more sporadic. Whereas before when they would spend long hours on the phone on the weekends when they didn't see one another, soon even his telephone calls became non-existent. The few times Ashela could afford to call him late at night, his roommate would tell her he wasn't available. But Ashela could swear she heard Parris' voice in the background.

It soon became apparent that he was avoiding her.

Ashela would lie in bed at night feeling dejected, as if her heart had shattered into a million pieces. She couldn't stop berating herself for not giving in to Parris' wishes to have sex with her. In her mind, she felt if she'd had the courage to "go all the way," he might still be hers.

***

Tracy Evers had blossomed into quite an attractive girl. She had almond-shaped eyes, thick long hair, dark complected skin, and a body that caused men to do a double-take.

She had her fair share of suitors, though the person she wanted most seemed to have eyes only for someone else. That "someone else" was the one person Tracy hated most in life: Ashela Jordan.

It seemed Ashela took personal pleasure in flaunting the fact that Parris Reed belonged to her. Everyone knew the Reeds were rich, with Mr. Reed being a big-time stockbroker. It appeared that Ashela wanted everyone to know that, of all the girls chasing him, she was the one he'd chosen. Everywhere Tracy turned, there the two of them were. Whether driving down Etchinson Avenue in Parris' shiny red convertible, huddled together sharing milkshakes through separate straws, or sitting cuddled up at the movie theater, Tracy had the unfortunate knack of running into them. Each time it only caused her to hate Ashela all the more, and dream about Parris even harder.

Tracy never forgave Ashela for setting her up that day long ago in Principal Jackson's office. In her opinion, she hadn't done anything egregiously wrong. But her father had thought otherwise. He had refused to speak to her for weeks after the incident. Tracy, who longed for her father's approval hated whenever he was displeased with her. His rejection of her deepened her hatred of Ashela.

Neither had she forgiven Ashela for the destruction she'd caused to her family. Tracy could look back and point to the exact time that "problems" between her mother and father arose. Before Ashela Jordan came to town, Tracy honestly believed that her parents had been happily married. But after Ashela's arrival, a breach occurred in Tracy's home life, and things were never the same.

Since then, her mother and father's relationship had shifted dramatically. Tracy lost track of the many times they argued only to stop abruptly when she'd come into the room crying. Her mother accused her father of sleeping with that "Charla Jordan" woman. And now that their "bastard" child was being flaunted right under her nose, how did he expect his wife to be respected by the very people to whom he preached hell, fire and damnation? All because of his philandering, she, a respectable woman, was the laughingstock of Durham.

An air of mistrust lingered in their atmosphere. Privately, her father acknowledged that Ashela Jordan was his offspring. To atone for his past indiscretion, he vowed to do everything he could to win back his wife's affection. But regardless of what he did or how much he sacrificed, it was never enough. It was as though Mrs. Evers could discern that in her husband's heart of hearts, his true love was Charla Jordan. She, First Lady of the largest Black church in Durham, North Carolina, knew she would always live in the shadow of another woman's memory.

It was inevitable that Tracy would put the blame for every imagined ill she suffered in life squarely upon the shoulders of Ashela Jordan. In her mind, Tracy had to make Ashela pay.

Tracy's cousin Dora Evers attended the same university as did Parris Reed. One weekend, Tracy and her parents were visiting NC State's campus. It was where Tracy decided she wanted to attend. While her parents were meeting with the president of the university, she and Dora took a tour of their own. As they stepped inside the student union building, who should Tracy spot but Parris Reed.

Tracy's heart skipped several beats. In the next second, she was standing in front of Parris, leaving the surprised, mouse-like Dora standing in her tracks.

Though he knew of her, in all his years in Durham, Parris had never so much as said hello to Tracy Evers. But as he looked over the bold young woman standing in front of him, he had no choice but to greet her and introduce her to his friends. Not that Parris didn't want to, Tracy was a looker. There was something about the deliberate way she clung to him and the knowing look in her eyes that intimated she could do incredible things in bed.

Though she was younger than he, Parris liked the mature way in which she handled herself. He had no way of knowing that the conniving machinations of Tracy's mind would have impressed Machiavelli himself. Before Tracy sauntered away, she had Parris' dorm number safely tucked inside her designer pocket book.

That next week, with Dora, who worshipped the ground Tracy walked on, safely ensconced in her corner, her courting of Parris Reed took on a full-frontal attack. Tracy gave Dora the impression that she was letting her into her world by entrusting her with a grave secret: Parris Reed was in love with her. The same Parris Reed whose parents were filthy rich wanted her as his girlfriend. Of course Tracy had agreed, but there would be no way for her to see him unless she could visit him on the weekends when he couldn't come to her. That's where Tracy needed Dora's help. Dora knew how strict Tracy's parents were, they kept her under lock and key. No way would they allow their daughter to visit NC's campus if they thought she was visiting a boy. But if they thought she were visiting her cousin, well, something might be worked out.

Carrying a juicy secret can be a delicious thing. For fat, homely Dora, it was just what she needed. She thought it was all so romantic. Of course she would do everything she could to help her cousin get away.

Just as she planned, Tracy visited Parris in his dorm every chance she got. When he started pressuring her for sex, she was all too willing to give in. Months later, Parris was hooked and had given her his promise that he would accompany her to her prom. His commitment to Ashela was already forgotten.

Meanwhile, when they couldn't be together, they burned up the phone lines. Whenever she sensed Parris waffling on the issue of Ashela, Tracy would casually talk of how Ashela was "seeing" someone else. Parris never had to recoup from unrequited feelings for Ashela. When he buried himself between the wet folds of Tracy's legs, Ashela Jordan was the furthest thing from his mind.

Chapter Six

Kyliah was the one who delivered the news of Parris' betrayal. Halfway into the school year, Ashela learned the reason why Parris had suddenly distanced himself from her as if she had the plague.

"Ash, have you heard from Parris?" Kyliah already knew the answer to her question. She knew Ashela and Parris were having problems but she hadn't known until recently to what extent. Neither one would talk about the other with her.

"No. Parris doesn't return my calls and I decided to stop badgering you about him. What else is there to say?" Though she was trying to hide her true feelings, inside Ashela was despondent. She suspected Kyliah was aware of it.

"Well, there's a reason behind it, Ash." Anger laced Kyliah's voice. "I just can't believe my own flesh and blood would betray us like he has. What a lowdown bastard he's turned out to be. You're better off without him."

Figuring Kyliah wanted her to know that she was on her side, Ashela smiled. Kyliah could be overly dramatic at times.

"I guess there's no way to sugarcoat what I'm about to say, Ash. So I might as well just come out and say it." Kyliah paused before saying, "Parris is marrying Tracy Evers."

The smile left Ashela's face and was replaced by a look of puzzlement. She figured Kyliah was joking, but it was unlike her to tease her about something so serious.

"Kye, I've already accepted the fact that Parris and I are history. But don't play with me like this. As much as I hate to admit it, it still hurts to think about him. So I just try not to. Let's talk about something else."

But Kyliah didn't sound like herself. Suddenly, she sounded teary-eyed and sad. Very sad. Ashela heard Kyliah sniffle and suddenly knew that she was telling the truth. When she spoke again, Kyliah's voice was hushed.

"She's pregnant, Ash. That no good Black bitch is pregnant by my brother. Her father is in such an uproar, you'd think that dumb ass Parris kidnapped the girl and raped her. The man's conveniently over-looking the fact that Miss Goody-two-shoes was the one sneaking off every Saturday to visit Parris in his dorm. Tracy's mother is refusing to let her have an abortion and insists the only way to keep politics out of this whole matter is for the two of them to get married."

Ashela felt as though someone had delivered a swift kick to her stomach. It all added up. Him not returning her phone calls, and never trying to contact her when he came to visit his parents. And to think he'd told her he loved her and wanted to marry her some day. Ashela had even made up in her mind that she would offer him her virginity, if he still wanted it. *Why was everything she loved snatched away from*

her so suddenly? she thought. Before she knew it, Ashela crumpled onto her bed as the pain made her double over. The phone fell away as she sobbed into her pillow.

"It's the oldest trick in the book, Ashela: Getting pregnant so a man can marry you. He loves you, Ash. I know Parris does. But it's just like Fredonia always said, pussy makes a man do strange things." Recognizing that she was being vulgar, Kyliah said, "I'm sorry, Ash. It's just that I'm hurting too. And, for once, I don't know what to do with my anger."

When there was silence on the other end, Kyliah realized she was talking to herself. She could hear the faint sound of Ashela sobbing. Kyliah's own eyes closed in anguish, she was grieving too. She hung up the phone wishing there was something she could have done to protect Ashela from further hurt and pain.

Ashela didn't have time for her wounds from Parris' rejection to heal. Just three days later, Grandma Julia suffered a severe stroke.

During fourth period, her home-room teacher tapped her on the shoulder and told her to come with him. Outside in the corridor, the teacher told her that her grandmother had had an accident. All he could tell her was that it was serious and that she needed to get over to the hospital right away.

Ashela rushed to Memorial Hospital where her grandmother was in the emergency room fighting for her life. Ashela was told to have a seat in the waiting room and someone would notify her of her grandmother's condition as soon as something more was known.

In a state of shock, Ashela sat with several other people who also awaited news about loved ones. Hours later, she inquired again about Julia but was told that there was nothing new to report. No word had come from either of her grandmother's doctors.

In the wee hours of the morning, a hand shook Ashela awake. A woman in a white coat stood before her. The nurse told her that Julia was very lucky to be alive after having suffered such a massive stroke. She was not yet out of the woods as she was still fighting for her life. She was too weak to have visitors.

The house seemed empty and devoid of life as Ashela closed the front door behind her. Physically and emotionally drained, she walked into her bedroom and slowly stretched out on her bed. She glanced at all the pictures of famous jazz singers plastered to her wall without really seeing them. Suddenly, an anguished cry tore from her lips. Ashela rolled to her knees and began to intercede for her grandmother's life.

When Ashela was finally allowed to see her grandmother, she wasn't prepared for the state that she found her in. The woman lying on the bed bore no resemblance to the healthy, vibrant person that she had known. This figure was twisted and gnarled.

Like a grotesque figurine from a horror movie, Julia's body lay limp like a rag doll. Ashela cringed at the macabre sight of the woman she had come to know and love. She was but a caricature of her former self. The smell of death overwhelmed Ashela's senses. Seconds later, she fell to the floor unconscious.

When she awoke, she found herself lying in a hospital bed. In a frenzy, she tried to throw off the sheets that covered her and struggled to loose herself. Finally, she fell to the floor, her breathing coming rapidly in short gasps. That was how the nurse found her, huddled on the floor with her head between her legs.

When she regained her strength, Ashela's only desire was to vacate the premises she had quickly come to associate with being a death trap. Regaining her composure, she walked to the nurse's station to inquire about Julia. Ashela knew in her heart that she couldn't bear to look upon her grandmother's twisted face and body.

She was told to wait because her grandmother's doctor wanted a word with her. A tall man approached her and told her to have a seat. A serious decision had to be made regarding her grandmother. Only the life support machine was keeping her breathing. In his opinion, it was just a matter of time before she expired regardless. As her only living relative, it was her decision whether to remove her now or later.

Ashela could only shake her head in sorrow. There was no way that she would contest the hospital's decision to remove her grandmother from life support. Not after seeing the state she was in. There were papers for Ashela to sign before she left the hospital.

Ashela returned to the house on Green Street filled with more pain and sorrow. She went straight to Grandma Julia's room and sat upon her bed. It was a hollow feeling to know that one was truly alone in the world. It gave a whole new meaning to the word loneliness. With no other relatives to call upon for support, Ashela felt as if she were staring into a deep, dark hole.

For the first time since the inception of their relationship, Ashela did not want to discuss her feelings with Kyliah. She hated the sense of powerlessness that engulfed her. To combat it, Ashela got up and went to her room. There, she pulled out her diary and began writing down what she considered to be her options. Next, she wrote down what she wanted to do with the rest of her life, no matter how far fetched.

Ashela reviewed her list and narrowed it down to two things: 1) bury her grandmother; and 2) move back to New York City.

It was the second item on her list that surprised Ashela the most. Always, in the back of her mind, she'd known that someday she would return to her home town. For the first time in her life, Ashela made the decision to buck conventional wisdom. She was aware that the town folk thought of her as the daughter of a trollop. They even went so far to say Ashela would never amount to anything.

As she made the decision to return to New York, she knew that one day she would prove each and every one of them wrong: Ashela was determined to follow in her mother's footsteps and become a famous singer.

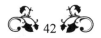

***

Tracy Evers sat in her bedroom oblivious to the goings-on right outside her door. Her parents were arguing again. It was all they seemed to do lately. Tracy could care less. A sardonic smile curled the corner of her lips. She'd gotten the desired result. She glanced down at the ring on her finger to prove it. In four months time, she would be Mrs. Parris Reed.

Now that Parris was hers, Tracy could gloat whole-heartedly. She had outwitted them all. Chiefly that bitch Ashela Jordan. Tracy wanted her, more so than any one else, to know of her impending marriage. She wanted her to hurt, bleed and feel utterly humiliated. The world must know that she, Tracy Evers, had won. Tracy couldn't wait to flaunt her diamond ring in Ashela's face. She would hand deliver the wedding invitation herself.

Parris would come around. Right now he was full of anger, too busy feeling sorry for himself and feeling nakedly manipulated. Who cared? Tracy had gotten what she wanted.

In time, she figured all parties involved would get over their feelings of antipathy. Already, her father's ruffled feathers were soothed because of the marriage arrangement. When he'd been given the news of her pregnancy, he had ranted and raved for days. But Tracy had wrapped him around her fingers by sitting before him and telling him the story of how Parris had convinced her to see him again and again with promises of marrying her someday. Though she knew letting him know her in the biblical sense had been wrong, she couldn't deny Parris because she loved him and knew that soon he would be her husband.

Bishop Evers believed his daughter because he *needed* to. He brushed aside the nagging feeling that his daughter was being disingenuous. Bishop Evers, fearless Man of God, knew that there was only one solution. He could not bear to see his unborn grandchild endure what someone else he knew had gone through. Just as quickly, he pushed his feelings of guilt about Ashela Jordan to the side.

***

Four months later, Dora Evers watched as her cousin walked down the church aisle to the tune of, "Here Comes the Bride." She was wearing the most beautiful wedding gown Dora had ever seen. Tracy looked to be at such peace with herself that Dora felt a momentary stab of guilt for thinking treacherous thoughts about her cousin. But in the back of Dora's mind, she couldn't rid herself of the notion that somehow Tracy had deliberately orchestrated this series of events. It didn't take a rocket scientist to know that Parris Reed was not happy about having to marry her cousin.

Dora suspected that Tracy had created the entire drama to "ruin" things between him and Ashela Jordan. When they had been younger, Dora too, had participated in the tormenting of Ashela. But she'd only done so to win Tracy's approval. As time passed, she couldn't bring herself to muster the same amount of hatred for her that Tracy had. Ashela had never done anything to Dora to spark feelings of ill will.

Dora looked around the church at all of the people in attendance. Kyliah Reed's absence spoke for itself. Dora knew Kyliah was Ashela's best friend and she wondered if Ashela's not being present diminished Tracy's victory in any small way.

***

Already standing at the alter, Parris Reed waited for his bride-to-be to reach his side. Parris still felt numb and afraid. He didn't want to marry Tracy Evers. He was still kicking himself for believing her when she'd told him she was taking the pill. Parris' eyes closed momentarily. He still remembered Kyliah's scathing words to him. True to her word, Kyliah had not attended his "shot-gun" wedding, as she called it, despite receiving orders to do so from their parents.

As Tracy reached his side, Parris did all he could to mask the anguish he was feeling in his heart. In his mind, he could hear Kyliah saying, "You were used, Parris. But you're too pussy whipped to realize it. That girl doesn't love you. She only pursued you because she knew you and Ashela cared about one another. But you haven't thought about Ashela have you, Parris? You bought that bullshit about her seeing someone else hook, line and sinker. You're my only brother, Parris, and God knows that regardless of what's happened, I still love you. But I never thought I'd see the day when I'd be embarrassed to claim you as my flesh and blood. One day you'll wake up and realize you threw away the chance to be with the one person who loves you for who you are and not for the money they know you're going to inherit some day."

These were the words that rang in Parris' ear. God help me, he thought. *What have I done?* Though he willingly acknowledged his wrongdoing, Parris could only hope that this one mistake didn't turn out to ruin the rest of his life.

***

The dream was a recurring one. Trapped inside a long, wide tunnel full of shadowy figures, she couldn't discern what was what. The chaotic darkness of the tunnel was broken only by the light at the very end of it. She sat huddled with her back against the wall, her knees raised to her chest. She lifted her hand to her forehead in an attempt to see more clearly. Whispery, hunched figures that had somehow come to life dragged to and fro. There was no sound inside the cave-like tunnel—only a pervasive silence. When the elusive, imp-like creatures came too close, she kicked and lashed out. Dodging the blows, they retreated for a short time.

Why didn't someone help her? Didn't anyone care that she was lost? Trembling from the cold, she edged toward the light, but it seemed so far away. If only she could gather the strength to make her way to the other end. Dragging her tired, ragged body, she lunged toward the light.

Recognizing she was trying to escape, the darkened figures converged upon her . . .

44

Part Two

Growing Pains

"The melancholy days are come,
The saddest of the year,
Of wailing winds, and naked woods,
Of meadows brown and sere."

– William Cullen Bryant

"...and with cunning craftiness they lie in wait to deceive."

– Ephesians 4:14

Chapter Seven

New York City was everything Ashela remembered it to be. She had arrived three months earlier on a wing and a prayer, feeling as though she'd left one life behind and was now fully prepared to begin a new one. Though elated over being back on the East Coast after so many years, she was unprepared for the culture shock she experienced as she exited LaGuardia Airport to hail a cab that would take her into Manhattan.

As the taxi cruised through traffic, certain aspects of New York were immediately familiar. The lack of trees, the way people piled their garbage in front of their homes, and the way all the houses were so closely grouped together. Ashela knew that she would have to reacclimate herself to the massive crowds of people and their close proximity to one another. For here in New York, groups of divergent races were thrown together in one huge melting pot.

Orientals lived next door to Nigerians. Jews lived across from Puerto Ricans. Vietnamese cohabited with Blacks. But it was this everyday hustle and bustle of the thriving, noisy metropolis that served to remind Ashela that Durham, North Carolina was far behind her now. For the first six weeks, she stayed at a hotel in the Midtown section of Manhattan. It took her that long to secure an apartment on Carmine Street in the section of New York commonly referred to as "The Village."

She traveled light from North Carolina, bringing with her only some clothes and a few personal items. She felt no need to hang on to any memorable keepsakes. Not even her grandmother's house.

Through selling the home, Ashela learned more about wills, trusts and probate court than she cared to. Having made the decision to put her grandmother's house on the market, she called an attorney to find out what the process entailed. The first thing he instructed her to do was to search for a will. Ashela knew of no such document and was told that probate court was her next step in order to have the property transferred to her name. She was forewarned that the procedure was costly and was guaranteed to take anywhere from six months to two years.

Such news was distressing. She needed money right away to have Julia cremated and there were hospital bills to pay. She also required money for the move back to New York. With no other alternative, she hired a lawyer who agreed to work pro bono until her grandmother's house was sold.

While sorting through Julia's things, Ashela found a small pouch labeled "important papers." The documents contained the solutions to a good number of her problems. Julia had established a revocable living trust which named Ashela as the beneficiary of her home and bank accounts. She also had health and interment insurance that covered the cost of her cremation and most of her hospital bills.

After the house was sold and all outstanding bills paid, Ashela breathed a sigh of relief. She had twenty-five thousand dollars remaining and she vowed to manage it wisely.

The only thing preventing her from leaving right away was the matter of her high school diploma. Graduating high school was a must for her. She'd come too far to leave before receiving her diploma. She knew that Julia would have wanted her to finish school as well.

As much as it galled her to do so, Ashela bided her time by counting down the days when she would no longer have to put up with the endless sneers and whispers from her peers and the rest of the town people. But as each day passed, her frustrations mounted. She hated passing Tracy Evers in the school corridors. It was obvious that Tracy went out of her way to deliberately run into her at every turn. To torment her the more, Tracy took to frequenting the McDonald's restaurant where Ashela worked in the evenings. With her sycophant friends in tow, she would boast loudly of being the woman Parris Reed had chosen to marry.

Neither could Tracy refrain from flashing her diamond-studded engagement ring in Ashela's face or from cattily reminding her that her wedding was only weeks away. She hinted sarcastically that if Ashela had the guts to show up, she would throw her her bridal bouquet as a gesture of sympathy.

Every time she thought of Parris and Tracy, Ashela forced the bile back down her throat. As anger toward Parris and hatred of Tracy seethed within her, Ashela now understood why her mother had never been able to contain her own incendiary rage. Fuming inwardly, Ashela charged from class to class bristling every time she thought of the smug look Tracy carried on her face.

There were days when Ashela could easily have murdered Tracy—and Parris, too, because of his betrayal. She found herself doodling in class, whiling away the time by dreaming of ways in which both of them would meet their demise. Because of the pain each had caused her, every imagined feat was more brutal than the last. To quell her increasing fury and resentment, Ashela threw herself into her music with renewed energy. Practicing on her instruments for hours at a time became her saving grace, and helped her maintain her sanity.

But with only two months left in the school year, Ashela reached her wits end and was ready to explode. She made an appointment with the school counselor to find out if there was any way she could receive her diploma prior to graduation. She explained her predicament—the death of her grandmother, having no other relatives in the city, having to be out of her home by a certain date because of its sale, and an overall inability to concentrate due to the compounding of recent traumatic experiences.

Empathetic, the counselor reviewed Ashela's records along with everything she had told him. After determining that she had amassed enough credits to graduate, he decided that her situation made her eligible for the school's "Dire Straits"

policy—an exemptive rule that allowed certain students to graduate early because of extenuating circumstances. After taking the mandatory exit exam, Ashela received her diploma a full two months in advance.

In the weeks following Julia's death, Ashela could feel her emotions hardening inside of her. Knowing that she was on her own made her feel a new sense of responsibility that she had not previously known. The old Ashela would have cried on Kyliah's shoulders every step of the way. But something had shifted, sparking a change within her. A new level of maturity caused her to view the world around her differently. Realizing she would have to rely solely upon herself if she was to make it in life, gave her a definite sense of purpose.

For once, she didn't want to burden Kyliah with her troubles. Her friend was probably having a wonderful time away at school doing all the things that college students do. So, Ashela forced herself to stand on her own. There was yet another reason why she was loathe to contact Kyliah. Though she loved her as a sister, Kyliah was a link to the pain and embarrassment Ashela had experienced over Parris. She was determined to stamp out every reminder of him, even if it meant separating herself from Kyliah for a period of time.

She realized that she had foolishly handed Parris her heart on a silver platter. Never again would she be so trusting of someone the way she'd trusted him. In the future, she would take considerable pains to guard her heart with all diligence.

***

Ashela spent her days exploring New York and familiarizing herself with the city. She rode trains and buses throughout Manhattan, Brooklyn and Queens, stopping to fill out applications for employment wherever she saw a "help wanted" sign. Every now and then, she'd spot a bargain that she couldn't resist and splurge on a knick-knack for her sparsely furnished apartment. With only a bedroom set and several papasan chairs, she promised herself a full set of furniture just as soon as she found herself a job. She didn't want to incur the expense of furnishing an entire apartment. Not when she'd had to shell out six months rent in advance to procure the place. Decorating her apartment piece-meal would allow her to stay within her budget.

Ashela soon found herself immersed in the ways of city life. Because there was always something to do, there was never a dull moment in the city that never sleeps. She took to frequenting various clubs on the weekends just to get a feel for the type of music they were playing. The open-mic jazz clubs invariably drew her attention. She loved sitting toward the back while listening to the different bands play. Ashela envied them and yearned to be a part of someone's group.

Though she wanted to get started on her career, it dawned on Ashela that she knew very little about the music industry. She'd tried locating Tanya because she knew her mother's old friend could give her guidance and provide her with valuable contacts. But she found no listing for her in any of the five New York boroughs.

Drawing on her memory bank, Ashela cased the neighborhood where she remembered Tanya had lived. After narrowing her search down to several buildings, she was told by the management of each one that no one named Tanya Redding had ever resided there.

Next, Ashela called Motown, hoping that someone there might know of Tanya's whereabouts. But, again, no one that she spoke to had ever heard of her. By calling repeatedly, she managed to catch the sympathetic ear of someone other than the secretary who normally answered the telephone. Ashela promptly took the opportunity to explain that her mother had once held a contract with Motown before dying at an early age. As her daughter, now that she was older, she too, wanted a career in the music industry. She had a good voice and knew she could be just as successful as her mother. All she needed was the chance to prove it.

Though the receptionist had never heard of Charla Jordan, Ashela's story was enough to get her put through to the Artists & Repertoire Department where new talent was screened. But while drawing on her mother's name may have elicited a response from the secretary, the A & R executive with whom she was eventually connected was not impressed. The man was brusque, hostile, and impatient. He only cared about whether or not she had a demo tape. Ashela did not, so he quickly ended the call by telling her to send him a copy of one when she got it. She was left holding the phone as the dial tone buzzed in her ear.

Shortly thereafter, Ashela landed a job as a runner for the New York Stock Exchange. She was essentially a go-fer for those in the trading pit. The environment was a chaotic madhouse where burn-out came swiftly. The turnover was high and few lasted beyond the first several months. But Ashela was able to endure because she viewed her job as a stepping stone, something to tide her over until her "real" job as a singer/musician came to fruition.

Ultimately, it was the evenings that Ashela looked forward to. She hung out at different clubs hoping to talk to some of the musicians after their performance. Even though none of the bands were necessarily of "superstar" caliber, many of them were still inaccessible. Most were surrounded by entourages that prevented people in the audience from getting too close unless permitted.

One night Ashela was hanging around the back stage entrance of the Blue Note hoping to snare one of the performers. A man approached the small group of people that she was standing with and handed them his business card. Someone asked him what he did since his card said only that he was an Independent Recording Consultant. He said he was a record producer scouting for new, up-and-coming talent and if they wanted a career in the music industry to give him a call.

Ashela studied the man's card after he walked away. While some of the people around her tossed his card to the floor, Ashela slipped hers inside her jean pocket.

"He's probably just another shyster out to scam somebody," a girl standing close to Ashela said.

The girl hadn't spoken to anyone in particular so Ashela didn't respond. She was reluctant to get drawn into a conversation with her or anyone else.

"Haven't I seen you here before?" the girl asked, speaking directing to Ashela.

Ashela shrugged nonchalantly and hoped that by ignoring her, the girl would get the hint that she didn't want to be bothered. But a lack of a response didn't seem to dissuade her.

"You'd think these guys were superstars with how arrogant they act. I swear, when *I* make it big, I'm never gonna forget where I came from."

While she continued to gripe about musicians and their peculiarities, Ashela glanced at her fully for the first time. She had a creamy complexion but it was the texture of her hair, which streamed past her shoulders in unruly waves, that signaled that she was of mixed heritage. Something vaguely familiar about her tugged at Ashela. And then it hit her. The girl's impatient attitude reminded her of Kyliah. Though she had been prepared to completely ignore her, Ashela changed her mind. Instead, she wound up introducing herself and learning that Stephanie was the girl's name.

The back stage door swung open and the six or seven people loitering outside it rushed the musicians as they poured out. Most of the loiterers had tapes that they were trying to hand to the players before they exited the building. While their entourages held the small crowd at bay, the band members swept outside and disappeared into their waiting vehicles.

"Hell! All that time we spent waiting and they couldn't even give us a few minutes of their time," was the general response after the musicians were long out of sight.

"There's got to be a better way," Ashela said as she moved toward the exit herself. It was one o'clock in the morning and she had to be at work by nine.

"There is if you can afford to make a quality demo tape and send copies of it to all the record producers. But who has that kind of money?" Stephanie fell in step beside her.

"How much does it cost to make a demo tape?" Ashela was curious.

"From what I hear, about seven or eight thousand dollars for a professional, quality tape." They had reached the subway station and Ashela paused at the top of the stairs, taken aback by the huge sum of money required to make something that seemed so simple.

"Maybe I'll see you around again," Stephanie said.

The sound of an approaching train snapped Ashela out of her reverie. "Yeah, maybe so," she replied before dashing down the stairs.

During her break the next day at work, Ashela called the number on the business card. She got an answering machine but because she had no way for him to reach her, she hung up without leaving a message. She tried calling Patrick Hart's number for the next several days but kept getting his machine.

When she finally connected with him a week later, he agreed to meet her after she got off work at Gemelli's, an Italian restaurant inside the World Trade Center. Though peeved because of the difficulty she'd had in reaching him, Ashela found Patrick Hart impressive nonetheless. He was articulate, well dressed and extremely knowledgeable about the music industry. He possessed a portfolio filled with famous singers whose careers he had helped get underway, as well as numerous photographs of himself at various awards ceremonies hugging famous entertainers. Ashela recognized every actress, actor, and singer that she saw in his book and immediately became star-struck.

While she continued to gaze at the pictures in awe, Patrick began to expound on the services he offered. "What I do, Ashela is take an aspiring artist, such as yourself, and craft him or her into a mega superstar. All of these people you see me with in the photographs, owe their start in this business to me. I've become so successful at doing what I do, that I no longer have to do it for the money. And I only work with special talent. From experience, I know just by watching a person whether or not they have what it takes to become successful. When I handed you my card, Ashela, I knew there was something unique about you."

They were seated at a table for two tucked away behind large, green foliage. Patrick Hart spoke almost conspiratorially, occasionally touching her arm. His touch was soft and reassuring, yet there was nothing intimate about it that Ashela could dislike. He explained that he was much in demand and that was why it was so hard to catch up with him. Because he worked for himself, Patrick made his own decisions about who he worked with. But first he had to know that person's background and how committed they were to actually succeeding. Periodically, if he was really eager to work with an individual or group, he invested his own money into them.

"While it's true that I am more interested in creating superstars than in gaining financially, I'm also a wise businessman. One who recognizes that people have the uncanny tendency to pay for what they want and then turn around and beg for what they need. How much time and money a person is willing to invest in their dream is an indicator to me of how serious they are about pursuing their goals." Patrick knew he had her full attention.

"Part of the problem in today's society, Ashela, is that people *say* they want success but they're not willing to put forth the effort that it takes. I believe it boils down to an even larger societal problem. You see, we're living in the age of two-family incomes, yet we still have more divorce. We have more time on our hands, but we enjoy that time less, we've managed to multiply our possessions, but we've also reduced our values . . ."

He's so wise, Ashela thought in amazement as her mind rushed to keep up with his philosophical expressions. So inured was she by what he was saying that she

never noticed how far off the beaten path he was straying. Challenging the validity of any of his statements never occurred to her. In her mind, she knew immediately that it would be an honor to work with him.

He was so easy to listen and talk to that Ashela soon found herself telling him her life's story. When he questioned her at length about both her mother and grandmother, she felt he was asking out of earnest sympathy. Patrick seemed to genuinely care about her when he told her how courageous she was for selling her grandmother's house and moving to New York on her own. It confirmed his initial opinion of her, he'd known from a glance, that of all the people she'd been standing with, *she* was the one who had what it took to make it to the top. With the proper guidance, it was just a matter of time before she catapulted her way into stardom. As a matter of fact, Patrick was so sure of her impending success that it would be *his* privilege to work with her to make her dream of becoming a major recording artist come true.

"You'll find as we embark upon our journey, Ashela, that today's version of the music industry is geared towards who you know over how well you do what you do. That's why I'm not particularly concerned with how much talent you possess or how well you can sing. Why? Because it's all about contacts. The right contacts can open doors that no man can close . . ."

Doors that no man can close? There! Ashela thought. Wasn't that particular saying a scripture from the bible? And if he knew the bible, didn't that count for something?

". . . doors that would otherwise take years to break through on your own. If you decide you want me to work with you, Ashela, I'll be your source. I know the right people, I have the right contacts."

He paid for both their meals and told Ashela she should consider getting a telephone so he could reach her when the time came for them to begin working together. Currently, he had one other project he needed to finalize, but as soon as it was completed, in approximately three to four months, she would be his next protégé. Before they left, Patrick gave her the phone numbers to several agents of major recording artists and invited her to call to verify his legitimacy. He told her, "My word is my bond, Ashela, and my work speaks for itself."

Ashela was in a state of euphoria as they parted to go their separate ways. All she could picture were lavish images of herself performing on stage in front of thousands of audience members.

So badly did Ashela want to become the next "overnight sensation" that she completely blocked out the need for caution. In her rush to grab the very thing she wanted most in life, she failed to consult wisdom. Not once did she question any of what Patrick Hart had said to her. Had she done so, Ashela might have remembered two truisms her grandmother had been fond of saying: First, *Even the devil, himself, quoted scriptures from the bible*, and secondly, *If something sounds too good to be true, it usually is.*

Chapter Eight

shela circled the upper floor of Club Excalibur looking down at all of the dancers on the lower level. Huge neon strobe lights swirled furiously bathing everyone in flashes of curious colors. House music blared at deafening decibels as Ashela's body swayed rhythmically to the beat of Junior's, "Mama Used to Say" mixed with Imagination's, "Just An Illusion." As she stood gazing down at all of the people, Ashela felt part of the crowd. Being among them was what she craved most. She could claim anonymity with so many others around her. It also allowed her to forget at least temporarily, that she was alone in the world.

She was leaning over the guard rail when a hand suddenly clamped onto her shoulder. "Ashela, I thought it was you! What's up girl?"

Ashela turned to find Stephanie wearing a short white wig, and dressed in a tight, black leather pantsuit that clung to her body like a glove. It was sleeveless and had a "V" neckline that extended all they way down to her navel. Circular patterns were cut out along the sides of the legs revealing taut flesh underneath.

"Wow!" was all Ashela could manage. Stephanie's outfit was daring to say the least, and Ashela knew that she would never have had the courage to wear it herself. Dressed as she was in her normal attire of baggy jeans and oversized sweat shirt, there was nothing about *her* garb that would draw anyone's attention.

"It's my work outfit, like it? How long have you been here?" Stephanie had to shout to be heard above the thunderous music.

"For a couple of hours." Ashela shouted her reply and wondered what kind of job Stephanie held that would allow her to wear such attire.

"I'm headed to Sweet Georgia Brown's. Wanna come check it out?"

Ashela had never heard of it. She shook her head, saying, "Maybe some other time. I don't have enough money with me to pay another cover charge." All of the clubs charged something to get in.

"Don't worry about the cover charge. I know the people there so you won't have to pay. You up for it?"

Since it would be free, Ashela agreed to go. They stepped outside and were greeted by catcalls and hoots from some of the males waiting to get in. Ashela was embarrassed by the onslaught of attention but Stephanie ignored them as she walked into the street to hail a taxi. When one screeched to a halt in front of her, she opened the door to climb in. She saw Ashela lagging behind indecisively and called out impatiently, "Come on!"

Rolling her eyes upward, as if to question what she was getting herself into, Ashela dashed for the taxi. She leaned back against the seat staring as Stephanie gave the driver their destination. With her heavy layer of makeup, Ashela found it hard to believe that this was the same girl she had shrugged off two weeks ago at the Blue Note. That girl had been makeup free, while the one before her now was a painted party animal.

Stephanie caught Ashela's look of astonishment. "Don't let the makeup fool you, Ashela. This is just my working face. You'll see what I mean when we get to the club."

Ashela saw exactly what Stephanie meant as Sweet Georgia Brown's turned out to be an Exotic Dance club. She stuck to Stephanie like glue as they walked inside and headed toward the back. They reached an entrance that was guarded by a huge, bald, strapping Black man. "How they hangin' tonight, George?" Stephanie asked, referring to the crowd of male patrons.

"Wild and heavy. Knock 'em dead and you'll make out like a bandit." Shouts and rowdy laughter filtered through to their area.

They stepped into a dressing room filled with women in various stages of dress. Some wore outrageous outfits that left nothing hidden, others were nude. Most of the women were seated at booths applying makeup to unusual parts of their bodies. Laughter and light banter filled the room.

"Over here," Stephanie called out.

Ashela realized she had been gawking when she looked up to find her friend on the other side of the room.

As she took a seat at Stephanie's booth, Ashela wanted to appear as though what she was seeing wasn't new to her, but she couldn't stop herself from gaping at the women. Some were white, most were Black, and all were well-proportioned. Though Stephanie was chattering away non-stop, Ashela hardly heard a word she was saying. She was too busy taking in her surroundings.

". . . know it's your first time. But the shock wears off. Trust me, you can make a lot of money stripping. Even more if someone requests a lap dance, a table dance, or a private audience . . ."

Ashela turned back to find Stephanie lacing up a pair of spiked ankle boots. She'd ditched the leather pantsuit for a dark blue micro-mini skirt. A sailor's cap and a jacket that was much longer than the skirt, completed her outfit.

George peeped his head inside and said, "You're up next, Steph! Let's go, babe!"

Stephanie's bored demeanor swiftly changed to one of excitement as she took a final look in the mirror. Hurriedly, she said, "I asked Keena to take you up to the

DJ's booth. Nobody'll bother you and you'll get a good view of everything." And then she was gone.

Ashela felt awkward and out of place as she followed Keena up to the next level. The DJ's booth was large enough to accommodate two people plus all of his records and equipment.

She watched as he flipped through dozens of LPs before queuing up "Maneater," by Hall and Oates. As the beat of the song ripped through the club, one had the impression that something wild was about to happen. Not knowing what to expect, Ashela braced herself. No sooner had she done so when Stephanie burst from behind curtains to a storm of encouraging whistles. Her confident strut resembled a tiger suddenly loosed from its cage. *No wonder she hadn't been moved by all the catcalls back at Club Excalibur,* Ashela thought, while struggling to close her mouth.

Stephanie was in total control as she dominated the stage. In a series of quick, fluid movements she teasingly divested herself of her cap and jacket. With provocative, suggestive gestures, she stirred the audience of mostly men into a frenzy before stripping down to a red string bikini that left little to the imagination. Her movements were sensuous as she slid to the floor and crawled down the runway on her hands and knees, stopping long enough only to extract money from willing patrons.

Stephanie reached for a silver pole that extended from floor to ceiling and clung to it like a drowning man latching on to a lifesaver. But the pole became her tool as she used it to gyrate her body spasmodically while sliding up and down. The men teetered on the edges of their seats as she crawled to every one of them who held money in outstretched hands. Each waived his money frantically, signaling for her to come claim it. Every man who tipped her received a few seconds of her personal attention: Cupped breasts thrust in his face or an equally tantalizing view of some other luscious part of her body. In return, the men lavished her with unrestrained lust.

As the song ended, Stephanie scooped up all the loose money thrown at her and pranced off of the stage.

For the first time in what seemed like several minutes, Ashela released her breath. No sooner had she regained her composure, though, when the next dancer vaulted onto the stage.

Though each woman had a different routine, ultimately, the ending scene was the same—they left the stage naked or semi-naked with fists full of dollars.

It was well into the wee hours of the morning before the patrons started winding their way out of the club. When Stephanie finally came to the DJ's booth to reclaim Ashela, she found her asleep in the corner. They left the club together, both of them tired in their own way. Stephanie suggested they stop to get something to eat and on impulse, Ashela invited her back to her place.

Stephanie walked through each room, somewhat awed by the fact that the entire apartment belonged to Ashela and that she lived alone. She specifically loved the mauve, burgundy, and peach colors that Ashela was using to decorate. They carried their Chinese food inside the living room and spread out on the carpeted floor. Between bites, they shared their personal stories of how they came to New York.

Stephanie was a mulatto. She was nineteen and had lived in New York for three years. She'd run away from her father's farm in Lewistown, Montana because he had been physically abusing her for years. Her mother was of African American descent. She had abandoned them when Stephanie was only five years old. In their small community, her father had been ostracized for marrying a Black woman to begin with. And, when she deserted both he and their child, he became a laughingstock among his peers and never fully recovered from their conjecture. With suppressed rage, he started lashing out at Stephanie as she grew older—beating her without provocation.

As her youthful body began to develop, his censure of her took on a different tone as he became aware of her in a different light. He appraised her budding breasts and curves much the same way he would a steer he was about to purchase. Stephanie could feel his eyes boring into her as he monitored her every move. At night, he would appear in the doorway of her bedroom, staring, watching her intently, as if biding his time. Though young, Stephanie was no fool as she feigned sleep each night. She knew her father wanted to do the same thing to her that the barnyard animals did to each other. She was eleven the first time he forced himself onto her. Afterwards, he began to treat her as if she were mere chattel rather than his daughter. He was cruel, using her nightly, never bothering to take precautionary measures. He became insanely jealous of her time as he sought to shape her life around his, forcing her into the position his wife had abdicated.

Stephanie bore the brunt of his punishing assaults, which worsened as she matured, until she felt she would snap. The beatings she could endure, but the forced sexual attacks—his using her as his personal receptacle—chipped away at her already eroded self esteem. Stephanie knew that if things continued, she would most likely kill herself.

She had lived in fear of her father all of her life and believed him when he threatened to "hurt her real bad" if she ever tried to leave him. But faced with the prospect of spending the rest of her life tied to him, and the horrible thought of becoming impregnated, she found the courage one night to run away while he lay in a drunken stupor from one of his many binges.

She hitched a ride with a white truck driver who listened to her fabricated story of "turning eighteen and wanting to explore the world" with feigned interest. His only requirement for giving her a lift was that she "take care of him" at intervals along the way to their destination, which happened to be New York City. Stephanie had agreed out of desperation, but it seemed to her that the man pulled over every hour on the hour. To his credit, he was patient and gentle with her and after their third or fourth stop, Stephanie grew accustomed to his heavy grunts as he relieved himself inside her.

When they arrived in New York two days later, she was stiff and sore, but at least she was alive and free. The truck driver tried to talk her into continuing on with him to Toronto, Canada. Stephanie declined. She was anxious to do something else with her life—something that didn't require her to be a conduit for men and their lust. Disappointed, he gave her three hundred dollars and told her to take care of herself.

With no place to go and certainly no "street smarts," Stephanie walked the streets for weeks afterwards. Eventually, her money ran out and she was forced, once again, to prostitute herself in order to survive. She consoled herself with the belief that what she was doing was temporary, just for a season until she made enough money to establish herself.

Whenever she "went out," money came quickly because her youth and good looks drew men by the dozens. She discovered that the younger she made herself look, the more she tended to draw white men as customers, and they were the ones who gave the bigger tips. Because she didn't want to be "tagged" by any of the cops or local pimps, Stephanie never stayed in any one spot for more than a couple of hours. Nevertheless, it didn't take her long to become acquainted with her peers or to discern that the life of a street-walking prostitute was harsh and unforgiving. What frightened her more than the every day violence that she witnessed, was that all the girls she knew to be her age looked twice as old, the bloom of their youth washed away in a cesspool of debauchery.

If asked, Stephanie would have said her body was her best asset—she had curves in all the right places. The trick for her was to make use of it wisely (and on her own terms) by not ending up like the others she'd come to know. It was an older, seasoned prostitute who suggested she try getting a job at a strip joint. The more Stephanie thought about it, the more she liked the idea. She had nothing to lose and such a job would surely beat living the life of a prostitute.

Stephanie decided to case all the strip joints on 42nd Street. She did so for days before settling on Sweet Georgia Brown's. With an all or nothing attitude, she sneaked inside to ask about a job and was promptly thrown out. But already, she'd glimpsed the women on stage and knew that, if given the chance, she could be just as good a dancer as they. For the next several weeks, Stephanie showed up like clockwork and hounded the man known only as "Krause" for a job. She was never obnoxious when she badgered him, just persistent beyond a fault. That same persistence was what caused Krause to finally give in and risk hiring her despite her being legally under-age. It was a decision he never came to regret, as she later became his best and most dependable dancer. That was two and a half years ago, and she'd been dancing ever since.

On a good week, Stephanie made as much as two thousand dollars in tips. Her needs were few, and the only thing that she enjoyed spending money on was clothing. So she saved the bulk of her money, convinced that one day she would need it. She had a room at a boarding house where the rent was cheap, though the place was none too clean. But at least it was hers.

From time to time, Stephanie thought about going back to school to get her G.E.D. As a child, she had enjoyed school and had always loved to read. Back then, books had been her only form of escape. But each time the thought of going to school crossed her mind, she'd talk herself out of it by convincing herself that the only thing she was really any good at was dancing. That and singing. She'd always loved to sing. People told her she had a sultry voice and that she should try to do something with it. Their words fueled her desire to want to someday become a famous singer. It was her only goal in life.

Ashela listened to Stephanie's story in awe and with compassion. Her own life suddenly didn't seem nearly as problematic. Nevertheless, she spoke of how painful and unpleasant it had been growing up amidst all the whispers and knowing looks from people because she was the illegitimate daughter of the town's most prominent preacher. Because her mother had died of a drug overdose, the town folks automatically assumed that she would amount to nothing. Though they thought failure was her destiny, Ashela was powerfully determined to prove them all wrong. She'd heard it said that success was the best revenge and she intended to let her own success avenge her.

The two girls openly fantasized about what their lives would be like when they became famous singers. They also talked honestly about not wanting to be involved romantically with anyone, albeit for different reasons.

A pact was sealed between them as they consoled each other with the knowledge that most superstars had, themselves, started out as nobodies. They both fell asleep on the floor dreaming about the time when they, too, would become major recording artists.

Just before she drifted off to sleep, Ashela remembered a particular saying she'd heard often back in Durham, North Carolina. The poignant phrase was aptly fitting for such a time as this: *Despise not small beginnings.*

Chapter Nine

ver the next several months, the late nights began to catch up with Ashela. Where before she'd get home at around 1:00 a.m., she still

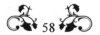

managed to get to work by nine. But ever since she'd started hanging out with Stephanie until after four in the morning, she found it increasingly difficult to get to work on time. Within the span of two week's time, she received three warning notices for tardiness. A fifth infraction was grounds for termination. The following Friday morning, when she picked up her paycheck, her supervisor terminated her.

Ashela was dejected over the loss of her job. She'd never before been fired. It made her feel irresponsible as well as immature. But along with the dejection came another feeling: A curious sense of relief that signaled it was time for her to do something else. It was nearly noon as she trudged home from work. She was filled with a restlessness, a need to make something positive happen in her life to combat the feelings being fired aroused. She dug out Patrick Hart's business card and dialed his number. As expected, she got his recorder.

"Hi, Mr. Hart. It's Ashela Jordan. I was calling to . . ."

The phone was picked up in the middle of her sentence. "Hart speaking."

He sounded groggy to Ashela, as if he'd just awakened. "Hi. I hope I didn't disturb you?" she asked hesitantly.

"No. I'm glad you called. As a matter of fact, I was going to call you soon anyway."

Adrenaline shot through her body. "Really?" she asked excitedly.

"Yes. I'm finishing up with a group of three young ladies who I was able to get a lucrative record deal with a major label. You'll soon be hearing about Sweet Sensation as they launch their new release. I wanted to give you a heads up that I'll be ready for you in a couple of weeks. Are you free to meet with me anytime before then?"

Ashela paced in circles to keep from shouting out loud. *Her dreams were finally about to come true!* "Of course I'm free. When would you like to meet?" She could hear him turning pages and she assumed he was thumbing through his planner.

"You're only available in the evenings, correct?"

"I'm not working at the Exchange anymore, so whenever's convenient with you is fine by me."

"It looks like I'm booked solid for the next couple of weeks. Tell you what, let's meet Monday, the fifth. That's a little over two weeks from now. We'll meet at A&M Studios on Horace Harding Expressway in Queens. How does 10:30 a.m. sound?"

"Fantastic. I'll see you there." When Ashela finally hung up the phone, she was much too hyper to stay inside her apartment. Needing to share her good news with someone else, she grabbed a jacket and swept out of the apartment in search of Stephanie.

Though Stephanie didn't have a phone, Ashela knew she stood a pretty good chance of catching her at her place on East 123rd in Harlem. Her nose wrinkled in distaste when she finally reached the tenement where her friend lived. Ashela didn't care how cheap the rent was, she could never see herself living in such a dump. The four-storied building was an eyesore. The owner was obviously a slumlord who did not believe in putting money back into the property, preferring to let it go seedy. A drunken man reeking of urine and stale liquor lay sprawled in the doorway. Ashela stepped over him and sprinted up to the fourth floor where Stephanie's room was located.

There were eight rooms to a floor and the traffic coming in and out of the building was heavy. Each floor was a hub of activity. Loud noises spilled from many of the rooms, filling the hallway with an assortment of sounds. Above the fray, Ashela heard music coming from inside Stephanie's room as she knocked hard on her door.

"It's me, Steph." Ashela called. She waited patiently while Stephanie unlocked the numerous locks she had securing her door.

"Well, well, well, for you to come to my humble digs, you must have either really good news or really bad. What's up?" She closed the door behind Ashela and relocked it.

Stephanie's "room" was only slightly larger than Ashela's bedroom in the Village. It served as her living room, dining room, and bedroom all wrapped in one. It had a small bathroom but no kitchen and was sparsely furnished with a bed, a dresser, a chair, and a small night stand with an even smaller television and radio sitting on its top. True to her word, Stephanie was a clothes horse and every available square inch of space was covered with clothing, including the walls.

Ashela cleared a space and took a seat in the chair as Stephanie waited to hear her story. "Well, I've got a little bit of both. Which one shall I tell you about first, good news or bad news?"

"Let's hear the bad news," Stephanie said as she yawned and stretched.

"Okay, the bad news is I got canned today. My supe gave me the boot. He said my tardiness couldn't be tolerated because it would send a negative message to the other runners. At first I felt like crap, Steph, but when I got home I called Patrick Hart. You remember the man we met at the Blue Note?" Excitement crept into Ashela's voice. "He'll be ready to work with me in two weeks. He just got another group, called Sweet Sensation, a recording contract and he's gonna do the same for me. Can you believe it?"

Stephanie lay on her side with her elbow bent and her arm propped on her hand. Ashela's enthusiasm was infectious and Stephanie sat straight up. "That *is* good news, Ashela. It looks like you're on your way, girl." Stephanie paused as she basked in her friend's good fortune. A thought occurred to her. "You're sure the guy is on the up-and-up though, right? I mean, didn't you say there was something about him that you couldn't put your finger on?"

"Yeah, at first there was. But since I've had the chance to sit down and talk with him and get to know him better, I must have been mistaken, Steph. Besides, he hasn't asked me for a dime. He's as eager to work with me as I am to work with him." Ashela hadn't yet gotten around to calling the numbers he had given her as references, but a part of her felt she didn't really need to because he had come across so convincingly as someone whom she could trust.

"Well, you seem pretty excited about it all so I'm sure everything'll work out. Maybe after he finishes working with you, you can put in a good word for me?"

"Of course. Besides, which ever one of us makes it first, we've already agreed to help the other, remember?"

Stephanie nodded and gave a slight smile. She had listened to Ashela sing on several occasions and felt that between the two of them, Ashela would be the one to make it. And when it happened, for some reason, Stephanie felt as though Ashela would soon forget her. The thought was almost painful because during the course of time, she had come to view her as a surrogate sister. To shake off the twinge of anxiety she felt, she said with a bit of humor, "Hey, I'm about to go to the dance studio. And since you're jobless and everything now, wanna come?"

"Sure. Can I use one of your leotards?" Stephanie rifled through her clothes, found one and tossed it to her. They dressed and headed out the door.

Sometime during her nightly excursions to Sweet Georgia Browns, a curious seed was sown for Ashela. She had become intrigued with the whole concept of stripping and nightclub dancing. She learned from watching that it entailed more than just removing one's clothes. But what struck her most was the women themselves. They ranged in age from 19 to 35. The oldest was a single mother who had been struggling to make ends meet. Some were college students who needed the extra cash. Others were ex-prostitutes who found the lifestyle much safer than the streets. They all were in excellent shape.

As Ashela watched them, she depicted an artfulness to the way they danced. They took considerable time to embellish and practice their steps.

Three times per week, Stephanie met with some of them at a dance studio in Harlem. They applied many of the moves they learned there to their nightly routines. The dance class also kept them limber and gave them an edge on the competition. All of them plied their trade with an artful eye towards seduction, but it was the combination of their creative movements that set them above strippers in other clubs.

Stephanie had once tried to explain why she enjoyed what she did. "There are sexual nuances to be taken into consideration, Ashela. You can't just hop on stage, strip, and hurry off. The men want and expect much more than that. They come here because they crave fantasy and they want to feel as if you're giving them a special treat meant only for them. But I'll tell you what turns me on. It's the *power* I hold over the men as I dance before them. It's like I have every one of them eating out of my hand. When I'm on that stage, I know they want me because I see it in their eyes. And the real high comes from knowing that no matter how much they want me, they can't have me. They can look, but they'll never be able to touch. Their weakness, Ashela, makes me feel empowered."

Ashela listened to Stephanie talk and wondered if she was venting some of her anger towards her father onto the men who came to watch her at night. But it was a thought she never voiced.

Ashela took in every step they made. She told herself that though she would never have the guts to get out on stage like Stephanie, it wouldn't hurt to know and be able to perform all their moves. During the next several weeks, she found herself practicing at home in front of her floor-length mirror. She'd twirl and gyrate her body in much the same ways she saw the other dancers doing.

One afternoon, Ashela eyed her nakedness appraisingly in the mirror. She knew Stephanie was right when she kept telling her, "You could be even more attractive if you wore your hair down sometimes instead of always pulling it into a pony tail. And why not ditch the baggy clothes? Do you have to dress like a boy *all* the time?" Stephanie ragged her constantly about hiding her curvaceous body beneath such dowdy clothes.

Since coming to New York, Ashela had totally changed her look, preferring baggy jeans and sweat shirts to the colorful things Kyliah had once given her. Besides, Ashela knew that by dressing the way she did, she drew less attention from others. It was exactly as she wanted it.

But as she surveyed her burgeoning breasts and sweltering hips, suddenly she longed to have a man look upon her in the same manner she saw them do to the women on stage. She cupped her ripe breasts and immediately the aureoles tightened as the nipples stood at attention. Her eyes closed as a wealth of sensations flooded her body settling in the pit of her stomach. Her right hand fluttered over her womanly contours and slid downward until it found the satiny thatch that guarded the entranceway of her being. When her finger slid past the tender lips, a sigh of pleasure almost slipped from her parted lips. She wondered what might it have felt like to let Parris have his way . . .

The mood was blown as Ashela's eyes immediately flew open at the mere thought of the one person she'd sought most to block from her mind. She didn't know what had come over her to spark such a hunger in her body. She certainly hadn't intended to think *him* up—and why fantasize about him of all people? Angry with herself because of her mental lapse, she spun away from the mirror to dress in another pair of her baggy jeans. She threw on an oversized sweatshirt and headed over to the dance studio to meet up with the girls.

Chapter Ten

shela arrived at A&M Studios precisely at 10:30 a.m. Theirs was a top-flight recording facility. Expensive in both its build and fees charged, it catered mostly to corporate clients and artists who were under contract with many of the major labels.

"Good morning. May I help you?" asked a woman from behind a granite curvature desk.

"Yes. I'm supposed to meet Mr. Patrick Hart."

The receptionist typed his name into her computer. "H-A-R-T? I'm sorry, I don't show anyone listed by that name. What company is he with? Or is he part of a band that's scheduled to record today?"

Ashela stood with a blank look on her face. She was glad she didn't have to try to answer either question as Patrick came striding into the building to join her at the desk.

"How are you today?" he asked the woman. "We're here for the Sony recording session." He handed her an identification card along with what looked like some kind of invitation.

The woman scanned them and passed both pieces back to him. "Thank you Mr. Butler. It's on the seventh floor." She threw Ashela a dirty look that implied she was an idiot for giving her the wrong name to look up.

Patrick grasped Ashela's elbow and led her toward the bank of elevators.

"Mr. Butler?" she asked inquiringly, wondering if he was using an alias.

"A friend of mine invited me to a private recording, one that's invitation only. Otherwise, we wouldn't have been given access to the session."

The elevator doors opened and they stepped inside. "Have you ever been to a recording session?" he asked conversationally, as if to change the subject.

"Nope." Ashela shook her head.

"Well then let me warn you, the initial part of it is chaotic because of all the people trying to set up all the different equipment. The sessions are broken into three segments: The set-up phase, the actual recording session, and then the mixing stage. The session we're about to sit in on will probably get underway in another fifteen minutes or so, assuming that the studio rats have had sufficient time to set up."

"What's a studio rat?" Ashela asked, eager to learn all that she could.

"The engineers and their assistants. They're the people who plug in and test all of the different microphones. They set sound levels on the mixing boards, load tape into the recorder, and set parameters for the many sound effects. Although we call them 'studio rats,' it's not meant condescendingly. What they do is invaluable because a recording session can't properly take place without them."

The room they entered was filled with people and diverse activity. Ashela noted that it was divided into three sections. The control room, which housed the masses of expensive equipment for the actual recording, was separated by a glass partition. Another section of the room served as the recording room, where the band would record their tracks. And about ten feet behind this area was a small section for the studio staff and a few visitors.

Introductions were skipped as the room's occupants were all too busy to stop what they were doing. Patrick ushered Ashela to a seat in a corner, where she watched the procession in fascination.

She had no idea who the group was that would be recording, but she could tell from the layout of the instruments that it was a five-piece band. She saw men tuning-up on drums, keyboards, bass, guitars and a sax, while two women harmonized into microphones.

The energy engulfing the room had her on edge. It was almost palpable as the studio staff, the engineers, and all of the musicians worked hastily to get everything in working order. She was busy taking it all in when the door opened and three additional people entered the room. Ashela's eyes nearly bucked out of her head when she recognized R&B songstress Chaka Kahn. The famed singer was all hugs and smiles as she embraced several people, including Patrick Hart. There was laughter before she was ushered into the recording room. From then on, the atmosphere was one of pure intensity as the session got underway.

As they were leaving the building, Hart said to her, "That will be you someday, Ashela. The sooner we get started, the better."

He was treating her to lunch at Tony Romas on Queens Boulevard. Since Ashela was still in the twilight zone trying to relive every moment of the recording session, he was the one to do all of the talking.

"The first thing I have planned for you, Ashela, is singing lessons. I know you took lessons when you were in Durham, but this will be different. The man I want you to work with is the absolute best. All the stars vie to work with him, but he's very selective. You've heard of Kathleen Battle, the famous opera singer? Even she was a benefactor of his tutelage." Patrick took a long sip of his gin and tonic as soon as the waiter set his drink on the table.

"It'll be difficult to get Lehmann to fit you in on such short notice. But he owes me one, so it shouldn't be too much of a problem. I realize that there are other instructors that we could work with, but they're not what I'm looking for. I've got a hunch about you, Ashela. You're going to soar right to the top. That's why Lehmann is the only one to instruct you. Trust me on this. My instincts are never wrong." He lifted his glass as if to toast her before taking another long gulp. The expression on his face remained serious.

"I want you tutored by the best, Ashela. As such, you'll find no one better than Leo Lehmann. So assuming I can get him to fit you in, you'll be able to say you studied under one of the best voice specialists of our time. Very few can boast of that. There's just one thing, though. His time is not free. His instructionals cost three thousand dollars." Without giving her a chance to respond, he continued. "I know that sounds like a lot of money. But when you consider what you'll be getting in return, three grand is but a drop in the bucket. I'm willing to put the money on the table if you don't have it, Ashela. But as I told you in the beginning, how much money, time, and effort a person is willing to invest in themselves proves to me how serious they are about their career and their future. Now," he seemed to be issuing her a personal challenge that hinged on the future of their relationship, "Can you afford it?"

Ashela stared at him across the table, nibbling nervously at her lower lip. She hadn't planned on giving him any money, but on the other hand, she wanted desperately to succeed. She thought it over for a split second before finally nodding her head in agreement. Once again, her common sense was over ruled by her desire and need for instant gratification.

Patrick Hart had done his homework efficiently. He'd dug into Ashela's background thoroughly, so he knew that she could well afford three grand. Breathing an obvious sigh of relief, he lifted his finger to signal for another gin and tonic. He needed that money. As it was, he was chasing Peter to pay Paul. Besides, Ashela need never know that Lehmann's classes were actually free.

***

Leo Lehmann taught Voice Theory 101 out of New York University on Tuesdays and Thursdays from 1:00 - 4:00 p.m. In his late sixties, he possessed a mane of white hair and thick, white, bushy eyebrows. He looked to Ashela like the absent-minded professor.

What surprised her most was her discovery that he was such a boring, *un*charismatic instructor. She couldn't believe he was the same man Patrick Hart had spoken about with such reverent enthusiasm. Ashela found his lectures even more tedious because most of what he taught, she already knew or either the information didn't apply to her areas of specialty, in particular, jazz and R&B. It certainly didn't help matters much when she would glance around only to find the rest of her classmates sound asleep.

Six weeks into the class, Ashela had had enough of Lehmann's tiresome lectures on vocal gymnastics and proper breathing techniques. Apparently these were the sentiments shared by ten other students who'd already dropped out, leaving behind just herself and two others.

The following week, instead of going to class, Ashela joined Stephanie and the girls at the dance studio. She found herself more excited about dancing with them than she was about the music lessons for which she had so unwisely paid three grand. She was angry at Patrick Hart and she intended to express her dissatisfaction the next time she saw or heard from him.

Ashela didn't know who among them first suggested it, but someone said, "Girl, as much as you practice with us, you might as well start dancin' at Sweet Georgia Brown's."

They were inside the locker room of the dance studio getting dressed to leave.

Another girl said, "You know she's right, Ashela. You've got the body for it, plus you know all the moves. What *are* you waiting for?" Everyone seemed to expect a reply. All except Stephanie, who had remained oddly quiet.

"She's chicken, that's why."

"Yeah, she thinks she's too good for it."

"All right, hold it. If I was as uppity as you all are trying to make me out to be, I wouldn't be hanging out with you in the first place." She turned to one of the girls who had spoken and asked, "How do you know whether or not I'm scared? Besides, if I really wanted to, I'd do it." Ashela slid into her blue jeans, irritated with the sudden turn of the conversation.

"Well then, that settles it," Stephanie said, bringing the subject to an end. "Whenever she's ready, we'll run it by Krause. If he gives it a go, Ash, you're on."

Ashela had met Jerrie Krause only once. He was a short, pudgy, fat little man with a triple chin and beady little eyes. He certainly didn't appear trustworthy to her, but the other dancers seemed to think he was okay.

That evening at the club, Ashela found herself scrutinizing the show more closely than usual. She was critical of each dancer, observing flaws in their routines almost as if she were making a mental note to herself about what steps worked and which ones didn't. She watched the men as well, noticing what tended to excite them and what moves elicited the least response.

By the end of the evening, Ashela's mind was made up—she was confident that she could give it a shot. She figured the biggest obstacle she would have to overcome was her own inhibitions. She knew she'd find it disconcerting at first, but if the others could overcome their diffidence, then so could she.

"You're way too tense, Ashela. Loosen up some. This is supposed to be fun, remember? If it helps any, think of it like this: You're not showing these guys anything they haven't seen before, you're just packaging yourself in a way that distinguishes you from your competitors. You've heard of the old saying, 'it's not what you have, it's how you use it?' Well, it's the same principle here. Your delivery, how you strut your stuff, is what counts most."

Inwardly, Stephanie was disappointed that her attempts to dissuade Ashela from dancing had been unsuccessful. It seemed the more she'd tried to talk her out of it, the more determined Ashela had become. Stephanie had finally given up and agreed to meet her at the dance studio to give her some helpful tips. "A private tutorial," as she called it.

Since it was just the two of them, Ashela felt at liberty to screw up as much as she needed to in order to get her routine right. She still wasn't one hundred percent clear about why Stephanie hadn't wanted her to join her on the stage. While she did know it had nothing to do with competition, try as she might, Ashela could not get Stephanie to reveal her reasonings. She was left to assume that Stephanie had her own pretexts for helping her in spite of her personal misgivings.

Ashela lowered herself onto the hardwood floor, angling her legs into a split. "You know Steph, the main reason I want to do this is because I've never done anything daring in my entire life." She lowered her torso forward until her forehead touched the floor. "But can I tell you what my worst fear is?"

"Uh huh," Stephanie said as she squatted on the floor with her back against the wall.

"I don't want others to know that I'm a virgin."

For a moment, Stephanie stared past Ashela as if she were looking at a distant object. When she finally spoke, Ashela couldn't tell if her tone was more wistful or sad. "Ash, I think it's great that you still have the option to choose who you want your first time to be with. I never had that luxury." Stephanie didn't want to dwell on the issue or else the ugly weights of her past would easily envelop her. She shook off the unwarranted memories, and said, "Besides, if you move your body like you've been doing, trust me, no one will suspect. The key is to block everything out. Everything except the desire to entice each man out of every dime he has. When you go out there, Ash, just pretend that each man there is that same jerk who dumped you back in North Carolina." Stephanie saw Ashela wince. "Pretend you're making every one of them pay by showing them what they're missing out on."

"You want to implant it in their minds that they've never had good pussy until they've had yours." Stephanie laughed at the grimace on Ashela's face. She held up her hand and said, "I know it sounds crude and raunchy, Ashela. But if you're gonna do this, you've got to be prepared. If you're to be successful, you've got to ask yourself, 'why are these men here in the first place?' You've noticed that the majority of the club's patrons are white, right? Well, most of them come because, in the confined atmosphere of the club, it's okay to openly lust for a Black woman. Some of them are just looking for something new and daring. Others are there simply because they need a break from their girlfriends or wives. I'm not saying you need to be a psychologist, but if you understand what motivates the men, you can use that knowledge to get them to dig even deeper into their pockets. It is, after all, a business, Ashela. Never forget that. If you don't remember anything else I've told you, remember to keep it strictly business. Never, ever, lct your emotions get tied up into what you're doing. It's only an act and that's what the men pay to see."

Ashela had risen to her knees. "I'll remember. But to tell you the truth, Steph, I just want the men to look at me the same way they do you and all the other dancers. I want to know what it feels like to be *desired*."

Stephanie stared at Ashela, observing objectively the shapeliness of her body. She didn't know why, but a part of her was saddened at the prospect of the changes she knew her friend was sure to undergo. She felt Ashela had no idea of the kind of world she was about to enter. On the outside, stripping may have appeared glamorous, but it wasn't all it was cracked up to be. It was one thing to observe them dancing on stage from afar, but to be an actual strip-tease dancer required one to deaden one's self to many factors. Stephanie knew this first hand.

To herself, she could admit that it was Ashela's honesty, her "I don't want to be hurt so I won't let you get close to me" attitude, and her overall *innocence* that had drawn her to her in the first place. Stephanie viewed her friend as the kind of person she, herself, might have been had her life been different. It wasn't that Stephanie resented the extra competition that she would get from Ashela. It was just that her greatest fear was that Ashela would change so drastically, that she would no longer resemble the person Stephanie had originally come to know.

***

A full two minutes had passed since the last dancer exited the stage. The men inside Sweet Georgia Brown's were growing increasingly restless as they waited impatiently for the next one. Suddenly, the club was doused with blue neon lights. Pale lighting bathed the entire place just as the beginning beats of a song familiar to every patron thumped through the air.

> *Tell us what you're gonna do tonight, mama*
> *There must be someplace you can go*
> *In the middle of the tall drinks and the drama,*
> *there must be someone you know . . .*

As the Eagles' hit, "Those Shoes," reverberated throughout the club, Ashela stepped from behind the velvet curtains. Dressed in a midnight blue ankle-length velvet cape, the loose folds of the garment swirled around her as she stalked the length of the stage. Her dark blue stiletto-heeled shoes shone underneath the glare of the neon lights. With her hair piled neatly on top of her head and a *faux* diamond necklace glistening at her throat, Ashela was the epitome of elegance. She gave the men the impression that they were about to receive a sophisticated treat, and she could sense them straining in their seats in anticipation.

She reached the end of the walkway and twirled, causing the cape to billow around her. A fleeting glint of flesh caused the shouts and whistles to commence. Unbuttoning the clasp that held the fabric together, she allowed it to fall to the floor. When the woman beneath it was finally revealed, the room became fraught with animal sexuality as the men took in the full display of her body. The briefest of a royal blue two-piece bikini barely encased the burgeoning flesh it was assigned to. Breasts that were heavy and firm begged to be released from their confinement. Her small waistline tapered into sweltering hips, and Ashela's strong, well-muscled thighs nearly caused an insurrection.

Oblivious to the mayhem, Ashela used her hands as sensuous tools, sliding them down the full length of her body, outlining her every curve. She squatted low and spread her knees wide, giving all a glimpse of sleek upper inner thighs. Snapping her knees shut with her hands, she drew herself upright while cupping her breasts—squeezing them to emphasize their thickness. Just as quickly, she twisted around and thrust out her rear, turning her torso slightly to stare over her shoulder. Slowly, Ashela bent low at the waist, extending her buttocks even further.

One moment, her hands were criss-crossed over her chest, in the next, she used them to palm the cheeks of her behind, slapping her left cheek loudly for the ensuing sound effect. The reddish-hued hand print left on her buttock was clearly discernible.

With her legs spread wide and her backside to the audience, Ashela was a stunning sight. Her bikini brief revealed more than it actually hid and the stiletto heels she wore defined her leg and calve muscles ostensibly. She placed her hands on the floor of the stage, resting her weight on the center of her palms. Bent low at the waist, her head was now perpendicular to the floor as she peered through the "V" of her legs.

Reaching up, Ashela removed the pins from her hair, shaking it out in its fullness. Where once she had been poised and elegant, now she was the seductive huntress stalking her prey. Seeing the men's barely restrained lust caused shivers to run up her own spine.

> *You just want someone to talk to*
> *They just wanna get their hands on you*
> *You get whatever you choose . . .*
> *Once you started wearin' those shoes.*

As the tempo of the song quickened, so did Ashela's movements as she sought to further arouse and incite the room full of men. Amidst the groans from her spectators, she plunged to the floor of the stage on her rear, hands behind her back and knees pressed to her chest. In sync with the music, she lifted her legs in the air one at a time, flexing them at the knee, before lowering them again provocatively, only to re-lift them and spread them into a wide "V."

Ashela raised herself to her knees. She stuck her thumbs inside the top of her bikini, pulling it downward. The men waited with baited breath for her to remove it completely. She started gyrating her hips, sliding her hands deeper inside the material, pulling it lower and lower. Bending backward, she eased her hands upward cupping her breasts, teasing them as if she were about to release them. When the men began to shout their encouragement for her to take everything off, Ashela snapped open the bra's clasp, allowing its straps to fall at her sides. With her hands still covering her breasts, before she could reveal them to her chanting audience, the song came to an end. Ashela scooped up her cape, holding it close to her chest and traipsed off the stage.

Though the full nudity of her body had been kept from them, the men were delighted nevertheless. They cheered as she exited. Some of them even called for her return.

Tingling from exhilaration, Ashela stood just backstage panting, listening to the men shout their approval. She saw Stephanie walking toward her and said out of breath, "I did it Steph! How was I?"

But Stephanie deadpanned, "Never ask another dancer how you did, Ashela. Always let the amount of tips you collected speak for itself."

Only then did Ashela realize she'd failed to collect a single tip. As she walked back to the dressing room, she forgot about her performance. Her only thought was, *"When will I ever get it right?"*

Chapter Eleven

tephanie sat listening in disbelief. "Ashela, weren't you just telling me how angry you were with yourself for giving that buzzard your money in the first place? Now you're trying to justify giving him even *more* money? Girl, come on! Where's your common sense?"

"But, Steph, he's promised to give me all my money back in a couple of days. Besides, I didn't commit to anything. Where's the harm in listening to what he had to say?"

"It sounds like you've already made your mind up, Ash, so why'd you ask my opinion in the first place?" Stephanie pushed aside the remains of her pizza and she reached for her soda.

"Because I needed someone else to bounce my thoughts off of, that's why." Ashela conveniently neglected to tell Stephanie the amount of money involved.

They were seated inside Sbarro's eatery near Times Square. It was a Tuesday night, one of the three evenings they had off each week. Three months had passed since Ashela's debut dance fiasco. Since then, she'd perfected her routine and collecting her tips was the most important part of her act.

Ashela was dancing Wednesday through Saturday. Though the money was good (she earned upwards of eight hundred dollars a week) she couldn't say she derived as much enjoyment from it, or hustled as hard to collect as many tips, as did Stephanie and the others. What went unspoken for Ashela was the fact that every time she danced, another small part of her heart was sealed off from emotional contact. It culminated in her most obvious change, an attitudinal shift towards men. The original need she'd had to be desired had spawned into contempt as she realized that to the men who patronized the club, she was merely a symbol of lust, a female object in possession of a great body. Ashela had fulfilled her wish to dance and be desired, but in the aftermath, she was left sorely disappointed.

Maybe that explained why it was easy for her to muster a strong dislike for the men as she danced before them. She'd developed a clear understanding of what Stephanie had meant when she urged her to channel her feelings into making the customers "pay." And pay they did as she flaunted her wares, spurning them while wooing them, taunting them up close with the knowledge that they could look but not touch. They could dream of having her, but would never have their fantasies realized.

Her impersonation of a wild, passionate, sex-crazed animal was just an act she performed while on stage. Offstage, sex was the furthest thing from her mind.

But strip-dancing had exacted its own price as well. Ashela's heart had become increasingly hardened towards men, ultimately causing her to move further away from wanting to be involved in a relationship. She completely rejected everyone who expressed the desire to "get to know her better."

There were some things about her that hadn't changed, though. Her determination to find success in the music industry hadn't lessened, despite her disappointment over the Leo Lehmann affair. She had maintained her anger towards Patrick Hart right up until the moment he'd come back into her world promising to return her money and to redeem himself by working with her at his own expense. Hart claimed Lehmann had grown senile in the span of time since he'd last worked with him. He said it was the only reason he could think of for the drop off in Lehmann's skills as a dynamic maestro of music.

Hart wanted her to complete a demo tape, free of charge, for him to distribute to all the Artists & Repertoire reps at the major labels. Ashela forgave all when she learned that he'd booked several slots of time at A&M Studios for her to begin making her tape.

He instructed her to sing three of her favorite songs and he wanted her to play the piano on at least one of them. He told her, "The singer who has sufficient skill to play a variety of instruments, Ashela, will be in great demand as a soloist. The fact that you play so beautifully will only add to your marketability."

Once they were set up to record, Ashela warmed up by running through all three of her songs. Though she was only practicing, after the last note had been sung, a quietness settled over the small studio. Both the producer and engineer had chills running up their spines. The purity and strength of her voice had mesmerized them. They were awed because they recognized they were working with someone of rare talent. Even Patrick, whose intentions were now shown to be less than honorable, couldn't help but think to himself, *"This girl really will make it someday."*

Three weeks passed as Ashela waited impatiently to receive her copy of the demo tape. When Patrick finally called her to come pick it up, she rushed over to meet him at A&M Studios. He was on the telephone when she got there, talking about "the deal of the century."

Ashela wasn't trying to eavesdrop but she couldn't help it when she heard him say, "Two hundred thousand is what he's planning to invest. Of course. Sam Ross is no fool. He knows the acquisition is worth millions. Okay, just let me know. We'll talk later because my protégé is here. The same one I was telling you about. She's got great potential and she's destined to go far. Yes, you must meet her. All right then, later."

Ashela tingled with pride when she heard his last remark.

"Sorry about that," Hart said as he hung up the phone. "I was finalizing an investment that will net me at least half a million dollars."

"That's great," Ashela replied. She was more interested in hearing her demo.

Patrick paused. "I suppose I can disclose it to you. I'm buying into a major record company. In a few days, the label will go public with its shares, and when it does, I plan to purchase twenty-five percent of its stock. Fortunately, not too many people know about it. I was just encouraging a friend of mine, who I know has fifteen to twenty grand to invest, to get in on the ground floor. You know, Ashela, it's a pity you don't have that kind of money. An opportunity like this not only would make you a quarter of a million dollars richer, but it would also make you co-owner of a major recording company." Patrick whistled sharply. "Imagine what a powerhouse you'd be."

He shook his head, saying, "Do you realize that in addition to becoming an instant superstar, you would also be part owner of your own label?" Sighing regretfully, Patrick said, "Oh well, that's enough wishful thinking. I called you down here to listen to your demo."

But Ashela's mind was still processing the information he had so cunningly supplied her. When she asked, "Can you tell me more about this investment?" Patrick honed in on his prey.

To participate, all Ashela had to do was invest $17,000. "Your investment's guaranteed and your money will be safe," he told her. But, if she planned to get involved, she would need to act quickly. There were already several music magnates attempting to gain exclusive control of the label. If she could somehow raise the money, her future would be guaranteed. She'd hold stock in the company and could, thus, direct her own music career. "Unlike most other artists who come into this industry grateful for whatever contract they get, you, Ashela, will control your own destiny."

Ashela left the studio some thirty minutes later in such heavy concentration over what she'd heard, that she completely forgot to ask for her personal copy of the demo tape.

***

As they got up to leave Sbarro's, Stephanie asked, "Wanna go check out a flick?"

"Not really, Steph. I've been working on this song that I'm writing. I think I'll just head back to my place."

"Okay. I'll come with you."

Ashela didn't mind, but her curiosity was aroused. Stephanie had been sticking to her like glue of late. It was almost as if she were squeamish about being alone. Ashela had noticed it a week prior. She could sense that her friend was jittery about something and wondered what was causing her to be on such edge.

She closed her apartment door behind them, but it was Stephanie who made sure it was locked. When Ashela came out of her bedroom, she saw Stephanie peeping surreptitiously through the living room curtains, as if she suspected someone was outside waiting for her.

Ashela said, "What gives, Steph? You've been acting so strange lately. Tell me, what's going on?"

Stephanie stepped away from the window. She shivered and clasped her arms around her chest. Though the temperature inside the apartment was perfectly normal, she felt cold. She came and took a seat on the sofa and momentarily stared into space. With her arms still laced around each other, she sat with her knees clasped together and her feet spaced far apart.

Ashela sat down next to her. "Steph?"

"Maybe I'm just paranoid, Ash. But lately I've been scared of everything, including my own shadow. Ever since . . ." Stephanie's voice trailed off as she nervously ran her hands down the sides of her face.

Stephanie looked pained as she continued. "Last weekend when I was on stage, I glanced out into the audience and thought I saw someone I knew. It scared me so bad, Ash, I lost my balance and fell to the floor. Oh, I played it off like it was part of my act, but nothing was the same afterwards. When I looked out into the audience seconds later, the man was gone. I know I probably imagined it, but still, I can't stop looking over my shoulder. I feel like someone's watching me all the time. I've never felt unsafe here in New York the way I do now, not even when I used to work the streets."

So hard were Stephanie's nails digging into the flesh of her arms, she was beginning to draw blood.

Ashela unwrapped them and clasped both their hands together. She didn't know why, but suddenly, she was afraid too. When she spoke, her voice held traces of nervousness. "You're frightening me, Steph. Who was the person you thought you recognized? Was it . . . Was it someone from Montana?" Ashela had the feeling that she already knew the answer.

"I could have sworn it was *him*, Ashela."

Stephanie's grip had become bone crushing and Ashela knew "him" was her father. She felt a flash of fear at the thought of him discovering Stephanie's whereabouts. If that were indeed the case, it would only lead to tragedy. Stephanie had reason to fear her father—he was sadistic, twisted and warped, and violent beyond measure. Though Ashela could empathize with some of what Stephanie was feeling, the brutal wounds that her father had inflicted upon her psyche seared far deeper than anything Charla had ever done to her.

"Maybe we should go to the police, Stephanie."

"And tell them what?" Stephanie laughed without humor, withdrawing her hands from Ashela's. "I could get a restraining order. But if it wasn't him that I saw, I'd just be stirring up a hornet's nest. It *is* possible that it wasn't him. Besides, how would he have found me?" At this point, Stephanie sounded more like she was trying to convince and reassure herself.

"I don't know, Steph, but either way you're staying here with me tonight. And you should have told me this sooner."

"I would have, but I kept hoping that what I was feeling would go away. You know, Ash, I know you've always wondered why I chose to live in the dump that I do. But I picked the place with a reason in mind. I feel safe when I'm in my own room. Nobody bothers me. Look at me." Stephanie examined the backs of her hands. "High yellow wench, is what *he* used to call me. I never did like my skin tone because of it. But now, I'm thankful that I look like I'm Black. As for him, that geezer's lily white and there's no way he's gonna come looking for me in Harlem, at least not without me hearing something about it."

Graphic clips of Stephanie's father molesting her when she'd been but a child superimposed themselves on Ashela's mind. The conjured images were too disturbing for her to ponder. Suddenly, Ashela didn't want to discuss anything more that had to do with Stephanie's father. In the days to come, she would make sure it was she who stuck to Stephanie like glue. She stood up and said, "Steph, I know just what you need." She went inside the bathroom and ran warm water in the tub. When she poured in a heaping of Vitabath gel, the aromatic scent filled the bathroom. She lit seven candles and placed them around the tub. Wanting to add mellow music to the setting, she brought in her portable cassette player and let Teena Marie whisper all about "Portuguese Love."

When Ashela ushered Stephanie into the bathroom, the delight on her friend's face was enough to let her know that she'd done the right thing by trying to alleviate her tension.

***

A week later, Ashela met with Patrick Hart at 110 William Street on the third floor. It was the first time she'd ever been to his office. He met her at the elevator and led her through a maze of empty desks and offices, until they finally reached his office. It was spacious and stately furnished with dark oak wood furniture. Ashela's eyes were drawn to a photo on the wall. A gorgeous silver-haired woman hugged two children. "Are those your children?" Ashela asked as she sat in one of the two chairs in front of his desk.

Patrick followed her gaze and glanced over his shoulder. "Uh, yes, that's my wife and my two children. As you can see, they favor her a lot more than they do me. Even in temperament, because I swear, sometimes they drive me crazy." Yet, Ashela could detect a note of affection in his voice.

"Did you bring the cashier's check?" Hart asked abruptly. He reached into his brief case and passed her an envelope.

Ashela took it before opening her purse to retrieve the check. She handed it to him and stared at the sealed envelope. "What's this?"

"It's a prospectus and bond which indicate that you now own fifteen percent stock in the Paramount Corporation." Hart took the check and quickly glanced it over before inserting it inside his suit jacket. As instructed, she'd had it made payable to Bestow Enterprises. "When you get the chance, review both of them. I'd like for us to get together soon so I can explain them in detail. I'm sorry to rush you, Ashela, but I need to take my wife to the doctor. She's seven months pregnant with our third child. Tell you what, are you free for dinner later this evening? My treat, of course. I could meet you at Leona's at," Patrick glanced at his watch, "How about seven o'clock?" He lifted his briefcase onto the desk and snapped it closed. He stood and came behind the desk as he waited for Ashela to rise from her seat.

Ashela nodded, somewhat relieved because she had the impression that he was taking her money and was about to run. "Is it okay if I bring a friend along? She's the one I've been speaking to you about."

"Sure. It's possible that I may even have my wife with me. I've been telling her about you as well and she wants to meet you. If I'm a couple of minutes late, go ahead and order yourself a drink or an appetizer, but I'll see you at seven or shortly thereafter." Hart closed the office door behind them and walked with her toward the elevator. Outside, he hailed a taxi and waived to her as he stepped inside.

For the first time since she'd made up her mind to invest the money, Ashela had strong doubts about what she'd just done. She hoped the gnawing feeling in the pit of her stomach was just an aberration.

At nine o'clock, Ashela and Stephanie were finishing their meal. At least Stephanie was. Ashela hadn't touched a morsel on her plate. Neither had she told Stephanie who they were there to meet. It was to be a surprise. But by ten o'clock, even Stephanie knew the person they were expecting had elected not to show up.

Ashela wasn't aware that the taxi cab had pulled up in front of her apartment building. She was completely numb. Hart may have had a perfectly legitimate excuse for not coming, but deep inside, Ashela was convinced she had been duped. Somewhere in the back of her mind, she was aware of Stephanie paying the cab driver and then she was unlocking her apartment door. Once inside, Ashela stumbled and nearly fell to the floor.

Stephanie wrapped her arm around her friend's waist. If she didn't know any better, she could easily suspect Ashela of being drunk. But she knew all that she'd had was two pina coladas. She pulled Ashela tighter against herself, saying, "Easy girl. Here, let's have a seat."

Stephanie knew something was terribly wrong. She didn't know who they were supposed to meet for dinner, but as time had passed, Ashela kept glancing at her watch and the frown on her face deepened with every passing minute. They'd ordered food, but Ashela hadn't noticed. Instead, she either stared out of the window or watched the door like a hawk. As the night drug on, she became quieter and quieter until finally, Stephanie felt as if she were having a one-sided conversation with herself.

No sooner had she situated Ashela on the sofa when she jumped up and ran into the bathroom. Stephanie could hear her regurgitating. Unsure of what to do, Stephanie approached the bathroom hesitantly only to find Ashela on her knees, hunched over the toilet, sobs wracking her body.

She stood just outside the bathroom door, not sure if she should be witnessing what she was seeing. She didn't know the details, but it didn't take a genius to discern that her friend was humiliated and hurting over something that had happened. When she thought Ashela was done, she stepped inside to grab a towel and handed it to her.

It was well into the night before Stephanie finally got the story out of Ashela.

The next morning, Ashela felt somewhat stronger, if still slightly sick to her stomach. She tried calling the number she had for Patrick Hart, but got no answer—not even an answering machine. She called Chase Manhattan bank to try to put a stop payment on the check, but because it was a cashier's check, she ran into problems. When the customer service rep pulled up her account information, she informed Ashela the check had been cashed the previous day.

Stephanie knew by the dejected look on her friend's face that she had received more bad news. She, herself, was still grappling with the amount of money that had been swindled. It never occurred to her to say, "I told you so," to Ashela. Stephanie knew that she was suffering enough as it was.

Ashela's mind was whirling. Unable to sit still, she dressed quickly to go to Hart's office and Stephanie was right beside her. They reached 110 William Street and took the elevator to the third floor. But, unlike the previous day, the building was swarming with people. All of the desks that had been empty only the day before, were now occupied.

Ashela made her way through the maze of cubicles and it was purely by luck that she found Hart's office. Before she could enter, she was stopped by a woman seated at a desk just outside his door. "May I help you?" she asked. Her tone was polite, but her demeanor clearly indicated they were intruding.

"I want to see Patrick Hart."

"There's no one here by that name."

Ashela was about to lose it. In her mind, she figured the woman was covering for him.

"Look, I know he works here and I intend to see him even if I have to kick the door in." Anger punctuated Ashela's voice.

"Miss, I'm telling you there's no one here named Patrick Hart."

Convinced the woman was lying, Ashela stormed into the office.

The woman quickly jumped up to follow her. "What do you think you're doing? Are you crazy?"

Ashela barged into the office and came to a complete stop. Seated behind the desk on the phone was the woman she had seen in the picture, Hart's wife.

The woman held the phone away from her ear and said, "What is the meaning of this?"

"I apologize Commissioner," said the secretary. "This young woman claims she's looking for someone named Patrick Hart. I've already told her there's no one here by that name but she ran inside before I could stop her. Shall I call security?"

The silver haired woman stood up before pressing a button to tell the caller she would have to call them back.

"Thank you, Jasmine. I'll handle it." Both Stephanie and the secretary were ordered to leave. After the door closed behind them, the woman said to Ashela, "Do you mind explaining what this is about?"

"It's about your husband, Patrick Hart. This *is* his office, right?" Suddenly, Ashela sounded doubtful.

"My husband is Dr. Larry Teele and I don't believe I know a Patrick Hart."

"But we met here yesterday. Right in this office. He said those were his children, you were his wife, and that you . . ." Ashela's voice trailed off as her eyes flew to the woman's flat stomach, ". . . were pregnant." She stared at the wall where the photograph had once hung. It was replaced by an even larger photo of the woman and her two children, but the picture included a man Ashela did not recognize. She suddenly felt light-headed and took a seat before her knees gave way.

Concerned, the woman came and stood over her. "I'm Robin Frazier-Teele, Commissioner of the Department of Business Services. This office was closed yesterday—it was a city-wide holiday." Commissioner Teele spoke rationally as if she were dealing with someone who was unhinged and was missing a few marbles. Though, she *had* noticed that several things in her office had been rearranged, she'd attributed it to Jasmine, her secretary. When the Commissioner questioned Ashela further, she was both amazed and saddened by what she learned.

By the time Ashela left, Robin Frazier-Teele had reviewed the so-called prospectus and bond that Hart had given her and declared them both fraudulent. She gave Ashela the address and phone number to the Better Business Bureau and urged her to file a police report against Patrick Hart for theft by deception.

***

As Ashela suspected, all the references Hart had given her turned out to be bogus. No one at any of the numbers she called knew of a Patrick Hart. Though she'd filed a police report, she faced the reality that he had neatly conned her out of $17,000, plus an additional $3,000 for music lessons that, for all their applicability, should have been free. It was doubtful that she'd ever see a penny of that money again. The $25,000 she'd had left from the sale of Julia's home was now gone. Ashela felt as though all of Julia's hard efforts had gone for naught because she'd failed to manage her inheritance wisely. Ashela could only wallow in her own stupidity, sure that all the heavens must be laughing at her. She couldn't stop herself from thinking over and over, *"What a fuckin' fool I've been."*

It was a Wednesday night, time for her to go back to work. But the thought of dancing was anathema. Both her head and her heart ached too heavily and all she wanted to do was sulk.

***

For the first time in months, Stephanie went to work by herself. It was business as usual at Sweet Georgia Brown's. But the dressing table next to hers belonging to Ashela didn't feel right being empty. Though Stephanie felt a spirit of camaraderie with the other dancers, she wasn't close to any of them. Ashela had filled that gap, quickly becoming the only genuine friend that Stephanie could say she'd ever had.

Stephanie knew the sadness she was experiencing was vicarious—it was just an extension of the pain that Ashela was feeling. She wished that there was something she could have said that would have prevented her from turning over her money. Stephanie knew that Ashela had simply been naïve and gullible, and that Patrick Hart had seen her coming.

She was staring in the mirror without really seeing anything when she heard George shout, "Yo, Steph! Krause wants you in his office." Stephanie turned to see that George had popped his head inside the dressing room and was searching for her.

"Tell him I'll be right there." Dressed in nothing but her underwear, Stephanie quickly threw on a robe and headed upstairs to Krause's office. He rarely mingled

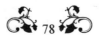

with the dancers. If he summoned any one of them, the news was either good or bad. The last time he'd called her into his office, he had given her a raise. But on this occasion, she had no idea what he could want.

His office was dark and cold making Stephanie wish she had grabbed a coat instead of her robe.

"Where's Ashela?" Krause asked brusquely as she sat in front of his desk.

Stephanie relaxed. "She's feeling under the weather but she'll be in tomorrow night." Thinking that was all he wanted, she was ready to leave. His penetrating and unblinking, beady little eyes always gave her the creeps.

Krause nodded. "See that she is. We're short staffed enough around here as it is." He lit a long cigar and exhaled the fumes in Stephanie's direction. "I've pulled you from the line up tonight." At Stephanie's look of surprise, he added, "Someone's requested a private dance with you. The man seems real fond of you, Stephanie. I told him you didn't do private dances and he paid two thousand dollars cash, plus thirty percent to me." Krause opened the drawer of his desk and placed the money on top.

Stephanie stared at the pile of bills. She should have been ecstatic that someone would offer her that kind of money just for a private dance. But something wasn't right about it and taking into consideration how unsafe she'd been feeling lately, Stephanie hesitated to accept. "Who is he?"

Krause shrugged. He hadn't a clue. All he knew was that the man's money was green.

But Stephanie wasn't satisfied, she probed further. "A white guy?" When Krause nodded, she said, "I want to see what he looks like before I agree."

Stephanie returned to the dressing room, relieved that the short, red-haired man that George had pointed out to her was no one she recognized. She locked the money inside her drawer and dressed for the occasion in a pink tasseled bikini that left most of her buttocks and breasts bare. She checked her makeup one last time and headed upstairs to her assigned private room.

The "private" dancing rooms were little more than small sections cornered off with long, floor length shingles draping each entrance. For safety reasons, there were no doors on any of the private quarters. Inside each one, the lighting was low and the only furnishings were a small table and a leather chair that could easily sit two. Stephanie parted the silver tensile that shielded the double doorway and stepped inside. But to her surprise, the room was empty.

The man hid in an adjacent room directly across the hall. With an evil glint in his eye, he watched everyone who went past. As he waited for his intended victim, he stilled himself against the impatience rising in his belly. For years, he'd thirsted for this moment. After nearly five years of expensive, futile searching, he had finally hit pay dirt. His search for his daughter had turned into a crazed obsession, causing him to lose pieces of his sanity in the process. He'd sold all but one acre of his property to raise the money needed to find her. Over the years, he exhausted every penny of it, hiring sleuth after sleuth who specialized in locating missing persons. But always, they'd come up empty.

It was by a stroke of luck that a truck driver recognized a picture he'd had posted in a Montana truck stop and called to say he'd given a young girl fitting the description a lift to New York City several years ago. It took the man an additional two years to hunt his daughter down. And now that he had tracked her, it was time to make her pay.

He should have known she'd turn out to be nothing more than the two-bit whore her mother had been—dancing in a whorehouse when he'd provided a decent home for her and a roof over her head. He'd worked hard for her, but that hadn't been enough. Instead, she'd run out on him just like that bitch of a mother of hers. *But she had paid as well.* He still remembered how she'd groveled for her life when he'd caught up with *her*. With each stab wound he'd inflicted, she had pleaded with him to spare her life. To this day, no one knew where he'd buried all the dismembered parts of her missing body.

He'd shown that bitch who was boss. Nobody used him and got away with it. Now it was time to do the same to Stephanie. The little whore may have thought she'd found safety, but now that he'd found her, he'd make her scream for mercy.

"I must have gotten the room number mixed up," Stephanie thought to herself as she surveyed the empty room. She could have sworn Krause had said room number four. Suddenly, the hairs rose on the back of Stephanie's neck as her sixth sense alerted her to an unseen danger. But as she swung around to leave, she crashed into the hulking figure behind her.

The rapid play of expressions sweeping her face pleased the man. Surprise, then a slow terror showed in her eyes when she saw the knife raise to strike. With no time to react, a terrified scream tore from her throat just as the first slash ripped her flesh from shoulder to belly. Sharp, excruciating pain sent her body into shock. Crimson tides sprayed the room with each ensuing slit and gash of flesh. As blow after blow reigned upon the fallen figure, flesh and bone were torn to shreds, until finally there remained only an awful silence mingled with heavy breathing.

George was the first to reach the room after hearing the blood-curdling scream. But even he was unprepared for the scene that he had rushed in on. Crouched over the remains of a tattered corpse was a demented man covered with blood. He wielded a huge hunting knife and it appeared to George that the man was mutilating his victim.

As George pulled his gun from his holster, the man charged him with knife extended. George fired, hitting his target head-on. A gaping bullet wound appeared in the man's forehead. Seconds later, he toppled over his victim.

The story made headlines for days afterward as each gory detail of the bloodbath leaked out. The National Organization for Women called for the removal of every business of ill repute along 42nd Street. Statistics were cited to show that exploitation of women led to further violence against them. Some activists were calling for stricter stalking laws, while local politicians waited in the wings to see if the murder case could benefit their own political agendas. But no matter which side of the issue people fell on, only one person remembered the girl *behind* the story.

Ashela would remember Stephanie as a friend, a confidante, and as someone whose smile could easily brighten a room. But above all, she'd cherish her as someone whose death would leave a huge, hapless void in her life.

Part Three

It's A Topsy-Turvy World

"Life is queer with its twists and turns,
As every one of us sometimes learns."

– Anonymous

"Chile, don't you know?
You got to go *through* something if you wanna get *to* something."

– Grandma Julia

Chapter Twelve

ora Evers awakened with her temples pounding. She sat up and pressed her palms tightly against the sides of her forehead. Only when the pain subsided did she ease the pressure and begin to softly caress the area. Another nightmare. Dora glanced over at the digital clock on her night stand, it registered two-thirty in the morning. The dream always occurred around the same time, followed by the blaring pain inside her head. But lately, the pain had intensified.

Swinging her feet over the side of the bed, Dora reached to switch on the night light. The blinding flash of pain was receding, leaving in its wake a dull, but not unbearable, thud. If only the dreams would dissipate as well, Dora thought. Though the chance of that seemed unlikely.

She got up and opened the miniature-sized refrigerator and withdrew a bottle of water. She was grateful that she had her dormitory room all to herself. The nocturnal hours she'd kept of late would be hard for any roommate to swallow.

A table laden with books beckoned her to sit down and journal her thoughts. Ordinarily, Dora would have done so, but on this occasion, she remembered all too vividly the dream's details as well as the significance behind it.

Dora approached the twin-sized bed and lay down on her side. With her knees drawn to her chest and her hands clasped together, she stared at the wall in front of her. The message behind the dream prevented sleep from claiming her.

Jonah was taken up and cast forth into the sea . . .

Dora buried her head in her pillow, as if to escape her clamorous thoughts. She knew well the biblical story of Jonah. A reluctant prophet of old, he'd been entrusted with a mission which he'd found sorely distasteful. However, rather than deliver his message, Jonah had chosen to run away. *But that was then and this is now*, Dora reasoned tersely.

At the slightest bit of tension, the drums began to beat inside her temples again. Angrily, she sat up and wrapped her arms around her legs. *Why me?* Dora questioned over and over. She lowered her head upon her knees knowing she was facing a dilemma. For months, she had been having the same nightmarish dream, only to awaken in the wee hours of the morning compelled to make note of its symbolism.

Some aspects of the dream were complex, although it always began simple enough. In it, a little boy walked along the side of a road. He seemed to know his destination for he veered not from the circuitous path. On either side of him were demonic forces disguised as worldly trappings that sought to deceive and draw the boy off course. Sometimes his path was well lit, at other times, it was dark and impossible to see. But always, there appeared to be a shield surrounding the little boy that protected him from harm.

83

As he traveled the road, he became a full-grown man, endowed with the finest things life had to offer. But somewhere during his journey, his path averted and the shield that once covered him was no more. The man faltered, seeming to lose his way. And one by one, he began to lose all the things he'd acquired along the path. Until finally, he imploded and became lost in an existential abyss.

It was the abyss that frightened Dora more than anything else. She saw the man trapped inside a tunnel of endless darkness that harbored ghoulish shapes and forms. Just before he disappeared, Dora would awaken from the dream. But not before she had the awareness that she was gazing into the pit of hell itself.

Dora was certain that the man in her dream would meet with some kind of ill-timed fate. But when she sought the reason for his demise, the overriding message she received was: *Because he took of the sacred things.*

At first, the dream and its connotation hadn't made much sense to her. A key phrase kept running through her head, *for we see through a glass darkly,* and it confused her even further. Yet, with each nightly occurrence of the dream, more details were revealed that made its interpretation all too clear. The man's face was undeniably one which Dora knew well: Belonging to none other than her uncle, Bishop Clay Evers. And the "sacred things" represented the misuse of church funds.

Dora soon understood that just as Jonah was given a message to deliver to the people of Ninevah, so too, had she been given a message, via her dreams, to deliver to her uncle, Bishop Clay Evers.

Months ago, when the visions first began, Dora was able to write them off as mere foolish nightmares. But then came the headaches which increased in intensity as she kept rejecting the dream and its contentions. After awhile, she knew in no uncertain terms the directive she was to deliver to her uncle. The problem was, Dora didn't feel worthy of the task.

Who was she to tell the great Bishop Clay Evers, pastor and teacher of the largest African American congregation in all of North Carolina, that he faced imminent doom if he failed to correct his ways?

Her uncle had literally put her through school and had provided for all of her needs. Were it not for him, her parents would never have been able to afford the high cost of tuition, books, clothing and food. In Dora's mind, she would be doing both him and herself a huge injustice by hinting that he was misappropriating church moneys.

So in the end, Dora berated herself. She wasn't some fearless biblical character—she was just a nobody. And even if her visions *were* dead on, it certainly wasn't *her* place to correct her uncle. Something of that magnitude belonged to his board members or the elders within his assembly.

Dora consoled herself with the knowledge that in a few short weeks, she would be graduating *magna cum laude* with a degree in chemical engineering. Though she'd received offers from corporations around the country, she'd made the decision to go with an East Coast firm whose acceptance package was by far the most generous. The opportunity for her to relocate to Washington, D.C., was merely icing on the cake.

With a little over three weeks to go before graduation, Dora was just biding her time. Rocking the boat with unfounded accusations that she'd received in a dream would be akin to biting the hand that fed her. She would be away from North Carolina soon. And maybe by then, the dreams and the headaches would cease.

***

Jealousy is an evil serpent that injects its venom into both the suspecting and unsuspecting. Tracy Evers-Reed seemed unaware that she was a victim of this insidious affliction. Not one given to self reflection, Tracy tended to overlook her own personal flaws by pointing out the inadequacies and errors in other people's ways. While her tactic served to absolve her of any guilt that she may have felt for wreaking havoc in the lives of others, it did nothing to diminish the anger and unforgiveness that begirt the core of her heart.

She pulled her BMW into the driveway of their home and slammed the door hard as she exited the car. Parris' Porsche was nowhere in sight and there was no telling what time he planned to return. This added to her anger. Already, she was livid and could hardly wait to tear into him the moment he arrived.

How dare Parris put her through the embarrassment that she had suffered today. It was bad enough that she'd had her good standing called into question, but to be subjected to rudeness from a low life ne'er-do-well such as Katrina Smith was unconscionable.

Nothing had gone right for Tracy on this day. She'd gone shopping with several of her peers, only to have the sales rep (scum bag and former schoolmate Katrina) tell her that her Visa credit card had been declined. Certain that a mistake had been made, for her credit limit was over $8,000, Tracy demanded that the witch run her card through again. Rage surged through her when Katrina snickered as she flippantly returned her card. Tracy fumed over treatment she considered disrespectful to someone of her stature. She figured Parris was somehow to blame for this. He had been threatening for months to curtail her spending by forcing her to adhere to a budget. If he'd reduced the limit on her charge card without informing her . . . Tracy would get to the bottom of things if it was the last thing she did.

She had an image to uphold. People around her looked up to her because the Evers' name was well respected. The Reeds may have had more money but they certainly didn't have the prominence that her family did. Why, even with all of their money, the Reed's were nothing more than rich hillbillies, Tracy thought spitefully. In her mind, Parris was the lucky one. If she'd had things her way, *he* would have been the one to change *his* surname.

Yet, Tracy admitted she had the best of both worlds—money *and* prestige. It was far more important to her that they live in the right neighborhood and drive the right cars than it was to Parris. Left up to him, he would still be driving the same beat up convertible Mustang he'd owned for years.

His entire family was so busy trying to be frugal, that they didn't know the difference between Gucci and K-Mart. How déclassé, Tracy thought. The Reeds had millions and could well afford to spend it. They had offered to buy Parris anything of his choice for his college graduation gift. To Parris' chagrin, Tracy had insisted they buy him a Porsche. That was Parris' problem, Tracy thought. He lacked gumption and originality. She shuddered to think what he would do without her. To hell with him and his family's frugality, Tracy thought. Though she feuded with Parris over what he chose to call her "wasteful, extravagant spending," she would continue to indulge her shop-a-holic tendencies as she saw fit. Besides, what purpose did it serve to have money if others didn't know you had it?

Tracy judged everything according to its price and she made sure folks knew _she_ was "in the money." Her home, her furniture, her clothes, her car, (she considered everything "hers") all were selected because of their price tag. Competitive by nature, Tracy was always trying to "outdo" everyone around her—she wanted to be the "Joneses" that people kept up with. Not long after Parris received his Porsche, she pitched a fit until he gave in and bought her the BMW. That was pretty much the way of their marriage. She ranted and raved, he silently sulked. But in the end, she always got what she wanted, compromise be damned.

Though Tracy invariably emerged the victor, what she failed to comprehend was that her marriage lay in ruins as a result of her self-centeredness and her constant need for dominance.

To say that her marriage was strained at times was an understatement. After the birth of their twin sons, Anthony and Kiante, Parris seemed to go out of his way to avoid her. Tracy wanted her marriage to work so she went through phases where she alternately tried to please and appease her new husband. But that had ended abruptly when she went through some of his things and found old photographs of him and that bitch Ashela Jordan. His holding on to them a year after their marriage confirmed that he still had feelings for her. When he refused to destroy them, Tracy promptly cut them to pieces.

Days later, Parris discovered his pictures in the garbage and the argument that ensued was ugly. For the first time, Parris saw how all-consuming Tracy's jealousy could be, and he didn't like what he saw. He took to keeping late hours, and soon arguing became their primary mode of communication. By the time the boys were two years old, Parris had entered grad school and he and Tracy continued to grow further apart.

Tracy was too busy to acknowledge the growing rift in their relationship, let alone her own misery. She had no intentions of becoming enslaved to some man the way her mother was to her father. To prove to Parris that she wasn't about to sit at home and try to be the happy homemaker, Tracy enrolled in college. Every Monday morning, she dropped the twins off at their grandmother Fredonia's house and left them there until Friday when either she or Parris would pick them up. Parris didn't like the arrangement at first, saying it burdened his mother who was getting up in age, but Tracy would hear none of it. Her mind was made up, and as far as she was concerned that was the end of the subject. Her parents were too busy to care for two small children, but Parris' mother, why all she did was stay at home and count her husband's money. She should *want* to look after her own grandchildren rather than see them put in day care.

With Parris working full time at a law firm and going to grad school in the evenings, and with Tracy busy with her own affairs, the two of them were like ships passing in the night. They shared a home but there was no warmth inside it. Intimacy was something they never learned to enjoy. They went months without touching one another and when they did, the sex was empty and meaningless, just a form of release.

It was a cold war that they waged upon one another. Parris bore no resemblance to the person Tracy fell for three years ago and, in turn, he felt he never really knew her. They'd had more fun during the brief time they spent courting in his college days whereas now, they were barely cordial.

Tracy didn't think in terms of divorce because that would be admitting defeat. She was accustomed to a certain lifestyle and being married to Parris allowed her to maintain it without having to rely upon her parents.

For her, the alternative to staying together was unacceptable. She would never allow Parris to divorce her, so she accepted the lines of demarcation that the two of them had silently drawn. *Once married, always married*, was her concept. If her parent's could stay together despite their marital problems, then so could she. Like it or not, Parris' tie to her was binding—theirs was a lifetime commitment. After bearing his children and putting her good name on the line, Tracy knew in her heart that if Parris ever left her for another woman, she would spend the rest of her life making sure that *his* was a living hell.

***

Kyliah Reed sat before Dr. Judy Gentry, Dean of Spelman's Office of Student Affairs. She had been summoned to resolve what should have been an open-and-shut case. Instead, she found herself embroiled in a power struggle.

Dr. Gentry glanced up from the papers she was perusing. "You've met with Vivian Terrell?" she inquired. When Kyliah nodded, she handed her the papers she'd been reading, saying, "Ms. Terrell has written quite an inflammatory letter to the president, the crux of which accuses you of discrimination. Please, tell me what happened."

Kyliah's lips tightened as she read the letter. She handed it back saying, "Her version of the facts differ significantly from what I recall. I met with her and two other students to give them a tour of the campus. It took about two hours and

afterwards, we ended the tour at the Student Union Building. Before we went our separate ways, I told them they should each consider participating in the mentoring program."

Kyliah was a strong advocate of Spelman's mentoring program, which Dr. Gentry headed. Through the program, Spelman liased with dozens of not-for-profit organizations, social service programs, and corporations to shepherd its mentees into entrepreneurship. In addition to providing personal coaching, those who served as mentors also showered students with strategic career and life planning advice. Just as she, herself, was currently being mentored, Kyliah mentored several freshman students each year. She took on no more than two at a time because of her activeness in other organizations. Between her studies and her many student activities, nearly all her time was accounted for. Her schedule was hectic and there were nights when she fell into bed exhausted, feeling as if she was burning both ends of her candle.

"At any rate, I explained the merits of the program and when one of the girls asked whether I was available as a mentor, I said no because of my workload. We parted ways when Vivian Terrell caught up with me and asked me to reconsider being her mentor."

"I gather you adamantly refused her."

"Yes. I reiterated that I had no spare time, but she refused to take no for an answer. When she realized I was not going to change my mind, she went to great lengths to tell me how it would be in my 'best interest' to mentor her because her parents were among Spelman's most eminent benefactors and were on first name basis with the president of this college. She told me that, if forced to, all she had to do was make a phone call.

"Dr. Gentry, I couldn't believe the girl had the nerve to come on so strong. So I told her I didn't care if her parents were on first name basis with the president of the United States. It still didn't alter the fact that I wasn't available to her. I told her if she wanted to be mentored, there was a host of faculty members and business leaders whom she could choose from. She said someone had told her that since I'm the only AKA participating in the program, if I mentored her, it would give her carte blanche to membership to the Alpha Kappa Alpha sorority. I told her how wrong she was, and that if her goal was to pledge AKA while she was an undergraduate, she'd have to go through the pledge process just like the rest of us.

"That's when she started threatening that 'people in high places' would hear of how I was turning her down, so I cut her short and told her that with an attitude like hers, she'd never make the grade."

Kyliah had thought that would be the end of it. It was unfortunate that Dr. Gentry, whom she had the utmost respect for, had somehow gotten dragged into the matter. Vivian Terrell wasn't interested in being mentored. She was more concerned with getting her way. She'd struck her as a petulant child and Kyliah had immediately viewed her as her nemesis, Tracy Evers.

"That's all there is to tell, Dr. Gentry. The only thing I'll add is that even if I were available, I wouldn't accept her as a mentee. I found her calculating and much too egotistical. Personally, I would recommend that a strong faculty member such as yourself take her on—someone who won't be swayed by her selfish machinations."

Dr. Gentry had been steadily taking notes while Kyliah talked. She had known Kyliah since her freshman year and had watched her mature into a confident, ambitious young woman of great potential. Her reasons for not wanting to mentor Vivian Terrell were valid and she accepted them without further question. To put a halt to the matter before it reached higher levels, Dr. Gentry decided to offer to mentor the young woman herself.

Kyliah walked back to the LLC2 dorm, her arms laden with books. Though she could well afford to live off campus, she'd elected not to. Living on campus made her feel as if she had her finger on the pulse of college life.

Kyliah was senior class president and was a Finance/Economics major with a minor in The African Diaspora of the World. As an active participant in most of Spelman's student activities, she was popular, outspoken, and was known as a leader. In her spare time, she headed numerous committees and her classmates had voted her "Most Likely to Succeed."

She slammed the door to her room, seething inwardly because Vivian Terrell had had the gall to imply that she had been the victim of discrimination at her expense. The girl didn't know the meaning of the word, Kyliah thought. Discrimination was having to sit in a restaurant with everyone around you getting served until you finally recognized that the management didn't want to serve you because your parents were a bi-racial couple, with children that were considered "zebras." Discrimination was walking hand-in-hand with your mother and being stopped by people who assumed she was your nanny so they could tell her how pretty her "charges" were. Discrimination was watching their faces change when your mother told them that her "charges" were her own children. Discrimination was watching the pain in your mother's eyes from the knowledge that her in-laws would never accept her, or her children, because they were Black.

Kyliah could tell Vivian stories for days about the real meaning of discrimination. Maybe then she wouldn't be as quick to use the term so loosely.

But Kyliah knew Vivian Terrell wasn't the real issue. She could handle her any day of the week. It was the dredged up memories of Tracy Evers that caused her stomach to churn. She didn't think of Tracy as her sister-in-law, and could not bring herself to call her a "Reed." That would take more time than Kyliah felt she had on earth.

Though several years had passed since her shot-gun wedding to Parris, Kyliah still carried unforgiveness toward her in her heart. She held Parris equally responsible for the mess the two of them were making of their lives. That he was still married to the witch was an affront to Kyliah's senses.

But it was his life and she was trying to let go of the past. Doing so, however, was a struggle. Kyliah felt the only good thing to come from their twisted farce of a marriage was the twins. She didn't want to see them hurt by the animosity Parris and Tracy directed toward one another. She was thankful that her mother, Fredonia, was raising the boys. Under her care, they were growing into two mannerable and well adjusted little boys. More importantly, they knew they were loved and they never lacked for affection. Kyliah thought that as long as her side of the family was heavily involved in their lives, Anthony and Kiante would turn out okay.

Kyliah acknowledged that behind her own range of accomplishments lay a thick wall of anger. Much of her activism was a result of the rage she felt—it was an indication that she was angry with the world. Racism enraged her the most. Over the years, she'd learned to celebrate the diversity within her family, though it still hurt deeply that her relatives on her father's side wanted nothing to do with them. *A wall of repressed anger*. Kyliah felt her stomach churn, and placed a hand on it to stop the rumblings.

Still, what hurt her more deeply than anything else was . . . Ashela. How could she go off and not contact her for these three and a half years? Friends forever was what they said they'd always be. She knew Ash had been hurt over Parris, but why had she closed *her* out of her life as well? *Get over it,* was the phrase that reverberated through her mind. Only God knew how much she was trying and only He knew the pain that she felt when she thought of having lost her best friend. Kyliah wondered how Ashela was fairing, how she was getting along, or even if she was alive.

This time, Kyliah didn't even try to stop the flow of tears that fell from her eyes. She'd rationalized the situation over and over to no avail. Ash hadn't even the decency to tell her that her grandmother had died. She'd had to hear it from Fredonia. Though Kyliah hated to admit it, she felt betrayed by Ashela, as if all the years of their friendship had meant nothing.

Feeling rage and sadness bottling within her, Kyliah grabbed her keys and reached for the door, slamming it hard behind her.

Chapter Thirteen

Werner Enterprises had offices on both the East and West coasts. Sam Ross stood in his West Coast suite gazing through vertical blinds that covered floor-to-ceiling windows. Expensive, sleek, and state-of-the-art furnishings dominated the huge office. Done in silver and black with gray undertones, the space was modernized in a "less is more" fashion.

Sam's mood was reflective as he peered down at all the traffic that lined Wilshire Boulevard. He'd just finalized a major record deal with the agent of superstar David Pennington. Pennington's contract had come up for renegotiation with his current label and Sam's goal had been to woo him over to Werner. He'd done so by convincing the agent that his client wasn't being promoted in the manner befitting him, and that unless he was with Werner, which was prepared to take his career in another direction *and* to another level, Pennington's performing potential would never be maximized. After receiving a promise that the signed contract would reach his desk the next morning, Sam hung up the telephone feeling satisfied.

He was a mastermind at engendering such deals. The key to his success lay in the swift and cunning way that he was able to structure mega-deals that his competitors couldn't match, and in his ability to make the most lop-sided deal appear to be a win-win situation for all parties involved.

Now that the Pennington deal was all but done, Sam planned to head back east immediately. Though he'd managed to spend a good chunk of his time in California, it was New York City that tugged at his heart. There was just something kinetic about the bustling metropolis that was unmatched anywhere else on the globe. In comparison, L.A. was a much more laid back, unhurried environment. Whenever he traveled west, Sam always found himself eagerly anticipating returning to the East Coast before long.

At one point, Sam had lived in California, running the L.A. branch of Werner Enterprises. But that was before his divorce of seven years ago. As part of the settlement, his ex-wife, Claudette, got to keep their Bel Air home and was awarded custody of their two boys. Sam thanked God that their divorce hadn't been a nightmare like so many others he knew about. They'd split everything straight down the middle, as was required by California Law. But Sam would have done the fifty-fifty deal even had it not been a necessity. Claudette had been good to him. She'd stuck by him when he hadn't had a pot to piss in nor a window to throw it out of.

The two of them had met and married in their early twenties. He was a promotion rep at the time, working long, grueling hours. The money he brought home was decent but when combined with what Claudette made on her job, they were able to make ends meet and eventually save for a down payment on a new home. In those days, Sam had been devoted to his wife. He promised her that if she stuck with him, one day he'd give her everything she'd ever wanted.

Their marriage lasted fifteen years. They had their ups and downs, good times and bad times. But as the years passed, they began to grow distant from one another and Sam was forced to shoulder the blame. Because of his long hours and his constant traveling, Sam became married to his job. His career eventually took its toll on his marital vows. The more successful he became in the record industry, the further apart he and his wife grew.

Claudette found that even with all of the money and rich trappings her new social status could afford her, it still was no substitute for the endless nights of loneliness. Where once Sam had been faithful, it wasn't long before he soon succumbed to the "fast-life" and Claudette saw it coming. Tired of playing the role of the "happy housewife," and frustrated over the amount of time Sam was spending away from home, she confronted him about being with other women while he was on his "business" trips. After awhile, Sam stopped denying it. He was no saint, nor had he ever pretended to be one. They separated for a brief period of time and once the initial bitterness faded, both agreed to the divorce. The one good thing that sprang forth from the ashes of his failed marriage was an improved relationship with his fifteen and thirteen year old boys, Ronald and Damael. His relationship with them was much better and healthier. He welcomed finding the time to spend with them, often flying them to New York and other cities in an effort to see more of them.

As for the women in his life, over the years, they had come and gone. Black ones, white ones, tall or short, Sam had had his pick. He found white women to be servile, taking whatever he doled out, while the sisters were the ones with spines, less willing to buy into his excuse that because he was recently divorced, he wasn't able to offer them anything but a temporary sexual satisfaction.

After his divorce, the women, parties and drugs, all suddenly grew old. Sam came to dislike the way he'd feel the morning after a night of drinking, women, rousing, and all the coke he could ever want. All Sam had to do was look around at the many wasted lives of "once beens" and "has beens." Stars who, in their heyday, had made a fortune and blown it just as quickly. Still others had had a couple of big hits and made some fast money, only to let it seep through their fingers like sand. Every one of them had their fifteen minutes of fame. And when the fame was over, ninety-nine percent of the time, the money was gone as well, smoked up in a haze of women, fast cars, or frivolous luxury items.

That's where the road parted for Sam. The difference for him lay in the fact that while money tended to cause many of his counterparts to fall prey to its deceptive trap, he never allowed himself to get swept away with the current. He wasn't about to wind up with nothing to his name but the memory of a few good times with people who claimed to be his friend all because he was part of the "in" circle. Sam knew also that the cardinal sin in his business was believing your own hype. The easiest way to lose everything in a downward slide, was to allow yourself to get caught up in what other people said about you. Regardless of what others wrote or said, you were never as bad and never as good.

Sam remembered all too well what it was like not to have anything. He'd spent more days with nothing in his pockets but two rusty pennies than he'd ever care to tell. He had no intention of going back.

Sam had grown up in the projects in the Watts section of L.A. Meager, poor, and bleak surroundings were all he could boast of. His childhood wasn't something he preferred to recall because it had been punctuated by poverty. One of eight children, Sam had had to hustle the streets ever since he could remember. As a kid, he'd felt the only things he had going for him were his height and a strong survival instinct.

Once, a scouting agent for a university picked Sam out of all the other boys on the basketball court. He approached him after the game and told Sam that he had something beyond talent that the others didn't possess: A hunger and a drive that didn't fade simply because the game was over. When the others were ready to call it quits, Sam was just warming up. While many tried to urge him in the direction of basketball, Sam couldn't flow with the idea. Basketball didn't do it for him. What the scouts failed to recognize was that he was a competitor by nature. No matter what the game, Sam hated to lose. Besides, b-ball was just a means to keep him from being recruited by the legions of warring gangs surrounding him. He learned that when he was in his own neighborhood, if he remained neutral and kept a b-ball in his hands, it was a signal to gang members that he was going somewhere other than where most of them were headed. Basketball had become Sam's out.

It was when he wandered outside of Watts, to the other sections of L.A., that Sam's dreams of a different life would begin. All he had to do was stand on Sunset Boulevard in front of RCM Studios watching the parade of fat cat performing artists roll up in their limos, and he knew what he wanted to be. Stuck in a quagmire of abject poverty, Sam just didn't know *how* to become what he wanted to be.

When star-studded musical events were held at the studio, like hundreds of other spectators, Sam would look on with wishful ideas, dreaming that one day, he too, would be a superstar.

One night, Sam was still on the basketball court shooting hoops long after all of the others had gone home. Around two in the morning, he was driving in for a lay-up when he saw a limo careen to a stop about half a block away. The door on the driver's side burst open before a man jumped out and started running like hell was after him. Sam stood with his ball tucked under his arm, debating whether to go check it out. When curiosity got the better of him, he headed in the direction of the abandoned limo.

The driver's door was ajar and the interior light was on. Sam cautiously peered inside. He could hear faint noises coming from the back. He crawled into the vehicle and looked through the glass partition that separated the driver's section from the

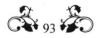

back of the limousine. Lying on the carpeted floor were two white men. One was face up, sprawled spread-eagled with a bullet hole in his forehead and a huge open wound in his chest, while the other was struggling to sit up against the leather seat. He was holding his hand beneath his breast. Blood was everywhere.

"Help me," the man pleaded in a weak voice.

Sam squeezed through the narrow opening into the back of the limousine and crawled toward the man. A calmness, akin to shock, stole over him as he knelt in front of him. "How? What can I do?" He shook his head as he stared at all the blood surrounding him. Instinct made him remove his own shirt and press it against the man's gaping wound in an attempt to staunch his flow of blood. He looked at the man and knew he would die if he didn't get urgent medical attention. "I'm going to call an ambulance." Sam started to back away to go call for help.

"Wait," the man rasped. He gestured to Sam. "Take these with you." He handed Sam a wallet and a little booklet that appeared to him to be an address book. "Take it! But don't give it to anyone." The man jerked in pain. "Please . . ."

Sam tucked the wallet and little book into his pants and crawled through the front window again. He grabbed his basketball and ran two blocks to the nearest payphone and dialed 911. When the police and ambulance arrived, a crowd of onlookers had gathered. Sam mingled with the curious bystanders and watched the paramedics remove the bodies from the vehicle. By the time investigators started questioning the onlookers, Sam was long gone.

The next day, Sam ditched school and hid in an abandoned warehouse to look over everything that was in the man's wallet. He first flipped through the address book, but it contained only names and dates with dollar amounts scribbled next to each one. The writing looked like chicken scratch and was meaningless to Sam. Inside the wallet were Visa, MasterCard, and American Express cards and a California drivers license with the man's picture on it. Every card had the name Ginovese Vitelli engraved on it. Because the name meant nothing to Sam, he had no way of knowing that the Vitellis' were heads of the largest organized crime family on the West Coast. Sam opened the middle of the wallet and counted out five thousand dollars in one hundred dollar bills along with two tens. Sam was in a daze as he stared at the cash. To him, it represented all the money in the world.

Hours later, Sam quietly entered his apartment to find no one home. He, his other sisters and brothers, along with his mother shared the three-bedroom unit. Though it was clean, it was still a dump by anyone's standards. Sam hid the wallet inside a hole in the bathroom wall before leaving the apartment. He turned and shoved a pink envelope with his mother's name written on it underneath the apartment door and disappeared.

That evening, Sam returned home to find his siblings surrounding his mother, who was sitting at the kitchen table sobbing hysterically. "What's wrong wi' ma?" Sam asked.

"Somebody left her a card with some money in it. They didn't say who it was from," one of his siblings replied.

Suddenly, through her tears, Sam's mother started praising God. She leapt to her feet and shouted, "Thank you, Lord! Thank you, Father! Thank you, Jesus!" Seeing her filled with such joy was something Sam would never forget as long as he lived. He never told his mother that he was the one who purchased the card with one of the ten dollar bills, and had asked a lady to write his mother's name on it so she wouldn't recognize his handwriting. Sam had put forty-nine hundred dollars in the envelope and sealed it.

Sam's mother would have beaten the devil out of him if he had just walked up to her and handed her the money. She would have thought he had stolen it. Even though his mother stood only five feet, five inches, she was a strong woman with a heavy hand. Her no-nonsense approach to raising her children and her favorite saying, which she was quick to back up, *"I brought you in this world and I'll take you out,"* had served to keep all of them in line. His mother was well aware of the pitfalls and dangers that surrounded her children. But daily, she prayed for each of them, primarily Sam, who despite all the beatings she gave him, remained the most rebellious. He was constantly ignoring his curfew, staying out till the wee hours of the morning. Daily, she lifted the names of her children up in prayer and always plead a hedge of protection around each and every one of them. Materially, it was true that they didn't have much, but they did have one another.

Five weeks later, Sam was on the court shooting hoops when he overheard some guys off to the side talking about two mob guys who had been found in a nearby limo and how one had survived while the other was shot in the head and all his body parts dismembered. Sam knew the dead man hadn't been cut up, but he didn't utter a word. Initially, he'd thought constantly of the man in the limousine, but as time passed he'd thought of him less and less, figuring him to be dead. To Sam, it was like carrying a small secret around inside him. He was neither fearful, nor worried. He knew the police couldn't trace him because he had never before been fingerprinted, and the shirt he'd left pressed to the man's body was so cheap, that nearly everybody in the 'hood owned one.

Hearing that the man whose money he had spent was alive caused Sam to think about him again.

The following weekend, Sam stealthily removed the wallet from its hiding place and left as usual to go play hoops. But instead of going to the b-ball court, Sam took a bus and headed up town. He caught a cab from there and gave the driver the address that was listed on the man's drivers license.

"Shit, boy. You think this is some kinda joke? It'll cost you sixdy, maybe sebney dollars to get out to Beverly Hills. You ain't got that much money. Git the hell outta my cab!"

Sam pulled out a hundred dollar bill and handed it to the driver. "Now, will you take me?" He slipped the wallet back into his pocket.

The man took the money and looked it over as if it had grown wings. Muttering underneath his breath, he put the cab in gear.

Nearly an hour later, the taxi pulled up to the address. Already in awe of the beautiful, scenic, and panoramic estates en route to his destination, Sam got out and walked up to the white wrought-iron gates. The cab driver didn't bother to ask if Sam wanted him to wait. Through the gates, Sam peered at the most beautiful home he had ever seen in real life. He stood there staring at the estate, nearly forgetting the reason why he'd come. Before Sam could press the intercom button on the gate, two white men were standing in front of him. It was as though they had appeared out of nowhere.

"You looking for someone?" one of the men asked.

Sam opened his mouth to speak but fell silent when he saw the gun in the man's holster just inside his jacket. He didn't know anything about the mob except for what he'd seen on television. But these men seemed to fit the general description.

"Maybe he's lost." the other man said.

"No. I'm not lost. I'm looking for Mr. Vitelli." Unsure of how to pronounce the man's first name, Sam shortened it saying, "Gino Vitelli."

The two men looked at each other. "Who wants to see him?"

"I do. I have something that belongs to him." Sam pulled the drivers license out of his jean pocket and handed it to the man through the gate.

One of the men walked away and spoke into a small radio. The other one stood looking at Sam, never blinking an eye. Moments later the gates parted and the men beckoned him inside. As they led him up to the house, Sam marveled over the beauty of the brick walkway and the huge, marble lions that stood just before the entrance. Sam wondered what it felt like to live in such rich surroundings.

The grandeur on the inside of the house was even more spectacular than he could have imagined. Everywhere he looked, there was marble and gold. Sam was so busy looking around him that he never noticed three thick, burly men in black suits come stand right beside him. Only these men wore no jackets and their holstered guns were obvious.

"Did you frisk him?"

Before anyone could answer, Sam was pinned tight by one henchman while another patted him down. "Hey!" was all Sam could muster in surprise. The man holding him was all muscle and Sam couldn't move, though he tried valiantly to jerk away. Suddenly, coming here didn't seem like such a bright idea. Gino Vitelli's wallet and address book were yanked from his pocket and handed to another guy who came to stand in front of him. He looked different from the other hawk-nosed men. He was taller, dressed casually and wasn't wearing a gun.

The man looked inside the wallet before looking at Sam. "Who sent you here?" Something about the quietness of his voice sent chills down Sam's spine. Where before he had been struggling, suddenly he went limp.

"Nobody," Sam whispered.

"Then how did you get this?"

Sam found himself trying to explain what had happened though he knew he probably wasn't making much sense. He told them about finding two men in a limousine and being given the wallet and address book by one of them.

The man looked Sam over carefully. He could sense the boy's fear and knew he was telling the truth. "Follow me." The man turned and walked away, expecting to be followed.

Sam's legs were weak. He couldn't move until one of the men pushed him along.

Sam no longer noticed the beauty of the home, instead he noticed its eerie quietness. They walked down a long, marbled hall that seemed endless. Sam's fear had not eased and added to it was a feeling of numbed uncertainty. They led him into a bare room with nothing but a table and four chairs and told him to have a seat. When Sam was seated, they left him alone inside the room.

Sam sat there for nearly thirty minutes with all kinds of thoughts running through his mind. He wondered if the men thought he was the one who had killed the man inside the limo. He wondered if they would kill him in retaliation. He was thinking of his mother and wishing he had never come when the door opened and the man, Gino Vitelli, walked through it on a cane, followed closely by two bodyguards.

Sam rose to his feet as Gino slowly advanced into the room. The man had a leonine face and a shock of white hair. He was dressed in a silk paisley robe with matching slacks. Even in his pajamas, he appeared to Sam to be a commanding figure. Someone who radiated power. "Sit down," the man said in a gruff voice.

Sam sat, his eyes never leaving the man's riveting face. He couldn't think of anything to say, so he remained quiet. They just seemed to sit staring at one another, neither of them speaking.

Finally, the man spoke. "Did you talk to the police or show anyone else the book that I gave you?"

Unnerved by the man's steely-eyed gaze, Sam could only shake his head.

"What happened to the money?"

Sam didn't need to ask what money the man was referring to. He swallowed and slowly opened his mouth to answer but before he could speak, the door opened and in walked the same man who had taken the wallet and address book. He dismissed all the other men and took a seat at the table. Just the three of them remained inside the room.

Sam looked at the older man and when he spoke, his words tumbled out. "I bought a birthday card and gave $4,900 to my mother. She thought it was a gift from someone. I spent the last hundred on the taxi getting here. Sam glanced at the younger gentleman before looking back at Gino. "I'm sorry. I thought you was dead and I figured my family needed that money a lot worse than you did." In the face of their silence, Sam added lamely, "I can pay you back."

"How did you discover he was alive?" the younger man asked. It was obvious the boy didn't have the wherewithal to pay anything back.

"The fellas where I play b-ball was talkin' about the incident, saying how the man was out of the hospital and that the police were looking for the ones who did it."

"How old are you boy?" They seemed to throw questions at him one right after another.

"I'm almost fifteen." No longer as afraid as he originally was, Sam just wanted to get the hell out the man's home. "Sir, I know I was wrong to spend your money, but like I said, I thought you was dead. I only came here today to return your wallet and the book. You told me not to show it to anybody, so I wanted to give it to you personally. I don't have the money now, neither does my ma'. But I'll get a job and I'll pay you back." Sam had the sudden thought that the man might send his henchmen after his family. "If you'll just . . ."

The older man raised his hand to silence Sam. He spoke slowly. "I'm not concerned about the money, boy. I wanted to know if you would tell me the truth. You saved my life and for that, I'm grateful. Think of the money as a small reward. Is there anything in return I can do for you?"

Sam could only think of one thing. "Don't kill me."

The two men laughed, and with their laughter all tension fled from the room. But Sam failed to see the humor, so he didn't join in.

"Tell me about yourself, what's your name?"

"Samuel J. Ross." Sam shrugged his shoulders. "There's not much more to tell you. I live in Watts. I'm a freshman in high school. I've got a mother and seven other sisters and brothers. That's it."

"And what do you want to do with your life?" Gino Vitelli asked.

Sam thought about it and said, "I want to work for one of the record companies and have money like the superstars. I want to be like you and someday own a limousine. But most of all, I want to move out of the projects and buy my ma' a house."

Gino watched as Sam spoke animatedly. It took guts for the boy to come here from where he lived, especially after he'd spent all the money, and Gino admired that. There was something different about him but Gino knew what it was. Unlike so many others of his kind whom Gino had met, the boy had dreams and aspirations. There was no resigned, hopeless stoop to his shoulders. Gino liked the fact that the boy had told the truth about the money and had said he was willing to work for something. Gino knew how he could help him.

"You look like a strong boy. Are you willing to work after school?"

"Yes, sir." Sam had no idea what direction the man was going in.

"I own a record company. How would you like to work for me?"

Shortly thereafter, Sam was driven home by two of the henchmen. Nearly sick with relief, he could care less about the job the man had offered him. He didn't believe him anyway and was just glad to escape with his life. Sam had the henchmen drop him several blocks from his door and then ran as fast as he could. He never saw the white-haired man again. Nor did he ever mention his visit to the mansion in Beverly Hills.

A week later, good fortune came his family's way. His mother received a letter notifying her that she had just won a six-bedroom home in East Hollywood, California, a much nicer section of L.A., along with $60,000. Sam's mother said it was "a blessing from the Lord," and added something about the wealth of the wicked being stored up for the just. But Sam had no doubt that it was a gift from Gino Vitelli. Yet again, he never said a word.

Instead, Sam decided to take the man up on his offer of a job and headed over to Werner Enterprises.

Sam was nearly fifteen years old when he first started working in the record business. He started out as a mail clerk in Werner's mailroom. Sam received no special treatment from anyone at the company. No one at his level knew how he had gotten his job, and his supervisor let him know on the first day that if he couldn't make the grade, he would be out on his behind quicker than the blink of an eye. Sam worked after school in the mailroom for four years. After he graduated high school, he was promoted to the Studio Department, where he ran errands for producers, managers, and other big shots. Sam's dependability garnered him high praises from his supervisors. He became familiar with management and eventually was entrusted with escorting the stars to and from airports in the company limousines.

For three years, Sam played the role of dependable go-fer, but he was always, always learning. He would watch with envious eyes, the big money, fancy cars, and beautiful women the music execs and stars had. Though he couldn't carry a tune if his life depended on it, Sam knew that one day he was going to be just like them.

As a newcomer to the industry, Sam wanted to be like the superstars he saw, but he would learn in later years that he didn't want to *become* like them.

He worked long hours fulfilling his need to learn everything there was to the business. There was so much to learn that in his excitement, he practically lived for his job.

Like a sponge soaking up every bit of liquid in its path, Sam continued to learn the ins and outs of the music world. He was in close contact with major performing

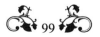

artists. Therefore, it was impossible for him to be content sitting behind a desk pushing papers and counting pencils, only to retire fifty years later with nothing but a gold watch to show for his time. Sam was soon recognized as a go-getter, someone who could be depended upon. And every time someone tipped him, they'd tell him, "Keep up the good work, son. You're going places."

Knowing there was money to be made at the top, Sam pushed himself even harder to get there.

By the time he was twenty-two, Sam had become a promotion rep, where he traveled all over the country scouting new acts. Predicting the public's waning interest and taste in music was a tricky thing, but it was a gift Sam discovered he possessed. What he liked best about the music business was the way the industry tides ebbed and flowed. There was never a dull moment, always new people to meet, new places to visit, new acts to be seen and heard. Sam's strong suit was his ability to recognize talent—raw talent. Sam could listen to a demo tape, see an artist performing in a smoke-filled room, or hear someone singing on a subway and he'd know immediately whether or not they had what it took to make it in the industry. It wasn't something he could explain, he just knew it.

Sam discovered that for some performers, it wasn't so hard to reach the top. One good hit and they were there, even if only for a moment. The hardest thing to do, Sam found, was to *stay* on top. That's why the music industry was so fickle. Here today, gone tomorrow. But Sam learned that as long as he trusted his gut instincts, he could make his own lasting impression.

Several years later, Sam went to work in the A & R (artists & repertoire) Department, where all the fresh, up-and-coming artists were previewed and considered for potential contract signings. This was where Sam thrived. He was capable of gauging talent, and more importantly, he possessed the ability to foretell industry trends. As a heavy hitter within A & R, Sam signed new acts to Werner's record label and worked with numerous producers. Over the years, he met so many people and cultivated so many relationships that his own reputation was being forged.

Sam took pride and pleasure in learning all phases of the business. He learned every aspect of the Promotion Department, the Marketing Department, the Artists-Relations Department, which covered tours and live performances, the Publicity Department, and one of his favorites, the Business Affairs Department, which handled royalties, contracts and financial arrangements.

The long hours Sam put in paid off in rapid dividends owing to his resiliency and the fact that he never lost touch with his people. As Sam continued to rise through the corporate ranks, he never forgot the importance of letting people know that *he* had not forgotten where he'd come from. He used his charm and charisma and always spoke to everyone—no matter how high or how low they were on the totem

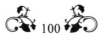

pole. The higher he climbed, the more people viewed and accepted him as "one of their own."

Sam recognized that the money to be made in the music business sprang from the development of new and budding artists. As one of the lone, Black A & R men, Sam had tremendous opportunity to give unsigned Black artists a shot at his label. He also thought of it as an obligation.

Sam knew that despite what the spin doctors wanted people to believe, it was Blacks who had crafted the music industry into the dynamo that it was. It was Black people whose music and lyrics were constantly being stolen and re-recorded to seem as though they were not the originators. Sam knew that popular music had always had its Black roots and he recognized that his people were the industry's heart and soul.

He watched in frustration as many artists, both Black and white, signed "dummy" contracts, unaware that they were signing away their lives being bought off with houses, cars, and whatever else gave them the temporal appearance of prestige. When these artists' hits dried up, so did their royalties from the record companies. Because of overly lavish lifestyles, many were left high and dry. Sam saw it happen over and over again. While others blew and frittered their money away, Sam became determined that the same fate would not befall him. He sought wise counsel and found ways to invest his money soundly.

Through the years, Sam grew in power and prestige. His hallmark was knowing the moment he was perceived as having clout, there were those who would inevitably come after him, doubly so since he was a Black man. Experience had taught him the value in knowing the difference between wielding his power and just making it apparent that he *could* use it. Sam knew when to hold and when to fold. And, similar to every other person who ascended to the top of his or her craft, Sam had created enemies along the way. He knew too, that invariably, it was always ones "friends" that one had to worry about—so Sam learned to keep his friends close, but his enemies even closer. He hadn't gotten to where he was without personal mishap. But he'd learned that if he took a personal interest in the lives of the people who worked with him, the mishaps could be minimized.

While the true artist creates, Sam recognized that it was the successful *marketing and management* of those creations that resulted in both the company's and artist's ultimate fame and fortune. With that premise in mind, and mostly through his own efforts, Sam saw Werner's revenue triple. He also watched as its stock increased exponentially. With the wealth of talent he'd brought to the label, he knew that much of Werner's success was attributable to him because he had positioned the company on the cutting edge. Sam had earned hundreds of millions of dollars for W. E. by

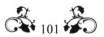

anticipating the public's musical appetites and by crafting undiscovered talent into mega-stars.

Now, Sam wanted a piece of the pie that he had helped to create. But owning a share of a pie that was controlled behind the scenes, as quiet as it was kept, by the *Mafioso*, for a Black man, was all but impossible. Acknowledging that Sam was a genius in bringing in the talent, increasing the company's revenues, and gauging the signs of the times were one thing, but to allow a *nigger* part ownership of the company was another. They'd just as soon kill him before they'd see such a thing happen.

When the board of directors brought back word to "The Silent Partners" (as the *Mafioso* was referred) that a Black man was making discrete inquiries into the whereabouts of the company's money, they immediately had Sam checked out.

The board of directors quietly called a meeting with Sam and asked him point blank if he had developed a sudden death wish. If not, he was advised that he would be wise to halt his inquiries into affairs that didn't concern him.

Without flinching, Sam explained to the board members exactly what it was he wanted. Sam held no illusions—he knew whom the board of directors answered to. He knew in whose hands the real power behind the organization was vested.

As Sam revealed his hand to the board members, he could see in every one of their faces that they were disquieted. Capitalizing on the element of surprise, he gave them his demands and relayed what he was willing to offer in return. Sam told them he expected an answer within a reasonable amount of time. He thanked them for their time before abruptly ending the meeting.

The board of directors did just what Sam expected. They met with their superiors.

To buy some time, The Silent Partners fashioned what was to become one of the most unprecedented moves of the decade: They appointed Sam Ross president of Werner Enterprises. Never before had a Black man been in charge of a major record label. There were several Blacks who owned indes (independent labels) but none had ever spearheaded a major. Overnight, Sam became one of the best lead stories of succeeding against the odds. His picture was plastered on the covers of all the major magazines. The mags vied to do feature stories on his life and his rapid ascent to power. Each magazine tried to chronicle his life and capture his rise to the top of the music mecca from a different and more specialized angle.

But there is an old adage among Blacks that has always rung true. *Once you let a spook through the door, it's not long before he's sitting at the head table.* Knowing they expected him to fail, Sam set out to prove they had underestimated him.

His presidential honeymoon period lasted only a few weeks and then all hell broke loose. Sam became a fireman because all he did was put out small "fires" within the company. But like cream which always rises to the top, Sam soon mastered the pitfalls of being president of a major label. And still, he wanted more.

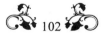

Sam knew that part ownership in the company was the only thing he'd settle for. He requested a meeting with The Silent Partners to tell them of his concerns. The Silent Partners stalled him for six months before agreeing to meet with him, but during that time, Sam had done his homework.

Impressed, but also nervous over the fact that Sam's hunger for more control of the company couldn't be satisfied with the usual trinkets that accompanied being president of a major record label, The Silent Partners decided to meet with him and weigh their options.

Knowing they were stringing him along, Sam began to discretely put out feelers about starting his own record label. He knew the ropes and with all the connections he had cultivated over the years, he knew that it would be a piece of cake to persuade some of the big-name stars to come along with him because he had garnered a reputation for being a man of his word. If Sam went to them and asked them to invoke what's commonly known as the "seven-year clause," a section of their recording agreement which gave them the option of terminating their contract, he had no doubt that many of them would do it.

Several days later, Sam was given a directive from the board of directors to attend a meeting at the Regent Beverly Wilshire Hotel on Wilshire Boulevard. No details about the meeting were forthcoming. Sam didn't fool himself, he knew it was a dangerous risk he was taking. But he had worked his entire life for this moment.

When Sam arrived at the hotel, he was ushered up to the Penthouse Suite. He seated himself and was alone in the guest room when he heard the door to the suite open and in walked a tall, white-haired man. Sam watched in fascination as Don Vitelli walked into the room. It had been over twenty years since Sam had been in similar circumstances, but he remembered sitting in the marbled mansion as if it were only yesterday. Sam stood to greet him, his manner respectful, and the two men shook hands before being seated.

Full of questions that he knew he could never ask, Sam noted that the man had become an exact replica of his predecessor. "Your father?" Sam asked.

Don Vitelli nodded his head. "Deceased. I run the organization now." Vitelli paused to light a thin Cuban cigar. "You've come a long way from the projects, Mr. Ross. And you appear to be a very ambitious man." Vitelli leaned forward to emphasize his next words. "Too much ambition can get a man killed."

Recovered from his initial surprise, Sam replied calmly, "Yes, but I'm also a man of wisdom, Mr. Vitelli. One who's wise enough to recognize that I'm of more value to you alive than dead." Sam flexed his hands. "If by some chance, an accident, involving myself, should occur, the same people I brought to this company wouldn't have a problem leaving to join another. Think of all the lost revenue this would mean to Werner. You could replace me, no doubt. After all, no one is indispensable. But who would you find to replace me that has amassed all of the contacts that I have?"

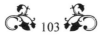

Sam knew a man of Vitelli's personage and character understood things in terms of dollars and cents. In order to communicate with him, he knew that he had to talk to him on his level.

When Don Vitelli inquired, "What, then, are you proposing, Mr. Ross?" and Sam laid it on the line, the true negotiations commenced.

Hours later, Sam left with what he'd come for—a thirty percent ownership of the company's stock.

Sam recognized two things: First, Don Vitelli had agreed to honor his request in part because of an old debt to his father. Secondly, because he had reviewed Sam's track record and found him more than capable and worthy of fulfilling the demands that he would now place on him.

Sam also knew Vitelli was testing the waters. But instead of flaunting and floundering the wealth of power he suddenly had, Sam dug in and worked that much harder. He sought to develop a powerful marketing and sales strategy that would position Werner as a superior brand record label—one that would substantially elevate and increase Werner's visibility and standing within the music industry. Sam envisioned a dynamic future for W. E. He developed a strategic plan to reorganize Werner as an enterprise of integrity, quality and commitment to its talent while becoming even more consumer conscious. Because he had profoundly increased the corporation's recognition as a market leader within the record industry, Time magazine ran an article that stated, "Werner Enterprise has become the dominant brand name in the music industry."

There were other aspects of the corporation that Sam wanted to change immediately. Foremost, no longer would artists be cheated of their royalties. Sam improved and upgraded the accounting procedures to give artists more frequent and accurate accounts of their royalties. If a company could not be trusted with an individual's money, Sam felt the person should conduct business elsewhere. Months later, the payoffs started rolling in in the form of even more artists bolting from other record labels to join Werner. Word got around that Werner was *the* company to be with if you didn't want to be ripped off. Sam was respected as a shrewd and hard-nosed businessman, and was known for his dazzling creativity in engineering lucrative deals. With uncanny business acumen, Sam protected his artist's money through tax shelters, IRAs and other creative, but legal, tax strategies. Sam taught his clients methods to ensure that they kept the bulk of their earnings, while becoming even more wealthier himself.

As the new talent and increased wave of financial gain flooded in, Sam had achieved something else: The grudging respect and approval of The Silent Partners—and he hadn't had to "sell out" in order to get it.

Chapter Fourteen

obust applause swept throughout the night-club as Ashela stepped to the mike. "Ladies and gents, give it up for the sweetest little sax player in all of Manhattan, Ms. Ashela Jordan! Let's show her some love!" She lifted her horn to her lips and her personalized rendition of John Coltrane's, "Take the A Train," surged through the smoke-filled crowd. When the rest of the band joined in, another rousing round of applause was heard.

Pandora's Box was located in Manhattan and catered to an after-work crowd. Its bar and tables were always filled with patrons who came for the live music, the festive atmosphere, and the happy-hour drinks. Throughout the week, The Ascetics, as the band was called, played an evening gig there. The quintet featured a lively forum of jazz melanges that included bits of swing, ragtime, bebop, free, and even mainstream jazz. Since joining the band, Ashela's imaginative vision had taken them to new heights. That the band could not be pinned down to any one particular jazz era was due to her creativity.

Ashela was celebrating her second year as the newest member of the group, which consisted of five members. Kerby Patterson, the leader, played drums; Janice, his girlfriend, was on guitar; Greg played bass, while Charles, his lover, played trumpet. Ashela had been selected to round them out by playing keyboards and sax.

Whenever she thought of the odd way in which she'd been recruited, a smile came to her face.

Her world had turned upside down in the aftermath of Stephanie's death. She was plagued by guilt over her friend's slaying and couldn't shake the feeling that had she been with her that night, things might have turned out differently.

Ashela never again set foot inside Sweet Georgia Brown's. After Stephanie's murder, she hung up her dancing shoes for good. With no funds left in her bank account (thanks to Patrick Hart) and no other means of income, Ashela was soon down to no money at all. Overcome by a mild state of depression, she slept throughout the days and played her saxophone by night. Days later, the tenants on her floor began complaining to management and Ashela was given notice to cease "disturbing the peace."

But playing her horn helped her to maintain her sanity. The next afternoon, she took her instrument to 42nd Street, to the Times Square subway station, where she played to the noon and evening rush hour commuters. To her delight, some of the passersby stopped to listen while others handed her dollar bills or threw change at

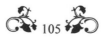

her feet. To catch every penny, Ashela flipped open her instrument case to form a make-shift bank. By the end of the evening, she was $56.78 richer.

For the next several weeks, Ashela hit the platform like clock-work. She'd entertain the crowds by interspersing blues and jazz melodies by legendary greats such as Louis "Satchmo" Armstrong, Duke Ellington, Thelonious Monk, Miles Davis, and Ramsey Lewis. Her music was sassy and dynamic, causing even oft-indifferent commuters to donate to her cause.

One Friday evening, Ashela drew a particularly large crowd of generous onlookers. The dollars bills in her horn case were piling up fast and she swooped down ever so often to stuff them into her pockets. Shortly before eight o'clock, she was packing her case when she looked up to find two people standing over her.

"Can I ask you a question? Why are you wasting your time when you could be earning much more than the crumbs these people throw your way?" She looked into the face of a tall, lean, attractive Black guy dressed in jeans and a leather jacket. Beside him was a short, medium built white girl, who in contrast, was dressed like a punk-rocker. They appeared an odd couple to Ashela. But she said nothing as she snapped her case closed and secured its belt around her waist. Without answering him, Ashela stood up and walked in the opposite direction.

"Wait, I'm serious. Have you ever thought of joining a band?"

He didn't seem threatening but just the same, Ashela was irritated that he was following her. Behind them, the girl he was with called to him impatiently, "Come on, Kerby. We're going to miss our train."

Paying no attention to her, he continued to follow Ashela up the stairs towards the exit. "Hey, will you hold up a sec? I'm Kerby Patterson and our group is called The Ascetics. You might have heard of us? We play every night over at Pandora's Box. Why don't you come check us out? Maybe you could even audition for us. We make good . . ."

They were at the exit when Ashela interrupted him. "Look, bud. Can't you take a hint? If I were interested, you would have known by now. Obviously . . ."

Neither of them had paid attention to the two guys who came ambling down the stairs. Ashela had her hand on the rail and one foot on the first step preparing to exit when one of them slipped behind her while the second one eased behind Kerby. Suddenly, Ashela went deathly still when she felt the butt of a gun press into her back.

"Give it up and nobody gets hurt," her assailant spoke gruffly from behind her.

"*What the . . .?*" Before Kerby could object, he too, felt the steel point of a gun against his own back.

"Y'all heard him, give us yo' money!" the guy behind Kerby said impatiently.

It was all happening so fast that Ashela never had time to react. But what followed was totally bizarre.

Kerby, the guy who had been hounding her, uttered in amazement, *"Willie? Willie Brown from a Hundred and Twenty-fifth Street? Is that you?"* Disregarding the gun in his back, Kerby spun around to face his assailant. Dismay swept across his face as he recognized his would-be attacker. "I'll be damned, it *is* you. Man, what are you doing out here stickin' folks up? You mean, you're just gonna take our money and *run*? Come on Willie, don't go out like that!"

Mutual recognition dawned on the face of the robber named Willie. He quickly put his pistol away saying, "Aw, *it's you*, man? What up dough, Kerby? My bag, man. We ain't knowed it was you. Swear ta God! We was just out to get some blow, man. Figured y'all prolly had big-time bucks. Tell you what, man, just spot us a couple of gee's an we outta here, man. No sweat."

Feeling as though she was trapped in someone else's nightmare, Ashela watched as the guy behind her stepped to the side and said, "Kerby? Kerby Patterson from B'ooklyn's Avenue U?"

"That would be me," Kerby replied reluctantly, not yet recognizing the guy who spoke to him.

"Man, it's me, 'member me? BooBoo Jones? We went to school together in the hood, man, 'member? Damn man, long time, no see!" BooBoo extended his hand to Kerby, saying, "Man, I thought you was dead! No shit, man, I thought you got popped by the Crips."

It had been nearly eight years since Kerby had stepped foot in the Brooklyn neighborhood in which he'd grown up, but he still remembered the Crips as a vicious, bloodthirsty gang of drug peddlers. Not wanting to renew acquaintances or press his luck with his old childhood friends, Kerby thought it best he immediately get rid of the now-turned hoodlums.

"Naw, BooBoo, it must have been someone else they knocked off," Kerby said. "But here, take this."

Ashela watched in amazement as Kerby reached into his jean pocket and took out a twenty dollar bill and handed it to the guy named Willie from 125th Street.

"For real, dough, man. We 'idn't mean no harm! Me and my boy, BooBoo here, was just tryin' to get a hit. Thanks, Kerby, man. Straight up dough."

"No problem, Willie, BooBoo. Take care of yourselves now."

Ashela couldn't move though the two punks scampered up the stairs and vanished just as quickly as they had appeared.

Kerby looked at her and said, "See, that's all the more reason for you to join a legitimate band. It's no telling what might have happened had I not been with you. You okay?"

Speaking slowly, Ashela said, "I'm not sure. It's not everyday that I meet stalkers like yourself with criminal friends named Willie and BooBoo from 125th Street."

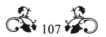

"The least you could do is say 'thank you.' After all, I did give up my hard-earned cash to save our lives."

"I could. But since they were your friends, consider the money you paid them a donation."

"Okay, so I'm out of twenty bucks, no big deal. Will you at least come check us out at Pandora's Box?"

They had climbed the stairs and reached street level when Ashela flagged down a cab. "I'll think about it" was all she said as she got in and closed the door in his face.

Ashela was too nervous to ever play at Times Square again. Though the money she'd earned there had kept food on her table, it did nothing to cover the cost of her mounting debt. Faced with the prospect of eviction (her rent was now two months past due) Ashela hit the streets looking for employment, albeit to no avail. Desperation forced her to seek out Kerby of The Ascetics weeks after the attempted robbery. She auditioned for the group and was offered a spot as soon as she completed it. Hoping it would be a step toward the fulfillment of her destiny, Ashela made the decision to join them.

The Ascetics shared a spacious, three-bedroom apartment in East Elmhurst, Queens. The money they earned during the week covered their living expenses and provided them with discretionary funds. In order to keep the group together, no member was allowed to play with any other band outside of the Ascetics. Moonlighting was grounds for dismissal.

After learning the ins and outs of the group, Ashela's only contention was with the way the group was run. She didn't always agree with Kerby, and whenever an issue came up, she was quick to let him know where she stood. However, the same could never be said for the other group members.

Janice abided by every word Kerby spoke and jealously monitored all that he did. For months after Ashela joined the band, she was subjected to suspicious looks from Janice. Only after she was assured that Ashela had no designs on Kerby, did her animosity towards her cease. Had Ashela known jealousy was the root cause of Janice's rancor towards her, she would have confronted her from the outset because regardless of how gullible she had been in the past, Ashela would never allow anyone to abuse her in the manner Kerby did Janice.

At least twice a week the two of them would go at it—him beating her and she cuddling up to him afterwards as though nothing out of the ordinary had occurred. Their off and on-again romance gave new meaning to the phrase "love/hate" relationship and their sadistic madness gave Ashela all the incentive she needed to stay out of their affair.

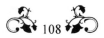

Greg and Charles, on the other hand, were little better when it came to standing up to Kerby. Greg, who was Black, was the more submissive one, while Charles, who was white, was the dominant one in their relationship. The two had been lovers for over four years.

Whenever a disagreement occurred, it was generally between Ashela and Kerby.

Kerby noticed that Ashela was the one who always added twists to the songs they copied from the superstars, so he encouraged her to write new material for the group. She wrote four songs which they practiced to perfection before playing them at Pandora's. The night they debuted the songs, the band was an instant hit and they easily doubled what they normally earned in tips.

From there on out, Ashela was constantly writing fresh material and before long, people started coming to the club solely to hear the Ascetics play. The weekly after-work crowd seemed to swell overnight. The bar had to be extended and more tables added to accommodate the growing number of patrons.

Ashela convinced Alicia Thomas, the owner of the club, to open the place on Sundays. It was also her suggestion to call it the Sunday Brunch Jazz Ensemble so that the band could play a strictly-jazz format. Alicia started advertising on WQCD radio and Sundays soon became her busiest day. She began to draw an older, eclectic crowd which had more discretionary income to spend.

Every Sunday, as a special treat to the audience, each band member performed a solo. Ashela drew the most tips whenever she performed, and tips were their bread and butter. One Sunday evening, instead of playing an instrument for her solo, Ashela chose to sing Crystal Gayle's "Don't It Make My Brown Eyes Blue." As she began singing, her eyes made contact with an older, salt-and-pepper-haired gentlemen who was seated up close at a table with three other companions. All Ashela noticed about him was that he had a pair of shockingly blue eyes. She caught and held his attention until the end of her song. When her solo was done, Charles was up next playing his rendition of one of Gene Hammond's tunes.

It was after closing time when Alicia handed her a sealed envelope. She wore a smirk on her face as she said, "Honey, the man said if I couldn't deliver it to you personally, I had to return it to him unopened the next time he came." Ashela thanked her and slipped the envelope into her pocket.

At home, she tore into the envelope. It contained three one hundred dollar bills along with a note that read, "Thank you for the serenade. Let's do it again sans the crowd." The note was unsigned. Ashela sat back on her bed, knowing it had come from the blue-eyed gentleman. It was too bad he wasn't Black, she thought. She didn't date white men. Ashela fell asleep recognizing that, other than Parris, she'd never dated *any* man. She was still a virgin.

***

109

On July 1 of the following year, Ashela turned twenty-two. It was a Sunday evening and as a surprise, Janice stepped to the mic and announced that it was one of the band member's birthday. Ashela was dragged to the center of the small stage while the audience joined in to sing happy birthday. Janice took the microphone and tapped into it. "Lift up your glasses everyone. Let's offer a toast to our birthday girl. Here's to the last virgin in the City of New York!"

Ashela's mouth fell open as the crowd started chanting and yelling birthday cheers. Though everyone around her was laughing and smiling, Ashela was thoroughly humiliated. To cover her embarrassment, she smiled and held up the plastic champagne glass that was handed to her. In one gulp, she drained it and tossed the glass laughingly into the crowd before accepting another one. She never noticed the man who caught it.

Ashela played her heart out that evening. But inside, she was fighting to cover up her mixed emotions. She was thankful when the evening finally came to an end. She packed up her instruments and told the rest of the group to go home without her.

As Ashela left the club, she noticed that a long, black, four-door Cadillac was parked in front of it. She paused for a moment, but continued walking when a man got out and called after her, "Excuse me."

Ashela turned and recognized the blue-eyed gentleman who had given her the three hundred dollars many months ago. She hadn't seen him since that time, or maybe he'd been there and she just hadn't noticed him.

Ashela waited for him to approach her. "Hi," she said when he reached her.

"Hello," he smiled. "I'm Randal Stein," he said, extending his hand.

"And I'm Ashela Jordan," she said, taking his hand.

"Can I give you a lift somewhere, Miss Jordan?" he asked after they'd shook hands.

"No thanks, I wasn't going anywhere in particular."

"Then may I buy you dinner and a drink?"

She seemed to mull it over and when she shrugged, Randal took her elbow and guided her to his vehicle. Before he could open the door for her, a big, giant of a man got out of the driver's seat to open and close the door behind them.

Starting to feel self-conscious and a little foolish for getting into his car, Ashela said, "Service with a smile," referring to his chauffeur. "It must be nice."

"What a beautiful southern accent you have. Where are you from?"

"How come you're so sure I'm not from New York?"

Randal smiled as he removed his suit jacket. "Bill, will you give us a tour of the city?" As the driver pulled off into the night, the glass partition between the front and back seats closed giving them an element of intimacy.

Randal turned to her and said, "You're too well mannered to be from around here. Besides, by now, a real New Yorker would have asked me for some kind of

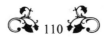

I.D." He was smiling as he reached into his suit jacket and passed her his wallet. "Go, ahead. Open it."

Ashela opened the leather wallet to see a photo bearing the name Senator Randal Stein. She looked up at him and said, "So you're a senator. Should I be surprised?"

"I don't know. Should I be surprised to find that you're a virgin?"

He would have to come to the club on the night of her public humiliation, Ashela thought. "I have no idea," was all she said as she handed him his wallet and turned to stare out the window.

"And now I've offended you." Randal lightly touched her face and turned it back in his direction. "I'll bet you're from Nashville."

Ashela smiled, already forgiving him. "No, I picked up my accent from North Carolina. And you? Are you a transplant too?"

"No, I'm afraid not. Growing up in Long Island makes me a native New Yorker." They were cruising in the heart of Manhattan when Randal pointed out the window and asked, "Have you ever been to Radio City Music Hall? Diana Ross and a host of other singers play there quite often."

Ashela shook her head, thinking to herself that one day *she* would play there as well.

"Are you famished? We could dine in my hotel suite." When Ashela hesitated he said, "Ms. Jordan, you have my word of honor that I will be nothing but a gentleman. Please, allow me to treat you to a birthday meal."

Staring into his eyes, Ashela said, "Mr. Stein, yours is the best offer I've had all night."

The driver drove into the parking garage of the elegant Presidential Plaza Hotel. Randal turned to her and said, "My driver will assist you to my suite and I shall meet you there shortly. There are a couple of things I have to take care of." Ashela was escorted up to his room by the chauffeur, Bill.

She walked through each expensively decorated room of the huge suite before settling in the parlor. She was sitting comfortably on an oversized sofa when Randal joined her some thirty minutes later carrying a Chanel shopping bag. "For you," he said as he handed it to her.

Pleased, in spite of herself, Ashela slid the box out of the bag. Inside, lay an expensive, floor-length burgundy velvet evening gown. The dress had a low U-back and a high slit up its side. In a separate bag was a set of gold, pearl-like earrings with a matching necklace and hair-clamp. A pair of high-heeled gold slippers completed the outfit.

"It certainly is beautiful," Ashela said as she laid it back into its box. She looked up at Randal and smiled. "Mr. Stein, I'm impressed. But really, you didn't have to go out of your way." Looking into his eyes, it was obvious what he wanted. The dress and jewelry were just his way of showing that he'd go to any lengths to get it.

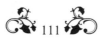

"I assure you it was no trouble." A knock sounded at the door. "That's our dinner. If you'd like, you can shower and change while the room service people set everything up. Remember, no strings attached." Randal got up to answer the door.

Ashela sat a while longer, trying to decide what she wanted to do. Despite what he said, she knew what would happen once she put on the dress.

She stood as she made her decision and was a bundle of nerves as she went into the bathroom to undress and step into the shower. Afterwards, she dried herself off and smoothed Coco Chanel lotion all over her body. Everything she needed was inside the accompanying makeup bag. Eye and lip liner, compressed powder, lipstick and blush. She took her time applying her makeup. Next, Ashela slid into the velvet dress. It was made of stretch material and fit her body like a glove. Her large breasts, her small waist and her wide hips were outlined appealingly.

After putting on the necklace and earrings, Ashela used the matching gold clamp to hold her hair atop her head. She stared into the mirror and nearly didn't recognize herself. She looked elegant and composed despite the fact that her nerves were screaming. Taking a deep breath at the thought of what she was about to do, Ashela opened the door and stepped out.

Randal Stein rose to his feet as she walked into the room. Even he couldn't believe how stunning she looked. Looking at her, he grew hard as a rock. It took every ounce of his self control not to rip the gown off her and take her right there in the middle of the floor. He walked toward her, took her hand, and led her to the dining room table. His fingers deliberately brushed her shoulders as he seated her. Her nervousness was obvious and Randal smiled at her across the table.

"Ashela." Randal had to repeat her name twice to capture her attention. When she finally looked up at him, he continued to smile at her. "Relax."

Though she was hearing his every word, Ashela's mind wasn't registering. Too many thoughts were filtering through her brain at once. Primarily, why was she doing this? *Because if you don't, you'll be an old maid before you lose your virginity,* her mind answered her. But it was her next thought that convinced her to go through with the evening. *And because you find him extremely attractive.* Having made her decision, Ashela lifted her glass and took a gulp.

Studying her, Randal was unable to believe he'd found such a gem. He continued to talk to her soothingly, aware that she wasn't comprehending anything that he said. Still, it was all part of the foreplay for him. After her second glass of wine, she was visibly relaxed and Randal made her eat. He didn't want her drunk, he wanted her ripe and ready for him when he made his move.

With his position, his wealth and prestige (not to mention his blue eyes and salt and pepper hair) Randal was as Caucasian as they came. An adventurous soul, his escapades had led him to scale the highest mountains on six of the seven continents. He'd swum the English Channel and competed in the Iron Man Triathlon. In his travels, Randal had sampled women from all over the world. And yet, there was

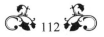

nothing he enjoyed more than being intimate with a Black woman. *The blacker the berry, the sweeter the juice. Once you go Black, you never go back.* All those idiotic, but most-true, sentiments ran through Randal's mind. They certainly were true for him—and for quite a few others whom he knew. Randal didn't mean to be crude, but if he possessed a kingdom, he knew he'd forfeit it all up just to have some *sweet black pussy* in his possession. Yes, he found his own race of women desirable, but when it came to pure, unadulterated passion, in his opinion, a Black woman couldn't be matched. Unable to control the trembling of his fingers, Randal knew it was time to make his move.

Ashela could see the bold look of desire on his face as he extended his hand. He was trying to be conservative, but she sensed it anyway. Her stomach felt queasy as he led her back into the parlor where they sat on the sofa and continued to talk. After awhile she grew comfortable again. Sensing her ease, Randal slid closer to her, his arm sliding over the back of the couch. When Ashela turned to look at him, his face was just inches from hers.

"Mr. Stein, you have such beautiful eyes."

"Please, call me Randal." He bent his head to whisper in her ear and his tongue lightly grazed her skin. Randal could feel the shiver go through her body. With his other hand, he cupped her chin and raised it before tracing his tongue down the length of her neck. Trying not to rush things, Randal slid one of the gown's straps off her shoulder. Her neck was arched back onto the sofa.

He could see the dazed and sensuous expression in her eyes. That was a good sign, he thought. She was enjoying it as much as he was. He slid his lips along her jawline and parted her lips with his tongue. She tasted like the Chardonnay wine. As his mouth pressed lightly to hers, he covered her breast with his hand, thumbing the taut nipple. Randal pulled his mouth from hers and reigned light kisses on her neck and chest.

The silky wetness of his mouth on her breasts nearly drove Ashela insane. Her gown was pulled down to her waist and his hands were rubbing her all over. Just when she had given herself over to the irresistible sensations, in the next instant, Randal was dragging her to her feet. With his hands pressed tightly to her well-rounded hips, he guided her dazed form inside the bedroom. In one quick movement, the dress was pulled over her head and she stood naked before him. Randal eased her onto the bed.

He stripped himself naked in world-record fashion and joined her, holding her, stroking her and disarming her. Unable to wait any longer for what he wanted, Randal stroked her core with his fingers until she moaned and parted her legs willingly. His male hardness probed her thigh. He pulled himself up and crawled between her legs. The sight of his whiteness against her browness was enough to almost make him spill himself all over her, but he was able to hold himself back.

He dipped his head down to her core and feasted on what he'd wanted all evening long. From her surprised gasps and the way she grasped his head, Randal knew she'd never had *this* done to her before.

The room was filled with his sucking noises intertwined with her ecstatic sighs. Several more pointed flicks of his tongue and Randal felt her entire body shudder uncontrollably. Afterwards, he held her limp form in his arms and once again parted her thighs. Only this time he inserted his maleness into her. First its tip, and then, little by little, more of himself as she welcomed him.

With his chest pressed to hers, he penetrated her until he reached her shield. Feeling its pressure, Randal nipped her hard on her ear to distract her from the pain as he thrust himself past it. He could feel her body jerk underneath him. But by this time, Randal had lost control. All he could do was grunt as he thrust himself back and forth inside her until finally, he pulled out of her and spewed his semen on top of her. Spent, Randal lay beside her and minutes later, he was fast asleep.

Ashela lay beside him, partly in shock and also in disappointment. Her body still tingled from the suddenness of it all. It had hurt more than she expected and it hadn't lived up to her expectations. The best part for her had come when he'd put his mouth and tongue in her vagina. Thinking that that was something that *had* to be repeated, Ashela too, soon drifted off to sleep.

At four-thirty in the morning, a discrete knock sounded on the door. Ashela shook Randal to wake him. He got up and went to the door but instead of opening it, he rapt lightly on the door in the same pattern that the initial knock had been.

Randal came back to the bed and sat down. Ashela lay naked on top of the sheets. Looking at her, his thick manhood hardened all over again. He slid next to her and wrapped his arms around her. "If only there was time," he kept whispering over and over.

There had to be time, Ashela thought. She just wanted him to do the thing with his tongue again.

Throwing caution to the wind, Randal kneaded and caressed her until he knew she was aroused. He flipped her over onto her stomach and slid on top of her, parting her legs with his thigh. He placed his hands underneath her and using his fingers, felt his way inside her. Spreading her tender lips apart, he slowly slid himself inside her, basking in the way she silkily closed over him in a most-tight manner. He groaned when he heard her sigh of pleasure.

The color of her skin against his excited him to the point of abandon as he rocked back and forth inside her. Randal began to lightly bite her on her shoulders. He squeezed her waist, pulling her to him more tightly. As the pressure began to mount, he kept whispering for her to squeeze him. She didn't understand him so he pushed her legs shut and continued to rock back and forth. Finally, he couldn't hold it any longer, and when he felt her shudder beneath him, he let loose with all he had.

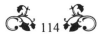

Randal lay gasping on the side of the bed, trying to gather his breath and steady his breathing. But this time, it was Ashela who fell fast asleep on him.

When she awoke from her exhausted sleep, Randal was long gone. There was a note left on the side of the bed telling her to order anything she wanted. It was already paid for. Ashela's eyes lit on the bills that lay underneath the note. When she counted out two thousand dollars, she didn't know whether to be flattered or insulted.

***

As she turned the key inside her East Elmhurst apartment door, Ashela picked up her horn and entered, shutting the door behind her.

"Well, well, look what the cat drug in."

"It's a bit early in the morning even for you to be a bitch, don't you think, Janice?" It was just shy of 10:30 a.m.

"Ash, can you whip up something for us to eat?" Kerby whined as he stood in front of her open door scratching his crotch through his shorts.

"Sorry, Kerb. I already had breakfast, and I'm just stuffed near to bursting. Why don't you have Jan fix you some grub? She's got to be good for something other than her daily beatings." Ashela shut her door in his face. She could tell all he really wanted was to ask her where she'd been.

The group held practice without Ashela that morning. She was busy car shopping, and hoped to find a used Volvo with the money Randal had given her.

That evening, there were flowers waiting for her at the club. Ashela smiled knowingly. She spent the rest of the week hoping to see Randal again but he didn't come. She eagerly awaited the next Sunday, expecting to see him then. But, again, Randal was a no-show. Ashela could barely hide her disappointment.

Randal Stein didn't come to the club the following Sunday or the one after that. Two months later, Ashela stopped looking for him. She had other pressing problems.

Because the club had started doing so well, Alicia had tripled their salary. The money was tax-free and should have been more than enough to last them as long as they budgeted properly. Things seemed to be going well and they were building their reputation, which was, after all, their primary goal. But then Kerby and Janice developed a slight habit—a drug-related one.

Ashela was forced to put a lock on her bedroom door because her money started coming up missing. Next, furnishings started disappearing from the apartment—first the VCR, then the television, followed by the microwave. Kerby also started beating Janice more violently than ever before and her performance started to suffer as a result. The bruises on her face were so obvious, she could no longer hide them with makeup.

When their drunken landlord, Mrs. Tayler, came looking for her rent money, claiming she hadn't been paid in months, Ashela knew she had to do

something—they'd worked too hard to let everything just fall apart. She told Alicia to start paying their weekly salary only to her. Alicia agreed, but already she, too, was complaining. Kerby and Janice were disrupting the show. They had started skipping practices and were so strung out on crack cocaine, they sometimes weren't able to perform once they reached the club. Alicia wouldn't tolerate their erratic behavior much longer because it affected her own income. She told Ashela that if things didn't change soon, she was going to have to let the entire group go.

One day, during the time when they were supposed to be practicing, Ashela knocked on everyone's door to call a group meeting. A half-hour later, they staggered groggily into the room. Kerby looked angry about being awakened.

Ashela stood facing them, staring hard at each one before she started speaking. Her sharp-eyed gaze caused several pairs of eyes to fall to the floor.

"Consider this meeting a reality check, guys. Someone has to step forward and point out the fact that we're pissing away everything we've worked for. Just when things were about to take off, just when we were off to a good start, we crash-landed. I mean, we were making a serious rep for ourselves, and now look at us. We don't practice anymore, there's no chemistry between us, no harmony, and no rhythm. And has anybody other than myself noticed that lately we sound like crap on stage?"

No one made eye contact with anyone. Everyone seemed to be staring at the floor or some distant object in space. "Last night, Alicia came to me and said she was giving us one last chance to get our act together." With none of them willing to say anything, Ashela feared her message was not getting through. She put her hands on her hips and shrieked loudly. "Guys! I need for you all to get this! If we don't have a job, there's no money. Hellooooo! Nooooo money! As in *no place to live!* Can somebody say H-O-M-E-L-E-S-S?" Ashela spelled the word out for them. Suddenly, they were all staring at her as if she'd grown two heads.

Trying to speak a little more calmly, Ashela said in a quieter voice, "Last month I used the last of my savings to cover the rent. I can't do it again this month, not even if I wanted to. So, from now on, I'm collecting the money from Alicia." Kerby looked at her with open hostility. Except Ashela didn't care. "And in two weeks, if we don't shape up, we won't *have* a salary to collect." She stared directly at Kerby.

"Who appointed you leader of this band? I'm the one who calls the shots around here!" But Kerby's words sounded feeble even to himself.

Ashela came and stood directly in front of him. "*You* made me the leader, Kerby. The moment you and Janice started stealing stuff from this apartment you signaled to me that *you* were no longer competent to lead anybody. Not even yourself. The minute you started blowing all the bill money was the same moment you said I was group leader. And now that the group is falling apart, I've decided to take you up on your offer. If you and Janice don't quit with the crack, there won't *be* a group for *anybody* to lead."

Ashela stood there looking at the two of them, feeling angry and betrayed. Already they had lost too much weight and the passion and fire for their music had died. But the problems had become bigger than them. The whole house was a wreck. With all the parties Kerby and Janice had been throwing lately, it looked like a pigsty. Ashela no longer bothered cleaning it up. She wasn't their personal maid. Their thievery had gotten so bad, she couldn't even take a shower without having to lock her bedroom door. It wasn't just them she couldn't trust, it was also their groupie friends. And topping it off, Greg and Charles were of absolutely no help. They were the most pathetic, passive males Ashela had ever met in her life.

She looked at Kerby who was whining about the fact that he would no longer be in charge of the money. It was obvious he needed clinical help—his face looked ashen.

Ashela sighed, cutting him off. "I'm having a problem, here, Kerby. Maybe you can help me solve it. You see, if I get *my* money and have to pay bills with it, and when you get *your* money, you spend it any way you want, that doesn't really make much sense to me. Not if we're sharing the same apartment and are *supposed* to be splitting all the bills—things appear extremely lopsided. What it boils down to Kerb, is that you're giving me responsibility without authority. And I will not *have* responsibility *without* authority!"

Ashela got in his face, "If you want *me* to pay the bills and keep everything operating properly, and when you get *your* money, you spend it all on drugs, well, once again, you're giving me *responsibility* without *authority*. And I will not take on the obligation of making things right without the *authority* to do so! If I've got to clean up your mess, Kerby Patterson, then I should have the power and the approval to do so!"

Angry, Kerby stood up and roughly pushed Ashela away from him. "Shut up, bitch!" Kerby had had enough.

Losing her balance, Ashela stumbled backwards to the floor. When it looked like Kerby was about to step to her, Ashela snapped. In a blink of an eye, she picked up an empty 40-ounce bottle of beer and jumped up and smashed it over Kerby's head before he even knew it was coming. Glass splintered everywhere and the violent impact felled him to his knees. Ashela stood over him holding the bottle's broken neck in her hand, daring Kerby to bust a move. She wasn't Janice. He must be stuck on stupid if he thought she'd allow him to kick her around, and she'd surely be damned if she ever allowed him to get the two of them mixed up!

Though he was much bigger and stronger, Kerby thought Ashela was crazy. Something about the cut-throat expression on her face as she stood over him, caused him to continue kneeling on the floor clutching his head, unaware of the blood that trickled down his cheek. The stupid bitch! He had only *pushed* her. Why'd she have to go and bust his head? With his pride wounded, Kerby turned away from her to look at everyone else, as if for moral support. But no one would even look at him.

Well, fuck 'em all! Kerby thought. Man, he needed another hit of that Blue Thunder! The rock was the only thing that really mattered. He didn't give a flying speck about whatever the little short bitch was bitchin' about anyway. Kerby sat there and continued to rub his forehead, ignoring all the blood on his hands. He just needed to think.

The others stared in horrified fascination, as though they were watching an action film. Charles had his hand clamped over his mouth and Greg and Janice were looking on in stunned disbelief.

Ashela stood gripping the broken bottleneck in her hand, her adrenaline still flowing. Looking around to make sure no one else was going to give her any trouble, she stared at each of them for several long seconds, daring any one of them to so much as crack a smile. When no one else challenged her, she stepped over the broken glass and walked into her bedroom, locking the door behind her.

Ashela leaned against her door and assessed her situation. She was nobody's fool. It didn't take a scholar to see that the band was finished. Kerby and Janice weren't in the right frame of mind to play. The two of them were so strung out, the only thing that would help them now was a serious detox program. They had become so desperate for drugs, they'd willingly steal the crack out of her behind. They needed help and Ashela wasn't about to stick around to provide it.

An hour before they were due to play that evening, Ashela went to take a shower. She walked into the bathroom to find Kerby sitting on the toilet seat with a belt pulled tight around his arm and a syringe protruding from one of his veins. Janice was sitting cross-legged on the floor and Charles was squatting on the edge of the bath tub. They were all staring at Kerby raptly, patiently waiting their turn for a hit of the Blue Thunder.

Ashela's nose flinched at the acridness of the smell. She might as well have been a fly on the wall for all the attention they paid her. Disgusted, she turned away from the door, shocked to find Charles with them. Frustrated, Ashela started packing her things. She had no idea where Greg was as she started loading her instruments into the trunk of her car. She threw some of her knick knacks and all of her clothes into a couple of garbage bags and loaded them into her car as well before driving off in the direction of the club.

Inside the club, house music blared from the overhead speakers. She found Alicia in the back, inside her office.

As soon as Ashela sat down, Alicia promptly told her the band was fired. She wouldn't miss them, there were too many other groups waiting for such a shot.

Seeing the look on her face, Ashela knew it was coming, but hearing her actually say it was another thing altogether. Her shoulders drooped dejectedly.

Alicia stood up and came over to her. She handed Ashela three hundred dollars, the last of the money that the band had coming to them and wished her good luck. Alicia liked Ashela, she seemed to be a good kid. Respectful, and not like the rest of

the group she played with. She shook her head as she looked at Ashela. Nowadays, it seemed like these kids were getting younger and younger before they left home. She knew some of them probably didn't even *have* homes. Though she knew Ashela's age, the girl barely looked fifteen as she sat with no makeup on her face, looking as if she were carrying the weight of the world upon her shoulders. Still, business was business to Alicia. She couldn't afford to develop a soft spot for any of the runaways who came through her doors. She helped Ashela to her feet. But prior to promptly showing her the door, Alicia said to her, "Look, kid. Do yourself a favor. Go home. If nothing else, find yourself a better group of people to work with."

With nowhere to go, Ashela drove aimlessly around Manhattan. She pulled up outside the Madhatter, another club that held open mics for bands, and pulled into an available parking space just as someone else was pulling out. They carded her at the door, verifying her age, before they let her in.

The place was packed but she managed to find a seat at a table in a corner of the room. She spent the next four hours nursing a sloe gin fizz while lamenting the demise of her group. If they just had stayed on track, she knew it wouldn't have been much longer before they snagged a recording contract. Ashela suddenly realized she sounded like Kerby: Optimistic without a clue.

Ashela liked the next group, Jaundice, the best. Though they were all white, she liked the rhythmic feel of their music. They were into their second song when she recognized it as one she'd written for her own group. When their allotted time was up, Ashela headed towards the backstage area intent upon asking them about the songs they had played. When they finally came from backstage, she cornered them and introduced herself as a member of the Ascetics.

Before any of the band members could speak, a Hispanic man stepped forward and said, "I'm their manager, Carlos Van Damm. Is there something I can help you with?"

Ashela's tone was friendly even though his was not. "I was curious about the songs the group played. They sounded like songs I wrote."

"Yes, I've heard your group play before. Kerby Patterson's your manager, isn't he? Well, we bought the songs from him for $4,500. If there's a problem, take it up with him. Otherwise, we really must be going."

"Wait. You don't understand. I'm not upset or anything." At his skeptical look, Ashela spoke hurriedly, "I was wondering if you needed a keyboardist or a sax player."

"Is Kerby still managing you?"

Irritation laced Ashela's voice. "No, Kerby's not my manager. Why do you keep saying that? And what do you mean he sold you my songs?"

Carlos was looking at her like she was on drugs. "How long have you been in this business? Cause you obviously don't know what time it is. I told Kerby months ago that your band had talent and that Alicia was ripping you off, but he told me he

had already signed the group up for several years. Did you ever sign a contract with him?"

Ashela shook her head, dumbfounded.

"Tell you what, if you're looking for work, why don't you give me a call tomorrow. I might know of another group that could use you." Ashela was handed his card before the man hurried out the door.

In the wee hours of the morning, Ashela pulled up to the 32nd block of 102nd Street. She could go no further because police had the entire street blocked off. Fire engines and television crews were everywhere. Even from her vantage point at the end of the block, Ashela could see blazes of fire and smoke. She just couldn't tell which house was on fire.

She parked her car the next block over and walked back to her street. She was squeezing her way through the crowd of onlookers when she realized it was her building that was on fire. Panicking, Ashela pushed harder through the throng of people, trying to make her way to her building. Unthinking, she ran forward, but a police officer grabbed her around the waist.

Hysterical, Ashela realized that nearly everything she possessed was inside the apartment. She was crying and visibly upset as the policeman led her to his squad car and let her sit in the back seat.

It took several hours for the firemen to extinguish the blaze. By then, Ashela was completely numb. Everything she owned, with the exception of her instruments, a few personal items and her clothes, had just gone up in smoke. But the worst was still to come.

The building was burnt to ruins, and even the two adjoining houses were heavily damaged. And, there had been casualties in the fire. One identified body on the first floor and three unidentified bodies on the second floor. Arson had not been ruled out. When the police chief discovered Ashela had lived in the building, she was taken immediately to the Manhattan precinct for questioning.

She was directed into a dark gray room furnished with nothing but a table and four chairs. Once seated, three detectives fired a barrage of questions at her. How long had she lived at that address? How many others occupied the apartment? Where did she work? Where was she at the time of the fire?

Ashela answered all of their questions in a dull, low, monotone voice. She was so numbed with depression that she didn't even realize that they suspected her of torching the place.

The detectives were notably interested in the part of her story about how she had busted Kerby Patterson's head with a beer bottle shortly before the fire. And how she thought Mrs. Tayler, the landlady, had been nothing but a mean, nosy, drunken old bitch. When the detective came right out and asked her if she had burnt up the place for revenge, Ashela looked at him uncomprehendingly.

"Revenge? Mister, are you sick or something? Nobody would do anything like that. Oh, but I forgot, this is New York. Everybody goes around burning up houses with people in them. Of course, I didn't set the house on fire! Are you crazy?" Ashela's voice rose with each word. "Everything I owned was in that apartment! Where am I supposed to live, Mister? Tell me that! Where the hell am I supposed to go without any money?" Seeing the deranged look in her eyes, the detective slowly backed away from the table.

His movement sent Ashela crashing over the edge. "What kind of sick fuck *are* you?" Filled with uncontrollable anger, she leapt across the table at him, wanting only to take out all of her frustrations on him.

The two other detectives grabbed her around her waist and tried to calm her down. At the nod of a head, the interrogating officer left the room.

"Ms. Jordan, we're sorry, please, calm down. The guy's a jerk. He should never have suggested what he did. We're just here to help you. Can we get you something? Coffee, tea, soda?"

Ashela was crying into her hands. With tears everywhere, she was unable to answer them. Finally, when she quieted her sobs, she was handed a handful of tissue to wipe her face.

On the other side of the two-way mirror, Detective Teferro McClodden watched her. He wrapped his arms over his chest and pulled at his chin with his hand. Thirty years on the force told him the girl was telling the truth. Not even the best actress in the world could feign such extreme histrionics. Touching the scratch marks on his cheek, he knew he'd better go clean them before they got infected. Turning to the other detectives beside him, he said, "Release her. She's clean."

Ashela was sitting with her palms pressed against her temples when another police officer stuck his head inside the room and said, "She's free to go."

Ashela turned to the policeman who was comforting her and said, "Free to go where? You all don't understand. I don't have anywhere *to* go!"

The policeman stood and said, "Don't worry, Miss. There are plenty of shelters that can put you up for the night. You'll be okay."

He led her outside into the hallway where there were people screaming at each other, swearing and even fighting. Ashela hadn't even noticed all the uproar and commotion upon her arrival. And despite the aspirin they'd given her, her head continued to pound.

At the front desk, the detective said, "Thanks for coming down here, Ms. Jordan. Take care of yourself." With no further mention of shelters or temporary housing, he turned and walked away.

Feeling abandoned, Ashela called after him, "Gee, thanks, Mr. Policeman. You could have at least told me to have a goddamned Coke and a fuckin' smile!" But the detective never looked back.

Outside on the step, Ashela had no idea of where she was. It was as though her sense of direction had deserted her. She asked another police officer and was told she was in Uptown and that she'd have to walk two blocks over to 34th Street, take any train to 42nd Street and transfer to the Number 7 train that would take her back to Queens. Great, Ashela thought. Just what she'd always wanted. To be lost in New York.

She paid her fare and got on the first train that came along. Lost in thought, she forgot all about transferring at 42nd Street. It wasn't until the train came from underground and the landscape changed from that of industrial buildings to that of burnt-out ruins that she began to panic. Looking around her, Ashela saw she was the only passenger on the train. She had no idea how long she'd been riding. When the train pulled up to the next stop, she wanted to get off, but looking outside at what appeared to be an abandoned station, common sense told her to stay on board. From the signs posted on the platform, she realized she was lost somewhere in the heart of the South Bronx.

At the next stop, the doors opened and four thuggish gang-bangers got on. They were mean looking, with red scarves tied around their heads to signal which gang they were affiliated with. Sensing that they intended to rob her, there was only one thing Ashela could think of to do.

Loud shrieks and wails of cackling laughter spread throughout the train car. Ashela began to laugh loud guffaws, smacking the empty seat beside her, as she pretended to be a raving lunatic. Never actually looking at any of the thugs who'd gotten on the train, she stared ahead of her, beside her, or out of the train's window. Just as suddenly, she stopped laughing and started rocking and muttering to herself out loud.

Ashela looked into the seat beside her as if someone were actually sitting there. In her most menacing voice, she said, "Dammit Dione, I told chu' not to ask me that agin! If you keep on talkin' to me, I'mma hafta cut chu' and kick yo' ass!" And then in the excited voice of a small child, she gestured toward the window and said, "Look over there, Dione! That's the building we're gonna live in one day." Excited, Ashela turned to her imaginary friend and said, "And that's the school and the playground we're gonna play at. Do ya' see it?" Suddenly, Ashela's eyes narrowed dangerously. "What the hell you mean, you don't see nothin'?" She slapped Dione hard, shaking her by the cuffs of her neck. "Now, look agin, dammit! Now you see it?" Ashela pressed her entire face and the palms of both her hands against the glass of the window, staring into the dark nothingness of night.

Ashela was correct in her assumption that the gang-bangers had intended to rob her—and rape her. But the moment they heard her laughing and saw her talking to herself, they changed their minds, deciding to amuse themselves with her, instead. The bitch was obviously crazy or either blowed out on drugs. Whatever the case, she showed no fear of them and that was the one element they required when they attacked someone: Fear. They didn't want to risk robbing her when she might be packing a knife or a gun. So, they sat back and watched her, laughing out loud at how she kept pointing out the window and asking the invisible figure if it saw the buildings, too.

So real and convincing did she come across, that the gang-bangers, themselves, looked out the window just to make sure nothing was there. But all they saw was a vast wasteland topped by a darkened sky. They turned back to find her choking and threatening to cut and shoot the invisible figure that was supposedly seated next to her. When the train pulled up to the next stop, the gang-bangers got off, still laughing amongst themselves at the stupid girl, unaware that they had just witnessed the theatrical performance of a lifetime.

Ashela's shoulders slumped the moment the train pulled away from the platform. Her lunatic impersonation had left her drained and empty. Though it had only been a charade, in those few minutes, she had actually *felt* crazy.

At least she hadn't been mugged or raped, Ashela thought. And at least she still had the three hundred dollars Alicia had given her hours earlier. It was all the money she had left in the world.

Chapter Fifteen

t was mid-morning when an exhausted Ashela finally made her way back to Queens. She picked up her car from the next block, grateful that no one had broken into it. Pulling up across the street from her building, she got out to study what remained of it. She'd never been a fire victim before. The feeling wasn't something she'd wish on her worst enemy.

The three bodies had been identified as Kerby, Janice and Charles. Ashela found it hard to believe that she'd never fuss, fight, or even play music with them again. She wondered where Greg was, and if he was aware of the tragedy.

The building had been completely gutted and was sealed off with yellow crime-scene tape. Huge shards of broken glass lay strewn about the sidewalk. Looking at the place now, one would be hard pressed to imagine that people had once inhabited it and that laughter had once graced its halls. Ashela took a final look before getting into her car and driving off.

She drove to a restaurant on Astoria Boulevard. While waiting for her order to come, she went to the pay phone and dialed Carlos' number.

"Hello." Gruff was the voice on the other end.

"Carlos? It's Ashela, we met last night, remember? Listen, I don't know if you've heard, but there was a fire at our house. Kerby and two other members of the band were killed." Ashela waited for a response. When none came, not even a "I'm sorry to hear that," she continued. "I was calling to see if you needed a keyboardist. Carlos, can you hear me?"

"Yes, I hear you. Why are you screaming?" Ashela heard him yawn. "It's not even twelve o'clock yet."

"Maybe not, but at least you have somewhere to lay your head. I don't. So what's up? You know anybody?" Frustration crept into her voice.

"Chill, baby, chill. It just so happens that I do know of someone. Do you know where Flatbush Avenue is in Brooklyn? Wait a minute. Scratch that. Go to Victor Street in the Bronx. Just ask for Lew. He'll be the one to set you up with digs. Be sure to tell him I sent you."

Grateful, Ashela got directions on how to get to the Bronx. She just hoped it wasn't near the bombed-out section of town she'd gotten lost in on the train.

When Ashela finally found Victor Street, she sat inside her car with her forehead pressed to the steering wheel. She hadn't known what to expect, but the neighborhood in East Elmhurst looked princely compared to the jaw-dropping poverty she found herself immersed in. She could feel a migraine headache coming on as she got out of her car, and went inside the dilapidated building.

In both Spanish and English, a sign on the door read, "Lew is on the fourth floor." Ashela hiked up the stairs slowly. When she reached the fourth floor, she encountered about ten to twelve people standing in the hallway. They were all Hispanic and were filling out forms. Ashela wondered, "What the hell is this? Immigration?" She pushed her way through to knock on the door.

It was yanked open by a man even shorter than herself. He stood about four feet tall. Ignoring the ferocious frown he wore on his face, Ashela said, "I'm looking for Lew. Carlos sent me."

"Ellos estan locos! Todos ellos estan locos!" Ashela had no idea what the man was saying as she followed him inside the apartment. But it didn't take a genius to surmise that he wasn't issuing compliments.

She was led into a room where a dark-skinned man with a long, wavy ponytail was sitting behind a desk.

"So Carlos sent you?" When she nodded, he asked in a heavily accented voice, "What can you play?"

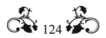

"Keyboard and sax. I write a little bit as well."

"Good. Here, sign this." He removed a sheath of papers and a pen from his desk and handed them to her.

Ashela read over the documents, ignoring the man's obvious impatience. After a long pause, she looked up at him as if he were crazy.

She tossed the papers onto the desk. "If you think I'd sign something like this, either you're a fool or you think I'm a bigger one."

"Look lady, everybody who works for me is required to sign this form. It's the only way we can do business."

Ashela stood up to leave. "Then I've wasted your time and you've wasted mine. I'm looking for a job, Mister, not a contract for indentured servitude. I'm not like the people you've got waiting on the stairs. I've already *got* a green card." She was turning the handle on the door when he stopped her.

Sighing heavily, he said, "Perhaps, we can work something else out, Ms. Jordan."

Ashela turned around and approached his desk. "Then talk to me, Lew."

In exchange for room and board and several hundred dollars a week, Ashela got to play for one or two Latin bands. All the clubs were located in the Bronx and featured La Bamba-type music. She didn't have to be a genius to play with the groups, she just needed lots of energy and the ability to read music.

She was given a small studio apartment in a three-storied building that was occupied by a host of Hispanic families. The units were packed like cans of sardines; there were approximately twenty people inside each studio apartment.

Lew paid Ashela her money directly. She worked six days per week and earned every penny. She found herself living from paycheck to paycheck and often wondered how any one managed to make money in the music business. Though she played with two groups at many different clubs, Ashela always had the feeling that she was an outsider.

The apartment building that she lived in was loud and had a heavy flow of traffic. It seemed the people who lived inside each apartment had an abundance of children. Ashela loved the children most of all. But it irked her that she couldn't understand what they were saying to her. She became determined to learn their language, so she bought teaching tapes on how to speak Spanish and within four months time, was able to speak the language fluently.

When she wasn't playing, Ashela kept to herself. While it was a lonely existence, what she learned during that stretch of time was how to be comfortable with herself and her innermost thoughts.

Ashela was on her way to the store one morning, when she discovered that her car had been stolen. She stood in the spot where she'd parked it trying to convince herself that whoever had taken it would bring it back.

After the theft, she became much more watchful and cautious. She wasn't easily frightened, but she had learned to trust the small voice that came from within. Whereas before when she would just jump in her car and drive wherever and whenever—with no car to drive at all, things changed because of her lack of mobility. Since each of her gigs ended so late into the night, Ashela would bum a ride back to her apartment with one of the band members. Before, she would brush it aside jokingly when some of the men in the clubs got too fresh with her. But now she was quick to set them straight. Having no car of her own made her very uneasy.

One night, she was sleeping soundly when something woke her up. As she laid deathly still, Ashela could hear someone, ever so slowly, turning the knob of her door. Quietly, she sat up in the bed and switched on her bedside lamp. No sooner had she done so when she heard footsteps quickly departing from her door. She didn't go back to sleep that night. Instead, she lay awake contemplating what she could do to make her small environment safer.

The next morning Ashela enrolled in a school for martial arts on Queens Boulevard. She also signed up for shooting lessons at a firing range in Long Island City. For the next several weeks, she spent her mornings learning how to protect herself in the event of an attack. She didn't walk in fear. She just wanted to be prepared.

Several days later, Ashela learned that a young Latino girl from the same building in which she lived had been found in a nearby abandoned warehouse sodomized, strangled and left for dead. As soon as she heard about it, she got one of her band members to procure a gun for her. She had already added two additional locks to her door, but still something was nagging her. She couldn't shake the feeling that she was being watched.

She took to wearing a leotard with green-beret pants that had deep pockets on the side of each leg. She bought several pairs in different colors and they became her new wardrobe. She also purchased two hunting knives and was careful to place one of the huge knives into the pocket of her pants. Her new outfits did nothing to enhance her femininity, but they gave her a feeling of security. Ashela felt that if she didn't want to be raped or robbed in the neighborhood where she lived, she had to sacrifice beauty and fashion for the sake of safety.

One night, after pulling a gig that lasted well into the wee hours of the morning, Ashela was dropped off at her apartment. She locked her door behind her and went inside the bathroom to shower and dress for bed. She had slipped between the covers and was nearly asleep when a noise inside her room awakened her. Suddenly, her closet door burst open and a man wearing a ski mask burst from inside her closet and threw himself on top of her. Her survival instinct overrode the fear in her body as she vied against the hands surrounding her throat. The two of them fought violently in the ensuing struggle, twisting and turning wildly on the bed.

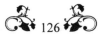

Battling for her very life, Ashela managed to turn onto her back, but the man was stronger and quickly straddled her legs and lower body. She twisted and flopped on the bed and when he tried to cuff her hands above her head, she bit hard into the flesh of his arm. Instinctively, the man yanked his arm away and slapped her across the face. But he made the mistake of relaxing his grip on one of her hands. Ashela lunged upward, twisting her body while reaching for the knife at her thigh.

As they each grappled for dominance, he shoved her hand away from her thigh causing the knife she'd almost held in her grip to fall to the floor. Bucking and using the strength in her legs to kick him backward, Ashela twisted off the bed and fell to the floor. Just before he could pounce on her, she snatched her .38 special from the holster she kept mounted underneath her bed and aimed it at his head.

Holding the gun steady with both hands, she whispered, "Don't move." The calm breathlessness in her voice signaled her willingness to fire the gun. "Now back the fuck up," she told him.

When the man didn't budge, Ashela said, "Please, *make* me have to repeat myself."

Just as she reached up to switch on her light, her assailant lunged at her. Ashela fired, capping three bullets into his neck and chest area. He fell backwards and thrashed momentarily before laying lifeless on the floor.

Ashela got up and stood over him. As blood seeped from his body, she bent down and snatched the ski mask off his head. Even in death, he looked menacing.

The gunfire had roused the other residents in the building. There were voices outside her door speaking loudly in Spanish.

Ashela went to the door and opened it with the safety chain in place. "Call the police," she told the people outside. When nobody moved, she repeated herself more harshly in Spanish, *"Llamar a la policia!"*

Ashela sat on her bed waiting for the police to come. The man was dead, yet she felt no remorse. Only exhaustion and sadness over the way her life was turning out.

Ashela found out that her attacker, a recent parolee who had a history of violence against women, had broken into her apartment through the vacant one above her and had waited for her to return. Since it was determined that Ashela had acted in self-defense, no criminal charges were filed against her—not even for having an unlicensed weapon. Out of fear, she'd told the police that the gun belonged to the deceased assailant.

***

After the attack, things shifted dramatically for Ashela. She wasn't sleeping well at night and had begun to lose weight. While her music was all she felt she had, she began to question if it was worth it. She'd been playing at local Spanish clubs for over a year now and was about ready to admit defeat.

When she called the insurance company to check on the status of her claim, they informed her that her car had been uninsured. Her policy had been canceled two days prior to its theft. Feeling as if she'd been hit with a sledgehammer, Ashela slunk back to her room. She had been counting on that money. She'd intended to use it to move to another city. But now that option had been eliminated. She couldn't afford it and she couldn't shake the feeling that she was trapped.

A deep depression gripped Ashela. She couldn't bear to leave her room. When different group members knocked on her door to signal it was time for their nightly gig, they got no response. By the end of the week, Carlos came to see her. He knocked on her door and when she refused to answer, he yelled that he would keep knocking until she let him in.

Dragging her tired body from the bed, Ashela unlocked her door. Carlos stepped into the room looking around him, but she had already turned away and was crawling back into her bed. He came and sat next to her. Lew had told him what had happened and that she had stopped showing up for all of her gigs. He had sent several people to check on her, but they'd gotten no response. Lew had too many other problems on his hands, so he asked Carlos to check things out.

Ashela didn't know it, but the two groups she played with needed her. They relied upon her energy and fed off of her intensity. She'd even written several songs in Spanish for both groups. With her sultry-sounding voice, she was a crowd pleaser. She also didn't know that both he and Lew were making a ton of money off of her. Attendance at the various clubs she played at had tripled since she joined the two groups. As she lay before him, her lackluster appearance and visible depression left Carlos unnerved.

Carlos had his own ulterior motives for coming to check up on her. He had a special gig coming up that he needed Ashela to be a part of. He got up and opened her portable refrigerator. There was nothing in it but orange juice. He grabbed the bottle of juice and smacked it against his palm before cracking it open.

"Here, Ashela, drink this." Carlos pushed her weak and flailing hands aside. He pulled her body upward and made her drink some of the juice.

It tasted sharp in her mouth and because she hadn't eaten anything in several days, it burned its way through her stomach. Ashela coughed loudly and turned her head away. She wanted only to go back to sleep.

"Come on, baby. We've got to get the ball rolling." Carlos lightly tapped her cheeks as if to bring color back into them. Recognizing that he had his work cut out for him, Carlos removed his suit jacket and rolling up his sleeves, pulled Ashela to her feet. He ignored her grumbles and led her to the bathroom, where he pushed her into the tub. Holding her head in a tight grip, Carlos turned on the cold water full speed.

As the overhead shower blasted her face and body with heavy jets of cold water, Ashela struggled to get loose. But Carlos held her firmly until the aggressive way she fought him back signaled that her passivity was gone.

Ashela cursed him and sputtered angrily. When he finally released her, she stood momentarily dazed before finally reaching down to turn on the hot water as well.

"Take your time in the shower. We've got some things to talk about." Carlos turned and shut the bathroom door behind him.

Nearly forty minutes later, Ashela came out wrapped in a towel. She stood in the doorway with a surprised look on her face. Sitting on the table in the corner of the room was a styrofoam tray of bacon, eggs, grits and biscuits with more orange juice. Realizing how hungry she was, Ashela sat down and gratefully stuffed her face. The food tasted so good her toes started curling.

Carlos talked animatedly while she ate. "The group that I'm managing, Jaundice, remember them?"

Ashela nodded her head as she plopped a half strip of bacon into her mouth.

"I've been giving it a lot of thought. The group is good, you know what I mean? But there's something missing. I was thinking about it when Lew called to tell me you hadn't been showing up for your gigs. And then it hit me. You're what the group needs, Ashela." Carlos looked as if it all made sense to him.

Spreading honey on her biscuit, Ashela was only vaguely listening to him. As she bit into the biscuit, her eyes closed lovingly. A deep moan rumbled from the back of her throat. She swore the biscuit was homemade.

"With you singing vocals and playing keyboards and sax, it would push us right over the top. You're what we need to take us to the next level."

When the smooth, buttery texture of the dough-like biscuit slid down her throat, Ashela's left hand raised slowly in the air. A quick wave of her fingers and an even quicker ball of her fist, signaled that she had a testimony: She was back amongst the living.

Carlos was looking at her impatiently, berating her for not paying attention. "Ashela, are you hearing me?" He expected attentiveness as he revealed what was on his mind and heart.

Replete, Ashela sat back in the chair and rested her head against the wall. All she could do was close her eyes and keep turning her head from side to side as she drifted away. She hadn't felt this good since that long ago night when Randal had gone down on her.

Moments later, she opened her eyes to find Carlos sitting on the very edge of her bed facing her. His elbows rested on his knees and his hands were clasped together at the fingertips. Carlos was repeating her name, over and over.

Ashela's eyelids had grown heavy and she was finding it difficult to stay awake. "*Si,* I'm hearing you, Carlos. You want me to play with your group."

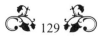

Carlos rose to his feet. "I knew you weren't listening to me. I'm not asking you to play with the band for a night or two, Ashela. I'm offering you the chance to become a *member* of the band. No more floating from band to band. This is a solid shot at the big time. We've got a gig coming up tomorrow night at the Marriott Marquee on Broadway. There'll be some big names and heavy hitters there. That's why I came here to get you this morning. You, and the rest of the group, need to spend some time practicing together. Tomorrow doesn't give us much time. So what do you say?"

Sensing the urgency in his voice, Ashela's sleepiness dissolved and was replaced by a glimmer of renewed hope at the chance for a new start. "I say let's get started." She pulled some clothes from her dresser and went into the bathroom to change.

When she reappeared, Carlos had removed from her closet the burgundy velvet evening gown that Randal had given her and laid it out on the bed. "You'll need something fancy to wear for the dignitaries at tomorrow's gig. Oh, and pack some other clothes in case you don't get to come back here for the next couple of days."

Ashela was silent during the drive from the Bronx to far Rockaway Boulevard in Queens. When they finally got to the house where the band lived, it was a mansion compared to the huts she'd been dwelling in.

She and the band members sat around talking and getting acquainted before they started rehearsing the songs they would play the following night. Practicing again felt good to Ashela. She liked knowing she would be playing with them for more than just one night. It erased her sense of transientness and gave her a feeling of stability.

They rehearsed for the next six hours, liking the overall synergy they were developing. Each of them could see the enhancement her presence brought to the group and they were all excited about it. They had long since claimed three songs that she'd written for her previous group, so they knew what she was capable of.

That evening, Carlos got around to discussing the contract she would have to sign in order to play with the group. He went over it with her, irritated by the fact that she read it in its entirety. She was quick to ask him about sections that she didn't understand.

Though Carlos patiently explained everything to her in layman's terms, it was the last contract Ashela would ever sign without having it poured over by lawyers. Unbeknownst to her, by signing, she obligated herself to play with Jaundice for the next two years and she signed away all rights to every song she would write within that time-frame.

When Ashela finished signing all the documents, Carlos told her that he wanted her to have a makeover the following day. He wanted her hair and nails perfect in case the group was caught on camera. He had very good vibes about their future. Gut instinct told him she was the missing link. She had good vocals and was dynamite on keyboards and sax. But above all, Carlos recognized that Ashela possessed the one

trait that could make or break any group: the intuitive sense of knowing when to lead and when to follow. She had come in willing to learn from the others, not thinking she was going to automatically be the group's star. Carlos knew the person who could sublimate their individual need for stardom while putting before them the overall needs of the group, was invaluable. Therein lay the reason for the failure of so many rising singing sensations: Everyone wanted to be the star.

The next evening, the band arrived at the Marriott at six p.m. sharp. The dinner affair, a gubernatorial fundraiser, didn't begin until seven, but they had to set-up and begin playing before the guests arrived. They were scheduled to play from six-thirty to nine-thirty or until the guest of honor, the Governor, got up to speak. Ashela was all smiles as her fingers flitted across the keys of the huge, white piano. With Peter Regas as drummer, Tim Ball as bass player, Dave Morton on trumpet, Scott Ashenfelter on trombone, and Shane Hopkins on guitar, they looked good as a group and sounded even better. The guys were dressed in white tuxedos while Ashela stood out among them, dressed in her purple evening gown.

At seven, when the first of the guests began to arrive, the band was playing a number of Count Basie tunes. By eight o'clock, the gathering was in full swing as the invitees patronized the open bar where the drinks and champagne flowed.

The band was set up on a small platformed stage just off from the throng of people. They were enjoying themselves as much as anyone in the crowd. Throughout the evening, guests would stop by and drop bills into a marble "tip" box set up on the edge of the piano for that very purpose. When they got to the trio of songs Ashela had written, she started singing softly into the mic.

". . . Thank you for the tip about Gibralter Securities, Senator. I'll certainly have my secretary issue a donation to your campaign fund."

"Thank you, Charlie. I was just doing my civic duty. It's not often that I get the chance to be of service to the president of Standard Oil, so I have to capitalize whenever I can. Excuse me." They shook hands again before he moved away.

"That was a bullish move by Microsoft. I hear it peaked at one seventy-eight and a quarter . . ." the conversation continued as he drifted away.

Senator Randal Stein was mingling amongst the guests, being stopped ever so often by heads of corporations and other constituents. Tinkling laughter sprinkled the current conversation he was having with two women and three men. Randal was flashing his brightest smile when suddenly he heard a familiar voice filter through the stream of conversations around him. Something about the voice grabbed his insides in a most delightful manner. He hadn't heard a voice like that since . . . Still giving the impression he was captivated by the story the woman standing next to him was recounting, Randal tuned her out and slowly turned his head in the direction where the music was coming from.

And then he saw her. All the way on the other side of the room. Sitting behind the piano crooning into the microphone. She was wearing the same outfit he had given her on her birthday. How on earth could he have missed her? Randal lifted his drink and took a deep sip before excusing himself from the conversation. He had long since ceased from listening anyway. Idly, trying not to draw attention to himself, he maneuvered through the crowd toward the area where the band was playing.

He was stopped by many people who wanted a word with him and it seemed to take him forever to reach his destination. Standing in just the area he wanted to get to was a group of lobbyists. Much to their surprise, Randal joined them, shaking hands with everyone in the group.

"Senator Stein, what a surprise! What do we peons owe to the pleasure of your company?"

"Who cares?" one of the men interjected. "Senator, have you seen the new bill the EPA has submitted?"

"Now, now, gentlemen. Let's not talk shop tonight. I'm just trying to enjoy the band." Randal directed his sole attention to the group of musicians.

"They're pretty good, aren't they?" someone commented.

"That they are," Randal concurred as he took another sip of his drink. He shook his head at the sight of her up close. She looked the same as he remembered her, slightly thinner with longer hair, but she was still breathtakingly gorgeous.

The morning after their delightful tête-à-tête, Randal had traveled to Washington, D.C. to return to Congress. As soon as it ended, he'd returned to New York and had sent Bill to look for her. When the owner of the night club told Bill she had no idea where Ashela had gone, Randal had kicked himself. After thinking of her so often, he couldn't believe his good fortune at having found her again.

Her second song was drawing to an end as Randal broke away from the group and strolled in her direction. She had her back turned to the audience and didn't see him until he stood near the edge of the platform where they were playing.

"I wonder if the band takes requests?"

Ashela spun around at the familiar sound of his voice. It had been so long since she'd seen or thought about him, she didn't know what to say. Regaining her composure, she stepped forward and asked, "What would you like to hear, Senator?"

Smiling, Randal said, "How about, Don't It Make My Brown Eyes Blue?"

Flashing a grin of her own, Ashela turned to the rest of the group, "I think we can play that, can't we fellas?"

"Sure, no problem," was the consensus.

Ashela sat down at the piano and led the others into the song. She glanced at Randal as the first of the lyrics fell from her lips. Her eyes were glued to his as she

sang for him. But only the two of them were aware that she was singing the song *to* him.

From the other side of the room, Kate Stein watched as her husband made his way through several groups of people. Something in that determined stride of his made her eyes follow his every move. When she saw him talking with several congressmen and stateheads, she relaxed. As an affluent woman of prestige, Kate wasn't as concerned about him as she was about *how* whatever he did made her look in the public eye. Though Randal was discrete, Kate was still aware that he had a roving eye. Nevertheless, it galled her that his flights of fanciful trysts tended to be with women of the darker persuasion.

Kate looked up a while later and saw her husband talking with a group of lobbyists. She thought it strange that he would be speaking to them since the two sides were always at great loggerheads. She decided to keep an eye on him, just in case. But someone touched her arm to capture her attention. When Kate finally looked over in the direction where Randal had been standing, she didn't see him. Her eyes cased the room until she spotted him by the band. Immediately, she excused herself and went to join him.

As the song came to an end, Ashela lingered on the last few words, her fingers finding the keys with ease. She smiled invitingly as Randal removed two bills from his leather wallet and placed them inside the lacquer tip box.

"Darling, I was looking all over for you." Kate Stein appeared out of nowhere and latched onto her husband's arm, guiding him back toward their table where other guests were also starting to be seated.

As they walked away, Kate said in a quiet but steely voice, "Randal, please tell me you were just complimenting the band. My mind must be playing tricks on me to think that you were conspiring with that . . . that . . ."

Eager to divert his high-strung wife's attention, Randal said placatingly, "Yes, love, if you thought I was doing anything untoward, then your mind *is* playing tricks on you. Dear, you know I only have eyes for you." He wrapped his arm around his wife's waist and led her to their table. But Randal's gesture was tenuous at best. While he had merely spoken words that he knew she wanted to hear, his thoughts were completely focused on Ashela Jordan.

The band knew they had been a hit and they smiled at Ashela knowingly. They were standing outside waiting for Carlos to bring the car around when a man came hurrying after them, calling Ashela's name.

Ashela recognized the tall and hulking figure immediately. As Randal's chauffeur approached her, he removed an envelope from his suit jacket and handed it to her. "My boss asked me to deliver this," was all he said before he walked away.

From that night on, Jaundice never lacked for work. Carlos saw to it that they were always performing at some function or headlining at a jazz club. Most of their time was spent practicing, crafting their image and chasing that elusive record deal. Always in the forefront of their minds, was the dream of snagging a recording contract with a major label. For Ashela, it was the only thing that made sense out of everything she was doing with her life. She discovered that a group could spend their entire lives playing in hole-in-the-wall digs and no one would ever know of their existence. While Jaundice's goal was to break beyond the barriers of mediocrity into the limelight of stardom, getting there was always the challenge.

Their lucky break came a year later when they had the opportunity to headline for Grover Washington, Jr. at the New Orleans Jazz Festival. They were a hit from the start and for three nights, they wowed the crowd with their songs. Ashela was already writing the band's music and with the smooth, rhythmic sound of their songs, by the time they left the stage each night, the audience was screaming for more. In essence, they set the tone in a spectacular way for Grover Washington's performance.

The money that they made from those three nights enabled them to buy studio time to record several professional quality demo tapes. They were proud of the finished product and felt they were close to signing with a label. In the meantime, their schedule was booked and they were beginning to make good money from all of the gigs they performed.

***

Ashela unlocked the door to her Brooklyn brownstone apartment. She had been living on Clinton Street for nearly two years, the same length of time she'd been a member of Jaundice. It was because of Randal that she had obtained the expensive loft. Right or wrong, the circumstances of her life had changed inextricably because of him.

The two of them had worked out an arrangement that many people would deem bizarre, but to them it was the perfect scenario. Because Randal was a married, high-profiled dignitary, he couldn't afford to be seen with her in public. Ashela's justification for seeing him was that she needed the thousand dollars he gave her as an allowance each week. She knew she didn't love him. She was just honest enough to admit she thoroughly enjoyed the wild and kinky sex life they had carved out.

Randal visited her at least twice a week, coming during the daytime so that his visits would never appear suspect. He'd call ahead of time on his private phone to give her time to get ready for him. There were times when he'd want her dressed in a

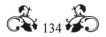

leather, one-piece bathing suit with fish-net stockings and high-heeled shoes; sometimes in black and white as a maid; or in a plaid school uniform as a student; in expensive lingerie; or at other times wearing nothing at all. Randal encouraged her sexual creativity by buying her books on the art of lovemaking, how to satisfy a man, and how to maximize an orgasm. Her spontaneity excited him and nearly drove him insane. He expressly enjoyed the times when she would dominate him and make him do things unheard of. Once, Ashela had bought a whip and dog collar, along with a can of whip cream. It took Randal nearly a week to recuperate from that particular odyssey.

But calling it like it was, Ashela knew that the bottom line was that she was Randal's undercover whore. He could afford to pay her the thousand bucks per week regardless of whether he visited her or not. Besides, Randal *wanted* to pay her. It made him feel as if he didn't owe her anything else. Sometimes, when Ashela reflected on it, she figured people would be dismayed at the prolific number of white men who privately enjoyed being with Black women. To them, women of color were the forbidden fruit, the apple they weren't supposed to reach for. Though few ever married Black women, unlike some Black men who jumped at the chance to marry a white woman, Caucasian men "crept" in disproportionate numbers.

After the fundraising affair when Randal had found her, Ashela had made it difficult for him to see her again. She brought back to her remembrance the disappointment she felt when he'd made no attempt to contact her after their initial encounter, and so she deliberately didn't contact him.

Assuming she was playing hard to get, Randal had Bill track her down. When she rebuffed his entreaties, he pursued her all the more. One night over dinner, in answer to his question, she told him there *was* no one else and that she hadn't been with anyone sexually since her first time with him. Randal listened in obvious disbelief. But after she described what her life had been like, he believed her. She explained that just surviving from day to day had been her primary goal—sex had been the furthest thing from her mind.

Randal knew that he had to see her again. He offered to pay her, even telling her of an apartment that he knew was available, that it was in the perfect area, not too far from the city, and how he could be at her place in no time at all. Ashela thought it over, and though she pretended otherwise, his proposition didn't really take much contemplation. All she had to do was use her imagination to remember how good it had felt with him the first time, and the deal was struck. She knew Randal could afford it. He came from an affluent background. Plus, he would probably write off the money he gave her through his taxes as a charitable contribution anyway.

He gave her money to furnish the apartment, even bought her a car. But everything Randal did for her came at a price. One day, Ashela could tell that he was feening for her badly. She, however, was not in the mood. Grumpy and irritated from the previous night's on-stage performance, she answered the phone and told him

flippantly she'd see him some other time. But in less than twenty minutes, Randal was at her door letting himself in with his personal key.

Once inside, Randal painstakingly reminded her who paid the rent on her apartment, who paid for her car, and whose money it was that enabled her to buy the things that she did. As she stood in the doorway watching him with an angry expression on her face, Randal had stripped naked, stretched himself out on her bed, palmed his erect manhood, and crooked his finger, an indication of what he wanted her to do.

Ashela had gotten the point loud and clear. His one-upmanship of her was a bitter pill in her mouth and it had galled her to the core.

Shortly thereafter, Randal started making strange requests of her. He had "friends" that he needed her to entertain in his absence. At first, Ashela flatly refused. It was bad enough that she had to do it with him when she didn't feel like it. She was not about to become involved with any of the ménage-à-tois she'd read about in the books he'd bought her. Randal begged, pleaded and implored her to change her mind. He promised her it wouldn't be that often and besides, if she'd commit to doing it every blue moon, he'd pay her an extra two thousand dollars whenever he needed her "assistance."

The money sounded too good to pass up and Ashela told him to give her some time to think it over. Two weeks later, Randal mentioned it again. But Ashela procrastinated, telling him she needed more time to think about it. Ever the opportunist, Randal slyly insisted that his first "friend" would be a piece of cake. With what he had in mind, she wouldn't have to do anything out of the ordinary. No one other than himself would actually touch her. All he wanted was for her to let his "friend" watch the two of them together.

Nervous, but also curious, Ashela had agreed. It was an experience that would turn out to be a disaster.

Randal showed up with his "friend" who looked to be at least a hundred and fifty years old. Randal spread out a blanket in front of the fireplace and positioned the old and wrinkled purveyor's chair about a foot away. Naked, he and Ashela lay upon the blanket and started coupling. But Ashela was feigning her arousal. She made the dastardly mistake of looking in the old man's direction. One glimpse of him leeringly stroking his small, withered, and shriveled up penis nearly made her gag. She automatically recoiled. Feeling her struggle to reject him, Randal grew overly excited. He pinned her on her stomach and held her down, slaking his lust between her legs, making sure the old man was getting a good view of it all.

From that point on, Ashela wanted out of the relationship. Even a dog had enough sense to hit the road when a brook dried up. Always an avid saver of her money, Ashela became even more frugal. She was to the point where she wanted to say to hell with the apartment and car, Randal could take them both and shove 'em up his blankety-blank-blank.

Soon, Congress was back in session and Randal's visits to her tapered off. One evening, he called her from Washington and told her he needed a favor. He had another "friend" whom he wanted her to see. Without hesitation, Ashela told him it would cost him seven thousand dollars and he would have to wire the money to her bank account the same day. Her plan was to take the money and end it all. The apartment—Randal could keep it. The spare bedroom in the group's home in Rockaway, Queens, would suffice. As for the new Lexus he'd bought her—well, he could keep that too. She didn't need a luxury car. With all the destructive pot holes in New York City, all she needed was a little piece of a car anyway.

Randal agreed to the dollar amount, but told her for that kind of money, he expected her to give his "friend" the royal treatment. Ashela hung up and made arrangements to meet the gentleman the following night.

***

She was required to dress in a white, full-length mink coat, which Randal had had delivered for the occasion. Underneath it, she wore an extremely skimpy, red two-piece leather thong bathing suit, red fish-net stockings and red patent leather shoes with four-inch stiletto heels. Assessing herself in the mirror, she had to admit that she looked like a straight-up ho'. She walked slowly and carefully in the high-heeled shoes, vowing to herself that she would never do this again.

When Ashela arrived at the Park Avenue address, she was already feeling a slight buzz from the Amoretto Liqueur that she'd been drinking at her own apartment. The door to the Penthouse Suite opened and a short, fat man dressed in silk paisley pajamas stepped to the side to allow her to enter. Ashela took one look at his frog-looking face and body, and her buzz vanished like vapor. The only expression she could think of to describe him was *"toe up from the flo' up."* With his quadruple chin, and funny shaped body, Ashela knew there was no way she could bed him. Quickly, she ran through a litany of things she could do to get out of having to screw him. Maybe she could go spasmodic by falling out and doubling up on the floor as she pretended to have a severe case of food poisoning; perhaps she could pretend she was choking; or better yet, maybe she could make like she was dead.

Meanwhile, the toadish little man was saying, "I'm so pleased and honored that you could fit me into your busy schedule. It's most gracious of you to delay your trip back to Italy just to see me one more time. Unfortunately, I have bad news: I cannot marry you. My wife has decided not to grant me a divorce. Penelope, can you please give me a bit longer to talk her into it?"

Penelope? Ashela managed to keep a sanguine smile on her face. But inside, she wondered what the fuck the little toad was talking about. Until it hit her like a ton of bricks. It was part of the charade! "Hey," she thought to herself, "If he wants to pretend like I've flown all the way from Italy just to screw his weird, fat little ass and was now suicidal because his old bird of a wife refused to leave him, well, hey, *who*

the fuck am I?" She was just there to help him get his groove on. And the quicker the better because she just wanted out.

Ashela was grateful she was wearing such a heavy fur coat. Though it was thirty degrees outside, it felt even colder inside the toad's suite. She had been instructed to sit meekly and quietly and to occasionally pretend to be distraught. Looking at his face, Ashela knew that part would be a piece of cake.

The toadish little man led her to a nearby sofa where he seated her and handed her some tissue. She sat there and stared at him blankly before remembering that she was supposed to be dejected. Ashela bent her head and dabbed at her eyes, wiping away the imaginary tears. She jumped when the toad came and sat beside her to hold and soothe her. He kept whispering over and over about how sorry he was and how he had never meant to hurt her. "You do know that I'd never hurt you, don't you? I realize how this must look, but I really do love you and I want to marry you. It's just that my damned wife is standing in our way." Suddenly, the toad had a brilliant idea. "We could have my wife killed," he said. "That way the two of us could always be together."

Ashela had drifted a million miles away. She had long since tuned the fat fuck out. But when she heard him say something about killing his wife, she stared at him long and hard.

"There, there," the toad was saying. "I know how to make it all right. All I need is your trust." He stood to his feet and gallantly extended his hand. "This time, it will be perfect. Just the two of us—no more mistakes." He led her inside a bedroom where, in spite of herself, Ashela gasped in surprised shock. The room was a bondage-lover's paradise. Iron chains and shackles dangled from the wall. In the middle of the room, was a round bed with red velvet sheets and pillows. Suddenly, Ashela heard the door lock behind them. She had the sinking feeling that she had just missed her last chance to escape.

Ever so gently, the toad removed her fur coat from her body. Ashela shivered in the coldness of the room. He guided her to the bed and gently pushed her onto it. From out of nowhere, he produced a set of handcuffs and a pair of red velvet ropes, wanting to either chain or tie her to the bed. Ashela had no idea which one. Shaking her head, she spoke for the first time since her arrival, telling him she would not permit herself to be tied up. As a matter of fact, she was ready to call it quits. She would have been game for tying *him* up or for beating *his* fat ass. But she didn't know him from Jack The Ripper, and from what she could tell by all the paraphernalia on the walls, he was probably into some heavy S&M.

Ashela made a move to get up from the bed. She was outtie. Randal could keep the seven grand.

She pushed the toad away from her, but in the next instant, he slammed his fist against the side of her forehead. Ashela was knocked unconscious. Minutes later, a dose of cold water thrown on her face brought her back. As she groggily came to, she

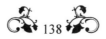

found herself handcuffed to the bed, spread-eagled. The toad was standing over her naked, with a huge, shiny, rubber, jet black penis protruding from his enormous belly. He was saying she had been a very bad slave-girl by trying to escape and that now she must suffer punishment.

Slow to regain her faculties, Ashela pulled at the handcuffs, testing their strength. When he moved to join her on the bed, she went berserk as she frantically tried to get away.

Her thrashing motions excited him. No longer was he the gentleman who claimed to love her as his precious Penelope. He had become the master who must punish the slave for trying to run away.

The next several hours were the most horrific of Ashela's life as the toad violently raped and sodomized her, causing her to black out.

When she came to again, she had been loosed from her chains. She was unable to move without pain gripping her body. When she heard the room's door open, she cringed, preparing for the worst. But it was only Bill, Randal's chauffeur. He came to the side of the bed where she was trying to sit up and helped her. Unembarrassed by her nakedness, Ashela was just glad to see a familiar face.

With his face expressionless, Bill retrieved her fur coat from the floor on the other side of the room. Back at her bedside, he assisted her in pulling it on. For such a huge, hulking figure he was surprisingly gentle. Attempting to stand, Ashela sobbed at the pain. She couldn't even shift positions. With her fur coat fastened from top to bottom, Bill easily lifted her into his arms and carried her from the Penthouse Suite.

Back inside her Brownstone apartment, Ashela locked and chained the door after the chauffeur had left. She limped and dragged her pain-filled body into the bathroom, grimacing at the sight of herself in the mirror. She had only one bruise on her entire face. But the lump on her forehead was the size of an orange. Not caring whether the combination could cost her her life, Ashela downed a handful of sleeping pills and another handful of Tylenol capsules. Taking her phone off the hook, she crawled between the sheets of her bed and slipped into blissful oblivion.

She was running through a maze of trees in a wooded area. She couldn't hear them behind her but she knew they were there, waiting to pounce on her the moment she stopped running. She stumbled over a rock in the grass, lost her balance and fell to the ground. She crawled to her knees knowing that they weren't far behind. A short distance away, she could see what looked to be an entrance to a cave protruding from the ground. She made her way towards it and crawled inside the rocky opening. It appeared to be a darkened, narrow tunnel. She was afraid to go deeper into it, but she was even more fearful of what awaited her outside. Weary and tired, she dragged herself onward, groping her way through the blackness of the

hole. She was scared and wanted so badly to rest, but she couldn't. She knew they were coming after her.

She felt like she'd been crawling forever when, up ahead, she could finally see a sliver of light. Maybe it led to an opening, a way out of the darkness. With the last of her strength, she crawled toward it. Suddenly, terror gripped her and she knew they had found her. Instantly, the darkness became filled with many hostile, invisible enemies—she could feel their evil presence lurking near her. Filled with fear and trepidation, she huddled against the brick surface of the cave-like tunnel. As the satanic-looking creatures surrounded her, she knew they were going to kill her. She lashed out in hysteria to save herself. She didn't want to die! As they prepared to attack her, she emitted a scream that pierced the darkness of her dilemma.

Chapter Sixteen

hen Ashela regained consciousness, her body felt numb. The only mobility she had was in her left arm. It took her a long time to maneuver, but she was finally able to reach her phone and get a dial tone to call 911. She was fading in and out of consciousness and her tongue seemed glued to the roof of her mouth. The last thing she remembered was hearing the paramedics break down her door. When she woke up again, she was in St. John's Hospital.

Ashela looked down at the intravenous tubes inserted into her arms. She lay there, disoriented, not even remembering how she had come to be there. At the sound of a voice at her bedside, Ashela looked over to see a nurse standing on the other side of her bed.

Her mouth was dry as she whispered for water. She was so weak that the nurse had to help her hold the glass to her lips. Ashela asked how long she'd been there and was told a week. They'd pumped her stomach and flushed her system out, hence her exhaustion. She'd also had some internal bleeding, but the nurse told her she should be fine within the next few weeks.

There was no phone inside her room. Later, she asked the nurse if she would call Carlos for her. The next morning, the whole group showed up to see her. Ashela wept at the sight of all the band members. It felt good knowing that *someone* in the world cared whether she lived or died. They brought her flowers, balloons and candy that she couldn't eat. They told her how much they'd missed her and how they'd been worried about her. They'd had to play several gigs without her and it just hadn't been the same. They were all full of questions and wanted to know how soon she would be back with them.

Three days later, she was released from the hospital and Carlos was there to take her home. All he could talk about was the band. He surprised her with the news that

a heavyweight in the music business, someone named Sam Ross, had seen one of their performances some months ago and was now prepared to offer them a recording contract with Werner Records.

Ashela smiled somewhat sadly and said, "I'm so happy for all of you, Carlos. You deserve it."

Carlos looked at her strangely. "What do you mean 'you're happy for us?' You are as much a part of this group as any one of us."

Ashela shook her head and said, "I want out, Carlos. I haven't decided what I want to do with the rest of my life, but whatever it is, it won't be here in New York. As soon as I'm up to it, I'm leaving town."

Carlos stared at Ashela as if she were missing a few screws. He figured she wasn't thinking straight because she'd just come out of the hospital. Her doctor had said that she'd tried to kill herself. Carlos reasoned it must have had something to do with the Senator she dated on the sly. But now that the group had finally snared a recording contract, he figured she could put all that behind her. He believed what she was saying now was merely the ramblings of someone who just needed to think things through.

After he left, Ashela lay on her couch unable to stop the avalanche of tears. She thought of the mess she'd made of her life. She had wanted to go places, experience things, and make a name for herself. But all she had done was waste time by becoming a murderer, a whore, and a failure. Bruised and beaten on the inside, Ashela didn't want to play with Jaundice anymore. She no longer wanted to do anything that was musically inclined. Her musical inclinations had brought her nothing but sadness and sheer pain.

After her tears subsided, she lay there formulating her next plan of action. She would sell everything inside the apartment, most of all the floor-length fur coat that wasn't even hers. She would take the money, pay her astronomical hospital bill, and head west—anywhere in the opposite direction of New York City.

***

Ashela drove to California filled with sorrow and condemnation. Many times, her eyes would cloud with tears and she'd have to pull over to the side of the road to weep. During one such stretch as she traveled through Illinois, she exited Interstate 90 in Chicago and pulled into a vacant parking lot not too far from the freeway. When she finally dried her eyes a short time later, she noticed it was seven o'clock in the evening. With her head resting against the seat of the car, Ashela saw groups of people filing into a chapel some distance away. The large, white overhead sign read, Bishop Noel Jones. Friday only. 7:30 p.m.

Ashela had no idea who Bishop Noel Jones was, but whoever he was, he seemed to have a huge following. People were standing in line, shoulder-to-shoulder waiting to enter the facility.

Before she knew it, she exited her car and headed toward the line of waiting people. Wearing a pair of tattered blue jeans, she stood in line trying to talk herself out of going into the chapel. She reasoned that it had been too many years since she'd been inside a church. And with all the things that she had been through, surely she was the last person who should be sitting in a church pew.

When she was finally shown to a seat, from the onset, the service was different from anything she'd ever experienced. The people were certainly louder and more vocal in their praise than what she was accustomed to. All around her, people were muttering in a strange language. When the woman seated next to her let out a ear-splitting roar, Ashela nearly jumped out of her skin. There was something electrifying about the atmosphere that reminded her of a scene from the movie, *The Blues Brothers*. Determined to stick it out, she sat rooted in her seat.

The music was what really held Ashela captive. It was modern, upbeat, and up-tempo. In the church where she'd grown up, she was used to songs like, I'm Climbing Up The Rough Side Of The Mountain. Not that there was anything wrong with the songs that she was used to, it was just that they were all she knew. These people seemed so *energetic*. Ashela stared around in wonder.

By the time the preacher stood to introduce the guest speaker, Ashela could actually say she was enjoying herself. Everybody clapped as a handsome, dark-skinned man of medium build came to the podium. He instructed everybody to stretch across the isles and join hands. No one was to be left untouched. As she listened to him, she didn't know what it was, but there was something oddly fascinating about his voice. He was saying that everybody was significant in the eyes of God and he talked about the woman with the issue of blood, how she hadn't wanted to actually *touch* the Savior, she'd just wanted to touch *something* that was touching Him. Likewise, the Bishop said he believed that they were holding the hand of someone who knew how to touch the Lord. Someone who knew how to intercede. Someone who knew how to get a word through to the Father, and that together, they could access the throne of God.

Ashela felt shivers travel down her spine. When they were told they could be seated, where she had originally intended to be cynical and judgmental, she found herself enthralled by the words the man spoke. Though he was speaking to the entire audience, Ashela felt as though he were talking directly to her.

She sat transfixed and listened to him preach about "The Reason I Survive." He brought back to her remembrance the fact that trials and conflicts come to test her resolve and commitment—and that no matter how great a pain they caused, it was only so far that her circumstances could take her before she bounced back. Every word the man spoke seemed directly related to something she had experienced or was presently going through.

She found herself squirming in the hot seat as he "read her mail." His words challenged her to stop blaming other people for her personal problems. *She* was

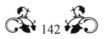

responsible for her individual happiness and success, no one else. She could no longer point her finger at Charla, Julia, Parris or Randal, or any of the bands she'd played with and blame them for her lack of success. She had to look within herself to find the answers. She had to face the person standing on the other side of the mirror and acknowledge that it was she *herself* who was in need of prayer. She was delusional if she was waiting for someone else to come along and right her wrongs.

She'd tried to run things and orchestrate the wheels of her life. However, left to her own devices, all she'd done was create a major mess. But after hearing the Bishop's message, Ashela now felt as though she could start anew.

All of the condemnation and self loathing she'd felt were gone. She realized that she wasn't a bad person, she'd just made some wrong choices. Her past was just that—behind her. With a feeling of elation, Ashela felt as though her past had been erased so that her future could be protected. Her faith would be the vehicle that would bridge the gap to her future.

Ashela now had courage to deal with the things she'd done in New York. No longer would she allow them to be held against her. She didn't have to *forget* what had happened, she just had to banish the feelings of inferiority and condemnation that remained. She would start by using her past as a stepping stone to rebuild her future.

As if a light bulb had illuminated itself in her mind, Ashela saw that in order to have a sound vision of what lay before her, she needed Someone to heal her past— Someone who could abolish the failures and pains of her yesterday so she wouldn't make a mockery of her tomorrow.

She realized that the goals and aspirations she'd had for her life were intertwined with her faith, and that if she were to see any of her dreams come to fruition, she would have to raise her faith to another level. More than anything, Ashela now knew that *untried faith was unreliable* and that only through her tests would she mature, develop and come to know what she had within her. Equipped with her newfound understanding, Ashela acknowledged that there *is* no such thing as success without hardship.

By the time she left the chapel, she recognized that she would never be immune to life's trials and afflictions, but she now remembered where the strength, wisdom and understanding to overcome them would come from.

***

Ashela settled in L.A. and for the next three years she mostly wrote lyrics and commercial jingles. In the beginning, she didn't have big name clout. But her sales were steady and the income helped to keep a roof over her head and food upon her table. She became a freelance musician, even snaring a temporary gig on Arsenio Hall's TV show. She played with many different groups but never signed with any of them until she snagged the coveted position as keyboardist in Grover Washington's band. It was then that she truly began to prosper. Under the guidance of her new

mentor, Ashela flourished as her musical abilities were honed to a fine point. Though the rag-mags and gossip-mongers tried to make more out of their relationship than what it was, there were never any romantic inclinations between them: Just one artist appreciating the alchemic magic of another. Grover Washington challenged Ashela to tap into and stretch her musical imagination in ways she'd never thought possible. Through him, she learned to create music that was timeless and enigmatic; music that held the hypnotic promise of lyrical richness.

If ever there was a time over the course of her career that Ashela could look back on and point to as the most meaningful and influential stage of her musical development, it would be the period of time she spent as a member of Grover Washington's band.

Life had taught Ashela many hard and rough lessons. Some of them had even hardened her heart. But one of the most profound ones she remembered was Julia telling her that life would give her what she demanded of it, and that people would only treat or do to her what she allowed them to.

Ashela made the pursuit of her goals the primary focus of her life. Not dating anyone was never something she consciously set out to do, it just happened that way. In her line of business, she met a slew of men. Just none whom she wanted to date.

As far as sex was concerned, to Ashela, it was overrated—she could satisfy herself. As long as she was taking care of herself, paying her bills, and busting her ass to make ends meet, she felt it would be sheer lunacy to allow someone into her life just for the sake of being able to say she "had a man."

Ashela didn't consider herself bitter, it was just impossible for her to experience all that she had and not be affected by it. She was determined not to end up a statistic like so many others who suffered traumatic experiences, or made huge mistakes and then lived the rest of their lives mired in regret.

In a world of fleeting diversions, Ashela couldn't say what her future held, but good or bad, right or wrong, she would learn to deal with life's challenges as they came.

Ashela firmly believed that she was destined for success. She had her detractors to thank for that. And after surviving everything that she'd been through, she knew she would make it to the top of her craft, in spite of it all

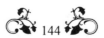

Part Four

The Meet

"...I walk into a room
Just as cool as you please,
And to a man,
The fellows stand or
Fall down on their knees...

...Men themselves have wondered
What they see in me.
They try so much
But they can't touch
My inner mystery...
I am a woman
Phenomenally.
Phenomenal Woman,
That's me."

— Maya Angelou

Chapter Seventeen

Los Angeles

CM's recording studio was located on Sunset Boulevard. But on this blistering, hot day, taking the usual short-cuts to get there proved a hassle. Driving through Beverly Hills into West Hollywood, Ashela was stopped at yet another traffic light. Her eyes cut to the digital clock on the dashboard. If the remaining street lights along the way were kind to her, she could make it to her destination in another ten minutes—fifteen max. Ashela hated to be late. Drumming her fingertips on the steering wheel in harmony with En Vogue's latest hit, she caught a frantic motion out of the corner of her left eye. Sitting next to her at the traffic light, two men in a black convertible BMW were waiving excitedly. One was holding a CD in one hand with an ink pen in the other.

Knowing she didn't have time to stop to give autographs, she rolled down the window of her silver Bentley. She smiled at them regretfully and pointed to her watch. When the street light changed to green, Ashela sped off.

Inside the RCM building, she signed in and headed past the security center for the third floor. Several production, studio and remix engineers were standing just outside the door to the recording room.

"Good morning, Ashela, they're waiting for you."

Ashela stepped inside smiling at the room's occupants. "My, my. How'd you guys get here so early? What'd you do? Sleep over last night?" Ashela pointed to the large oval clock on the wall which displayed 9:35. The meet had been set for 9:30 a.m.

Already inside the glass partition was Toni Braxton. TB was to record two songs which Ashela had written precisely for her. Ashela was to provide the background instrumentals and Kenny "Babyface" Edmonds was producing them. Face had gotten to the studio shortly after nine o'clock and, along with the engineer, was testing the state-of-the-art digital sound system. Laughter spread around the room as Ashela sat piecing together her sax and clarinet. With horns ready to blow, she too, started warming up.

As she and TB began harmonizing together, the jocular atmosphere changed to one of intensity. The session was not open to the public and only a small number were allowed to witness the production. The less spectators present, the fewer the distractions. The first song was a slow tune, similar to Stevie Wonder's, Ribbon In The Sky. Once the actual recording got underway, Face had them start over several times trying to get the tracks just right. After awhile, the many retakes increased the tension in the room exponentially.

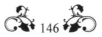

By 1:30, the take was going so well that no one wanted to break for lunch. By four, they were really into the groove of the songs and at seven o'clock sharp, just when everybody was completely exhausted, Babyface signaled that the session was a wrap.

***

Ashela was dog tired during the drive back to her home in Malibu. With its prime beach front-property, the majestic enclave where she dwelled was home to many of the rich and famous. She pulled into her garage and unlocked the connecting door that led directly to the inside of her home. With five bedrooms and three-and-a-half baths, her place was as spacious as it was lavish. Fifteen-foot high ceilings, two giant fireplaces, windows that spanned from floor to ceiling. Bright skylights, wooden parfait floors, beveled brick glass walls and arched doorways were the custom. Decorated in light-colored hues, the entire house was sunny and bright. Her living room was filled with a variety of African art, huge abstract paintings, large Chinese urns and decorative divider screens. Lladro statues (imported directly from Spain) along with several gold and brass knick-knacks complemented the cream over-sized, stuffed sofas. Huge exotic plants were placed strategically throughout the entire home, giving it an overall lush, tropical effect. A winding staircase led to her upper level.

Ashela walked upstairs to her bedroom and stripped before stepping inside the shower. Refreshed and hungry, she slipped into a simple but sexy, peach colored satin boxer pajama, pulled on her oversized bunny rabbit slippers and headed downstairs to find something to eat. Afterwards, she stuck in a Bartók CD, savoring the soothing effect that classical music had upon her.

With a glass of white zinfandel in hand, she stepped outside onto her deck and reclined in a fold-out wicker chair. The California night breeze was warm and gentle as it flitted over her body. Staring up at the reddish-hued skyline, with its twinkling diamond-like stars, she reveled in its beauty. The roar of the sea combined to give a serene effect to her atmosphere. Ashela couldn't help but compare her current lifestyle to that of her past. Rough times made her appreciate the things she now had in her possession.

In stark contrast to her days of yesteryear, Ashela's world was now filled with opulence and superstar celebrities. She saw first-hand how difficult it was for many to keep from succumbing to the vagaries of decadency. In the eight years since she'd been in L.A., four-star hotels and restaurants, limousines, and $500 bottles of champagne had become the norm for her. Drugs were as prevalent in the circles she frequented as was the hard core liquor and Rémy Martin champagne. Now that she had become such an overwhelming success, Ashela also had to contend with the difficulties of living her life under the microscopic gaze of the public eye.

Because of her frenetic work schedule, it was serene moments like these that Ashela cherished. Time spent alone where her problems seemed non-existent. Over

the past several years, she'd worked with so many industry "superstars," and was surrounded by so much superficiality that she treasured her solitude. It allowed her to go inside herself to access a place where there was no deception—only the naked truth about who she was and what she had become.

Over the years, Ashela had earned the reputation as someone who was tough to work with. But she felt otherwise. She was a perfectionist and if her name was to be attached to a project, she wanted it done right. If she hadn't become one of the best songwriters and musicians in the business, she wouldn't be as successful and prosperous as she was. Her no-nonsense approach to her work made it clear to everyone with whom she worked that professionalism and pride in her accomplishments were the cornerstones of her career.

Staring at the stretch of sand that lined her beach front, she watched the water crash onto the sandy shore only to leave its imprint in the sand as it receded.

She thought it amazing how one moment a person could be at the bottom of the mill and then in the blink of an eye be transported into an entirely different lifestyle. Though people had the misguided impression that achievements and goals evolved overnight, Ashela knew otherwise. She didn't believe in overnight success stories. Maybe it happened for a lone few, but that surely hadn't been the case with her. She knew that dreams and aspirations took time to come to fruition. She'd had to learn that firsthand.

Ashela had learned that success was not just recognizing one's inherent gifts. It was a combination of hard work and timing; a result of preparation meeting up with opportunity. When Ashela discovered the vast amount of money to be made from the writing/producing side of the music biz, she'd concentrated her efforts on developing her talent for creating lyrics. As more and more of her music began to sell, people noticed that it was her songs that were consistently rising to the top of the charts. Regardless of who was singing them, Ashela's songs quickly signaled a success. So much so that the demand for her lyrics and her time became extraordinary. When Rolling Stone magazine dubbed her as the "hottest songwriter of the year," the roof was blown off of her earning potential and the money and royalties from her music began to flow like rivers of living waters.

***

The next morning found Ashela hard at work at her baby grand piano. She was working on the composition of a series of new songs. When her creative juices were flowing, Ashela could hear a song in her mind's eye. The type of voice she attached to the lyrics gave her insight as to who the song would be ideal for. Once the song was just right, she'd play it back for Mikyra Toney, her arranger, to help craft the song into perfection. She'd then hand the lyrics over to Adrienne Dantley, her agent, always letting him know who the person was that she envisioned singing the song. Adrienne would copyright it and get on the horn to the publisher, specifying the artist or group that the song was for, giving them first crack at purchasing the lyrics.

If they were interested, and they most always were, a price was agreed upon. If not, the song would be marketed to someone else. Every artist craved that elusive number one hit. And many saw Ashela as a means to that end.

Ashela had also been commissioned by both TV producers and large corporations to create jingles for television programs and marketing campaigns. She found that ideas for her music tended to flow best in the wee hours of the morning. Experience had taught her that when the inspiration for a new song hit, she had to get it down on paper immediately. Otherwise, the vision and the song would become a figment of her imagination.

When it came to creating music, even her critics concurred, Ashela had the "Midas touch." But TV music supervisors and large corporations weren't the main entities vying for her creative talents. The top names in the music industry approached her as well. Ashela's lyrical depth sprang from a cauldron of musical creativity and the uniqueness of each of her songs caused people to pursue her all the more. Because there were so many demands on her time and not enough hours in each day, she had to structure her time carefully. The amount of money offered was not always the bottom-line factor that determined whether she wrote for someone exclusively. It mattered to her more what vibes she got from a particular person or group.

Once, she dropped everything she was working on when she received a call from Luther Vandross. Luther was one of her favorite artists to work with. He was a demanding perfectionist but he wasn't hung up on his enormous stardom.

When the chemistry was right, Ashela could work with a group or individual and the music would flow effortlessly. Though jazz was where her heart lay, she could make the transition from writing jazz ensembles to pop music swiftly and easily. Whether her songs would be instrumental or vocally inclined, merely depended upon what mode she was in.

***

Later that afternoon, she went upstairs to switch into her workout gear and headed into the spare bedroom that housed all of her exercise equipment. At 5'5", Ashela maintained her rounded, well-muscled physique by working out three times per week.

Breathing hard and drenched with sweat, she was in the kitchen washing down a bottle of distilled water when the doorbell rang. Draping the towel over her shoulder, she went to the intercom. Ashela opened the door and Kyliah Reed, her long time friend and now Public Relations Advisor, swept through. Dressed in an orange Donna Karan top and matching velvet mini-skirt, Kyliah wore her long hair parted down the middle with one side swept behind one ear. Both of them had come a long way since the days when they'd played hopscotch and tag in Durham, North Carolina. But repairing the strained breech in their friendship had been most difficult, if not all but impossible.

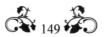

***

Kyliah stood waiting in line at the American Airlines departure gate of Houston's Inter-Continental Airport. There were approximately fifteen people ahead of her, each waiting patiently for their turn to receive assistance. There was only one customer service rep manning the desk, so Kyliah stilled herself against her rising impatience. En route from a corporate client site, she'd made a last minute decision to detour to North Carolina to surprise her folks.

Since the line she was waiting in was moving rather slowly, she busied herself by jotting notes into her weekly planner, occasionally glancing up to observe passersby. Minutes later, as she tucked away the leather book, Kyliah noticed that the line had come to a virtual standstill. She stepped to the side to get a view of the number of people ahead of her and to see if she could discern what the holdup might be. A small-sized woman wearing an expensive, floor-length fur coat was speaking to the customer service representative. She was surrounded by Gucci luggage and was motioning her hands as if expressing anger. It appeared to Kyliah that the small woman was giving the service rep a hell of a time. Though Kyliah couldn't hear their conversation from where she stood, visible signs indicated that the representative was near to tears.

Sighing and shifting impatiently because the woman was taking up so much time, Kyliah halted herself from barging to the front of the line to demand to know what the problem was. When another ten minutes passed with no apparent resolution, Kyliah snapped. She headed to the front of the line fully intent upon insisting that the customer representative call a supervisor and request additional help. In the time the rep had spent servicing the one customer, the line had all but doubled.

". . . I don't care that you have no record for me in your system. Here's my ticket and I'm telling you I'm confirmed for a first-class seat!" the small-sized woman declared tyrannically.

"Excuse me, miss. Can you call a supervisor, or someone who's in charge, and tell them you require additional help? You've been assisting this same customer for the past twenty minutes. Isn't there . . ."

"Kyliah!"

She had paid no attention to the small woman standing next to her other than when she'd viewed her cursorily from the back of the line. As she turned to give the woman her full regard, her breath was taken away.

"Ashela Jordan." Kyliah uttered the name quietly, shaking her head. Though she'd envisioned seeing Ashela again a thousand times, never had she expected to run into her inside an airport.

Ashela moved to embrace her and Kyliah could feel the years drop away as they became children once more. But just as quickly, her mind fast forwarded to the present and all she could recall was the persistent agony she'd endured when her

friend had left her high and dry. Kyliah never raised her arms to hug Ashela in return.

Happy as all get-out and completely unsuspecting, Ashela released Kyliah and stepped back with the biggest of smiles on her face. However, she was totally unprepared for what followed.

Using as much force as she could muster, Kyliah swung her hand back and whacked Ashela hard across the face. All the years she'd spent pining and wondering about her welfare was funneled into the one blow.

The force of the slap propelled Ashela backwards. As she stumbled, the people waiting in line gasped at the unexpected melee.

When Ashela recovered, she stepped toward Kyliah holding the side of her jaw, wearing a confused expression on her face. Suddenly, her look of confusion turned to anger. In a soft voice that seethed with rage, Ashela said, "Kyliah, trust me when I tell you that you're the only person on this planet I'd allow to get away with what you just did to me."

Filled with a rage of her own, Kyliah replied, "Is that right? Well, fuck you too, Ashela." Abruptly, she turned and walked back to her place toward the end of the line. Too many memories were rushing through Kyliah's mind, and on top of it all, she could feel tears of anger threatening to burst through their ducts.

Along with everyone else who stood in line, the customer service rep was momentarily at a loss for words. Ignoring the shocked expressions from the on-lookers, Ashela stepped over her luggage and went in pursuit of Kyliah. When she drew near her, the people waiting in line parted like the red sea, almost as if they didn't know what to expect but didn't want to be involved if a brouhaha ensued.

Ashela stood in front of Kyliah and said, "I don't know what that was all about, Kye, but can we talk?"

Without looking at her, Kyliah replied, "I think not Ashela. I've got a plane to catch."

"So do I, Kyliah. I've also got a concert that I'm scheduled to play in within the next several hours. And if I'm willing to be late for it, then surely you can grant me a few minutes of *your* time."

"You know, Ash, you've got mega nerve stepping to me after all these years of not contacting me. Do you have any idea of just how inconsiderate that was of you?"

Suddenly, a light bulb exploded in Ashela's mind. Finally realizing what the entire incident was about, the winds of indignation left her sails. Only then did she sense what Kyliah was trying to express. Immediately, she humbled herself out of respect for the many years of their friendship. Putting her pride aside, she said, "You're right, Kye. I can't even argue with you. I was wrong, I know that now. And there's probably not much I can say to change that, except that I'm sorry."

"Yeah, well, so am I, Ashela. Believe me, so am I."

With Ashela no longer tying up the line, it was beginning to move forward again. As Kyliah pushed her carry-on luggage forward, Ashela inched along with her.

"So how have you been, Kye?" Despite what had just transpired, Ashela knew Kyliah would never believe how good it was to see her again so she didn't voice her thought out loud.

"Look, Ashela, what's done is done. But don't expect me to stand here and make polite conversation with you because I can't and I won't. Whether you realize it or not, you took your friendship away from me without asking what I thought. I know what happened between you and Parris was hard to swallow, but why take it out on me? Even if you needed space, I could have understood that too. But you don't just up and leave the people who really love you."

Feeling thoroughly chastised, Ashela remembered something Kyliah had always said to her back in high school. " 'Men come and go like underwear. But friends are supposed to be forever.' I learned that from you, Kyliah. And I guess I violated a code of our friendship. There was to be nothing we couldn't talk about with each other. Didn't think I remembered that, did you?" Though Kyliah still wouldn't look at her, Ashela said, "You know, Kye, in all the years that I didn't call or speak to you, there wasn't a day that went by that I didn't think about you or see something that reminded me of you in some small way. True friendships are forever, Kyliah. Even when one party violates any aspect of it, you never stop loving that person. I was wrong to shut you out. I realize that. And just like I said before, there's nothing that I could ever say that will erase the damage that's already been done. We've wasted too many years as it is. So I'm asking you, Kye, can we put the past behind us and start anew? God knows, you're the only true friend I've ever had. And I'd surely hate to lose you because of my own stupidity."

When Kyliah raised her hand to wipe away the tears that were streaming down her face, it was the only opening Ashela needed. She stepped forward and again embraced her childhood friend. Only this time, Kyliah didn't reject her. She enfolded her in her arms as well.

Wrapped in bear hugs, the two of them laughed self-consciously as the people around them started clapping.

***

Over the next several months, Ashela sought to make up for lost time as she moved to renew the bonds of their friendship. When she found out that Kyliah was living in Atlanta and worked as an actuary for PricewaterhouseCoopers, she began attempts to lure her away to California.

After they brought each other up to speed with the past and current events of their lives, their conversation turned to public relations. Ashela spoke of needing a publicist desperately. Though Kyliah was and had always been a whiz with numbers, Ashela knew that she was also a great "people" person. So she convinced her to come to L.A. and give it a shot.

Four years later, Kyliah's role had expanded to include executive assistant duties as well. As a PR advisor, Kyliah cultivated a great number of professional relationships and over time built up a sizable contact base. She became so proficient at promoting Ashela that she started taking on additional clients until she eventually started her own PR firm.

***

Kyliah took a seat in the living room while Ashela ran upstairs to take a quick shower. She came back downstairs to find Kyliah studying a black, Hermès Bugatti leather planner. She had helped herself to something to drink.

Ashela caught Kyliah's accusatory glance as she sat on the arm of her sofa. "Why are you looking at me like that? What have I done now?" Ashela asked when Kyliah gave her a look that indicated she was fed up with her.

"For starters, you obviously haven't checked your messages. Secondly, you had a three o'clock hair appointment with Derrick. And thirdly, tonight you have a seven-thirty dinner engagement at Debbie Allen's house."

Ashela clapped her hand to her forehead. "Ohmagosh! I thought that was tomorrow! Man!" Ashela looked up guiltily. "Debbie will never forgive me if I miss tonight's dinner party. Not after I missed her last two. Do you think Derrick can still take me?"

Kyliah wiggled her pen between her thumb and index finger. "I called Derrick and told him you were running an hour behind schedule, and I confirmed with Debbie last night." Kyliah gazed at her friend with no sympathy. "You know, Ash, all of this could be avoided if you simply turned on the ringer to your phones around this house. And we would really have our problems solved if you checked your answering machine," Kyliah paused with lifted eyebrows, "Oh, maybe, say, something other than every blue moon?"

"Honestly, Kye. I checked my messages last night when I got in." Ashela got up to show Kyliah her message pad. "See? I just haven't had time to call anybody back."

Kyliah flashed a "talk-to-the-hand" gesture and gave Ashela a look that said she'd heard it all before. "Go change, please. Derrick is going to try to fit me in, too. So can we be on our way?"

Ashela stood up to go get dressed. "You're coming with me tonight?"

Kyliah smiled. "No sweetie. I can't do the party thing tonight. I've got places to go, people to see, and things to do."

"Yeah, right, you bum. The only people, places and things you've got to see is probably some new vanilla ice cream stud."

Kyliah laughed as Ashela left the room. She knew Ash was trying to slip in a dig about the fact that she preferred to date white men. She called after her, "That's all right. At least *I* got a life. Unlike some people!"

***

When they arrived at the No Gossip hair salon, it was fifteen minutes till four. As usual, Derrick, friend and beautician to many celebrities, was fussing up a storm. Getting him to fit you in at short notice was virtually impossible. The demand for his services was so great that appointments had to be made sometimes months in advance. If he did squeeze you in on short notice, you could expect to pay and pay heavily.

Sitting in his chair, Ashela stared into his mirror and told him, "Derrick, I'm ready for that new style you've been trying to sell me. Go ahead, love, make me beautiful."

"Feeling daring today, are we, darling? Well, let's see what we have to work with." As gay as a two headed frog, Derrick's voice was high-pitched and everything about him was effeminate. Nevertheless, when it came to hair, the man knew his stuff. Ashela's thick hair was well past shoulder length. But lately, Derrick had been challenging her to go for a shorter look. As he started clipping away, she closed her eyes, unable to watch as long clumps of her hair littered the floor around her.

Seated in the next booth across from her, another patron was being serviced. Both the hair stylist and client talked non-stop. For the life of her, Ashela could not comprehend why they named the salon "No Gossip" when in fact it was a hotbed of exactly that. Maybe the name was meant to be an oxymoron. All around the marbled shop women were sharing the latest juicy tidbits.

". . . and I saw Eddie Murphy and . . ."

". . . well I heard that Madonna was . . ."

". . . Van Peebles is taking my sister to the premiere of Denzel's new film . . ."

". . . well, yeah, but I was told Wesley turned down the script and that's how Tyson Beckford got . . ."

". . . I ran into Robert DeNiro's new girlfriend. She had . . ."

". . . I can't confirm it, but rumor has it that Dennis Rodman . . ."

". . . I heard that Tyra Banks and Halle Berry were arguing over Sam Ross . . ."

On and on it went. Some who weren't engaged in conversations had their eyes glued to The National Enquirer, The Star, or some other news mag. Ashela had discovered long ago that for some people, there was nothing more enjoyable than basking in another person's misery. For a short period of time, it enabled them to forget about their own inadequacies. By shining the glaring light of examination onto someone else's activities, they could fool themselves into believing that they were more fortunate or better off than the next—that just maybe they weren't doing as badly as they thought they were. Ashela knew, too, that it didn't matter who someone was, no matter how high or how low they were on the totem pole, that everybody had kinks and quirks in their armor. Those who thought they didn't just needed to examine themselves a little more closely.

Permed and shampooed, Ashela was under the dryer when two nail technicians came to service her. One worked on her nails while the other tech proceeded to give her a pedicure. As was customary for her, the drone of the hair dryer and the muted voices around her, lulled Ashela to sleep.

***

In her dream, the years fell away and once again she was a child basking in the games that only children play with such abandoned innocence. She, Kyliah, and Parris. Playing hide-and-go-seek in the wooded area behind the Grand Oaks estate. Running from tree to tree with wild, unrestrained recklessness, as if their very lives depended upon not being caught, they laughed and squealed delightedly.

They ran until they reached Briar's Pond, a small stream of water that ran through the forest. The three of them sat near the rippling water and threw rocks into its midst.

"What are you going to be when you grow up Parris?" Ashela asked him.

"I'm gonna be a pilot when I grow up. That way, I can fly all over the world." Parris stood up to throw his rock as far as he could.

"What about you, Kye? What are you going to be?"

"I dunno." Kyliah raised her knees to her chest and wrapped her arms around them. "I guess I could be a lot of things cause my teacher says I can be whatever I wanna be."

"Well, I'm going to be a famous singer, just like my mother."

"How you gonna be a famous singer when you sound like a scratched chicken?" Parris flapped his arms, jerked his neck back and forth and started clucking, "Bock, babock, babock . . ."

Shouting childish obscenities at him, Ashela and Kyliah jumped up to chase him. Hot on his trail, they ran until they reached the house. Laughing, they raced up the stairs and fell onto the porch.

Friends to the end is what they said they'd always be.

An hour later, Ashela stared into the mirror with amazement. "Derrick, babes, *you* are a phenomenal creature!" She turned her head in both directions and ran her fingers through it. Short curls on the sides and top of her crown fell forward to feather-frame her face. The back had been cropped close to her head in waves. A midnight black rinse gave her hair vibrant shine and luster. The style heavily accentuated the squareness of her jaw. She looked good if she had to say so herself. Ashela stood and pecked Derrick on the cheek and slipped him a $100 tip. She looked around for Kyliah and was told she was in the back having a body massage. Pressed for time, Ashela quickly headed home.

Chapter Eighteen

ressed to the nines and looking like a ten, Ashela stood in the foyer checking her dress in the mirror as she waited for her limo driver to pick her up. She wore an elegant, black Givenchy halter-dress that tied at the neck and emphasized the muscled tone of her arms. The sleek, long dress was made of crepe material and was cut to flatter her shapely form. Three-inch, patent leather T-strap Manolo Blahnik sandals completed her outfit. Her jewelry consisted of a pair of long, dangling diamond earrings, a diamond tennis bracelet and a slim gold Fontaé watch.

At the sound of her doorbell, Ashela grabbed her Chanel bag and matching black satin shawl and locked the door behind her.

It would take forty-five minutes to reach her destination. Debbie Allen frequently entertained guests in her sprawling, multi-million dollar Beverly Hills estate. Happily married since day one, she and her hubby were well liked by everyone. Known for their exclusive parties, they were used to entertaining the rich, the famous, and the powerful. People vied to be included on their guest list. Tonight's affair had been limited to a mere fourteen guests.

Actors, actresses, doctors, politicians, singers, models and producers completed the mixture. Everyone brought something to the table.

As the limo pulled into the driveway of the estate, Rolls-Royces, Ferraris, and Lamborghinis were already in line formation waiting for the valets to open the door for each guest. This was not Ashela's first time inside their residence, but as always, she was in awe of its decor. As she walked through the grand marbled foyer with its huge crystal chandelier, she found the mansion all the more impressive because she knew that Debbie had done the decorating herself. The predominant color scheme was a mixture of sorbet pastels, and despite its size, the mansion was warm and inviting.

Debbie looked ravishing in a purple silk, back-plunging, floor-length gown. Around her neck, she wore a glittering diamond and ruby necklace. She was greeting Angela Bassett as Ashela approached. Debbie and Angela loosely hugged one another, touched cheeks and blew kisses in the air—the standard Hollywood greeting. Ever the delightful hostess, Debbie did the same with Ashela.

"Ashela, I'm so glad you could make it this time." Debbie introduced her to Angela and said teasingly, "I've been trying to get this busy lady to my last several dinner parties, Angie. But it seems she's too busy for us little people."

Ashela rolled her eyes and shook her head. "Deb, you know that's not true. I always clear my plate when you call." Debbie gave her a "don't-even-try-it" look.

She shooed them away, and with a silken swish of her gown was off to greet her next guest.

Ashela and Angela were led by servants into the miniature ballroom where pre-dinner drinks and hors d'oeuvres were being served.

"It is truly a pleasure to meet you, Ms. Bassett. I must admit that I've seen all of your movies and I've become quite a fan." A waiter, dressed in a tuxedo with white gloves, approached them carrying a tray of glasses filled with Cristal champagne. Ashela and Angela each took one. "The scene in *Waiting To Exhale* where you lit the match and torched all the man's things . . . Now that was classic."

Angela laughed. She was dressed in a pink chiffon Lacroix evening dress that highlighted her skin color and showed off her legs. "Why, thank you. But you must call me Angie. All my friends do. You know, I've heard your name mentioned as well but I couldn't attach an association."

Ashela smiled, "Pleeeease tell me you didn't see me on the latest edition of 'Hard Copy.' "

Angela laughed. "No. I was flying back from filming in Jamaica when I came across an article about you in Emerge magazine. It helped me make the connection. I found it quite impressive, the way most of the songs you write become number one hits."

Before Ashela could comment, a deep, masculine voice spoke from behind her. "Good evening ladies. You two are looking extremely enchanting." With champagne glass in one hand, Larry Fishburne joined them. Sliding his other arm around Angela's waist, he placed a chaste kiss on her forehead. The two had worked together on several film projects and had become good friends.

"Larry, what a pleasant surprise. I thought your latest shoot had taken you out of the country. How did you finish filming so soon?"

"Piece of cake, sweetheart. That's why they pay me the big bucks." Larry's eyes never left Ashela.

Noticing with amusement the way Larry was staring at Ashela, Angela made the introductions. "Have you met Ashela Jordan?"

Larry looked Ashela up and down and said in a slow sexy drawl, "No, I can't say that I've had the pleasure. How *do* you do?" Larry gave her a 100-watt smile as he extended his hand.

Ashela laughed as she shook it. "Angie, is he always this charming?" She stared at the gap in Laurence Fishburne's teeth, unable to believe how incredibly good the man looked up close. Television obviously didn't do him justice. She took his hand, thinking that he was the epitome of *savoir debonair*.

"Yes. Even at his worst, I'm afraid he's always quite the charmer. Larry, just as you joined us, I was telling Ashela how impressive it must be to have had seventy-

five percent of the songs she's written reach number one." As impressive as Ashela's musical accomplishments might be, Larry Fishburne didn't seem to be interested.

Still smiling, Ashela tried to pull her hand from Larry's grasp but he wouldn't allow it. She said to him teasingly, "Mr. Fishburne, in a few seconds, you and I are going to look foolish standing here holding hands."

"Never." Larry said as he raised her hand to his lips and kissed it before gently releasing it. "You can tell so much about a woman from her hands."

Ashela tilted her head. "Is that right?"

"Certainly. And, you, Ms. Jordan, have very strong hands. There's also a soft, tenderness to them. Which tells me that you're a romantic at heart but you take considerable measures to hide it with cynicism."

Amused, Angela Bassett said, "You two are getting way too deep for me. I think I'll go and mingle with some of the other guests."

"Angie, please, don't go." Ashela didn't trust herself to be left alone with him. "I believe Mr. Fishburne is simply displaying his great charm and wit. And being the charming globetrotter that he is, I'm sure he's going to promise to behave himself. Isn't that so, Mr. Fishburne?"

"Only if you promise to call me Larry."

Just as he finished speaking, supermodel Patricia Howard joined them. She gave Ashela and Angela a perfunctory greeting. Patricia literally had eyes only for Larry and she made it plain that she intended to monopolize his time. Ashela took advantage of the model's presence by making an impromptu exit.

"Please excuse me. I *must* say hello to Regina." As Ashela quickly departed, she made a mental note to stay away from Mr. Laurence Fishburne.

"Gina, you look gorgeous!" Ashela approached Regina Belle and her hubby John. Hollywood hugs commenced. Dressed in a navy blue, off-the-shoulder, Halston dress, with her hair swept on top of her head, she did, indeed, look stunning.

"Ashela Jordan, surely, you're not going to play me like I haven't been calling *you* for the past several months." Regina shook her head like she wasn't having any of it. "See, Ash, I could get real homegirl on you. But I'm not going to go there tonight. No, it's okay. Just treat me like a bald-headed step child. I know when the joke's on me." Regina pretended to be mortally offended.

"Gina, Gina." Ashela looked to John for support. John shook his head.

"Don't look at me, Ash. I just got here." He swiped a champagne glass from a nearby waiter and went to mingle.

Ashela had written material for Regina's past several albums. Each song she'd written for her had been an overwhelming success. Word had it that Regina was currently in the studio working on her next release.

"Gina, I'm so very busy. Honestly, girlfriend, I haven't been ignoring you. I've just been swamped. Tevin Campbell's, Keith Washington's and Phil Perry's projects

have zonked every bit of spare time that I've had. I'm telling you, it's been a virtual madhouse. Keith Sweat's producer called me last week, pleading for me to do something with Keith's new CD. But I had to say no. I simply don't have the time. And then, Gina, about thirty minutes later Keith called me himself, *begging*. And girl, you know the brother can beg. I had to explain to him, with all that I've got on my plate, there's no way I can squeeze his album in."

Ashela was finally able to wring a sympathetic look from Regina.

"But the good news is that I was able to complete TB's project. So now I'm on to the next one, which happens to be Maxwell."

"How did Toni's project go? Is it finished?" When the top artists were about to come out with a new release, word got around.

"My portion of it is. But I'm pretty sure she and Face have some more editing to do." Ashela took a sip of her champagne. "Okay, okay, please stop looking at me like that. When's the deadline for your new release?"

"Two months from now."

"I'm only doing this because it's you, Gina. Give me a couple of weeks. I'll see what I can come up with. But you owe me, Regina. Big time." Ashela knew she'd kick herself in the morning. Where would she find the time? An old adage came back to her: If you want something done, give it to someone who's already got too much to do.

Regina said teasingly, "Awe, AJ. You're going to fit me in. You really *do* love me."

Regina laughed when, in return, Ashela held up her middle finger against her champagne glass in such a way that only Regina knew she had flipped her the bird.

Lynn Whitfield arrived at the same time as John Singleton. Next came Senator Carol Moseley Braun with her guest, cardiologist, Frazier Klein. Vivica Fox arrived on the heels of basketball superstar Grant Hill. And looking good enough to eat, came actor Richard Lawson. Everyone was mingling, getting acquainted, and enjoying themselves when the last guest arrived.

In walked Sam "Money" Ross, looking like Mr. GQ, himself. Maybe it was her, but Ashela could have sworn that when he entered the room, the tone of the gathering shifted, as if royalty had just walked through the doors. Even Debbie seemed to greet him with an extra bit of fondness. As she led Sam into the room, several of the guests gathered around him.

Sam Ross, President and CEO of Werner Enterprises, was one of the most powerful and influential figures in the music industry. Insiders whispered that he had mob connections. True or false, anyone who knew anything about the "behind the scenes" aspect of the music business recognized Sam Ross's name. When Sam Ross spoke, people listened, and when he snapped his fingers, they jumped to attention. Ashela had never met him in person. Their paths had never crossed. Though she wanted an introduction, there were too many others clamoring for his attention. She

looked on as he held court with Senator Braun, Frazier Klein, Grant Hill and Norm Nixon.

At precisely eight o'clock, all of the guests were led into the dining room where elegant white and gold name cards were placed in front of each setting. Part of the allure of attending a Debbie Allen affair was that she never gave advance notice of her guest list. Each guest had no clue as to who else would be attending the affair. All one knew was that they would be given the opportunity to hobnob with other people who were famous in their own right.

Ashela smiled at the match-making tendencies of Debbie Allen. As the seating arrangements for the evening's affair unfolded, she could see Debbie's hand at work. She found her seat and was about to take it when someone behind her said, "Please, allow me to get that for you."

Ashela glanced over her shoulder as Sam Ross pulled her chair out for her. Up close, he smelled divine. Dressed in an Italian, tailor-made, teal-blue Corneliani suit, his clothing highlighted the rich darkness of his skin. His broad shoulders gave Ashela the impression that with him, she could lay all her burdens down and find comfort in his arms.

"Thank you, Mr. Ross. That's kind of you." Ashela couldn't believe that he was going to sit next to her.

"My pleasure," Sam murmured as he pulled out his own chair just to the right of hers.

Ashela wondered why on earth Debbie was trying to kill her. First Larry Fishburne and now Sam Ross. Didn't Deb know that having these many gorgeous Black men in one room at one time was enough to give even the healthiest woman a heart attack? Ashela glanced over at Grant Hill, John Singleton and Richard Lawson. Since most of the gentlemen in attendance were single, Ashela sincerely hoped that some lucky women somewhere would hurry and snatch them up. With all of these single men about, the world wasn't safe.

Ashela considered it a privilege to be seated next to Sam Ross. The man had a self-assurance like no one she had ever seen or met. It was different from the other men in the room. His was a confidence that seemed to come not so much from what he had, but from who he was. She could see it in the warm and assertive way in which he spoke to those around him.

"It's an honor to finally meet you, Mr. Ross." Ashela said as she turned toward him.

"I return the compliment, Ms. Jordan. My compatriots tell me that you are continuously working musical miracles. I'm also told that you are a very, very busy woman. It is *Miss* Jordan, is it not?" Sam thought the simplistic elegance of her evening gown made her look all the more alluring.

Ashela smiled at his obvious flattery. "Yes it is. And please, call me Ashela."

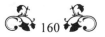

A sense of power exuded from him, so much so that Ashela wanted to call him "sir." She thought of the earlier conversation she'd heard at the beauty salon. The one where the woman said she'd heard that Tyra Banks and Halle Berry were seen arguing over Sam Ross. Ashela had to put a clamp on her sudden desire to smile. She took a sip of her water and covertly glanced at him as he turned to speak to the guest on his right. Oh, yes, Ashela thought. She could easily understand *and forgive* two grown women of their caliber for fighting hog wild in the middle of the street. A man like Sam Ross could make a woman lose every shred of decency she even thought she might have had. Not one to believe every rumor in the mill, Ashela had the sudden feeling that there might just be a whiff of truth to that particular one.

Patricia, the supermodel, was seated on Sam's right. She was holding his arm possessively in an attempt to garner his attention, just as she'd done earlier with Larry. Again, Ashela couldn't blame her. Between Sam Ross and Larry Fishburne, a woman could easily forget her vow of celibacy. They were both men whom Ashela had no intention of standing in line to fight for.

Not wanting to battle for Sam's conversation, Ashela turned her attention to her left, to the good doctor and the guest seated next to him, Senator Braun. She listened in on their conversation and laughed as he told the ending of his story for her benefit as well.

Soon, the waiters began serving the first course.

Ashela nearly jumped out of her skin when Sam touched her wrist and said, "What a beautiful watch."

"Oh, thank you. It belonged to my mother many years ago." Ashela lifted her wrist to show him the watch, trying to downplay the smooth softness of his touch. "And it hasn't given me much trouble either. If only everything else in life were so simple."

Sam spread his napkin on his lap and tasted his soup. "Delicious," he murmured. He turned to her and said, "Tell me, Ashela, what would you know about the hardships of life? You can't be more than a baby."

Ashela laughed and smiled enchantingly. *If he only knew.* "Surely, Mr. Ross, you don't believe that age is anything but a number? Besides, looks are deceiving. I could tell you some stories that would raise the hair on your neck."

Sam fastened his eyes on her and smiled. "I'm very interested in hearing these stories."

Ashela's gaze slowly flitted over his face, her eyes lingering on the whiteness of his teeth. Attracted to him yet not wanting to appear obvious, she spooned some of the soup into her mouth. Ashela froze when she heard Frazier Klein say, "Sam, I'd like to hear these stories as well. So, please, Ms. Jordan, share one with us."

Having been backed into a corner and put on the spot, Ashela smiled and said to both men, "Well, I've never been one to monopolize the conversation. Not when there are so many other people present whose stories would far outweigh anything I

could ever tell. Mr. Ross, why don't *you* share a story with us. I'm sure it would be much more entertaining." Smiling as if she'd scored a point, Ashela spooned more of the soup into her mouth.

Before he could speak, the pesky Patricia Howard chimed in. "If it's a story you want, I've got them up the ying yang. I see *many* horrible things in my line of work everyday. But even the newspapers don't seem to want to write about them." Patricia went on to bemoan the conditions of the dressing rooms which models had to deal with and how many times she, personally, had had to change clothes right out in the open. Ashela was glad the woman had purposely jumped in and unknowingly spared her. She even pretended to be interested in what the model had to say.

The main course arrived, followed by dessert. Once dinner was completed, the last course having been served, Debbie announced that she had a surprise that she wanted everyone to stay for. They were led into a huge drawing room, where in one corner of the room sat an awesome ruby red baby grand. There were two microphones sitting on top of it.

"Actually, it's as much a request as it is a surprise. I've just purchased this wonderful piano and I was hoping that Ashela could try it out for me. And then I thought that if she's going to play for us, why not take advantage of one of the most talented voices of our time, Ms. Regina Belle."

Ashela's and Regina's widened eyes connected from across the room. Neither of them had had any idea that Debbie would spring this on them.

"Let's show them some love." Debbie started clapping and the other guests followed suit.

Given no choice, Ashela walked over to the baby grand and seated herself. She started strumming her fingers over the keys and the room became filled with the soft cadences. Regina came over and sat down next to her. She took one of the mics into her hands and tested its sound.

"Debbie, I'm going to get you for this," Regina said in a mock threatening voice. Laughter sprinkled the room.

Ashela piped in, "Make sure you get her for me too. I guess this is my payback for missing two of her previous affairs. What did *you* do, Gina?"

"I don't know. I think I was fifteen minutes late tonight." Regina crooned pleadingly into the microphone, "Debbie, I'm soooooorrry." Laughing, everyone started gathering around the piano with an air of excited expectation.

Ashela dipped her head toward her microphone, still playing a slow jazzy number. "It's a good thing Regina has been working on her new album, otherwise she might have been caught off guard." Ashela looked out at every one. Her eyes roamed until they found Sam Ross's. "But I've got the easy part, Sam. All I have to do is sit here and wing it." Ashela looked at Regina, smiling. "It's all on you, kid. Is there anything in particular you'd like me to play?"

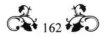

Debbie came and sat on Ashela's left. She moved the mic closer to her and put her arm around Ashela's shoulder.

"You all, Ashela *thinks* she's got it easy, but not tonight. As hostess, *I'm* making the request. And tonight I'd like to hear Ashela and Regina do their rendition of Billie Holiday's God Bless The Child. If you've never heard the two of them sing together, you're in for a real treat."

Ashela laid her head on Debbie's shoulder for a quick moment as she continued to play. She knew she couldn't sing Holiday's song. It wasn't that she was bashful, it was just that that particular song reminded her too much of her mother. If she sang it, she was guaranteed to cry. And she wasn't about to do that tonight. Over the years, so many people had told her that she reminded them of her mother and that when they heard her sing, if they closed their eyes, they wouldn't know she wasn't Charla. For that reason, these days Ashela rarely used her voice in song. She stuck to writing and playing her instruments. She looked at Debbie and Regina before speaking into the mic.

In a husky voice, Ashela said, "This has been such a wonderful evening. As Debbie can tell you, because of the demands on my time, I don't get out much. But tonight has been special. Meeting so many new and genuine people who I know will be in my life for years to come." Ashela looked over at Angela Bassett and Lynn Whitfield. "I want to keep it that way—special. Holiday's song has significance for me because it reminds me of my mother. What I'm really trying to say is that there's no way I can sing it without thinking of her and crying. I won't do that tonight. Instead, I want to give all of you something special to take with you that you'll remember for a long time." She reached over and quickly pecked Debbie on the cheek. "Debbie's such a sweet woman, isn't she?" Everyone murmured and shook their heads in agreement.

Even as she spoke, Ashela's fingers continued to flit over the ivory keys. "A couple of years ago, I had a song come to me. And as I was writing it, I could picture as clear as day, Regina Belle singing this song. I thought of how nurturing Regina is, not just with her own children, but with so many others. As I completed the lyrics for the song, I knew that Regina was the only one who could sing it." Ashela's gaze flitted over everyone who gathered around. "Needless to say, we recorded it. When her album was released, the song immediately catapulted to the number one spot. It's still one of my favorite songs. I'm going to ask Regina to sing it tonight." Ashela turned to Regina and nodded her head.

Regina let Ashela play the first verses of the song. As the notes filled the room, recognition dawned on everyone's face. She lifted the microphone and started singing softly. As her voice rose and fell with every note, the pleasure on the gatherers faces was obvious.

If I could stop every hurt,
If I could shelter you from every pain,

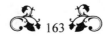

I would shield you from the storms of life, if only I could . . .

As Regina ended her song, seeing the satisfaction on the faces of the onlookers was pleasure in itself. To know that she possessed something so valuable and yet so intangible and to be able to share it with others—that's what made it all worth it.

***

The following morning Ashela was seated outside soaking up the sun on her deck which overlooked the majestic Malibu waters. Seated at her wicker table, soft breezes grazed her temples and the gentle roar of the sea sounded in the background. She wore a pink, striped, sleeveless vest over matching baggy pajamas. Wicker furniture was neatly arranged on the spacious verandah. In the middle of the table sat a Chinese tea set. Ashela was sipping hot tea and writing checks to pay her bills when her cordless phone rang. She checked the Caller ID before answering.

"May I help you?" Kyliah was on the other end of the line.

"Whatever happened to hello, good morning, or even how are you? Of course you can help me. Give me the goods about last night."

Ashela adopted a British accent and said, "Hellewww, who would you like to speak tooo? I con't hear you verdy well. I think you hov the wrong nomber. Please don't call here agane. Click!"

"Ashela, girl, would you quit playing and acting silly? Give me the 411 in a 911 fashion!"

Still maintaining her chirpish British accent, Ashela said, "Let's see, old chap, where do I begin?" Her voice suddenly changed to a slow, sexy southern drawl. "Would you like to hear about how Larry Fishburne kissed my hand or about how *foine* Sam Ross and Grant Hill are in person?" By the time Ashela finished her sentence, there was no trace of a British accent.

Kyliah gasped. "Ugh, ughn. Sam Ross? Larry Fishburne? Girl, where was I? Who else was there?"

"Let's see if I can remember." Ashela paused, taking her time.

Kyliah was about to scream into the phone. She *hated* trying to get details about anything from Ashela. As musically inclined as she was, when it came to re-telling a story, she tended to get all the details out of chronological order. It was like pulling teeth from a tiger.

Ashela's doorbell rang as Kyliah waited breathlessly to hear what she had to say.

"Kye, should I be expecting anyone today?"

"No. Not that I'm aware of. Did you order something?"

"No." Ashela went to inquire who it was through the intercom.

"FTD," came the reply.

"FTD?" Kyliah was asking on the other end of the phone. "Who sent you flowers?"

"I have no idea," Ashela replied as she opened the door.

"Delivery for Ashela Jordan."

Ashela signed for the flowers, tipped him, and closed the door. Inside the box were huge red roses surrounded by mounds of fresh baby breath. "Kyliah, they're beautiful! A dozen red roses." A small card lay on top. Making herself wait to read it, she went into the kitchen and found a vase to put them in. Back on her deck, she placed them in the center of the wicker table.

"Who sent them? Will you hurry up and open the card? What does it say?"

Ashela slowly opened the card and read, "Red roses to compliment the romantic side of you. Please have dinner with me. I promise to be good. Larry Fishburne."

"Get outta here! Ashela, look, let's start from the beginning. Take a deep breath and begin by telling me, who . . . all . . . was . . . there."

Before Ashela could recount the evening's details, the doorbell rang again.

"Who could that be?" Kyliah asked, impatient to get the previous night's details.

Ashela opened the door for yet another FTD man. "Ashela Jordan?" he inquired.

"Yes."

The man went back to his van and returned carrying in each arm two dozen flaming white roses in separate vases. Ashela stood at the door with her mouth hanging open. "Kyliah, you're not going to believe this."

"Look, rockhead, do I need to hang up and just drive over there? What *is* it?"

Ashela stepped to the side to allow the delivery man to bring the flowers inside. On his way out, she asked him if he needed her to sign for them and was told that she could sign when he finished bringing *all* the flowers in.

Ashela laughed in disbelief, guessing they were more flowers sent by Larry. "Kye, let me see where I'm going to put all of these flowers and I'll call you back."

"Why can't I just hang on? Goodness!"

In exasperation, Ashela said, "I'll call you right back, I promise."

Kyliah reluctantly hung up the other end.

In total, the delivery man brought in twelve vases, each filled with a dozen white roses surrounded by more baby's breath. She signed for them, gave the man a $20 tip, and took the card he was handing her. Assuming it was another one from Larry, she slipped the card into her pocket and began to distribute the vases of flowers around the house.

Seated once more outside on the wooden deck, Ashela opened the card. "To a woman of grace, style, wit, and excellence. I'm looking forward to hearing the stories you didn't have an opportunity to share with me last night. Fondly, Sam Ross." She was sitting there staring blankly at the card when the phone rang again.

"Being the forgetful scholar that you are, I figured you must have misplaced my phone number. I'm just calling you back so you won't have to look for it." Kyliah wanted the goods, and this time she was not to be put off.

"Okay, okay! Sooooome people." Ashela recounted for her the details of the previous evening. Describing for her how the evening had ended with everyone congratulating her and Regina Belle. She remembered shaking hands with Senator Braun and Vivica Fox, exchanging numbers with Angela Bassett and Lynn Whitfield. She'd held hands longer than was necessary with Sam Ross, and finally, she'd touched cheeks with Larry Fishburne as he whispered in her ear that he was aware of how she had avoided him all evening.

"And that was it. Honestly." Ashela had to convince Kyliah that she wasn't leaving anything out.

"Wow. Sam Ross. Larry Fishburne." Kyliah's voice was a hushed whisper. "Which one are you going to call first?"

"I don't know. To be honest with you, probably neither."

"Duhhhh," Ashela could hear the sarcasm in Kye's voice. "Probably neither? Okay, Ash, look. Let me help you out here. After all, I'm just here for you. Okay?" Kyliah adopted a homegirl monologue. "Remember, this is me you're talking to. So we can cut the crap and be real." Kyliah started counting on her fingers. "First off, it's not like you're seeing anyone. Secondly, it's not like you get out much. And thirdly, it's not even like you've got any prospects."

"Kye . . ." Ashela tried to interrupt.

"Wait, wait, wait, rockhead. This is *my* story, remember? So please, let me tell it how *I* see it. I promise, you'll have your turn." Kyliah continued to break it down for her. "As I was saying before I was rudely and crudely interrupted. You *ain't* got no man. You *ain't* got no kids. And outside of your music, you *ain't even* got a life!" Kyliah was doing the stop sign thing with her hand. "But, not to worry, because as I said earlier, I'm here for you. If it were me, this is what *I* would do. Larry Fishburne is *foine*. Do we agree on that?"

Smiling, Ashela said, "Agreed."

"Okay. Larry could wine you, dine you, and valentine you. And make you feel like there *is* no tomorrow. But Sam Ross. Well, Sam is . . ." Kyliah stopped because she felt her own toes curling just thinking about the man.

Ashela was busy remembering the smoothness of Sam's touch. She said, "Yes, my sistah, I, I do see where you're going. I mean, I know this is *your* story and all. Trust me, I'm not trying to steal your testimony. But, ugh, let me just help *you*. You see, a man like Sam Ross, well I'm sure he would *definitely* treat a woman right."

"Mmmmmm," Kyliah said, with a visual image of Sam plastered to her mind.

"I'm sure a man like him would even keep a woman swept off her feet."

"Mmmm, hmmm."

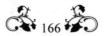

"Maybe even glued to the bed."

"Yesssss, go right ahead." Kyliah was in la la land just thinking about it.

"Well, that's my point, sweetie. I'm not looking to be swept off my feet. Nor am I looking to be wined and dined *or* sixty-nined."

"Wait, wait, wait. You see, you had me, Ash. My, sistah, I was *with* you. I was *feeling* you. I mean, we were almost *there*. But see, now you done started talkin' cray-zie. Ash, what is wrong with you? Help *me* understand. I know you love your music . . ."

Ashela interrupted her. "That's right. And every time I look at my bank account, I can *see* the money."

Kyliah tried a different tactic. "Look, Ash, the money is great. You're living large, so how can you complain? You got it like that. But what about a little entertainment on the side? What's wrong with enjoying yourself from time to time? Ash, when was the last time you've even had dinner with a man that wasn't because of business?" Kyliah sat up in her bed. For some reason, the tone of the conversation had shifted.

"Ash, babes, all kidding aside. I know that money is good. Who wouldn't feel good knowing that they had millions in the bank? But what about *living*? What about vacations? These last few years, you've sent me on several *paid* vacations each year, so I can't complain. But why can't you come with me some time? Heck, for that matter, you could go somewhere by yourself." Kyliah knew she was treading thin ground, but she said it anyway. "Okay, forget about going out to dinner with a man. Forget about vacationing in the tropics somewhere. Why not take a break, sweetheart? You deserve it. How many hits have you had in the last two to three years, Ashela? Over a hundred? What's there left to prove? *How much money do you have to have before enough is enough?*"

A steely silence detonated the air. "I didn't ask for your opinion, Kyliah. And I think this conversation just came to an end."

"Yeah. I'll talk to you later." Kyliah hung up with an attitude. She couldn't say that she and Ash saw eye-to-eye on everything. What Ashela did in her private life was her own business. But Kyliah could say that, as friends, they were always honest with each other. They were at a point in their relationship where they could agree to disagree. Right now, Ashela was probably fuming and cursing her out, thinking who the hell did Kye think she was to tell her how to live her life. Kyliah knew she probably wouldn't hear from Ash again until the next day or so.

She didn't stand in judgment of Ash. She just thought she took life too seriously. How had they even gotten on such a touchy subject anyway? But Kyliah felt that life was too short and precious. She couldn't understand how Ashela could let stuff that happened years and years ago, block out any chance for happiness in the present. It seemed to Kye that too many times, people, herself included, majored on the minor

things in life. And in the meantime, life was passing them by. Time was forever slipping away.

Kyliah was grateful that she was not hurting financially. And that she had a sizeable nest-egg stashed away. But money wasn't everything. She thought a person's happiness should be just as important. Kyliah saw nothing wrong with accumulating wealth. Still, she wondered, what sense did it make to harbor a boatload of the stuff if it didn't bring you any pleasure?

Chapter Nineteen

he MSI Corporation was an agency constantly scouting for new talent. The company comprised a litany of agents who were known for their representation of the most well-known artists in the music industry. Adrienne Dantley was one of MSI's top music agents and his client list included a string of notable celebrities. Inside his plush, cherry oak office, his secretary, Evette Pearson, greeted Ashela as she entered.

"Go right in, Ms. Jordan. Mr. Dantley's waiting for you."

Adrienne was on the phone when Ashela entered his office. He motioned for her to have a seat. With the phone pressed to his ear, he leaned back in his chair and ran his fingers down the length of his tie. "Nupe, you're not hearing me. I'm your agent, not a social worker. What you need right now is immediate damage control. You want to pull out from me to climb in bed with somebody else, fine. You'll get no complaints here—you'd be doing *me* a favor. But, as your *current* agent, let me warn you, Nupe, with this latest incident, you won't find a dog willing to touch you. And it gets worse. If you don't go back and straighten this situation out—you will never, *never*, get a decent gig anywhere again. Even Mickey D's wouldn't use you after this. You want my advice? Have your lawyer call Sam Ross directly. Tell him to say it was all meant to be a joke. A stupid prank that got out of hand and that you had no idea your boys would fuck up a ten million dollar set. Next, have him ask Sam Ross what it's going to take to smooth things over. From there, you and your crew start sucking up. Find yourselves a couple of children's hospitals and some homeless shelters to visit. You need as much positive PR as you can get right now and doing community service work will help provide it. You don't like it? Well, that's the best advice I have to offer, Nupe." Adrienne glanced at his watch. "Take the rest of the day to think about it. Call me tomorrow and let me know what you decide. I've got another client so I'm outta here."

Adrienne slammed the phone down and ran his hand over his shaved head in frustration. "These stupid bastards will never learn. Give them money and a little notoriety and they think they own the damned world." He stood and walked around

to seat himself on the corner of the large desk. "AJ, if all my clients were like you, I could set up shop in Aruba. All I'd need is a phone in one hand and a tall drink in the other."

Ashela was sitting on his leather couch, irritated that she'd been summoned on such short notice. She said unsympathetically, "Adrienne, please dispense with the drama. You know you love it. All day long, you get to sit on your throne and be king, play with people's lives and then take twenty percent of everything we earn. Who wouldn't love a job like that?"

"If that's all you think of me, AJ, then I'm hurt. What credit do I get for busting my ass all day long just so you can sit around and boast that you're the hottest piece of property this side of the planet?" Adrienne reached around for his packet of cigarettes. He removed one and was about to light it up.

"Ah, ah, ahhh. You know I can't stand the smell of cigarette smoke! Look, Adrienne, it's obvious you're having a bad day. Or maybe you just need a tampon. I don't know. But you must realize I have better things to do than sit here and listen to you gripe about some of the screwballs you call clients. Now that I'm here, why don't you go ahead and tell me what was so urgent and confidential that you couldn't discuss it over the phone."

Evette buzzed him and he picked up the phone. "Thanks. Call me the moment he gets here." Something about Adrienne's attitude quickened. Suddenly, he was back to all business, the head-aching problems of his previous client forgotten.

"I asked you to come on such short notice, Ash, because I just got the news myself. I know it sounded cloak and daggerish, but that's why I couldn't give you details over the phone. I simply didn't have any. All I know is that it's a deal where you would stand to make fifteen to twenty million dollars." When Ashela sat up even straighter, Adrienne knew he had her attention. "Sam Ross called me last night to say he was putting together a proposal that involved big names and even bigger money. You happen to be one of the players he wants involved in the deal. He asked if I could have you here for a conference-call, but Evette just said he called from his cellular to say that he'd be here in a few minutes. I guess he decided to come in person."

Adrienne picked up his phone again. "Okay, send him in." He got up to go open his door. Seeing the wide-eyed, open-mouthed expression on her face, he said, "Ashela, I've got as many questions as you do. Why don't we just hear him out?"

Talk about being taken by surprise! Ashela was totally at a loss for words. The only thing she could do to prepare herself was to stand to her feet before the man came through the door.

Sam Ross entered the room followed by another gentleman whom Ashela had never met. "Sam, good to see you." Adrienne shook hands with him before greeting the man behind him.

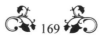

"Ashela, how are you?" Sam walked over to her and extended his hand. As he took in the length of her, he was reminded that there was something about her that he found irresistible. Sam just wasn't sure yet what it was. Dressed in a leopard-print silk blouse and long brown wrap around skirt, Sam thought she was gorgeous.

Ashela clasped both her hands around the one he extended, once again struck by his powerful aura. She was trying to maintain some semblance of self-composure, but feared she wasn't doing very well.

"I'm in my finest hour, Sam. It's good to see you again." He just had no idea how good. All kinds of sparks were going off inside of her. It was a struggle to remain calm and focused. *God, he looked good.*

Three weeks had passed since the night of the dinner party. Ashela had mailed him a thank you card on which she'd written, "Thank you for the flowers. How incredibly sweet of you." She'd signed it and hadn't heard from him since. Neither had she tried to reach him.

"Ashela, I'd like you to meet my financial advisor, Arron Davenport."

Ashela shook hands with Arron, a tall, somewhat thin, but very broad-shouldered man. "Pleased to meet you, Mr. Davenport."

"Please, call me Arron."

They seated themselves around a conference table, and as if on cue, Evette entered carrying a tray of coffee and breakfast rolls. She served the men and when Ashela waived her hand to say no thanks, left the room.

Sam began the discussion. "Ashela, thank you for accommodating me on such short notice. Adrienne informed you of my proposal?"

Ashela stared at him unblinkingly. "About thirty seconds before you walked through the door. I know about as much now as I did then."

"I apologize, that's my fault. I wanted to feel both of you out before revealing my entire plan." Sam opened a briefcase and took out a packet containing four color proposals.

"Why all the secrecy, Sam?" Ashela glanced at the cover of the packet she'd just been handed before looking at him as she waited for his answer.

"I couldn't afford for news to spread before I've had a chance to discuss it with all of the proposed players. We, Werner Enterprises and myself, are looking to form a Limited Partnership which would comprise the top songwriters in the industry. I envision this consortium as a futuristic paradigm that other labels will seek to duplicate in the years to come. If word leaked out too soon of what we're trying to do, someone else could get a jump on us. Also, we don't want to be brought up on charges of tampering with another label's property. Consequently, you can understand our need to 'feel out' certain prospects before we extend an offer. As I said before, we're interested in only the top people. Obviously, your name is high on

that list, Ashela, and we'd like you to be a part of our future when we launch this new venture."

Ashela carefully reviewed the packet. She was primarily interested in the numbers. "It looks good, Sam. But talk to me. Why would I sign a two-year deal with Werner when I'm doing just as well on my own?"

"That's where I come into the picture, Ashela." Arron leaned forward and folded his hands. "It's my duty as financial consultant to Werner Enterprises to spearhead the economic side of the proposed merger. I'm here to ensure that you understand our commitment to making this move worth your while."

"Then what are the figures you're proposing?" Adrienne asked.

"Since Werner wants Ashela to work exclusively with them, they're offering twenty million for two years. The catch, of course, would be that you would write only for Werner's talent. No one else could talk to you within the two-year period."

Ashela nodded. "Arron, that's very admirable of Werner, and Sam, I'm honored that you thought to include me. However, at the risk of slighting all parties involved, understand that I'm not trying to champion anyone's cause. I'm a *free-lance* songwriter. By year's end, I will already have grossed close to ten million. So why would I be willing to give up my freedom just to work with one company to make the same amount of money I'd make if I stayed on my own? Doesn't make sense, does it? Besides, I like being able to pick who I write for."

"Ashela, while our initial offer was twenty million for two years, that figure is open for negotiation. And you'd still be given much leeway as to who you'd write for."

"I'm glad to hear that Arron. Because I'd hate to think that my intelligence as well as my creative talent was being insulted, especially after Sam has just recognized me as a luminary in my field."

Adrienne interceded. "In light of what she's just told you, Arron, what new figure are you proposing?"

Arron loosened the notch on his tie before offering another amount. Adrienne looked at the figure he'd written and showed it to Ashela. She shook her head in disagreement. Ashela had learned from past experience that the first person to put money on the table did not always come out on top. She knew she wouldn't take less than thirty mil.

Sam watched in silence, admiring how well versed she was in the art of negotiation. He shouldn't have been so surprised, though, because she had warned him, telling him that age was just a number.

When they reached an impasse on the dollar amount, Sam intervened. "Does this mean that we at least have your interest, Ashela?"

"What it means, Sam, is that everyone, including myself, has their price. You want me to join your team, make it worth my while." Ashela glanced at her watch.

"Gentlemen, I'm sorry that I have to leave so soon, but I have a noon recording engagement that I cannot cancel." When Ashela stood, the men stood with her. "Sam, let me say this. My track record speaks for itself. I *am* the cream of the crop. If you want the best, put your money where your mouth is." She put her purse on her shoulder and reached her hand out to shake theirs. She was at the door when Sam spoke.

"Can we discuss this over dinner?" Sam wanted to see her again. Deal or no deal.

"Why not? Have your people call my people and we'll schedule an appointment." Ashela closed the door behind her.

Inside his office, Adrienne finally lit up one of the cigarettes he'd been dying to smoke. "I should have been able to tell her about the proposal and your coming here long beforehand, Sam. Right now, she's pissed and I'm afraid it's going to cost you."

"I can see that. But since it's OPM (other people's money), I think I can live with it. How old did you tell me she was again?"

Adrienne dragged another puff. "She won't tell me, but I think she's a very old thirty. I'd say she's been here before."

"She is something else, that's for sure," Arron ran his hand over his head.

Sam sat drumming his fingers on the table. Yes, Ms. Ashela Jordan was a puzzle, he thought to himself. Normally, any other woman who received flowers from him called to thank him the same day she received them. But not Ashela. She hadn't bothered to call at all.

During the subsequent weeks after the dinner party, Sam had become preoccupied with a myriad of other issues. He hadn't thought about her again until her name came up in his meeting with the Werner people. He recalled how arresting she was as she played the piano, and how her voice seemed to caress him when she'd singled him out from the rest of the guests, calling him by name. His overall impression of her up to that point was that she was somewhat shy and reserved. But all of that changed the moment she sat at the piano. Once she started playing, that's when he'd glimpsed it: A wellspring of passion that lay just beneath her surface. Sam found himself forcefully drawn to her and knew then that he wanted to see her again.

After the Werner meeting, she had crossed his mind frequently. He had even gone so far as to do his homework by trying to find out as much about her as he could. He and Adrienne Dantley went way back—they both had started out as go-fers on the low end of the business. As Ashela's agent, Sam figured that if anybody knew anything about her, Adrienne would be the one. Instead, he came up empty-handed. Sam knew that in this industry, everyone's life was pretty much an open

book. If he couldn't find any dirt on her, it meant either there was none or that she took careful pains to hide it. He'd reviewed the number of songs she'd written over the past several years. To amass so much in such a short period of time, a person would have had to practically work around the clock. Sam was impressed and also intrigued. He had made signing her to the Werner label his personal priority—getting to know her better was also a definite part of his plan.

***

"Can you believe he didn't even warn me why I was coming to his office?"

"Of course, I believe it. The guy's an asshole whose only concern is making sure he gets his twenty percent."

Ashela and Kyliah had long since patched up their disagreement and were back as thick as thieves.

"I can't get over how they thought they were going to railroad me. I guess Sam figured he could send me flowers, sweep me off my feet, and then turn around and screw me both ways before I even knew what time it was."

"Ash, no, girl. Not Sam, the money man. Puh-lease, say it ain't so. Maybe he really didn't have an idea of how much money you made per year. At least give him the benefit of the doubt."

"We'll see. If I do decide to sign the Werner deal, it's going to cost him thirty million. Not a cent less. Kye, if we get thirty, we can *all* take a tropical vacation."

Kyliah wasn't going to touch that statement with a ten-foot pole. "So what do you want me to tell him when he calls?"

"Stall him. Tell him I'm in the studio and that I can't be disturbed but that you'd be more than happy to deliver any messages he may have."

"Ash, this is Sam Ross we're talking about. Are you sure you want to play him?"

"He tried to play me, Kye. Why not give him a taste of his own medicine?"

Three days later, Ashela was working feverishly to complete the lyrics to three songs for Regina Bell's upcoming album. For the past several days, she'd worked unceasingly. Knowing that she refused to be disturbed when she was in her "creative flow," Kyliah had left several messages on Ashela's answering machine saying that Sam and Adrienne were calling constantly each day.

In the wee hours of the next morning, Ashela finally completed the trio of songs. Drained, she lay spent on her bed and seconds later was knocked out cold.

***

Another benefit to Kyliah's public relations career was that she got to work from home. She had turned the downstairs bedroom into an office, complete with the whole nine yards of equipment. She was sitting in her living room reading the last chapter of *Preconceived Notions*, when her business line rang. Emotional from

seeing the characters in the novel all get back together, she dried her tears with the tissue that she was holding in her hand, trying to pull herself together. After all, it was only a book. She answered the phone on its third ring. "Five, two, eight, nine. May I help you?"

"Yes, five, two, eight, nine, you may help me." Ashela recognized Arron Davenport's voice.

"Mr. Davenport, I've already told you, Ashela's in the studio until the end of the week. She's not available."

"I understand that. That's not why I'm calling. I wanted to know if you would have dinner with me."

"Excuse me?"

"I'm asking you to have dinner with me." Seeing that she required an explanation, Arron said, "You sound like such a wonderful person that I'd like to take you to dinner to see if my assumptions are accurate. Besides, after three days of calling and being given the brush off, not only should you feel like you know me by now, but you should also be feeling a little sympathy. And please, call me Arron."

"Okay, Arron. Let me help you out with your preconceived notions and save you some money in the process. I *am* a wonderful person and you don't need to take me to dinner to discover that. All you need do is take my word for it."

"So is that a 'yes' or a 'no'?"

Kyliah considered it. "It's a 'I haven't decided,' which means you'll have to give me a moment to think about it." She didn't have anything on tap for the evening and he *did* sound interesting. Finally, she said, "It depends on what type of food you like to eat and where you'd like to go."

"I like meat and since you know this city better than I do, why don't you suggest a place."

"Arron, how do I know that I can trust you?"

"Trust me to do what? We're just having dinner. Look, I'm from Boston but I'm not the Boston strangler. Nor am I a serial rapist. I just want to have dinner. I promise to be on my best behavior. I'll be the perfect gentleman."

Kyliah smirked. "We'll see. Do you like seafood?"

"Love it.

"Then pick me up at seven o'clock sharp. Don't be late." Kyliah gave him her address, along with directions and hung up.

Later that evening, Kyliah stood before the mirror undecided as to what to do with her hair. She finally clamped it on top of her head and hot-curled the several strands which she let hang down. She slipped on a beaded, Chloé red silk mini-dress whose wide V-neckline rested at the tips of her shoulders, the sheerest of sheer off-black stockings and her red Salvatore Ferragamo pumps. Her overall visual impact was dazzling.

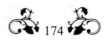

At seven sharp, Kyliah answered the door to find a six-four, paper-bag brown-skinned, curly haired man. With his wire-framed glasses, he looked handsome in a border-line nerdish way. But when he shook her hand, the size and length of his fingers made her quickly re-think her nerdish impression.

"Woah! Well, *I'm* hooked. What's next?" On the other hand, Arron felt like he had hit the jackpot. She was all legs and stunning.

Attracted and liking him already, Kyliah smiled at his gawking expression. "I thought you promised to be on your best behavior. Let me get my purse." Leaving the door cracked instead of inviting him in, she scooped up her things and locked the door behind her.

Inside his Jaguar, Kyliah stretched out. "You have no idea how thankful I am that you didn't show up in a two-seater scruncher."

Arron glanced over at her long shapely legs. "So am I. I wouldn't have wanted you to think you couldn't trust me."

"I'm still not so sure. And keep your eyes on the road."

"Yes, mam," he replied playfully.

They arrived at Chasen's, known for some of the finest seafood in L.A., and were shown to their table. For a Thursday night, the restaurant was crowded.

They ordered seafood platters, martinis and virgin pinà coladas.

"Tell me about yourself, Kyliah."

"Not fair. Didn't you know? Ladies don't have to go first anymore, so you tell me about yourself. And give me all the dirt and gory details."

"Bold, abrupt and forthright. I think I can live with it." Arron told her what it was like growing up in Boston with three sisters, all older than himself. Before long, their dinner arrived and they were biting into succulent shrimp and cracking open juicy crab legs. They never ran out of things to talk about and their entire conversation was punctuated with laughter. Long after their food had been removed from the table, they sat talking and drinking. Kyliah told him of her childhood in Durham and of how she had longed to see other parts of the world.

All during the course of the meal, what went unspoken was the intense chemistry that weaved itself between them. Every now and then, their hands would lightly touch, offering them revealing glimpses of passionate promises. Implicitly, both of them sensed the animal attraction hidden beneath their spoken words. Each wondered if the other was feeling the same way.

Arron started imitating his mother, who was always trying to fix him up with someone, telling Kyliah how at thirty-five, his mom kept badgering him about getting married and starting a family like his three sisters.

After Arron's third martini, even though he appeared unaffected, Kyliah appointed herself the designated driver. Around midnight she drove them through

fog-filled streets till she reached the Beverly Hills Hotel. She allowed him to talk her into coming up to his suite.

As they stood outside his room, Arron saw the look of doubt on her face. He said softly, "If you'd like, I can call you a cab." Unlocking his room door, he stepped inside and waited for her to decide.

Taking a risk, Kyliah entered and shut the door behind her. She was in full control of her senses and felt she was in good hands. Sex between the two of them was out of the question, at least for the moment. It was much too soon. He'd made no passes toward her and as attracted as she was to him, Kyliah didn't know whether to be flattered or offended.

He led her inside the large parlor adjoining his bedroom where they sat on his sofa continuing their conversation. When she emitted the first yawn, Arron promptly invited her to stay. He was enjoying her and was reluctant to see the evening end. He got up and disappeared for a moment and came back holding a Georgio Armani robe for her to put on.

"You can sleep on the bed if you like." Arron added with a boyish grin, "Scouts honor, I promise not to bother you."

Kicking off her shoes, Kyliah stood to take the robe from him. Feeling its softness, it smelled and reminded her of him. With a half smile on her face, she said softly, "This has been a lovely evening. Thank you very much."

In response, Arron tenderly stroked the side of her face. His intentions had been honorable when he'd told her that the evening would be platonic. But with her standing before him looking like a golden goddess, he couldn't resist the temptation. In a spellbound daze, with his other hand he removed the clamp from her hair, letting it fall in a tumbled mass. He stared at her hungrily before sliding his hand around the back of her neck. With gentle insistence, he pulled her toward him and planted a slow kiss on her lips. What was meant to be a test-the-waters, friendly kiss, turned into a burning desire for the both of them.

All throughout the evening, there had been hints that this might happen. His touching her now aroused feelings that neither could deny nor ignore.

Kyliah felt a warm flush flare over her body. She, too, had had no intentions of making so fast a move. But the way that Arron looked at her, and the gentle-yet-demanding feel of his touch, aroused her in a way that couldn't be resisted. It was too easy to allow herself to flow with the desires he was stirring within her. She now needed him to quench the thirst he'd created.

Before either one could say anything, they were on the bed, stripping naked, exploring one another, tasting one another, filling one another, satisfying each other. Their lovemaking had a wild urgency to it. Hot, passionate embers needing to be slaked over and over and over.

***

Arron's phone rang early the next morning. "Aren't you going to get that?" Kyliah raised herself up to look down at him.

"You get it. Please. You're closest to it." Arron's voice was gruffled. Kyliah also detected a bit of a hangover.

"Arron Davenport's room. May I help you?"

Sam thought the voice on the other end sounded awfully familiar. "Yes. Arron, please."

Kyliah looked down at him and smiled. "I'm afraid he's not available. Care to leave a message?"

Sam now knew where he'd heard that voice before. He was used to being told by the same voice that someone else was also unavailable. "No. But thanks." Sam hung up.

Kyliah hung up as well, convinced that she had the right cure for Arron's hangover. She slid her leg along his thigh and her hand down over his buttock.

***

Later that afternoon, Arron met Sam downstairs in the restaurant for a late lunch. Kyliah was long gone. When the waiter asked if he wanted something to drink, he specifically asked for water.

Recognizing Arron was in no mood for small talk, Sam said, "Based upon the voice I heard earlier, I'd say things went okay and that you had your hands full. So what did you find out?"

Unable to manage even a crooked smile, Arron came right to the point. "Naturally, she talked more about herself than her girlfriend. They happen to be long-time friends since they were kids. What I picked up was that Ashela is someone who's driven right now to achieve and accumulate all that she can. It appears that she's not dating anyone and hasn't for the last several years. The two of them lost contact with each other right after high school until Ashela offered her a position that led her to start her own public relations firm. The only man she could tell me about was some guy they grew up with. Harris, Parris, Travis, something like that." Arron thanked the waiter and dug into his omelet.

Sam sat stroking his chin, pleased with himself. "What of the friend? Do you plan to see her again?"

Arron took a sip of his water. "I'm in, so why not? And speaking of being in, pay up."

Sam pulled his wallet from his jacket and removed one thousand dollars, the amount he bet Arron when he challenged him to try to find out whatever he could about Ashela Jordan.

***

Ashela woke up later that afternoon, her body still tired from the recent strain to which she'd subjected it. She reached for the phone and was trying to dial Kyliah's number but she was unable to get a dial tone. She put the phone to her ear and said groggily, "Hello?"

"Ashela? It's Adrienne."

Ashela yawned and laid back down in the bed. "And?"

"Were you expecting someone else?"

"What's it to you?" she snapped. "You're awfully nosy this morning. What do you want?" Irritation sprinkled Ashela's voice. "What time is it, anyway?" She looked around her room for her digital clock.

"It's four o'clock. If you had called me back I wouldn't be tracking you down. I've got someone here who wants to speak with you." Adrienne put her on speakerphone.

"Good afternoon, Ms. Jordan."

Recognizing the voice, Ashela sat straight up. "Good afternoon to you too, Sam. What do I owe to the pleasure of this call?"

"Wait," Adrienne interjected. "Why is it a pleasure when Sam calls? I'm your agent and I always get cursed out when I call."

"Adrienne, that's because you deserve it. Would you two mind explaining what this call is about?"

"Two things," Sam said. "Number one, I want you to agree to the contract I offered you and number two, I want you to have dinner with me."

Ashela stretched and yawned loudly, not trying to suppress it. "You sure do want for a lot, Sam Ross, given that you're a man who's not bringing the right amount of money to the table. Tell you what." Ashela proceeded as if Sam weren't listening. "Adrienne, you claim to be my agent, so do your job. Get Mr. Ross to bring his numbers up to thirty. Then, *and only then*, are you to let him know we'll sign. As for you, Sam, dinner is on me—my treat. Just hop right over to your favorite restaurant, order anything on the menu and then send yourself the bill. That way, when you tell Werner that you signed me, you'll be able to say you wined me and dined me. In the meantime, allow me to introduce both of you to my old friend, Mr. Dialtone. Hang on a moment while I get him." Ashela clicked the off button on her telephone and placed it back in its stand.

Sam laughed as he heard the line go dead. Though it may have seemed otherwise, slowly but surely, he was making progress.

***

Ashela called Kyliah early Monday morning to get squared away for her appointments that week. A very tired and worn down voice spoke into the phone. "Hello?"

"Girl, you sound *whacked*! What's up?"

Kyliah said in a slow, weary voice, "What I can't figure out is why you're all up in my kool-aid."

"Well, actually, I'm not. But when a person who's usually up singing with the birds answers the phone at 9:00 a.m. sounding like her butter's been whipped, well I consider it my civic duty to find out what's going on. Excuse me. Maybe it's me, but if I caught you at a bad time, just speak the word and I can call you back later. After all, I'm just *trying* to be here for you."

Kyliah turned over in her bed and groaned into the phone. "If I had the energy, rockhead, I'd read you like a cheap dime store novel. But I don't, so I'm just going to politely ask again what you want. And when you finish telling me, don't be surprised to hear the phone go 'click.' "

"Oooookay. Since it's clear that *you* woke up this morning with a serious attitude, a decent conversation seems to be out of the question. So let me just ask, do *you* have a story that *you'd* like to share? Obviously, you do. So go ahead, tell it."

"Ugh, ugh. It would take too long. Just know that after partying at Helena's and Vertigo's, my body is out of it. Drained to the max."

"I see. So who was the lucky man? Elliott?" For a change, Ashela saw that she was going to have to drag details out of Kyliah, who had suddenly grown taciturn.

"No. Elliott's history, remember? Anyway, I had a *new* date that turned into a week-end get-away. One thing led to another and before we knew it . . . Hey, what can I say?"

"Wait a minute." Ashela had the feeling she was being played. It wasn't like Kyliah to be skimpy with the details of a juicy story. "Maybe it's just me. I know, recognize, and understand that there are times when I'm slow and just don't get it. It seems like now is one of those times. But, do I know this person? How long have *you* known this person? And where did the two of you 'get-away' to?"

"Well, tell you what. How about you tell me the latest on those Chicago Bulls?" Whenever either of them didn't want to discuss something, they changed the subject by talking about something totally and entirely different.

"Hold up. *Surely*, this is not the same person who jumped down *my* throat weeks ago because she felt like I couldn't handle the truth about *my* life? All I'm trying to discover is when did you become so tight-fisted with the details about yours? Help me understand here because I thought you and me were like that." Ashela held her first two fingers together tightly. "I thought we went way back. I thought I was there for you and you were *supposed* to be there for me. I mean, any other time, you'd be bubbling over *begging* me to listen to the details of a new relationship. Maybe I'm just not talking to the right person. This is 867-5309, is it not?"

"You've got the right number, you silly shrew. But I'd still like to know what's up with those Bulls."

"Girl, fogedaboutit." Irritated, Ashela became business-like as she changed the subject. "What do I have on tap for the week?"

"Ash, please, give me fifteen minutes and I'll call you right back. I've got to get the calendar. Plus, I've got to get *myself* together."

"Fine. Just leave it on the machine." Ashela hung up.

Kyliah's body was in blissful agony. Moving in any direction only increased the knawing soreness between her legs. She stretched languorously as she acknowledged that it had been years since she'd had these particular sensations. Kyliah hadn't felt this good since she'd dated . . . a brother. Ever since her early college days, she had found herself drawn exclusively to white men. Maybe subconsciously she was searching for someone like her dad. If that were the case, she'd come no where close as she found herself in and out of one relationship after the next.

She sat a full minute thinking about Arron, about how different he seemed from other men she'd dated and how gentle, considerate and insatiable he was as a lover. She liked him even more because he was educated, degreed, came from a good family and appeared to have bank. All that and he wasn't even hung up on himself.

Kyliah gingerly shifted toward the edge of the bed. She didn't know why she couldn't tell Ash that it was him that she had been with. Maybe because she hadn't sorted her feelings out for herself.

One thing Kyliah did know was that she wasn't about to sit at home entertaining herself when there were plenty of others willing to do it for her. Unlike Ashela, Kyliah had no problems finding a date each weekend. It wasn't that she was hung up on her good looks. She just recognized that if you were looking for something, in order to find it, you had to search for it. And that was what she was doing—searching for her mate—and sitting at home and being anti-social wasn't going to get the job done. While she considered herself a very goal-oriented person, she also believed in such a thing as work/life balance. Lately, she'd found herself thinking more and more about marriage and a family. Already she was thirty-one, her clock was ticking and she wasn't getting any younger.

No, she didn't hop into bed with every Tom, Dick or Harry. She had standards—high standards. But she was a long way from being like Ashela, who was celibate and had been for some time. That was Ashela's bag, not hers. She suspected that Ashela was still hung up on Parris, even though she denied it. Time was too short and Kyliah couldn't afford to waste it hoping that the right man would stumble along and knock on her door. If a relationship didn't work out, Kyliah moved on to the next. She didn't deceive herself, she knew the score. Some men were looking for a good lay while others just weren't ready to make a commitment *or* a sacrifice. Even so, there were still many good men out there that were doing things for themselves. Men who had degrees and were businessmen, doctors or lawyers or whatever and who happened to be making a pretty good dollar. There were even some who were looking for the right sistah to marry. Kyliah just wanted to find the right one for her

before time ran out. And now that Arron had re-opened her eyes to Black men, who knew, he just might be the lucky one.

***

Sam lifted his head from the stack of papers that littered his desk. He signed the last form awaiting his signature before gathering them all up and delivering them to his secretary, whose desk was just outside his office. Closing the door behind him, he came and stood in front of the huge office window holding a copy of the L.A. Times.

A quick glance at the financial section gave Sam cause to review parts of his life.

Hard work and gut instinct had gotten him to where he was. That and blind intuition had molded and forged him into one of the most powerful forces behind the music industry. After all these years, he could still smell talent a mile away. Now, more so than ever before, his words weighed heavily within the industry and if he said an artist or group didn't have what it took to make it to the top, the insurmountable onus was on them to prove him wrong.

In addition to his power and notoriety, Sam also possessed great wealth. Over the years, diversifying his money and investments had paid huge dividends. He had made Forbe's list of wealthiest Americans for the past five years. He owned his own private Gulfstream 18-passenger jet and while he could afford estates all over the world, Sam chose to live modestly in his hacienda-style home in Hollywood Hills, his mini-mansion on Martha's Vineyard, or in his upper east side penthouse suite in Manhattan.

At forty-six, Sam was still a relatively young man. His life was full and he wanted for nothing. He'd shared his wealth with those less fortunate, creating scholarship funds for students, programs for the homeless and needy, and aid to the elderly. Sam had two healthy, beautiful sons. So in many respects, he had it all. And yet, there were times when he felt something was missing from his life, an aching void that yearned to be filled.

Sam tossed the newspaper on his desk as he stepped away from the window. He pressed a button on his phone and spoke into it. "Lee Ann, get me two front-row-seat tickets to the Brahm's Symphony. Next, get Ashela Jordan on the line. If Ms. Jordan can't be reached, return the call of the actress, Lela Rochel, the one who's been calling here all week. Find out which of them is available tonight."

Chapter Twenty

he studio engineer was definitely starting to trip. He was irritable and cranky. But so were the rest of them. Only they weren't disrupting the session every fifteen minutes in order to run to the bin for a quick fix. They'd spent the last five hours mixing the

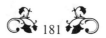

background vocals and instrumentals on several different tracks, and in Ashela's opinion, nothing had been accomplished.

She'd told Jimmy beforehand that she didn't think it was a good idea to use Marshon. Word on the street was that he was into some heavy blow. Though Marshon was known for being temperamental, his drawbacks were offset by his genius on the sound boards. Yet and still, his current antics were wreaking havoc on the recording session *and* on Ashela's nerves. Since Jimmy was producing the album and had worked successfully with Marshon on a couple of other occasions, he had insisted upon using him anyway—and now disaster had struck. They were running way over budget on the album and their studio time was nearly up. Marshon was a prime example of why many albums weren't cut on schedule and why good demo tapes became terrible songs. Ashela felt that studio engineers like him were the main reason many artists failed to recognize their own songs after they recorded them.

Tired, Ashela stood up from the synthesizer. "Look guys, I'm cutting out. Y'all work out the logistics without me." Everyone stared at Ashela as if she had just grown horns. "Jimmy, my part is nixed, so I'm done. What you're arguing over has nothing to do with me. Besides, I've already stayed an hour beyond what I originally agreed to." Ashela didn't wait for a reply, she started packing up her gear. Her time was money and was much too valuable to be wasted on lost causes.

Jimmy excused himself to help Ashela carry her things to her car. As they exited the building he said contritely, "Okay, so I blew it, big time. Bad case of character judgment. Whaddaya want from me?" He gave Ashela a look that was meant to evoke sympathy.

Ashela unlocked the trunk of her hunter green Jaguar and said, "I don't want anything from you, Jay. I'm not a priest so you don't owe me a confession. It's not my money you're blowing. It's Def Jamm's, remember?" Ashela could see he still wanted sympathy, but she wasn't in the mood to play wet nurse.

"Hell, Jay, I told you not to use the guy in the first place. He may have been at the head of his class once upon a time—but that's history. Right now he's flashin' so bad, he can't even think straight! How much you wanna bet that by the time you get back up there, he's already in the bathroom again snorting three or four lines?" Ashela opened the driver's door as Jimmy closed the trunk.

"I realize the guy's your friend and all, but are you going to let him screw up your album just because you *feel* for him? Make him grow up, Jay. Don't pacify him just because he's yo' dogg." Ashela rested her purse on the passenger seat before turning back to Jimmy. "If you really want to save your boy, encourage him to get some help. Maybe you can start by teaching him to just say no to drugs."

"So, Ash, you're just going to leave me hangin'?" Anger was now added to his frustration. He knew how difficult it would be to get her to reschedule, and as much as he hated to admit it, he needed her help if the album were to achieve any success.

"Like a rope twistin' in the wind, my brotha." Ashela closed her door and rolled down the window, angry that her time had been wasted. She started the car and put it in reverse. "Next time, tell Marshon to leave his nose candy at home. Maybe then you'll get your tracks done right *and* on time." As far as Ashela was concerned, this was now his personal problem. At their level, such unprofessionalism was intolerable. When she glanced in her rear-view mirror he was still standing there watching her turn the corner.

It was nearly five o'clock when Ashela pulled into her driveway in Malibu.

There was a message from Kyliah on her answering machine saying that it was imperative that she call her the moment she got in. Still irritated, Ashela shook her head, wondering why everything had to be an emergency with Kyliah. "This is why I refuse to wear a pager," she thought to herself. She knew people would hunt her down everywhere she went if she allowed herself to own such a contraption.

Ashela grabbed the cordless and headed for the kitchen to prepare herself something to eat. Lasagna and a breast of lemon chicken sounded good to her. She dialed Kyliah's number as she gathered all of the necessary ingredients.

"What's up?" Ashela asked brusquely.

Kyliah could tell by the sound of Ashela's voice that she'd had a rough day. Recognizing that she needed to vent her frustrations, Kyliah asked, "How did the session go?" Kyliah also needed to smooth the way for what she was about to lay on her.

Ashela spent the next ten minutes griping about the fact that nothing substantial had been accomplished, all because Marshon, the studio engineer, had been flying on ice. She told Kyliah that if Jimmy called, no matter how much he begged and pleaded, to tell him she would not be available again any time soon, not even for help with minor remakes.

Kyliah listened with honest sympathy. She knew that while people embraced the illusion that working with stars must be the life, reality was far from it. Many had egos the size of an ocean, others were straight up loonies and then there were some who were just totally strung out. And people wondered why many stars didn't sound as good live, on stage, as they did on their records. Kyliah knew the half of it wasn't told.

"That's my story, kid. So what was so urgent that you needed me to call?" Ashela switched the phone to her other ear as she grated a lemon to sprinkle on her chicken.

"I had a call from Lee Ann McKnight wanting to know if you were available this evening."

"Who's Lee McKnight?"

"Lee *Ann* is Sam Ross's Executive Assistant. She wanted to know if you were free for the evening. Are you?"

183

"Free for what? What's she want? A tour of the city? Tell her to call a travel agent."

"No, rockhead. Sam Ross has two tickets to the Brahm's Opera and he wants to know if you'd like to attend with him."

"Tonight?"

"That's right, my sistah. You should go, too. It's not like you've got anything else to do. Shall I call him to confirm?"

"No can do, chump. I may not be painting the town red like you and your *mysterious* date, but I do have other things of import to occupy my time."

"Ash, girl, you've got to go!" And then Kyliah added sheepishly, "I mean, I already told Lee Ann that you would."

"Then you lied, and that's too bad, isn't it? Guess you'll have to call ol' Lee Ann back and tell her that you should have conferred with me *before* you said yes. Better yet, ask her if you can go in my place." Ashela heard Kyliah sigh heavily. "Hey, I'm not trying to give you grief. It only serves you right." Ashela wiped her hands on the dish towel and laid it on the counter. She checked the temperature on the oven before heading upstairs.

Desperate, Kyliah said, "Ash, this is Sam Ross we're talkin' about. You just can't leave him hangin'!"

"Seems like somebody *else* said those exact words to me just a short while ago, too, and I don't see him around anywhere either. Look, you're the one who screwed up, Kye. You should have asked me *first*. How do you know I'm not cooking a meal for two right now, preparing a seven-course, candle-lit dinner for me and *my* man?"

"Oh yeah? And who's yo' man, Ash? Casper the friendly fuckin' ghost?" Kyliah laughed at her own crude humor. "My bag, I forgot. His name's 'the shadow,' right?" Kyliah tried a different angle. "Look, okay. Maybe I did screw up. But could you please forgive me and go out with the man at least this once? Please?"

"Kye, there's no maybe to it, sweetheart. You *did* screw up. But you're a big girl, and being the match-making scholar that you apparently are, I know you'll find a way to get yourself out of it. Do what you have to do, my sistah. But I'm not going anywhere with Sam Ross." Ashela shook her head just thinking about the man's magnetism. "Girl, you've got to be outta your mind."

Kyliah smiled, "Admit it. You're scared of him, aren't you?"

Ashela smiled to herself as she walked into her bathroom to run some bath water. "Maybe, maybe not. But you'll never know, will you? Anyway, I don't know why you're wasting your time shooting the breeze with me. Yo' butt needs to be callin' Lee Ann whatever her name is so she can find a replacement date for the man." Ashela started undressing. Naked, she stared at herself in the full-length mirror. She clamped the phone between her shoulder and neck and cupped her breasts. She squeezed them until her nipples were taut. She admired their round

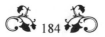

firmness before running her hands along the contours of her body. What *would* a man like Sam Ross do with all of this, she wondered.

"Okay. Be that way. I'm just going to call and ask my buddy Lee Ann if I can speak to the man directly. I'll think of something to tell him, all right." Kyliah paused to think of what she would say. "Maybe I'll just tell him that you wanted to go, but the thought of sitting next to all that *gawjous* dark honey and muscle . . ."

"Hey, hey, hey!" Ashela clutched the phone in one hand as she spun away from the mirror with her other hand on her hip. "Blockhead, have you lost your mind? You'd better *not* tell him anything like that!"

"Look, you said I was a big girl, right? You *did* tell me I could handle it, am I right?"

"Yeah, bonehead. But you ain't gotta go out like a punk and start lying to make *me* look foul! Why not just tell the truth? And why do you need to speak directly with him anyway?" Ashela started to feel a momentary sense of panic. She knew how bold and brash Kyliah could be at times, so she knew she had good cause to worry.

Kyliah laughed. "What are you getting all uptight about? I got cho' back. I'm there for you, remember? Look, if you can't see him tonight, who am I? It's *yo'* world. I'm just the stupid squirrel tryin' to get a nut! Anyway, I'd love to hang on the line and listen to all the great stories you've probably got to tell. I mean, you're such a great conversationalist and all. But once again, I've got things to do, places to go, and most importantly of all, I've got people to call and talk to."

Hearing the impish note in her voice, Ashela screamed into the phone, "Kye, you'd better not . . ." But the line was already dead.

***

Kyliah used her most professional voice. "Hi, Lee Ann? It's Kyliah Reed. Is it possible for me to speak with Mr. Ross?" No trace of any kind of "homegirl" accent here.

A few seconds later, Sam Ross came on the line.

"Ross speaking."

Whatta voice. My God, whatta man! "Mr. Ross, I'm Kyliah Reed and I wanted to call to apologize to you personally. I realize I informed your assistant earlier that Ms. Jordan would be available tonight. However, I'm calling to tell you that that's not going to be the case." Kyliah was just loading her gun.

"Oh? Is she okay?"

"Yes, sir. She's fine. It's just that . . . How can I say this tactfully?" Kyliah cleared her throat. "In my haste to play the part of the matchmaker, I spoke for her. You see, I never conferred with her about your request. To tell you the truth, I was so elated that you'd called I just automatically spoke for her. I guess I wanted her to go

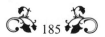

out with you tonight so badly that she probably developed cold feet." Kyliah paused to see what kind of effect she was having.

"Go, ahead. I'm listening." Sam was listening *very* attentively as he relaxed into his chair.

"Well, at the risk of breaching confidentiality, Mr. Ross, I must say that you're someone whom Ashela, as well as myself, admires very much. A woman could certainly be forgiven if she finds herself intimidated by you. I mean, it's not every day that *any* woman gets invited to dinner by one of the most attractive and richest men in the world."

Sam laughed. "Ms. Reed, I do believe you're trying to flatter me. It isn't necessary. You can speak freely with me."

"Okay. Then may I be very candid?"

"By all means." Sam's curiosity was definitely peaked.

"Well, you seem to be a man of great stature. And please, I'm not saying this to score any points. While I do happen to be Ashela Jordan's PR advisor, I'm also her best friend. As such, the last thing in the world I would want to see happen to her is for her to be hurt, even by you Mr. Ross."

"Please, let's dispense with the formalities. Call me Sam."

Kyliah knew that she had him now. "Thank you. As I was saying, Sam, Ash is a genius with regard to her music. Everything she feels is in her songs. But on a personal note, I'd like to see her get out more, and sad to say, that's not happening. It probably has a lot to do with the fact that she's so choosy. I mean, she refuses to date anyone she works with. And since all she does is work, well, where can a woman like herself find time for romance if all she does is work and exclude all forms of play?

"Well, that's where you come in, Mr. Ross. I think you'd be ideal for Ashela. I'm not expecting you to run out and buy the biggest engagement ring there is, but what I'd like to see happen is for the two of you to spend some time alone together. I know I said I was her friend, but when it comes to matters of romance, she rarely shares my views. So even if I did try to get her to go out with you, I doubt very seriously that she would listen to me. Are you following me?"

"Yes, Kyliah. I'm with you. Essentially what you're saying is, if I want to snare a date with her, it's going to take more than just your approval. It seems I'm going to have to be very unorthodox as well as persistent to get her to agree to go out with me." Sam appeared to be in thought. "Let me ask you something, Kyliah. Do you think she's attracted to me?"

Attracted to you? Are you crazy or what? Instead, Kyliah replied, "Oh, most definitely. You're all she talks about ever since the Debbie Allen affair, and you certainly were a big hit after all the flowers you sent." By now, Kyliah was in way too deep. She felt she might as well go for broke.

"You see, Sam, ever since Ashela's heart was broken years ago, she's been too afraid to love and trust anyone again. But you seem like the type of man that could make any woman forget about every type of heartache, past or present." Kyliah searched for the right words. "I mean, you seem so understanding, so sensitive, so . . ."

Sam laughed. "Kyliah Reed. I can see that Arron definitely has his hands full with you. Lady, you are something else. Perhaps, once I've persuaded Ashela to have dinner with me a couple of times, the four of us can go out together."

"I'd like that very much Sam. Tell you what, why don't you give Ashela a call, right now." Kyliah gladly gave him Ash's phone number.

After they'd hung up, Kyliah snuggled into her couch with a grin on her face that was so big, she could have stuck her entire foot in her own mouth.

***

Ashela was relaxing amidst a whirl of bubbles and soothing jetstreams listening to the mellow sounds of Jeane Carne blowing in the background. Kyliah and every other problem she may have had was a million miles away. She lifted her muscled calf and watched as the soapy suds cascaded downward.

"Just let me get to know you, before you break my heart . . ."

Ashela's head bobbed and her neck craned from side to side and she whispered along with the song.

The soft ring of the telephone was an unwelcome intrusion. Ashela reached for the cordless.

"Yes." Ashela's voice was as silky as the water she was soaking in.

There was a pause before a deep voice said, "You don't sound like a woman who's tired, drained, and empty to me."

Ashela's breath caught in her throat. "Sam?"

"Were you expecting someone else?" A laid-back and somewhat provocative quality edged his voice.

"I . . ." Caught off guard, she replied, "Actually, I wasn't expecting anyone at all." How had he gotten her number? *That Kyliah . . .*

"I just had some disturbing news. It's most unfortunate that you can't join me this evening. But dinner at your place later this week sounds most enticing." There was an obvious, seductive ebb to his tone.

"Excuse me?" Ashela could only imagine what Kyliah had said to the man.

"Oh, I spoke to Ms. Reed and she informed me of what a gourmet cook you were. But then, I shouldn't be surprised. You see, I'm learning that you're full of small wonders, Ashela."

Something in his voice was causing her stomach muscles to knot. Maybe it was the way he was pronouncing her name. As though he were whispering it into her ear. Ashela said haltingly, "Sam, I have no idea what Kyliah . . ."

"Say my name again. I like the way you say it." Sam had taken a seat by his office window. He could hear the soft sway of the water around her. The image of her naked in a pool of water was too enticing to resist.

In that instant, the shift was made from a business relationship and that of a much more intimate one evolved.

"No." Ashela laughed softly. But in spite of herself, her nipples hardened and her toes curled in the water.

Sam leaned forward and slowly passed his hand over his chin. "No, what?"

"Sam, are you cra . . ."

"That's it." Sam spoke ever so softly. "Say it one more time."

Tingling sensations crawled up the sides of Ashela's stomach and her nails automatically scraped the side of the tub as she shifted her position. "I'm taking the fifth, Mr. Ross. Mainly because I have no clue as to what you're talking about. What do you mean about being invited to dinner? I don't recall ever asking you." Still, her voice was soft and intimate.

"No, but your trusted advisor explained that I needed to go very slow with you because it's been a long time since you've allowed yourself to be swept away." Kyliah actually had said no such thing but he wanted to gauge her response.

Ashela gasped, as he had hoped she would. "I'm going to kill her," was all she could manage to say.

"Ashela, why are you fighting me? All I want is to have dinner with you. I promise you I'll not ask a thing more of you than you're capable of giving. How's that?"

Ashela was still trying to close her mouth. She couldn't say anything.

Encouraged by her silence, Sam added even more softly, "I can't remember the last time I've had to beg so hard just to get a woman to go out with me. Woman, what must I do?" The tone of his voice indicated he would do anything she asked.

Ashela was trying to collect her scattered thoughts. *What was happening to her?* "Sam . . ."

The way she pronounced his name was music to his ears. He could hear her take a deep breath.

"I . . . I guess I should inform you that I don't date the people that I work with." It sounded lame even as she said it.

"That's okay. I just want you to have dinner with me. We can work out all the other tactical issues at a later date. When are you free? Tonight?"

Ashela laughed. The man just didn't give up. "Sam, even if I wanted to, tonight is out . . ."

"What about tomorrow?"

". . . And as for the rest of the week, I . . ."

"The day after that. The week after that. How about the next lifetime?" Sam's persistent patience was admirable.

Ashela laughed because he wouldn't let her get a word in edgewise.

"Sam, you and I both know that there aren't many women who would resist the opportunity to have dinner with you. I'm sure that I'm sure that I'm sure that your Rolodex must be filled with women just waiting longingly by their phones hoping for you to call. You're doing them a grave disservice by pursuing someone who's not even in their league. You should stick to the Sam Ross groupies."

"I didn't know that such a legion of women existed. What does one have to do to become a member? I want to induct you."

Ashela's senses were still reeling from the sensuous quality of his voice. *Did he just say "induct" her, or . . .*

"Well, from what I hear, membership has its privileges. It's also hard to come by. First, you need to be tall and willowy and you have to be one of the top models in the industry."

"Ahhh, Ms. Jordan. I'm wounded. In reality, I like my women about 5'5", of medium build, sweltering hips, short hair and knock-'em-dead dimples. There's something special about a woman who gives the appearance of being demure, when she's actually just tempering her aggression. And a woman's who's hard to get just sends me to the moon. Did I peg you right?"

"Sam, do you realize that you're going to be late for the opera?" Anything to change the subject.

"Since my date is standing me up, my tickets are just going to be wasted."

Ashela lifted herself from the tub. On the other end, Sam swallowed a deep intake of breath and silently shook his head as he envisioned her naked.

"Sam Ross. You are incorrigible. If I didn't have to go check on my dinner . . . Let's just say that I'm letting you off the hook this time." Ashela patted herself dry.

"I'll let *you* off the hook this time. But know this, Ashela Jordan. You can run, but you can't hide."

"Sam, did you know that I was once a long distance runner? I've been known to elude even the best of them."

"Baby, you've never come up against Sam Ross before either. That's a warning." With a smile in his voice, Sam said, "Expect to hear from me very, very soon."

"Ta taaaaaa," Ashela chimed before disconnecting him. But she was still trying to recover from the masculine and sexy way he'd called her "baby." That Kyliah! *Her ass was grass!*

 189

Chapter Twenty-One

shela tried calling Kyliah but she kept getting a busy signal. The bum had probably deliberately taken her phone off the hook. But that's okay, Ashela thought. There'll be plenty of opportunities to get even. She kept trying until she finally got her on the phone.

"Hello?" Kyliah asked. There was dead silence on the other end of the line. But Kyliah was well aware of who was there *and* why she was calling.

"Well, if it *ain't* Junebug! Wassup? Wassup?" Kyliah started speaking in her most down-home southern accent. "Chile, I ain't seen you in a *coon's* age! Baby, what chu' wont? You wont somthin' t'eat? Go head, speak up now, mamma ain't got all day!" Laughter was all in her voice.

"Ah'ight. You can play stoop, if you want to, but I know where you live." Ashela spoke with an "it's payback time" note in her voice.

"What? What? What did I do? I'm a law abiding citizen. I pay my taxes. What more you want from me?"

"Oh, yeah? Think I don't know you played me like a punk with Sam? Ah'ight, keep playin' stoop. But just remember that the next time *yo'* butt is in a sling and you need me to bail *you* out. Babes, I ain't even gon' know you. But I got cho' back, though. I ain't mad atcha."

"Why are you taking this so personal? It was only a joke, Ash. The man is obviously feelin' you right now. So, jump on it, my sistah. What's up with the 'I'm-playing-hard-to-get-so-I'll-get-back-witcha' role? Girl, a man like Sam Ross isn't going to wait around forever. You've got to take decisive measures."

"Okay," Ashela said the word slowly, stretching it out. "And I suppose 'taking decisive measures' means droppin' my drawers in the blink of an eye? Kye, do I look like I'm desperate for a man to you? Be honest, please. Cause on this one issue, you and I don't seem to be on the same page."

"Ash, sweetie, you make it sound as if I'm trying to be facetious about this whole matter. It's not that you're feening, hon. You seem to pretty much have things in their proper perspective. I mean, you're *'all that.'* But what you need is a little somethin' somethin' to smooth all the rough edges, you know, to round out the total picture. And being the 'I've-got-to-take-my-time-so-we'll-wait-and-see' scholar that you are, I just thought I'd help you out. No harm done, right?"

Ashela was very quiet on the other end.

Kyliah ignored Ashela's sullenness and said, "So tell me, what did you two talk about?" Curiosity was getting the better of her.

"Let me get this straight, Kye. You set me up, leave me caught out there with my tail blowing in the wind—I mean, after all, you *are* supposed to be my girl—and then you expect me to tell you everything we talked about? Kyliah, don't play me, play Little Lotto."

"Ash, come on now, don't be like that. After all the trouble I went through, the least you can do is tell me what happened." Kyliah was starting to whine.

"Who's the guy you're dating?"

"Excuse me?" Kyliah was taken aback by the sudden change of subject.

"You heard me. I want to know who you're seeing. You want to hear what Sam and I talked about? Well, I want to know who you're dating and why you're being so secretive about it." Ashela strongly suspected Kyliah was seeing a certain rock star who had been sweatin' her royally. Maybe she had finally given in and was just too embarrassed to fess up in light of the way the two of them had dogged him out over the phone.

"Wait, wait, wait. What's that got to do with anything? We seem to be mixing apples and oranges here."

"No, my friend. *We* don't seem to be mixing anything. I know what I'm asking. I'm just waiting for you to start talking. So who is it this time? I'll bet it's Ken Vander . . ."

"No, it's not." Kyliah interrupted her, knowing who she was about to say. "It's someone you'd never think I'd be with. Someone who's gorgeous, strong, intelligent, ambitious, caring, committed . . ."

"Save the drama for yo' mama. Who is it?"

"Excuse me, but do I rudely interrupt you when you're in the middle of one of your famous soliloquies? Can I at least have my moment of glory? Thank you. As I was saying . . ."

Ashela interrupted her again. "All I want to know is if he's Black or white."

"Excuse me, you *did* change the subject and ask me who was in *my* life, didn't you? Well then, can you at least be quiet for a moment and let me tell *my* story? Do you want to hear this or not? All right then." Laying on her bed, Kyliah rolled over on her stomach and crossed her calves at the ankles. She breathed heavily into the phone and with a serious tone in her voice said, "Ash, I realize I might have said this before, but I really think I'm falling for this guy."

"Okay, so that means he must be white. No big deal. But let me ask you this: Does he have money?" When Kyliah's silence spoke for itself, Ashela started singing into the phone. "What's love got to do . . . got to do with it? What's love but a sweet old fashioned notion . . ."

"Ugh, ughn, Ash, you're wrong. Don't slam my past dirt in my face. So what if I prefer men with ducats. Where's the harm in that? But for all you know, I could really be in love this time."

"Kyliah Reed, I haven't said a word. How can I render an opinion when you haven't even told me anything major about the person yet? *You still haven't told me who he is.*"

"Okay. Do you promise not to go off on the deep end?"

"Uh, oooohhh. This must be serious. Are you sure you're ready to tell me?"

"I guess. I mean, you're bound to find out sooner or later anyway. Now is as good a time as any. Are you sitting down?"

"Go ahead. Shoot."

"It's Arron Davenport."

"Arron Davenport? Who's Arron Davenport? Wait, you mean the guy who works with Sam?"

"The one and the same."

"Well I'll be darned. A Black man! No wonder you didn't wanna tell me. I mean, he's attractive and all, and I guess, on one hand, he's no different from all the other 'Wall Street/pinstripe' type of men you've ever dated. But at least he's a brother so I'll admit that I'm proud of you." Ashela shook her head in wonder. "Since when did you re-develop the hots for brothas anyway?"

"Ashela, do not tease me on this. I'm sensitive and also I'm being real."

"Okay then, let's be real. What do you want to see come out of this relationship?"

Kyliah pursed her lips and slowly shook her head. "For once, I'd just like to take my time. I don't want to force anything and I certainly don't want to expect too much too soon, but I like the way I feel with him. There's something gentlemanly about him that I can't explain." At a loss for words, Kyliah shrugged her shoulders self-consciously and said, "That's it."

"You know, kid, there's a note of vulnerability in your voice that I've never heard before. Normally you're flippant about the guys you date. But suddenly you sound hesitant and unsure of yourself. It's as though you're afraid of revealing how you really feel about him." Ashela was grateful that she wasn't the one with a love jones dilemma. "You know him better than I do, Kye. I just remember him being conservative and bookish. I guess, too, it's just a pleasant surprise to see you dating one of our own. But, hey girl, what do I know? I'm the last person you should consult for relationship advice anyway. I ain't even got a man, remember? So what kind of vibes are you getting from him?"

"It's the strangest thing, Ash. Usually I can tell right off the bat how far a relationship will go. But with Arron, I can't gauge anything. I know he likes me, but that's about it."

"And of course the sex has you swinging from the chandeliers."

"Yeah, so what's your point?"

"Well, maybe you should give the juice a break to see how the two of you get along without it. Who knows? Maybe it'll also give you time to sort out your feelings for him."

"That sounds good, Ash, believe me, it really does. But this stick that I've gotten ahold of is just too big and sweet to give up right about now. Plus, I don't know how much longer he's going to be in town, so I've got to milk him for all he's got. And I ain't talkin' about his money either." Kyliah started shaking her head at the memory of how good it felt being with Arron. "Ash, girl, if you only knew like I knew. Celibacy ain't got a *thing* on this. *Can we just be real?*"

"Kyliah, you know what the difference is between you and me? Let me help you. You see, you need a man to help you get your groove on. But me? Baby, when I want to go to the moon to taste some of its cheese, I can get there all by myself. And when I'm done, babes, I'm off to la la land with a big smile on my face. But wait, it gets even better. The best part is that when I wake up the next morning, I ain't got no hangover, no headaches, and most importantly of all, no heartaches from having to deal with somebody else's mad drama."

"Hey, I hear you, girl. When you please yourself, you *do* wake up without any problems. But it's just that, for me, I need to feel a man's rough hands on my body. I need to wake up with that delicious feeling between my legs that let's me know that I've been made love to. Don't get me wrong, though, I ain't got nothing against satisfying yourself. I've even tried it once or twice. But I felt so lonely and empty afterwards that I just decided it wasn't for me. What sense does it make for me to wind up needing someone beside me even worse than I did before I decided to go there in the first place?"

"Girlfriend, you don't have to explain, I understand completely. Different strokes for different folks. In my case, after I hit the moon, I'm rejuvenated, feelin' like a million bucks, and looking forward to the next trip. The key is knowing what turns you on and what doesn't. So, back to Mr. Arron. What are you going to do about him?

"Girl, I guess I'm just going to have to wait and see. Man, do I hate that!"

The next morning, Ashela was on her car phone while talking to Adrienne's secretary, Evette. She was trying to remain calm in light of the fact that Evette had misplaced the Werner contract that Sam had sent over to Adrienne's office. Adrienne had looked it over and had found everything to be in place. However, Ashela still wanted her attorney, Peter Corti, to also look it over. Pete was *the* sharpest, brightest, most high-powered attorney in the entertainment business, with a whopping one-thousand-dollars-per-hour fee to boot. He often remarked jokingly that there were only seven people running the music business: Himself and six others. Ashela didn't

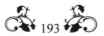

doubt him. She'd seen the near billion-dollar deals he negotiated for some of his clients. She signed nothing without his approval.

Adrienne was out of town for the next day or so and Ashela wasn't about to wait for his return just to take a look at her own contract. She told Evette to forget about it. She would have someone pick up a copy of the contract from Mr. Ross's office. Ashela hung up and called Kyliah, who promised to pick it up ASAP.

***

Kyliah dressed with care for her trip to Sam's office. She could just as easily have sent a messenger for it, but she wanted to go herself. The likelihood of her actually seeing Sam was slim, but just in case she should run into him, she wanted to be prepared. She wore a simple but elegant, belted sheath mini dress the color of sea mist. Pearl earrings and cream T-strap dress sandals completed her outfit. She hot-rolled her hair for fifteen minutes and let it fall to feather frame her face.

It was after one o'clock when she parked her Benz in the visitor's lot and headed inside the offices of Werner Enterprises. Kyliah entered the building and took the elevator to Sam's floor. She could see immediately that the receptionist was having a crazy day because the phones were ringing off the hook. The girl looked up and greeted her with a harried smile, signaling that she'd be right with her. She took five more calls during the time Kyliah stood there waiting. Finally, she put another caller on hold and said to Kyliah, "I'm so sorry. It's just that there are supposed to be four receptionists and they all called in sick. I'm just a temp but already I can understand why they wouldn't want to work here cause I'm about to get the hell outta here myself. But enough about me, how may I help you?"

Kyliah laughed sympathetically and introduced herself saying, "I'm here to pick up a contract from Mr. Ross."

"Oh yes, I spoke to you earlier. Tell you what, hold on a minute." She dialed an extension and said, "Mr. Ross, someone is here to pick up the contract for Ms. Jordan. Yes sir. Thank you."

The receptionist hung up and said to Kyliah, "He said the copy is on his desk and I can come and get it. Can you do me a favor? I can't possibly leave this area right now. Can you go and get it yourself? I'm sorry to have to ask this of you, but since I'm just a temp, I don't even know where his office is anyway. I think it's somewhere to your left though."

"That's okay, hon. I don't mind. You stay put and I'll be right back." Kyliah happily headed off in search of Sam's office.

Kyliah walked down the long corridor which supposedly led to Sam's office. At the end of it was a tall oak door that was left slightly ajar. Kyliah could hear voices coming from inside the office. She quietly stepped closer to the door and heard the unmistakable sound of Sam's deep voice.

". . . about time you answered the phone. Another late nighter with Kyliah Reed, huh? You'd better watch yourself, Arron, that one just might take you out."

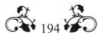

Kyliah could hear papers rustling in the background and figured Sam must be on the speaker phone. When she heard the sound of Arron's voice, she quietly pushed the door open, almost stepping into the room.

"Yep, she's a gem all right," Arron was saying. "And like most gems, she's expensive. The thousand dollars you paid me for our first date has long since been spent. At the rate I'm going to places like Mr. Chow's, Spago's, Orso's, The Bistro Gardens, and L'Ermitage, Werner is going to get charged a pretty hefty expense tab."

"No fault of mine. You're the one who elected to see her again. The grand you got from me was strictly for the information you provided."

"Listen, Sam, she's so good till she's worth that much and more. The woman is a virtual tigress in bed. I've got scratch marks all over my body that I'll never be able to explain when I get back home. Speaking of home, I've been here for nearly three weeks and as much as I hate to see all the fun, sun and good times come to an end, I've got other accounts that I've got to handle. How soon do you think we'll be wrapping up here?"

Sam's back had been turned to the door. He swiveled around in his chair, preparing to sign a document, when he looked up and noticed Kyliah standing in the doorway. Sam had never met Kyliah before, but based on Arron's description and the ashen look on her face, he knew beyond a shadow of a doubt that it was her. Their eyes locked from across the room.

Without removing his eyes from hers, Sam said, "Uhm, I've got someone standing here. Let me call you right back." His fingers reached for the release button on the speakerphone.

Before he could release the button, Arron said, "Hold up a sec, Sam. I've only got one more question."

Kyliah could not recall another time in her life when she had ever felt so humiliated. She stood inside the doorway trying her best to keep a composed look on her face. *If you listen at closed doors, you'll only hear things you won't like.* She had no idea where the saying came from, but it certainly applied right now. She stepped into the room and said calmly, "This, Mr. Ross, is what is invariably known as an awkward moment. If you have the contract handy, I'll just take it and be on my way."

"Kyliah?" The surprise in Arron's own voice was apparent even through the speakerphone.

Kyliah ignored Arron as she approached Sam's desk to retrieve the manila envelope he was handing her. She turned and walked out the door, closing it behind her. At the front desk, she waived the envelope in the air as she passed the receptionist who was still alone and was still trying to handle the barrage of telephone calls.

***

Inside his office, Sam said angrily, "She's gone Arron, I'm sorry. I had no idea she was even standing in the room. But I promise you, heads will roll because of this screw up. Let me go up front to find out who's responsible. Meanwhile, I could tell by the look on her face that she heard everything we said. Yeah, man, I know. I'm really sorry. But if you intend to see her again, I think you'd better get on the horn and do some damage control. Right." Sam hung up and headed to the front of his office.

Inside her Mercedes Benz, Kyliah felt numb as she got on the expressway and headed for Ashela's home in Malibu. She wanted so badly to cry, but no tears would come forth. *What a fool I've been,* she kept thinking over and over. All she could do was replay the conversation in her mind.

The thousand dollars you paid me for our first date was spent long ago . . . Kyliah's car phone rang, but she turned it off and reached into her handbag to retrieve her sunglasses. She needed desperately to take her mind off the hurt and embarrassment she was feeling inside.

And just when she thought she'd found the right one. *The best laid plans of mice and men . . .*

Kyliah pulled into Ashela's driveway, but she didn't get out of the car right away. She sat there debating whether or not to just dump the envelop into Ashela's mail slot and keep on going. Truth was, she didn't really have anywhere to go. She was supposed to meet Arron for lunch around 2:30, but that was now totally out of the question. Kyliah knew she could talk to Ash about her feelings, but she wasn't ready to face the ugly reality with anyone beyond herself.

Ashela hadn't been home too long herself when she heard a car pull up. She opened the door to see Kyliah sitting inside her car wearing sunglasses, looking straight ahead. Not yet sensing that anything was wrong, she stood in her doorway biting her apple waiting for Kyliah to get out of the car. Minutes later when Kye hadn't moved, Ashela's preceptory senses kicked in and she walked outside towards the car.

Inside the car, Kyliah's eyes were closed behind her glasses. Tears trickled down her face. She jumped at the intrusive knocking upon the driver's window. Turning to see Ashela standing there, she pressed the button that rolled down the window.

"What's wrong?" Ashela asked.

Kyliah shook her head, removing her sunglasses to wipe her tears. Taking a huge breath, she said, "I've been such a fool, Ash."

Concerned, Ashela said, "Tell you what, why don't you and I go inside and talk about whatever's happened. Come on, get out."

"No. I think I need to be alone right now. I just came to bring you your contract." Kyliah reached over to the passenger side to get the envelope and hand it to her.

Not taking no for an answer, Ashela reached inside Kye's vehicle and pulled her key out of the ignition. She twirled the group of keys around her finger and said, "Guess you'll *have* to come inside now. But lighten up, chump, I've been told that my company ain't so bad." Ashela was merely trying to ease Kyliah's tense and sorrowful mood. "Now get out of the car, Kye, and come inside."

Cracking a crooked smile in spite of herself, Kyliah got out and followed Ashela into the house.

Ashela went into the kitchen and turned on the tea kettle. When she looked up and saw Kye standing in the doorway, she said, "Go have a seat out on the verandah. I'll be there in a second." Minutes later, Ashela carried the tea set outside and placed the tray on the table. She poured a cup of peppermint tea for each of them.

Ashela didn't have to say anything to prod Kyliah to talk. She knew she would tell whatever story she needed to tell as soon as she was ready. The two of them sat sipping tea, watching the waves of the ocean crash against the shore when Ashela had a funny thought.

She laughed as she said, "Hey, can you picture the two of us as old women sitting in rocking chairs watching the hunks stroll by?"

Kyliah smiled. "Yeah, but at least *I'll* still look good. While you on the other hand will probably be walking on a cane."

"Oh, I don't think so, my sistah. I'm the one who works out three times a week, remember? While you, well, we both know the only exercise you get is probably between the sheets."

In jest, Kyliah said haughtily, "Hey, don't hate *me* because I'm beautiful." She placed her cup on the table and clasped her arms around herself. She tilted her head back, closed her eyes and started rocking back and forth, ever so slightly.

"I don't think I've ever been more embarrassed in my life, Ash. I got all dolled up just to go over to Sam's office, and when I got there, the girl at the front desk was so busy with the phone lines that she asked me if I could go and get the contract from Sam myself. And, being the over-eager scholar that I am, more like the dummy that I am, I ran off to his office.

"But when I got to his door, Ash, I heard him talking on the speakerphone. So I just stood there listening. The next thing I heard was Arron's voice—him telling Sam that . . ." Kyliah's voice trailed off as she began to cry.

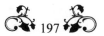

Ashela got up and went inside the house to get a box of tissue. She came back out and handed some to her. Kyliah wiped her eyes.

"He was saying how the money Sam had paid him to go out with me was long gone. It seems that he only went out with me to get information about you for Sam. Then he started telling Sam what a good lay I was." Kyliah gave an ironic laugh. "To think I actually thought he liked me. What a poor judge of character I made."

Ashela sat on the other side of Kyliah taking it all in. Now, she was steamed with anger. "That low down, slimy bastard! Men! White or Black—girl, you just can't trust them." Ashela took what Kyliah said so personally, it might as well have been her that had just gotten sprung.

Kyliah lifted her legs into the chair and wrapped her arms around her knees. She smiled bitterly, "Well, kid, it looks like it's just you and me again. Just like old times."

Ashela stood and walked to the edge of the porch, still angry. "It's a damn shame! Even *liking* somebody can be painful. I mean, this whole business of learning to love and trust, it's for the birds. Who needs all this senseless drama?" Ashela sighed disgustedly. "But I guess that's just taking the easy way out. You know what I've always admired about you, Kye?"

"No. Tell me." Kyliah was feeling so down that she would accept any compliment that bolstered her bruised ego.

"You're never afraid to risk failing when it comes to love. I mean, I know we're both feeling like shit right now, but a couple of weeks from now you'll have forgotten all about this creep. By then, you'll probably even have someone else knockin' at your door. Think about it, Kye. It takes guts to keep trying again."

Kyliah smirked and flipped her hand at Ashela.

"No, come on. I'm serious, Kye. Most people give up after the first couple of times. Look at me. It's been years since I've been romantically linked with someone. Why? Because I don't want to go through the pain and headache that being in love breeds. You have no idea how much easier it is to just channel all that energy into my music. And the strangest thing, Kye, is that I don't even miss it. I figure that one day, somebody's gonna come along that I just can't resist. But until then, I'm content just as I am. All that emotional drama is for the birds." Ashela came back and sat down. She stared out into the pale blueness of the ocean and after awhile, said, "Remember Smokey, Kye?"

Suddenly, Kyliah laughed the first real sounds of laughter since the day started. "Yeah, I remember him. How could I forget?" Smokey was the old gray horse that her family had owned.

Ashela said, "Remember when you would ride him, if he threw you, you'd get up and get right back on him? But after that one time when he flipped me, I never rode him again. And when they finally had to put him to sleep, you cried somethin' awful. Me? I hated that sombitch of a horse."

198

"That was because you were too rough with Smokey. But wait, girl. I've got one better than that. I said I'd never been so embarrassed before, right? Well, remember Ricky Howard?" At the puzzled look on Ashela's face, Kyliah said, "Girl, come on, you remember Ricky! One-legged Ricky?"

Ashela screamed with laughter. "Girl, you mean Ricky Howard only had one leg?" She suddenly recalled that Ricky had gone to the same high school as Kyliah.

"That's right, baby." Kyliah did the stop-sign thing with both her hands. "Girl, the brotha was *foine*, wasn't he?"

Ashela threw her hands up, shrugged and said, "Hey, if you say so. Who am I?"

"Don't play stoop, Ash, cause I know you remember his fine butt. Anyway, I pull up to this bus stop one day and I see him standing there with all those bulging muscles and biceps. I was mush, okay? So we exchanged numbers and hooked up later for a date. I mean, I liked what I saw and so did he. There was no need to pretend that we were going to do anything other than get our groove on.

"So we're finally at the hotel and before I know it, the brotha wants to turn out all the lights. I'm like, 'what's up with this?' The reason why I'm here is because I want to gaze at his body. Him turning out all the lights would defeat the purpose. So I talk him into leaving one of the lights on. Girl, there we are, going at it. I mean, having a ball! Naturally the brotha was loaded so I had no complaints. Well, we wound up on the floor—me on top of him. Suddenly, I turn around to change positions and happened to look down and there's this stump twistin' on the floor! It scared the crap outta me and took me by such surprise that before I knew it, I panicked. I jumped right off him and hopped onto the bed.

"Well, girl, Ricky started trippin'. Talkin' bout why did I have to go and ruin everything. Couldn't I at least have waited till he came? Ash, girl, no lie, the brotha got up off the floor and started *hoppin'* around the room. *The man only had one leg!* What the hell did he *expect* me to do? I mean, I look down and there's only one leg plus another half of one that looks like a big snake that's floppin' all over the floor. Girl, that thing scared the hell outta me."

"Wait, wait." Ashela was pounding her hand against her leg succumbing to gut-splitting laughter while trying to picture Ricky Howard with one leg. "Naw, Kye! And you never even told me? What chu' do next, girl?"

"Ash, girl, I told the brotha he was wrong. He should have told me from the get-go that he only had one leg. Not waited till we were in the heat of the moment and then I happened to look down and freak out because of what I see, only to hear him say, 'oh, yeah baby, by the way, I only got one leg. But you can hang with that, right?" Kyliah imitated him speaking in a "doofus" voice, and shaking her head. "Babes, I got up, calmly put my clothes back on, and left his one-legged, hop-along, naked ass, standin' right in the middle of the room lookin' like he was stuck on stupid."

Ashela was laughing and snickering so hard that she had traces of spittle on her face.

"Don't laugh Ash. Because from that moment on, I started asking. I'd come right out and say, 'baby, is there anything I should know? You got any missin' parts that you need to tell me about? If so, tell me *now* cause I don't want no surprises.' That's right. You can laugh if you want to, but I ask. I don't know about you, my sistah, but as for me and *my* house, I need to know up front."

"Ah'ight, I got one for you." Ashela told Kyliah about the time she had collared Randal like a dog and chained him to the tub before she beat him with a paddle. But not before making him lick a can of whip cream off of her you-know-what.

The two of them howled in gut-grabbing laughter as they shared their most raunchiest memories. Hours later, they went inside and Ashela cooked dinner for the two of them. In the process, Kyliah was able to get a better handle on the pain and hurt she was feeling over Arron. Before it was over she wound up spending the night as they rolled on the living room floor, laughing and reminiscing about the good ol' days.

The next morning, Kyliah turned the key in her lock and closed the door behind her. She was greeted by her huge, black Persian cat, named ET. He rubbed himself zealously against her leg, purring and meowing loudly as he followed her every step. Kyliah nearly tripped trying to avoid stepping on him.

"Go home, ET!" Kyliah used the expression whenever he got on her nerves. Seeing that he wasn't about to be ignored, she picked him up and carried him into the kitchen to feed him. With ET eating his fill, she walked back into the living room and checked the messages on her machine.

". . . Kyliah, it's me. I've been trying to get you on your car phone, but you wouldn't pick up. Listen, it's not the way it seems. If you'd just give me a chance to explain . . . Just a minute." Arron shouted to someone in the background. "It's room service so I'll call you back. Kyliah, can you just call me so we can talk about this?" Beep. Monday, 1:20 p.m.

". . . Why aren't you answering your page. Look, Kyliah, I know you're angry. But will you at least let me explain what happened? The conversation was just an inside joke. Sam and I were only talking men's talk. Will you please call me as soon as you get in?" Beep. Monday, 1:55 p.m.

". . . Kyliah, don't do a brotha like this, please. I know you're upset and you've got every right to be. Hell, I would be too. But you've got to let me explain my side of the story. I'd like to see you so we can talk this over. You've got all my numbers, so call me, please." Beep. Monday, 2:20 p.m.

". . . Look, woman. I've been standing outside Pagano's for the past half an hour hoping you'd show up for our lunch date. You could have at least called to say you

weren't going to make it." Irritation was in Arron's voice as he hung up. Beep. Monday, 3:00 p.m.

There were several other business related calls for which Kyliah jotted down their numbers. There were even more hang-up recordings on the machine. She checked the Caller I.D. and saw that in total, there had been eleven calls from Arron throughout the previous day and night.

Kyliah went upstairs to shower and change. She was just stepping out of the shower when the phone rang. She answered it on the third ring.

"Yes?" She was all business.

"Kyliah, why didn't you call me back? Did it ever occur to you that I might be worried about you?" Arron asked.

Continuing to dry herself off, Kyliah took a seat on her bed and applied lotion to her body. Brusquely, she said, "No, Arron, it never crossed my mind that you might be the *least bit* concerned about me. Yesterday, I may have been feeling hurt about what I overheard, but today is a new day and I'm over it. I suggest you get over it too. Cut the bullshit, Arron. Don't even bother wasting your time." Click.

Arron was left staring at the receiver he was holding. He knew she had a right to be angry. But damn! Was she hard on a man. What he'd done was wrong and he was prepared to admit it. He was even willing to beg if he had to. But how could he even do that if she kept refusing to listen to what he had to say? Frustrated, Arron sat there wondering what he could do to get back into her good graces.

Kyliah didn't waste time getting dressed. She had business-related things to do, places to go and a female broker whom she was due to meet for lunch in less than forty minutes.

When the phone rang again, she checked the Caller I.D. Seeing it was Arron, she let him get her machine.

It was after six o'clock when Kyliah returned from running her errands and shopping. She'd gotten back just in time to beat the sudden onslaught of rain. She was cooking greens and baking turkey wings while talking on the phone to Ashela. She gave her a rundown of the different ways her broker recommended she diversify her funds.

"By the way, Ash, Michael and the Chicago Bulls will be in town tomorrow to play the Lakers. Remember last month, you promised to go to the game with me? Or have you forgotten that too?" Mostly, Kyliah attended the games with whomever she was dating at the time. But since she wasn't seeing anyone steady at the moment she'd gotten Ashela to commit to going. Only Ash was now trying to play stupid.

"Of course I remember. It's just that you know I'm in studio tomorrow morning with TLC. Or have *you* forgotten?"

"Since I'm the one who scheduled the session, no, dearie, I haven't. But that's at 8:00 a.m., my sistah. You'll be finished, at the very least, by five o'clock. That leaves you two and a half hours to get to the Forum before the 7:30 tip-off. Don't fake me out, Ashela Jordan."

"Okay, okay! Man, do I ever give you this type of grief whenever I want something?"

"I know you don't expect me to answer that. Anyway, this body of mine needs a bath, so I'll hafta get back witcha."

Before Kyliah could hang up, Ashela said, "See ya, chump," and hung up on her first.

Thirty minutes later, Kyliah was bending over the oven, turning the two turkey wings. They were basting a golden brown but Kyliah wanted the meat tender enough to fall off the bones. The delicious smell of turkey wafted throughout the whole house and ET meowed loudly at the prospect of getting his fair share.

She had just closed the oven door when the doorbell rang. She wondered who the hell would be foolish enough to venture out into such torrential rain. Without opening the door, Kyliah peered through the peephole and saw Arron. Too bad, she thought. His dumb ass could drown for all she cared. She promptly turned around and went back into her living room.

Most of the lights were on inside her duplex. Anyone peering in from the outside would assume that she was home. Knowing she was there, Arron continued to ardently ring her doorbell.

Kyliah calmly sat on her sofa flipping through several magazines. She figured that if he got drenched enough, he would give up and leave, which was just what she wanted. She was inside the kitchen cutting up the turnips for her greens when Arron appeared at her back door and started knocking on the window. With a turnip and a knife in one hand, Kyliah went and stood in front of the door and just stared out the window at him. Though Arron was drenched, with water pouring from his face and clothes, Kyliah didn't crack a smile.

"Come on, Kyliah. You see I'm drowning out here. At least let me come in so we can talk." Arron placed both his hands on the kitchen door window and said, "Please, Kyliah. Have some *mercy* on a brotha."

Pulling down the decorative shade in his face, Kyliah calmly turned away from the door and cut up the rest of her turnip, dropping the pieces into the greens. After washing her hands, she slowly went upstairs to her bedroom to get her door keys from out of her purse. She had to use a key to unlock her kitchen door and if Arron was gone by the time she finally got back down stairs, well then, so be it. She trudged back, humming as she went along with ET following her every step of the way.

She raised the shade and there was Arron looking for all the world like he'd lost his best friend. Kyliah unlocked the door and opened it to let him in. As soon as he stepped inside dripping puddles of water, she said, "Ugh, ughn. Hold it right there, buster. There's no way you're going to track up my clean floor."

"You didn't care whether I lived or died out there, did you?"

"Sounds to me like you already know the answer to the question. I'll be right back. You might as well get out of those things, they're soaking wet."

When she returned to the kitchen, she handed him an oversized bath towel and said, "I'm running you some bath water, so wipe your feet before you go upstairs. Here, give me your clothes and put this on. I'll throw your things in the dryer." Kyliah's manner towards him had not softened one bit. She stepped out of his way to let him pass.

When Arron came back into the kitchen less than a half hour later, Kyliah was lifting the cast-iron skillet out of the oven and onto the top of the stove. He stood in the doorway admiring her from afar. He could gauge her mood and sensed that she was still too angry for him to even try to get near her.

"As good as your food smells, I hope you have enough for two."

Kyliah turned to see him leaning against the doorway, his arms crossed over his chest. With him dressed in nothing but the towel she had handed him, one look at his body's golden-brown muscularity and Kyliah knew telling him to take his clothes off hadn't been good thinking on her part.

When she approached him, Arron straightened up against the door. She stood directly in front of him, staring into his eyes. While the tongue was capable of espousing many things, Kyliah knew the eyes never lied.

Arron wanted only to touch her and to take her into his arms. He lifted his hand to caress her face but she stepped away from him saying, "Your being dressed like that is not such a good idea. Come, let's find you something else to put on."

Following behind her, Arron happily watched the sway of her hips beneath her black silk chemise.

Inside her bedroom, he casually stretched out on her bed with his head propped on his elbow. The room was tastefully decorated in bronze, black and gold undertones. It was beautiful and he thought it suited her well.

Arron sat up as she rifled through her closet. "Kyliah, will you stop acting as if I don't exist."

Kyliah came out of her closet, prepared to bite his head off, when he said, "Please, just hear me out, okay? That's all I ask."

Kyliah stood a few feet in front of him, ready to snap, but saying nothing for the moment.

Sitting on the edge of her bed, Arron rested his elbows on his knees. "Before I ever met you, Sam bet me a thousand dollars that I couldn't find out any info on

Ashela. I accepted the bet and asked you to go out with me. But during our first date, it was obvious that we were hitting it off so well, the money didn't even matter. I didn't go out with you because I needed the money, Kyliah. It was just a simple bet. By the end of the evening, when you came up to my room, I no longer even remembered the bet Sam and I had made."

"That's because you were drunk, Arron." Kyliah was still holding on to her hurt feelings.

"No, Kyliah, you and I both know there was more to it than that. Even had we not made love that night, I would have found a way to see you again, even if it was just to make sure I hadn't dreamt or imagined the chemistry we'd developed for one another." Arron reached out and taking hold of one of her hands, slowly pulled her between his legs.

"On principle, what I did was wrong, Kyliah, but wanting to see you and be with you again," he shook his head as he looked up at her, "There was nothing wrong about that. I wasn't being deceptive during the times we spent together. I was having just as much enjoyment as you were. Do you really think a sane man would drive all the way here and stand outside in the pouring rain while you openly dissed him? When you didn't return any of my calls yesterday, I *had* to see you. That's why I came here tonight. I had to explain."

Kyliah pulled away from him and sat down on the bed beside him. "It sounds good, Arron. But all that business about my spending your money and me being like some wild animal in bed. I can't tell you how humiliated I felt. I wasn't with you because of whatever money you do or do not have. I was with you, Arron, because I *liked* you and I was foolish enough to think you liked me too. I certainly didn't expect to be some joke for you to laugh about with your cronies." Kyliah shook her head vehemently, remembering the way he and Sam had discussed her.

"Kyliah, look at me." He turned her face in his direction. "I haven't lied to you, not even once. The one thing I know is that no matter how good the sex is between us, we can't have a relationship without some form of truthful verbal communication. So if I lie to you, then the only thing we have is sex.

"I'm not hurting for money. If I couldn't afford to take you out the way I've been doing, believe me, I'd tell you up front. I don't pretend to be something I'm not. What I said to Sam was just male locker-room talk. I enjoy it when we're together. Not just when we have sex. If you've noticed, we've spent more time talking than we have making love. I don't know about you, but there've been many times in my life when I've been with someone and afterwards, we didn't talk at all."

"What about your comment of having to explain where your scratches came from? You told me you weren't seeing anyone."

"No, Kyliah. I told you I wasn't seeing anyone *seriously*. Again, I didn't lie to you. Maybe you heard what you wanted to hear . . ."

"No, Arron, I'm not the one who's hearing-impaired here." Kyliah's anger flared up again. "I heard what you *wanted* me to hear. If your relationship is not serious, then what the hell would you call it?"

"It's just someone whom I've taken out several times. We've never even been intimate."

Kyliah was suddenly remembering what Ash had once said about loving someone being so risky. Right now, with her heart feeling as if it were in tatters, she had to agree. She pulled her legs up on the bed and sat cross-legged with her arms behind her.

Arron stared at her, his hunger for her apparent in his eyes. She was just a few inches away from him and he couldn't resist nuzzling her waist with his nose. She smelled like Escape perfume.

Though Kyliah's senses were aflame the moment he touched her, she didn't want to sleep with him tonight. Her heart ached too badly. She placed her hand on his head and said, "Arron, please, I really don't want you to touch me right now."

Not taking her rejection of him lightly, he said, "Okay, then I won't. But just let me hold you. Come here." She didn't resist him when he stretched out on the bed and pulled her towards him. With her backside pressed against him, Arron wrapped one of his arms around her.

Unbeknownst to him, tears dripped from Kyliah's eyes. She could only lay there wondering how things had gotten so far out of hand in such a short span of time. She'd only known him for three weeks. How could he have stolen her heart so quickly? As a rule, she called the shots. When a relationship was over, she was always the one who ended it. Take 'em or leave 'em, Kyliah was the one who set the boundaries for all of her relationships. But this time, from a simple bet, she had fallen for this man who, ironically, was not even the type that she would ever have dreamed of dating. Kyliah hadn't gone out with a brother since her early college days. *What goes around comes around. You reap what you sow.*

When Arron touched her face and felt the wet tears on her cheeks, he didn't sit up and look at her, he just smoothed them away using his fingertips. He couldn't understand why she was so hurt from the conversation she'd overheard, but neither did he cast her feelings aside. Whatever was going on within her was something he couldn't comprehend, but it didn't take a scholar to detect that she was hurting. Arron was truly sorry about that. He wasn't some unsympathetic ogre. He imagined how he would feel if he discovered someone had gone out with him because of a bet.

Though he could certainly be categorized as a solitary person, Arron thought he knew something about women. And what he did know was that there were times when they had to be kept at arms length. This was what he felt with Kyliah. He didn't want to give her the wrong impression. When the women he dated became too clingy, he tended to pull away. He hadn't lied when he'd told her that he was seeing someone else. It was just that there was no "someone else" in particular. There were

quite a few women that he occasionally took out to dinner, just none that he wanted to make a commitment to. This was just his master defense, his safety mechanism—his own way of keeping all women at bay. He wasn't sure of how he felt about Kyliah. He liked her. He enjoyed her company, and he definitely craved their sex life. But beyond that, well, it was just too soon to judge. Besides, they lived worlds apart, and he couldn't say what their chances were of seeing one another again. He just wanted to enjoy the moments they now had. Smoothing back the hair on her head, Arron placed light kisses on the side of her face.

Feeling herself weakening, Kyliah asked, "Are you hungry, Arron?" She sat up and looked at him.

"You mean you're going to feed me?"

Kyliah smiled. "Don't get too happy. If your clothes aren't dry by now, you're going to have to eat up here alone. ET and I will just have to eat by ourselves."

"Pleeeease, clothes, please be dry," Arron said in jest as he lifted his head toward the ceiling.

While Arron dressed, Kyliah set the dining room table for two. There was a candle centerpiece on the table but she removed it, not wanting to give him the wrong impression. When he came back downstairs clad in his sleeveless undershirt and pants, the table was set before him.

"You cooked such an elegant meal just for yourself?" Arron asked. They had eaten out so much over the past several weeks that he was amazed she could cook.

"You've obviously never dated a southerner before, have you? We don't need a special occasion to prepare a home-cooked meal. Oh, I get it. You didn't think I *could* cook, did you?"

"You've got me."

Without waiting for him to do it, Kyliah blessed their food and gestured for him to hand her his plate so she could serve him.

After dinner, they were in the kitchen washing up when her phone rang. Knowing she'd left her cordless upstairs in her bedroom, Kyliah dashed up the stairs. "Hello?" she asked breathlessly.

"Will you accept the charges for a collect call?" Kyliah inquired as to who it was and said yes.

"Fade? How ya doin'? It's cuzin Puddintang." Because she had been so light-skinned when she was born, Fade was the southern nickname Kyliah's folks on her mother's side of the family had given her.

And she'd run all the way upstairs for him? "Hi, Cuz. What's up?" Kyliah already knew.

"Fade, can you loan me a hunnerd bucks? You know I'll pay you back as soon as I can."

Kyliah knew he wouldn't pay her back. But she'd send it to him anyway simply because she liked him. "Sure, Cuz. I'll wire it tomorrow. But I've got company now, Cuz, so I've got to go. We'll talk later, okay?" Kyliah knew she had to stop him before he started talking or else she'd never get him off the phone. She disconnected the line and sat on her bed.

"Everything okay?" Arron asked behind her from the doorway.

"Everything's copecetic, Arron. All is well." As he slid onto the bed beside her, Kyliah knew what he wanted. The problem was she wanted it just as much as he did.

She offered no resistance when he pulled her down beside him and kissed her lightly on her face and neck. With gentle insistence, he untied the silk robe and ran his big hands all over her body, caressing her roughly, but slowly and gently, just the way she liked it. Before she knew it, he had removed the night gown from her body, leaving her completely naked.

This time, Kyliah lay on the bed completely passive, the exact opposite of the aggressive woman, he'd come to know. But as he slid his body on top of hers, Arron didn't mind at all. He palmed her buttocks, spreading them and planted himself against her. He didn't enter her, he just needed to feel her warm moistness against him. When she purred into his ear, he muffled his groan into her neck.

As she wrapped her arms around him, Kyliah just wanted to feel him inside her. She knew he'd take her heart with him when he left, but at this moment she needed his closeness, his fieriness, his passion. She lifted her legs and locked them around him in a butterfly grip, nudging him to satisfy her and give her what she wanted.

As her sweet hisses and sighs filled the room, Arron poured all of himself into her, basking in her slippery wetness. He reveled in her abandonment, losing all track of time.

Filled with only the desire to satiate both of their urgent needs, together they rode the waves of passion, rising and falling with every crest, quenching and satisfying the fiery thirst of a lifetime.

Part Five

"...The Hunt, The Chase,
The Capture..."

"What's this whole world coming to,
Things just ain't the same,
Anytime the hunter gets captured by the game."

– "Captured by the Game"
Song by the Marvelettes

Chapter Twenty-Two

shela exited the American Airlines terminal at New York's LaGuardia Airport and headed for the baggage-claim area. She was trying to peer above the crowd in search of her escort who would be holding up a sign marked "AJ" to distinguish himself as her limo driver. Ashela had learned from past experience to warn companies in advance not to use her last name alone when picking her up from airports or any other place. People saw the name Jordan and automatically assumed it was the basketball icon. She retrieved her luggage and finally met up with her driver and was taken immediately to the Ritz-Carlton.

Ashela's purpose for coming to New York was a mixture of business and pleasure. She had come to discuss and finalize the Werner contract with Pete Corti, her attorney, but also, to play a gig that she had agreed to months before.

She, Patrice Rushen, and Richard Elliott would be performing together live, in concert, for two nights only at Sweetwaters in Manhattan. Ashela purposely didn't come to New York often. The city held too many unwanted memories for her. But every blue moon, when business prevailed, she capitulated and returned to the place that had helped shape her into the person she now was.

Before she'd left L.A., Ashela had spoken to Sam only once. When he found out from Adrienne that she was traveling to New York, he had called her at her home and offered to fly her there on his private plane. Ashela was terse with him and adamantly refused. She was equally as angry with him as she was with Arron Davenport for what had happened to Kyliah. She ended her conversation with him in the same manner it had begun, by addressing him as "Mr. Ross." In a sense, Ashela was thankful for the mishap. It afforded her the opportunity to once more raise the barrier she'd so easily allowed Sam to penetrate.

Sam could tell from her icy professionalism that he was back to square one with her. While on the surface it may have appeared to be a huge setback, Sam was unperturbed and felt nothing but confidence—that it was only a matter of time before the small crack he had once managed to produce in her armor became an unobstructed entrance with his name tattooed upon the door. Sam was both ruthless and relentless in his pursuit of a challenge. His tactics were methodical and he never ceded until he had conquered and claimed anything that he considered his.

All tickets to the performance were sold out. The event had been well publicized on most of the New York and New Jersey radio stations. Disappointment awaited all who failed to purchase their tickets in hopes that the performing dates would be extended.

Friday night's show opened to a packed house. But that was the beauty of Sweetwaters. It allowed for a large-sized crowd, while enabling performers to give the impression of being up close and personal with every person present. The large area was oval-shaped with a square stage in its center. Surrounding rows of candle-lit tables dominated the room. Low-lighting projected a soft, cozy, romantic ambiance.

By Saturday morning, all of the New York papers were filled with rave reviews of their impelling Friday night performance. They had wooed the crowd with every song they played, putting on an unforgettable, show-stopping production.

***

Kyliah had opted not to make the trip to New York. She sat with her back pressed against her bathroom wall as she towel-dried ET. Despite the great myth of how cats abhorred water, ET was one of the lone throwback animals who didn't put up too big of a fuss whenever she bathed him. The big Persian purred loudly as she brushed his long hair. The huge amount of hair he managed to shed was his only drawback. Kyliah was rubbing flea powder into his fur when the telephone rang.

As she stepped inside her bedroom, she was surprised to find that it was her business line that was ringing. Most people limited their calls to the weekdays and she wondered who would be calling on a Saturday. Nearly an hour later she retrieved the message and was surprised that the call had been from Sam.

Kyliah sat on her sofa holding the phone in her hand wondering what angle Sam was trying to come from. Any trust he may have previously inspired in her was completely gone. Despite how personal and pleasant sounding his message had been, she intended to keep her association with him impersonal—a far cry from the manner in which she'd originally approached him. She wouldn't return his call. He probably only wanted more info on Ashela anyway.

Arron had departed for Boston a week ago and Kyliah hadn't spoken to him since that time. Though he'd left his phone number with her, she refused to call him. For the life of her, she couldn't understand the sinister void and aching need his departure had caused within her. Never had she undergone such inner turmoil over a man, particularly in light of how brief the time was that she had known him. How it was possible for such strong emotional attachments to develop in so short a period of time, Kyliah had no clue. But she remembered something her mother had told her years ago about "soul ties," and how they were established whenever a man and a woman slept together. It had sounded deep to her then and was still too deep for her now.

The one thing Kyliah could attest to was that while she was adamant about resisting the urge to contact Arron, she was likewise decisive about directing all of her emotional energy into getting over him. Her first step along the way was to *believe* her way out of her current state of forlorn prostration. Regardless as to what it took, she was determined to believe her way past her feelings of broken-

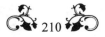

heartedness, and to at all costs protect herself from allowing something like this to happen to her again.

On the final night of the show, the trio brought the house down with yet another spectacular performance. As the three of them bowed before the crowd, several people in the audience threw roses onto the stage. Breathlessly, Ashela stepped to the mic one final time and invited everyone to join them for cocktails at the after-set.

A pathway was cleared through the crowd for the on-stage performers. They were led to a suite in the back of the building where they could relax and mingle before the afterset. A group of industry people were already waiting inside the room. Dom Pérignon champagne, Chardonnay wine, and all kinds of sparkling juices flowed as freely as did the laughter. With her adrenaline still flowing, Ashela held up her glass of wine and took a long sip when another group of people entered the rapidly-filling room. With a wine-glass in one hand, and a small, round, palm-sized purse in the other, Ashela donned the hat of social butterfly and flitted from person to person, thanking several people for coming and receiving in return their profuse congratulations.

Her back was to the door as a record exec leaned down to whisper a private invitation into her ear. Ashela gave him a tempting smile and patted him on his cheek before turning away from him. Never in a million years, she thought. As she stood facing the door, her heart leapt inside her chest as Sam Ross strode purposefully towards her carrying a bouquet of white roses. Try as she might, Ashela was incapable of invoking anger toward him or of stopping the warm smile that suddenly spread across her face. Unconsciously, she stepped forward to meet him thinking that the man didn't have a right to look so good.

When Sam reached her, time seemed to stand still. Later, she wouldn't remember him handing her the roses or taking them from him. There was just the memory of her lifting and arching her neck to welcome a kiss that she knew was forthcoming. And then her eyes closed as his lips slowly grazed her skin. Naked shivers streaked down Ashela's spine. The other people inside the room seemed to vanish along with all the ill will she was supposed to be feeling toward him. As a languorous sensation settled in the pit of her belly, her only thought was of how good it felt to see him again. She didn't know how he had found out that she would be here tonight, but she was grateful that he had taken the time to come. Feeling as though she were in a haze-filled daze, Ashela knew that she was near to being swept off of her feet. It had been much too long since any man had inspired these types of feelings in her. She held her bouquet of roses against her chest to mask her obvious signs of arousal, willing herself to come back to her senses.

As she slowly began to fade back to her present surroundings, she noted that several people were milling around them, all of them talking to Sam. With a slight

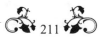

smile plastered to her lips, Ashela glanced about, mindless to the hubbub of conversation going on around her. There were only about twelve to fifteen people in the room but because of the high energy and enthusiasm of every person present, there seemed many more than that.

Ashela brought her gaze back to Sam and languidly took all of him in. Dressed in a charcoal Hugo Boss pantsuit, his outfit was accentuated by his yellow rib mockneck sweater. She took in the broadness of his shoulders, the size of his neck, the shape of his jaw, and especially the grooves in his cheeks that deepened whenever he smiled. She even envisioned herself softly stroking his face. By the time her eyes reached level with his, a half smile had curled her lips. He was so at ease with his surroundings and his magnetism had completely drawn her in. Though she stood directly in front of him holding the flowers he'd just given her, two other women standing amidst their small circle were still trying to get their bids in.

Staring into Sam's eyes was like looking into a liquid pool of deep, dark molasses. Seeing his look of intent assessment, Ashela was neither equipped nor prepared for what she saw mirrored in the depths of them. She slowly pulled her eyes away from his to regain her composure. And for the first time since Sam's entrance, she wondered where the man who had been about to whisper sweet nothings in her ear had disappeared to. With four others around her monopolizing his attention, now was the perfect time for her to break the spell that had completely fallen over her and make her great escape.

It was as though Sam could read her mind. In the brief moments when he'd first entered the room, he'd seen the unguarded expression in her eyes. A look that told him that she was as glad to see him as he was to see her. He'd caught the rampant look of desire and the quick catch of breath in her throat before she'd had a chance to mask it with her usual nonchalant, carefree stance. As his eyes raked her body intently from head to toe, his gaze managed to pierce through her every defense. Sam's look displayed possessive ownership of someone that he already considered his. She wore a bright orange, iridescent, mini-dress. With its clusters of satin spaghetti straps, the dress rested just above her knees. Muscled thighs and well shaped calves gave clue to her many workouts. Her only jewelry was a pair of large, button-shaped orange earrings. Knowing she had tuned the other conversationalists out, Sam saw her look towards the door and he could measure the exact moment when she would excuse herself.

Just as Ashela prepared to make her way out of the room, Sam surprised her by catching hold of her wrist and detaining her as he excused both of them from the current group of people. Knowing she had been caught in the act of leaving, Ashela looked up at Sam and smiled guiltily.

She said softly, above the din of conversation, "Sam, I wouldn't dream of pulling you away from so many adoring fans. Shouldn't you go back and console them?"

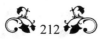

Sam shook his head with a determined look. "Woman, I flew over three thousand miles to get here to see you tonight. I'm the one who's the adoring fan—and also the one who happens to have a strong case of jet lag. Shouldn't you be trying to console me?" Ashela could only stare at him, losing herself in the smile he gave her.

A few feet away from them, the door opened and in walked several more record execs, promoters and managers. Ashela was still half smiling at Sam when a woman approached them. Something about her was vaguely familiar and Ashela quickly searched her mind for some clue as to where she might know her from.

As it all came back to her just where and how she knew the woman, Ashela broke away from Sam and the other guests who were quickly surrounding him to hug her mother's old friend.

"Tanya! My, but don't you look the same." Ashela hadn't seen her since the day of her mother's funeral. Tanya was fifty-something now, but time had obviously been good to her. With her long, silver-gray hair and flawless skin, she hardly looked her age.

"Ashela, you flatter an old woman. You, on the other hand, are beautiful. Do you know you're the splitting image of your mother?"

"It pleases me to hear you say that, Tanya." Ashela was trying hard to suppress the sudden barrage of memories. So much about Tanya was bringing back images of Charla to her. "How have you been?"

"I've been well, Ashela. When I found out this morning that you were in town, I had to call in several favors just to get tickets. How long are you going to be in town?"

"Just till the beginning of the week. Do you still live here?"

"Yes. Manhattan is still my home. We must get together before you leave New York. There's so much for us to talk about." Tanya was already writing her home number on the back of a business card.

Ashela had so many questions. Of course, she would *have* to see Tanya before she left town. As she held the card examining it, Sam came and stood beside her. Ashela was quick to make introductions.

"Sam, this is an old friend of mine. Tanya Redding, this is Sam Ross."

Neither Tanya or Sam spoke or shook the other's hand. Instead, when they looked at one another coldly, Ashela immediately picked up on their obvious signs of hostility. She looked from one to the other with curious intent, but tactfully, ventured not a word.

Ignoring Sam, Tanya asked Ashela, "Will you be attending the after-set?"

Sam said to Tanya, almost as if he were challenging her, "I'm pretty sure we'll both be there."

Tanya continued to stare at Ashela as if Sam were not even present.

To ease the growing tension, Ashela said, "And even if I don't attend, Tanya, I'll definitely call you tomorrow."

As more people began to join their small circle, Sam aggressively nudged Ashela towards the exit and said loudly over his shoulder, "We'll see everybody at the after-set."

When the two of them departed together, the rumor mill was activated as whispered innuendoes and raised eyebrows circulated throughout the room. If Sam Ross and Ashela Jordan were an item, it was newsworthy and might even be worth something to a number of the gossip mags. While a few contemplated the best source to deliver the juicy tidbit to, only Tanya continued to watch the two of them balefully as they left the crowded room of well wishers.

Outside in the hallway, Sam led them through the throng of people all the way to his limousine. In all the years that Ashela had been performing, it never failed to amaze her the way people swarmed and pressed their way just to touch or get a glimpse of an entertainer. She laid her roses and her purse down and leaned back almost wearily against the limo's soft leather seat. She sat directly across from Sam.

Smiling, Ashela said, "Don't pull off yet, Sam. I've got to tell Cedric to pack up my equipment and then I've got to let my own limo driver know not to desert me."

Eager to have her remain with him, Sam whipped out a super-thin cell phone from inside his jacket and dialed a number. When the person picked up, he said, "Dwayne, it's Ross. I need you to have someone paged." Sam glanced over the phone and said to Ashela, "What's Cedric's last name?" She told him and he went back to speaking to the person on the other end. "When you get him, have him call me on my cellular." He lightly placed the phone down on the seat next to him.

As Sam leaned forward with his elbow on his knees, Ashela couldn't help but smile at his take-charge attitude. He was watching her again with an intent look upon his face.

Sam was just happy that he'd been able to sneak her away with such relative ease and he wanted to know what thoughts lay behind her lazy smile and beautiful dimples. "What are you thinking?"

"Actually, I was trying to remember how I even came to be here. One moment I was on stage performing and in the next, here I am alone with you, staring at you as if I have no other place to be. You have a remarkable way of moving so fast, Sam. It takes me a minute just to put things in their proper perspective."

"It was really quite simple. All we did was fight tooth and nail to push our way through the crowd and, 'voila!' Here we are."

Ashela shook her head. She knew the dynamics were much more compelling than that. His cell phone rang and he picked up on the first ring. As he spoke into the

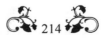

phone, Ashela looked around her, admiring the beauty of the limousine. Its dark gray leather interior and oak wood paneling was offset by brass trimmings, a built-in, high-tech television, a state-of-the-art stereo system, and a well-stocked bar. Like the man himself, his limousine was expensively furnished and power-laden.

Her eyes met his when she heard him say, ". . . Cedric, I have Ms. Jordan here with me. I need you to pack up all of her stage equipment. Make sure it's delivered to her hotel room before you and the limousine driver take the rest of the night off."

When Ashela heard him dismissing her own hired help, her eyes widened and she was off her seat and sitting next to him in a flash. Sam leaned away from her as she tried to take the phone out of his hand.

Half irritated and half flattered, Ashela leaned into him trying to reach for the phone, saying, "Samuel Ross . . . If you don't . . . Who gave you permission . . .?"

Sam had already released the line. As she looked at him in exasperation, he sat back and said to her with a smile in his voice, "Will you relax and let me take good care of you?"

Ashela twisted her mouth and bit the inside of her lip as she looked at him assessingly. In a move that surprised him, she sat back and calmly lifted her legs onto the leather seat, tucking them underneath her. With her elbow resting on top of the seat, she stared at him. Though she was relaxed and not the least bit sullen, her tone was frank as she said, "Sam Ross, I know you're used to simply taking over and taking charge. But so am I when it comes to my own personal affairs. Don't ever do that again. Next time, ask me first. Contrary to what you may believe, I don't like being whisked off my feet. You'll find that I'm much more . . . pliable . . . when you make me a part of your decision-making process." Ashela's gaze never wavered from his and she spoke quietly but firmly.

Sam loved the way she chastised him. She was sitting inches away from him and he turned to her without touching her. Ever so softly, he said to her, "You're right, some things I do out of habit without even thinking about them. I apologize. Will you be with me tonight, Ashela Jordan? Can we make this our first date?" Sam's eyes strayed over her face. She wore that half-smile of hers again, that look that hid her emotions.

Already forgiving him, Ashela stared at the shape of his lips, memorizing the angles of his face. He was so close to her that she couldn't resist the urge to reach out her hand and using the back of it, stroked her knuckles and fingers down the length of his jaw. His freshly shaved skin was semi-rough underneath her touch. Ashela's eyes locked with his as her fingers slid to the nape of his neck. Soft and slowly, she pulled his head down to hers and whispered into his ear, "Didn't I tell you that I don't date the people I work with?"

As Sam lifted his head and stared down at her, the faint touch of her fingers against his skin was tantalizing. Her demeanor was all silk and satin. But he sensed an underlying toughness to her femininity. Sam knew he was staring at a woman who

215

knew how to temper her aggressiveness, mixing it with the right amount of womanliness. Her hand was still resting lightly at the nape of his neck, her fingernails caressing his skin and Sam had the distinct impression that she was testing his self-restraint.

"Since you haven't yet signed my contract on the dotted line, officially, that makes us mere acquaintances, not co-workers." Though he considered himself to be in possession of much self-control, Sam didn't even try to resist the need to be closer to her. He removed her hand from around his neck and turned her into him, lacing his fingers with hers. With her back pressed into his chest, his palm easily swallowed her hand in his. Casually, he slid his left arm over the back of the seat. "Although I have you under lock and key, I'll be a man of my word and let you help call the shots. So tell me, Lady, where would you like me to take you?"

Ashela was too busy looking at the way his hands entangled and over-lapped hers. The size of his fingers and the way they shielded hers caused too many intimate mental images of the two of them to run through her mind.

Sam continued to stroke her hand with his as he said, "We could go to the after-set and socialize with all the highfalutin jet-setters or we could dine at any restaurant of your choice and spend this time getting to know one another better."

Ashela's mind was way ahead of Sam's. In her imagination, dinner was already over and done with. She had catapulted him back to her hotel room where she had him stretched out on the bed underneath her while she straddled him and held him captive.

In reality, though she had already melted against him, Ashela suddenly needed to clear her mind and think. And the only way she could do that was to put some space between them. She pulled away from him and got up to sit across from him, once again on the opposite side. But the atmosphere was still rife with sexual tension. "I like your last suggestion best. Let's dine at B. Smith's, shall we?"

In reply, Sam hit a button and the smooth, jazzy sounds of Dave Crushin filled the limousine. He was willing to let her name any place she so desired, and for now, he would even allow himself to dance to her tune. It had been a long time since Sam had played the game of cat and mouse. Normally, what he wanted from a woman was offered before he could even ask for it, and with no regret he either took it or turned it down without looking back. But there was something different about Ashela Jordan or perhaps it was just the chemistry that had evolved between them. Regardless, there was an air about her that invited him to unlock and tap into her hidden, epicurean mysteries.

Never one to turn away a challenge of his liking, Sam stretched his legs out in front of him and crossed his Gucci leather shoes. "B. Smith's it is then." He picked up a nearby phone and gave the driver their destination. Sitting across from him with her long, shapely legs and alluring thighs, Ashela looked the part of the sexy starlet. As she sat with one leg tucked underneath her and the other one dangling over her

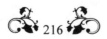

seat, Sam obliged her by taking all of her in. The roundness of her breasts, the way her hips were accentuated by the narrowness of her waist. There was so much about her that Sam desired to know—she was the quintessential puzzle that he yearned to solve.

"How old are you, Ashela?"

"Old enough to separate the men from the boys," she quickly rejoined. Still, his question surprised her. With a lifted eyebrow, she said, "Sam, why do you pry? Haven't I already told you that age really is but a number? It's only a person's maturity level that really counts." She tilted her head and stared at him, unconsciously wetting her bottom lip with her tongue.

Following her movement with his eyes, Sam leaned forward and once again rested his elbows on his knees. "Then tell me what makes Ashela Jordan tick."

Ashela shook her head at him. "Sam, I think you're rationalizing too much. By trying to figure me out, you're making me into someone who's deeper than I really am. I'm just an ordinary girl, full of idiosyncrasies and many inadequacies. I'm a loner, but I'm content with my solitude. Not many people can say that, Sam. Can you say it? Or do you feel contentment only when there's a bombshell dangling from your arm? Not that I fit that description." Ashela shrugged before she lifted her other leg under her and stretched out on the seat, resting her head against the palm of her hand.

"Do you *have* to have a woman in tow, Sam? By no means am I judging you if you do. I wouldn't dare do that when there are so many women throwing themselves at you all the day long. But me, Sam? I need the aloneness to hear myself think. I can't waste time trying to figure out people's motives or be bothered to take the time to decipher whether or not someone wants to be with me for me, or whatever they think I may have to offer. And even though I'm like everyone else who desires to be loved, I'm unwilling to settle for the temporary hypocrisy that a one-night stand provides. I do quite well satisfying myself, Sam." Smiling at him through half-closed lids, Ashela continued, "So you see, in many respects, I'm no different than the next person. But on the other hand, I'm an enigma unto myself. I choose to be alone not because I'm rejected or can't find anyone else, but because I'm unique and consider myself in a class all by myself."

Sam could only stare at her in wonder. He'd asked her about herself but felt as though he'd had his own mail read. She was so inviting as she lay stretched out on the leather seat. Pensively, he pressed his fingertips together and rested them against his lips. A pint-sized dynamo was what she was. Self-reflection from a woman was something he hadn't encountered since his days with Claudette.

As Ashela stared at him with challenging glints in her eyes, Sam wanted nothing more than to undress her and pull her down on top of him. He knew that with ardent persuasiveness, he could eradicate her self-controlled facade and arouse her in the exact way she was now arousing him. Sam sensed that she could be gentle and that

217

she would require tenderness in return. Suddenly, he ached to have her whisper once more into his ear. But only this time, he wanted her to whisper sweet signs of her desire. Sam felt the incessant need to possess her and to make her forget all her talk of intellectualism. Right here and right now, Sam wanted nothing more than to have her underneath him, totally submissive to his sweet, seductive, but merciless care.

For once, Ashela could read *his* mind. She could tell by his motionless stance and by the dark look in his eyes just what he wanted of her. As her breathing rose and fell rapidly, Ashela no longer tried to deny it—she wanted to give him what he wanted to take. She stretched out her arm and rested the side of her face on it, her thighs shifting as she turned completely on her side. With her voluptuous and sensuous posture, she issued him a silent, but wanton directive.

In a flash, Sam was sitting beside her. His arms locked on either side of her. As he glanced down at her, he sensed the willing permissiveness behind her demeanor. He saw the yearning in her that invited and tempted him to touch and explore her every crevice. But still, Sam knew she was holding something back—and that "something" was what he needed from her. Some emotion that he couldn't describe.

When Ashela opened her eyes to gaze into the fires that smoldered in his, unconsciously she arched her chest, begging him to touch her, urging his hands to caress her body. As Sam stared at her, he knew at that exact moment what it would take to please her. But not here, someplace else. Not inside his limousine where he had cheaply seduced so many others before her. As he lightly stroked her jawline, she was turning her face into his hand, almost purring, when a discrete tap sounded on the front panel signaling they had arrived at their destination.

With the moment interrupted, Ashela sat up self-consciously, trying to hide her embarrassment. So much for all of her talk about needing to be in control, because in the blink of an eye, she had lost her self restraint. In a matter of mere seconds, she had all but parted her legs and begged him to . . . What must he think of her? If she could have turned red, Ashela would have been the color of a beet. For the moment, she was unable to even look at him.

Sam detected some of what she was feeling and knew that if he didn't handle her or the situation right, she'd never allow him the opportunity to get this close and intimate with her again. He wrapped his left arm around her waist, pulling her close to his chest before whispering into her ear, "I sure hope you're hungry, Lady. Because I'm starving. I haven't eaten since this morning." With his right hand, Sam lightly kneaded the nape of her neck.

Ashela rested her cheek against his arm, still trying to regain her composure. "Sam, Sam, Sam. Ohhhh, but are you dangerous. I suddenly remember why I warned myself to avoid you. I even told Kyliah that you were the type of man who could make a woman lose every stitch of her dignity. I was just trying to ensure that it didn't happen to me."

Sam smiled and said, "Ashela, you've not lost your dignity. And the only danger you're in right now is of being eaten alive." He dipped his head and nibbled on her neck, squeezing her in a ticklish way, causing her to laugh and lean away from him.

But his teasing manner afforded her the opportunity to pull herself together. Ashela collected herself and finally said to him, "Come on loverboy, let's go order some food."

No sooner were they seated at their table when Barbara Smith, the owner of B. Smith's, came and greeted both of them. She hugged Sam as if the two of them were old friends. Minutes later, a chilled bottle of their best Opus One wine arrived at their table, compliments of the owner. Several business associates and industry friends also stopped by their table to say hello. They all seemed to be paying homage to Sam and Ashela knew that he received this kind of treatment everywhere he went. In some respects, Sam was more high-profile than many well-known entertainers.

Ashela took a sip of her wine and leaned her elbows on the table. "It must be quite a task heading up the largest record label in the world. So tell me, Sam, how then does it feel to have the entire music industry tattooed to your behind?"

Sam laughed. He didn't answer her right away. He lifted his glass and swirled his wine around in it. Finally, he stared up at her and said, "Right at this moment, Ashela, sitting here with you, it feels damned good. Other times, I feel like I need a proctologist."

Smiling gleefully, Ashela said, "Everywhere you go, people seem to kowtow to you. It's incredible. I thought *I* had it bad, but after being with you tonight, I'll never complain again."

Sam shrugged. "You get used to it. Once you learn how to read people and weed out the seekers from the potential offerers, it's a piece of cake. No one stays on top forever, Ashela. Remember that. That's why whenever you're there, you've got to make the most of your time. If you grease the right people's palms along the way, they'll remember you when you most need it."

"Is that how you've managed to stay on top for so long, Sam?"

"That and because I've been able to change with the times. The key to longevity in this business, as you well know, is being able to reinvent yourself so that when the winds do blow in the opposite direction, you can change stride mid-stream. And not get caught with your pants down."

"That's true. But still I marvel at how swiftly our marketplace changes at the drop of a hat. I've noticed that today's music industry is producer-driven as opposed to several years ago when it was artist-driven. I don't know whether the change is good or bad. I mean, from what I can see, all it's done is made it that much harder for our yesteryear's artists to even get a recording contract. It seems as though all the labels are only signing young, teenage acts. Your label included, Sam. On one hand,

I welcome the young talent, but on the other hand, I still prefer working with those who are older than myself. I find that I don't have to reach inside as deeply with them as I do with the teenagers. It's as though the gifts I have within me are more accessible to older artists because they know how to tap into them and pull them out of me. With them, recording sessions become a piece of cake."

"I understand," Sam said. "But I don't set the trends, Ashela. I just make money by spotting them. You'll find that at Werner Enterprises, we have more older artists with us than at any other record label. That's because I've encouraged those at Werner to be flexible and to be willing to reinvent themselves. If you've noticed, we've even taken to teaming up several older artists with the younger ones. By doing so, we introduce the older ones to a whole new marketable age group. We've produced many such combinations and several of the duets have even topped number one on Billboard. For instance, the song you wrote, "Forever More," featuring Aretha Franklin and Mary J. Blige, that hit was incredible."

Ashela didn't know why it surprised her that Sam was aware that she had written the song. After all, as president of the world's largest record label, it was his job to stay abreast of industry trends. Even so, she was impressed all the same.

"The bottom line, Ashela, is that those who are willing to re-shape their images will survive, thrive, and prosper. But those artists who sit back and bemoan the fact that the younger artists are getting all the recording contracts and making it big by sampling their music, they're the ones who'll be left behind."

In the next moment, the waiter arrived and served the couple their meal. When he departed, Sam said, "Tell me why it is that you choose to get out so infrequently. Didn't anyone ever tell you that all work and no play makes Jill a very dull girl?"

"I've never really been one to listen to all that people tell me, Sam. Anyway, I don't even think of it as 'not getting out much.' I really enjoy what I do. And like you, I'm committed to doing it. The time that I spend writing and perfecting my songs seems to fly by without my even noticing it. My music sustains me, Sam. It goes back to what I said earlier about enjoying working with older artists more so than the younger ones. They're much more professional and they're also more serious about their work. It's as though having struggled to get where they are, they appreciate it more. And I like that. I can also relate to it because when I'm in the studio with Face or Luther or Janet, the hours zoom by like seconds on a clock. Why? Because they're consummate professionals. Like myself, they're perfectionists who take what they do just as serious as I do."

Ashela took a bite of her Chicken Parmigiana. "When you love what you do to the degree that I do, Sam, when there's no time to quote, unquote, *play*, your work *becomes* your play. It's like a marriage of sorts. Wherein if you don't make your marriage bed your playground, then your bedroom becomes a battle ground. That's why I've made *my* work my playground, Sam. Do I miss the dating scene?" Ashela stared into her wine glass, shaking her head. "I have to say no because there doesn't

seem to be anything worth missing." And then she threw him a glaring smile. "So there you have it, Mr. Sam Ross. My life in five words or less."

As he bit into his shrimp, Sam said to her, "I'm not letting you off the ropes that easily. There's much more to Ashela Jordan than that and we both know it. Here, taste these shrimp. I say they're the best in New York." Sam speared one onto his fork and guided it all the way through Ashela's parted lips.

She nodded her head, smiling. "That is good," was all she managed to say between bites.

Ashela was chewing the succulent shrimp when an old friend appeared at their table.

"Ashela Jordan." Senator Randal Stein stood before her and whispered her name with reverential longing.

Trying to remain relaxed in the face of his intense demeanor, Ashela extended her hand and said, "Hello Randal. How are you?" He lifted her hand to his lips and kissed it. Though Ashela was surprised to see him, she hid her mixed emotions well.

"I've missed you. That's how I've been. And it's been much too long." His eyes were plastered to her and he never even bothered to acknowledge Sam as her date. Randal's interest in her was so overt that Ashela was forced to introduce him to Sam.

Trying to correct his oversight, Ashela introduced the two of them. Both men shook hands with powerful grips.

Randal turned back to her and said, "I looked for you, Ashela, but they told me you'd left town. It's good to see you obviously looking and doing so well." He handed her his business card and said, "Please call me." Randal pointed to the card he'd just handed her. "My home number is there as well." He turned to Sam and said finally, "Nice meeting you, Mr. Ross."

After Randal walked away, Sam stared at her with an impassive look on his face. A look that plainly told her that he expected an answer. But Ashela continued eating her meal.

Finally Sam said, "Are you or are you not going to tell me where you know the good Senator from?"

"I'm afraid there's nothing to tell, Sam. We happen to be old friends who just fell out of touch with one another."

Sam laughed outright. "Right. And I'm Donald Duck." The memory of how hungrily Randal had stared at Ashela made Sam angry. The man had been so blinded with lustfulness that he had been downright disrespectful.

Ashela didn't like the tone in his voice. "Sam, let's call a truce, shall we? Rule number one: I won't ask you about your past indiscretions and neither will you ask me about mine. Suffice it to say that Senator Stein was once an adoring fan of mine. But we lost touch with one another because one of us felt the need to move on.

Besides, Randal is old news. Can I have another bite of your shrimp scampi? You're barely touching it."

Sam swirled his wine around in his glass before taking a sip. As much as he hated to admit it, he felt twinges of jealousy at the thought of her being with someone else. Maybe it was the way the man had looked at her that he didn't appreciate.

"When are you returning to California?" he asked.

"I'm scheduled to return Tuesday, the day after my meeting with my lawyer. I'm meeting with him on Monday to go over your contract."

"Yes. I hear Pete Corti is representing you. He's certainly one of the best entertainment attorneys in the business. You've chosen well for yourself. Since you're going to be here, I could get us a pair of tickets for tomorrow night to see August Wilson's Broadway play, *Jelly's Last Jam.* Are you interested?"

Ashela smiled at him. "Yes, Sam. I'd love to attend. Do you know that in all of the years that I lived in New York, I never once saw a Broadway play?"

Sam leaned forward. "I didn't know you once lived in New York. You must tell me all about it. Is that how you met Tanya Redding?"

Their waiter again came and asked if they were interested in dessert. Sam shook his head, but Ashela promptly replied, "I'll have a slice of your New York cheesecake topped with strawberries." The server bowed and hurried away.

Not answering him right away, Ashela spread a clean napkin onto her lap. She didn't really want to discuss Tanya with Sam and unlike her earlier response, she no longer was even curious about the hostility between the two of them. "Tanya happens to be an old friend of my mother's. I haven't seen her since I was a child at my mother's funeral." The waiter placed her cheesecake in front of her. Glad for the diversion, Ashela happily bit into it. It was delicious. Just like old times, she thought.

Sam smiled just watching the delighted expression on her face. She forked another piece and lifted it to his lips. He shook his head but when she insisted, he ate it. "It's good," he, too, nodded his head.

"It's my fondest memory of New York."

"Why won't you talk to me about it?"

"Because I choose not to remember much of what I went through while I lived here. It wasn't all bad, Sam, but by no means was it all good. So I choose to have a selective memory about my time spent here. I will say this, though. After I met you at Debbie's dinner affair, I couldn't stop thinking that I knew you from another place and time. But I kept telling myself that that was impossible. Until it dawned on me that you were at my mother's funeral many years ago. I was the little girl you found on the terrace that night and carried inside to tuck away."

Sam searched his memory bank to recall the night Ashela referred to.

"I never forget a name, Sam. Many years later, a con man used your name in order to dupe me out of my life's savings. But there's also another twist to the story, Sam. I was once part of a group called Jaundice. You were the one to offer us our first recording contract. But because I was quitting the group, I understand the deal was never struck. It's funny, though you never knew me, you've been a part of my life for many years.

"At any rate, Sam, New York is where I grew up. Not in the literal sense of being raised here, but in terms of coming into my womanhood. As in *welcome to the real world.*"

Ashela finished eating her dessert. She pushed the plate away from her and with her elbows resting on the table, clasped her hands. "Shall I cover this, Sam?" She nodded towards the table. "Or at least let us do separate checks."

Sam looked at her with raised eyebrows, unable to believe she was for real. Recognizing that she was serious about paying for her portion of the bill, he could only shake his head, wondering how it was that she would even ask such a thing of him. Sam would be insulted and mortally offended to let a woman he had invited to dinner pay for the meal.

Ashela stood up and excused herself to go to the ladies' room. By the time she came back to the table, Sam had settled their bill. As the waiter left with his credit card, Sam asked her if she wanted anything else.

"You're sure? Coffee, tea, another slice of cheesecake to go?"

Ashela smiled. "No, Sam, I'd better not. Another time, perhaps."

The waiter returned Sam's credit card and he stood up to pull her chair out for her. "Another time, it is then. I intend to hold you to that."

They walked out of the restaurant unaware that Randal Stein was watching Ashela's every move. Just before they got into Sam's waiting limousine, a tall man called Ashela's name. She hesitated and then waited as Bill, Randal's chauffeur, approached her. He handed her an envelope. She didn't have to ask what was inside.

"Excuse me for a second, Sam." Ashela walked several steps away from the limo signaling for Bill to follow her. Out of earshot from Sam, she said to Bill, "Tell Mr. Stein that I've buried my past, Bill. I outgrew my days as a 'kept woman' the second you rescued me that long ago night. Please return the envelop to him and tell him that I said no thanks." When Bill nodded his head almost respectfully, Ashela walked away to step inside the waiting limousine.

Sam stood leaning against the limo and got in behind her before they pulled off.

When she sat on the opposite side of him again, Sam knew that it was her way of putting distance between them. She appeared reflective, almost distracted, as if a part of her were no longer with him. Though he was curious, he knew better than to ask her what the incident had been about.

 223

Ashela sensed the air of protectiveness that emanated from Sam. She knew, too, that he was full of curiosity about her relationship with Randal. She wouldn't discuss it with him, but neither did she want him carrying around some myth that she needed to be protected. "Sam, I don't want you to have any preconceived notions about me. If you do, you'll only be setting yourself up for disappointment. I may be younger than you are, but I'm not some snot-nosed kid who just got off the banana boat. I've worked hard to get where I am today. I've paid my dues and I've earned my stripes.

"I'm only telling you this because I don't want you thinking that I'm typical like the women you have chasing after you, Sam. I'm not trying to be with you so I can climb your *golden ladder of success*. I'm capable of paving my own way. I'll admit that you make me nervous and you remind me *why* I haven't been out on a date with a man in . . . years. I didn't mean to offend you when I suggested we opt for separate checks. It's something that I've grown accustomed to doing. It makes me feel comfortable, like I've paid my own way so I don't owe anybody anything." Ashela tilted her head, looking at him as if she really needed for him to understand where she was coming from.

"When I look at you Sam, I see a man who has enough money to burn up a wet elephant. No, don't laugh, I mean it. I see a man who's confident and self-assured, but surprisingly, not self-centered. You want to know the real reason I decided to accept your invitation tonight, Sam?" Ashela got up and slid next to him again. But she didn't touch him. "Not just because you're so persuasive, or incredibly handsome, or even because you're extremely rich. But I did so because of the simple fact that you don't wear an earring in your ear." Sam laughed as he shook his head in dismay.

"I'm very serious, Sam. I know it sounds crazy. But I love to see men without earrings in their ears. It's so refreshing. While it's just my own personal pet peeve, it tells me so much about a man. For instance, it tells me he's someone who's willing to dare to be different, someone who doesn't succumb to following the crowd—no matter what his surrounding peer pressure is like. But most of all, it tells me that he possesses rare qualities that, these days, are extremely hard to find." Ashela reached over and took Sam's hands into her own, resting them on her leg. She flattened his fingers and slowly ran her palm over his as she studied his hand. "These, Sam, are the hands of a man who's not afraid to get them dirty. There's great strength in your hands. But, Sam, you also know how to hold a woman with gentleness. I found that out tonight." She lifted his hand and placed it along the side of her face. Whispering to him softly, she said, "These hands belong to a man who knows how to give love and how to receive it in return." Ashela rubbed her face into his hand, longing to tell him so many other things.

What a juxtaposition, Sam thought. With her simple honesty, she had broken through *his* every line of defense. With her piercing words, he felt as though she were peering into his very heart, seeing into the essence of his soul. Her skin felt like

silk against his hands and she reminded him of a sultry cat. With seemingly little effort, Sam pulled her onto his lap and asked her at which hotel was she staying.

Chapter Twenty-Three

shela awoke the next morning with a smile on her face. She lay wrapped amidst the blankets with one arm behind her head reliving all that had transpired the night before, right up to the moment when Sam had delivered her safely to her hotel room.

As she'd inserted her keycard into her door, he had leaned against the wall waiting for her to step inside. Ashela stood just inside the door with her hands and her roses behind her back, smiling up at him with a look of fondness. Surprisingly, Sam bent down and planted a soft, lingering kiss upon her lips. He lifted his head and watched the play of expressions on her face before glancing at his watch and saying, "I'll see *you* this evening."

As he turned to walk away, Ashela said to him softly, "I know your moves, Sam Ross."

"Do you?" Sam turned around to face her but still continued to walk backwards towards the elevator.

"Yes. And I'm prepared for you." Her statement was almost a warning.

Sam stopped and walked the short distance back to stand in front of her. Resting one arm above the doorway, he cupped her face in his other hand. "Ashela, I don't know if you're prepared or not. But, woman, you'd better be." Sam was smiling and his look held promising allure.

Ashela stretched before she sat up in the bed and reached for the telephone. She had the distinct impression that she'd just crossed a line with Sam that made it impossible for her now to turn back or change the coming course of events. She dialed Kyliah's number, but her line just rang until finally it kicked into voice-mail. Without leaving a message, she hung up to retrieve Tanya's card from her purse.

There were buoyant greetings after Tanya picked up on the third ring. She invited Ashela over to her place for lunch. They agreed to meet at one o'clock.

Tanya lived in an expensive loft near mid-town. She gave Ashela a tour of her lavishly furnished home. It was bright and sunny and to Ashela's surprise, her home was decorated all in white. Everything, including the carpeting, was either white or gold. Though Tanya said it wasn't necessary, Ashela insisted upon removing her high-heeled shoes. Everything was so neat and clean that Ashela felt as though she were inside a glass house, fearful of touching or sullying anything.

Tanya led them into the dining room where she had prepared Caesar spinach salads with chunks of chicken on the side, along with baked potatoes.

"I'm a vegetarian, but I cooked the chicken just for you. Come, have a seat."

All of the dishes and eating utensils were gold as well. Even the napkins had gold linings. "Tanya, you didn't have to go to all of this trouble for me. We could easily have eaten out."

"Honey, believe me. It was no trouble at all."

They made small-talk during the meal, having agreed to defer all heavy-laden questions until after they'd eaten.

Afterwards, Tanya cleared away the plates, refusing to let Ashela help. Inside her living room, Ashela promptly took a seat on Tanya's carpeted floor. Her furniture was so *white* that Ashela didn't want to sit on it. She sat cross-legged waiting for Tanya to return.

"Ashela Jordan, honey, if you don't get off of that floor, I will not be responsible for my actions."

Ashela laughed at Tanya, who stood with her hands on her hips. "It's okay, Tanya. Really, I'm comfortable here. Please, I've got so many questions to ask that I don't even know where to begin."

Tanya appeared just as eager to talk about the past as Ashela was.

"Before you ask anything, let me show you something." Tanya led her upstairs to a door that Ashela assumed was another large bedroom. As Tanya slowly opened the door, what struck Ashela right away about the room was its color. Instead of being white like the rest of the house, it was a deep purple. The same color which had been her mother's favorite.

A king-sized, maroonish lacquer bed was offset by purple wall-to-wall carpeting. A royal purple satin comforter with matching pillow shams donned the bed. But above it, hanging on the wall, was a huge, gold-framed photo of Charla. Her image seemed to leap out of the picture. Her hair was piled on top of her head and wisps of it hung down from the nape of her neck. She was half smiling and her eyes seemed to glow. Ashela had never seen this particular picture of her mother before, but sensed that it must have been taken during a happier time of her life.

Tanya entered the room behind her and stood beside a wide dresser. Covering the dresser was a long sheath of purple lace topped by gold-framed pictures. Ashela stood in front of it in awe, feeling as if she were beholding a shrine. Pictures of herself as a child playing underneath her mother's baby grand piano. Pictures of her with ribbons in hair, laughing as she played with her dolls. And pictures of her and Charla together.

"Charla would have been so proud of you, Ashela. You have no idea how much your mother loved you. She loved Julia, too, in her own way. But you'd never know it by the way the two of them fought."

With her eyes closed, Ashela became a child again, remembering how she would wait by the door for hours for her mother to come home from a tour. Sometimes

she'd fall asleep while waiting, only to be awakened by Tanya who would lift her and carry her up to her bedroom.

"Charla always felt that she was not fit to raise a child. Although she wanted to have you with her on the road, she loved you too much to subject you to the vagaries that most musicians' children experience."

"And I thought she never wanted me."

"That's not true, Ashela."

Ashela shook her head, wiping away her tears. "I'm a grown woman, Tanya, but the hurt and sense of betrayal I felt when you made no attempt to contact me or claim me as your own feels as fresh as if it were yesterday. After all these years, you'd think it wouldn't hurt anymore." Ashela fingered one of the photographs. "Why have you kept all these pictures, Tanya?"

"Haven't you figured it out yet, Ashela? Because I loved your mother, that's why. I loved and cared for your mother more than I've loved anyone else before or after her. You still don't get it, do you? Your mother and I were lovers, Ashela."

Despite Ashela's stunned look, Tanya continued, "Your mother wasn't perfect, honey. But she was the type of person who'd give you her last of anything if you asked for it. But it wasn't until after your birth that she and I became lovers. We were friends first because she was still in love with your father even though she still dated and saw other men. After you were born, we just grew closer and closer until she finally realized that her feelings for me were stronger than she cared to admit. I know what I'm telling you is scandalous but try not to think too unkindly of your mother, Ashela. There are much worse things that can happen to a person other than loving someone of the same sex."

Ashela had sat down on the bed. "Right now, Tanya, I really don't know what to think. But believe me, I don't love my mother any less because of what you've just told me. I'm shocked and I don't understand, but . . ." Ashela's voice trailed off as she searched for words to describe her emotions.

"All these years, I've held on to these . . . things because they were Charla's. She was taken from me so swiftly that I needed them as reminders that she was actually here. But later, I learned to view her death as if she were still a part of me."

Tanya picked one of the pictures up off of the dresser and stroked it lovingly. "These pictures were my only reminders of you. I wasn't allowed to see you after you went to live in North Carolina, but still, you were never far from my thoughts. You know, Ashela, I never wanted to see your mother hurt and I wouldn't want to see you hurt now." Tanya came over and sat on the bed next to her. "Tell me something. Are you seeing Sam Ross?"

Ashela was feeling so many conflicting emotions. And her mother was on her mind too heavily to give Sam Ross a single thought.

"Why?" Ashela asked. "I mean, I noticed that you two didn't exactly hit it off."

227

"I just ask because I want you to be careful where he's concerned, honey. I've known Sam Ross for many years and I've found him to be nothing more than a cold-hearted bastard."

Though Tanya spoke with much venom in her voice, Ashela was reserving judgment. She didn't know what all the dynamics were concerning Tanya, Sam and even her mother. But she needed time to sort through her feelings.

"I met Sam a few years before I met your mother. I'd heard of him beforehand, who hadn't? He was a big exec at Werner even back then. Things were going well between us until . . . What I'm trying to tell you is that he and I became enemies the moment he tried to . . ." Tanya saw Ashela's narrowed look and said, "I know all of this seems like a bit much, Ashela. But where Sam Ross is concerned, just stay away from him, honey, he's bad news. Sam Ross uses people, namely women, and then throws them away at the blink of an eye. The man changes women like underwear and he has more recipes for screwing them over than Prego has for making its sauce."

They heard a door open and close on the first floor and then a woman's voice called out Tanya's name.

"Up here," Tanya yelled.

Seconds later a tall, beautiful woman stood in the doorway almost angrily. She was about to speak when she saw Ashela sitting on the bed.

"Sweetheart, this is Ashela Jordan. Charla's daughter."

Instead of advancing into the bedroom, she said from the doorway, "Has she come to claim her mother's things?"

Neither of them answered her. Certainly not Ashela who was stunned because she recognized the woman as a very famous actress. She'd even seen many of her movies. Ashela couldn't begin to fathom the notion that the woman and Tanya were lovers.

Ashela stood up. "Maybe I'd better be going, Tanya. I wouldn't want to distress your . . . guest."

The woman entered the room. "Please, don't leave on account of me. I'm sorry about my outburst. But you have to understand my point of view. You have no idea how difficult it is trying to live up to a dead woman's image."

Tanya interrupted her. "Sweetheart, please, Ashela doesn't need to hear this."

But the woman ignored Tanya and said to Ashela, "For years, I've been fighting Tanya to get rid of all this stuff. It's unhealthy the way she's hung on to them. Ever since Tanya found out you were in town, you and your mother are all she's talked about. When I saw you sitting on the bed, the first thing I hoped was that you had come to take it all away. I'm not an insanely jealous person—I just want what's best for Tanya. So I'm asking you to please take everything with you. Do what you have

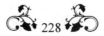

to, but help her to see that she can't continue to blame herself for what happened to your mother."

If Ashela had any doubts that the two of them were lovers, the lover's tiff they were now engaged in erased them.

"Can I speak to Tanya alone please?" Ashela noticed how the woman refused to speak Charla's name and she did not want her privy to what she now needed to say to Tanya.

By the time Ashela left, Tanya had agreed to part with Charla's things. She had cried horribly at first and Ashela had just held her, comforting her. She, too, had loved the same person, only for different reasons and in a different way. After she'd departed, Ashela felt strangely sad, but also strengthened in a manner that she couldn't quite define.

It was nearing three-thirty when she left Tanya's place. Sam wouldn't be picking her up until six-thirty that evening so Ashela went shopping. She felt the need to placate herself by buying a new outfit for tonight's affair, and maybe even some jewels to go along with it. Two hours later, she had spent close to seventy-five thousand dollars. Focusing on the enormity of her bill allowed her issues surrounding Tanya and her mother to slowly recede to the back of her mind.

Back inside her hotel room, she laid her purchases out on her bed. She sat on the opposite edge and with her elbows resting on her knees, she cupped her face in the palms of her hands. So many thoughts filtered through her mind that an eerie sadness enveloped her. She couldn't identify all of the reasons behind her sudden melancholy, but she did know they had a lot to do with her mother and grandmother.

Ashela fingered the magnificent Christian Dior, red silk evening gown that lay on the bed behind her. With its intricately beaded patterns, the dress' tab had been a mere six thousand dollars. The red sling-back evening pumps had cost a thousand and the Marquise, Princess-Cut diamond necklace and matching heart-shaped diamond earrings had cost upwards of sixty-five thousand dollars. Outwardly, she would look stunning for her date with Sam. But inwardly, her heart was burdened with an inexplicable grief. All the money in the world couldn't salve the wounds that she bore in her mind and heart. Internally, she grieved for the unredeemable time she'd lost with Charla and Julia. No amount of money could bring either back from the grave. And certainly, no amount of money could heal the seething, searing wounds that Charla and Julia had etched into one another's psyche.

Nor was there any sum of money that could erase the sudden feelings of insurmountable loneliness that converged upon Ashela. Her heart felt so heavy within her that her mind suddenly began to replay and recount all of the negative things that she had either witnessed or experienced in her lifetime. Before she knew it, she dropped to the floor. Huge sobs that had lain chained in dark isolation for

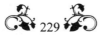

many years escaped her body. She cried not just for herself, but for the multitudes of people who, like herself, were hurting all over the world because of lost loved ones, unreconciled relationships, and irreparable estrangements that had been forged because of grave misunderstandings. Ashela's heart ached so profoundly that she found herself doing something that she hadn't done in years: She curled into a fetal position and prayed to God. She didn't want to work the rest of her life to accumulate hoards of money that she would never enjoy. She wanted her life to count for something. She wanted love and a family and above all, she didn't want to face the rest of her life alone.

***

Dressed in a wine and black Richard Tyler suit, Sam stepped off of the elevator and walked down the short hallway to Ashela's penthouse suite. He was running about five minutes late as he rang the doorbell.

Sam's whistle was loud and sharp as he closed the door behind him. He knew an expensive, designer gown when *he* saw one. Surveying her elegant but snugly fitting, off-the-shoulder ensemble, Sam said with amusement, "Well, go ahead and turn around so I can see just what we have here." With her jutting breasts and sweltering hips, she was all body.

Smiling, Ashela twirled around in a quick circle. "Do you like it?" she asked, extending her hands with her palms facing upwards.

"Do I like it? Woman, with this outfit, we *must* make a change of venue. And I know just the place to take you." Sam came and stood in front of her and, using his thumb, traced the outline of the diamond necklace that encircled her neck. He rested his thumb on her rapid pulse at the base of her throat. "Beautiful," he whispered before bending his head to kiss her lips.

Before his lips could touch hers, Ashela turned her face against his jaw. Sliding her hands upward along his jacket, she said teasingly, "If you kiss me, Sam, I'll have to re-do my lipstick and that might make us late."

"Who cares?" Sam replied, as he lowered his hands and clasped them around her waist. "You know, if you've changed your mind and perhaps don't feel like going anywhere . . . well, we could stay right here or maybe even go to my place. I can entertain you just as well as any Broadway play ever could."

Shaking her head, Ashela said with a smile, "Sam, I have no doubt that you could do just that. But do you really think I'm about to waste this outfit? You're taking me *somewhere* tonight, even if it's around the corner to McDonald's."

Standing before him, she looked so appealing and inviting that Sam felt the sudden urge to lift her into his arms, lay her on top of the bed and just . . .

Ashela could tell by the look in his eyes and by the way his grip tightened on her hips what direction Sam's mind was going in. She firmly unclasped his hands, saying, "Mr. Ross, may I remind you that you promised me a night at the theater? When I told you that I'd never before been to Broadway, you *promised*. And being

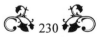

the honorable man of your word that I know you are, I'm sure that you're not about to renege on me now." Ashela felt the warmth of his hand in hers and knew that the best thing for the two of them to do was to leave her hotel room immediately.

"Let me get my purse," she told him before releasing his hand.

Sam watched her every move as she turned away.

Inside his limousine, he made sure that she sat next to him instead of far away. "Can I get you something to drink?" he asked. When she shook her head, Sam whet her curiosity by saying, "I received the invitation to where I'm taking you several weeks ago. So, if you can bear with me and try to fit me into *your* busy schedule on tomorrow evening, I promise to take you to Broadway. But for tonight, I think you'll enjoy where we're going even better."

Ashela knew he was being facetious. Though she tried to get him to reveal their destination, Sam remained tight-lipped.

Traffic slowed to a crawl as they neared Radio City Music Hall. Looking out of the window, all Ashela could see were flashing light bulbs as people got out of limousines in front of them. She nearly had her face pressed to the glass window as she strained to see out of it. Suddenly, Ashela recognized Debbie Allen.

"Look, Sam, there's Debbie!" Excited, Ashela turned to glance at Sam, but he only smiled slyly, as if he'd known Debbie would be there all along.

Catching his look, Ashela said, "Sam Ross, tell me what affair this is."

When she turned to glare at him, demanding an answer, Sam caught her off-guard and clasped his hand around the nape of her neck. He pulled her to him and kissed her slowly as though he'd been wanting to do it for some time.

There was genuine need behind the subtle urgency of Sam's kiss. His mouth was warm and demanding, signaling his desire for her. Melting against him, Ashela found herself clasping her arms around his neck, wanting him just as much in return.

When he finally released her, Ashela was scrambling to bring her dazed senses back under control, but Sam could easily discern the air of latent sensuality that enveloped and emanated from her.

"Sam, *now* look what you've done. I've got to hurry to get my lipstick together all over again. And look at you. You've got lipstick on your lips as well. Here, let me . . ." Ashela's whispery voice trailed off as she pulled tissue from her purse and wiped Sam's lips. For some reason, she couldn't quite look him in the eye yet, so she busied herself with her small compact as she freshened her lipstick.

No sooner had she pressed her lips together when a red-tunicked valet opened the door of the limousine, proffering his hand to help her exit. Red carpeting lined the curb of the street and stretched all the way to the entrance of the building. Steel gates were placed on both sides of the walk-way to the entrance. Screaming fans and photographers (held back by uniformed policemen) were on either side of the gates

straining to get a look at all of the entertainers and Hollywood movie stars as they walked by.

Ashela proudly slipped her arm through Sam's as they walked from the limo into the building.

"Hey, look! It's Sam Ross with Ashela Jordan! Over here, Sam! Look this way, Ashela!"

Blinding flashes of light bulbs went off as the paparazzi aimed their cameras in their direction. With a smile plastered to her face, Ashela was relieved when they finally reached the safety of the building, away from the glare of the cameras. Greeters arrayed in black tuxedos welcomed them as they made their way inside.

The function turned out to be the premiere of Steven Speilberg's latest film *Dancing On A Smooth Edge*, based on a story line from the book, *Preconceived Notions*. Debbie Allen, one of the producers who was actually starring in the movie, was present along with the entire all-star cast of characters: Morgan Freeman, Angela Bassett, Samuel L. Jackson, Wesley Snipes, Vanessa Williams, Lynn Whitfield, Lisa Raye, Morris Chestnut, and basketball superstar, Rick Fox. The two mystery guests were the actress and actor who were starring in the leading roles of Imagany Jenkins and Elliott Renfroe. A host of celebrities had come out in support of the movie's premiere.

As they mingled with the crowd, Ashela was content to remain by Sam's side. It felt good standing beside him and she loved it when he slid his hand possessively around her waist.

Before the movie's showing, Piper's champagne and other expensive wines and sparkling juices were served. Everybody was urged to serve themselves from the cornucopia of food that was available. A huge buffet with a magnificent ice carving of a five-foot swan was placed in the center of a long table, surrounded by Buluga caviar, crab, lobster, shrimp, and a variety of meats and salads.

By the time they had eaten and were seated in the theater awaiting the raising of the curtain, everyone was filled with a sense of anticipation. With Sam's arm resting over the back of her seat, Ashela was truly enjoying herself. From the onset of the movie's opening scene, she was riveted. She laughed, she cried and when the love scene between the lead characters finally unfolded, she grew decidedly uncomfortable. It was passionate, it was raw, it was tastefully vivid, and it was all too real.

Trying to appear unaffected by the heated embers the characters were creating on screen, Ashela had to physically restrain herself from squirming in her seat. She closed her eyes, not wanting to witness the way the characters were lighting up the screen with their fiery lovemaking. But even the sensuous sounds generated by their intimate coupling were too much for her to handle. She took a deep breath and tried to force herself to relax but couldn't do so because in her mind, the characters on screen had ceased to exist and it became she and Sam who were starring in their own

version of their own sensuous production. When Ashela felt Sam lightly caress her wrist, she nearly jumped out of her skin.

So aroused had she become that Ashela began quietly speaking and reasoning with herself. "Okay body. Yes, it is true that it's been a long time since you've made physical contact. And yes, it's true that you've never been quite as tempted by a man like you are by Sam Ross. And yes, I even know that the way Sam just touched you feels exceedingly good, but body, I'm telling you that right now, at this very moment, I need you to *sit down*, to *shut up* and not to embarrass me. I cannot allow you to willfully imagine yourself being with Sam as if you'd like to lick the very hair of his . . . Hey, hey, hey! Over here, body! Come back over here to the *left* side. I promise you, if you'll just behave, I will take care of you *as soon* as we get home. So please, please, please, just remain calm."

Ashela's mental soliloquy managed to quiet her senses and allowed her to refrain from making a complete idiot out of herself. Only then was she finally able to bring her focus back to the movie and its cast of characters.

When the picture was over, a thrilling euphoria seemed to permeate the building as people began to react to the movie. En route to their limousine, Black Entertainment Television stopped Sam and Ashela for an interview to get their reaction to the film.

Ashela wiped traces of tears from the corner of her eye as she searched for the words to describe it. "Dynamic, funny, and wonderfully romantic. It was just an awesome film."

Sam on the other hand was composed as he gave his opinion. "Powerfully dramatic. The ending was spectacular. It's definitely a must-see movie." As he spoke, BET's cameras were rolling. The two of them looked good together and though Ashela wasn't aware of it, Sam's stature and her near-weeping reaction made for good television footage.

Inside his limousine, the two of them spoke more about what they either enjoyed or disliked about the film, and about twenty minutes later the limo pulled to a stop on Park Avenue in front of the Fairmont Towers.

"This is my humble abode, Ashela. Will you come up for an after-dinner drink?"

Ashela's heart started racing inside her chest. She'd known that this moment would come. The problem was, even though she'd known it, she still wasn't prepared. A part of her wanted to say yes, but the other half of her knew that she should decline.

"Sam, I . . ." The beginning of an acute headache was starting to develop inside Ashela's temples. *How could she explain to him that it had been so long since she'd been with a man that she was actually nervous and scared?*

Sam could see that she was having a bit of a problem making up her mind. He relaxed, threw his arm over the seat and crossed his leg over his knee. "Did you know that I have two sons?"

Ashela shook her head. She didn't mind or question the sudden change of subject. She was grateful for it.

"Well I do. I have a fifteen year-old named Ronald and a thirteen year-old named Damael. I bring them here many times during the year so that I can spend as much time with them as I can. We also spend a lot of time in the Hamptons on Long Island, or in Massachusetts on Martha's Vineyard. But whenever I want to spend time with a lady-friend, I take her to a condo that I own in lower Manhattan. Never have I brought a woman back to my Park Avenue home. To be honest with you, Ashela, I'm not sure why I've invited you. So, you can come up if you'd like to, or if not, my driver can take us anywhere else you'd prefer to go."

Feeling reassured by his simple honesty, Ashela said, "I think I'd like to see your home, Sam. Maybe it'll reveal something about you that you haven't yet told me."

Sam's Park Avenue apartment was a beautiful, six- bedroom duplex. It had a manly decor to it and was deliberately bereft of a woman's touch. There was a slight chill inside the place and Sam slipped his jacket over her shoulders as he went to turn up the heat inside the apartment.

While he was gone, Ashela curled up on the soft, plush velvet sofa in his living room. And when Sam returned, he was carrying two flute-shaped wine glasses and a bottle of wine. He sat beside her and uncorked it, waiving away her refusal of the drink. "I've noticed that you're not a heavy drinker, but just try this. I think you'll like it. It's a very fine wine. Extremely light and delicate. Here, taste it." Sam poured her a glass and waited for her reaction.

Ashela took a sip and then another one. "It's very good, Sam. It tastes faintly of cranberries and peaches, yet it's not too sweet."

"Have you ever been to a wine tasting ceremony?"

"No, but I bet it would be fun. I'd probably wind up drunk as a skunk."

"No you wouldn't. The trick is not to swallow the wine but to just swill it around in your mouth so that you can sample the essence of the wine."

"I see. So you're a connoisseur, I take it?"

"I dabble every now and then. It also helps that I own shares in a wine manufacturing company. That's how I came to know all about the wine-making process."

Ashela held her glass out for him to refill it and pulled his jacket tighter around her. Sam refilled her glass and then rose to light the fireplace. Minutes later, small flames began to leap against the slowly kindling wood.

After stoking the fire, Sam left the room to wash the ashes and soot from his hands. He came back and assumed his seat on the sofa. It seemed only natural for Ashela to curl up against him, her back pressed to his chest. They talked for a long while thereafter, and even grew comfortable with the occasional silence that fell between them.

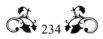

Neither of them knew who made the first move, but the sudden desire to make love to one another was strong. Maybe it was the way his hand rested possessively against the flat of her stomach, or maybe it happened when he started nuzzling the nape of her neck. But in the next instant, she was seated in his lap. He was kissing her and she was holding onto him.

Whispering, Ashela said, "I suspected I'd wind up in big trouble if I came back to your place, tonight."

Sucking her lips with his, Sam said, "Don't say that. You're not in any trouble."

"Yes I am, Sam. Right now, I can't even think straight. I barely know my own name."

"What's your name, baby?"

Ashela melted at the way he called her "baby." In a tiny voice, she whispered huskily, "I think my name is Sam. It must be, because Sam is all I can think about at this moment."

Sam laughed softly. "Talk to me, baby. Tell me how long it's been since you've been made love to."

His name became a whispered caress as she lightly trailed her tongue along his stubbled jaw. "It's been . . . years. Much longer than I'd care to admit. Are you offering to help solve my dilemma?"

"Sam Ross is at your service. Whatever help you need, Daddy aims to please."

Ashela slid herself alongside him on the sofa. She whispered to him, "What else will Daddy do for me?"

Her sexy voice whispering in his ear thoroughly aroused him. "Whatever you want. Just name it." Sam was already pulling her on top of him as he lay stretched out on the sofa. His hands found the hook at the back of her gown and slowly, he unzipped it. His hands stroked the silkiness of her skin.

Holding his face between her hands, Ashela said, "Sam, sweetie, do you know why we're just going to cuddle with one another tonight?"

As he nipped her playfully on her chin, Sam knew they were going much further than that. He knew he wouldn't call it a night until he had her underneath him begging him to give her exactly what she needed. But he bided his time and shook his head anyway.

"Because neither one of us came prepared for this night." Sam knew she was referring to birth control and he groaned into her neck. Knowing he couldn't have her in the manner he now desired, his aching need for her increased.

"But I'm going to take pity on you tonight, Sam. The last thing in the world I intend to do is leave you hanging. Do you know what 'Lap Dancing' is, Sam?" When he smiled, she knew that he did. "Then you also know the rules? No touching, Sam. I mean it. I can touch you, but you may not touch me. Got that?"

Sam slid his hands down to her hips and palm-squeezed her well-rounded buttocks. "What happens if I accidentally cheat? Can a man be condemned for making a simple mistake?"

Ashela loved the firm and demanding way in which he gripped and kneaded her buttocks. Just the feel of his strong hands caressing her body created havoc with her senses. "Sam Ross, you have no intentions of abiding by the rules, do you? Well, I know just the thing to ensure that no 'simple mistakes' occur." Ashela reached up and loosened the bow tie from his shirt and pulled it from around his neck. She said to him, "Put your hands behind your back."

Sam laughed when he saw that she actually wanted to tie him up. "I mean it, Sam." Ashela got off of him and made him sit up and put his feet on the floor. In the next instant, she hiked her six-thousand dollar dress up past her thighs and straddled him before whispering into his ear, "Come on, Daddy. Let me do you right." When she bit teasingly into the side of his neck, he melted and it was no problem getting him to clasp his hands behind his back. Ashela hurriedly and expertly tied his hands together tightly. Just as quickly, she unbuckled Sam's belt and unzipped his pants, pulling them open to reveal the whiteness of his underwear along with the imprint of his throbbing manhood.

Unable to resist the temptation, Ashela slid to her knees and lowered her head all the way down to lightly trace the outline of his manhood with the edges of her teeth. Sam pulsated as she nipped into his male hardness ever so gently. She left a lipstick-trail of teethmarks on his underwear when she finally lifted her head. Ashela raised herself off of the floor and stood in front of him, her figure spotlighted by the glowing embers of the cackling fires in the background. Slowly sliding her gown off her shoulders, it fell to the marbled floor in a heap around her ankles and she was left standing arrayed in her red silk, strapless bra and red panty-like stockings. Sam feasted his eyes upon her luscious breasts and hips.

Emboldened by the fact that she could touch him but that he could not touch her, Ashela used her own hands on her body as if they belonged to Sam. In a series of quick, supple movements, she gyrated her hips in front of him, getting close up to him. With her hands cupping her breasts, she slid them down her waist to her thighs and used them to quickly spread her legs for him as if she were squatting.

She turned around with her backside facing him and spread her legs. Ashela bent forward and leaned down to the floor, peering at Sam through her slightly parted legs. Quickly, she lifted her torso upward and spun around to raise her heel onto the back of the sofa. She placed her foot right next to his head, almost as if she were inviting him to drink from the fountain of her most secret part.

Just as quickly as the dance had begun, it ended. Because in a flash, Ashela lowered herself to straddle Sam and pressed herself tightly onto him, feeling his largeness underneath her. With her arms encircling his neck, she outlined his lips with her tongue. In a move that demonstrated her litheness, Ashela leaned back and

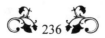

raised her legs onto Sam's shoulders, clamping his neck between her calves. Reaching up, she encircled his neck with her hands, pulling his head down to hers.

Sam was on another realm. As waves of desire filtered through him, he could feel the searing heat of her loins through his own underwear. He could only imagine how hot and moist she must be. Sam longed to taste her, but unable to do so, he satisfied himself with tasting her lips instead.

Ashela re-arranged herself, once again seated on his lap. Her bra unclasped in the front and unhooking it, she grasped her breasts and kneaded them in front of Sam's face. Lifting them and teasing her already hardened nipples.

The need to touch and possess her intensified. Abruptly, Sam had had enough of this "no-touching" game. He had to feel her with his own hands and he needed to taste her even as she continued to press herself downward, gyrating on top of him. But as he tried to unclasp his hands, he realized for the first time just exactly *how* expertly Ashela had bound him. Even with all his strength, he could not break the knot.

Knowing he was struggling to get loose, Ashela teased him further. She completely removed her bra before pushing him back hard against the sofa. Still straddling him, she turned around on top of him. But this time her backside was pressed against him.

At the feel of her hips and buttocks pressing into him, Sam groaned for mercy and called out her name. He could literally *feel* her through the bare nothingness of her silk stockings, and he knew she was wild and hot.

Ashela rested her palms on his knees and using her hips and her pelvic muscles, stroked him rapidly. The huge length of him throbbing hard against her had aroused her far beyond a turning point. So Ashela felt no shame as she gyrated and ground herself down on top of him until finally, she felt him climax underneath her. Still needing the same release for herself, she turned around and faced him once more, encircling his neck with her arms. Whispering into his ear the words she needed to hear that would help her reach her own orgasm, Ashela refused to cut Sam any slack until she finally slaked her own passions. Afterwards, she purred into Sam's ear as her body trembled with quaking responsiveness.

Feeling her relaxed state, Sam inhaled deeply before expelling a long release of breath. Shaking his head in wonder, he said softly, "Ashela, baby, untie me."

Ashela huskily whispered something unintelligible into his ear.

Sam wasn't sure, but he could have sworn she was speaking in Spanish.

"We have to go to your kitchen, Sam. The only way I can untie you is to cut it off."

"Woman, are you kidding me?"

Still feeling weakened and slightly drained, Ashela said, "No, sweetie. I'm dead serious. So let's do it before I fall asleep." She eased off of him and put back on her bra before helping him to his feet.

With his hands tied behind his back, Sam felt nearly ridiculous, almost like a hardened criminal in handcuffs as he led her into his kitchen. After she cut his bow tie from around his wrists, Sam rubbed and massaged them to bring back the circulation. "I think I need a drink. Care to join me?"

Dressed in nothing but her bra and stockings and high-heeled shoes, Ashela shook her head. "This is what happens, Sam Ross, when you tangle with a woman who hasn't slept with a man in a very long time. I know you had this 'I'll-treat-her-like-a-princess' concept going, and I'm really sorry I disappointed you. But as much as I wanted to live up to that 'princess' image, unfortunately, you just happened to unleash the beast in me. Try not to think too poorly of me, Sam. I'm only human. And at this moment, I'm also sleepy. So I'll be retiring to your bedroom now. You're welcome to join me, though. I promise you, Sam, I'll behave myself this time and I'll even be a *very* good girl."

Chapter Twenty-Four

shela awoke in Sam's bed a few short hours later. She'd slept fitfully, probably because she was in an unfamiliar bed. She was wearing one of his shirts and it hung low and loose on her body. Sam was nowhere in sight. Not that Ashela expected him to be. After he had shown her to his bedroom and offered her a shirt to sleep in, he had disappeared. As she sat up in the bed, Ashela felt irritated and her body was still tired. Possibly jet lag and the time difference had just caught up with her, but whatever the reason, Ashela just wanted to go back to her own hotel suite. She got up out of the bed and went in search of Sam.

She found him inside his living room, stretched out on the same sofa that the two of them had occupied earlier. Sam had picked her gown up off the floor and had laid it over a nearby chair. Ashela took a seat and pressed her knees together, her calves and feet spaced wide apart. She clamped her hands together and pushed them between her thighs. Though she was ready to leave, she didn't want to awaken Sam, so she just sat there looking at the banking embers of the fire.

Sam's eyes opened to find Ashela sitting in the chair not too far from him. She appeared to be lost in thought as she sat staring into the shadows. Sam bent his arm and rested his head in the palm of his hand. "Penny for your thoughts."

A dimple appeared in the left side of her cheek as she crooked a half-smile at him. "I thought you were sleeping."

"I was. Couldn't you sleep?" Sam glanced at his watch and saw that it was 1:30 in the morning.

Ashela shook her head. "I think I'll have to go back to my hotel if I plan on getting any sleep. Is your driver still outside?"

"I released him several hours ago. Is it urgent that you leave?"

"Not really, but look at you. You're sleeping on your own couch because of me. I didn't intend to put you out."

"You didn't, Ashela. The only reason I didn't sleep in the same bed with you was because I knew there'd be no way for me not to touch you. As a precautionary measure, I thought that by sleeping here, I'd safeguard us both."

Ashela turned back toward the fireplace. "Have you ever been dog tired but just unable to wind down and sleep? I haven't slept well since I arrived in New York. Too many memories, maybe. I can't wait to return to California." A note of longing crept into her voice.

Sam threw the comforter off of him and sat up on the couch. He stood and walked over to her, and stretched his hand out to hers.

"What?" Ashela asked him. She was conscious of his bare chest as he stood before her clad only in his pajama bottoms.

"I'm going to put you to sleep the old fashioned way, Ashela. Let's go." Ashela took Sam's hand and he led her back upstairs to his bedroom. She hesitated inside his doorway, but Sam released her hand and went to draw back the covers on his bed. He sat down and crooked his finger, beckoning her. "Come here, Ashela." Sam's voice was demanding.

She came and stood before him and he pulled her between his legs. She was naked beneath the shirt but she made no move to stop him from unbuttoning it. "We've already agreed that we wouldn't make love tonight, so I'm just going to help you get to sleep."

When her shirt fell to the floor, Sam took a moment to simply behold her nakedness before sliding beneath the covers and pulling her down onto the bed with him. He laid on his side and pulled her to him, with her back against his chest and her buttocks pressed into his loins. As she rested her head upon his out-stretched arm, Ashela unconsciously basked in the feel of his warm and strong body against hers. As he began to softly caress her body, she grew stimulated but was very relaxed. Just the feel of his large hands caused all tension to leave her.

Sam started rubbing his hand on her stomach in small circular patterns. His hand felt course against the softness of her skin. He gently eased his motions upward until he reached the small area between her breasts. When his hand cupped and squeezed one of her rounded globes, teasing her nipple, pleasure oozed and coursed through her veins. Ashela sighed in ecstasy as she melted against him. She could feel his largeness throbbing behind her, pressing into her. When his hand slid to her hip, Ashela was glad Sam was a man of his word, because if he had sought to have his

way with her, protection or no protection, she would have been powerless to stop him.

His knee pushed itself slightly against hers, forcing her legs apart, and when Sam's hand slid downward through her bushy pubic hairs, the pleasure was so intense that Ashela nearly curled up into a ball. Sharp, pleasurable sighs emitted from her throat area, but Sam held her tightly as he continued to press himself against her. By the time his middle finger delved into her steamy, creamy core, Ashela was all but begging him to finish her off. When Sam pulled his middle finger out of her, he raised it to her lips and guided it inside her mouth. As she sucked and twirled her tongue around his finger, he whispered into her ear, "That's it, baby. Taste it for me."

Suddenly, Sam's mouth was where his finger had once been. His lips were kissing hers as he turned her onto her back and slowly eased himself on top of her. Her legs widened on their own accord to accommodate him. With her breasts flattened against his chest, Sam ached to plant his throbbing manhood inside her. But he knew he couldn't, so he settled for palming her behind and imprinting himself against her. Sam wanted her to know just how much he had to offer her. And then, slowly but surely, he began to lower his upper body until he was between her legs and finally able to sample her warm, sweet moistness.

A very, very short time later, Sam was gripping and holding her hips as she convulsed against him. As he lifted himself alongside her once more, her arms encircled his neck. As if in thankful appreciation for the wonderful service rendered, Ashela gave Sam the kiss of a lifetime, lapping her juices from his lips and chin. And in what seemed like only seconds later, she was fast asleep.

***

When Ashela woke again, Sam was long gone. He had left a note pressed to the dresser mirror stating that his driver was waiting outside to take her anywhere she desired. He would track her down later. It was 9:30 a.m. as Ashela dressed hurriedly. She needed to get back to her hotel and change clothes for her eleven o'clock appointment with her attorney.

Inside Pete Corti's Madison Avenue office, Ashela's mind was only half tuned to what he was saying. The other half was another million miles away.

Finally she said irritably, "Sam, is it a good contract or not? All I need to know is whether or not there are any concessions that need to be made."

Pete came and stood in front of her. "Sam? As in Sam Ross? No, Ashela, it's me. Pete Corti, your attorney. You haven't been listening to a word I've been saying, have you?"

Ashela rolled her eyes contritely and shook her head at her obvious mistake. "I'm sorry, Pete. Please forgive me. My mind is totally in another place."

"Hangover?"

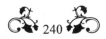

Ashela threw up her right hand. At that moment, she didn't care what Pete thought. All she knew was that she was feeling irritable.

"It's a good contract, Ashela. Werner Enterprises has been more than generous with you. I've negotiated several contracts for three other writers who'll be joining you in the Werner deal, and I must say that your contract is unique because it grants you a certain amount of autonomy. I'm pleased with it, and I think you should be too. Sign it and go home, Ashela."

Ashela picked up her coat and went to Pete's desk to sign the documents.

Back inside her hotel suite, Ashela started packing. She called American Airlines to change her flight arrangements and having done so, checked out of the hotel to head back to California.

***

The limousine service was awaiting Ashela when her plane arrived in Burbank. The chauffeur delivered her to her doorstep and she tipped him generously before unlocking the door to her home. She stepped inside, sweetly relieved to be back. *There's no place like home.* She unpacked her things right away, preferring to do it while she had the time rather than putting it off. The second thing she did was to strip naked and soak for a long time inside her jacuzzi. More than an hour later, she toweled herself dry and promptly went to curl up in her own bed. In no time at all, she was fast asleep.

The incessant ringing of the phone stirred Ashela hours later. When her answering machine didn't pick the call up, she answered it on the eighth or ninth ring. "Hello?" Her voice was still slightly groggy.

"You really know how to break a man's heart, don't you?"

"Sam." Ashela turned over onto her stomach as she whispered his name. "What have I done now?"

"Just blow me off like a leaf on a tree. Not only was I stood up again, but I'm having to fight off feelings of rejection."

"Sam Ross, you really know how to pour it on thick, don't you? I know you won't believe me, but I really did forget all about our date for the Broadway play tonight. All I could think of was getting back home and sleeping in my own bed."

"Was my company that unbearable?"

"Far from it, Sam. I just needed to get myself together and coming back home was the only way to do so." Ashela turned over onto her side, drawing her knees up. "It's nine o'clock here, Sam, and twelve midnight there. What are you doing up so late?"

"Would you believe that I miss my dinner partner?"

"Wow. For you to miss someone, that person must really be awesome."

"Oh, I think she is. But I'm still trying to figure her out, though."

"Maybe she's so simple that she doesn't have to *be* figured out."

"I don't think so. See, on one hand, she's all lace and satin. But then on the other, she's got a little street in her."

"Sporting a bit of a thuggish streak, is she?"

"Remember, those were your words, not mine."

"Doesn't matter. We're just calling a spade a spade, Sam. But yes. I'm all that, and so much more. But now, it's your turn to tell me something."

"Go ahead. Shoot."

"Don't you get tired of the 'different-girl-every-week' scenario? I mean, we're just talking here, Sam, so let's be real with one another. I'm a believer that when you share your affections with more than one person, all you're really doing is spreading yourself too thin. Mind you, I'm not judging you. But then, I guess I just don't get it. Surely you're not trying to be like these assholes who . . ." Ashela started snapping her fingers, trying to think of an example. "You know the one jerk I'm talking about. That brain-dead athlete who boasted of all the women he slept with?"

Sam laughed because he was aware of who she was referring to. Maybe it was because he knew that Ashela didn't want anything from him that he found himself wanting to open up to her. He thought of how for several years after he'd gotten divorced, he had used women so that he wouldn't have to feel alone. And then, they had became almost like a habitual drug. He seemed to always be searching but never finding fulfillment and so the women had become a sea of faceless, nameless people who all had lent a hand in helping him eliminate his loneliness. But he didn't tell Ashela that. All he said was, "I don't know if there's a woman out there who could put up with me."

"Is that a round-about way of saying you're not a monogamous person, Sam? Okay then, fine, but what about AIDS? Don't you worry about the multitude of diseases out there?"

"I'm always mindful of them, Ashela. That's why I never sleep with a woman without a condom. Is that why *you've* remained celibate for so long?"

"That's part of it. The other part is that I stopped sleeping around because I felt empty and unfulfilled whenever I awakened next to some stranger who I knew I wouldn't want to see again. I just made the decision one day that I'd rather go it alone than have to deal with all the emotional drama and baggage that you get as a consequence of allowing someone to be intimate with you. So I've been celibate for some years now, Sam. And if I can do it, anybody can do it. All it is to me is proof that I've conquered the senseless desire of needing to jump in and out of different people's beds just to satisfy a fleeting hunger or a passing feeling of loneliness."

"And here I was thinking that you were afraid to trust because of a past failed relationship."

"Sam, you're so busy dissecting women in an attempt to find out what angle they're coming from, that you never get to know any of them."

"All women want something, Ashela."

"You're right, we do. But look at it like this, Sam: All *people* want something. And that *something* is that we all desire to be loved. So much so that we willingly subject ourselves to a series of dead-end relationships and one-night stands just to be able to say we're 'in love.' Everybody's looking for love, Sam. The trouble is, half the people look for it in the wrong places and the other half wouldn't know what it was if it jumped out and bit them."

"And I take it that you're one of the rare people who *do* know what love is?"

"It's not so much that I know what it *is* as what it *isn't*. I'm no expert, Sam, and I've never taken any psychology classes, but I do enjoy observing people. In my opinion, love isn't the way you're able to make my heart beat faster whenever I see you. Nor is it the way I respond to you sexually when we're together. Ugh, ughn. All that is is straight-up, plain old-fashioned chemistry. I believe love is work, Sam. Real love, that is. Think about it. When couples with wonderful relationships make it happen for one another, they don't do so based on luck. Nothing and no one becomes successful based on *luck*. And so it is with relationships. You have to *work* on being happy, Sam. I'll give you a perfect example, you've spent time around Debbie and Norm. Haven't you noticed the way the two of them act like little kids whenever they're together? I mean, they're so *into* one another. And it's genuine and sincere. That's why many people can't receive the fact that they're so happy with each other. But they work at it, Sam. I've spent time with them, and whenever I'm in their presence, I find myself saying, *that's the kind of relationship I want.* The kind where I want to make my man feel like a king and because of it, he's striving to make me feel like his queen.

"But romancing one another is an easy thing to do at the beginning of a relationship because you're both trying to make a good impression. The problem comes, Sam, when people fail to parlay those feelings over a prolonged period of time. After the newness wears off, people don't try as hard as they once did in the beginning. And then before you know it, disappointment sets in and they're taking one another for granted. That's where the 'work' part comes in, Sam. It takes commitment to keep a relationship fresh. And whenever you bring children and other emotional factors into the mix, well, then you've got to work that much harder."

"It sounds good, Ashela. But what happens when the relationship becomes lopsided, with one person giving more than the other?"

"I'd say that somewhere along the way, there's been a breakdown in communication. One or the other party has stopped expressing effectively what it was that each needed. It's like the wife who yells at her husband for spending too much time at work or with his friends, or even for watching too much television. What she's really trying to say is, 'I need attention, too, and I want you to spend some of that quality time with me.' The problem in such a situation is what the wife *didn't* say. We, women *and* men, sometimes expect our significant other to read our

minds. No matter how you look at it, Sam, it's still a breakdown in communication. Severe breakdowns don't have to take a long time to develop, Sam. They can start overnight, but then in a few days or weeks become huge chasms that suddenly seem too hard to overcome. People often forget what it was about the other person that they fell in love with in the first place. You want to know why *I* believe men cheat, Sam?"

Sam was enjoying just listening to her. "Tell me."

"Because they like the way the other woman makes them feel, and more importantly, they like the way *they* feel about themselves when they're with that other woman. Almost as if they're saying, 'I feel good about *me* when I'm with you.' I'm no expert, Sam, but I really believe that most problems boil down to communication or the lack thereof. When people say, 'we just grew apart or this happened or that happened' what they're really saying is that 'we just lost the desire and ability to communicate.' You show me a relationship that fell by the wayside and I'll show you a couple whose ability to communicate with one another became impaired. Somewhere, a breach occurred in the channel that once allowed them to be receptive to one another. Money, affairs, in-laws, children, simple misunderstandings, you name it, Sam, it all boils down to communication."

Ashela turned over onto her back and rested her arms behind her head. "You know, Sam, men are such visual creatures. You all see an image of a woman who looks good, or maybe has a body like "bam" and your attention span is captured immediately. But the second you tap into a woman's mind and discover her thoughts, wham, you're gone. Most men don't want to think in terms of a relationship. They want to be made to feel good and then go about their business. But in the back of their minds, they're searching for that elusive woman who's going to slay them in bed and then mother and support them outside of it."

"I'm not sure that I agree with that."

"Don't sweat it. Consider everything I've just told you as bits and pieces of 'Ashela-ology.' Just my own twisted brand of thinking."

"Okay, Dr. Ruth. If you're so knowledgeable about men and relationships, how come you're not married or even in a committed one yourself?"

"Because I'm simply waiting for the right one to come along. I'm patiently waiting for my king, Sam. That man who's feet I'll be proud to sit at. I'm not looking for sex, Sam. I've become an expert at satisfying myself. That's why I've been able to go for years without laying with a man. I need more than just brief interludes filled with melodramatic moments. I want what Debbie has, and like her, I want what I want all wrapped up inside one man. Not two or three. Just one. Plus, there's my music, Sam. I've often heard it said that music reveals the hidden psyche or soul of a person. It must be true because by emptying *my* soul into my music, I'm able to love through my songs. That's why I *really* enjoy writing love ballads. Of all the songs that I've written, Sam, do you realize that most of the ones that have reached number

one on the charts have been love ballads? Not all of them, mind you, but the majority of them."

Sam was impressed, but he wanted to get back to what they were talking about before. "Ashela, did you know that I do a great impression of a king? Just call me King Sam."

Ashela laughed. "Sweetheart, I *know* that you do. That's why you've got so many women losing their minds trying to become your queen. Ever met a person, Sam, who brightens a room by *leaving* it? Well, you're on the opposite end of the spectrum. You light a room up with your presence. Everyone wants a piece of Sam Ross. But there's also a cruel streak in you, Sam. I'll tell you how I know it. I watched you with that model when we were at Debbie's party. I watched the way you toyed with her. She wanted to be seen with you and you just wanted to screw her. I said to myself, 'I'll bet any amount of money that he sleeps with her tonight, and afterwards, I doubt that she'll ever hear from him again.' And Sam, I'm sure that I'm sure that I'm sure, that if you didn't bed that woman the same night, then you've already slept with her by now. That's why, the next day, when you sent me all those flowers, they didn't mean a thing to me. Because, as attracted to you as I was, Sam, I didn't want to be just another notch on your belt."

Sam was at a loss for words because Ashela had hit the nail on the head. Just as she'd called it, he *had* slept with the model that very same night. And even now, he couldn't even remember the woman's name. She'd called his office numerous times after the fact, but Sam had never returned her calls. Ashela was on it, all right. Or was it that he was just so obvious?

"When Kyliah shared with me what happened with you and Arron—how she overheard you two on the phone—I vowed not to speak to you again. But then, here you come sashaying through the door with another bunch of roses in your hand and what do I do but melt all over you. So you see, Sam, on one hand, while I can be just as . . . predictable . . . as other women, on the other hand, I'm waiting for the man who makes me want to work at a relationship. He'll be someone whom I can call . . . 'Daddy.' Not that I'm assuming that you're even applying for the position, Sam, but I'm not so sure that you're the one. You don't strike me as the 'one-woman' type of man. But I will say this in your favor, Sam. You don't wear an earring in your ear. And that, my friend, is requirement number one."

Sam took a deep breath. "Well, what possibly is there left for me to say except that I can't wait to see you again, Ashela Jordan."

"What? You mean, even after I've talked your head off and you've discerned that I might be missing a lube or two, you still want to see me again? Well, gol-lee gee! Methinks the man likes me!"

Sam smiled at her silliness. "Yes, I think so, too. So, when can I see you again?"

"When are you coming back to California?" Ashela's voice was challenging. New York wouldn't see her again for quite some time.

"In about a week or two."

"Make it two weeks. And Sam, I want you to do something for me. It may be difficult for you, but I want you to try it anyway. I want you to fast for me, Sam. Not a food fast, but a sexual fast. Don't even *touch* a woman until you see me again. During these next two weeks, I want you to build up an appetite for me, Sam. I want it to be that the next time you see me again, you'll be bursting with anticipation. And if you feel like you can't make it, well then, you just call me. I'll take you on a trip to the moon right over the phone.

"Remember how aroused you had me last night, Sam? I couldn't even think straight. Well, that's how I want you to be when you see me again. If somebody asks you what your name is, I want you to be thinking about me so hard that before you know it, you'll be telling people that *your* name is Ashela Jordan."

A lopsided smile blanketed Sam's face. "Okay, Ms. Jordan, that's all fine, well, and good, but tell *me* more about this phone thing. I could stand a trip to the moon right now."

In a low, husky, and sexy voice, Ashela whispered, "Could you, Daddy? Then tell me what it is you want. Does my baby want some pussy?"

Sam's eyes widened as he swiftly took a deep intake of breath. As his insides tightened, he could tell right away that by the end of their conversation, he'd be able to notify NASA that *he* had found a short-cut to the moon.

Chapter Twenty-Five

n Tuesday evening, Ashela had just finished up in the recording studio with Kashif and was making the journey from L.A. back to her home in Malibu. Over the next three days, she was scheduled to spend time working with R. Kelly on an album that the two of them were putting together for a motion picture being released by Mandalay Films. Ashela knew that as soon as the word got out that she had signed a new deal with Werner which prohibited her from working with artists outside the Werner label, she would be swamped with last minute calls from people wanting to avail themselves of her services.

She was inside her bedroom removing her high-heeled shoes when the phone rang. She saw by way of the Caller I.D. that it was Kyliah. "May I help you?"

"How ya doin', my sistah?"

"Hey, I'm hangin' on strong." Ashela sat on the bed and began to massage her feet.

"Apparently you are. But one would *think* you could at least call a person and let them know you're back in town. Oh, I forgot. I'm the low man on the totem pole, so I

don't have the luxury of being kept informed of your whereabouts. I have to find out from other people that you're back on the coast."

"Okay, I stand corrected. My bag, so sue me."

"Hmph. I might just do that. For emotional deprivation. You don't know how to pick up the phone and put a call in? Sheeze! After all the years we've been friends, to think this is the thanks I get?"

Ashela was busy reading between the lines. "Kye, maybe you should just tell me whatever it is you're trying to say. Is this the part where we need to have one of those heart-to-heart chat things?"

"I was hoping you could tell *me* what's up. After all, I'm the one who got stuck with answering all the questions when I didn't have a clue about what was really going on."

"Are you going to tell me what this is about, or do I just need to hang up until you get *yourself* together?"

"What it's about, chump, is that I had to field several calls from people wanting to know if you and Sam Ross were an item. Word is already on the street that the two of you are thick as thieves. I just thought that if anybody should have been the first to know, it should have been me. I thought we were like that and all." Kyliah was pressing her first two fingers together and waiving them in the air.

"Well, actually, if there had been something to report, I would have reached out to you. But then, as a matter of fact, I did try calling you a couple of times and you weren't around. So who's fault was that?"

"Then where were you Saturday *and* Sunday night? I know you weren't in your room cause I kept trying your number well into the wee hours. Not that you bothered to retrieve your messages, I'm sure."

"Well, Mother Dearest, it just so happens that I was invited to several after-parties. Even *I* have to occasionally hobnob and network with the jet-setting crowd."

"Okay, Ash. It's obvious I'm not getting any straightforward answers here, so let me just bust you out. Sheila Taylor called from Vibe magazine claiming that she'd heard from an extremely reliable source at BET that not only were you and Sam Ross spotted dining *very* cozily at B. Smith's after your concert on Saturday night, but then on Sunday evening at the premiere of *Dancing On A Smooth Edge*, the two of you *supposedly* were seen sticking together tighter than crazy glue on a hair weave. But wait, that's not all, missy. Then the one and only Maggie Z. calls from the L.A. Times wanting to know if I had the low-down or maybe a four-one-one scoop for her to print in her Sunday gossip column."

Ashela had long since stopped massaging her feet. She sat straight up in the bed, totally at a loss for words. At that precise moment, she could have been bought *and* sold for a penny.

"That's okay, dahlin', you can close your mouth now. I must admit that *my* mouth was hanging open for a long time too. But, being the dependable girl-Friday that I am, once again, I covered for you like I always do."

Ashela groaned. "What did you tell them, Kye?"

"I said I covered for you, didn't I?"

"Kyliah, I'm asking you: *What* did you tell them?"

"Calm down, please. Seeing that I didn't even warrant the benefit of a phone call to apprise me of the sudden turn of events in your life, what was I supposed to tell them?"

Ashela whispered in a barely discernible voice, "I'm only going to ask one more time, Kye. *What did you tell them?*"

"You know, Ash, I really need some time to try to remember exactly what it was that I told them. Just give me a moment to . . ." Suddenly, the line went dead. Ashela had hung up on her in the middle of her sentence.

Undaunted, Kyliah whistled a tune as she re-dialed Ashela's number. And of course the line was busy. The shrew obviously had taken her phone off the hook.

Ashela was still sitting on her bed, stunned. She knew she shouldn't have been, not with today's technology and how everybody's business was an open book. But the lightning-fast way in which Sheila and Maggie Z. had gotten the goods on her and Sam was still disconcerting. All she'd done was have dinner and attend a movie premiere with the man. Well, maybe she'd done just a *little* more than that. But even so, it was still her business. What if she hadn't wanted the whole world to know about it?

Kyliah tried Ashela's line again and surprisingly got through to her. "We seemed to have somehow gotten disconnected, but I ain't mad atcha, so go ahead, give me the four-one-one scoop."

"Like you did when I was trying to find out about you and Arron?"

"Ashela, Ashela, Ashela. I thought we had matured to the point where we could let by-gones be by-gones. Arron is history, so why are we still discussing him?"

"Maybe because I want to remind you of how you left *me* out in the cold when I wanted details about *your* love life."

"Okay. So you've reminded me. *Now*, may we move on to bigger and better things? So it's a 'love-life' that we're singing about these days, is it? Instead of telling Sheila and Maggie that you and Sam were just good friends, maybe I should have spiced it up a bit. Is there anything more I should know in case someone *else* calls?"

"Kye, I guess I'm just not ready to talk about Sam right now and I definitely wasn't ready for the world to know about us. But enough about Sam. Let's talk about the Werner deal."

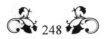

Kyliah had caught the "us" in Ashela's statement. "Ugh, ughn. Not so fast. How could you even think that you could appear *anywhere* in the public domain with Sam Ross and *not* have the rag-mags find out about it? That's a sudden case of intellectual near-sightedness on your part, isn't it? Look, Ash, if you don't want to discuss Sam, so be it. But why take me all the way around the mulberry bush just to tell me that?"

"Probably for the same reasons that you couldn't come right out and tell me that you didn't want to discuss Arron Davenport. Or, is this simply a case of the pot calling the kettle black? When I'm ready to talk about Sam and whatever my thoughts or feelings are toward him, you'll be the first to know."

"Got it." Kyliah could tell that Ashela was getting testy so she dropped the subject. "So back to the business end of things. There's an article in today's L.A. Times about the deal with Werner Enterprises. It's written from a 'devil's advocate' point of view. It starts out by lauding Sam as a shrewd and hard-nosed businessman who's known for his consultant-management of the top superstars. The article even goes on to list the names and salaries of several artists whom he's been able to snatch away from other labels and woo over to Werner.

"Listen to this: 'Dynamic deal maker, Sam Ross, is once again blazing trails and setting the music industry upside down with his dazzling creativity. With the same uncanny business acumen he uses in cutting deals and negotiating mega-superstars' recording contracts, Ross has begun to make acquisitions by purchasing majority shareholdings in eight of the ten independent labels. While Ross is to be commended for single-handedly parlaying rap music into the phenomenon that it has evolved into today, has the ultra-rich music mogul gone too far in his bid for control of the music mecca? Our industry sources have learned that Ross is preparing to corner the music market by consorting with the top music writers and lyricists under the Werner label and barring them from writing for anyone not under the Werner umbrella. If this monopoly materializes, how will the major and few remaining independent labels survive?' There's more here, but I'm afraid the rest of the article is not so complimentary."

"Fax me a copy of it. I want to read it."

"Done. Another thing, earlier today I fielded several calls from industry insiders wanting to confirm whether you were part of the Werner deal. They admitted to being taken aback by the notion that they wouldn't be able to utilize your services under the terms of the Werner contract. I'm also getting a barrage of calls from agents and managers who're also concerned about booking you before the contract goes into effect."

"I knew this would happen. That's why I lobbied to have until the beginning of the year before the contract took effect. That gives us a good six months to tie up any last minute loose ends."

"Well, at least you'll be able to fulfill your current contractual obligations. I'll comprise a list of artists whom I think you'll want to work with before year's end. One last thing to cover. Pamela, Stevens called. She's the producer for Tavis Smiley's talk-show on BET. They want to put together a show with you, Sam, Tony Gray and Babyface to talk about how the Werner deal will impact the music industry. I've got to tell you, Ashela, there aren't going to be a lot of happy campers outside of Werner Enterprises who'll want to see Sam's deal get done. I just hope things don't get ugly."

"We'll just have to deal with it, Kye, even if it does. Unfortunately, this is the age of 'me first' and 'who cares as long as I get mine' attitudes. In the long run, I'm just looking out for me. What I think people are overlooking is the fact that the Werner deal is going to open up the market and make way for a slew of new writers and lyricists—people who otherwise might not get a chance to showcase themselves. But now, with the big-named writers tied up in one segment of the market, it's going to open some doors and force many of the artists to give these new writers a try. Mark my words, Kye. Since everybody is always on the lookout for fresh, new material, by the start of the new year, it's definitely going to be a writer's market."

"So do you want to do Tavis's show?"

"Let me talk to Sam first. I need to know how much he wants to reveal to the public about the deal. Let Pamela Stevens know that you'll get back with her shortly. We definitely want to do everything we can to keep Tavis smiling."

Kyliah was far from finished with talking about Sam. "So you and Sam are like that now, huh? Tighter than a flea's butt and closer than two peas in a pod. All I know is that you flew to New York over the weekend for a concert and now that you're home, all you can seem to talk about is consulting Sam Ross for this or talking to him about that. I guess you just have to forgive me because there seem to be a lot of gaps and holes in the story that I'm trying to piece together. And if I don't seem to be comprehending it all that well, well then, I'm sure you can understand where I'm coming from."

Ashela knew Kyliah was irritated by her tight-lipped stance. "Kye, if it was all that, I'd still be in New York and not here in California."

"Mmmm, I don't know about that. I happen to know how low your tolerance level *is* for good ol' New York. Just tell me this: Did you sleep with him?"

"Kyliah, Kyliah, Kyliah. You of all people should know that you can't believe everything you hear and then only half of what you see."

"I think I'm just miffed because I had to hear it from someone else instead of from you. And you still didn't answer my question. Did you sleep with Sam Ross?"

"Technically, Kye, the answer to your *very* personal question is both yes *and* no."

"So now you're the queen of double-talk?"

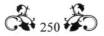

"You know, Kye, I feel like *I'm* dancing on a smooth edge here and it's been too long of a day. So on that note, I'll catch you tomorrow."

Kyliah threw both her hands up in a "I'm through with it" gesture and said, "Then tomorrow it is."

***

The ensuing weeks saw Sam don his fireman's hat and cape. He seemed to be spending an inordinate amount of time in board meetings as a result of the writer's consortium he had put together. Sam had anticipated the sudden fallout he was now receiving from foes and competitors alike. His opponents had chosen to thwart him by using the media to voice their opposition to his new-found alliance. But despite their insidious verbal campaign, Sam's spin doctors were already launching their own counter-attack. Putting the plan together had been a brilliant, strategical ploy on his part that would leave all the rival labels reeling, thereby, guaranteeing Werner's foothold on the music industry for many years to come. Sam knew he would do whatever it took to bring the merger to fruition.

The hypercritical backlash generated by his adversaries' negative press about him would have devastated a lesser man. But Sam had been graced to handle the resulting turmoil. To relieve the mounting stress, he worked out in his private gym and when he found himself working well into the night, he even slept in his office. His office contained a full-sized bathroom and his walk-in closet was filled with tailor-made Giorgio Armani, Ralph Lauren, Donna Karan, Ermenegildo Zegna, Prada, Richard Tyler and Hugo Boss suits.

By the end of his second week in New York, when he was due to return to California, Sam knew he was too swamped to make the trip.

Women were another form of stress relief for him. But because of the pledge he had made to the delectable Ms. Jordan, he refrained from his normal dietary supplement. Much to his surprise, Sam could say that he was enjoying the budding relational aspect of their acquaintance. And as badly as he wanted to see her, he would savor and prolong their upcoming "meeting" for a few more days.

***

Arron Davenport was in deep trouble and he knew it. In the three weeks since his return to Boston, he had been chasing unsuccessfully—and among Arron's peers, "chasing unsuccessfully" was a cardinal sin. "Chasing" was what he and all the other men he knew did to hasten a woman's exit from their lives while ushering another one in. But only this time, the usual fail-proof process wasn't working. Arron couldn't sleep, he was extremely irritable, and at times, couldn't even think straight. All this despite the fact that he had submerged himself in his work.

It didn't help matters any that Kyliah had not bothered to call him at all, and on the one occasion when *he* had broken down and called her, she hadn't even returned his call. At work, Arron found himself feeling that hopeful tinge whenever his phone rang. But it was always a business-related call. Worse yet, it would be some other

woman whom he didn't feel like being bothered with. The problem was that all the women he'd seen since his return to Boston somehow fell into that category. He'd had two dates in the last twenty two days (but who was counting?) and had turned down far more.

Arron likened his situation to being offered a blueberry muffin when what he really craved and wanted was blueberry pie. Sometimes, there was no substitute. Outside, it was a clear and beautiful summer day in Boston. He stood up from his desk and walked over to the window, leaning against it with his arms folded and his ankles crossed. From his vantage point on the eighth floor, he could see all the way down to the cobbled stone pavement that lined Briers Square. Arron glanced over at the pile of papers on his desk and then at the phone which sat next to them. In spite of himself, he walked over to the phone, picked up the receiver and dialed Kyliah's number.

***

Kyliah was swamped by a surge of calls from all over the country. Many were from the media, who were trying to get to Ashela with questions about the Werner deal. But most of the calls were from frantic agents and artists alike trying to book time on Ashela's schedule. Kyliah was just about to switch the line so that all calls would be forwarded to the messaging service when she decided to take one last call for the day.

"Five, two, eight, nine." There was nothing but silence and Kyliah wondered if the caller had dialed the wrong number. And then, the person finally said hello and his voice was sweet music to her ears.

As much as Kyliah had inundated herself in her own work trying to forget about Arron Davenport, knowing that it was him on the other end of the line tugged at her heart-strings. Her eyes closed longingly as she lowered her head to shake it slowly from side to side. Kyliah's heart had melted the moment she heard him speak.

When Arron said, "I was wondering if you were holding up any better than I was," sweet relief flooded her senses.

In a soft voice, Kyliah managed to reply, "I didn't know that you cared."

"But I do, and if you had taken the trouble to return my call, you would have known that."

"Maybe, Arron, you had the best intentions of calling me, but you and I both know I haven't heard from you since the night you left my home."

"Kyliah, that's not true. I called you last Friday afternoon. But your answering service picked up and said the office was not available. I left my name and number and then never heard back from you. So here I am, now, sitting here holding my shredded heart in my hand."

Kyliah smiled. "No. Not you, Arron Davenport. I'm not so sure that you have a heart."

"Kyliah, there's only one way I know of to convince you. Have you ever been to Boston?"

***

It was fast approaching ten o'clock as Ashela made the evening trek through Malibu Canyon. The drive just off I-101 was one of the most breathtaking scenic routes in Los Angeles. A wave of brilliant colors washed the night sky. It was the beauty of the mountains and the surrounding area that helped make her long drive such a tranquil and surreal experience.

Ashela pulled into her garage and entered her home. The first thing she did was check her machine to see if there were any calls from Sam. There were none and she was unable to mask the quick flicker of disappointment. Still needing to unwind from her day-long recording session, she poured some cranberry-grape juice into a flute-shaped wine glass and went out onto her verandah. Setting the glass on the wicker table, she walked to the end of the deck and leaned against the wooden rail. Ashela wrapped her arms around herself as she deeply inhaled the smells from the nearby sea. As gentle breezes floated over her, a feeling of restlessness nipped at the edges of her senses—an inherent longing which she was reluctant to define.

It would be early evening on the East Coast. But regardless as to the time, Ashela knew her restlessness would not dissipate until she had at least spoken with Sam. She went inside to retrieve her cordless phone and came back outside to dial the 800 number that he had given her. She was disappointed when she got his paging system, but she left her name and number anyway before hanging up. She grabbed her wine glass and drained the remaining juice in one gulp. If she couldn't have what she really wanted, she'd capitalize on her jitteriness by channeling her energy into creativity. There was no better time for her to write a new song.

Four hours later, Ashela was still strumming away on her baby grand, her fingers sliding, gliding, and flashing over the ivory keys. Humming and occasionally whispering the words, she'd stop only to jot down several strings of notes into her songbook. Many times she would close her eyes and tilt her head downward, as if lost in deep concentration. When she completed the love song, she felt that it would be another colossal hit. But she would make it an early Christmas and birthday gift to her good friend Vesta.

She showered and changed into a black lace teddy and was lying on her bed flipping through a Harper's Bazaar magazine when the phone rang. Hoping it was Sam, Ashela snatched up the receiver. "Hello?"

"What are you doing up at this early hour?" Sam asked.

Ashela relaxed when she heard the sound of his voice. "Sleep, my friend, does not define us good people out here on the West Coast. *We're* too busy doing things. Unlike you East Coast folks who keep bankers' hours, that is. How are you?"

"Busy, baby. Just trying to fight off the wolves."

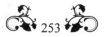

Her heart did a somersault at the way he called her "baby." *Fool that I am,* Ashela thought.

"I figured as much. You've been in the papers quite a bit lately. It ain't easy is it, sweetheart?"

"If it were, everybody would be doing it. The deal will get done, though. With or without opposition. Right now, it's still stinging the competition and they're all crying foul because they didn't think of the concept first. But, they're learning. They now *know* they have to get up early and stay up late to hang with the big dog."

Ashela shook her head. "Sam Ross. Always on the cutting edge preparing for that next major deal. Admit it, Sam, it's the thrill of the hunt that you enjoy. Well, what happens *after* the hunt is over? Agh, don't answer that. I already know the answer. When you slay one giant, you simply move on to the next. And that's the good thing about New York, isn't it, Sam? There's always a new giant to be slain."

"It's very similar to you and your songwriting, Ashela. The same reason you don't stop writing when one of your songs hits number one on the charts, is why I keep doing what I do. What we do has ceased to be work for both of us and the issue of money was solved long ago."

Ashela was glad that Sam had spotted the victory for his new deal. She was happy for him. But it still didn't do anything to ease *her* craving. "So when are you coming back to L.A.?" Enough about business.

Sam's voice deepened. "When do you want me to come to L.A.?"

Ashela remained quiet, as if in thought. An intense *hunger* for him had crept over her. She had an insatiable need to touch him, to hold him, to hear him, *to feel him* . . .

"I wouldn't want . . . anything . . . to get in the way of your business, Sam."

Sam could hear the slight hesitation in her voice and he knew he would capitalize on her vulnerability. "But?" he asked, almost encouragingly.

"No buts, Sam. I'd just really like to see you again." *Why was admitting that so hard?*

The soft firmness in her voice caused a silky thread to weave it's way through his body, all the way to his loins. "So when I see you tonight, Ms. Jordan, where are you taking me?"

"Sweetheart, if you get here tonight, I'm not taking you anywhere. You'll be right here with me, held tightly under lock and key. You'll dine a sumptuous meal a la carte, compliments of chef Jordan. You'll sample the fairest wines of Cordon Bleu. And your dessert . . . my king . . . Well, let's just say that your dessert will be sweeter than the honey from a honeycomb."

Sam's toes curled rigidly inside his Gucci leather house slippers. "Woman, good *googlee ma-golly*! Baby, I'm hungry right *now*! Isn't there *anything* you can do for a starving man before the main meal?"

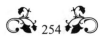

Laughing at him, despite herself, Ashela shook her head. "No. No, baby, I'm afraid there isn't. You'll just have to get here and experience it for yourself. Just be sure to be on time. Oh, and Sam? Be hungry, darling. Be *very* hungry." Ashela couldn't help herself. She started singing the lines from *Get Here*, a hit she had written specifically for Oletha Adams.

You can reach me by railway . . .

You can reach me by Trailways . . .

I don't care how you get here, just get here if you can . . .

"Ashela, I'm only surprised you don't realize that I'm *already* there with you. I may not be with you physically, but trust me, baby, I'm with you in spirit."

Part Six

Lover's Lane

"Let those love now,
who never loved before;
Let those who always loved,
now love the more."

– Thomas Parnell

"The course of true love never did run smooth."

– William Shakespeare

Chapter Twenty-Six

board his private Gulfstream jet, Sam was pouring over a host of documents that required his immediate attention. He anticipated that his stay in California would be for two weeks at most. But during that time, there was still much work to be done on a multitude of deals that he had going simultaneously.

It was noon pacific mountain time when his plane landed at the private airstrip. Sam stepped into the waiting limousine and instead of going to his home in Hollywood Hills, he had his driver take him to his offices on Wilshire Boulevard.

"Good afternoon, Mr. Ross." Surprised greetings and glances were thrown his way as Sam walked through the building heading for the executive suites. Normally, whenever he traveled to either office, the news of his impending arrival filtered through the company grapevine faster than a speeding bullet. But this time, Sam had informed no one—not even his own secretaries, so no one had prior knowledge of his plans. But Sam knew the moment the elevator doors closed, people would be circulating the news of his arrival frantically, especially since it was Friday when everybody either wanted or planned to leave early.

"Hello, Mr. Ross. Is there anything you need, sir?" Lee Ann stood ready with her tablet and pencil in hand. She knew better than to say that she had had no idea he was coming. Or, that she had intended to leave early herself.

"Hi, Lee Ann. I'll be dictating several letters that must go out immediately. I'll give you the tape as soon as I'm done."

Inside his office, Sam made light-work of the letters and documents that needed to be overnighted. There were also many calls that he had to return. Several hours later, he left a message on Claudette's machine letting her know that he was in town, and that if she didn't have anything planned, he'd like to pick the boys up tomorrow so they could spend the entire day with him. Minutes later, Sam was on his way out the door.

***

Earlier that morning, Ashela had conferred with Kyliah. She dialed her number and was surprised to get her instead of her machine. "Kye, I need a dinner menu. Come on, wake up, kid. What should I cook?"

It was six o'clock in the morning. Very groggily, Kyliah said, "Ash, if I didn't know any better, I'd accuse you of being on drugs. That's the *only* reason I can think of that you'd call me at this ungodly hour to ask me something so stupid." Click.

Laughing because *she* was wide awake, Ashela redialed her number. "Kye, I'm serious now. I've got a guest coming over tonight and I need your opinion on what I should cook."

Seeing that her nemesis would not go away, Kyliah snuggled deeper into her pillows. "Ashela, don't you know what time it is? At six in the morning, girl, I don't care what you cook tonight. Throw some Pop Tarts in the microwave and some bologna in the oven and, 'presto!' You've got yourself a meal. And that's free advice that I won't even charge you for. So look, kid, take it light and do it right. I promise, I'll get back with you."

"Kye, if you hang this phone up, I'm calling the police. I'll tell them that I'm your sister and that I haven't heard from you in over a week, and then I'll ask them to go check on you. You know they'll come banging on your door, so get up, girl."

"What, what, what?" Kyliah was struggling to get the sleep out of her eyes. "See, this kind of abuse is why mugs go *postal* on folks. And here I was dreamin' *so* good! Oh, why me? What did *I* do to deserve such horrible treatment . . ."

In the midst of Kyliah's whining, dramatic temper tantrum, Ashela said, "Well, since you feel that way, go ahead and be like that. I guess there's no need for me to tell you that Sam is coming over for an intimate, candlelight dinner. Guess I dialed the wrong number—it looks like I'll just have to call my buddy Martha Stewart. *She'll* give me a dynamite menu. *See ya!*"

Suddenly, Kyliah sat straight up. "What? You? . . . Sam Ross? . . . For goodness sake, girl, why didn't you say so? Wasting my time like this. We could have had the meal already cooked by now! Look, my sistah, of course you dialed the right number—and yes, you're talking to the right person. Now, let me think." Kyliah was suddenly wide awake. Excitement laced her voice. "I've got it! Here's how I see it, Ash. See, Sam is used to the finest, most expensive foods in the world. I mean, there's probably not a gourmet meal that you could cook him that he's not already tasted. That's why we've got to go a different route. You know, go through the back door instead of the front—homestyle instead of gourmet. So, how about some fried chicken, turnip greens, some succotash and candied yams?"

Ashela was lightly nibbling her thumbnail between her teeth. "I don't know, Kye. Don't you think that's a little *too* down-home?" After all, Sam *was* a connoisseur.

"Okay, maybe you've got a point. Let's go to Plan B. It's Friday, right? What did *we* used to eat on Fridays when we were back at home?"

Suddenly, Ashela snapped her fingers loudly. "You're right! Fish Friday! It's perfect, Kye." Then her brow furrowed. "But what kind of fish should I cook?"

"All kinds, baby. All kinds. Go to Marlins and buy a variety of fish: Buffalo, catfish, perch, flounder and maybe even throw in some shrimp to mix it up."

"But what about sides. What do I make for those?" Ashela felt as though she'd lost the simple ability to think.

"Let's not sweat the small stuff, hon. Why not go with the same thing Billie would cook?"

"Kye, what would I do without you? Remind me when this is over to give you a raise."

"Didn't I tell you? Now that we, as in you and me, have just signed this Werner deal, my raise is already in the bag. Rodeo Drive? Get ready cause . . . Here . . . I . . . Come!"

***

From ten to two that Friday afternoon, Ashela was slotted for studio time with Teddy Riley. But as soon as the recording session was over, she planned to hit the ground running. There was food to be purchased and cooked, and a complete evening-wear ensemble that had to be put together.

But just as the best-laid plans often go awry, so did a snag occur in hers. Instead of finishing up at two o'clock, the session didn't end until after four. Pressed for time, she hurried over to Marlin's to pick up the uncooked fish and the other side items. Once she was on the expressway, her usual hour-long drive was reduced to thirty-five minutes as she pushed the Lincoln Navigator to speeds of near 100 m.p.h. Already, it was five o'clock and Sam was expected to arrive at 7 p.m. Two hours didn't give her a lot of room to play with.

Inside her kitchen, Ashela scrubbed her hands before beginning to prepare the food. Once all of the fish was seasoned and frying in several cast-iron skillets, she started preparing the hush puppies and coleslaw. She would wait until last to steam the mixed vegetables. She'd chosen a Cabernet wine as a perfect backdrop to their meal. It's rich redness would enhance and bring out the flavor of all the dishes.

Like a madwoman, Ashela raced upstairs to quickly hot-roller set her hair with some Aveda styling gel. The curlers were good and hot from when she'd first turned them on. With a scarf tied around her head, she raced back downstairs into the kitchen to finish the cooking. It was 6:30 by the time all the food was ready. The burnished ivory lacquer dining room table was arrayed with her finest linen and china, while two cream candles were placed in the center.

Vaulting up the stairs again, Ashela quickly showered and stood in front of her wall-to-wall closet, trying to make a quick clothing decision. Should she go for the knock-out impression with something haute couture? She sifted through her clothes, fingering gowns by Coco Chanel, Oscar de la Renta, Ralph Lauren, Karl Lagerfeld, and Gianfranco Ferré. Nope, they were *too* dressy. Maybe she should go for the jugular with something soft and sinewy. She had dresses, both long and short, by Calvin Klein, Isaac Mizrahi, Mila Schön, Richard Tyler, and Perry Ellis. But were they *too* suggestive?

Narrowing her selection, she finally pulled out a body-hugging chocolate tube dress made of lycra and silk by Kenar. She looked it over and shook her head again. She replaced it and in the end settled for something with charming simplicity. An apple green, Nicole Miller crushed velvet mini-dress. It had a scooped neckline,

reached her mid-thigh area, and flared at its bottom. Sheer Giorgio Armani silk stockings and apple green Chanel flats would give her outfit added elegance.

Ashela donned her Bobbi Brown makeup. Her parfum was the soft and sensual fragrance, Cashmere Mist, by Donna Karan. The Natasha hand-crafted, 18-karat, diamond heart-shaped earrings were her only pieces of jewelry. With an all-or-nothing attitude, she removed the curlers from her hair and did the best she could to create a "Derrick" effect. It wasn't the best hair style she'd ever had, but with some Aveda mousse, it would get her through the night.

At precisely fifteen minutes past the hour, her doorbell rang. As she went to open the door, Ashela couldn't remember ever being so nervous, even when performing on stage.

Sam stepped into the foyer with a huge smile on his face. But Ashela's grin was even bigger because the thought was running through her head that he was finally here in *her* home. She imagined that the numerous women preceding her had probably felt the same heart flutterings that she was experiencing now. But all of the other women didn't matter right now. Ashela would enjoy *her* ride while it lasted.

Surprisingly, Sam was dressed semi-casually in a lavender Ralph Lauren blazer, and a black crew-neck shirt with black slacks. He was holding an expensive bottle of wine encased inside a decorative gold carton. Sam handed it to her as she closed the door behind him.

"Boy, am I glad that I didn't get super dressed-up." Ashela stood with her back to the door holding the bottle of wine in front of her.

"It would have been okay if you had." Sam bent down and placed a light kiss on her lips. "Something sure smells good."

"Let's hope it tastes as good as it smells. Come." Ashela stepped away from him, feeling giddy from his kiss. She walked ahead of him and then stopped and turned around with a puzzled expression on her face. She started to say something but then abruptly changed her mind.

Sam caught the look. "What?" he asked, smiling.

"Nothing. Just . . . an observation." She was about to continue walking when Sam caught hold of her hand and stopped her.

"Tell me what you were about to say."

Ashela laughed as she shook her head at him. "I . . ." She spread her hand almost self-consciously. "It's just dawning on me that I've never had a . . . male guest in my home. But then, Adrienne's been here several times so I guess I can't quite say that. Besides . . ." Now her smile was becoming sheepish. "Nothing, forget it, Sam."

Sam was still holding her hand in his and he pulled her closer to him. "I'm honored and really very flattered to be here, Ashela. Thank you for inviting me."

Ashela looked down at the bottle in her hand. "Well, you're welcome. Let's go into the kitchen to put your wine on ice. Do you know it was a struggle for me to

figure out what to cook for you?" Ashela was fighting her way through her nervousness.

"I'm just shocked that you know how to cook. I thought most successful women of today considered cooking déclassé."

Ashela gave him a scolding look. "Sam, you should know better than that."

As she started removing her bakeware from the oven, Sam could tell that she was feeling more at ease now. Her earlier awkwardness had amused him and he was charmed by her apparent bashfulness. "Can I help with something?"

Ashela threw a smile his way. She seemed to be full of them tonight. "No, but what you can do for me is give yourself an unguided tour while I set the food on the dining room table. Would you like a glass of wine as you show yourself around? No? Oh, well, off with your head. Be gone from me, my child. I've work to do."

Banished from the kitchen, Sam strolled through her home. It was large and spacious and so beautifully decorated that he assumed she'd hired a designer to do it for her. He roamed through the living room admiring the decor but got no further because he heard her calling him from up front.

She met him in the hallway and ushered him into the dining room. "What I was saying earlier was that when I was growing up, every Friday was Fish Friday. On that particular day, nearly everybody in the entire city of Durham ate some kind of fish. So I thought I'd give you a sample of what it was like."

"So, that's where you grew up?" Sam pulled her chair out for her as she sat down. He sat directly across from her.

"Yep. The deep hills of North Carolina. What about you?" Ashela was already filling Sam's plate.

"I came from the jungle. Right over in Watts."

"Wow, Sam." She paused from serving his food. "That must have been quite an existence."

"It was. Sometimes I drive by there to remind myself of where I came from, and to also show others that there's hope."

"And look at you now. Did you ever dream that you'd be as successful as you are?"

"I used to dream about making it big ever since I was a kid." The fish was cut in small sections and Ashela let him sample some of each. Sam forked a piece of the catfish and then tasted the coleslaw. "This is very good, Ashela."

"There you go again, Sam Ross, pulling my leg." She was happy to hear him say it just the same.

"I wouldn't say it if I didn't mean it. Tell me how you got from Durham to New York."

"I was young, starry-eyed and very foolish. I had dreams of becoming a famous musician so I high-tailed it to The Big Apple. But, like so many people who come

into the business with more talent than common sense, I got hooked up with others who weren't as serious as I was, or who weren't going in the same direction that I wanted to go. Then, I got hooked up with a manager who took me for a ride of an entirely different kind—a financial holocaust. I lost millions because I wasn't aware of the value of copywriting my work for future royalties." Ashela shrugged nonchalantly. "I didn't know any better. I wrote songs and then just gave them away. But the one good thing that came out of all my difficulties in New York was that I discovered I had a love for writing music even more so than playing it. When I think of everything that I had to endure while I was there, I don't know if I'd say it was worth it, Sam, but I *can* say it's a big reason why I'm where I am today."

Nodding, Sam said, "Unfortunately, it's almost a rite of passage for newcomers to get railroaded in their attempts to break into the music business. It's a practice that's been going on since this industry's inception. Wherever there's money to be made, you'll always find people of mercenary and unsavory character. And even *if* you do manage to get your foot in the door, there's still no guarantee that you're safe from the sharks. What I try to tell newcomers to the industry is not to get involved if they're not prepared to starve before they make it. And when they do, to always read the fine print. But the most prevalent mistake I see made by those in the business today, is spend-thrift waste. An act gets signed to a label, never bothering to get an attorney to review their contract, and then when they cut a record, the money is gone as soon as they get it. I'm afraid almost everyone in the business has a horror story about how they managed to break into it. Everything else in life has its price, why not success?" He seemed to change the subject. "Are you satisfied with your contract with Werner?"

"Yes, I am. Thank you, Sam."

"Good. I wanted you to be happy."

Ashela didn't know how to take that statement so she opted not to touch it. They finished the meal with more "shop" talk and laughed about how they could still enjoy the pleasures of simple things like hot sauce on their food. Ashela tried to get Sam to talk more about his childhood, and he told her about what life had been like for him growing up with seven crazy sisters and brothers. He had never known his father, and when Sam finally spoke of his mother, he seemed to sadden visibly as he described how she had died of cancer several years earlier.

A connection forged between them as Ashela, in turn, began to share her childhood with him. What it was like for her without a father, with no other siblings, and a mother who had died when Ashela had been just a child. As she related her experiences, a mental bond was formed, one that needed no voice to articulate its existence.

Once their appetites were sated, Ashela stood to remove the dishes from the table. Sam got up to help her. She chided him, "Do you honestly think I'll have it said of me that I invited you here to help me with my dishes?"

"Woman, do you have any idea of how many dishes I've had to wash in my lifetime?"

"Yes, Sam, I do. Probably not more than two."

They were inside the kitchen when Sam said, "I've figured out what the problem *really* is. You think I'll break your precious china, don't you? Go ahead, admit it."

"Okay, you've got me. So, let's call it a truce. We'll put away the left-over food and just load the dishes into the dishwasher. How's that?"

"Fine. I'll never have it said of me that I don't pull my weight wherever I go."

"Sam, no one would ever accuse you of that." Ashela poured them both a glass of the wine that Sam had brought with him. "Come on, let me show you where I work my magic."

Sam eagerly rubbed his hands together with a big smile on his face. "It must be dessert time."

"Sam Ross. What's a girl to do with you?" Ashela handed him his glass and led him inside the room where she created all of her songs. She took a seat at the ivory baby grand and smiled at him as she patted the area next to her. Sam sat down close beside her, but his back was facing the piano keys.

"Do you play, Sam?"

"No. I've always had to admire from afar those who could."

Ashela nodded, her fingers lightly strumming the ivory keys creating a soft, romantic melody of their own. "I've always loved music, Sam. Ever since I was a child. I used to sit underneath the piano and listen to my mother sing and play. Whenever she would be away from home, I'd sit at our baby grand and pretend I was her. And then when I got older, I started pretending I was Teena Marie. I never imagined a time when I would be without music. Sometimes, Sam, my music was all I had." As she talked, Ashela's voice was very low.

Sam watched her as she talked. Her voice was so . . . magnetic, that he thought he could sit and listen to her all night. There was a warmth emanating from her. A genuineness that attracted him to her. Everything about the setting pleased him as well. The huge room had a beautiful waterfall at one end of it. Behind the softly cascading water sat large, tall tropical plants. Gold flood-lights shining just inside the waterfall gave it a colorful effect. Skylights bathed the room in a warm glow and even the gigantic, picturesque, abstract paintings that hung on the rest of the walls seemed the perfect complement. Sam had the incredible feeling that somehow, somewhere he'd seen her place before.

As she continued to play, Ashela smiled at him as if she were privy to a secret that he didn't know. Soon, Sam recognized the tune. Almost prophetically, it was Teena Marie's "Deja Vu." Feeling most comfortable, he crossed his legs and leaned against the piano, bracing his arm on top of it.

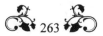

Ashela smiled at him invitingly. She knew that he recognized what she was playing, and she surprised them both by singing the song itself.

"I used to be a queen, you know . . .

on an island by the sea, with rainbow colored people, happy as can be . . .

and I can feel this for sure, for sure, for sure, for sure

. . . I've been here before. . ."

Sam felt her eyes float over his face as her voice rose with the high and low notes of the song. But when his eyes caught hers, she glanced down at the keys. Regardless, Sam had already glimpsed the passion that lay behind them. She wouldn't look at him again as he wanted her to and so he stared at her, willing her to meet his gaze.

Ashela *couldn't* look at Sam, so she hid behind her song. A feeling of warmth had washed over her and she could feel the butterflies fluttering in her stomach again. Maybe they were caused by the pending thoughts of all that she was sure that he would do to her, and what she wanted to do to him in return. When she felt his hand at the base of her throat, her fingers stilled upon the keys. Though she knew Sam wanted her, somehow, the feeling was with her that the timing for their coupling was not yet ripe.

"Let me show you something." Her voice was so husky that it was barely discernible. She stood and took his hand in hers and led him through the door and out onto her verandah. Outside, the glare from the full moon danced upon the ocean waters. Even at night, the view from her deck was spectacular.

"It's beautiful."

"Yes. Whenever I need to clear my head, this is where I come."

Sam took a seat in one of the large wicker chairs and stretched out his legs. Ashela stood against the railing for awhile longer and then came and stood next to him. She folded her arms across her chest and stared down at him. "How can you trade such tranquility as this for the high speed drama of New York?"

Sam reached out and guided Ashela onto his knee. He placed his hand on the small of her back. "There's no denying the beauty of California. And you're right, it is peaceful. But having grown up here, I know first hand that when you scratch beneath the surface, there's nothing really there. I prefer New York because it's *real*. A person can burn out fast here in L.A. because of the ascetic and surreal surroundings. I moved to New York after my divorce and then wondered what had taken me so long. Now, because I'm a visitor, I enjoy Cali much more than I ever did when I lived here."

Ashela shivered. "New York was unkind to me during my years there. I don't have any fond memories of the place. Only scars and bruises that I got from The School of Hard Knocks. So I wonder what it is that draws you there."

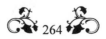

Feeling her tremble, Sam tightened his hold on her. He didn't like the idea that she'd been through rough times. "New York can be anything you make of it, Ashela. But if you can make it there, you can make it anywhere in the world."

"Look at you, Sam. You even sound like a Yorkie—the whole East Coast accent and all."

Sam only smiled at her. He relaxed deeper into the chair, still holding on to her. Turning to look again at the waves, there was something hypnotic about the way they crashed onto the shore. He continued to stare out into the blackness of the sea.

Minutes later, Ashela leaned into Sam's chest and looped her arm around his neck. Her nervous jitters had passed away. The shyness was something that she couldn't quite explain. When she had been on his turf, she had all but molested him. But now that he was in her home, instead of feeling even more comfortable and playing the role of seductive huntress, she had retreated behind a wall of reticence.

Sam was aware of her silent struggle. From the moment he arrived he had been ready to make love to her. Dinner was delicious, but if he had had his wish, they would have bypassed it and gone straight to her bedroom. Even when she'd sat at the piano and played for him, the moment he touched her, he could feel her withdrawal. Not physically, but mentally. Intuitively, Sam had known that she wasn't ready for him. He also knew that for most women, the foreplay began long before they ever made it to the bedroom, and so he was willing to wait for her—to take things slowly at her pace. Even when he felt her body slide against his, he made no move to touch her. His face was still turned away from her as he watched the rushing waves.

Ashela's senses were suddenly ablaze as she rested her head against his shoulder. She could smell a hint of the cologne that he was wearing. His skin was warm and its color so dark and rich. Before she knew it, she was trailing her nose upward along his neck, inhaling his scent. With a half smile, Ashela placed her hand lightly on his jaw and pulled his face toward her. He seemed lost in thought, as if he were miles away. She would have been surprised to know he'd been thinking of her.

With nimble fingers, she traced the shape of his lips with her thumb. Too many thoughts were filtering through her brain at once. She wanted to *do* too many things to *him* at once. Her fingers trailed from his jaw to his neck, to the base of his throat, down to his chest and then to his waist. Aroused, suddenly Ashela was off his knees and pulling Sam to his feet. Her demure attitude completely vanished as she acknowledged the fact that she was ready to make love to him.

Silently, she led him upstairs to her bedroom where she hit the dimmer switch that lowered the lighting inside the room.

The king-sized bed with its russet-colored, satin pillows and sheets invited Sam to sink into it. He sat down on the bed and watched as Ashela stood before him, stripping off her dress. With ease, she removed her silk stockings. She slid onto the bed beside him wearing a strapless, green and black zebra-print bra with a matching thong bikini.

With his elbows resting behind him, Sam was silent as she climbed on top of him, straddling him. Her knees were tucked under her as she sat atop him and wrapped her arms around his neck. Again, she inhaled his scent, basking in his smell. Ashela released her hold on him and reached around her back to unhook her bra. Released from their confinement, her breasts seemed to thrust themselves at him, begging for his touch.

In the next moment, she was pushing him down on the bed, kissing him deeply. Her need of him an admission in itself. Mentally, she tried to stop herself from moving too fast. But physically, all she could fathom was the desire to have him on top of her, inside of her, filling her . . .

Recognizing her need for total domination, and understanding that it tied into her comfort level, Sam appeased her by letting her control the tempo. He relaxed, content to enjoy the languid, sensuous sensations that she was stirring within him, for he knew the time would come when he could seize the momentum. When he felt her tongue trail along his neck and jaw and up to his lips, he kissed her passionately before slowly turning her over onto her back.

Her arms were above her head as Sam partially rested his weight on her body. His lips swept over her neck and chest. When his warm mouth covered her nipple, her arms entwined about his neck. His hands were everywhere and Ashela loved the feel of them sliding all over her body. Her leg lifted to encircle his waist and Sam's hand fastened around her knee to lock it in place.

Leisurely, Sam pulled himself away from her and stood beside the bed. He reached down and slowly removed her panties from her hips, leaving her naked before him. In an unhurried manner, Sam slipped out of his shoes and began to unfasten his belt buckle. He pulled his shirt out of his pants and within seconds, his chest was bare.

Ashela lay stretched out on the bed with her head resting upon her arm. As Sam divested himself of the remainder of his clothes, her legs curled and her nails dug into the bed at the sight of his nakedness. As he met her on the bed, there was nothing left to separate the two of them—nothing left for either of them to hide. Flesh to flesh, bone to bone, their bodies melded together. With quivering sighs, they wallowed in the erotic feel of their nudity.

Sam lay on his side and pinned her body beneath his. Again, Ashela laced her arms around his neck and pulled his head to hers. She tasted his lips and capitalized upon the nakedness of their bodies by fitting herself even closer to him. Next, Sam turned her completely onto her back and slid his body on top of hers, fitting himself between her legs. Her senses dazed, Ashela melted as a searing heat poured through her veins. They lay entwined, skin upon skin, in anticipation of the exotic vortex of passion that awaited them. But their dance of love was unrushed in its tempo, and a languidness seeped throughout the both of them.

Her breasts were crushed beneath his chest and her legs were spread in a wide V-like pattern with her calves and curled toes pointing downward. Sam's hands were on either side of her face as he held her, his tongue assaulting hers. His lips played havoc with her senses as they trailed downward to her neck and chest. When he bit gently into her collar bone, a soft, pleading whimper escaped through her lips, belying her weakened and malleable state. She felt his hips ease off of her ever so slightly while his hands lowered to palm the cheeks of her buttocks. His hands seemed to deftly spread her apart as he rested himself fully against her, planting his large maleness upon her moistened center. Immediately, sharp pangs of ecstasy careened through both of their entire bodies, almost as if nerves and tendons had been jolted by electricity.

So great and intense was the pleasure that he was inflicting upon her that Ashela was nearly unconscious. Feverish tremors continued to race through her. Her fingers dug deep half-moon impressions into the sinewyness of his rich, dark skin. It was all just her way of transmitting her silent need of him, just her way of persuading him to delay no longer, and just her attempt to sway him to sample the waiting wet, pulsing, and tight treasure that she had to offer. When her hand weaved itself between their bodies to slide downward and catch hold of his virility, his thickness filled her hand with ease. It was the last thing she needed to do because knowing there was so much of him, and needing to know how it would feel to have *all* of him inside her, Ashela lost all vestiges of shame. With no remaining inhibitions, she began to plead her case before him as she whispered his name with newfound insistence, all the while writhing underneath him.

The bold and knowing way in which she caressed and stroked him served to heighten Sam's senses, forcing him to another plane. Her wild, hot, and hungry demands nearly drove him over the edge, tempting him to plunge himself into her with no remorse. But he would wait and make her wait as well. Her whispered sighs of pleasure were but sweet sensuous music to his ears. He knew of her unhidden need and her intense longing, but his needs were equally as strong.

Sam had the hardest time disentangling himself from her. As she bit into the corded muscles in his shoulder, her hold on him was similar to that of a vice-like grip. But he caught hold of her hands and eased himself from between her legs. On his side, he pulled her to him, fitting her backside against him and resting his weight over hers. Ashela's arm reached upward behind her to wrap around his neck. Sam's hand trailed from her stomach to her chest to firmly squeeze her breasts. A sharp sigh of pleasure emitted from her and he gently gripped her throat while his knee prodded itself between hers. He shuddered when his manhood probed the moistened area between her cheeks. Sam was trying to hold out—he really was. But his insides were straining to the breaking point and the way she kept quietly whispering his name over and over—"Sam, please?"—pleading with him to satisfy her, was beginning to torch his nerves.

His finger was in her mouth now, and he removed it to probe the hot lava of her substance. Sam felt and heard her toes scrape the satin covers on the bed. The timbre of her beseeching sighs gave clue to the severity of her need for him. He knew that what he was doing to her was like pouring gasoline onto a raging fire. And then he was turning her limp body around to face him. He planted a deep, lingering kiss on her lips, before whispering in her ear, "Are you with me, baby?"

When she wilted against him, her silky whimper was the only reply he needed. He took her hand and guided it downward and urged her to massage his throbbing manhood. As he sucked her lips with his, pulsating spasms gripped his innards. Sam roughly palmed her behind and lifted her leg onto his side. He knew all too well what she really wanted, what even *he* wanted at this point, but he was determined to make her wait. And then he whispered his demand into her ear.

Ashela knew exactly what he meant the second he whispered for her to "taste him." Knowing that *her* needs would not be met until she appeased his, Ashela needed no further prodding to slowly slide downward to taste and sample *his* goods.

Her mouth was a warm and wet delight to Sam's senses as she took him easily into her silky confine. When her teeth lightly grazed him, euphoria reigned through him and Sam couldn't refrain from whispering, "That's it—yeah, baby, that's it."

Sam pulled her up to meet him once more. As his mouth clashed with hers, it was apparent that her needs would now be met because there was a sudden urgency about him that had been latent before. He swiftly turned her over, placing three pillows underneath her stomach, positioning her to now meet *his* need. And then he was behind her, sliding on his condom before sliding himself on to her. With the palm of his hand pressing down onto the small of her back, he applied light pressure. He spread her knees with his and with his weight resting on one arm, Sam began to stroke her with his manhood, teasing her until she moaned and hissed. Even through his protection he could feel the heat of her as she urged him inside. And then, with no further delay, he guided himself into her. Slowly, Sam entered her, little by little, inch by inch. He basked in the feel of her heated, tight womanhood as she enveloped him greedily. Sam groaned loudly himself, because being inside her felt like being immersed in a very hot, tight apple pie.

Ashela was surely on a level that she'd never been on before. It was all she could do to contort her body to allow him to have his way with her. With each gentle push, each piercing thrust, Sam was causing a tidal wave of pleasure to cascade over her. And then he was resting his weight on her back, pressing her further into the bed. Her hands clutched the satin comforter and when one of his hands made its way up to her mouth, she latched onto his middle finger, sucking it like a pacifier.

The pleasure that he was inflicting upon her body was the kind that no self-generated orgasm could ever achieve. And because Sam continued to whisper and probe his tongue into her ear, all the while stroking her flesh and satisfying her generously, Ashela was in a frenzied state of bliss. Her senses were under intense

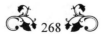

attack and Sam took advantage of her pliability by lifting her upright and pulling her against him, while kneading her breasts and biting into the soft area of her neck. His rhythmic dance behind her never ceased. In one instance, her neck craned to the side and she arched her chest as her arms stretched upward to lock around his neck. But it wasn't long until Sam was forcing her down onto the bed again, strapping his hands around her waist, pulling her hips to his as he insistently ground himself into her.

On and on it went, his hips clashing against hers, while he palmed her buttocks with ease. Ashela knew that she couldn't stand much more, because every time his hips made contact with hers, she felt as if her senses and nerves were being dealt a pulverizing blow of ecstasy. The pleasure was too much and too extreme for *any* person to withstand all at one time. Even the pitch and tone of her passionate cries changed as well. Each husky groan she emitted now begged and pleaded with him for release. Each sensuous gasp and moan entreated Sam to have mercy on her, by helping her to expel her pent-up frustrations in the form of an orgasmic release. But it wasn't to be because Sam was far from finished with her.

With primitive pleasure he continued to consume her, groaning aloud himself as ecstasy oozed and coursed its way through *his* veins. Weaving his fingers through hers so they could grip one another's hands, Sam refused to relinquish his gentle but punishing assault on her senses. With every rise and fall of her hips, Sam was there to meet her, thrusting deeper inside her to fill her even more. And then he was gripping her waist again, compelling her to meet him at every turn. Filling her emptiness with his largeness, coercing her body to adjust to his size. Mercilessly, he wouldn't cut her any slack until she was on the same plateau as himself.

As their sighs filled the room, the beat and pace of their bodies was the only music that was needed. Their timed movements were collectively in sync, and as they performed their own harmonic din, he satisfied her, appeased her, filled her, *loved* her.

The moment had come long ago when Sam had recognized that her surrender was complete. But now, her intensified moans resonated deeply in her throat as his strong hands locked her in place. He moved behind her generating a rhythmical pattern all his own, and then he wrapped the crook of his arm around her neck, pushing her down on the bed as his other hand cascaded downward to weave its way through her pubic hairs. His fingers sought to tweak and tease the button that was her love auricle. But the moment Sam touched Ashela's most private part, she went flying over the edge. In wild abandon, she nearly fought him for her release. The pleasure was now *too* intense, yet her sudden thrashing tempo was what Sam needed himself. So, he held her tightly, pinning her to the bed, forcing her to take and endure the last of what he had to give her.

With their bodies drenched with wetness, sweat poured from everywhere as the two rose to a pinnacle of ecstatic bliss. Lost in the smell and heat of each other, there was no turning back. True and raw intimacy pierced the depths of their souls. When

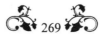

the impact of their union finally played itself out, so powerful was the aftermath that Sam's knees nearly buckled from the intense, final pleasure that ricocheted through him. Only then did his pace slacken. Only then did his crescendo ease as his body finally rested in languor upon hers. Spent and replete, Sam lay atop her feeling as if he'd found paradise, holding onto her while his heart returned to its normal rate.

Fulfilled as well, Ashela couldn't yet stop the shuddering waves that racked her body. She was only thankful that Sam continued to hold her tightly. She knew that she wasn't in control of her senses yet. Her breathing was rapid and both her mind and her body were still struggling to adjust. So she just lay there with her eyes closed.

In another second, she would turn over and ask Sam how it had been for him, whether he had derived as much enjoyment and pleasure as she had. She would tell him explicitly how good it had been for her and make him describe in vivid detail what emotions he had felt. But just for these next few seconds, she would rest her eyes and wait until her body and nerves returned to normalcy. Then they would talk.

Within those few, short seconds, a state of indolence swarmed over her and she succumbed to it, nodding off, well on her way to dreamworld, la la land—maybe even to the moon.

***

Sam lay there recuperating for a while longer and then got out of bed to shower. He came back into the bedroom and put on his underwear. He bent down and picked all the clothes up from the floor, and placed them on a nearby chair. Ordinarily, this would be the part where Sam would don his clothes and exit via the front door. But he sat down on the bed and looked over at Ashela, who was completely knocked out. A smile lit his face and silent laughter shook his body at the way she lay sprawled all over the bed. He didn't want to wake her, but the comforter upon which she lay was completely soaked with the sweat of their lovemaking, so Sam got up and stripped it from the bed. He folded it and lay it on a nearby table. Out of habit, even as a grown man he continued to fold items when he was done with them, simply because it was something his mother had instilled in him as a small boy.

Unable to sleep, Sam pulled on his pants and went downstairs, stepping outside on Ashela's deck. It was just shortly past mid-night. Though he was relaxed and enjoying the feeling of lethargy that filtered through him, he knew that sleep was far from him. So he lay in the fold-out wicker chair listening to the sounds of the ocean, and letting the breeze drift over him until finally, sleep overcame him.

Hours later, Ashela's eyelids fluttered open. She could easily have turned over and gone back to sleep but something told her Sam was no longer in the room. Gradually, she sat up in the bed looking around while her eyes adjusted to the room's low lighting. Her heart quickened a beat because she assumed he'd left. As she stared at the folded comforter on the table, she couldn't mask her disappointment. She'd gotten what she'd wanted, so why the feeling of discontent?

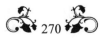

She got up to use the bathroom and it was only then that she saw Sam's shoes peeking out from beneath the bed. Ashela stood in the doorway to the bathroom, relieved to know that he hadn't left, but concerned about the fact that already the thought of his leaving troubled her. Mentally, she took herself to task for allowing her emotions to get in the way. No doubt, countless women before her had tried to "capture" Sam with clinging tactics. She determined right then and there that she would not wind up like so many others had—totally devastated when he walked away. Not *if* he walked away, because Ashela knew that with Sam, it was only a question of *when*. No. She would be the one person who came out of this thing on top. She didn't want anything from him, nor did she need Sam to give her anything. Well, maybe just a little more of what he'd given her tonight. But other than that, she would require nothing of him. The last thing she wanted to do, as Kyliah would put it, was *go out like a punk*.

When she came out of the bathroom, she brushed her hair and donned a white, silk chemise and went in search of Sam.

He stirred when he heard the sliding glass doors open and close. As she approached him, Sam said, "I thought you were out cold."

"I was. But then nature called." Ashela joined him on the wicker cot. It was spacious enough for the two of them. She slid her body alongside his. With her hand against his face, she said to him, "When I didn't see you at first, I thought that you had left." Immediately, she felt his body grow still.

"What would make you think that?" Sam's gaze was piercing as he waited for an answer.

"I don't know. My instincts tell me that you're not the type to hang around." Ashela wrapped her arm around his neck. "Don't be offended Sam, I'm just happy that you stayed."

While his still being here *was* out of character for him, her keen perception of his routine ways never failed to startle him. "How happy *are* you?" Sam's look was intent.

"Happy enough to fall asleep right here in your arms." She didn't think that she could stand another round of his lovemaking. In fact, she wasn't sure if she had recovered sufficiently from the first episode.

"I know of something that will make you even happier than that."

She could feel him harden against her thigh. "Sam, I don't think I want to know what it is."

"That's okay, baby, then I won't tell you. Just let Daddy put you to sleep the old fashioned way."

Ashela's insides contracted at the very thought of it. Against her will, she melted as the feel of that old, hot, molten lava poured through her body.

One look at the way her eyelids closed in slow languor, and feeling her body wilt limply against him, Sam knew that it wouldn't take much to persuade her. He kissed her lips several times and then whispered his knowing words into her ear. As she stirred sensuously against him, Sam leaned his body over hers.

Ashela's toes were locked in a curled position. The moment Sam started whispering all that he wanted to do to her *"sweet pussy,"* her body betrayed her. It was all she could do to prevent herself from climaxing on the spot.

With no further objections from his lover, Sam picked Ashela up and carried her back to her bedroom.

Chapter Twenty-Seven

he next morning, Ashela walked Sam downstairs. He was dressed and prepared to go on his way. "Sure you don't want me to whip you up something to eat?"

"No, I'm fine." They were standing inside the foyer, in front of her door. "What have you got planned for today?"

"Actually, Sam, because of you, I'm extra busy these next several days—months, if you want to know the truth." Ashela clasped her arms around herself. "You understand, with everyone vying to get their last minute dibs in before I come on board with you. But, as for today, I'll be in the studio from noon until five. Same ole, same ole. What about you?"

"I'm spending the day with my boys and after that, I've got some paperwork to go over." Sam lightly tugged at the silk belt of Ashela's robe, wrapping it around his hand.

Ashela smiled at him as she leaned over to unlock and open the door. "Try not to work too hard then."

Sam didn't make a move to walk out of the door. She was wearing that half-smile of hers again. The one that did nothing to reveal her thoughts. Was she rushing him?

In the face of his silence, Ashela said, "I had a wonderful time last night, Sam. Thank you for coming." But now it was time for him to leave. Ashela understood that and wanted to make it easy for him to do so. She'd be damned if she'd stoop to asking him when or if she would see him again. She preferred for him to just leave. No need to stick around and wind up making promises that couldn't be kept.

Sam definitely felt as if he were being kicked out. Wasn't *this* quite a change? "Ms. Jordan, do I at least get to see you again?"

"I certainly hope so, Sam. I would hate to have to wonder if what I savored last night was only a dream."

At least now she was giving him a full smile. "There's only one way to find out." He bent down and kissed her lips. "I'll call you."

Ashela smiled as she nodded her head. She wouldn't hold her breath. If anything, common sense told her that she'd better begin gathering the blocks to start rebuilding her world.

***

At noon time, Kyliah was luxuriating at the Beverly Hot Springs Spa on Oxford Avenue. She'd tried calling Ashela several times but when she couldn't reach her, she figured her dinner date with Sam had turned into an all-night fiesta. She hoped that Ash would keep her noon studio engagement. Regardless, Kyliah was just dying to get the juicy details of the previous night's excursion.

True to her word about hitting Rodeo Drive, as soon as she left the spa, Kyliah was on her way to a round of shopping. Gucci, Umberto, Chanel, Armani, and maybe even Prada, would each receive a visit from her. Kyliah never really needed an excuse to go shopping—any occasion would do. She even knew some of the shopgirls by name. Since she had decided to go to Boston to visit Arron, she would *have* to pick out a few new outfits for the occasion.

Ashela was working with Boys II Men on their new album. Her portion of the project was estimated to take at least two weeks. When she left the studio that afternoon, she headed north on Sunset Boulevard. She drove to the No Gossip Hair Salon and twisted Derrick's arm to get him to fit her in. Much to her surprise, she found herself dodging a slew of questions from Derrick as he grilled her about all of the rumors he'd been hearing regarding her and Sam Ross. Ashela played the dumb role, assuring Derrick that there was no truth to any of the rumors. She convinced him that it was all a move on the part of the rag-mags to stir up dirt where none existed.

Ashela may have fooled Derrick, but as soon as she was placed underneath the dryer, she wasn't able to fool herself. Instead of falling asleep, as was her usual custom, all she could do was replay in her mind's eye all that had transpired the night before between she and Sam. What surprised her most about him was how gentle—yet demanding—and considerate he was as a lover. Sam was legendary for his savvy, cut-throat business dealings. So, for him to be so *giving* and demonstrative a lover was a reality that would take some getting used to.

Her eyes closed and she relaxed deeper into the chair as she recalled how rough, but gentle, Sam had been. And how was that even possible? How could a man of his strength be so *masterful* at assuaging a woman's needs? Maybe the saying was true

after all that practice made one perfect. Ashela's toes curled inside her patent-leather shoes as she remembered how Sam had gripped and held her breasts and buttocks. And the part where he had pulled her upright so that she could lift her arms backwards and lock them around his neck—that had been the ultimate. Sam had forced her torso and stomach outward while pulling her behind toward him, riding her in an upright position. That had been sheer ecstasy. But what had *really* blown Ashela away above all else—was the fact that Sam's hands actually were callused. It wasn't the first time she had noticed that about him.

But a man of Sam's caliber with *calluses* on his hands? How could it be? Ashela knew that to some people it might seem odd, but for her, a man with rough hands and no earrings in his ear, well watch out! Cause *that* type of man, for her, was worth fighting for in the streets. In light of all the mitigating circumstances, maybe she *could* see Sam at least one more time. One for the road and another for old times sake. All Ashela knew was that the slow, unrushed and unhurried manner in which Sam had ridden her last night reminded her of back-alley dogs mating in the heat of the moment.

As a powerful flashback hit Ashela, a lingering pang gripped her stomach muscles and a mouse-like squeak escaped her lips. It was the kind of flash-back that comes from remembering how good it feels when a person touches you a certain way, or bends and contorts your body into a certain position to maximize the pleasure. Ashela's hands tightly gripped the arms of the chair—she desperately needed something to hold on to while the sensual spasms passed. As Ashela's breathing quickened and then returned to normal, her eyes popped open to look around and see if any one had witnessed her brief orgasmic-like reactions. Thank goodness no one seemed to be watching her!

It was slightly past seven-thirty as Ashela walked into her home and disengaged her security system. Though she was hungry, she was much more tired. So she went upstairs, undressed and soaked in her huge whirlpool bathtub. An hour later, she was inside her bedroom, massaging some Guinot body lotion onto her skin and looking forward to climbing into bed. The phone rang and Ashela figured it had to be Kyliah. She'd seen numerous calls from her already on the Caller I.D. But whoever this person was, their number was coming up as private. "Hello?"

"Hello to you too. How're you feeling?"

"Tired, sweetheart. Very tired."

"I was hoping we could go somewhere and grab a late-night snack."

"I don't know, Sam. Maybe another time. I just got out of the shower and right now, all I can think about is sleep. My mind and my heart might be willing, but my body is telling me that it needs rest.

Sam leaned forward in his chair, unable to stop himself from hardening at the thought of her stepping naked from the shower. "I want to see you, Ashela."

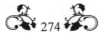

Ashela could tell by the silky tone of his voice that that wasn't all he wanted. She lay stretched out on her bed. Her eyes closed and her nipples standing at attention. That lava-like substance was weaving through her body, betraying her once again. In a husky whisper, she said to him, "Sam, please . . . I don't think my body can take any more right now."

Her soft, whispered plea caused Sam's insides to tighten. He, too, had been having flashbacks of his own. And now he began to stroke her with his voice as he closed in for the kill, convincing her to see him. "I'll be gentle with you, baby. I promise."

"Sam . . ." Ashela could only shake her head. What was he trying to do to her? "How about letting me take you to the moon over the phone tonight?"

"Not a chance, baby. Not while I've got the real thing just minutes away. Look, Ashela, I'm on my way." And then the line went dead.

Ashela lay there, her body tingling all over, trying to believe that he had hung up on her. So much for getting a good night's sleep.

In what seemed like minutes later, Sam was ringing her doorbell.

Dressed in an exquisite, floor-length, champagne-colored nightgown that had a thigh-high slit in the front with a matching silk and lace robe, Ashela met him at the door. She wore no makeup and the diamond studs in her ears were her only jewelry.

Nevertheless, Sam was swept away at the sight of her. He came in and closed the door behind him. When he went to hug her, Ashela held up her hand in a stop-sign gesture.

"Sam, wait. We've got to talk." She started backing up as he approached her with a slight smile on his face as if he were stalking her. "Sam, I'm serious, now. Wait, listen to me."

But Sam was already picking her up and her arms were now wrapped around his neck. "I'm listening, but you're not talking," he said. He headed upstairs to her bedroom. Inside, Sam lay her on the bed and sat down beside her.

In spite of herself, Ashela *was* happy to see him, so she clasped his face in her hands and kissed him. Sam returned her kiss with forcefulness.

Seeing that his kiss could lead to much more, Ashela said, "Sam, wait. Let me say something." She was melting fast and she needed to say what she had to say before she either forgot it or changed her mind. Sam was untying her robe, kissing her neck and sliding his hands over her body, all at the same time, and Ashela was finding it hard to think straight.

"Talk to me, baby. I'm listening." He was, but his lips were busy sampling her skin and body.

Ashela grabbed his face and brought it back in front of hers. Her voice had a sensuous whine to it. "Sam, I'm serious, now. I really do need you to listen to me. What I'm trying to say, baby, is that I'm still sore from last night. Sam, stop smiling

like that and listen to me. I just want us to talk tonight, okay? Nothing more. Now her arms were around his neck again. "Remember when I told you it had been a long time for me? Well, now I need to get used to you. You're not 'Tiny Tim,' Sam, and my body has to have time to adjust." Though Ashela was baring her soul, she could tell by the dark look in Sam's eyes that he still wanted to make love to her.

"Ashela, you know I wouldn't hurt you." His hand was on the side of her face.

"I know you wouldn't, baby, but . . . Not purposely, that is. But still, Sam, let's just cuddle and talk tonight. Do you know that when you left this morning, I honestly didn't believe I would hear from you again?"

Sam looked at her disbelievingly.

Ashela gave him a "don't-even-try-it look." "Sam Ross . . . You know good and well that based upon your track record, I had every right to think that."

"Ashela, you make me sound as if I'm some monster. I'm not. Look, if I don't have a good track record, it's because I've wanted it that way. And I've always chosen women who knew the score. That's why I can walk away with no strings attached. So here I am with you—and whether it'll be different or just more of the same, remains to be answered. But this afternoon, all while I was with my boys, I kept thinking about you. I took them to The Museum of Jurassic Technology, then to The Museum of Contemporary Art, and finally to a late lunch at Chez Jay's. Do you know I kept wanting to call you? Do you have any idea how unusual that is for me? Well it is. All I'm asking is that you don't shut the door without finding out if there's something between us." Sam leaned forward and kissed her lingeringly. "Have you eaten at all?"

"No. I was too tired and I just wanted to go to bed."

"Come on. Let's go heat up some of that fish you cooked." Sam was pulling her to her feet. "I don't want you to pass out on me tonight. You're going to need every bit of your strength."

"Sam!"

He smiled. But he meant it. Oh, they would talk all right. But by the time he finished with her, she would be begging him the same way she'd pleaded with him last night. All the way downstairs to her kitchen, Sam marveled at her. She was such an odd mixture of woman. Satin and lace on one hand and hard as nails on the other. Sam knew that he would have to watch himself carefully with Ashela. Or, he just might end up getting caught in his own snare.

They were sitting at her kitchen table eating some of the re-heated leftovers. With chairs turned sideways, they sat on the same side of the table. Ashela's legs were stretched out and her feet rested in Sam's lap. He was smiling as she told him of how she'd been interrogated by her hairdresser, who had wanted to know if there were any truth to the rumors surrounding the two of them.

"How did you answer him?"

"Like any level-headed person with a smidgen of common sense would have. I told him the rumors were false."

"Why? Is it so hard to fathom that you and I could become involved?"

Ashela took a sip of her wine. She forked a piece of the flounder, leaned over and lifted it into Sam's mouth. "It's not a question of whether or not I can envision it, Sam. It's just that the likelihood of it is slim. Not because we wouldn't click or couldn't get along. But, the truth of the matter is that for you, Sam, it would only last until the next person came along." She held up her hand to stop him from interrupting her. "I don't hold any false illusions. That's why I'm determined to enjoy whatever time we spend together. The only catch, Sam is that, when you leave my door to be intimate with someone else, don't come back. Be with me, *and only me*, while you're with me, Sam. I mean that. Be monogamous with me. If it's only for a day, a week, a month, a year, however long we're together—just do it.

"I told you before that I don't spread my affections, Sam. It's too dangerous a thing to do. I'm not speaking of just the physical dangers, but of the *mental* dangers. Oh, yes, they exist as well. Don't you realize that for every person you sleep with, they take a part of you with them when they leave? I don't care, Sam, even if you do say you'll never see them again. It doesn't matter. Because that person can still lay claim to some small portion of you. Besides, sharing myself with several people at the same time, or worrying about whether you're doing it, would only drain my creative juices."

Ashela stared at him over the top of her glass. "I've worked hard to get where I am, Sam, and I've had to fight to get here. I'm not willing to throw it all away just to be with you. These last few weeks, I've thought about you more than any man I've known in my entire life. And . . . even though this is just our second night together, I have to think ahead. Maybe I'm being presumptuous by telling you all these things, but I'm only being honest. The thought of being with you is a heady notion, Sam. Any woman would jump at the opportunity. Many already have. But I'm not just any woman, Sam. I'm unique in and of myself. All I'm asking is that you think about what I'm saying to you."

"Why do you think you'd have to throw everything aside in order to be with me?"

"Because. The way you've pursued me over these last few weeks has been . . . dizzying. But now that you've got me, Sam, I know I'd be making a grave mistake by thinking it could last. What I'm saying to you is, if you intend to chase other women while you're with me, then make this next trip out my door your last one. I don't want to look up and see myself in the newspapers being listed as one of your latest castaway victims. If that's asking too much . . ." She gave him a sardonic smile. "Then let the door knob hit cha' where the dog shouda bit cha,' my brotha."

277

Sam was massaging her feet. He was silent for a long while, as if reflecting upon or weighing his options. "Tomorrow's not promised or guaranteed to any of us, Ashela. All we have is right here and right now. I told you earlier, the women that I've been with have all known the score. So I can understand your need to lay down your own by-laws. While I'm not able to say how long this will last between us, what I can say is that you have my . . . word that as long as I'm with you, there'll be no others. But if it turns out to be only for a week or two, then so be it."

Ashela was watching and listening to him intently. With his words, she nodded her head. Her deep-set dimples were on full display. "Sam, do know that I'm suddenly feeling . . . refreshed?" Ashela wiggled her feet out of his hands. "And I was soooooo tired. But now? I think I can even walk up the stairs on my own."

Sam merely grinned in anticipation. *What was he getting himself into?*

Hours later, they were entwined in each other's arms when her telephone rang. She started to let the caller kick into her answering machine, but reached over Sam and picked it up. "Hello?"

"Well, look who made it back from the moon!" Kyliah kicked her own feet up on her couch. "How the hell are ya?" It was after midnight.

"I'm fine. Thank you for asking."

Kyliah laughed outright. "Wait a second. Hold up. *'I'm fine. Thank you for asking?'* Girl, don't even try it. Give me the four-one-one scoop. What happened between you and Sam last night?"

"Yes, Sam is fine too. As a matter of fact, he's lying right beside me. Fast asleep, I might add. Is there anything you wanted in particular, Kye? Cause if not, we really must continue our conversation another time."

"Girl, get the *fudge* outta here!" Sam was still there from last night? As bad as she wanted the details, Kyliah said, "Look. As soon as the man hits the door, you need to call me and give me the goods. I don't care where I am—*find me!* You know all my numbers, right? My pager, my cellular, my home digits, my fax, my e-mail—you got 'em all, right?"

Ashela laughed. "Yes, love, I do. And I promise to call you later. Ta taaaaaa." Ashela turned the ringer off on the phone.

"Let me guess. Kyliah?"

"Bingo. She thought you were still here from last night." Ashela snickered sarcastically. "Wouldn't I be a dead woman."

Sam pulled her back down to lay on top of him. "Didn't I promise to be gentle with you?"

"Yes, baby. And you were. I have no complaints." She kissed him on his nose.

"I'm the one who's complaining. Don't you know I'm an old man?"

"Yeah, right. You don't carry me up the stairs like you're an old man."

"That's easy. You're a lightweight. Just don't get any heavier or we'll have problems."

"Go back to sleep, Sam. In my older days I plan to grow as big as a house."

The next morning Sam came downstairs freshly showered. He could smell the strong aroma of freshly brewed coffee. He had slept extremely well the night before. He went into the kitchen in search of Ashela but didn't find her. After pouring himself a cup of coffee, he headed in the direction of her music room. She was inside playing the piano and recording notes in a song book. She looked up when she saw Sam in the doorway. "Good morning."

"The same to you." He came and sat beside her on the piano bench.

"How's the coffee?"

"It's good. Did you go to all this trouble for me? I've yet to see you drink coffee."

"Can't stand the stuff, but I love the smell of it. And it was no trouble at all. Are you always a grouch in the mornings, Sam?" He appeared slightly surly.

"My ex-wife used to accuse me of that." He sipped his coffee.

"Mmmmm. I wonder why," was all Ashela said as she stared at him.

"Come walk me out the door. I've got a load of paperwork awaiting me."

"How about dinner tonight?"

"Your place or mine?" Sam asked.

"Oh, I had the II Ristorante de Giorgio Valdi in mind."

"That's daring. I thought you didn't want to be seen in public with me."

"Why, Sam Ross, I never said that. What I said was that I didn't want to be *humiliated* publicly by you. Big difference love."

Women! Sam shook his head as he stood to his feet. "Reservations for seven o'clock?"

"I'll be ready." Ashela got up and walked him out.

Later that afternoon, Ashela put in a call to Kyliah.

"It's about time! Sheese. I thought about calling the paramedics. I figured you guys must have become glued together from the waist down."

Ashela had just gotten off her stepper machine and taken a shower. Now she lay on the living room sofa.

"Unfortunately, I'm not as insatiable as you are Kye. Nor do I seem to have your stamina."

Kyliah was shaking her head. "I don't know, my sistah. You seem to be holding your own pretty well—considering the fact that it was *you* telling *me* a couple of weeks ago that I needed to lay off the juice-pipe. So, how was it?"

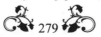

Ashela was grinning from ear to ear as she laced her hands together behind her head. She caught her bottom lip between her teeth before saying, "Kye, the man is dangerous. I mean, now I understand why the women are out there fighting in the streets over him."

"Ugh ohh. Don't tell me you intend to become one of them?"

"Not if I can help it. I told him that I couldn't be with him if he were going to continue to see other women."

"Get the hell outta here! For real? What did he say? I mean, how did he respond?"

"At first, he didn't say anything. But then he said okay. I know it sounds weird, but I just wanted to be honest with him, Kye. I can't run around worrying about who he's with and what he's doing with them."

"Do you believe him though, Ash? That just sounds too good to be true. We are talking about Sam Ross—the same one who's rumored to last no more than a week with any woman."

"Kye, our agreement is that while we're together, we won't see other people. Now, who's to say how long we'll last? *I* certainly don't have a clue. And oddly enough, I do believe him. Call me crazy, stupid, gullible, whatever. But I've peeped a side to him that's just really gripping my attention right now. It's like, having glimpsed it, I've got to peel away every layer that's there until I get to the real him."

"Ash, I was afraid this might happen. I mean, I should have known that once you got a little juice out of the bottle, you would want to drain the whole jug. While I say go for it and all, just be careful with him, kid. Don't let him steal your heart. I like Sam, but neither do I want to see you get hurt. I certainly don't want to see you go through what I did with Arron." Kyliah hoped that she wouldn't come to regret the fact that it was she who had urged Ashela to go out with Sam in the first place.

"Yeah, I hear what you're saying. It's been a long time since I've been with a man and now that I have one, at least temporarily, I'm just trying to keep myself from falling overboard."

"It's all one day at a time, babe. So, tell me, how did he do it to you?"

Ashela laughed. "Kye, you are sick. Do you know that?"

"Yeah, I know. But tell me anyway."

"Girl, the question should have been how *didn't* he do it to me." Ashela's toes locked just thinking about it. "Kye . . ." A low growl escaped Ashela's lips.

"I'll bet he was big wasn't he?"

"Mmmm hmmm. And *real* sweet. Kye, he's even got a slight curvature to his tip."

"Awww, nawww." Kyliah's own toes curled tightly. "Ash, say it ain't so."

"It's true, girl. But what I really like, is the way he takes his time when he loves me. I mean, he was driving me out of my mind! Kye, you *know* I love it when a man

grips my hips. Well, Sam . . ." She spread her hands. "It's like he knows how to apply just the right amount of pressure. Girl, he kept givin' it to me and wouldn't let me go. At one point he even had his arm locked around my neck so I couldn't move. I had to just take it, girl." Ashela put her hands back behind her head again. "And, Kye? Are you sitting down, girl?"

Kyliah's stomach was knotted and she was curled up into a ball as visions of Sam rocking Ashela flashed through her mind.

"Are you there, Kye?"

Two tiny mouse-like squeaks slipped from Kyliah's lips as her teeth bit into the knuckle of her finger.

"Girl, the man has calluses on his hands!" Ashela was almost yelling.

Kyliah rolled to the middle of her bed. Her knees were tucked close to her chest. Flash-back spasms shot throughout *her* body. *Where was Arron when she needed him?*

Now Ashela was whispering again as she brought her own emotions back under control. "How is that possible, Kye? Can somebody please tell me how a man like Sam can possibly have *calluses* on his hands? Where'd they come from? I know he works out, but he's got to be doing something more. Maybe a hobby that I don't know about yet. Whatever it is, the man roams his big hands all over my body and I just lose it. And, Kye, no lie, my sistah, the brotha likes to whisper in my ear while he strokes me. My sistah, can you believe it?" Ashela was screaming again.

Kyliah was finally able to pull her knuckle out of her mouth. In a small voice, she whispered hoarsely, "Did you taste him?"

"Girl, you *know* I had to!" Ashela spread her hands as if she were talking to a simpleton. "So yes, my sistah, I'll admit that I sucked the *lead* off his pipe. He was sweet too, Kye. Big, thick, long and sweet." Ashela couldn't stop shaking her head from side to side.

"Mphm, mphm, mphm," was all Kyliah was able to murmur. Every muscle in her body was rigid.

"I know, girl. But close your mouth *if* you can. Kye, I just need you to do one thing for me. I mean, you got my back, right?"

A small, squeakish murmur came from the other end of the line. Ashela knew Kyliah was still trying to regroup and regain her senses.

"Just do me this one favor, Kye. If you see me going off on the deep end. I mean, if I appear to be losing it, you've got to step in and slap me and make me get myself together. You've got to be my safety net. I can't lose everything I've gained because of Sam. And Kye, you know what I'm talking about. How many times have we seen sane women go berserk over a man simply because he's laying the groundwork in the most awesome way? Kye, don't play stoop. You know where I'm coming from. How many times have you brought me a newspaper article about some high-ranking

woman of good, *noble* character snapping the "F" out because some man caused her to get strung out there? Sometimes the lovin' can be so good, it'll make an intelligent, hard-working woman lose her mind. I don't want that to be me, Kye. I *cain't* go out like a punk. So I'mma need your help here, girlfriend. If you see me drifting too far out to the left field, just tap me on the shoulder and say 'come on back, my sistah. Cause you're losin' it.' I promise, I won't be mad atcha. I'll even thank you in the end."

Kyliah could finally talk again. *"Whatta man, whatta man, whatta man!* Salt and Pepa knew exactly what to say!"

"I know. Tell me about it. We're even going to Giorgio Valdi's on Channel Road for dinner tonight."

Kyliah took a deep breath. She was sufficiently recovered now. "Ash, you know that's where all the movie stars dine. So if you go there, just be prepared to see your picture in the paper tomorrow morning."

"I'm ready. I went by Derrick's yesterday and even he was trying to get the four-one-one."

"Well, sweetheart, after tonight, all of L.A. is going to know that you and Sam Ross are an item."

"And I can't wait." Ashela screamed into the air, "All you Sam Ross groupies . . . eat your heart out!"

When they finally hung up, Kyliah was left shaking her head. She certainly had some new techniques that she intended to use on Arron. So into Ashela's story had she been that she'd forgotten to tell her that she was going to Boston for an entire week.

They arrived at Il Ristorante de Giorgio Valdi in Sam's candy apple red Lamborghini. Valets assisted them out of their vehicle before driving off to park it. They entered the restaurant looking glamorous and stunning as a couple. Both were dressed in black. Sam in his tux and white shirred shirt and Ashela in a long, body-hugging, one-shouldered gown that had a very high side split. Harry Winston diamonds sparkled at her ears, neck, and wrist.

Throughout the meal, friends of Sam's stopped by their table to speak. Actors and actresses, movie producers, most of whom Ashela had heard of but had never met. What stood out the most for her was just how well connected Sam was.

"Sam, how do you know all of these people?"

He shook his head as he swallowed a bite of his filet mignon. "I've been around a long time. Also, about ten years ago, I was able to buy a large chunk of stock in several film companies. So I got to know quite a few people in the industry. You know, I used to be a regular at this restaurant, but it's been years since the last time I've dined here." Sam took a sip of his wine. "The food is excellent, but most people

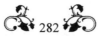

come here to preen, be seen and have their photographs taken by the paparazzi. For the last couple of years, I've tried to avoid having my picture taken with so many different women. People see it and tend to think that I'm sleeping with every person I'm photographed with. It only fosters the same kind of misconceptions as the ones even you have about me. But, primarily, I'd stopped coming because I didn't want my boys to get the wrong impression either."

"And here I was thinking that you were forced to hobnob with all these good people because of your position at Werner."

Sam laughed. "Years ago, when I was first appointed Vice-President of W. E., they used to refer to me as 'the eating vice-president' because I got sent to all the minority-hosted functions. At first it was fun because, even there, I got to meet so many different people. But then it got to be old news because I quickly recognized that I didn't have the kind of authority and clout that I really wanted. That's when I began to groom myself to move up even higher. It wasn't easy. I've found that many times when you become a high-ranking black person in a corporation, that's all you're expected to be *is* a good knife-and-forksman. But, either way, if you want to get ahead in corporate America, you have to learn to play the game. And knowing who's who in your industry helps to build your arsenal. I'm just surprised that it's taken me all of this time to meet you. I'd seen your picture and knew who you were by name. But I never saw you at any of the industry functions."

"I told you I didn't get out much. I've always wanted it that way, Sam. I prefer to do whatever it is that I do and remain in the background. I don't have a hunger to be in front of the camera. Although, I did want to be seen with you tonight."

Sam was smiling at her over his glass of wine. "Why?"

"I'm not one-hundred percent sure." With her elbows on the table, Ashela folded her hands and leaned forward to ask him softly, "Would it surprise you to know that a part of me wants to brand you? Asking you here tonight was just my attempt to stamp my own name across your . . ." Her dimples were flashing again.

"Uhn, huh. Don't stop—you were saying? You wanted to stamp your name on my what?" Smiling, Sam pressed for an answer.

"Your . . . chest. That's safe enough, don't you think? That way, *you* know my name is there, but it's not out in the open where everyone else can see it."

"But, surely, Ms. Jordan, that's not wise of you. Since you've obviously given us a time frame of only a week or two before we go our separate ways."

Ashela tilted her head and smiled at him. "Who knows, Sam? I might just get lucky."

"There's an old adage that's been around for eons, Ashela. It's one that I've personally tried and tested and have found to be quite true."

"And it is?"

Sam peered at her over the top of his wine glass. "Be careful what you wish for, you just might get it."

"That sounds like a warning, Sam."

"It was *meant* to be."

Ashela took a spoon of her tapioca pudding and lifted it into Sam's mouth. "I think I'll take my chances."

After dinner, they returned to her home and came through the front door laughing over how Maggie Z. had cornered and begged them to pose for a picture.

Ashela went into her kitchen and poured grape juice into two wine glasses. She met Sam outside on the deck. It was another warm and breezy night. Sam had removed his jacket and was leaning over the railing. She handed him the glass.

He tasted it. "Grape juice?" His eyebrows were raised. "It's different."

"Hey. When you run out of the real thing, you have to get creative."

Sam placed his glass on the wicker table. "Let's go for a walk on the beach."

"Now?"

"Sure." Sam kicked off his shoes and removed his socks. He opened the wooden rail gate and walked down the stairs to the landing. "Come on." Sam stood looking up at her.

Ashela didn't mind walking in the sand, but not dressed as she was. Finally, she stripped off her dress and sheer stockings and walked down to meet him wearing only her strapless bra and panties.

Hand in hand they walked through the sand, laughing underneath the moonlight. Ashela danced into the wet area of the sand where the waves washed onto the shore. Laughing and still holding on to Sam's hand, she started singing mockingly in a high-pitched voice like the little mouse, Fievel, in the movie, *An American Tale.*

Somewhere out there,

Beneath the pale moonlight . . .

Someone's thinking of me,

And loving me tonight . . .

"James Ingram and Patti Austin. Didn't think I knew that, did you?"

"No, I didn't. How'd you know that? You don't strike me as one who'd watch an animated flick."

"James is under the Werner label. I try to stay abreast of what our artists put out." He pulled her onto a drier part of the sand before sitting down. Ashela sat behind him and wrapped her legs and arms around his waist. Staring up at the moonlight, Sam said, "Tell me where you get the inspiration for your music."

Ashela came around in front of him and straddled him, forcing him to lean backwards on his elbows. "All I know is that it comes from somewhere deep within

me. In a way, Sam, it's almost like magic. Sometimes, I think of it as a springwell of untapped passion that's waiting patiently for the right moment to be brought out. I put all of myself into my music. Love, pain, fear, hurt, anger, sorrow, joy. My music is the stage in my life. It's the avenue that allows me to release everything, Sam. It's where my emotions can flow unchecked, unhindered, and uninhibited. Songwriting can't be taught. You have to *feel* your way into it." And right now, Ashela was starting to feel him. She leaned down and whispered into his ear, "Let's go take a shower and make love, Sam."

"I'll race you back to the house," he said. But Ashela cheated. She was already off of him and running.

***

Soft jazz by Gerald Albright played in the background as Ashela massaged Calvin Klein body moisturizer into Sam's skin. Both of them were fresh from their shower and now lay across the silken sheets. He, on his stomach while Ashela sat atop him taking her time as she languished him with the fragrance-free lotion. She caressed his neck and applied pressure to his shoulders and arms. Her fingers glided over his body, spreading the lotion evenly. All over his back and waist, his buttocks, thighs and calves, even massaging his ankles and feet.

As she urged him to turn over while easing herself back on top of him, Sam was in a relaxed state of blissful indolence. He relished the feel of her hands sliding over him, applying light pressure to his sensitive areas. Her fingers felt like featherweights as she lowered herself to caress his inner thighs. And then surprisingly, but most delightfully, Sam felt the tip of her tongue glide over his erect manhood. Then her lips were guiding him into her warm, wet orifice. Tawny sensations seared throughout his body. Only this time, it was *he* who needed to grip and hold on to something as intermittent spasms gripped his insides.

Ashela eased herself upwards to sit on top of him again. With her hands planted firmly on his chest, she stared down into his eyes with a powerful look of seduction. In a voice that was barely above a whisper, she said to him, "You make me feel so soft and feminine, Sam. You make me want to love and be loved in return. It's almost like you've become embedded in my mind so that I can't stop thinking about you. And it's dangerous for me to feel this way. *You're* dangerous, Sam."

Ashela leaned down and kissed him, slipping her tongue past his teeth. And while he was unsuspecting, she reached between them and slid him inside of her moistness. As she slowly sat upright, bit by bit, like a sponge, she absorbed his length and thickness into the warmth of her taut and cream-filled nucleus.

Sam groaned aloud. Instinctively, his hands gripped her hips as she performed a rocking dance of her own. He couldn't have asked for more as her body slowly gyrated and reeled on top of him. Erotic shivers coursed through his bloodstream, and in order for him not to release himself into her so soon, Sam sat up with his arms

outstretched behind him, his head thrown back. But Ashela used the opportunity to lace her arms around his neck and tease him by pressing her breasts to his chest.

In the blink of an eye, she had turned the tables on him. At the snap of a finger, she had taken command. And by turning the tide, *she* was now the masterful navigator in charge of steering them toward their sensual destiny. She was biting softly into his chin, and the low, stimulating, near-guttural noises that she was making as she rocked his world were causing Sam to lose it. He could feel his insides pulling downward with the force of gravity and he knew he wouldn't last much longer. She constricted her vaginal muscles tightly against his throbbing, pulsing and aching tool, whispering over and over for him to "give it to me, baby" and telling him in no uncertain terms how much she loved and needed "Daddy's big, sweet, black stick." Sam could no longer hold out.

As naked spasms gripped him, Sam cried out as intense waves of pleasure overcame him. His senses dazed, he released himself into her. Finally spent, he lay back on the bed and felt Ashela slide alongside him. "That wasn't fair," was all he managed to say when he caught his breath.

Her leg rested over his and she trailed her fingers down his chest. "*All* is fair in love and war, Sam. You can't always expect to be the enforcer. Sometimes you've got to lay back and learn how to let someone else give to you for a change. You know something, Sam? For a long time, I could only enjoy making love from two positions. Either I had to be on top or my lover had to take me from behind. The missionary style never did it for me. And then I discovered why. Whenever I laid on my back, I couldn't enjoy it because, to me, it made me feel like I was being submissive. It felt like I didn't have any control over what was happening to me. And so I learned to avoid having sex in that position. But guess what, Sam? Tonight, you're going to give it to me missionary style because I want to play the submissive role right now. I want you to dominate me and love me like you did that very first time."

Ashela didn't have a chance to say much more because Sam, listening to her whisper her words, had become thoroughly aroused again. And then he was kissing her, sliding her onto her back, spreading her legs in a V-like fashion, and penetrating her voluptuous and womanly depths. But this time, Sam needed to possess *her*, to own her, to *brand* her as his own.

As he took his time, stroking her cavity with gentle insistence, Ashela was immobilized with pleasure. In her weakened state, it was all she could do to wrap her arms around his neck and her legs around his waist. She clung to him, her body rising and falling in timed sequence with his. As she whispered her own sweet words of encouragement into his ear, her nails scraped his back without drawing blood.

In those moments as he pleased her, he *became* her king. Loving her as she urged, prompted, guided, and begged him to. Once again, Sam found himself unable to resist the whispering whine in her voice—unable to withstand her sensual,

pleading, vocal expressions. And so he satisfied her craving, gave her what she needed, and fulfilled her like she wanted. But what enthralled Sam was the fact that, as he pleasured her, he gratified himself.

Once again, he palmed her in the manner that she'd come to love so much, thrusting himself deeper into the juicy core of her being. And when the time came for him to empty himself into her, he did so with no holds barred. With her teeth locked into his shoulder and his hands gripping the fleshy area of her hips, both clung to each other as hypnotic spasms loosed through both of them. And in blissful satiation, they sunk down to bed content to float off to separate, but similar, destinations.

Chapter Twenty-Eight

am wound up staying in California for two months—a far cry from the two week time-frame he had originally planned. During that time, he and Ashela unintentionally embarked upon a whirlwind romance. Like lovers exploring a city for the first time, they uncovered places that neither of them had been before. Up-and-coming art galleries, museums, comedy clubs, and many, many, restaurants. Ashela had never been adventurous enough to try Japanese food, so Sam dragged her to Ginza Sushi-Ko. For lunch, they sampled cuisines from Valentino's and Drai's. For dinner, Locanda Veneta and The Little Door. And for Sunday brunch, The Ivy.

They also took one another to their favorite personal hideaways as well. He took her to the Getty Center and horseback riding at the Tao of Riding. In return, Ashela took Sam to her favorite nook and cranny jazz spots. To The Jazz Bakery, The Catalina, Marla's Jazz Supper Club, and to The Cinegrill in the Hollywood Roosevelt Hotel. She even surprised him by taking him to several of her favorite lingerie stores. Playmates, Fredericks's of Hollywood, Fred Segal and to The Pleasure Chest.

The two of them were spotted dining intimately at expensive restaurants such as L'Orangerie, and were seen huddled together sharing a whispered secret over a glass of Kahlúa at many of the popular bars. On evenings when they just wanted to spend time alone, they strolled hand in hand along Ashela's beachfront. The gossip columnists had long since linked them romantically and rumors were further exacerbated when Maggie Z. reported that the "M" word had been rumored between them.

One Wednesday afternoon, she and Sam agreed to meet for lunch, but Ashela had gotten hung-up in the studio. She called him on his cell phone to tell him that she was running late and on impulse, invited him up. She and Face were working on a

single release for Karyn White. As Sam stepped into the room, pleasantly surprised glances were thrown his way. It was rare that he got the opportunity to sit-in on a recording session, but when he did, everyone wanted to shine for him.

Ashela was behind the glass partition with Karyn and she didn't see Sam when he first arrived. She looked up in time to see him and Face clasping fists like old-time friends. When he looked her way, she blew him a kiss and he smiled at her in return. Soon afterwards, the session became even more energized and when Ashela finally looked up again, an entire hour had passed. She glanced over at where Sam had been sitting but he was gone.

It seemed to both of them that the weeks were flying by because before they knew it, two months had expired and the time had come where Sam was now forced to return to the East Coast. There was sadness on Ashela's part. She'd grown accustomed to having him around. She teased him about the need to get a dog now that he was leaving her. But Sam didn't like the way she'd used the term "leaving her." So he reassured her that he would only be a few hours away and any time she wanted to come to him in New York, he'd send for her in his private jet.

Before he left, Sam bought her a huge Great Dane puppy. But Ashela was afraid of dogs and she made him return it, convincing him that she wouldn't begin to know how to care for the animal and neither would she be home often enough to train him.

Sam spent the night before his departure at her place. It was mid-September as she pressed him for an answer about when he planned to return to California. When Sam told her that he'd be back in time for Christmas, the weeks until then seemed like an eternity. Their lovemaking that night had a deep-seated urgency to it, and afterwards they held and caressed one another with tenderness. But despite all of Ashela's assurances of how much she'd miss him, try as he might, Sam was unable to get her to commit to visiting him in New York.

***

Early Saturday morning, Kyliah was having a shiatsu massage and a cucumber facial at the Hahm Rejuvenation Center. As she relaxed under the expert hands of the masseuse, thoughts of Arron drifted through her mind. Three weeks had passed since she'd returned from her trip to Boston. She liked Arron and definitely enjoyed being with him, but the nagging voice inside her head told her that she'd only be setting herself up for more heartache if she tried to pursue a relationship with him. The two of them had had a wonderful time during her stay. There was much laughter, fun, and spontaneity that had been shared between them. But little things had also occurred during the trip that gave clue to the many barriers that would have to be overcome, and distance was the least of them.

She'd spent ten days in Boston. He'd met her at Logan International Airport in his Jag and had taken her back to his Cyprus Hills duplex. Arron's condo was located in a chic, high-rent district where well-to-do yuppies congregated. He returned to his office that same afternoon but was home by five-thirty to take her out

to dinner. They dined at Biba's and it didn't take long for Kyliah to discover just how popular a Bostonian Arron was. Several women stopped by their table to ask why they hadn't heard from him in a while and to let him know that their phone numbers hadn't changed.

Angered not in the least bit, Kyliah simply smiled and told him that before he started thumping his chest and thinking that *she* was about to get bent out of shape, he really needed to take into consideration that only women of low class and no character would stoop to doing what they'd done. It was merely an indication of their desperation.

Arron didn't correct her. But Kyliah would have been shocked to discover that the very women she'd just labeled as "low class" were considered the "crème de la crème" of Boston society, specifically because they came from moneyed backgrounds.

It was with immense pride and pleasure that Arron showed her around his illustrious city and Kyliah soon found out that he possessed a great deal of civic pride. He was a history buff and had an incredible love for buildings with majestic and historic architectural structures. With lavish detail, he described the history behind every place he took her. Places such as the African Meeting House, the Bunker Hill Monument, the Paul Revere House and Boston Common. His enthusiasm and eye for detail, allowed her to view the city through his eyes.

Arron had been right on target when he'd advised her to bring comfortable shoes. Because of its twisting, winding, and narrow streets, Boston was a city made for walking. It was also a bastion of tradition with a strong African American heritage. She spent five days touring the city with him, visiting the art galleries, museums, and main attractions that Arron felt every first-time visitor to the city must see. On the sixth day, Kyliah made him promise to take her shopping. She didn't need him to pay for anything, she just wanted his presence.

It was a Tuesday afternoon as they strolled through Copley Place before winding up at a jewelry counter inside Tiffany's. Arron stood looking into a glass casing that held beautiful diamond wedding and engagement rings while Kyliah was a few feet away talking to a saleswoman. She was pointing to a diamond tennis bracelet when she heard a female voice behind her say, "I *thought* it was you, Arron. But I had to find out if I was mistaken. What brings *you* here during working hours?" By this time the woman stood between she and Arron, and Kyliah turned around to get a look at her.

She was a slim, expensively clad woman who appeared to be in her early fifties. She also seemed waspish in her mannerisms. The look on her face suggested that she'd just caught Arron red-handed and demanded that he tell all.

Arron bent down and touched his cheek to hers before saying, "I'm here with a friend."

Making the assumption that he was with Kyliah, the woman gave her a sweeping glance from head to toe. She cleared her throat, expecting to be introduced.

Arron threw his arm around her shoulders and took several steps in Kyliah's direction. "Kyliah Reed, this is my aunt, Sasha Downer." Kyliah extended her hand.

"It's a pleasure to meet you, Ms. Reed. Please forgive me, I'm just taken aback to find my dear nephew, of all people, shopping for an engagement ring. Why, Vanessa didn't even mention to me that you were even thinking of marriage." Surely her sister would have told her had she known about it. A thought crossed her mind. "You two wouldn't be planning on eloping, would you?" She looked up at Arron. "Think of how heartbroken your mother would be, Arron."

"With all due respect, Ms. Downer, I don't believe wild horses could force your nephew to put a ring on *any* woman's finger." Kyliah detected a bit of snobbery behind the woman's prying attitude.

Ignoring her remark, Sasha was determined to get to the bottom of things. "What a pleasant accent. And such . . ." Sasha searched for a non-offensive word. ". . . lovely eyes you have. May I ask where you're from?" What she really wanted to know was of what origin she was.

"No, Aunt Sasha. You may not. Kyliah's here on vacation. And since she's not applying for membership at any of our high-society clubs, there's no need to grill her." Arron spoke kindly but his voice was firm. He knew that if Kyliah answered one question, twenty more would follow.

Though Arron was trying to brush her off, Sasha strongly suspected that something was going on between them that they didn't want anyone to know about. But give her time and she'd find out—whatever it was. "Oh, shush, Arron. If you're planning on getting engaged, surely your own aunt has a right to know about it." She looked Kyliah over even more intently, examining the shade of her hair.

As the sales clerk motioned to Kyliah to hand her the diamond bracelet she'd asked to see, Kyliah turned back to the counter. She focused on what the sales clerk was saying, deciding to let Arron handle his aunt alone. "This one is normally fifteen. But right now it's on sale for twelve. As you can see, the diamonds are of an excellent and flawless cut. Here, try it on."

Kyliah waved her hand back and forth as the diamonds sparkled and shone on her wrist.

"De Beers' diamonds are so beautiful, don't you think?" Sasha offered, continuing to watch Kyliah closely.

"Oh, yes. No woman's wardrobe is complete without one." Kyliah wanted Sasha to know that she was not a novice when it came to purchasing diamonds. She turned back to the sales clerk and said, "Thank you, I'll take it. Can you wrap it for me, please?" Kyliah reached for her wallet to hand the saleswoman her credit card.

Irritated that his aunt was still standing with them watching Kyliah's every move, Arron said, "Put your money away, Kyliah. I'll get that for you."

Kyliah turned to him and said, "No, baby, I wouldn't dream of it. Save your money for our engagement ring. I've decided to get the one with ten carats." A rash of irritation swept over Arron's face as Kyliah gave his aunt more fodder for the family rumor mill.

Sasha missed Arron's facial expression, but she'd caught everything else. The way Arron quickly offered to pay for a twelve thousand dollar bracelet and the fact that she now knew they were *definitely* shopping for an engagement ring. Imagine that! Tight-fisted Arron buying a *ten carat* diamond ring that could easily feed an entire family for a year? Sasha couldn't wait to run and tell it. But first she intended to get a little more information.

"Is this your first visit to Boston, Ms. Reed?"

"Yes it is. Please, call me Kyliah."

"Then you must be enjoying yourself. How long have you two been engaged?"

"Very cute, Aunt Sasha, but Kyliah was only jesting. Shouldn't you be finishing whatever shopping you were about to do?"

"Oh, I'm in no rush. Reginald's birthday isn't until next week but I just thought that I'd pick out his gift ahead of time. That reminds me, you still haven't R.S.V.P.'d for the party, Arron. You will be coming, won't you? Particularly now that you're engaged. It would be the perfect opportunity for you to introduce Kyliah to the family."

"Auntie, Kyliah and I are not engaged. We're just friends, so please, do not go spreading false rumors."

But Sasha was convinced otherwise. Why else would he look so guilty while trying to hide his anger? It could only be because he hadn't yet told the rest of the family. *To a mixed girl of all people!* "Yes, Arron. Whatever you say. But then, I really shouldn't be surprised. You always did say that when you chose to get married, it would be to someone none of us knew." She glanced at Kyliah again. "Well, I won't keep you, dear. I'm sure you two have much more shopping to do. Nice meeting you, Kyliah. I'm sure I'll see you again." Sasha hurried away. Probably to the nearest pay phone.

Arron was irritated, Kyliah could see it all over his face. She wouldn't have said a word if his aunt had not appeared so pompous and uppity. If the rest of his family was anything like her, it would do Kyliah nicely to meet nary another one of them.

As she figured he'd be, Arron was silent during the ride to his home. Finally, Kyliah turned to him and said, "Arron, will you get over it, please? How do you think *I* felt standing there with you looking for all the world like I was the last person you'd choose to be with? You should be grateful I insisted on paying for the bracelet myself. If not, you'd have really had something to call Sam Ross to complain about."

Kyliah debated whether to bring up the issue that his aunt had been taken aback simply because of her mixed heritage, but decided against it.

"Oh, so you're reminding me of that again, huh? Now I'm Mr. El Cheapo? You think I wouldn't have sprung for a twelve hundred dollar piece of jewelry?"

"Excuse *you*, Arron. But it was a De Beers bracelet and it was twelve *thousand* dollars, not twelve *hundred*. No wonder you volunteered to pay for it so fast. You weren't even listening when the saleswoman quoted how much it was." Kyliah looked at the open-mouthed expression on his face and laughed.

"Kyliah, you went into that store and plopped down twelve grand for a *bracelet*?"

"And? What's your point?"

"Look, I know it's your money, and it's not the amount that troubles me. What bothers me is that you only purchased that bracelet to impress Sasha. Not because you saw it and fell so in love with it that you had to have it. And yes, you're damn right. Had I known it was twelve grand, I wouldn't have paid for it. I probably wouldn't have let you buy it either."

"You know, Arron, you're right—it *is* my money. But if you think I bought the bracelet just to impress your aunt, you're dead wrong. I don't give a flying fuck about what your aunt thinks of me. And whether or not she thinks I'm good enough for you, is the least of my concerns. I'd made it up in my mind to buy the bracelet before she even came on the scene. For your information, it was twenty percent off, so for me, it wasn't just a purchase—it was an investment. What we *need* to discuss is why you felt the need to play me like 'orphan Annie' in front of her."

"I did no such thing. I just don't want her passing misinformation on to my mother and the rest of my family. You have no idea of the kind of flak I'm sure to get from this. Besides, *I* invited *you* to Boston. So as your host, I expected to pay for your trip, including your shopping excursions."

"Arron, that's noble of you. It really is. But can we just change the subject?" Kyliah turned her head to stare out of the window as they headed toward the Callahan Tunnel. She could tell that money was just one more issue that they would argue over, and it seemed as if her mixed heritage and his family's social status were others. Unfortunately for her, the blood in her family's veins was a *mixed* red. Not the true blue kind that was apparently required by the Davenport brood. As good as the sex was between them, it wasn't enough to compensate for the growing number of differences she was beginning to see between them.

Later that evening as they made love fiercely and passionately, so good was it to both of them that neither was willing to admit that there were *any* potential problems between them. As they held, caressed and savored one another's body, it was all good as they lay basking in the sweat of their exertion. By the next morning, they were laughing again and back to chasing each other around the house like little kids.

Kyliah now knew from Arron that his family came from money. After meeting at least one of his family members, what struck her most about him was that he wasn't as snobbish as she suspected the rest of his family was. With his education and cultured background, she now understood why his parents were impressing upon him to marry someone on their social "level." While Kyliah was nowhere near as versed in the social skills and graces that his family obviously was, neither was she a backwater hillbilly. She was just a simple, down-home southern girl and she saw no reason to try to change or put on airs to appear to be something that she wasn't. Kyliah just appreciated the fact that when she and Arron were together, their conflicting personalities meshed well with one another. Sure, they argued and had their differences, but still, they enjoyed each other's company without false pretenses and, little did she know that this was the very thing that attracted Arron to her.

Sure enough, Sasha went back and informed the rest of Arron's family that she'd seen him at Tiffany's with a bi-racial woman whom no one in the family had ever met. That same evening, the phone calls started coming in. But Arron knew that it was his family calling him with questions about his alleged engagement, and he let the answering machine take all of his calls.

The rest of her days were spent taking side trips to Lexington and Concord. There was so much to see that she couldn't possibly cram it all into the few remaining days she had left. On her last night there, she cooked a light meal for them at his home and they spent a quiet night together.

After dinner, they curled up on his sofa to watch an old, classical film, Imitation of Life. He lay in her arms when halfway through the movie, the telephone rang. Arron had turned the ringer back on hours ago and it was the first time the phone had rung since their return to Boston earlier that day. Kyliah picked up the receiver and pressed it to his ear. She could tell immediately that it was his mother.

"Yes, I'm fine. I was just out of town for a few days."

Obviously, she was grilling him about why he hadn't been answering his phone.

"No, Mother, I'm afraid I have nothing to report. While I have met someone, we're hardly to the point where we're discussing marriage. No. She was just purchasing a particular bracelet that she wanted. Yes, I assume so."

Kyliah unwrapped herself from him to go upstairs. When he tried to pull her back onto the sofa, she skipped away from him. She didn't want to hear whatever excuses he was about to make.

Arron watched the sway of her hips beneath the long, satin nightgown as she walked away.

"She's from California, mother. And I would love to bring her for dinner but I'm afraid she's leaving tomorrow morning. Yes, I do intend to see her again, so you'll get to meet her the next time she comes. I have to go now, mother. Yes, I'll call you later."

Arron got up off the couch to go and find Kyliah. She was inside his bedroom packing some of her things into her suitcases. He stood inside the doorway. "I thought you weren't going to pack until early tomorrow morning."

"I'm just getting a head-start, so I won't have that much to do tomorrow."

"That was my mother wanting to know why I was shopping for an engagement ring." Arron was watching her closely.

"I have no doubt that you set the matter straight." After all, what son would want his elitist mother thinking that he was about to marry some country hick? Kyliah changed the subject. She wasn't about to let him peep her newfound feelings of inadequacy. "You know, Arron, I didn't get a chance to wear half the stuff I brought with me." She zipped up one of her garment bags.

Arron stepped into the room, picked the bag up off of the bed and hung it back in the closet for her. "Guess you'll just have to come back again then won't you?" He sat on the bed as he watched her kneel down to zip up her suitcase.

She didn't answer him on that one. She just continued to buzz around the room while engaging him in light conversation that avoided discussion of marriage and wedding rings.

Arron watched her, thinking that she would make some man a wonderful wife. He just didn't think it would be him. He wondered if he would now be able to forget about her when she left, or if he would at least be able to bring his feelings for her back into check. All he knew was that he wanted to make love to her several more times before she left, and then afterwards, Arron hoped that she wouldn't dominate his thoughts the way she had during the past several weeks. He was determined that his relationship with her would become nothing more than the good friendship that it was.

***

As the masseuse urged her to turn over onto her back, Kyliah didn't fool herself. She knew that Arron preferred to date women in his own circle. A circle which did not include her. So be it, she thought to herself. Life goes on. Kyliah had had time to do some deep soul searching since her return to Cali. After an in-depth inventory of all of her plusses and minuses, she hadn't liked what she'd learned about herself. Acknowledging her flaws was very much like looking at a ragdoll with all of its stuffing hanging out of it, only in this case, the doll was none other than herself.

She'd sat cross-legged in the middle of her bed with her head thrown back, as she looked up at the ceiling. Like it or not, there were many areas in her life that were in need of serious repair. It had taken a failed relationship to make her notice them. At least in that respect, she owed Arron a note of gratitude. His subtle rejection of her forced her to realize that it was time to re-evaluate her priorities and get herself together.

Kyliah started remembering all of the things she'd enjoyed doing before she'd unwittingly let the pursuit of men consume her. She acknowledged that for the last

four years, in many respects, she had simply spent the time being unproductive. Sure, her changing careers had been great, and so was the money she'd accumulated in the process. But there were so many other things she could be doing with her spare time other than shopping to keep abreast of the latest fashions. She definitely could afford to further her education and it wasn't like she didn't have the time to do it. Kyliah figured that's where she could start the process of restructuring her life.

Yes, she was honest enough to admit that she still wanted a man in her life, and yes, she still had a desire to be married. But only this time, she'd relax and let it come to her. Hadn't Fredonia always told her that when a *man* finds a wife, *he* finds a good thing? And to top it off, look at Ash. She was all work and hardly no play at all and someone had found her—Sam Ross of all people! That's it! Kyliah thought. Maybe she would take a page out of Ash's book and let the men find her for a change. And in the meantime, she'd forget all about Arron and concentrate on other things like getting her master's degree. But God, even thinking about him hurt. The longing for him was like a needle piercing her heart. She knew it was going to take some time to get over him. But get over him she would. Her self respect depended upon it.

Chapter Twenty-Nine

hristmas in L.A. is just as spectacular as it is in the winterest wonderland. With eighty-degree weather, the absence of snow does not lessen the festive atmosphere. The street lamps lining the boulevards are gaily decorated with pine green trellises and large, bold-red ribbons. All of the stores vie to have the best, brightest and most attractive displays, while the streets become filled with people who scurry about, shopping for gifts and presents.

With the holidays barely two weeks away, Ashela and Kyliah were having dinner at the Bar Marmont on Sunset Boulevard. It was after six o'clock on a weekday and only the cognoscenti were present. Seated at a private booth, out of listening range from any would-be eavesdroppers, they joked as they discussed their resolutions for the upcoming year. Soon, fits of laughter prevailed as each took turns poking fun and reminding the other of the previous New Year's resolutions that they had failed miserably to keep.

In the weeks since she'd last seen Sam, Ashela had been busy clearing her calendar. Her spare time was spent channeling her energy into songwriting. In the past, most of her songs had been the product of days or sometimes weeks of hard work, but Ashela suddenly found herself driven and inspired like never before. Music that was now tinged with a newfound sultriness and laced with an even heavier dose of passion, flowed rapidly from the heart. Compliments of Sam Ross,

her love-life had blossomed into a spicy affair that energized her creativity in ways she had never dreamt of.

It was customary for her songs to evolve into best-selling singles or albums. Rarely did she write one that did *not* make the Hot 100 Singles or Top 200 Albums Chart. But the music she composed during her relationship with Sam Ross proved to be some of the most phenomenal of her career. Each song, when produced, would rocket up the charts like lightning. Saucy love ballads that would top Billboard for weeks on end were the result of her relationship.

Ashela talked to Sam daily. And nightly. Taking him to the moon smoothly, encapsulating him with sheer sensuality, and arousing him in ways that even he had never previously experienced. Knowing he couldn't get away, she teased him all the more, denying his beseeching requests for her to join him in New York. Meanwhile, Ashela put every emotion she encountered into her music. Holding nothing back, she told the world of her need of her man, her desire to hold him and just *be* with him again. With intense longing, she sang of the heartache she felt during each second of time that was spent away from him.

But through it all, Ashela was still reluctant to admit that she was much happier than she had been in years. It was as if such an admission would prevent her from hanging on to the remnants of her heart. All Ashela could do in light of the transformation she found herself undergoing, was watch as the icy particles were melted away from around her heart.

***

For the past several weeks, Kyliah had been studying hard and her efforts had paid off as she'd just passed the GRE days prior and was preparing for entrance into graduate school. Her fierce determination was admirable as Ashela had rarely seen her so committed. With uncharacteristic valor, Kyliah spoke of wanting to do something else with her life instead of just hoping to be married. Finding a hobby and maybe even volunteering to tutor kids in math as she had done in New York, offered promising rewards. She spoke frankly of needing to guard her romantic inclinations much more carefully, and openly admitted that what frightened her the most, was not knowing how long it would take for her to find her mate. But for right now, she intended to focus on getting her master's in Finance.

With Christmas just around the corner, Kyliah made plans to return home for the holidays. She wanted to visit her nephews. And because she hadn't seen or spoken to him in years, maybe even sit down and talk with Parris.

Ashela swirled her wine around in her glass, staring intently at the circling liquid. Parris. Tracy. All of that was so long ago. She was just glad that none of it mattered anymore.

They changed the topic as Kyliah prompted her to talk more about her feelings for Sam. She liked hearing Ashela discuss her relationship with him. She had never known her to speak with such alacrity about a man. Ash had never said it outright, so

Kyliah wondered if she loved him. Over the past several months, her entire attitude seemed to lighten and even her laughter was infectious. On impulse, Kyliah asked her what it was that she liked most about Sam.

Immediately, Ashela's eyes closed and her head turned to the side. Her nails were already digging into the wood of the table. With a grin on her face, Kye reached out and covered Ash's hands with hers. She, herself, knew a thing or two about flashbacks and a restaurant that was equipped with ever-curious onlookers was *not* the place to have one. Trying to appear low-key, she whispered patiently for Ashela to come back to earth before she cracked a nail or damaged the good folk's cherry wood table. The last thing in the world they needed was to get thrown out of a posh establishment in an area where media hounds were forever lurking. Several deep breaths later, Kyliah could tell that Ashela had gotten a grip, and had landed safely back on Earth. The answer to her question needed no further clarification.

***

Sam Ross was feeling a serenity he had never known. Though the past several months had been filled with hard-fought battles waged by his competitors, Sam had come through it all without so much as a scratch. He was looking forward to seeing Ashela again. She had stirred emotions within him that had lain dormant for many years. He smiled when he thought of their nightly conversations. He shook his head thinking of how the woman had a way with words. She had the incredible ability to create an exotic oasis in his mind. Sam also noted in fascination that he hadn't been with any other women in the six months that they'd been dating. The surprising factor was that he'd been faithful without even trying. Maybe it was because his schedule had been so hectic that he hadn't had time to really think about anyone else. Or, perhaps it was because he hadn't felt the need. Excuses, excuses. Sam knew the cold truth was that he was hooked and enjoying it. So much so that he had even gone shopping, personally, for a certain woman and had spent quite a bit of time selecting her gift. With the small fortune he'd spent, she was sure to be pleased with what he'd chosen.

When Sam's plane landed at the private airstrip, instead of having his driver waiting for him with his limousine, he stepped into his elegant Rolls-Royce Silver Seraph. Inside, enveloped by the Seraph's Scandinavian leather, he picked up the phone and dialed his ex-wife, Claudette's number. To his surprise, she picked up and not one of her servants. "Hi, where're the boys?"

"They went shopping with your sister. But, Damael just called. They should be back shortly. Where are you?"

"I'm just getting in from the coast and thought I'd check in with them. Everything okay?"

"Everything's dandy. You're welcome to come and wait here until they get home. They should be here in another twenty minutes."

"Thanks, that would be great. But only if it's not an inconvenience." Sam knew that Claudette was seeing someone and he certainly didn't want to intrude.

"Sam, you know me well enough to know that I'd tell you if it were."

Sam smiled as he replaced the phone on its hook.

Thirty minutes later he pressed the intercom on the front gate and drove through as the huge wrought-iron posts parted to allow him entrance. He pulled up the long driveway and Claudette stood at the door waiting for him to exit his car. Time had certainly been kind to her, Sam thought to himself as he approached her. She looked too damned good to be in her late forties. She wore a double-breasted Dolce & Gabbana houndstooth pant suit. Matching black & white Calvin Klein pumps completed her ensemble. Her hair was cropped closely to her head.

As he walked up to her, Sam said, "You're looking well, Loon." "Loon" was the petname that Sam had given her when they had first started dating over twenty years before. They'd shared so much fun and laughter back then that he started calling her "Loon" in jest. The name stuck.

"Thank you. I'm feeling well. The boys haven't made it back yet, so come, have a seat." Claudette closed the door behind him and led him into the living room.

It had been months since the last time Sam had seen his ex-wife and years since he had stepped foot inside the home they had shared while they'd been married. Whenever he had the boys, Sam had his limo driver come and pick them up and bring them to his home. On the times when he had dropped them off himself, he never entered the house. It was his way of keeping distance between himself and Claudette thereby, ensuring that he didn't encroach upon her life. Though they spoke occasionally over the phone, all of their conversations evolved around the boys. They had forged a working relationship, with each of them being extremely polite and cordial to the other.

Sam often wondered why Claudette hadn't yet re-married. She was still a beautiful woman. But judging from what he'd heard from his sons, that could all change. Suddenly, Sam wondered if that were the reason for her generosity in inviting him over. Maybe she wanted to tell him she was planning on re-tying the knot.

Without asking, Claudette poured Sam a glass of Dom B&B, a smooth, but very expensive cognac-liqueur combination. It was one of his favorites. Sam now knew that there was something she wanted to discuss with him. He took the glass from her and looked around him, his eyes alighting on an original Van Gogh painting. "The place is beautiful, Loon. From what I can see, you've outdone yourself." Embellished in soft grays and even softer pastels, it had probably cost her a fortune to have it decorated. Correction, it had probably cost *him* a fortune.

"My home has always been beautiful, Sam. You were just never around long enough to notice it." She sat across from him on the loveseat. She held her glass with both hands as she elegantly crossed her legs.

Ouch, Sam thought as he lifted his glass to his nose to inhale the rich aroma of the Dom. Choosing not to respond to her statement, he merely took a sip of the drink. He recognized the challenging tone of her voice and figured that if he remained quiet, she would eventually tell him what had put a bur in her cap.

"You've been in the papers quite a bit lately, Sam. It seems as if the entire town is buzzing about you and your latest conquest."

"Why should that concern you?" Sam leaned forward and placed his glass on the marble cocktail table.

Ignoring his question, Claudette continued. "There's even talk about a possible marriage. Surely, even an ex-wife has a right to know about these things in advance, Sam. Especially if they're true."

Sam smiled. Now he knew where she was going. "Since when did you start believing what you read in the papers, Loon?"

"Oh, I don't know. Maybe when people started questioning me about whether or not it was true that you were getting married. All I keep hearing these days is how you've never been seen with one woman as much as you're being seen with whomever this current person is." Claudette stared at Sam, expecting him to offer her some kind of answer.

"I'm seeing someone. But no, we've no plans to get married. Don't tell me you're concerned about my well-being."

"Who knows? Maybe I'm just trying to protect our assets from some would-be predator. She seems a bit younger than you, Sam. Robbing the cradle these days, are we?"

Sam shook his head. "I don't think so, Loon. You're taken care of royally, if I must say so myself, and so are the boys. Even if I do eventually re-marry, you're still covered financially. Go ahead and say what this is really about. Because she's younger? So what. She's also quite rich in her own right. Does that reassure you? As she'd be quick to tell you, in her case, age really is nothing but a number." Sam changed the subject. He hadn't come to fence with her. "Speaking of marriage, how are things going for you and Vince? I thought you two would have taken the plunge by now." Sam knew Vince Stanton, the man she was dating. He was a V.P. over at Universal Studios. Still, it made Sam wonder how she had time to be concerned with his relationships.

Claudette reached for her drink. She'd caught the part about him "eventually getting married" and for some reason it didn't sit well with her. She shrugged. "Vince is fine. Unlike you, he seems to know that he wants to be married. I'm just not sure that I'm ready to be tied down again."

"Why not, Loon? Vince is a great guy. He'd be good to you. And the boys certainly seem to think a lot of him."

Because Vince doesn't move me like you did! Claudette wanted to scream at him but she was determined to keep her composure. Suddenly becoming irritated, she got up and came to sit on the couch next to him, lifting her feet underneath her.

The angry, frustrated look she gave him was a familiar one to Sam. In fact, the entire scene felt familiar to him.

"Who is she, Sam?"

At that moment, Sam knew who he was involved with was the furthest thing from both of their minds. In past times, such energized anger would have led both of them straight to the bedroom where all frustrations would have been eliminated between the sheets. But only this time, things were different—weren't they? For a brief moment, a flashback hit Sam and he turned to face her, staring into her eyes.

"Why?" Sam's gaze penetrated the emotion behind hers. It wasn't that he was not drawn by what he sensed in hers, it was just that he had more of a need to understand the dynamics behind it all. He knew one "last hurrah" between them would only re-open a Pandora's Box.

In the face of his calm stance, sanity seemed to return to Claudette. She leaned back against the sofa and said, "All these years of hearing about this person or that person, Sam, I knew you weren't serious about any of them. I guess I just got used to the idea that you'd never settle down. And now I hear differently. Maybe I just want to know more about this person who appears to have tamed you. She looks a *lot* younger than you. Could that be it, Sam? Are you pussy whipped?" Claudette was clearly baiting him. But she knew also that she had evoked a response in him moments ago, even if he was trying to hide it.

"*You* decided that you didn't want *me* anymore, remember Loon? You're the one who filed for divorce because you couldn't take being married to me any longer. So is this a case of 'I don't want you but I don't want anybody else to have you either?' I'm surprised at you, Loon. That's not your style."

Claudette snapped at him. "You don't know what my style is, Sam. You should have . . ."

"Dad!" Ronald and Damael came bounding into the room. They were surprised to see him.

"Hey, fellas." Sam stood up to embrace his sons in a bear hug. He believed in the positive reinforcement that physical contact with them provided. His sons were intelligent, handsome boys and Sam was proud of them.

"How long are you going to be here, Dad?"

"Just for three or four weeks. But I got us court-side tickets to the Lakers-Bulls game. Just like I promised."

Completely composed again, Claudette watched as Sam threw his arms around their shoulders, leading them out of the room. She liked the fact that he remained such an integral part of their lives. Looking at her boys was like staring at a very

young picture of Sam. They were destined to be as tall as their father and equally as handsome. Already, she was having to fight off the girls with a stick.

At the entrance to the living room, Sam turned and said, "I'll talk to you later, Loon."

Claudette would make sure that he did. She was nowhere near finished with their little conversation.

Outside, Sam leaned against the Lamborghini while Ronald and Damael sat inside it fingering the controls. Knowing the answer in advance, still, they begged to be allowed to take his $300,000 toy for a spin. The top was down when Damael, his younger son, looked up at him. "Dad, mom says you might be getting married to that singer. Is it true?"

Sam folded his arms across his chest. "No, son. There's no truth to that at all."

Damael glanced up from the driver's seat. "Vibe magazine had a picture of you and her at some movie premiere. Man, is she fly! Can we meet her, Dad?"

Sam laughed, shaking his head. His son's were growing up right before his very eyes. It was almost frightening. "I make no promises but I'll see what I can do. Come on, I've got to be going. Ask your mother if you can spend the weekend with me. We'll go sailing Saturday morning. Cool?"

"Yeah, Dad."

Sam got inside the car and they took turns lightly pounding their fists on top of his. Sam marveled at them. At fifteen and thirteen, they were evolving into young men and they needed him more so than they ever had. Needed his guidance, his direction, his leadership, his tutelage, his time, and yes, most of all his love. Sam was proud of the fact that his boys didn't have to grow up like he did. He was grateful that they would be well educated and equipped to operate in a society that dictated that if you were black, you were already behind the eight ball.

His sons were taught to understand and appreciate the value of money. Things weren't just handed to them because of whose children they were. They had chores and had to earn their allowances and bonuses. Claudette ran a tight ship and Sam was grateful for that. She was an awesome woman and he tipped his hat to her. It was because of her firm hand and tough-love stance that the boys were as respectful as they were. And they didn't give her much flak either. Sure, they went through their ups and downs as all teens did. But for the most part, his sons were good boys and Sam was a doting father.

Sam found himself reflecting on what had transpired between he and Claudette when she'd sat on the couch beside him. Yes, they were both wiser now. But he knew that he would be treading on thin ice if he ever allowed himself to become entangled with her again. The physical part of their marriage was the one aspect that had never diminished even though everything else around them had. The timing was wrong to even begin to entertain such a notion. A side affair with her would only

complicate his life in ways unimaginable. It was best that both of them leave things the way they currently were.

Chapter Thirty

yliah would be gone for nearly a month, so she insisted that Ashela drive her to the airport. En route, she rattled off a litany of things that Ashela was to swear to remember to do. All this, in addition to a ten-page list of things she already expected Ashela to have completed before her return to the coast in January. Most unfortunate for Ashela was the fact that Kyliah was the type of person who would get halfway to the airport and suddenly wonder aloud if she had forgotten to make sure the gas was turned off or whether she'd locked her door. Her ramblings made Ashela want to stuff a sock in her mouth.

"Look, chump, do I look like Big Bird or something? You make it seem as if I'm not capable of making it on my own while you're away. Will you calm down and just relax? Sheese!"

Kyliah continued as if Ash hadn't even spoken. "And whatever you do, do not let ET trick you into overfeeding him. He knows he's only allowed one can of salmon per day. I'm warning you in advance not to feel sorry for him and feed him every time he starts following you around batting those eyes of his. Believe me, that cat knows every trick in the book. Oh, and don't forget his appointment with the vet on the 5th." Kyliah started digging in her purse looking for something. Probably another list, Ashela thought.

"Also, try to remember to brush him at least once a day, Ash. If not, ET'll get all knotted up."

"Look, the sooner I get you to the airport, the sooner I can say good riddance! Both you *and* your cat are already getting on my nerves. I don't understand why he can't eat regular cat food like every other normal cat. A can of salmon everyday? Do you know how much that stuff costs per can? The fur ball eats better than I do! And on top of all that, you expect me to chauffeur him back and forth to the vet, brush him every day, *plus talk* to him every day? No wonder no animal boarding house would take him in. He's just a *cat*, for God's sake! Rockhead, *you* should be paying *me*!"

Kyliah normally took ET with her to North Carolina whenever she went home. But ever since a couple of years ago when Kye had come back ready to kill somebody, ET was no longer allowed to travel with her. All because her little nephew, Kiante, had chopped off huge tufts of ET's hair. Kiante had called himself giving ET a haircut that would make him look like a *"playa."* He thought he'd surprise his aunt by turning her cat into what a *real* "home-boy cat-from-the-hood"

should look like. He'd surprised her all right. When Kyliah saw her ribbonless, once-upon-a-time well-groomed, pedigreed cat, she flipped the fuck out. She nearly had to be sedated as she went storming through the house with a thick paddle in her hand, in search of the culprit who had committed such a heinous act.

At first, Ashela had thought that Kyliah was exaggerating. She knew how protective Kye was of ET. But when Kyliah dragged her over to her place to see him, Ashela had to admit that the child had gone a tad too far. Poor ET looked like a sheared sheep with a mangy, fucked-up do!

And now, Kyliah had conveniently waited too long to book ET into a pet hotel. Needless to say, Ashela was stuck with baby-sitting him.

They arrived at LAX and as she helped Kye retrieve her things from the Navigator, it was all she could do not to kick her out and throw her bags out with her before speeding off.

At home, Ashela brought ET's pet carrier into the kitchen where she set up his litter pan. As Kyliah had instructed, she lured him out of his cage and put him into it. She was standing looking at him with her hands on her hips wondering how, with his size and girth, anyone could categorize him as a cat when her phone rang.

As soon as she picked up and said hello, Sam said, "Hi, baby. I was expecting to get your answering machine."

A huge smile lit her face. "Hey, bay. You would have but I had to take Kye to the airport."

"Oh, yeah? Where's she off to? Boston?"

"Not by a long shot. Where are you?"

"Just came from seeing my boys and now I'm heading home for a bit. Will I see you tonight?"

Ashela's voice deepened. "Why wouldn't you?"

Sam paused before saying, "I just needed to make sure. Would you like to go somewhere for dinner?"

"Sweetheart, didn't I tell you? *I am dinner.*" She heard Sam's laughter.

"Well, in that case, maybe I should swing by Coleman's and pick up some dessert."

Ashela had all the bases covered. "Not necessary. Didn't you know? *You* are the dessert."

With a huge grin on his face, Sam pulled on his chin. "Baby, what kind of comeback can I supply for that? I *know* when it's time to surrender. So what time is my presence required?"

Ashela leaned against the counter as she eased away from ET, who was displaying signs of friendliness by rubbing up against her velvet jeans. "Well, I figured I could fix us something light. You know, maybe a Caesar's salad with a couple of chunks of chicken in it. But whatever I fix, it'll be something light, quick

and easy. After all, who needs food when an a la mode dessert is about to be served?"

"It sounds like I'm being put on a diet tonight."

"You could say that. I just don't want you weighed down with food. You've got a lot of physical work ahead of you tonight, Mister."

"Ashela Jordan! You're making me blush! Don't you know I'm on the expressway? Have some compassion for a brother."

"Sam, you get no sympathy from me. Now, what time are you coming so we can be ready for you?"

"We?" Surprise was evident in Sam's voice.

Ashela laughed at the question mark in his tone. "I'm sorry, bay. You'll have to meet ET when you get here. Now hurry up, cause I wanna see you."

"Okay, okay. I'm on my way. But I have to stop off at home first. Do you have any of my favorite wine?"

"Oops. Sorry, love. You'd better stop by Du Vin's and pick some up."

With a smile in his voice, Sam said, "I thought you were supposed to be taking care of me. Now I've got to drive all the way out of the way to pick up my favorite wine. I thought you were in a hurry to see me?" Actually, it wasn't that far out of the way, Sam just wanted to give her grief.

"I *am*, bay, you know that. But I can't be relied upon to remember everything, can I? That's why they say two heads are better than one."

"Hmmm. I don't think I'll touch that one."

"Oooh, Sam! Get your mind out of the gutter. Anyway, I've got to go. See you when you get here."

***

With the receiver pressed to his ear, Arron Davenport was trying desperately to come up with a reason, or even a cockamamie excuse, as to why he was unable to see Mrs. Thorpe. Though she had come without scheduling an appointment, Mrs. Edwina Huntington-Welsington-Thorpe was not used to waiting for anyone, and Arron knew that he had to think quickly. Incapable of conceiving anything remotely believable, Arron told his secretary to send her up.

Arron berated himself for not recognizing that the situation would escalate to what it had. Realistically, he'd had no way of knowing that a one-time business transaction would turn into such a fiasco. Edwina Huntington-Welsington-Thorpe was every bit as wealthy as her name implied. Having survived as many as three husbands, Mrs. Thorpe was left wealthier with the passing of each spouse. Financial powerhouse, Chase-Bardeaux Securities—the brokerage firm where Arron worked—was fortunate to manage some of Mrs. Thorpe's money. The lone account that Arron handled for her itself was in excess of sixty million dollars.

Prior to being awarded the account over a year before, Arron had been called into a meeting with the three senior securities brokers at CBS. He'd walked into the meeting and there sat the indomitable Edwina Thorpe, surrounded by three of her own attorneys. Arron knew of Mrs. Thorpe and was vaguely familiar with her account. On this day, he had been summoned to shed light on an account of hers that had been previously handled by Smyth Whithers, who was no longer with the firm. Arron was considered among the best of the securities brokers at the firm and if anyone could provide immediate answers to Mrs. Thorpe's lawyers, it was he.

As he stepped into the room, Arron promptly assessed the situation. The body language of every person sitting at the table made it fairly obvious that Mrs. Thorpe was threatening to pull her account from CBS. As soon as he was introduced and seated, Arron's summation was confirmed.

Mrs. Thorpe was stating that she hadn't been kept informed by her advisor as frequently as she liked, and it seemed that CBS was no longer providing her with the hands-on treatment it had once accorded her. Arron knew that what Mrs. Thorpe was really saying was that her present advisor hadn't been kissing her ass lately in the manner and to the degree which she preferred.

Before Arron had sat down, he was handed a copy of Mrs. Thorpe's portfolio. He glanced over it while his fellow associates continued to placate Mrs. Thorpe and her legal cadre of lawyers.

Arron finished briefing himself on her account and interjected after one of her attorneys finished speaking. The first thing Arron said as he began to mollify Mrs. Thorpe was to reaffirm her value as a customer. By all means, he told her, she had every right to feel slighted. But could she please bear with the company as they shifted her account to another securities broker, in light of the fact that Mr. Whithers was no longer with the organization? Whithers had resigned after a series of personal misfortunes had struck him—the most serious being that his entire family had perished in a recent airplane crash. CBS's condolences were regrettably with Mr. Whithers as he recuperated from the devastating tragedy.

In reality, Arron suspected Smyth was probably relaxing on some remote island like Antigua Bay, sipping tall pina coladas and flipping the bird sign at all of the head honchos back at CBS. It was rumored that Smyth had pilfered millions from many of his client's accounts, but CBS currently was unable to prove that Smyth was the actual culprit. However, Arron knew that where ever Symth was, he had better watch his back. If CBS found him before the Securities Exchange Commission did, he was as good as dead. Theft in the securities industry was a potential landmine. And whenever it occurred, such a caveat was not information that a brokerage firm disclosed to any of its clients.

At any rate, Arron went on to direct Mrs. Thorpe's and her attorney's attention to her portfolio. If they would be kind enough to turn with him to page seventeen, they would note that Mrs. Thorpe's account was actually yielding a high-interest rate

that was earning for her market-breaking returns. Arron pointed out that the bottom line was that even though Mr. Whithers had suffered an extreme setback, Mrs. Thorpe and her account had not. Arron stressed with pride that even in the face of terrible tragedies such as Smyth Whithers', Chase-Bardeaux Securities was still turning a profit for one of its most valued customers.

After Arron finished speaking, her lawyers threw a barrage of questions at him and he skillfully answered them all with facts straight from Mrs. Thorpe's portfolio. Mrs. Thorpe was impressed. He had allayed everyone's concerns and now that Edwina Thorpe was happy with the outcome, so were her attorneys. Suddenly, everyone around the table was all smiles as Arron ended his presentation, driving home the fact that Mrs. Thorpe would be hard-pressed to find another company that would work as hard as CBS to generate such advantageous returns on her money.

Arron's colleagues were quick to heap high praises on his shoulders when Mrs. Thorpe inquired just who Mr. Davenport was. She added that since Mr. Davenport was so knowledgeable about her account, why had *he* not been handling it to begin with? Furthermore, Mr. Davenport was to be put in charge of her account immediately.

Later, when his fellow co-workers patted him on the back, telling him that he was "the man" and how original the "plane crash" story had been, Arron should have known from their teasing laughter that everything was not what it seemed.

The next morning, John Furcon, the president of Chase-Bardeaux Securities called Arron into his office to commend him on his quick thinking and innovative approach to dealing with Mrs. Huntington-Welsington-Thorpe. However, there was one minor detail left unspoken. It seemed from time to time that Mrs. Thorpe required "extra special" attention. Would Arron be able to have dinner with Mrs. Thorpe, who would tell him all about her specific needs? After reminding Arron that Mrs. Thorpe's account would yield him a six million dollar commission over the next year, Mr. Furcon ended the meeting by telling him that he had every confidence that Arron was the perfect man for the job.

Sure enough, that afternoon Mrs. Thorpe had called and asked if Arron could stop by her estate that evening. She would be serving dinner and it would please her if he would join her. On his way to her home, Arron had a funny feeling in the pit of his stomach. Something about the way Furcon had hinted at the "extra special" attention Mrs. Thorpe would require, didn't sit well with him. But he couldn't exactly come out and ask his boss if he were suggesting that he screw a sixty-something year old widow just to keep her happy. An image of the pale and corpulent Mrs. Thorpe came to Arron's mind. The very thought of such a transaction made him nauseous.

As Arron drove through the gates of Mrs. Thorpe's Windsor-style estate, he was aware that only families who came from "old money" inhabited this section of Boston. Though he was driving a Jaguar, Arron would not have been surprised to

have been pulled over by the local police. In fact, he was more surprised that he *hadn't* been stopped.

It was early evening as a servant whom Mrs. Thorpe referred to as Hobbs, showed him into her drawing room. Arron sat patiently for about fifteen minutes, occasionally glancing at his Rolex watch. To kill time, he started walking around the room looking over the paintings hanging on the wall of men and women whom he assumed were part of Edwina Thorpe's family tree. He was strolling from painting to painting when Mrs. Thorpe swept into the room with a cloud of perfume trailing after her. She was dressed in a yellow chiffon evening gown and was bedecked with jewels as she walked toward him clutching a cigarette attached to a long, ivory stem.

Watching her, Arron couldn't shake the feeling that he was viewing an old movie from the "silent film" era. Edwina Thorpe took a seat on one of the cherry leather sofas and patted the seat beside her. Arron retrieved his briefcase and sat on the sofa with her but he made sure there was distance between them. He lifted his briefcase onto the sofa and opened it, intending to remove the portfolio that he had discussed with her and her attorneys the day before.

The double-doors to the drawing room opened and Hobbs stood at the entrance asking if Mrs. Thorpe would care for an apéritif. She nodded, and Hobbs quickly returned with a tray which held a small glass of cognac for Arron and an entire decanter of whiskey for Mrs. Thorpe. If straight, hard-core liquor was considered an apéritif, then Arron must have just escaped from the pen. Since when was a bottle of 100-proof bourbon considered a cocktail?

As soon as Hobbs closed the double-doors behind him, Mrs. Thorpe handed Arron his glass. She poured herself a double shot of the bourbon and turned the glass bottoms-up. First one and then another. It was all Arron could do not to stare with his mouth open. The strong smell of the liquor confirmed its 100-proof label. *Anybody* who could drink it straight-up *had* to have hair on their chest and be a bad mother sucker . . .

So that he wouldn't appear awkward, Arron asked softly, "Is there anything in particular you wanted to discuss about your account, Mrs. Thorpe?" Arron gave her a look of deference as he stared into her green pupils, while avoiding looking at the taut leathery skin of her face which appeared to have seen far too many cosmetic surgeries.

Edwina patted her auburn hair before pouring herself another drink. She leaned toward Arron and said, "No, dear boy, there is not." At first, Arron thought she was drunk but there was no trace of a slur in her voice as she added, "I do not wish to talk about money at all. In fact, fuck the money. I want to talk about *you*." She calmly drained her glass and proceeded to pour herself another drink.

It was perfectly safe to say that Arron was shocked speechless. To hide his dismay, he looked down and fumbled with his papers. All he could think about was how he'd been educated at Harvard and held a master's degree in Finance from Yale.

Arron served as an investment advisor to many of the top Fortune 500 companies in America, and as such, he held court with the presidents of them all. But as educated as he was, none of it had prepared him for a ball-buster like Edwina Huntington-Welsington-Thorpe.

As Arron continued to ruffle his papers, Edwina said, "My lord, dear boy, I do believe I've made you blush. You *must* tell me all about yourself."

This was the second time that she had called him "dear boy." So, what was he now? The family *pet*? Arron gathered himself and finally said, "Mrs. Thorpe, there's very little to tell you about myself. Surely a woman of your," Arron paused delicately, "Stature and caliber must want to discuss the rate of return on your money or perhaps even . . ."

"Baloney, Mr. Davenport! I have no desire to discuss further anything relating to finances. You've already impressed my legal hounds so I'm satisfied as well." Edwina clapped her hands and in strode Hobbs who must surely have been waiting with an ear pressed to the door.

"Dinner is served Madam." Arron stared at Hobbs and *knew* that this entire scenario had to be a drawback from an old flick.

Hobbs led the way into the dining room followed by Edwina Thorpe. Feeling like a lamb being led to the slaughter, Arron stood up to join them.

The meal consisted of three tasteless courses that Arron didn't even remember eating. But Mrs. Thorpe certainly seemed to be enjoying herself. With Hobbs constantly keeping her wine glass filled and with Arron the apt pupil, she reminisced about the "good ol' days." With no appetite himself, Arron ate sparingly. He was just becoming comfortable with his role as financial "listener." He would certainly bill Mrs. Thorpe for this time, and if she wanted to waste it by telling him her life's story—his time was hers.

After a cream-filled dessert, she led them into another drawing room that was even larger than the first. This one was equipped with a fireplace that was lit—probably compliments of Hobbs as he was the only servant Arron had seen all evening long. Sitting on the table next to a chintz sofa was a fresh decanter of bourbon and another small glass of cognac. Good thing he wasn't that much of a drinker, Arron thought. Hobbs sure was stingy with the cognac. He probably wanted to ensure that at least one of them remained sober. Nevertheless, Arron planned to nurse his drink throughout the rest of the evening which he hoped wouldn't last too much longer.

As he watched Edwina gulp down drink after drink, Arron answered all of her questions politely. He'd made sure he sat on the couch across the room from her. When more than three-fourths of the decanter of bourbon was consumed, only then did Arron begin to detect a slight slur to Mrs. Thorpe's speech. As Edwina poured herself another drink, she belched loudly. With it, her entire body quaked causing some of the liquor to spill to the floor. Arron could only watch in fascination as she

threw her head back once more and sucked the last drop of bourbon directly from the crystal decanter. When she wiped the back of her hand across her mouth, he noticed that her auburn colored hair was suddenly tilted slightly askew.

Thinking that now was the opportune moment to make his great escape, Arron was about to stand up when, with surprising strength and accurate precision, Edwina Thorpe threw her shot-glass into the blazing fireplace. With a loud crash, the glass shattered into a million pieces as the flames leapt around it. Arron jumped in surprise. Appalled, he could only stare into the fireplace with his mouth open. When he turned back, Edwina Thorpe was standing in front of him demanding that they "get down to business."

With her red wig now lying on the floor, in the blink of an eye, Edwina snatched her teeth out of her mouth and commanded Arron to unzip his pants.

An entire year had passed since Arron had heard from Ms. Huntington-Welsington-Thorpe. He had heard in passing that she had gone "abroad." Whatever. Arron had been thankfully relieved. Less than a month after "that night," Arron had started getting calls from at least six "friends" of Edwina's who needed his "financial assistance." To his credit, Arron was traveling quite a bit during the time when they were calling and he had quickly referred them all to CBS's president, John Furcon. One evening, Furcon came to see Arron personally, tactfully suggesting that he take on Edwina's referrals. After all, each of the widows were worth an estimated one-hundred million dollars. Couldn't Arron imagine the commission?

No he could not. And Arron knew that no amount of money on God's green Earth could persuade him otherwise. When Arron declined, though he wanted to, Furcon didn't press the issue. He knew what "special services" Edwina and her friends required and it certainly wasn't something he could "make" Arron do. After all, they hadn't hired him on the basis of his sexual prowess. But oh, if only he would reconsider.

As far as Arron was concerned, there would be no repeat occurrence. "That night" was a one-time event that he would take with him to his grave. After thinking about it long and hard, personally, Arron was convinced that Mrs. Thorpe's three husbands were not dead. He firmly believed that they were somewhere hiding.

Now, Mrs. Edwina Thorpe came through the door with her silver fox stow wrapped loosely around her neck. Ever the gentleman, Arron showed her to a seat, even pulling it out for her. But he quickly put distance between them by retreating behind his desk.

Edwina eyed him coldly. Direct and to the point, she asked brusquely, "Why have you not returned my calls, Mr. Davenport?"

In spite of himself, Arron smiled at her. She was the proverbial "toothless tiger." "Mrs. Thorpe, you know that's absolutely untrue. When have you ever called me that I did not drop whatever I was doing to return your call?"

"Hmph! Well, you certainly haven't attended any of my dinner parties. I've invited you at least six times, you know. And what about all my friends that I referred to you? To think, after I gave you such wonderful ratings! How can you conduct business with me so shabbily after all that I've done for you?" Edwina demanded an answer.

Suddenly, Arron knew how he would handle the situation. He spoke in a most sincere but regrettable manner. "Ms. Thorpe—Edwina, if I may. You have truly been most kind to me. And I will eternally be grateful for all that you've done. Why, without your account, I could never have achieved all that I have." Though Arron was just stroking her ego, admittedly, in the year that she'd been away, Mrs. Thorpe had regularly sent him money, jewelry and other trinkets totaling close to a million dollars. Arron had put the money into a separate account and the other items he had put inside his safe. Arron had been too embarrassed to tell a soul about her and her "gifts." He wasn't some kind of pet that Edwina Thorpe and her friends could keep just to call upon whenever they were in "dire straits."

Arron continued. "But the fact of the matter is, Mrs. Thorpe, I'm engaged to be married. You can understand what kind of position that puts me in." Arron got up from his desk and went to the safe inside his office and removed the box that contained all the items Edwina Thorpe had sent him over the past year. "I even kept all of the gifts that you sent me. Everything you gave me is here, Mrs. Thorpe. It would be unethical of me to accept them."

In the face of Arron's unrelenting "gee-my-hands-are-tied" attitude, Edwina Thorpe conceded. "Well, I guess if a man is getting married and insists upon remaining faithful, who am I to spoil the plot? But you don't know what you're missing out on, Arron Davenport." Edwina stood to her feet and walked to the door. "And don't give me that mumbo-jumbo about not being able to accept my gifts. They were gifts, dear boy, so do keep them." With that, Edwina Huntington-Welsington-Thorpe slammed the door in his face.

Arron exhaled a deep sigh of relief. With one less headache to deal with, he sat down with his hands behind his head. He stared out of the window and almost out of habit, started daydreaming about Kyliah. He had been doing a lot of that lately thinking about her. Wondering what she was doing, whether she was thinking of him, and why she hadn't bothered to call him. Before he could talk himself out of it, he picked up the phone and dialed her number for the third time in as many days, but once again, he only got her machine. He hung up without leaving a message and picked up one of the jewelry cases that Edwina Thorpe had given him.

Inside, Oppenheimer diamond cufflinks rested against a black velvet background. He estimated their value at well over eight thousand dollars. Snapping

the case closed and shaking his head, his thoughts turned once more to Kyliah. In spite of himself, Arron was forced to admit that he missed her. Missed having her in his home. He missed her warmth, her laughter, and her ascerbic wit. And he especially missed having her nakedness next to his. For the first time since she had left Boston some months ago, Arron quietly acknowledged to himself that he was in love.

Chapter Thirty-One

hen Sam finally arrived at Ashela's place, it was well after seven-thirty. She was already dressed in her night-gown. A long, red, sheer mesh number. The slinky, one-shouldered gown comfortably hugged her body's curves and left her feeling stunningly sexy.

As soon as Sam closed the door behind him, he went to wrap Ashela in a bear hug but she danced away from him. Smiling, he lunged forward to grab her again but she skipped away and darted through the house, running upstairs to the bedroom. With her squealing with laughter, Sam was hot on her trail. Inside, she threw herself onto her bed.

"Woman, why are you running from me?" Sam slid onto the bed beside her.

"Why were you chasing me?" She twisted around and wrapped her arms around his neck.

Bending his body over hers, Sam kissed her lingeringly. "Because . . ." he whispered between kisses. His hands were already caressing her body as if he were familiarizing himself with her every curve and contour for the first time.

Quickly losing herself in the slow tidal wave of sensations he was stirring within her, Ashela soon forgot what it was they were even discussing. "Because what?" she whispered. Her hands cupped his face before sliding down to his shoulders.

"Because I missed you." Sam sensed the languor that was pouring through all of their members. As her eyes closed and her head turned to the side, he took advantage of her exposed neck area by trailing kisses on it and lightly nibbling it. Suddenly needing to feel her bare nakedness against him, he stripped her gown from her body. Sam wasted no time. He climbed off of the bed and disrobed.

Ashela turned to watch him. Her body had grown listless in stark anticipation of what he was about to do to her—about to *give* her. When he slid his nakedness partially on top of hers, it was all she could do to lock her arms around his neck. She whispered into his ear, "Did you miss me, bay?"

Without replying, Sam began to demonstrate what mere words could not describe. He slid his body atop hers and loved her as strong and fiercely as she had come to know, cherish and expect.

Afterwards, they lay holding one another and Ashela stroked her hand over his face. "Did you eat, bay?"

Sam laughed. "What do you mean, 'did I eat?' You were supposed to feed me."

Ashela stretched and yawned sensuously. "Oh, yeah, that's right. Come on, let's go see what's for dinner."

After a light meal that consisted of baked perch and salad, they were seated inside her living room. She on her sofa and Sam on the floor between her legs. They were watching a tape of their appearance on Tavis Smiley's talk show. It was the first chance they'd had to view the program even though it had already aired.

Ashela found it fascinating to watch, because even on screen Sam came across as a powerful and dynamic persona. With simple clarity he disputed the fact that he was trying to corner the market and used relevant statistics to show how his new alliance would even benefit the music industry in the long run. In comparison, Ashela came across as very personable and articulate. She was in support of Werner's songwriter's consortium and she praised Mr. Ross's innovation in creating the deal. She saw many in the industry prospering as a result of it and pointed out that other writers would now be given chances that they'd otherwise be denied.

They sipped chilled wine that Sam had brought with him and continued to talk long after the tape had rewound. They were watching "BET Tonight" when Sam said, "Whoah. When did the stork bring *him*?"

Ashela looked over to see ET sitting several feet away from them licking his paws. "He belongs to Kye. I keep telling her he's really a dog masquerading as a cat. Have *you* ever seen a cat that big?"

"Yes, but only on "Wild Kingdom" or The Discovery Channel. What's she feeding him? Steroids?"

As if sensing that he was the butt of their laughter, ET got up and walked away, swishing his humongous tail behind him.

Some time later, Sam was seated on the couch on the opposite end of Ashela. As his hand continued to stroke her foot, he said to her, "My two sons want to meet you, Ashela."

She had been listening partially to the TV and also to Sam, but when it finally registered just exactly what he'd said, she turned and stared at him with wide eyes.

Sam could only smile at her open-mouthed expression. "They saw your picture In Vibe magazine and now all they can talk about is meeting my new 'fly' girlfriend."

Ashela didn't know why such news should take her by storm, but it did. A part of her felt that she already knew Sam's boys because he spoke about them so often. But never did she ever think about the prospect of meeting them or of them wanting to meet her. "I don't know what to say, Sam. What did you tell them?"

"That I couldn't make any promises because I had to check with you first. I think what really has them curious, is that they've never known me to be with anyone this long *except* their mother. They even asked me if I intended to marry you." Sam watched closely as Ashela gulped, looking almost like a deer in headlights.

"Bay, why don't we go for a drive." It was all Ashela could think of as she lifted her legs off the couch and onto the floor.

"That's a good idea. Who's driving, you or me?"

"Me," Ashela replied. She needed the cool air to clear her head.

Ashela was dressed in the same provocative nightgown that she had worn earlier. But that was the beauty of L.A., no one questioned what you wore. Style was what you made it. She drove Sam's Lamborghini and they started out toward Desert Hot Springs. With the car's rooftop down, they rode in silence underneath a panoply of bright and brilliant stars. She slid a Whitney Houston CD into the compact disc player.

Sam reclined his seat back and lay with his hands cupped behind his head. They were driving for at least twenty minutes before either of them spoke.

"Tell me why you're apprehensive about meeting Ronald and Damael."

Ashela reached down and lowered the volume on the sound system. "Partly because the thought of it makes me nervous. Then the other part of me worries, what if they don't like me?" She shook her head slowly before turning to glance at him. "I guess I just don't want to tamper with what we have. I get it too, you know. Questions from people about what's going on between us. I even told BET's producer that the only way you and I would agree to do the show was if we weren't asked any personal questions. I keep reasoning to myself, Sam, that we get along so well because we don't live together and also because we don't have children. When you think about it like that, how could we not hit it off?"

"You think meeting my boys might throw us off key?"

"I don't know. The whole family bit just kind of scares me."

"Don't you want to be married with kids someday?"

"Well, yeah. If it happens, great. And if not, it wasn't meant to be." *Why couldn't she admit that she wanted a family more than anything else in the world?*

"They'll like you, baby. Damael even fancies himself a singer. So he's probably got ulterior motives for wanting to meet you anyway."

Ashela smiled. "You know, Sam, I'll be the first to admit that I don't think I've ever been in love before. So all of this is pretty heavy for me. In all honesty, I don't know that what I feel for you *is* love. But what I do know is that you awaken the feminine side of me. Right now, there's not much that I *wouldn't* do for you. And I can only hope that if I give you what you need, you'll respond by giving me what *I* need. If I please you, Sam, and I see that you're striving to please me in return, you can rest assured that I'll break my neck trying to go the extra mile for you. I don't see

you as someone that I'm just sleeping with. I see you as someone who I happen to be sharing my life with."

"Ashela, it's been a long time since I can remember even *enjoying* someone as much as I have you. It's not just the physical part of our relationship, either. We can only spend so much time in bed anyway. That's why it's good that we click outside of it even when we're just spending time together. It's really good knowing that I matter to you, baby. Not because of what I've accomplished or what I possess, but simply because of who I am."

"Really, bay?" Ashela was all smiles. "So when do I get to meet your sons?"

"We're going sailing this weekend. I think it would be nice if you came with us."

"Let me look at my schedule first. Sam, I've been wondering about something lately. At first I told myself I didn't want to know, but now I do. If it's too personal, you don't have to answer."

"What is it?"

"It's obvious that you and Tanya knew one another long before I came into the picture. What happened between you two to make you dislike each other so?"

He was silent for a good while, just staring ahead of him. Sam shifted onto his side and stared at her. "You could say that Tanya and I go way back. We . . . dated for over a year and a half. I was still married at the time, so I was the one really taking all the risks. She didn't seem to mind my being married. She was older than I was but that didn't matter either. When I met her, I could tell she was still trying to get over someone before me and I was determined to make sure she did just that. I guess I got caught up. For a while, I even thought about divorcing my wife to be with her."

Sam shifted in his seat. "She was a consultant manager so I helped her out financially and even steered quite a few groups her way. But then, one day, the bottom dropped out. I had keys to her place and she had keys to mine. Early one afternoon, I came back from the West Coast a couple of days ahead of time and I went to her place to retrieve a brief case that I'd left there. Once I went inside and climbed the stairs to her bedroom, there she was making love to some other woman." Sam started shaking his head as if reliving it all over again.

"I don't think I'll ever forget the sickening feeling in the pit of my stomach. From that moment forward, I couldn't stand the sight of her. I just had one question for her, though. I wanted to know how long she'd been seeing other women while she was with me. And man, was she brutally honest. *All* along, she claimed, and every chance she got. She even told me I was just the one she'd chosen to see if she could go straight. After that, I dumped her. Oh, she tried to get back in with me, but I wouldn't allow it. I was finished with her and I didn't want anything more to do with her. To this day, she claims I blackballed her in the industry. But that's just not true. When her clients started dropping away from her like flies, it wasn't because of me.

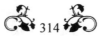

She'd started drinking too much, and the rest is history. All that she went through, Tanya brought on herself."

"You must have loved her, Sam, for it to have affected you so harshly. Either that or your ego was just wounded."

Sam shrugged his shoulders. That was all history. He faced Ashela again. "Now it's my turn. Tell me how you *really* know her."

Ashela asked in surprise. "What do you mean, 'how I *really* know her?' Like I told you, she and my mother were friends. I grew up knowing her as 'Auntie Tanya.' All I knew was that she was helping my mother with her singing career. After my mother passed, I didn't see or hear from her again until that night backstage in New York. She gave me her card, I called her and then went by to see her. It was only then that I discovered that she and my mother were once lovers. I mean, to find out that my own mother was a *lipstick lesbian?* What the hell was I *supposed* to say?"

"Wow. Nothing, I guess. I remember your mother, but only vaguely. I can recall once hearing her sing a jazz club in D.C. She was a natural, too. And everybody was scrambling to sign her. I was still a rep at the time but I think she went on to record several duets with a couple of the big guns. I don't recall hearing anything more about her until years later when I read that she had overdosed. Man, it's a small, small world."

"It's also a rough business, Sam."

"Yes, I agree. But at least you're making it, Ashela. And I'm sure that your mother would be proud."

As she turned the car around to head back home, Sam made her pull over so he could drive back. When he clasped one of her hands in his, no words were necessary as they rode in silence. His fingers laced with hers, offered her all the comfort that she needed.

Part Seven

Games People Play

The truth game,
The lying game,
The loving game,
The hurting game,
The honesty game,
The denial game...
...Are all games that people play.

– Sheri R. Faulkner

"Aye, now the plot thickens."

– George Villiers

Chapter Thirty-Two

ith only two days before Christmas, Ashela found herself full of excitement. For the first time since her arrival in California, she had decorated her home with Christmas paraphernalia. While her decorations were nothing close to spectacular (lights, wreaths, velvet red bows, colorful candles and an assortment of other Christmas objects), they energized her holiday spirit.

One advantage for Ashela during the Christmas season was that she didn't have a long list of people to shop for. She bought gifts for Kyliah and several other people in the entertainment industry whom she was fond of. But this year, she looked forward to buying a gift for Sam. And as an afterthought, she added his sons to her list as well.

Ashela had met Sam's boys when she'd joined them for an afternoon sail. She hadn't known what to expect because her experience with children was limited. What struck her most about them at first, was how incredibly similar they both looked to Sam.

At fifteen and thirteen, the boys were impressionable and had asked a lot of questions. She could tell by their speech and mannerisms that they were highly-educated and well trained. But the biggest surprise was that she enjoyed being around them as much as she had. As the day wore on, she insisted that they call her by her first name and not "Ms. Jordan." As Sam manned the boat, she couldn't help but admire how easily he slid into his role of loving father. He also surprised her with his knowledge of sailing. The expert way in which he hoisted the boat's sail, answered her long-awaited question of how he'd managed to get calluses on his hands.

The day ended with her promising to let them come visit her while she was in the recording studio, something they rarely got to do with their father.

***

As Sam and Ashela had planned, Sam would spend Christmas day at his ex-wife's home with his two sons, and afterwards come back to her place in the early evening. He asked her if she wanted to come along as his guest, but Ashela declined. However, the amount of jealousy she felt at the thought of him being with his ex-wife surprised her.

She found herself feeling extremely possessive of Sam and when curiosity about his ex-wife got the better of her, she said, "Sam, I think I *will* come with you. But clear it with her first, will you? Women don't like men showing up at their homes with other women they've never met before." When Ashela heard Sam sigh into the phone, she said, "Trust me on this, Bay, I know what I'm talking about."

It was a quarter to two when Sam pulled up in Ashela's driveway. She was a fetching sight as she locked the door behind herself and met him at his car. Dressed in a lime-colored Liz Claiborne jacket dress, the dress itself was short, about mid-thigh level while the jacket overlapped it and extended below her knees. A black silk scarf was wrapped expertly around her neck and matching black and lime pumps completed her outfit.

Ashela was carrying the gifts she had purchased for Sam's two sons. He opened and closed her door for her and as soon as he locked his seatbelt in place, Ashela slid her hand behind his neck and pulled his head to hers. "Hi, Bay," she said before planting a succulent kiss upon his lips.

Grinning from ear to ear, Sam asked, "Happy to see me, huh?"

"Maybe," she replied with a smile.

Sam put the car in reverse and they set out on their way.

A while later, they arrived at his ex-wife's Bel Air estate. "Nice," Ashela said nodding her head as they pulled through the entrance gates. "Very nice."

Sam pulled behind an assortment of luxury cars that were already in the driveway. He got out and opened Ashela's door for her. "Thank you, Sam."

The front door was snatched open and Ronald and Damael came bounding through it.

"Dad!" Damael ran toward Sam and grabbed him around the waist. He received a reciprocating bear hug and then Sam reached for Ronald and hugged him as well. As soon as he released him, he reached for Ashela who was standing just behind them.

Both boys greeted her and she handed them their presents. "Thank you, Ashela," they replied graciously.

With his arm around her waist, Sam guided them into the house.

Ronald seemed to hesitate when he'd first spotted Ashela. Though his hesitation had been quick, Ashela caught it nonetheless. When Sam closed the front door behind them, his sons went ahead of him to spread the news of his arrival but Ashela stopped him and asked, "Sam, remember when I told you to check with your ex before inviting me? You did clear it with her, didn't you?" *Why else would his son seem surprised to see her?*

Sam detected the seriousness in Ashela's tone. He stared down at her and said, "Actually, I didn't. You're my guest, Ashela, so that makes it okay."

Ashela rolled her eyes, unable to stifle the groan that fell from her lips. "Aw, Sam. Didn't I ask you to trust me on this?" Without provocation, Ashela sensed that she might as well prepare herself for a battle. Sighing heavily, she looked at the front door suddenly wishing she was anywhere but where she was at the present moment.

"Baby, I'm telling you, it's okay. Claudette won't mind." Sam could feel Ashela's withdrawal as he sought to reassure her.

"Hello, Sam. I came to find out what was taking you so long to come inside. And now I know." A nondescript man of medium build stepped forward and extended his hand. "Aren't you going to introduce us, Sam?"

"Ashela, this is Vince Stanton, Claudette's fiancée. Vince, this is Ashela Jordan."

"Ms. Jordan, I'm charmed."

"It's a pleasure. Please, call me Ashela." Though he was nothing along the order of Sam, Ashela was just pleased to discover that Sam's ex had someone else in her life. Maybe she didn't have anything to worry about after all.

"So you're the young lady Damael's been raving about. One thing's for sure, he didn't exaggerate. Aren't you two coming inside?"

Ashela was soon introduced to three of Sam's sisters, their husbands and two of his brothers along with their wives. Children seemed to come out of the woodwork to clamor around "Uncle" Sam.

Ashela was standing near the fireplace talking with Sam's sister-in-law, Lavon. Minutes later a tall light skinned woman stepped into the room wearing a deep purple Donna Karan belted pantsuit. Ashela didn't need to inquire who she was. Her eyes seemed to zero in on Sam the moment she walked into the living room. In the few seconds that it took her to saunter over to where he was standing, Ashela summed everything up in one glance. Though Vince was standing next to Sam, Ashela noted that it wasn't *him* that Claudette gravitated toward as she sidled up to Sam and intimately wrapped her arm around his waist. Too intimately, Ashela thought. When she lifted her cheek for his kiss and afterwards *still* didn't release her arm from his waist, Ashela needed no further confirmation of the thoughts which ran rampant through her mind.

Sam, Vince, and everyone else around Ashela may have been blind to the obvious, but any impartial observer could see that there stood a woman possessively holding onto a man whom she clearly considered hers, still. At a glance, Ashela knew that Claudette may have been divorced for a number of years, and Sam may have moved on with his life, but regardless as to what he could ever say, Ashela knew his ex had only given the *appearance* of having moved on with hers. Suddenly, Ashela felt a twinge of sympathy for Vince Stanton. He seemed clueless to the unmistakable signs of desire that his fiancée was emoting for Sam *while standing next to him*. Ashela figured the man had no idea his impending marriage would only be a mere substitute for what Claudette really wanted. Sam had never discussed his marriage at any length with her, but Ashela couldn't wait to uncover the details. She thought, *if she loved him so much, why in the hell did she let him get away?*

But as always, Ashela realized there were two sides to every story. She wondered about the version Sam's ex-wife would have to tell.

Suddenly, Claudette's head swung in Ashela's direction and she found herself being swept from head to toe with a glance that was full of barely masked

vehemence. Ashela knew she was the subject of conversation when Sam led his ex in her direction. Claudette's eyes never left Ashela's.

"Loon, this is Ashela. Ash, this is Claudette," Sam said when they stood in front of her.

There are times when men can be so ignorant to facts that appear glaring to women. Whether deceptively obtuse or not, Ashela had no idea as Sam disengaged himself from his ex and latched on to her, drawing her forward.

Sam may have been mindless to the displeasure his ex felt at Ashela's presence, but Ashela was not. Disregarding the woman's vexation, Ashela extended her hand, saying, "Hello."

Ignoring Ashela's greeting *and* her outstretched hand, she turned to Sam and said, "You should have told me you were bringing a guest, Sam. Now I have to try to muster up another table setting." Claudette turned and walked in the opposite direction. But she threw over her shoulder, "I stand by my earlier words, Sam. She's a bit young for your tastes."

For several seconds, Sam, Lavon, and Ashela stood looking as if they'd been harpooned. Until Ashela stepped forward. "Don't bother setting a place for me. I won't be staying for dinner."

As Claudette continued out of the room, Ashela turned to Sam, who for all purposes, looked as if he could have been bought for a penny. "Give me your car keys, Sam."

Sam's lips had tightened ominously. "No, I'll go talk to her."

"Not on my behalf, Sam. Now give me your fucking car keys before I embarrass you by creating a goddamned scene." Though only Lavon was standing near them, everyone inside the room had to be aware of what had just transpired.

"I'm not giving you the keys, Ashela. So just hold on a second." Sam walked away to go after Claudette. He thought to himself, *Women, you can't live with 'em and you can't live without 'em!*

"Lavon, I'm sorry to put you on the spot, but would you be kind enough to point me in the direction of the front door?"

At a loss for words, Lavon said, "Of course."

Outside, Ashela set off walking off of the property. Here it was Christmas day and Ashela had no idea where she was going or how to get there. She walked until she saw a Mercedes Benz 600 SEL pulling out of the driveway of a neighboring home. She approached the car and was surprised to find a teenager behind the wheel. "Hello there. Can I beg you for a lift?"

"Sure. Where're you headed?"

"No where in particular. So I guess I'm going as far as you'll take me."

"Well, I was going into the city. If you don't mind riding bogus, you're welcome to come along." Ashela hopped in and they set off.

"Riding bogus? This isn't a stolen car, is it?" she asked jokingly.

"Nope. I just don't have a driver's license."

"Well, I do. So if we get pulled over, I'll tell them I'm your legal guardian. What's your name?"

"Tyrone."

"So tell me, Tyrone, why is a nice young man like yourself about to go joy riding on Christmas day?"

"I just needed to get away for awhile. My parents are such a drag. All they do is fight. I figured they won't even know I'm gone." He threw a look her way and asked, "What's a nice girl like you doing walking down the street?"

"Let's just say I got mixed up with the wrong people."

Tyrone played with the buttons on the sound system until he found a rap station. He turned the volume up high and they rode in silence, each lost in their own thoughts.

They were approaching River North Mall when Ashela asked, "Want to check out a movie?"

"Sure. But I'm afraid I don't have any money."

"That's okay. It'll be my treat. I'll buy you some gas as well so you can get back home."

It was after eight o'clock when the taxi dropped Ashela off at her home. She and Tyrone had checked out two movies and had dined on a sumptuous Christmas fare of hot-dogs, nachos, popcorn and soda. Ashela couldn't recall a time when she had spent an entire afternoon hanging out with a teenager outside of the recording studio. It was different, but it sure had been a lot of fun.

Inside her kitchen, she took out two small cans of salmon and poured them into ET's dish. "Merry Christmas, ET. Kyliah would kill me if she knew how much I've been feeding you lately. But any cat that's as skilled as you are at begging, deserves every bit of food he gets. It'll just have to be our secret."

She went upstairs to shower and slipped into a silk teddy before heading into her music room. As always, when Ashela was troubled, there was no better antidote than music. Before she could even sit down, her doorbell rang.

Sam stepped through her door looking very irritated. "I've been calling you for hours. Where have you been?"

Ashela locked the door behind him. "I just got in." As he stood staring at her, she walked around him and headed back into her studio. She was turning the sheets of her music book when Sam appeared in the doorway. Ignoring him, Ashela started to play.

"So where've you been, Ashela?"

"Out and about," she answered surly and noncommittally.

Sam had gone in search of her the moment he found out that she'd left the party. He had cased the area for nearly an hour looking for her, wondering where she could have disappeared to. Sam was angry with her because he'd been worried about her and he was not about to let her shield herself behind her music. He came and sat on the bench beside her and took hold of one of her wrists.

"Out and about isn't a sufficient answer, Ashela. Try again."

She snapped, "Well, I guess it's going to have to be, Sam. Because that's the only answer you're getting from me." Angry herself, Ashela snatched her wrist from his grasp. She moved to get up from the bench, but Sam, who was sitting with his back turned to the piano keys, wrapped an arm around her waist and prevented her from leaving. He yanked her body against his.

"I want to know where you've been." Sam's voice was low, but the anger he felt penetrated it.

"None of your damned business. You should have thought about it before you took me some place where I'd be humiliated, Sam. Maybe you *should* get yourself someone older. And you can start with that bitch of an ex-wife of yours."

Again, Ashela tried to pull away from him but he held her too tightly. "Let me go, damn you!" She raised her hands to pummel his chest and when Sam tried to kiss her, she slapped him hard across the face.

Sam stood up and pulled her up with him and thrust her body on top of the piano. With his hands on her waist, he nudged her legs apart and forced himself between them. Ashela's hands pushed against his shoulders. "If I wanted to be with someone older I would be. But I've chosen to be with you. Is that not good enough for you?" Roughly, Sam's hands slid from her waist and raised to cup her breasts through the silk of the material. Though his touch was far from gentle, he could feel her nipples harden beneath his hands.

Still angry with him and in no mood for his games, Ashela slapped his hands away from her. But Sam easily grabbed her wrists and held them behind her back. When he bit into the flesh of her collar bone, Ashela's struggles ceased. She could feel her anger evaporating as quickly as snow in a Nevada desert. As he fit his body closer to hers, bending her over the piano, her lava began it's traitorous descent through her body. "Stop it, Sam," she whispered as she desperately tried to sustain her anger. His lips reigned kisses up along her throat. But already Ashela was melting and wanted nothing more than for him to continue his assault.

Sam slid his hands downward, underneath her, lifting her up. He palmed her behind and pulled her closer to him, making her aware of his arousal. In a heartbeat he removed her chemise and threw it to the floor. His tongue traced a slippery trail along her flesh from her breasts to her navel. In the next instant, Ashela's legs were thrown over his shoulders as Sam bent to taste the creaminess of her center.

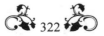

When Sam's lips finally locked again with hers, Ashela was putty in his hands. She heard him release his belt and unzip his pants. In the next second, with her arms wrapped tightly around his neck and her legs clamped around his waist, she discovered exactly why he was *the* master puppeteer, pulling her strings at will. Her musical sighs were his confirmation that she needed him, *wanted him* as the two of them whirled amidst a delirium of sensations. With plunge after gentle plunge, Sam's hardness filled her fierce dampness. When he finally queried her about whose lovin' it really was, Ashela had no qualms telling him that it was his and that it belonged only to him. His hands spread her buttocks apart and she clung to him for dear life. Her tongue trailed wet kisses down the sides of his neck, inside his ear, and back to his lips in an effort to reward him for the honor he was bestowing upon her, while embroiled in the heat of the moment.

She whispered his name over and over, pleaded with him to bring her satisfaction to an end, and finally clung to him helplessly as he released his life-force into her pulsating moistness.

With very little energy left in her body, Ashela whispered into his ear, "What do you want from me, Sam?"

Out of breath himself, Sam replied with no hesitation, "I want you to love me, Ashela. But love me for who I am, not for who or what you need me to be."

***

For New Year's Eve, Werner Enterprises threw a big bash in the posh ballroom of L.A.'s Waldorf Astoria. It turned out to be a huge media event as big-name artists and entertainers from both the music and movie industries were in attendance. With pride, Ashela flaunted her new quarter-million dollar Loree Rodkin diamond and ruby jewelry. She made sure that everyone who complimented her on the necklace and earring set knew that they were a "Christmas gift" from Sam Ross.

***

It wasn't until the end of February that Ashela could say that she was fully adjusted to working within the confines of her contract with Werner Enterprises. She had to acclimate herself to the fact that she was now working within their timeframes, and with only their artists. After reviewing their roster of talent, she created her own list by highlighting the artists she preferred to work with and eliminating the ones she absolutely *refused* to work with.

Months later, problems began to surface when several of the groups she had vowed not to work with continued to request her services. Because Ashela was one of few, brilliant lyricists whose mind surged with hooky grooves, soulful melodies, stylish verses, up-beat tempos, and sexy, provocative rhythms, she was highly sought after. As a Black female songwriter, her songs stood out because they were thought-provoking and tended to stay with people long after the song was over, unlike most other songs that were forgotten as soon as they ended. Because her lyrics were substantive and never meaningless, Ashela's music tended to evoke emotional

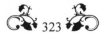

responses from listeners. While it was an honor to have the majority of the artists within the label clamoring for her to write material for them, Ashela was unwavering. She held fast to her personal standards and refused the requests of many. Soon, artists began jockeying for the right to be next in line for her written material. While all of the artists under the Werner label were free to utilize material written by writers outside of the writer's consortium, many wanted to take advantage of the fact that they could now have their music written for them by the renowned Ashela Jordan—particularly those who had never been fortunate enough to work with her in the past.

As she continued to deny certain artists' requests, she gained the reputation of "Ms. Queen Bee." Soon, someone leaked news of her selectivity to the press. Since all of the other labels were continually denouncing the Werner writer's consortium to begin with, they tore into the slightest bit of negativity like sharks gathering for a feeding frenzy. When the artists Ashela refused to worked with started labeling her as a "Prima Donna," in addition to "Ms. Queen Bee," the nay-sayers and gossipmongers were there to capitalize on it.

Many of the magazines and rag-mags started running quotes from one group in particular, The Kool Souljas, who lambasted Ashela at every turn. They claimed they were being denied an audience with her on the grounds of a past incident which she was the cause of. While their complaining to the media cast aspersions on her public image, ironically, the media attention also caused the demand for her professional services to soar. Artists outside the Werner label, whom she'd enjoyed working with in the past, were begging for her to slip a song or two their way.

Most castigating of all were the accusations that Ashela received preferential treatment within the writer's consortium because she was the bedmate of the president of the label.

One particular evening, Ashela was at Sam's home in Hollywood Hills. They had just finished playing tennis on his out-door court and she had taken a royal thrashing. Tennis wasn't her forte, but after being beaten like she'd stolen something, she was determined to learn the game. Inside, they showered and were eating a light meal when the discussion turned to Werner Enterprises.

Six months had gone by since the inception of the songwriters' consortium. By all accounts, the deal had already proven its success by the number of records topping the charts by Werner artists. As Sam had some of the best writers in the business now working exclusively for him, hit after hit was being recorded by his stable of artists. To counteract the initial wave of negative publicity generated by the media, Sam sent letters to all of the artists under the W.E. label that forbade them from talking about the songwriters' alliance in "any fashion that could be deemed as counter-productive." In effect, Sam's command served as a gag-order that stopped anyone from using language considered defamatory to the alliance.

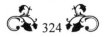

Thus far, Ashela was still the most sought after of all of the Werner composers. She had a waiting list a mile long that extended even beyond the two-year time line of her contract. And yet, despite all the distractions she had been faced with over the past several months, she was still cranking out the music left and right.

As they sat at the dining room table, Sam wanted to talk to Ashela about the group, The Kool Souljas. Their manager had requested a meeting with him in which he demanded to know why "AJ" was allowed to dis his group by writing songs for every other group except his. Before Sam responded, he decided to find out *why* Ashela was so adamant about not writing for the group. After she revealed her reasonings, Sam was thankful he'd gotten the story directly from her.

Ashela told him she knew the group well. And why she would quit writing all together before she ever wrote a note for them to sing.

She had been commissioned to work with The Kool Souljas more than four years prior. The only reason she'd agreed in the first place was because she owed their producer a favor. After he'd twisted her arm, she listened to a couple of their tapes to get a feel for their sound. Based on that, she wrote five songs for the group. Kyliah had set up the recording session and it wasn't until that very day that Ashela met the group members in-person.

At the time, the group had consisted of four twenty-something year olds as opposed to the five members they currently had. The four men were high on drugs when she got to the studio that day. Ashela had long since learned to trust her instincts. Immediately, her preceptory senses kicked in and she didn't like what she saw. Wanting to begin the session so she could get it over with, she told them it was time to get started.

First, Ashela had wanted them to warm up so she could get a feel for them. Suddenly, one of the guys in the group popped off, saying that he knew of a damned good way that she could get a feel for *all* of them. She could start by sucking their dicks. Seated in a leather chair, he proceeded to grab his manhood motioning it up and down. As laughter spread around the room to include the rest of his boys, he became even more emboldened. Just as quickly, he unzipped his pants and, because he was wearing no underwear, whipped out his organ and started stroking it in plain view.

Though she was appalled and highly insulted, Ashela stood deathly still as the rest of the group continued to laugh at their fellow member's antics. It may have been a joke to them, but it was no laughing matter to her. And on that particular day, they had chosen the wrong girl to play with. With a stern glare, Ashela pulled her purse strap onto her shoulder and stood up to leave.

As she walked to the door, she casually slipped her hand inside her large Coach leather bag. She continued toward the door when another guy in the group wanted to get in on the fun. He rose to his feet and barred her from leaving the room. As he

moved to obstruct her exit, before he could get any closer to her, Ashela spoke to him in a low voice seething with anger.

"Get the fuck outta my way." Something about her tone and the way she spoke put him on the defensive.

"What's the matter bitch, ain't enough of us for you?" He spread his arms wide as he spoke.

Looking into his eyes, Ashela knew he was high as a kite. Just as he took another step towards her, without blinking an eye, she yanked her 8 millimeter Glock out of her bag, uncapped the safety, and aimed it right between his eyes.

Staring down the barrel of the Glock, looking death in its face, the guy's high quickly evaporated. Ashela tilted the gun to the left at a 90-degree angle and said in a menacing voice, "Now back up off me." Suddenly, another kind of tension filled the air—a deadly silence that harbored the potential for violence.

The door was on her right and her back was to the wall. As the guy she was pointing the gun at began to back up, the door opened and in walked their producer carrying a dozen donuts in one hand and a cardboard box filled with soft drinks in the other.

All he saw was Ashela pointing a gun at one of the group members.

Allen froze in his tracks. In a split second, his eyes took in the entire scene. The guy who had initiated the entire incident was still sitting in the chair, his hand covering his now-flaccid genitals.

"You're late, Allen. And that's unfortunate. Maybe you forgot to tell yours boys that I came here to conduct a recording session, not to be gang-raped by a bunch of doped-up convicts."

Only when the band members had backed up against the studio equipment did Ashela lower her gun. Seeing that the situation was defused, she slid the safety back on the gun and slipped it into the holster inside her purse, all while edging out of the door. Her eyes never left the four guys.

Allen finally found his voice. "Will somebody tell me what the hell just happened here?"

Allen directed his statement toward his group. Just then, three other people came up behind him, hoping to sit in on the recording. Noticing the tension in the room, they too, had puzzled looks on their faces. Knowing something had to be done, Allen handed his packages to one of the guys standing next to him and hurried after Ashela.

Ashela had long since slid past him and the men standing behind him. She was halfway to the elevator when Allen came out running after her.

"Ashela, wait!" he shouted. It didn't take a genius to figure out what had just gone down inside the studio. And all Allen could see before him were lawsuits and lost revenue.

Ashela was pushing the down button for the elevator when Allen approached her.

"AJ, I'm sorry. I don't know what the fuck happened back there, but I'm really sorry. Are you okay?"

Ashela looked at him, emotionless. "I'm fine. I can take care of myself. Look, Allen, I didn't want to work with those nuts in the first place. You know that. But I did it as a favor to *you*. Consider the favor done."

"Ashela, please. I know they fucked up, but you can't leave me hangin' like this. You signed a contract, remember?" The elevator doors opened and Ashela stepped in. She turned to face him.

"Very true, Allen. But read paragraph nine of that very same contract. It gives me the right to terminate same without written notice. I'm choosing to exercise that option as we speak."

Before the elevator doors could close, Allen stepped inside. He ran his hand over his head and sighed heavily. He knew he'd have to take a different angle. "Damn, what is the world coming too?"

Ashela made no comment. When the elevator doors opened again, she strode briskly towards her car.

All kinds of thoughts were running through Allen's mind. He thought of the timeframe in which he had to deliver a new album to the label. He knew that at this short notice, it would be next to impossible to find another top-notch writer or producer to replace Ashela Jordan. If she didn't stick this out, millions of dollars would be forfeited. Allen walked with her to her car pleading his case.

"Allen please. I don't need this bullshit right now. If I were you, I'd go back upstairs and have a long talk with every one of them. I'd take great pains to make sure they realized the severity of what just happened and what else will happen if I decide to press charges. I don't know, maybe they're *used* to pulling stunts like that. But that's on you, Allen. Good luck in finding yourself some tunes." Ashela unlocked her Lincoln Navigator, got in and drove off.

The next day, both Allen *and* his attorney called her office repeatedly. When they finally reached Kyliah in an attempt to have the group issue Ashela a personal apology, it was too late. They were informed that an apology would not be needed. A police report had been filed and the five songs Ashela had written for them had all been purchased by the groups Boys-II-Men and Naughty-By-Nature.

Ashela looked up at Sam. "There you have it, Bay. Ever since then, I check out whomever I write for beforehand. If I don't like an act, I don't work with 'em. I'm told that The Kool Souljas has a new producer and a couple of different members. Doesn't matter, Sam. I *still* won't write a note for any of them."

***

Claudette Ross was about to become the new Mrs. Vincent Stanton. But, inside, tucked away from watchful and knowing eyes, was a searing anger that was made evident by the recurrence of a small patch of hives. An angry group of bumps had broken out in the area just below her breasts. A tell-tale sign to her that she was under some form of stress.

Though Claudette had agreed to marry Vince, in her heart of hearts, she knew that a part of her still loved her ex-husband. And it was something that she was trying to come to grips with after all of these years. Yes, she would marry Vince because he was safe and she'd never have to awaken in the middle of the night wondering where he was. Sam had been right about one thing, she *hadn't* wanted him any more. She had become too frustrated with his antics. But it wasn't so much *him* that she hadn't wanted as much as it was what he had put her through. The late nights, the traveling, and finally, the other women—all of these combined had been too much for her to overlook. But just because he'd chosen to walk out of her life all those years ago, why couldn't he understand that *she hadn't stopped loving him?*

Maybe in the back of her mind, Claudette had even held on to the frivolous notion that one day they would get back together. Even if such thoughts were fanciful thinking, what irked her to no end was the fact that Sam had chosen someone younger. Someone whom he would, in all probability, marry and start another family with. Claudette had seen the way Sam looked when he'd made the introductions. She knew the look well—his was the look of . . . *a man in love.* Abruptly, she got up from her chase lounge and stood in front of the mirror. She wasn't some shallow woman with nothing better to do with her time than to sit around and long for the past. She was a wealthy, beautiful, intelligent woman who simply recognized that she could not step into her future unless she'd resolved her unfinished business with the past. If not, she knew she'd go into her new marriage living a lie.

Chapter Thirty-Three

 s the months quickly rolled by, it was the following Thanksgiving before everyone knew it. Kyliah had originally intended to fly home for the weekend, but an unexpected visitor caused her good intentions to fall by the wayside.

Arron had been calling incessantly during the course of the year. Each time, Kyliah would have very little to say to him and would promise to call him back as soon as she found the time. Though he'd waited, she never called. From what he could gather, she was enrolled in night school at UCLA and in the daytime, she was still doing PR and other related things for her friend,

Ashela. Arron knew the best time to catch her was during the day or late at night. If he got her machine, he hung up because she never bothered to return his calls.

At first, Arron had thought Kyliah was seeing someone else, but when she told him of her hectic schedule he believed otherwise. He found it hard to accept that she simply didn't have time—not even for him. With their positions juxtaposed, Arron was the one feeling a sense of urgency. When he spoke to her, she was never cold to him, yet he sensed the distance that lay behind her words. Where once she had been willing to fit him around *her* schedule, now he felt as if *he* was the low man on the totem pole.

He had been wanting to see her for quite some time, but she always offered an excuse about "now" not being a convenient time. Back in July, he had asked if she would like to come visit him. Kyliah quickly declined. Then, he'd asked her if she would like *him* to come see her. She hesitated at first but then said evasively, "Maybe sometime in the future." He pressed her for a specific time and she eventually said Thanksgiving. Arron had the sneaking suspicion that she'd said it only because it seemed like eons away. But he was desperate to see her, so like a starving man begging for a morsel of food, he was thankful for the tiny scrap she'd tossed his way.

***

Two days before Kyliah was scheduled to board the plane to North Carolina, her classes let out for the Thanksgiving holiday. Tired and hungry, it was after nine o'clock at night when she headed for her home in Brentwood. Forty-five minutes later, she pulled into her driveway behind a Jeep Cherokee. From her vantage point, she couldn't tell who was inside and she had no idea who it could be. As she walked up the driveway, the driver's door opened and out stepped Arron.

Kyliah stood rooted to the spot.

With a hesitant smile on his face, Arron said, "You could greet me and at least tell me that you're happy to see me."

"Arron! I . . . What a surprise!" Kyliah closed the distance between them, but she made no move to touch him.

Finally, Arron bent down and placed a light kiss on her lips. "Am I invited inside?"

"Oh, sure. Come on." He reached for her book bag and they walked inside her house after she'd unlocked the door.

Although she was taken aback, Kyliah was still struggling to act cool and collected. A million questions were running through her mind.

She shut the door and said, "Arron, I won't pretend I'm not surprised to see you. Are you here on business or something?"

"Actually, no, Kyliah. I came with the express purpose of seeing you. If you recall, you *did* tell me I could visit you around this time." Arron knew he'd caught her off guard. He also discerned that she wasn't "pleasantly" surprised to see him.

Kyliah searched her memory banks. "Okay. But I thought we'd at least talk about it before you came."

Arron spread his hands. "So now I'm here. Do you want me to leave?" She hesitated a bit too long for him, so Arron turned and walked toward the door. Even he knew when to leave well enough alone.

When the door closed behind him, Kyliah was still standing there undecided about what she wanted. It was only when she heard his engine start up that she approached the door and opened it. She stood in her doorway staring at him before she realized he wasn't going anywhere. Her car was blocking his exit.

Trying to contain her mirth, she walked to his Jeep and stood in front of the driver's side window. "Gee, Arron, looks like you're in a bit of a quandary, doesn't it?"

Inside the Jeep, Arron continued to stare straight ahead of him.

Seeing that he wasn't in a humorous mood, Kyliah wrapped her arms around herself and lowered her head. She stared at the ground before flipping her head upwards to look at him, her long hair framed her face. "Tell you what. Why don't we go inside and discuss this over a sandwich and a cup of Cappuccino?" When he turned his head away from her, Kyliah threw her hands up in the air. She'd suddenly become irritated, too. "It's your call, Arron. You decide. *I've* had too long of a day, and I'm not about to stand out here all night. If you want to come inside and talk, fine. If not, after I get finished eating, I'll come back out and move my car and then you can be on your merry way." Kyliah turned and walked back inside her home, slamming the door behind her.

Halfway to her upper landing, her door bell rang and Kyliah went back downstairs to open the door for Arron. She stood to the side and waved her arm beckoning him through. She excused herself and headed back upstairs to shower and change into her pajamas. Dressed in a pair of black silk pants and a matching sleeveless v-neck vest, she walked into the kitchen and started fixing two turkey sandwiches.

She carried everything into the living room on a tray and set it down on her coffee table. She sat on the floor cross-legged while Arron sat on the couch with one leg crossed over the other. She offered him one of the sandwiches, but he only shook his head.

She raised her knee and rested her elbow on it. "So talk to me, Arron. Because obviously, I'm the one who's clueless here."

He stared at her with a sullen look upon his face. "What do you mean?"

"Please, Arron. Let's be real with each other, okay?" Kyliah got up and came and sat down on the opposite end of the couch. "When you and I first met, for

whatever reasons all I was to you was some joke that you tossed around with your pal, Sam Ross." She lifted her hand to stop him when he was about to deny it.

"I had feelings for you, Arron. And because of it, whenever you called, I was Johnny-on-the-spot. But after I visited you in Boston, any illusions I had of you and me as a couple got thrown by the wayside. The way I see it, I don't have a degree from Harvard or Yale. My mother doesn't have a membership to the Boston Society Club, neither does my father belong to the Insiders' Circle, and to top it off, I happen to be mulatto. So, all in all, I guess that makes me the proverbial country bumpkin. Well, woop-dee-fuckin'-do, Arron. I don't knock you for your upbringing. But at the same time, I'm not sittin' around any more bemoaning the fact that I don't come from the same background as you. I'm not beating myself up anymore, Arron, because my mother is Black and my father is white.

"When I wanted to be with you, you didn't know I existed because my name isn't Buffy or whatever else your Boston girlfriends call themselves. You knew I cared about you and all you did was never miss an opportunity to remind me that I didn't possess the social graces of all the other women you've ever dated. I mean, you all but practically died when your Aunt Phoebe, or whatever her name was, saw us in the mall together. And when your family started asking questions about me, the next thing I knew, I was on the plane so fast, *my* head was spinning. In the meantime, Arron, you handed me my heart back after it was torn to shreds."

Kyliah was thumping her fingers on the sofa. "This past year, I've spent my time bettering myself. Not for you, Arron, or for any other man. But for myself. The silver lining in my relationship with you is that it forced me to recognize how shallow I had allowed myself to become by sitting around bitching about the fact that I'm not married. I may not have been good enough for you, Arron, but it doesn't matter anymore. I'm good enough for myself.

"Finally, now that I've picked myself back up and gotten on the right track, here you come out of no where trying to waltz back into my life as if nothing has changed between us. I'm proud to say that this entire year, you, Mr. Davenport, have been the furthest thing from my mind. I don't understand you, Arron, and believe me, I'm done trying. You show up tonight without even calling and I'm supposed to *welcome* you with *open arms*? What nerve—what sheer gall you must have. Tell me, what gives? The Boston girls aren't freaky enough for you, so you decided to go slumming?" Kyliah had talked herself into a fit. She sat staring at him with sheer venom in her eyes.

"Are you finished? Can I speak now?" Without waiting for her to reply, Arron said, "It's never occurred to you that I have feelings, too, has it? No? Then I guess that's why it never dawned on you that I cared for you as well. I may not be able to express my feelings and emotions as well as you do, Kyliah, but that doesn't mean that I don't have them. You make it seem as if I was embarrassed to be seen with you. Did I not introduce you to the few people that I consider my friends? Did I ever

disrespect you in the least way? Since the time you overheard Sam and I discussing you, I've had to preface every conversation I've had with you by saying how sorry I was for that particular day. If you had your way, you'd have me feeling sorry that I was ever born.

"No, I *didn't* introduce you to my family when you came to Boston. I didn't feel that it was appropriate. Though you claim otherwise, I never lorded it over you about where I came from or what my background was. And I've never even bothered to *ask* about your background. As far as I was concerned, your being bi-racial didn't matter. *It simply was not important.* Let me remind you, Missy, that *you* were the one who always talked about all the hard knocks you took as a child of a mixed couple. All along, it sounded as if *you* were the one with the sour grapes to me. And now, you sit here and pretend that *I'm* the one with the social-class consciousness hangup? I don't think so, Kyliah.

"I never made you feel lesser than who you are. You made *yourself* unhappy by always comparing this person to that person. You were the one pointing out your own inadequacies, silly things that didn't even matter to me. You meet *one* member of my family and then you judge every one by that one person, thinking they must all be snobs. *You're* the one who needs to take a look in the mirror, Kyliah. When you can answer the question of what it is you're running from, *then* come back and talk to me about not knowing how to treat people."

Arron stood up to leave. He was suddenly just as sick of her as she was of him. "Don't bother moving your car. I'll do it myself. Where are your keys?"

Kyliah could only purse her lips. She didn't look at him when she said, "Maybe we both needed to let out some steam, Arron. It seems we both had some issues that needed to be addressed. Misunderstandings, private concerns, and disappointments." Kyliah pressed her hands together between her clinched thighs. "That's what's going through my mind right now, Arron. But even above all that, is the thump of my heart that's telling me that I don't want you to leave. If you're hurting right now, a part of me wants to say 'good.' Because at least now you know what it feels like to want someone when they don't really want you."

"Kyliah, I'm sorry. But this isn't a tit-for-tat game for me. If I didn't care about you, I wouldn't be standing here right now. Yes, I strung you along in the beginning, but only because I wasn't sure of how I felt about you. Was it wrong? Absolutely. So yes, I'm hurting and since you've made it clear that you 'really don't want me' I'm not going to hang around. If I've caused you any hurt, I apologize for that. But just as your heart healed, so too, will mine." Arron's eyes fell on her car keys on top of a near-by table. He went and picked them up and tossed them up and down in his hand before heading towards the door. As he closed her door behind him, his own heart was heavy in his chest. Whoever started the stupid myth that men don't cry, never had their heart ripped to pieces.

Kyliah used the back of her hand to wipe her tear-stained eyes. She felt ET's paw on her leg and she looked down at him. He was looking up at her as if to say that *he* still loved her. She lifted him into her arms and wished she could be like him—no pride whatsoever. However she treated him, ET's love for her never diminished.

As Arron came back inside to hand her her keys, she placed ET on the couch and got up to take them from him. When he turned and walked away without saying good-bye, Kyliah said, "Arron, please stay."

Arron stopped but he didn't turn around to face her. "Kyliah, we've both had our say. Let's just call it a draw." He continued toward the door.

"Don't make me beg, Arron."

He could hear her sniffling behind him and finally, he turned around to face her. "I can't think of one good reason why I should stay, Kyliah. But all I know is that I don't want to leave."

"Then don't. We've fought enough for one night. So, can't we just try to get along?"

"I'm not the fighter that you are, Kyliah. Keeping the peace is all that I know *how* to do."

"Then will you stay with me?

"Aren't you supposed to bribe me?"

"Uhm, yeah. But all I've got is those wilted turkey sandwiches on the table."

Arron shook his head. A hint of a smile was beginning to form on his face. "That's not good enough. What else have you got?"

Kyliah walked over to a nearby table, grabbed a Kleenex and blew her nose. She walked back over to stand in front of Arron and tried to hand him the snotty tissue. "How about a peace offering?"

Arron shook his head again. "No way, lady. One final try. What else you got?"

Kyliah wrapped her arms around his waist and rested her chin upon his chest, leaning into him. "I can offer you my heart."

"Now that, I'm willing to accept." Arron cupped the sides of her face and lifted it to meet his.

Chapter Thirty-Four

*A*s the spring of the following year gave way to the summer months, Ashela celebrated the fact that she and Sam were nearing their second anniversary. During that time, she had practically moved into Sam's abode and when either of them referred to "home," they both knew they were referring to his house in Hollywood Hills.

As a power couple, she and Sam attended many social gatherings together. Occasionally, she would entertain his business associates and she even hosted a number of fêtes in his honor. In the eyes of the media, the two of them were as good as married.

Ashela's thirty-second birthday was fast approaching. This year, Sam insisted that she meet him in New York. He had a surprise for her, and try as she might, she couldn't pry so much as a hint out of him. A part of Ashela strongly suspected that Sam was planning to propose to her. Such a thought made her tremble. It was one thing for them to be together constantly, it was even something for them to share all that they did, but marriage?

It was a heady notion for Ashela. In the time that they'd known each other, Sam had been her everything. Her lover, her friend, her sounding board, and her shelter from the storms of life. With him, Ashela felt as if she had it all. But the one factor that stood out was the glaring truth that neither of them had ever told the other that they loved them. Ashela had thought a lot about that over the past year or so. Of course she loved Sam, how could she not? When you cared about someone, when that person mattered to you, when your heart fluttered at the very thought of them and a smile came to your face every time they entered a room, when you willingly shared everything you had—if that wasn't love, then Ashela certainly didn't know what was.

She was constantly being told by her friends and associates that she "had it all." Love, money, happiness. If that were true, then why the hell did she feel as if there was still a huge void in her life? The constant, insatiable craving for something that she couldn't define or describe would not go away.

It nagged her as she boarded Sam's private airplane. Each time that she sat in the plush, leather seats that enveloped her, Ashela was impressed with the royal elegance of the plane's interior. It's expensive build and decorous layout was befitting of a king. Several hours later, Ashela was whisked by limousine to Sam's Manhattan condominium.

An unusual excitement tinged the edges of Ashela's nerves as she closed the door behind her. She hadn't seen Sam in close to two weeks. She called him to let him know that she'd made it from the airport and asked him to wait at his office for her. She had some shopping she wanted to do and would come to him afterwards.

Ashela was feeling very Gucci today, so she dressed herself from head to toe in the famed designer's clothing. A simple black stretch lamé slipdress with black leather pumps. To add an aura of mystique to her outfit, Ashela donned a strand of cultured pearls around her neck with matching pearl earrings and a black, wide-brimmed straw hat.

She directed the limo driver to drop her off on Fifth Avenue, and gave him instructions to pick her up from the same spot in one hour.

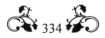

Ashela stood gazing into the display window of Saks Fifth Avenue, admiring the shining raincoats which the emaciated mannequins wore. Thank goodness her figure was far from that of any stick-like model, but despite her rounded voluptuousness, the raincoat she could still play. She walked closer to the display window oblivious to the stares of passersby. New York was filled with stars and bums alike strolling down its Manhattan streets. So it was without intent that she happened to snub a dirty, grungy bum that passed her by.

***

It was her all right. Greg was sure of it. Even through the drunken haze of his stupor, he could tell it was her. But he had walked past her just to be sure. The bitch hadn't even bothered to say hello. Guess she thought she was too good to speak to him now. More than ten years had passed since he'd laid eyes on her. But in that time he'd seen her picture plastered all over everywhere and Greg swore he'd kill her if he ever ran across her again.

It was *her* fault that his life had turned out the way it had. Everything that had gone wrong for him, everything that he had lost had all been because of her. The night of the fire was as fresh in Greg's mind as if it had happened yesterday. In one night, he'd lost his lover, Charles, *and* his promising career as a bass player. The way Greg remembered things in his misaligned world, his star had been about to rise. If it hadn't been for her, a record company would have signed him to a multi-million dollar record deal long ago. Greg knew that he had been the best damned bass player in the world. Now, dressed in her finery, she couldn't even give him the time of day.

Years earlier, Greg had barely escaped the fire with his life. He had third-degree burns everywhere on his body, including his face. He remembered being rushed to the hospital where he'd undergone emergency surgery to save his life. Weeks later, he had been transferred to a burn center where they had tried to rehabilitate him for his return to "normal" society. Just prior to his release, the doctors had recommended he get psychiatric treatment. But with no money and no health insurance, Greg became just another New York statistic.

At first, he figured no one wanted to hire him because he was scarred everywhere on his body. After seeing people's horrified looks, he took to wearing long-sleeved turtle-neck shirts and pants—even in the dead of summer. Hatred and the desire for revenge had literally caused Greg to lose his mind. In the years since the fire, he had been in and out of jails, asylums, *and* mental institutions. At night, he'd comb the dangerous streets looking for a way out. Turning to drugs and crime was just a means to get him through this life.

But drugs and crime had exacted their toll on him as well, and his face and body proved it. Greg was a carrier of the deadly HIV virus and it had ravaged both his mind and body. As he stood in the middle of the sidewalk staring at his intended victim, passersby stepped around him. Dressed in a thick, dirty winter coat, torn-up

pants, a ripped turtleneck shirt, and filthy high-top tennis shoes with no laces, he wreaked of urine and feces.

Greg stood in the middle of the sidewalk trying to think through a suddenly clouded mind.

***

As Ashela started to walk into the store, someone called her name. She looked in the direction when suddenly a photographer flashed her picture. Knowing he would probably use it for one of the tabloid journals, she raised her hand against the glare and hurried into the store.

***

Having obtained his pictures, the photographer walked past the stinking bum and headed on his way.

"Hey!"

Knowing the man was crazed, the photographer kept walking.

"Hey! I'm talkin' to you! Cum 'ere!"

The photographer paused at the corner for a streetlight. But that was all the time Greg needed to slowly catch up with him.

Out of breath, Greg said to the man. "Yo, man. I was talkin' to you. How much you'll gimme for some candy on Ashela Jordan?"

***

Inside the store, Ashela fought to shake off her annoyance over the photographer. They were animals, the paparazzi. Always looking to dig up dirt, even where none existed.

She took the elevator up to the fifth level where she walked through several different stores fingering gowns and a variety of scarves. As she approached the Emanuel Ungaro Parallele boutique, she went inside intent on purchasing one of the raincoats on display. She was waited on attentively and finally selected a shiny, red iridescent raincoat. Several purchases later, she had picked up a red, sequined, strappy G-string, some Bvlgari body crème and a pair of red, patent leather Paco Rabanne stiletto-heeled shoes.

Nearly an hour later, Ashela headed out of the store. She walked towards the corner where her limousine was to pick her up to take her to Sam's office. When she heard someone call out her name, she kept walking thinking it was the same photographer. But when she heard the voice call her again, she stopped and turned around. There was something oddly familiar about it.

Approaching her as she turned around was Parris Reed.

The years since she'd last seen him seemed to melt away. More so than the shock of seeing him was the reminder that fifteen or so years of her life had gone by in a flash.

"Hello, Ashela. Wow, is it ever good to see you again." Parris was dressed in a business suit and tie. He was all smiles. "What are you doing in New York? I thought the West Coast was your territory."

"It is, but I'm here visiting someone. Here comes my ride now." Ashela hesitated and then asked, "Can I give you a lift somewhere?"

"Unfortunately, I'm not alone. Besides, I wouldn't want to inconvenience you."

"I understand. And it wouldn't have been an inconvenience, Parris." Ashela assumed he was traveling with a female companion.

Parris read her mind. "I have three of my fellow associates with me."

The two of them were standing at the corner when Ashela's limo pulled up.

She walked toward it and her driver got out to open the door for her. "I've got plenty of room if you change your mind."

Parris grinned when he saw the limo. "I think we will take you up on your offer. Wait one second."

As Sam's driver helped her into the limo, Parris hurried to get his companions. He brought back with him three other gentlemen, two white and one Black. They were all older than he.

They had come to New York City to settle a court case and were staying at the Omni Hotel. Inside the limo, though they were corporate men Ashela could tell by the way they looked around that they were impressed. It was Sam's limo and Ashela knew they would be. There was nothing feminine about the vehicle. The limousine spoke of power. After shaking hands and making introductions, she offered them something to drink. They declined, but one of them complimented her on a bottle of Krug champagne that was amidst Sam's stock. The particular brand was three-hundred dollars a bottle.

As an act of kindness, Ashela reached for the bottle of Krug and handed it to the man. "Parris tells me you gentlemen are in town to settle a court case. Take this to celebrate your victory before you return home. Is North Carolina home for all of you?" The man accepted the bottle with gratitude.

After confirming that it was, it was only natural for them to ask her what line of business she was in.

"I'm a songwriter, Mr. McFarrin. Right now, I'm under contract with Werner Enterprises." She spread her hands to indicate the limousine. "The good thing about them is that they take care of their own."

Parris said, "Ashela and I grew up together. She's come a long way since then. I've been keeping up with you, Ash. I read about your deal with Werner. Thirty million? Gentlemen, wouldn't you all agree that she's come a long way?"

"Of course, I feel as if I know you already." As Mr. McFarrin's remark was meant to be humorous, they all laughed.

Minutes later, the car pulled up in front of their hotel. They shook hands and as they departed the limo, Ashela emptied out one of her small shopping bags and handed it to the man carrying the champagne bottle.

"It was a pleasure to have met you, Ms. Jordan. If we can ever be of assistance to you, please don't hesitate to call." Mr. McFarrin was the senior partner at their law firm and he was obviously impressed.

Parris didn't get out with the rest of them. Ashela said to the driver, "Give us a moment, Fred." He nodded and closed the door to give them privacy.

For the first time since entering the limo, Ashela removed her hat, laying it on the seat beside her. "You look well, Parris." She meant it too. He was as gorgeous as ever.

"So do you."

Ashela smiled at him. "How's your family, your mother?" She wouldn't dare mention Tracy's name.

"She's well. She and Kye speak of you often. I'm the only one who has to get my info about you from what I read in the papers." He looked away from her before turning back to say, "I guess I keep up more than I should."

When she looked at him with a raised eyebrow, he said, "I'm just really proud of you, Ashela." Parris wanted to add more, but he didn't.

"Thank you." Ashela was still trying to decipher what seeing him meant to her.

"Where's your ring? I'd heard you were married."

She flashed her fingers. "No, Parris, I'm not married. You shouldn't believe everything you read, you know. Kye will probably be married before I will."

"Think so?"

"Definitely." Ashela had the feeling that both of them were lightly treading water, as if being mindful not to offend the other.

"Well, I guess I should be going." Yet Parris made no move to exit the limo. Taking a deep breath, he said, "You know, Ashela, all these years, I told myself if I ever saw you again, I'd tell you how sorry I was for how I treated you years ago, and for how everything's turned out. Tracy, she and I never loved each other. We were doomed from the start. Did you know she and I are getting a divorce? No, I guess you wouldn't know. I'm sure Kye never even mentions me to you. I don't know why, but seeing you again makes me feel like I owe you an apology. Why haven't you married, Ashela?" No matter how illogical the thought, Parris wanted desperately to hear her say she'd been waiting for him.

"Oh, I don't know, Parris. I guess I was waiting for that special person to come along. I'll admit that years ago, I was devastated when I found out that you were going to marry Tracy. It felt like my heart had been ripped from my chest. I think that was my first lesson in betrayal. I won't say it was the best thing that ever happened to me. But, if things hadn't turned out the way they did, I probably wouldn't be who

338

I am today. A long time ago, I used to dream of different ways that I could exact revenge on the two of you, but the problem with revenge, Parris, is that it's far from sweet. I've learned that it leaves a bitter taste in your mouth. Seeing you today, Parris, has helped me put a period behind some places in my life where before there were only question marks. I really am sorry about your marriage. It's too bad it didn't work out. Everybody deserves to be loved. Even someone as miserable and twisted as Tracy."

Suddenly, Ashela wanted badly to be with Sam. It was as though seeing Parris had brought closure to her life, making her recognize that she really did love Sam. "Don't hold any illusions about me, Parris. I'm not the same girl you knew all those years ago. Although things change and people change, we can't change the past. I'm not hurting anymore, Parris, so don't beat yourself up over something that's done and over with. It was good seeing you again. Take care of yourself."

Parris opened the door to the limousine. But before he stepped out, he said to her, "I know it's too late, Ashela. But for whatever it's worth, I really did love you."

As the door closed behind him, Ashela sat looking down at the purchases she had made. More so than ever before, she felt the need to be intimate with Sam. Right now, she needed him inside her, reaffirming what her body knew but what her mind was slow to catch up with.

***

Karen Mitchell was Sam Ross's girl-Friday. It had been a long, grueling day. She glanced at the clock on the wall and knew it would be another hour and a half before she'd be able to call it a day. She was rubbing her temples when the door to the suite opened. As Ashela Jordan walked through the double doors, her first thought was that she had to be a bold sistah to wear such a short number. "Good evening, Ms. Jordan. I'll buzz Mr. Ross to let him know that you're here."

"How are you, Karen? Do me a favor, don't buzz him. I'll just surprise him. By the way, go home, Karen. It's almost six o'clock. I'll let him know I told you to leave." Ashela stepped to the door of Sam's office. She turned back to Karen. "Oh, one last thing, Karen, forward the rest of his calls into voice-mail." She winked her right eye at Karen and walked through Sam's door, locking it behind her.

For a moment, Karen sat staring at the closed office door. Four-inch stiletto heels? It didn't take a brain surgeon to figure out what was about to go down inside Mr. Ross's office. Some women had all the luck! Quickly, Karen gathered up her things, activated voice-mail, locked the doors to her boss's executive suite and headed for home.

Sam was seated behind his desk on the telephone. As he looked out at the New York skyline, he squeezed tightly the exercise hand-grip in the palm of his left hand. When he heard his office door open and close, he turned around in his chair, expecting to see Karen.

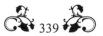 339

As Ashela leaned against the door, Sam tried desperately to stay in tune with the conversation he was holding. He watched as she began to slowly parade around his office. One by one, she walked to each window and drew every blind closed. Her shiny red raincoat encased her hips and showed off her legs to perfection. The stiletto heels added a stalking feel to her steps. She dimmed the lights inside the office and took a seat on his couch. Untying the belt from around the raincoat, she opened it slightly to reveal a red-sequined bikini.

She's a little leather, but she's well put together. It was a phrase Sam had heard older men say when he had been just a little boy. Now, he knew just what they meant.

"Andy, I'll call you tomorrow afternoon. I promise you, we'll reach an agreement that will be amenable to all parties. Fine. Then tomorrow it is." Sam hung up.

He sat with one leg crossed over his knee. His elbow resting on his desk, fingertip on his chin, his thumb rested just underneath it. Sam's gaze was fastened to hers. Ashela stood up and removed her raincoat, allowing it to drop to the floor. Her sleek, well-oiled, muscled body stood a short distance from him. Shapely arms, melon-like breasts, narrow waist tapered off into smooth, solid thighs, and long legs gave way to shapely calves. Sam was the helpless fly caught in the black widow's web.

As she sauntered toward him, Sam saw the intensity in her eyes. He knew what she wanted and knew what he had to give her. Motionless, he sat before her as she stood with her feet spaced far apart. No talking, no words needed. Resting both palms on his desk, she bent forward as if expecting to be strip-searched. His breath coming rapidly, Sam got up from his chair and stood behind her.

The slow sound of his pants unzipping caused her breath to catch in her throat.

Temperatures rising, Sam released his large manhood from its confinement and guided it to the edges of her waiting lips. Teasing her. Long, soft hisses escaped her lips. He shifted the G-string, leaning his hips against her buttocks. Reaching around her to gently pull apart her tender lips. As his size filled her hot and tight love tunnel, her teeth gritted and he knew they were bared.

Then he pushed her down onto the desk, his hips crashing, grinding against hers as he urgently plunged himself roughly into her. Sam lifted one of her legs onto his desk and guided himself in and out of her silky, tight wetness until finally, he finished her off.

***

Sam's birthday surprise for Ashela turned out to be a ten-day vacation to a thirty-five room Chateau in Sintra, Portugal. For $2,000 a night, they rented the well-kept, century-old edifice. The Chateau overlooked a medieval royal palace, it had an ocean view, magnificent chandeliers, and a natural pool which was fed by a waterfall. The romantic hideaway came complete with an English-speaking staff of twelve ready to wait on them hand and foot. For ten days they slept late and feasted on the finest of

foods, zesty dishes that were surprisingly low in fat. In the evenings they sipped grappa as they waited for the sun to die down. In the afternoons when it was blistering hot, they fled to the neighboring towns of Pyrenees, Province, Normandy, Ticino or to Donegal.

They laughed as the locals stared at them curiously but without malevolence. Peasants on one-speed bicycles, toothless ancients hawking obscure vegetables, sulfite-free wines, and unpasteurized cheeses. These people reminded Sam and Ashela of how simple life once was. Another delightful surprise was how much fun Ashela actually had as she dabbled with a variety of paints attempting to create her own Impressionist masterpieces. It was also good for her to see Sam relax and unwind. He did so by swimming, horseback riding and, of course, making love to her until she begged him to stop.

It was a time for them to relax, enjoy one another, and to experience how people lived on the other side of the world.

Though she'd expected Sam to propose to her, he hadn't. The rising disappointment she felt caught her off guard. For such a time as this, Ashela told herself she was happy. But if that was truly the case, then why was she constantly plagued with the nagging feeling that something in her life was missing?

***

Three days after Sam and Ashela departed for Spain, Kyliah was steaming with anger. She had gotten a call from Marlene Bowens who worked for Maggie Z. at the L.A. Times. Marlene was a friend of Kyliah's and she was calling her under the strictest of confidence. Marlene wanted to tip Kye's hand to a feature story that Maggie Z. was about to run on Ashela Jordan. While The Times would only run pieces of the story, Marlene was calling to warn Kyliah that the rag-mags were about to have a field-day. Marlene had a lucrative side deal going in which she sold personal details about stars to interested rag-mags. She was only hipping Kyliah to the fact that something was about to go down because she owed Kye a favor. Marlene gave her bits and pieces of what would be in the article.

The next day, Kyliah went to the newsstand and as much as she hated to support the bastards, she bought copies of all the rag-mags.

Sure enough, the tabloids were lambasting Ashela in a big way.

Unidentified sources claimed to have first-hand knowledge that singer/songwriter/jazz musician Ashela Jordan was once a crackhead during the time she lived in New York. She was also a reputed pyromaniac who had committed murder by way of arson. The unidentified sources said Ashela later became a high-class prostitute who had once even murdered one of her johns. The article went on to hint that her main client had been none other than a certain wealthy senator of longstanding prominence.

After quickly reading the article, Kyliah leaned her head back against the seat of her car. With pursed lips and her eyes closed, all she could do was shake her head.

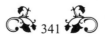

She didn't know how much truth the article contained, but the one thing she did know was that even if she managed to pull a rabbit our of her magical public relations hat, the press was still going to have a field-day with her best friend and confidant, Ashela Jordan.

Chapter Thirty-Five

yliah's worst fears were confirmed as the torrid stories made headlines in all the gossip columns across the country. Magazines and newspapers were now labeling Ashela's music as the work of a twisted and psychotic genius. As the media continued its feeding frenzy, Kyliah's phone rang off the hook, non-stop, day and night. She was so busy issuing "no comment" disclaimers until she finally stopped taking calls all together.

As Kyliah continued to deny all versions of the stories circulating about her friend, she was also getting requests from a variety of sleazy talk-show producers who were inviting Ashela to come tell her side of the story. Also frustrating Kyliah was the fact that Ashela had never really discussed with her what had happened during the years she'd spent in New York. She'd talked in generalizations, but never in detail. If what the gossipmongers were saying was true, Kyliah could understand the reasons behind Ashela's secrecy.

***

When Sam and Ashela returned from their vacation, they were unaware of the media fallout and the controversy it was causing at Werner Enterprises. Sam disembarked from the plane in New York while Ashela continued on to L.A. where a limousine waited to pick her up and deliver her to her Malibu doorstep.

Hours later, the limo rolled up her driveway and she got out carrying her purse and a small makeup case. As the driver retrieved the rest of her luggage, Ashela was searching through her purse for her keys to unlock the door to her home.

From the time the limo pulled into the Jordan driveway, two media trucks were waiting to see exactly who would exit the vehicle. Just days before, a number of trucks had been stationed outside her residence, but after several days of no activity, all but two of the vans had departed. As Ashela Jordan alighted from the limousine, the remaining news crews knew they had hit pay dirt. At a drop of a hat, they entered the gates and pulled up behind the limo with their cameras rolling. All at once, they ambushed and besieged her with questions.

Catching the stunned singer/songwriter by surprise, they sprayed her with questions regarding her sordid past.

"Ms. Jordan, is it true that you used to be a high-class prostitute when you lived in New York City?"

Robyn Williams

"Ms. Jordan, is it also true that you once murdered a man for one of your pimps?"

"Ashela, tell us about your drug use. Is it true you had to be hospitalized because of your strong drug dependency?"

"Ms. Jordan, tell us the name of the senator you used to prostitute for."

Ashela felt like she was in the twilight zone as they crowded around her on her doorstep. With her mouth hung open, she stood motionless until her limo driver shouldered his way to the front and shielded her with his body. As he blocked her from the view of the cameras, he elbowed her to break the state of shock that had completely fallen over her.

"Open the door!" he hollered at her.

With trembling fingers, Ashela inserted the keys into the lock and pushed the door open. He closed it hard after hauling the luggage in behind him. After several seconds, her alarm went off, effectively scaring everybody on the outside away.

Ashela stood looking at the driver in amazement. "Okay, what just happened out there?"

But he didn't hear her over the blare of the alarm system. He only pointed to the gadget on the wall, gesturing for her to disarm it. Ashela walked over to the unit and punched in the alarm code to silence the loud and reverberating sounds. She was *still* in a state of numbness.

"Look, are you going to be okay?" The driver was edging his way to the door. He had other rounds to make.

"Yes, I think so. Do you have to leave?" Suddenly, Ashela didn't want him to go.

"Yeah, I'm afraid so. I've got other people to pick up."

"Oh. Well, here, take this. Thank you for all your help."

"Nothing to it. The media's nothing but a bunch of vultures." His eyes bucked as she handed him five one-hundred dollar bills. "Wow! Thank you. This is very generous of you."

"What's your name?"

"Perry Boyd." He reached into his jacket and handed her his business card. "Any time you need anything, just let me know."

As he opened the door to leave, a police vehicle was pulling up behind the limo.

"Is there a problem, mam?" the police officer asked as he got out of the squad car.

"No. Yes. I mean, I was just accosted by the news media. Can you please make them leave my property?"

After the police cleared everyone from her property, she turned away from the window and dialed Kyliah's home number.

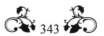

With a trembling voice, she spoke into the answering machine, "Kye, it's me. If you're there, pick up." When she got no response, she hung up and paged her. Five minutes later her phone rang and she picked up on the first ring. "Hello?"

"Welcome back." Kyliah was calling from her cellular as she drove down Sunset Boulevard enroute to her home.

"Yeah," Ashela said with anger. "And what a fucking welcome it was." Ashela proceeded to tell Kye everything that had transpired, but Kyliah stopped her.

She didn't want to say much over the phone. She told Ashela she'd be to her place within an hour.

Ashela was still angry after she'd hung up. She walked back into the foyer and grabbed her suitcases to unpack. All while doing so, she steamed with rage at the lies that the reporters had thrown in her face.

Ninety minutes later, Kyliah's voice spoke through the intercom on Ashela's door.

She opened it to admit Kyliah, who was carrying an Italian leather briefcase. They went into the living room and took a seat before Kye snapped open her briefcase and took out five different rag-mags. She tossed them all on the table.

Without saying a word, Ashela picked one up and skimmed it.

Kyliah watched the exasperated, angry look that ran across Ash's face. Inside, she too, was angry. But part of her anger was directed at Ashela, whom she felt could have at least explained to her some of what had happened to her while she lived in New York.

Ashela threw the paper onto the table, refusing to read anymore. "This is a bunch of bull. It's all lies. There's no truth to *any* of this." She stood up and started pacing vehemently.

"Then you're saying that all of this is just a bunch of make-believe bullshit? Someone sure went out of their way just to screw you over, Ashela."

Ashela didn't like Kyliah's tone of voice. She stared at her with narrowed eyes. "Are you calling me a liar, Kye?"

"I'm not calling you anything. How the hell do I know what's a lie or what's the truth? Did you ever so much as hint at what happened to you while you lived in New York? For all I know, everything that's in there could very well be the truth."

"Well, I'm telling you that it's not."

"Then fine. You try telling that to a hungry media for seven days straight without fail. All I've *been doing* is covering for you while you've were away. If nothing else, I deserve to know the truth."

"Handling my PR is part of why I pay you, Kyliah. And if that's suddenly become a problem, just let me know. Furthermore, I don't owe *you* or anyone else an explanation about my life *or* anything that goes on in it."

"Agh! Wrong answer, Ash. As your publicist and your *supposed* friend, I have a right to be in the know about *everything*. In the event that I'm left to defend you against the wolves, I damn *sure* deserve to know about everything."

Ashela stood up. In addition to her anger, she could now add frustration and intolerance. "Well then, I guess this is just another one of our philosophical differences. You don't like it, Kye, then you're welcome to get the fuck out."

Snapping her briefcase closed, Kyliah stood up and did just that.

Ashela stalked upstairs to her bedroom and called Sam. She tracked him down at his office and in a whiny, petulant voice, started telling him everything that had happened, ending her story with how Kyliah had accused her of it all being true.

On the other end of the phone, Sam listened with a half-smile. His poor baby needed pampering and cuddling right now, and to top it off, she couldn't even cry on her best friend's shoulder. But Kyliah was right in one sense. The stories circulating about Ashela were pretty damning. Sam could certainly understand where Kyliah was coming from because the stories managed to raise several questions in *his* mind. He always had wanted to question Ashela further about the incident involving The Kool Souljas' recording session. Anyone who pulls out a Glock and uses it with the skill she had implied, had to be a pro. He couldn't help but wonder where Ashela had gained such knowledge. Sam also had no doubt that the good senator in question was none other than the extraordinary Randal Stein. He had even heard recent whispers that the Senator was preparing for a presidential run. If his name was ever associated with the now "infamous" Ashela Jordan, his chances might be completely ruined.

Lastly, although Sam would never admit it, he could damn sure picture Ashela in the role of a high-class madam. Sometimes she *could* be a little "out there" with her sexual proclivities. But Sam hadn't complained yet and he wasn't about to start now.

To placate her, Sam said, "Look, baby, I'm pretty sure this will all blow over in a couple of days. Don't even worry yourself about it. In the meantime, look on the bright side: In the ten days we've been gone, look how the record sales of all the songs you've written have soared. That's good news, sweetheart." Sam couldn't prevent a smidgen of amusement from tingeing his voice.

In a shrill voice, Ashela said, "Sam, this *isn't* a laughing matter. *You* don't have reporters camped out in front of your home. Fuck the record sales. My rep is being trashed here and all you can talk about is goddammed record sales?"

Sam's voice lost the amusement as he became firm with her. "Look, Ashela, the damage has already been done. Now I suggest you just lay low until this all blows over. Why don't you rest or do some more painting. Better yet, go work off your steam by writing some more songs. I'm not unsympathetic about what you're going through, baby. I'm only saying that if you respond to them, you'll only be adding more fuel to the fire. Even if you try to sue them, you still won't get anywhere. Look at how long Carol Burnett's case took. Do you really want to spend ten years in

addition to millions of dollars trying to defend what you say is a pack of lies? Just let it go, baby."

"Yeah, right. And fuck you, too, Sam." Ashela slammed the phone down in his ear.

Sam sighed heavily. He hated it when she was in one of her temperamental moods, which seemed to recur often of late. He got a dialtone and called Kyliah. When she picked up, he thanked her for helping him arrange their trip to Portugal. She'd gotten the passports and made all of the other arrangements as well. He told her about his conversation with Ashela. As he listened to Kyliah's side of the story, he could tell that the two of them were still angry with each other.

Sam shook his head as he listened to how Kyliah herself was embracing the role of matyred victim by claiming that Ashela rarely told her anything about her personal life. Now that she was fed up with it, Kyliah felt that she *should* just quit.

Running his hand across his forehead, Sam convinced Kyliah to just hang tight. Ashela was going to need her badly in the next few weeks until she got over the slew of negative press. After soothing her, Sam hung up. He called Karen inside his office and had her make arrangements for him to return to the West Coast. It seemed Sam would have to, once again, don his fireman's cape. This time, he would be squelching a blaze that Ashela Jordan had caused with her own fiery past.

Over the next eight weeks, Sam proved incorrect in his assumptions that the whirlwind rumors about Ashela would die down. In the ensuing furor over her horrid past, new and even spicier details emerged causing everyone to clamor to find out just who the mysterious senator was with whom Ashela had had such a hot and spicy love affair/pimp and prostitute relationship. Whoever the man was, he was rumored to be the only man she had ever loved and because she could not have him, she had turned to the strong and supportive arms of Sam Ross, president and CEO of Werner Enterprises.

Completely irritated, Kyliah wondered in frustration just who the hell was thinking these stories up.

Meanwhile, a beleaguered Ashela was beginning to show signs of her own distress: She was starting to drink a bit too much. After she'd first returned from her vacation with Sam, she had released her anger towards the media by writing several rap songs. Rap was just another form of expression anyway, so Ashela used it as an outlet to vent her pent-up emotions and feelings. But as the media continued its onslaught, shadowing her every step, she stopped going places, preferring to stay inside either Sam's or her own home. Soon, she stopped scheduling recording sessions and before long, fell into a full-fledged depression.

She and Sam began to have horrible arguments until he, too, eventually started avoiding her.

The National Enquirer and TV's Hard Copy were by far the worst of the bunch as they painted her as a tramp who had slept her way to the top of the music industry.

In addition, they were also drawing comparisons of her to her mother, Charla, who had died of a drug overdose. With hurt feelings, Ashela struggled to deal with the onslaught of media scrutiny. Though her public image was now mud, people demonstrated their hypocrisy by rushing to the stores to buy everything that displayed her name.

Through the haze of her depression, Ashela could not figure out who the "unidentified sources" were who had masterminded this entire fiasco. But she did know that it was just a matter of time before Randal's name surfaced.

***

It took Arron to point out to Kyliah the error in her thinking towards Ashela. So what if Ashela didn't feel as though she had an obligation to share every detail of her life with her. She was still her "employer," since Kyliah continued drawing a salary. But beyond that, Arron told her that he thought they were supposed to be "friends." If she thought the way to show her friendship was to fight off the media on Ashela's behalf, that was nothing. She was *supposed* to do that—it was part of her job description. But as far as the friendship aspect was concerned, in Arron's opinion, Kyliah had blown it big time.

Arron had admired the camaraderie that the two of them had with one another. It was genuine and sincere. Their closeness went a long way toward dispelling the myth that women could not get along or work together. Arron was extra rough on Kyliah as he told her that she was being down right unfair in her approach to the entire matter. *She* was not the one on trial. It was one thing to sit behind a desk and deny charges over the phone, but it was all together another matter to be the actual one that all of the rumors were about.

Kyliah admitted that Arron was right. She hadn't been a friend to Ashela. She'd been more like her judge and executioner. She'd condemned her right along with the media and the rest of the world. She hadn't bothered to offer Ash her solace, nor any comfort or even a shoulder to cry on. Suddenly, Kyliah was immensely ashamed of herself.

***

Sam Ross's patience was wearing thin. For the past two months, he had done nothing but cater to Ashela as she "went through hell" with the media. He was supportive of her, he was there for her, he was encouraging of her, but he was also becoming increasingly frustrated. This clinging, temperamental, hesitant, and unsure-of-herself person was nowhere near the strong, independent creature he had come to know. He wanted Ashela to get on with her life regardless of what the media creeps were saying about her. The demand for her musical services were up two-hundred fold. What more could she ask for?

The two of them had been bickering even more as of late. So much so that Ashela had decided to go back to her home in Malibu until things cooled off. Sam

 347

agreed with her that he didn't think it was such a bad idea either. It would give them both a chance to regroup.

Chapter Thirty-Six

here wasn't another bottle of wine anywhere in the house. Ashela had searched everywhere. In angry frustration, she swept everything that was on the kitchen counter onto the floor. Dishes, toaster, mixer and silverware went crashing to the ceramic-tiled floor. After the initial sounds of broken dishes, clanging silverware and electrical appliances, she could hear the doorbell ringing. Thinking it was the news media, Ashela had a sudden vision of herself getting her gun and blowing someone's head off. She didn't even bother to answer the door. As she sank to the floor to huddle in a corner by the kitchen counter, she was unaware that she had become such a pathetic sight.

Kyliah used her spare key to open the door to Ashela's home. Shutting the door behind her, she disarmed the code, noticing that there was a stale smell to the air, as if the place hadn't been aired out lately. Kyliah drifted further into the house, calling out to Ashela.

Ashela heard Kyliah calling her. She scrambled to her knees, attempting to lift herself up, but suddenly she felt extremely lightheaded. She could only kneel on her kitchen floor on all fours until the dizziness passed.

That was how Kyliah found her, kneeling on the floor with her head tucked into her chest. Alarmed, Kye went and kneeled beside her, lifting her up and sitting her in a nearby chair. Kyliah pulled her head back so she could get more oxygen into her system.

"What are you doing here, Kye? Nobody invited you."

"I know. I decided to invite myself. You're not answering your phone these days."

Kyliah placed a wet towel over Ash's head. "You stink Ash, And this place is a mess. When was the last time you ate? Never mind. Let me just fix you something." Kyliah proceeded to pick up the fallen objects from off of the floor.

"Yeah? Well fuck you too." Ashela got up off the chair and made her way into the living room. She threw herself onto the sofa.

Minutes later, Kyliah came into the room carrying a tray of toast, eggs, bacon and orange juice. At the smell of food, Ashela's senses didn't know whether to be

hungry or nauseated. She stared at the plate for a while and then lifted the fork to nibble at the food.

"Good eating, huh? Sure beats all the empty bottles of wine in the garbage."

"I told you before, Kye. You don't like it, get the fuck out."

"I didn't come here to argue, Ash. I came to apologize—to say I'm sorry for the way I mishandled this entire matter. I was angry that you didn't trust me enough to tell me about what went down in New York. It was wrong of me to disrespect your right to privacy. I'm sorry." Kyliah stood to pick up a broken Lladro statue which lay on the floor. She didn't bother to point out it's value to Ash. "I've been demanding to know who the unidentified sources are for all the rag-mags. Naturally, they won't say. So I've just been counteracting them by stating that this is all an attempt on the part of Werner's competitors to sully your name. Tavis Smiley has extended an offer for you to come on his show to defend yourself and to tell your side of things. That is, if you choose to do so."

Ashela finished eating. She placed her fork on the tray and picked up the glass of orange juice. "Thanks for the food, Kye. It was good of you to stop by. But I'd like for you to leave now. I'll think about Tavis Smiley's offer and I'll get back to you." Ashela stood up to show her out of the house.

Kyliah's feelings were hurt. But maybe she deserved it. Admittedly, she had acted like an asshole. "I'll leave now, Ashela. You don't have to show me out. You have a right to be angry with me, and I know that our friendship has taken a blow. But until you fire me, I'm still just doing my job. I have one more thing to say though, Ash. You and I have always talked about the repetitive cycles in our own and other people's families. Well, right now, I'm looking at you repeating your own mother's cycle. You don't have to go down the same path that she did, Ash. Do yourself a favor, baby. Don't touch another drink. I mean that. I'll see you tomorrow. But at least think about what I've said."

After Kyliah left, Ashela went upstairs to take a shower, her first one in days. It was a long while before she stepped out. She searched for her phone book, found the number she was looking for and dialed it.

***

Inside his company-issued vehicle, Senator Randal Stein accepted the transferred call from Ashela Jordan. He was aware of how the media had been attacking her lately. He was certainly watchful of his own name being mentioned in light of him about to announce his presidential candidacy. So it was with interest that Randal listened as she informed him of her suspicions that his name would soon surface. Ashela told him that if he didn't find out who was behind all of her recent troubles, his name would soon be brought into the media foray.

After replacing the receiver, Randal sat back and contemplated his next move. Aware that his career would certainly be besmirched and his presidential bid finished

before it ever started, Randal had no choice but to investigate the situation. His only option was to call on an "associate" to eliminate his problems.

Several days later, Greg Starks, a drug addict and former musician who had once played alongside Ashela Jordan, was found dead inside his Harlem SRO. There was a single gunshot wound to his head. On the floor lay the gun which he'd used to kill himself and beside his bed was a suicide note addressed to Ashela Jordan apologizing for all the lies he had fabricated about her to the media. He had been jealous of her success and had blamed her for his own failure. Greg Starks had ended the note by asking for her forgiveness.

***

In an unrelated incident, three days after Greg Starks was found dead, Carlos Van Damm's body was found floating in the Hudson River. It was widely known that Carlos had been in deep with several loan sharks, but despite the marks covering his severely beaten body, his death was recorded as an "accidental drowning."

***

Unaware of the deaths of her former nemeses, Ashela determined that it was, indeed, time for her to get on with her life. She couldn't continue to live her life in fear and dread over what the media wrote or said about her. She appreciated what Kyliah had said to her, but she still wasn't quite ready to forgive her. As a friend, she felt as though Kye hadn't been there when she'd really needed her.

The next day, Ashela got up and cleaned her entire house. She opened windows and doors to let her place air out. She knew that she had fallen into a terrible slump and she no longer blamed Sam for not wanting to be around her. She hadn't heard from him in weeks.

Ashela picked up the phone and dialed his home in Hollywood Hills. To her surprise, a woman answered the phone. At first, Ashela didn't say anything. She must have dialed the wrong number. "I'm sorry. I must have misdialed."

"Who did you want to speak to? Sam?"

"Yes, I did. Who's this?"

"I don't believe that's any of your business. But I'm his wife."

What the fuck? Ashela abruptly stood to her feet. "I *must* have dialed the wrong number because the Sam Ross I need to speak with doesn't *have* a wife. He has an *ex*-wife. But *I'm* the closest thing he has to a wife. Anyway, let me hang up and dial the *right* number." Ashela hung up but instead of redialing the number, she hit the redial button to display what number she had actually dialed. It was Sam's number all right. And now Ashela was pissed. She had no doubt that the person she had spoken to was Claudette.

There were no traces of any kind of depression as Ashela hurriedly dressed in jeans, a sweatshirt and sneakers. As she pulled a baseball cap onto her head, she grabbed her car keys and hit the door running. It would be unfortunate for any media person who got in her way. Ashela was on a mission.

As soon as she hit the driveway, several media people stood in the middle of it, as if to block her exit. Enraged, Ashela gunned the engine of the Lincoln Navigator. She hit the gas pedal and the Jeep took off at a galactic speed. As she neared the end of the driveway, she fully intended to run over anyone in her path.

The reporters had hoped to block her exit. But seeing that she had no intentions of stopping, and in the nick of time, the three of them threw away their equipment and lunged out of harm's way, hurling their bodies to safety. By the time they picked themselves up off the ground, Ashela was long gone.

She made the drive from Malibu to Hollywood Hills in record time. She entered Sam's access code and the wrought-iron gates parted to allow her entrance. With trembling fingers and a racing heart, Ashela sped up the driveway. A single car was parked there, one that she didn't recognize. She hopped out of the car and hit the pavement, nearly running to the door. If what she suspected was true, somebody's ass was going down.

Without knocking on the door, Ashela used her key and went inside. Slamming the door shut, she started calling Sam's name at the top of her lungs. The nature of her voice indicated he'd have some explaining to do when she found him. She took the winding stairs two at a time. Just as she hit the top level, a woman was walking down the hall. "Who are you?" she asked the intruder.

"No, who the fuck are *you*?" Ashela's tone was hostile as she prepared to fight.

"I, I . . ." The woman was taken aback. It was obvious that this short little woman standing in front of her was *looking* for a fisticuffs brawl. *How had she gotten inside the house?*

"Look, lady. I don't know who the hell you are, but you had better start talking, and I mean fast." Ashela started unzipping her purse.

Horrified because she thought the woman was reaching into her purse for a gun, she said, "I'm Jeane, Sam's sister." Even though Jeane was older and much taller than the woman on the stairs, she had the sneaking feeling that she was staring at a deranged woman, certainly someone who was missing a couple of screws.

Hearing her words, the wind seemed to blow out of Ashela's sails. She took several steps toward the woman, intent on apologizing, but Jeane stepped backwards. Ashela stood her ground and said, "Hi, Jeane. I'm sorry. I truly apologize from the bottom of my heart. I'm Ashela Jordan, Sam's girlfriend. It's just that I called earlier and a woman answered the phone. She said she was Sam's wife. Knowing that Sam doesn't have a wife, I just panicked."

"You probably spoke to Claudette. She was here earlier. But she's gone now. Look, Sam's not here either. Would you like to come back when he gets home?"

351

Jeane wouldn't dare ask her to leave. Even though she had apologized profusely, Jeane strongly suspected that this girl was wound a bit too tight.

"Let me just get some of my things, Jeane. Afterwards, I promise you, I'll leave." Ashela walked past her to the bedroom that she and Sam shared.

Inside it, Ashela immediately sensed that something wasn't right. She could feel it the moment she walked into the room. Her sixth sense told her something was not as it should be. She looked at the bed which hadn't been made and approached it. As she drew closer, hidden half beneath the covers was a black, silk teddy that didn't belong to her. Ashela looked up at the door at Jeane, who was hovering just inside it.

"Are you sleeping in this room, Jeane?" Ashela's voice was deathly quiet. The woman had her hand clasped to her throat. "Jeane, I don't know you, and I'm sorry that you had to meet me under these circumstances. Trust me, I'm not normally so. . . temperamental. But right now, I need to know if you slept in this bed."

"I think you should leave, Ms. Jordan." Her voice trembled as she spoke

Ashela knew there and then Jeane hadn't slept in Sam's bed. Someone else had. Angry adrenaline flowed through Ashela's veins. Ignoring Jeane who abruptly left the room, she began to walk around the bedroom. Though she saw nothing else that did not belong to her, Ashela was still enraged. Since nothing else in the room was out of its place, Ashela knew the person who left the gown had *wanted* her to find it.

Suddenly, Ashela heard voices coming from downstairs. With her head pounding from her anger, she walked out of the room. At the top of the stairs, she heard Jeane talking to someone so Ashela flew down the stairs. Coming through the door were Sam and Claudette. *She* didn't seem surprised to see Ashela. But Sam, who had seen her vehicle parked outside, definitely looked "caught."

"Ashela, what are you doing here?"

"Agh! Wrong answer, Sam. I thought I *lived* here. The correct question is, what are *they* doing here. I've already met Jeane. But who's she, Sam? Your mother?" Ashela's voice was heavy with sarcasm as she threw a dig Claudette's way.

"Well, well, well. Quite the uncouth one aren't you? But what can one expect when a much older man picks a much younger woman of trailer-park caliber such as yourself?" She turned to Sam. "I take it you haven't told her about us."

"Be quiet, Loon. Ashela, why don't you leave and we'll talk about this later."

"Fuck you, Sam. You've been sleeping with her behind my back? No wonder I haven't heard from you these last two weeks. Been a busy boy, haven't you?"

"Ashela, I asked you to leave."

"Maybe she can't hear you, darling."

In the span of a snapped twig, Ashela flew across the room. With a Tae Kwon Do kick, her foot landed in the middle Claudette's chest. Claudette went flying backwards and finally crashed into the cherry oakwood table against the wall. The

huge lamp fell on top of her head and everything on the table plummeted to the floor and toppled around her. Claudette was out cold.

Horrified, Jeane screamed. Sam lunged to grab Ashela. But before he could grab her, she spun around and delivered a severe blow to his neck. Sam yelped in pain. As he clutched his neck, his back was turned to her. Ashela reared back and within a split second, she drop-kicked Sam in his back and sent him reeling to the floor as well, gasping for breath. Jeane flew up the stairs to dial 911. Convinced that the woman was a threat to their safety, she called the police.

With only part of her anger released, Ashela picked up vases, lamps, statues, and figurines and hurled them all against the wall. She then walked to the door and slammed it behind her.

Ashela didn't go home right away. Instead, she drove to the beach. Pulling a pair of sunglasses out of her glove-compartment, she parked her car, took off her gym shoes and walked the rest of the way. Within a short distance from the sandy shore, she took a seat on a nearby bench and watched the surfers, artists, hippies, athletes, skateboarders and the amazing in-line skaters. It had been much too long since she'd been a casual spectator at the beach. After watching the people go by seemingly without a care in the world, Ashela knew she had been taking life much too seriously.

Hours later, she made her way back to her car. She dashed across the street and was unlocking her car door when suddenly she saw an old, blind woman jaywalking across the street right into oncoming traffic. Without thinking about her actions, Ashela flew across the street and threw her body onto the old woman, effectively knocking her to the ground. With mere seconds to spare, Ashela had saved the old woman's life.

Around them, screams were heard as one car crashed into one another. In a few minutes, a crowd had gathered around the area where she and the old woman lay. Ashela lay stunned for a moment, flexing her body parts to ensure that she was unhurt. Without thinking of herself, she crawled to her knees and looked at the old woman who lay lifeless on the ground. Seeing no movement, she lifted the woman's wrist to check for a pulse. Ashela didn't feel one. Panicking, she administered CPR to get her breathing again. She blew into her mouth and pumped her chest, oblivious to the curious bystanders. When the old woman finally gasped for breaths of air, Ashela sat back on her heels exhausted. Only then did she notice the sharp pain in her ankle. It felt almost like it was broken. Ashela became aware that the elderly woman was now crying and she pulled her into her arms to offer what little comfort that she could. As an NBC news van pulled onto the scene, that was how their camera caught the pair just before the ambulance came to rush the two of them to the hospital.

Ashela left the hospital later that day with a cast on her right foot which extended all the way up to her mid-calf. X-rays had revealed a hairline fracture of her right ankle—probably the result of saving the elderly woman, the doctor had said. But Ashela knew otherwise. If she hadn't played the part of a Ninja Turtle back at Sam's place, her foot would have been just fine.

Standing in the hospital's lobby on crutches, she dialed Perry Boyd's number to have him pick her up as she was unable to drive herself. She asked him if he could bring along another driver who could follow them in her car. After she was seated inside the limo, Ashela's thoughts turned to Sam and Claudette. Admittedly, anger was the dominant emotion she was feeling. But it was followed by hurt and a strong sense of betrayal. Suddenly, Ashela wondered if Claudette would press charges against her. She didn't think Sam would, but with the ex, she couldn't be so sure. And wouldn't the media have a field-day with that, Ashela smirked.

After Perry and his friend helped her inside her home, she paid them and locked the door behind them. Ashela immediately turned on her alarm system and climbed the stairs to go to bed. It was still early evening, but the day's activities had drained her and left her exceedingly tired. She lay on her bed unable to sleep, thinking about Sam, Claudette, and the elderly woman.

Ashela had told the hospital to bill her for the woman's stay in the event that she did not have health insurance. All she had thought of while holding the woman was what if it had been Julia? Wouldn't she have wanted someone to do the same for her grandmother? When Ashela's mind drifted back to Sam, she didn't want to think about him anymore. Didn't want to analyze what the day's events had meant, and she certainly didn't want to accept the notion that she hadn't meant anything more to Sam than just a brief fling. Two-and-a-half years wasn't exactly brief, but the length of time didn't change the fact that he had chosen to sleep with someone else when she'd thought she, herself, was his only one. No wonder Sam hadn't called her lately. Maybe he hadn't known how to tell her it was over.

Later that evening, as she watched television and ate a sandwich while lying in bed, Ashela flipped to the local news. She was shocked to suddenly see her own face flash across the tube. NBC was featuring her as a heroine for having saved an elderly woman from being run down by a hit and run driver. The commentator shifted to a New York scene where Greg Starks, a former drug addict, had been found dead in a Harlem SRO. He had a long history of mental illness and had reportedly committed suicide. Prior to doing so, he had confessed to lying about Ashela Jordan to all the news-media outlets for money to support his drug habit, and because he was envious of her success and had been enraged by his own personal failure. Seconds later, the news shifted to another story.

Guess I'm not newsworthy anymore, Ashela thought. In a matter of hours, Ashela went from being the town's biggest scandal and goat to that of a courageous heroine who was now being heralded as an unselfish superstar who'd risked her own

life to save someone else's. Gone were all the recriminations about her being a prostitute, a crackhead and a murdering arsonist.

Ashela flipped off the television and tossed the remote onto the bed. She continued to ignore the phone which had been ringing off the hook for the past several hours. A quick thought came to her mind. Just before she dozed off, she knew what her next course of action would be.

***

As she awakened from her sleep, she was aware of the eerie silence which surrounded her. If only she had something to combat the prevailing darkness. Maybe then she could find the strength to climb out of the hole that had enveloped her. Why did no one care enough about her to search for her? Didn't anyone realize that she was alone and lost? Did everyone hate her so? If she had time, she could change. If she could stop the tiny creatures from sucking her dry, she could summon the energy to escape. But freedom was too far away when she'd wasted so much energy fighting off the demon-like creatures. Why didn't they just end it instead of tormenting her? In despair, the dreamwalker reached out. But what she latched onto was slimy and sticky. As more terrified screams tore from her throat, her tormentors converged upon her with fatal tendons.

Part Eight

Endings

"All farewells should be sudden."
– Lord Byron

"Lest I face... a wretched twist of fate!"
– Miguel de Cervantes

Chapter Thirty-Seven

drienne Dantley sat behind his desk rubbing his forehead with the palms of both hands, an obvious sign that the pressure was starting to get to him.

Ashela paced the area in front of his desk like a caged animal, her arms wrapped around her chest. Suddenly, she halted and placed both palms flat on his desk. "Adrienne, I don't care what it costs me. I just want out of the contract."

"AJ, you don't understand the enormity of what it is you're trying to do. You may be a millionaire many times over, but you *don't* have the money required to go up against a conglomerate like Werner Enterprises. Even Pete Corti admits that the contract you signed is airtight. Yes, technically you *could* buy your way out. But I've already talked to Business Affairs and they say that a termination will cost you roughly two hundred mil. Now, if you had deep pockets like a Bill Gates, we wouldn't be having this conversation. But since you don't, AJ, there's not much else we can do."

Ashela had been pacing for nearly an hour as Adrienne made calls to Pete Corti and to Werner's Legal Department to see if there was any way she could terminate her contract. Every call had ended with the same verdict: Pursuant to the agreement, Ashela would be in breach if she failed to live up to its terms.

With a look of defeat on her face, she took a seat in a nearby leather chair and rested her head in her hands.

Adrienne sighed heavily. He was sorry to be caught in the middle of a bad situation that in his opinion was nothing more than a lover's quarrel gone awry. "Look, Ashela, I know it's none of my business, but when you signed the two-year contract extension, things were going great between you and Sam. Now, all of a sudden, you want out of it? What reason could you possibly give a judge for wanting to haphazardly terminate such a lucrative contract? What I'm saying to you is, why don't you try patching things up with Sam? That seems a hell of a lot simpler than trying to end a contract that would probably take you longer to get out of than it would to fulfill it." It was certainly obvious to Adrienne that she and Sam still had feelings for one another. Why else would they wage such a cold war against each other? Meanwhile, it was middlemen like himself and Pete Corti that got caught in the ensuing crossfire.

Ashela's head jerked upward at the mention of Sam's name. "Fuck Sam, Adrienne. From the day you started representing me, haven't I made it clear that I don't write for anyone that I don't want to? Well, that includes Sam Ross."

"That may be true, AJ. But technically, you're not writing for Sam. You're being paid *by him* to write for his stable of artists."

"If I wanted a list of your fucking technicalities, Adrienne, I would've hired a goddamned technician," Ashela snapped.

Ignoring her agitation *and* her sailor-like colloquialisms, Adrienne said, "Like it or not, AJ, that's the way things stand. Since your signature's on the contract, it seems to me you've no choice but to abide by its stipulations. Either that or risk facing a lawsuit."

A momentary silence hung in the air.

Finally, Adrienne said, "Here's my last piece of advice, Ashela, whether you want to hear it or not. If you want out of the contract as badly as you say you do, then go talk to Sam. In all the years that I've known the man, I've never known him to be unreasonable. If the two of you came together, I'm sure something could be worked out. If all else fails, you've still got yourself a hell of a lucrative contract. Even you have to admit, AJ, that Sam has been more generous with you than with any writer in his consortium. As a matter of fact, if you look at what *any* songwriter is making in these other copy-cat consortiums, you'll find that you come out way ahead." As Sam had predicted, a paradigm of writer's consortiums had sprung up within the music industry. But none came close to matching the standard of excellence that W. E. had trailblazed. Adrienne shook his head when he thought of all the money Ashela would forfeit if she walked away from the contract. Why she insisted on doing so, to him, defied logic.

Ashela was despondent as she made the journey back to Malibu. By all appearances it looked as though she were locked into her contract with Werner. Yet, a small part of her was not ready to concede defeat. Somehow, there had to be a way for her to extricate herself without losing everything she'd worked so hard to attain. Sure, she could live out the terms of the contract. But two years was too much time to spend wrapped up in something she no longer wanted to be a part of.

Damn Adrienne and his advice, Ashela thought. Because the last thing in the world she wanted to do was hold a conversation or be in the same room with Sam Ross. She hadn't seen him in the weeks since the incident at his home in Hollywood Hills. Surprisingly, his ex had opted not to file assault charges against her. Ashela wondered if that had been Sam's doing or whether she'd chosen not to do so because of the publicity that was sure to follow.

Ashela was still all too angry with Sam. Hence the reason for her determination to get out of her contract with Werner. When thoughts of him sleeping with Claudette ran through her mind, something destructive grabbed hold of her that made her want to annihilate everything in her path. This type of vengeful jealousy was new to Ashela but no matter what she did, she couldn't seem to shake it.

There was something else that Ashela couldn't ignore. Something that was too frightening to admit to anyone other than herself. The magic behind her music had

ceased to exist. Since her breakup with Sam, the wellspring of her creativity that had once been her mantle, had evaporated. Sweet, timeless musical lyrics that once had come forth in an extraordinary display of synchronicity, no longer tinged the membranes of her imagination. It was as though her brook had dried up. It was a phenomenon Ashela had never experienced before and it unnerved her. She would sit for hours at the piano playing listlessly with one hand, hoping that the inspiration for a new song would overtake her. Met by an endless silence that reverberated through her mind, Ashela soon found herself avoiding her music room altogether.

While she may have had a temporary lid placed on her musical gifts, the demand for her services had not lessened. Because she continued to be bombarded with requests, Ashela informed the persons who handled scheduling within W. E.'s writer's consortium that she would be on vacation for two months. She was stalling for time but hoped that eight weeks would give her ample time to get out of her contract. Ashela convinced herself that all she needed was a break from the norm and that once she "got over" Sam, her music drought would end.

But forgetting Sam was becoming harder to do with each passing day. Nearly everything in her house reminded her of him now. Whether it was some object that he had purchased for her or some errant place where the two of them had made love, memories of Sam enveloped her.

The following week, Ashela found herself beset with cabin fever. She was sitting on her bed contemplating an overseas trip when her telephone rang. At first, there was silence on the other end. Her heartbeat fluttered at the thought that it might be Sam.

"Hello, Ashela?"

"Speaking. Who's this?"

"It's Parris. I know this is a surprise, my calling out of the blue and all. But I'm here on business and I was hoping to see you before I left. Please tell me that's possible."

"Where are you?"

"I'm staying at the Hyatt Regency on Hope Street. No pun intended, I swear. Can we meet for a drink?"

"I think I'd like that, Parris. Tell you what, give me an hour and then meet me downstairs in your lobby."

It was shortly after six o'clock when Ashela entered the Hyatt Regency. Parris stood and embraced her before placing a quick kiss on her cheek. "You look marvelous, Ash."

"So do you, Parris." Tall, light-skinned with naturally curly hair, he looked extremely handsome dressed in a dark blue suit with a gray tie over his white wing-tipped shirt. "Want to grab a bite to eat?"

"I'd love to."

Ashela chose an Italian restaurant, Maggiano's. They were shown to a booth that was much too intimate for her liking but because it was all they had available in non-smoking, she accepted it without complaint.

The waiter took their order for a bottle of white wine and an appetizer that the two of them could share. When he departed, Ashela said, "I was surprised to hear from you Parris. How did you get my number and how long will you be staying in L.A.?"

"I had to twist Kyliah's arm to get your number from her. My own sister treated me like I was a potential rapist, can you believe it? As for how long I'll be staying in L.A., well, that depends on you."

Ashela took a sip of her wine. "How so?"

Parris took a deep breath. "No matter how crazy this may sound or seem, Ashela, just hear me out first. I know I should let the past go given how I screwed up so many years ago. But we're both older and more mature now. I can only say to you that for all the time I spent married to Tracy, I never loved her. I stayed married to her out of a sense of obligation. Nothing more. Because she was pregnant, I felt *obligated* to marry her since I was as much at fault as she was. But it never changed my feelings for you, Ashela. For years, I was miserable so I lost myself in my career and with raising our sons. In the meantime, I fantasized about you. I've always told myself that if I ever saw you again, I'd tell you how I really felt about you."

Parris gave a short laugh that held no traces of humor. "The only good thing to come from our union is my boys. Can you believe they'll be sixteen soon? Sometimes I find myself asking where did all the time go."

"Don't I know it," Ashela said while listening to him with an open mind. Part of her was flattered. The other part was . . . mournful because she still was hurting over Sam's betrayal. The waiter came and took their orders and refilled their wine glasses.

"Our divorce will be final any day now. It's not been pretty either. I've met every demand that she and her lawyers have made only to be faced with a new one at every turn. Alimony, our savings, the house, you name it. Everything we owned jointly, she's getting in the settlement. The only thing I wanted was custody of the boys. She fought me on that as well, even though we both knew she didn't want them. Since Fredonia and I have practically raised them, it's clear to all that it's in their best interest to stay with me and my family. When she balked against that idea, that was when I finally recognized that it didn't matter how much money Tracy got in the settlement. It still wouldn't be enough, because for her it was never just about money. Tracy is out for blood—my blood."

"Why? I mean, I don't doubt her capability. But do you think she's suffering from 'the scorned woman' syndrome?" Ashela knew a thing or two about that herself.

"I don't know. I've tried to analyze it but I don't get it. I'm practically giving her everything that I've got to the point where I'll literally have to start over from scratch, but that still hasn't satisfied her. It's like she's become *obsessed*. There's no way these divorce proceedings should have taken as long as they have, not when I've been so accommodating. At our last court date, Tracy made an outburst that was filled with so much vitriol that the judge ordered her to get counseling as part of our settlement. Because of the judge's intervention (the judge is a woman by the way) our divorce will be final in a couple of days."

Parris took a long sip of his wine. "But do you want to know what the cruelest twist of fate is that's taken everyone by storm?"

"Sure, tell me." Ashela was still visualizing an image of Tracy spewing hateful rhetoric while seated in the courtroom. Regardless of what anyone believed, Ashela knew Tracy was battling her own host of psychotic demons. And as sad as it was to admit, Ashela understood some of what Tracy was feeling now that Sam had dumped her. After all, some of that Evers' blood ran through her veins as well.

"Her father has lost his ministry."

At first, Ashela didn't seem to hear Parris. When what he said sunk in, she said, "Excuse me?"

"You heard right. The good Bishop Clay Evers has been removed as pastor of his once great congregation." At Ashela's stunned expression, Parris continued. "It appears that Clay Evers pilfered millions of dollars from the church coffers over the years. It's a given that they'll seek to have him prosecuted. Can you believe that he had the audacity to ask my family to bail him out? The man is in hock for millions of dollars and he expected us to just cough up the money like we owed it to him." Parris shook his head in disbelief.

"My gosh! When did all this happen?"

"It's been in the papers for weeks now. I'm surprised Kyliah didn't mention it or that you haven't read about it given the media's preference for stories laden with controversy and sensationalism. But then again, I guess you wouldn't, California being so star-conscious."

Ashela was in a state of shock. "But how did they find out? What put them on to him?"

"Remember Tracy's cousin, Dora?"

"Vaguely."

"Well, she's an engineer out of the D.C. area. The papers claim that a few years back she paid Bishop Evers a visit to tell him about visions that she'd been having of him stealing money from the church. He supposedly became so enraged by her accusations that he threw her out of his office. Anyway, his secretary was in a position to hear every word of their conversation. She reported it to one of the board members who started a secret investigation. In the end, it was discovered that the good Bishop had been having an affair with the church treasurer for years. That's how he was able to get his hands on all the money without anyone else knowing about it.

"It's gotten so much publicity in North Carolina, that I'm surprised the man hasn't been stoned. He certainly has become a pariah. The worst part, Ash, is that no one comes out ahead in a case like this. With all the negative press, that church is just a shell of its former self. As a result, membership has declined drastically. Where before there were at least ten or fifteen thousand, I'm told that now Clay Evers' has had to resort to preaching to the few remaining members in the choir stand. Everybody else has defected."

"My God!"

"Yeah, it's sad. But I feel no sympathy whatsoever for the man. Do you have any idea of how many people will lose faith in the church because of his actions?"

"You're absolutely right, Parris. Not only that, but even for people who *don't* believe, something like this just gives them further incentive not to *ever* join a church."

"Well, they won't be joining that one because the city is about to foreclose on the property."

Ashela pictured city inspectors nailing boards to the windows and doors of the building. Just before driving off, she imagined one of them removing a can of spray paint from his pocket and scrawling the words, "Ichobod and Beelzebub were here." As she continued to shake her head in amazement, the waiter came and removed what remained of their barely touched appetizers.

Once the table was cleared, with no knowledge of the future calamity his actions would cause, Parris did something that totally surprised Ashela. He removed a tiny case from his jacket pocket. He reached for her hands and cupped them while sliding the case between her fingers.

"Parris, what on earth is this?" Smiling, Ashela opened the tiny case. When she saw what was inside, she threw her head back and laughed.

"I take it you like it?"

"It's precious. Where did you find it?" Tucked inside the velvet case was the friendship ring Parris had given her when they had been mere teenagers.

"It was among the things you returned after you found out about my marriage to Tracy. I've held on to it all these years. I wonder if it still fits."

"There's only one way to find out." The small piece of gold jewelry fit like a charm. "Well, who'd have thunk it?" Ashela said smiling. Before she could say more, the waiter appeared with their food.

The two of them spent the rest of the evening reminiscing about their childhood antics. It wasn't until later when Ashela was driving him back to his hotel that he asked her whether she thought they had a chance together.

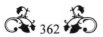

"Parris, this is all too new for me. Here it is, you come waltzing back into my life after all these years. What do you expect me to say? We're friends, Parris. That hasn't changed. But what happened between us was so long ago that I'm not sure it can be recaptured. I'm truly sorry things didn't work out between you and Tracy. But that's a choice you made. I don't feel the same way that I did back then. We're both different people now, Parris. Besides, how would it work anyway? We're worlds apart, plus you've got two sons. And me? Why, I don't know the first thing about raising kids. So I'm afraid all I can commit to right now, Parris, *is* friendship. Friends forever is what we said we'd always be, remember?"

But Parris wasn't ready to let her slip away so easily. "We don't have to be worlds apart, Ashela. That's why I wanted to see and talk to you. My job has offered me the chance to relocate here to L.A. At first I was against it. But then I thought of you and I just knew I had to meet with you to see if there was anything there after all these years. I think there is, Ashela, but only if you're willing to give it a chance."

"Parris, I can't say yea or nay, simply because I don't know what I feel. I'll be honest with you. Right now, I'm in love with someone else. Even though it's obvious that he no longer wants me, I still need time to heal from that relationship. So don't move out here to the coast, Parris. That would only mess with my head. Give me some time to think things over first. Right now, the best thing for both of us is to not rush into anything that we'll only end up regretting later on."

Parris accepted her answer. But only for the moment. The man that she was pining for obviously didn't know a good thing when he had it. Whoever he was, all Parris knew was that he had to be a fool for letting her get away.

***

Two days later The National Enquirer came out with their latest edition. The headlines screamed, "Songwriter Dumps Music Magnate for High School Flame!"

When Kyliah received a copy of the magazine, she clapped her hand to her forehead. A picture of Ashela and Parris sitting cozily inside a restaurant was plastered on the front cover. Parris was sliding a ring onto her finger while Ashela looked the part of the gushing bride-to-be. The rag-mag left no stone unturned as they talked about the devastating breakup of the once-famed power couple, Sam Ross and Ashela Jordan. Sam was supposedly taking the breakup so badly that he had retreated to his mansion on Martha's Vineyard.

The story went on to report that Ashela was not the least bit upset about her recent split with the music mogul because she had already set her sights on wealthy businessman, Parris Reed, who wasn't allowing the ink to dry on his own divorce papers before proposing to the sexy songwriter. Reportedly, Reed was dumping his wife of fifteen years just to be with Ashela Jordan.

Kyliah sat reading with her hand clamped over her mouth, hoping that Sam Ross would not see the edition. And if he did, she hoped he'd recognize that there was no

truth to the story. To ensure that there *wasn't*, Kyliah picked up the phone and dialed Ashela's number.

Mrs. Vincent Stanton read the article with obvious glee. *It serves Sam right*, Claudette thought maliciously to herself. Sam should never have gotten involved with such trashy riff-raff as Ashela Jordan in the first place.

When Adrienne Dantley read the piece, he was not the least bit amused. His only thought was, *Sam's not going to like being made a fool of.* He, too, could only hope that Sam wouldn't see the article.

Karen Mitchell sat outside her boss's office pouring over a copy of The National Enquirer that someone had so thoughtfully sent to Sam. Karen debated whether or not to include it with his morning mail. She didn't know what had happened to cause their breakup, but she did know that Ashela Jordan was a classy lady whom Sam had deeply cared for. Karen placed the magazine at the bottom of the stack and carried it into his office.

It wasn't until late in the evening that Sam got the opportunity to go through his mail. When he saw the copy of the National Enquirer, his first reaction was irritation. Karen knows better than to include this in with my mail, he thought. Sam picked up the copy and was about to toss it in the garbage bin when the headline caught his attention. Before he knew it, Sam had read the entire article word for word.

***

Days later, Pete Corti reviewed Werner Enterprise's letter of contract termination with surprise. He knew that Ashela had expressed the desire to be released from her contractual obligations with the writer's consortium, but he never thought for a second that Sam Ross would agree to it. At least not without there being hell to pay. Pete read the letter through for the second time. It was clear as day. He buzzed his secretary and said, "Ambi, get Adrienne Dantley on the line."

When Ashela heard the news that Sam had released her from her contract, her immediate reaction was, *never look a gift horse in the mouth.* She sat in Adrienne's office with a stupefied look on her face. "Adrienne, are you telling me that I'm free to write of my own accord again? That I can work with anyone of my own choosing with no repercussions from Werner Enterprises?"

"I know it sounds too good to be true, AJ, but that's exactly what the termination letter says. There aren't even any strings attached. All you have to do is sign it."

Ashela re-read the two-paragraph letter for the third and final time before signing it on the dotted line.

As she reached for the door to leave, Adrienne said, "AJ, I'm glad you decided to talk to Sam about releasing you from your contract. Did you ever imagine it would go as smooth as this?"

"No, Adrienne, I never thought it would be this easy. I'm just glad it's a done deal. But I never talked to Sam, though. I thought you did." Thinking no more of it, Ashela closed the door behind her.

Inside his office, something nagged at Adrienne about the letter of termination. He just didn't know what it was. He remembered something he had told Ashela during her last visit to his office. *"I've never known Sam to be unreasonable."* Though he'd known Sam for what felt like a lifetime, in all that time, neither had Adrienne known him to be *too* reasonable. Whatever it was that was bugging him about Ashela's expulsion, Adrienne was sure it would eventually come to light.

***

"That's great news, Ash! The folks at Werner must have had a sudden change of heart, you think?"

"Either that or they're really eager to have nothing more to do with me. Doesn't matter to me which one it is. Now that the contract's terminated, I feel like a new woman, Kye. Believe it or not, I've decided to go abroad for a while." Ashela and Kyliah had settled their differences over the media blitz incident and were back as close as ever.

"Get out! You? Taking a break? This, I've got to see. It's not that I don't believe you, my sistah, it's just that you'll have to call me from your intended destination before it finally sinks in. So where are you going?"

"London, England. I'm going to stay for about a month."

Kyliah shook her head. She was proud of Ashela for taking time off from her work, being the workaholic that she was. But she had a surprise of her own. Before springing it, Kyliah had to ask, "Ash, have you thought about calling Sam to say thanks?"

"Calling who?"

"Sam."

"Who? I can't hear you? There must be static on the line." Ashela tapped the bottom of the phone on her bed stand.

"Okay, scratch the question. I'm changing the subject. Guess what?"

"I'm listening."

"Yeah, yeah, yeah. Listening, but not guessing. So I'll just out it. Arron has asked me to marry him."

"Gethefudgeouttahere! You go, girl! Now, *that's* great news, Kye. Wow. I'm so happy for you. Did you say 'yes,' dingbat?"

"You know I did. But I gotta tell you, Ash, it's a little overwhelming. Wait before you say anything. I know I've been wishing and praying for this since day one, but now that it's here, I'm scared shitless. Man, Ash, I get goosebumps just thinking about it. Me? Married? Girl, what the hell do I know about being a wife?"

"Hold on, my sistah. You know a lot. How long have Fredonia and your pops been married? Since dirt was dirt, right? Well that goes a long way. You run into any problems, all you have to do is give ol' Free a call. Besides, it's just all right, Kye. Good things *do* come to those who wait. Am I going to be the best girl?"

"Of course, knucklehead. And the correct terminology is 'maid of honor.' Your being there goes without saying."

Ashela's call-waiting kicked in. "Okay girl, I've got another call coming in. It's my playmate, so I'll talk to you later."

"Poor Parris. Try to go easy on him, Ash. The poor boy probably has no idea that he's only a mere stand-in for the real McCoy."

"Now I know it's time to hang up. See ya!"

As Kyliah released her end of the line, she marveled over Ash's budding relationship with Parris. Though Ash swore they were only friends, Kyliah saw through the guise to the bottom line. Ashela was hurting and was missing Sam in a big way. So if Parris was available to help ease her pain, why shouldn't she make the most of a bad situation? Kyliah didn't blame her. After all, she too, knew what it felt like to suffer the wounds of a broken heart.

***

Ashela had no way of knowing that her trip to London would yield one of the most interesting and exciting times of her life. Or that she would encounter someone of larger-than-life stature whose influence would help change the course of her life.

She arrived at London's Heathrow Airport and was escorted directly to the luxurious Blake Hotel in Kensington. Known for its opulence, as well as its personalized service, the hotel catered to the wealthy and featured a full line of amenities that few other hotels in the royal city could match.

Rich in an historical and a traditional sense, Ashela found London to be a mass of startling contradictions. For all its living and ancient history, the city was very much alive and on the cutting edge of originality. Where once London had been known for its medieval staidness, the city had come a long way in launching itself as a major competitor in the tourism industry, thereby gaining the reputation as the "hottest, coolest city in the world." Ashela found that London offered the very best in cuisine, fashion, film, the visual arts and even music. Because of its innovative trend-setting, the capital of Great Britain was a connoisseur's paradise.

And because her stay was an extended one, she didn't have to try to cram all of her sight-seeing into a day or even a week's time. Unburdened by time constraints, she could take her time leisurely exploring the place which, up until now, she had

only heard and read so much about. Thus, Ashela alternated her sight-seeing between tour packages and exploring the city by foot.

The bus tours that she did venture out on took her on exotic excursions to the Tower of London, where she was fortunate to hear Big Ben chime. She viewed the Houses of Parliament from Westminster Bridge before moving on to Westminster Abbey. Ashela had her photo taken by another tourist at Trafalgar Square where she seemed to be the only tourist unimpressed with its hundreds of pigeons. Next came the fabled and illustrious Buckingham Palace where she lined up to view the "changing of the guards."

As a music gourmand, and because she was in Beatles' Country, she took the Beatles' Mystery Tour twice to ensure that she hadn't missed out on anything the first time around.

But it was when Ashela explored the city on foot that she fell in love with its great museums, its royal pageantry, and its history-steeped homes. Armed with energy and curiosity (along with a good map), Ashela set out to glean its hidden mysteries.

Everyone warned her from the outset that she'd get lost. And she did. Ashela found London's maze of streets terribly confusing to follow because, unlike the United States, London was not given to a rigid grid system. She'd find herself strolling down a street peering at one address while the building next to it, or directly across the street from it, would be labeled totally out of sequence. Street names and addresses inconsistently collided one into another with no obvious pattern or rationale. Ashela soon wondered what the authors of such confusion were thinking when they created the maze of streets.

Each day, she randomly meandered the city's backstreets and mews. She'd walk around Park Lane and Kensington and the Kew (the smallest of the royal palaces) with its beautiful botanical gardens.

Ashela visited the London Symphony Orchestra at the Barbican Centre, the London Philharmonica at the Royal Festival Hall, and she attended many of the lunchtime concerts held throughout the city in smaller concert halls, arts-center foyers, or even in churches. In between, she'd stop for lunch at one of the many pubs along the way, while at night she had her choice of an array of theaters, operas, and ballets.

Her Sunday mornings were spent at Speaker's Corner in Hyde Park, where she'd listen briefly to spectators share their opposing political views and ideologies, strolling through Covent Garden, or treasure hunting for antiques at a variety of shops.

Ashela had just finished examining the treasures of the National Gallery when she decided to grab a bite to eat. She hailed a taxi and told him to take her to The Ivy, one of London's premier restaurants. Because there was a forty-five minute wait, she was waiting to be seated when a familiar figure walked through the door.

"Walter!" Ashela asked hesitantly. Walter Dutton was a member of Tina Turner's band and it had been years since she'd last seen him.

When he looked her way, a huge grin spread across his face. "Well bloody Mary, look who it is! Ashela Jordan, how are you?" Standing well over six feet, Walter dwarfed her as he embraced and swept her off her feet.

"Walter, listen to you. You sound as though you've lived here all your life. With such a thick brogue, who would guess you're originally from Philadelphia?"

"No one and that's just fine by me. Why, the last time I saw you, AJ, you were on stage performing with Najee. What brings you to London?"

"Has it been that long, Walt? My goodness!" Ashela shook her head. "I'm on vacation. I've been here for three weeks already and I have to tell you, old chap, that I could get used to living here. What about you? Are you still with Tina?" Before he could answer, she asked, "How *is* T.T.?"

"She's as swell as ever. Listen, I have reservations. Would you care to join me?"

"I'd love to."

A waiter escorted them to the rear of the restaurant which was even more opulent than its front. Once he saw her seated, Walter excused himself. When he returned, Ashela was studying the menu.

Avoiding the beef dishes because of England's Mad Cow disease scare, Ashela placed her order and was immediately regaled by Walter with stories about his life in London. She was laughing at one of his adventures when her eyes were drawn to someone who was striding toward their table.

As Tina Turner came waltzing through the restaurant, all eyes turned to her. With her flamboyant but elegant style of dress, she looked beautiful and awesome in a short, bronze mini-dress. Ashela stood to greet her before she even reached their table.

"T.T.!"

"Ashela Jordan! When Walter told me you were here I almost didn't believe him." They embraced and were seated when a flurry of waiters rushed to assist them. Tina was given royal service everywhere she went.

She wanted to know everything that Ashela had been doing since they'd last seen each other. Word of the U.S.'s growing number of writer's consortiums had spread to England where they weren't quite sold on the concept. She wanted Ashela's take on the rapidly spreading alliances. Tina flattered her by telling her how much London could use someone with her genius for songwriting. Even more so since Elton John and Bernie Taupin were nearly their only preeminent songwriting team. She felt that if Ashela ever chose to relocate to London, she would surely give them a run for their money. Before their lunch was over, Tina insisted Ashela commit to working with her on her upcoming project. In doing so, she had no idea of how dangerously close she came to wooing Ashela over to her side of the globe.

Ashela's remaining days in London were filled with visits to a variety of entertainment venues. Because Walter insisted that she hang out with him while he took her to his favorite haunts, Ashela wound up staying an additional two weeks. But still, the days flew by in a whirlwind of activity.

The morning before her scheduled return to the U.S., Ashela awoke from her sleep gripped by nausea. Her vaginal area felt as if she had cramps, but her stomach was turning somersaults. She barely managed to make it to the bathroom in time to empty the contents of her stomach. Ashela's first reaction was that she had contracted a case of Mad Cow food poisoning, but she knew she hadn't eaten any dishes containing beef. Fear came later as she lay on the bed holding her stomach. A quick mathematical tally of the number of days between her last menstruation had led to thoughts she could neither fathom nor accept.

Ashela lay there a while longer until her weakness passed. When she felt steady on her feet again, she dressed hurriedly in jeans and a sweatshirt and left to make a special purchase. Back in her hotel room, she removed the three pregnancy kits (two wouldn't suffice—she needed a *third* opinion) from their packaging and took them into the bath room. Less than an hour later, Ashela sat on the edge of the marble commode holding her face in the palms of her hands. To say that she was devastated over the positive results from all three of the pregnancy kits was an understatement.

Just as quickly, Ashela's disbelief turned to anger. Anger at herself for her own stupidity at not having the foresight to take preventative measures at *all* times. *Of all the idiotic things to do! How could she have let this happen?* Her mind was ablaze with self recriminations as she sat in a trance-like state. Convinced that there was a possibility that each kit could have yielded an inaccurate result, Ashela told herself that when she got back to the states, she would pay her gynecologist a visit. If her doctor's test came back positive, there was only one solution to her problem. It was an unfortunate but necessary evil that Ashela didn't want to contemplate.

While it was true that she wanted a family, Ashela wanted it on her own terms. She didn't want to give birth to a child whose father she wasn't even on speaking terms with. Even more embarrassing was the knowledge that the general assumption would be made that her actions had been premeditated in a deliberate attempt to trap Sam Ross. As she sat rocking herself back and forth, gut instinct told her the tests were accurate—that the only mistake made was on the part of her and Sam. Unfortunately for all parties concerned, it was a mistake that would have to be corrected. Ashela would never give Sam Ross, or anyone else, the satisfaction of thinking she would stoop to such deplorable tactics just to have him in her life.

Ashela's thoughts turned to the unborn fetus she carried in her womb. Saddened by the prospect that it would never reach maturation, or fulfill its unknown destiny, she brushed the falling tears from her eyes. Feeling burdened by her predicament and

ɦer intended actions, she squared her shoulders, stood up and began packing her things.

Chapter Thirty-Eight

shela had come to Adrienne's office to get a definitive answer about a recent series of troubling events. "So what exactly are you saying, Adrienne? Are you telling me people are backing out of projects previously agreed to because they suddenly no longer want me involved?"

She had been back in the states for three weeks now and was scheduled to begin production work with a number of artists under contract with several of the major labels. There was only one problem. Each of the seven projects she'd had lined up had either been scratched or postponed indefinitely.

Ashela found the timing of each cancellation odd because she didn't have signed contracts with any of the artists. They were still in the process of being drawn up. One by one, their agents had contacted Adrienne to say the proposed deals were off. It didn't make sense to Ashela, who normally had people jockeying for her time. It was as though she had suddenly become a pariah and now she wanted answers.

"I'm afraid, AJ, that that's exactly what I'm saying. I received a call under strict confidentiality about a month ago while you were in London. The person told me that all of the projects you had going with artists under their label were being nixed. Though the person I spoke to was a reliable source, I still felt compelled to check it out. What I discovered was that none of the studios are producing anything that your name is attached to. My source then confirmed that when each of the artists agreed to eliminate you from the equation, their deals were miraculously approved with no further delays."

Ashela sat in stunned anger. She spoke with bitterness in her voice. "Naturally, the labels in question all fall under the umbrella of Werner Enterprises."

"Exactly. But it's no longer confined to W. E., Ashela. This ban has apparently and effectively spread to all the other labels as well. Hoping that my worst suspicions would not be confirmed, I made more calls only to find out that this sanction *is* industry wide. I knew whoever was behind this was in a position of power because a number of strings had to be pulled at each label to accomplish this."

"Sam." Ashela uttered his name with deep regret.

"My sentiments exactly. That's why I took the liberty to call and ask him directly. He said he had no comment on the matter and suggested you get yourself a lawyer if you could prove that he was black-balling your name in the industry. But he didn't sound like the Sam I've known for so many years. He sounded . . . cold and very calculating. At any rate, the way things stand now, AJ, even the indes wouldn't

accept you as a part of any of their writer's alliances. It's a shame that this has happened, but if you intend to work again in this industry, I suggest you *do* get a lawyer. I don't know where this will lead to but it's your only recourse. Sam has definitely overstepped his bounds, for I have no doubt that he's behind this entire fiasco."

An overwhelming sense of sadness had enveloped Ashela. To think that all the times she'd shared with Sam that things between them had sunk to this level. He was the only man she had ever truly loved in her life, and after all that they'd been through, he was treating her as if she were lower than a dog on the street. She thought they had loved one another. She had done things to and for him that she'd done for no other man, and it hadn't meant a thing between them. Here was the man whose child she carried in her womb and he thought nothing more of her than to destroy her career, her livelihood, everything that she'd ever worked for? How was it possible that two people who had once loved as avidly as they did, could turn around and become such vicious adversaries? Thinking that what she'd shared with Sam was something out of the ordinary, she found herself awakened to one of the grim realities of life. The bitter truth was that both of them had allowed their egos to smother rationality and in the end only she and Sam's human frailties remained. To Ashela, these were the facts that had become stranger than fiction.

And what of her unborn child? Ashela had had her pregnancy confirmed by her doctor, but she lacked the conviction to go through with an abortion. A child was not a pawn to be used in a game. So while she certainly could stay and try to fight Sam and "the powers that be," she had to first ask herself if it was worth it. Was going through a court of law worth enduring all the negative energy and emotions required for such a battle? Ashela thought not.

Coupled with her sadness was now a feeling of tiredness. She could feel her shoulders slump as she leaned back against the sofa.

In all the years that Adrienne had known Ashela Jordan, both as a client and on a personal level, he realized he had never seen her cry. As he watched the tears trickle from the corners of her eyes, he could only sit quietly not knowing what to say to her. Her head was thrown back and her eyes were closed but somehow tears still flooded from them. Unconsciously, Adrienne could feel her silent pain. He had the inalienable feeling that what she grieved for had nothing to do with the devastating news he had just delivered to her about having become an outcast in an industry that in her own way, she had helped to define.

Damn, Sam! Adrienne thought. He had no doubt that Sam's actions to date had stemmed from jealousy, spite and vengefulness. It then dawned on Adrienne why Ashela's sudden release from her contract hadn't sat well with him. Sam must have intended to do this all along. Adrienne was convinced that somehow, The National Enquirer's story had played a part in prompting Sam to act as he had.

 371

Ashela removed tissue from her purse and wiped her tears from her face. She said to him, "Forgive me, Adrienne. These days I'm so emotional that it seems as if I cry at the drop of a hat. While I understand what you're saying about fighting Sam in court, I don't want to do that. I'm tired of fighting Sam, Adrienne. I just want some peace in my life. God knows I haven't had any lately. Over the past six weeks, I've had a chance to revisit some of my mistakes in life and I can honestly say that ever since the negative press I received months ago, I don't like the person I've become.

"See, Adrienne, I have this problem where I don't like to admit when I'm wrong. Well, I made some mistakes in my dealings with Sam. But I'll never admit that to him. While I can't change the past, there are certain aspects of my character that I do intend to change. Plus, I know how Sam thinks. Fighting him in court is just what he wants because it would keep us tied together, locked in a battle that would prohibit either of us from coming out on top. I'll not do that. What hurts most, Adrienne, is that the people who reneged on their contracts with me are long-time associates, people whom I admired and had deep affection for. But then, there never was loyalty among thieves, was there?"

"No, Ash. Not in this business. People are more concerned about making a dollar than taking sides in any battle that doesn't concern them. If that means having to disassociate themselves from you, then unfortunately, that's the way it will be."

"Yes, I understand that. But Grover of all people? He was my mentor, Adrienne. If any one could have stood up to Sam, it was him."

But even *he* has to eat, Adrienne thought to himself. Sam's influence was powerful and far-reaching in this industry. No one wanted to piss him off.

Ashela rose to leave. "I'll be seeing you, Adrienne. Thank you for all that you've done."

She sounded as though he wouldn't see her again for a long time. Subconsciously, Adrienne sensed that that would be the case. He embraced her and found himself saying, "Take care of yourself, AJ."

For the first time since she entered his office, she smiled, "I always do, AD. I always do."

***

"I don't know what to say, Ash. You're springing a lot on me all at once. Are you sure this is what you want to do?" Kyliah sat on her sofa next to Ashela who had stopped by to pay her an impromptu visit.

Ashela had just given her the news of what had transpired in Adrienne's office. When she had finished, all Kyliah wanted to do was kick Sam's butt. She wasn't feeling this new kinder, gentler Ashela and she definitely wasn't in the conciliatory mood that Ashela seemed to be feeling. Who the fuck did Sam think he was anyway? The Black bastard! As if he were bigger than the music industry itself. His actions galled Kyliah to the core. All she knew was that while he was free to attend her

upcoming wedding, he would *not* be allowed to be Arron's best man. Particularly in light of what Ashela had just revealed.

"There's something else as well, Kye. I find myself almost too embarrassed to tell you what it is after all my speeches of how children belong in two parent homes and how they should be planned for. I'm pregnant Kye."

Kyliah gasped and was speechless for a change.

"Close your mouth, dahlin' because my first thought was to have it aborted. But I couldn't go through with it. Now, all of a sudden, I want this child, Kye. Maybe it's because I don't know if I'll ever have another one."

A thought occurred to Kyliah. Tentatively, she asked, "Whose . . ." but her voice trailed off.

Ashela smiled. "Kye, I've never been intimate with Parris, so there's no question of who the father is."

Kyliah's disappointment was obvious. A part of her had secretly hoped that Ashela and her brother would get back together again.

"Ash, whatever you decide to do, you know I'm here for you."

"I know that, Kye. And I'll always love you for it." As she embraced her lifelong friend, tears fell from Ashela's eyes.

***

Sam sat inside his semi-darkened office staring into the distance. It was well after seven in the evening and he had asked Karen to dim the lights on her way out. He had just finished nixing a deal with one of Pete Corti's clients. Had the artist had anyone else as his attorney other than Pete, Sam knew he would have been much more flexible in his negotiations. As it stood these days, it was either Sam's way or the highway—take it or leave it.

Admittedly, Sam had been a tyrant of late. Like a shark in a feeding frenzy, he was devouring everything in his path. Every deal he put together, he somehow had to come out on top. Sam knew he would have to soon reign himself in because he didn't want to gain a reputation for ruthlessness.

Even more surprising was the fact that Sam had not been with other women since his breakup with Ashela. Normally, he would have appeased himself by now with any number of them. But Sam merely convinced himself that he had just become more discriminate in his tastes, and that he needed a break from the female species. After all, it was a female who was the cause of the rage he felt roiling through his body at times.

When Sam had read of Ashela's romance and impending marriage to her childhood sweetheart, he had experienced jealously like he'd never known before. He could have throttled her over the incident with Claudette, but for her to run into another relationship so soon, was unforgivable. Sam had deliberately sabotaged her career as an act of revenge.

But even those actions couldn't remove the dagger from Sam's heart. If revenge was supposed to be sweet, he wondered why he felt only a disparate sense of emptiness and dissatisfaction. *Lingering unhappiness kills in slow motion...*

Abruptly, Sam stood and reached for the light. He threw some papers into his briefcase, grabbed his coat and headed out the door.

***

In a bizarre twist of fate, Clay Evers sat inside his attorney's office trying to mastermind a deal that would allow him to avoid going to jail for embezzlement and grand theft. As more and more charges were brought against him, things didn't look good for the home team. Not since Carolyn, his mistress and the church treasurer, had turned state's evidence against him. She'd copped a plea saying that she had been inured and hypnotized by Clay's magnetism. Her defense was that since Clay was a "man of the cloth," she had trusted him blindly and in doing so, had been led astray.

Silently, Clay's lawyers thought that by thinking he would never be caught simply because he was "God's man," their client had immersed himself in a hopeful swirl of delusion.

But Clay Evers soon received a cogent dose of reality when his lawyers informed him that the least amount of jail time they could plea bargain for him was two years plus probation. Clay's lawyers advised him to accept the settlement because if the case ever went to trial, in lieu of all the sordid details his mistress was willing to testify to, the jurors would eat him alive.

As he buried his face in his hands, Clay thought to himself, *"This is the abyss Dora warned me about."* But he had ignored her prophetic warnings just as he had ignored the seeds of lust and avarice that were sown in his heart that long ago day when he'd made up his mind to consummate his desire for Charla Jordan.

For the first time, Clay acknowledged his many years of wrongdoing. With regret for the destructive consequences his actions had caused, Clay Evers agreed to take the shortened prison term.

***

Blood-curdling screams tore from the throat of the dream walker.

They were upon her. She knew this time they would kill her but she didn't want to die. Not when she had so much to live for, so much more she needed to do. Tracy thought she could see a ray of light . . .

A nurse rushed into the hospital room where the patient had been brought in only hours earlier suffering from a nervous breakdown. As the nurse hurried to the side of the bed to restrain the patient, she knew something wasn't right. The woman appeared to be having violent seizures. The nurse shouted for assistance.

They were all over her now. She was trying to fight them off, but they were much too strong for her. Why wouldn't they leave her alone? Tracy struggled valiantly, but

she could feel her strength slipping away. She could change, she had so much to live for, and so much more to say. She would show her love this time. She wouldn't fight it as she had in the past. If she could just get the slimy creatures off of her. With a final lunge, Tracy twisted away from them. But instead of running, she felt her body slump, becoming liquid as she melted away . . .

It had taken six nurses to subdue the woman on the bed. Though they had pumped sedatives into her bloodstream, she had fought them as if demon-possessed. As the medication took its effect, the patient slipped into a coma-like state. Only later would it be determined that Tracy Evers-Reed had suffered from debilitating seizures. Had she taken her medication as prescribed by her doctors, her aneurysm might have been avoided. As it was, her brain had ceased functioning. Tracy had become little more than a vegetable.

Epilogue

Three Years Later

shela Jordan stepped to the platform and accepted her fourth Grammy Award of the evening. Her solo album, *Giving It My All,* had already won Grammys for Contemporary Jazz, Pop Instrumental, Record of the Year, and now, Album of the Year. She basked in the applause, and as the sound waves of appreciation washed over her, this was the way she hoped it would be.

She was trying desperately not to shed tears, but it was such a phenomenal night for her. Primarily because of all that she'd had to endure just to get there. She thanked her Creator and told the audience that mere words could never describe the joy that was in her heart. Most of all, she wanted to thank the fans who purchased the album, because they were the ones who had made this happen for her tonight. Finally, she told them that with their continued encouragement, she looked forward to doing it all over again.

As she walked back to her seat in the audience, Ashela suddenly knew what it meant to have one's "cup running over." Memories of Julia and Charla flitted through her mind. Her greatest wish was that they could witness her achievements tonight. However, she felt no sorrow, only a gentle reminder of the times when laughter had once lived in both her grandmother's and her mother's faces.

Ashela clasped tightly the golden statuette in her hand. Memories of what it had taken for her to get where she was flashed before her eyes. Her album had exploded onto the European scene long ago, but efforts to release it in the states had been met with resistance. But Ashela's detractors soon discovered that, because of the prevailing spirit of capitalism, a legitimate hit will override anything, even the widespread influence of a conglomerate like Werner Enterprises. Because Ashela had the money to back herself, she circumvented the "system" by releasing her album underground in the U.S. At first, she'd sold the album much the way drugs are sold, not in stores but on the streets of Anytown, USA.

She gave away the first hundred thousand CDs. But the strategy worked to her favor. People on the streets were hawking her records and word spread like wildfire about the jammin' new release by *internationally*-acclaimed artist, Ashela Jordan. The critics soon hailed her for showing them her genius and the depths of her mind. They said her music was more powerful than anything she had previously written and that it lulled one into a euphoric trance. One could hear any number of hits from Ashela's album playing on radio stations all across the country. As demand soared, record outlets scrambled to get the CDs in stock. By the time the album was finally sold in stores, it skyrocketed onto the music scene; first achieving gold, then platinum and then multi-platinum status.

***

Hours later, Ashela finally made her way back to her dressing room. She tipped one of the security guards and told him that she was not to be disturbed. Ashela just wanted to catch her breath in solitude before she returned to the circus-like atmosphere. She had been invited to a litany of after parties, but had no intentions of attending any one of them. She wanted to go home to be with Ramsey. Nearly three years old, her son had already stolen her heart and he was the splitting image of his father. He would be sleeping now, but Ashela wanted to get back to him nonetheless.

A discreet tap sounded at the door. "Come in," she called, assuming it was the man standing guard at her door.

"Hello, Ashela."

Hadn't a part of her hoped he would come? She turned to face him. "Hello, Sam. What do I owe to the honor of your visit? Come to take back the awards, perhaps?" Ashela ignored the pounding of her heart.

"No one will ever do that, Ashela. You've ingrained yourself upon our hearts and our memories. No, I came to offer my sincere congratulations."

"Yes, well, as you can see I was just about to leave, so thanks for stopping by." Suddenly the dressing room had become too small for the both of them. His closeness was starting to play upon her nerves and Ashela knew that she had to make him leave.

Sam knew he was being thrown out. But he couldn't leave before saying what was on his mind. And not before he admitted . . . "You were sensational tonight, Ash. You charmed them all. Namely me." Sam stepped closer to her. He needed to look deeply into her eyes. He needed to . . .

Ashela took a step backwards. She didn't trust him, or herself. "Sam, please leave."

But Sam only shook his head as he stepped even closer. "I've missed you desperately, Ashela. I came here tonight only to apologize for my actions toward you. I acted purely out of jealousy. The thought of you being with someone else nearly drove me insane. You couldn't have gotten married because I would have heard about it. And, I don't see any rings on your fingers." Sam's eyes glided over her.

Why did he have to appear so apologetic? So sincere and humble? And why did her heart want to melt at the sight of him? Ashela couldn't look him in his eyes. "Sam . . ."

But suddenly, he was cutting her off as his hand reached out to cup the side of her face, forcing it upward. "I love you, Ashela. Whether you believe me or not, it's true. I think I always have. I was just too stubborn and filled with too much angry pride to ever admit it. But now I can say it freely: I love you, Ash, and I want you to marry me."

It was strange, almost surreal to be standing so close to him, hearing him utter such tender words. Ashela's jitteriness vanished the moment he took her into his arms. When his lips found hers, rapturous sensations possessed her. Why did he have to be the only man capable of leading her to that paradise that only they shared?

Suddenly, Ashela pulled away from him trying to regain control of her senses. "Sam, you have a lot of nerve waltzing in here and dropping all of this on me like nothing's changed between us. Especially after everything you've done to me."

Sam grinned. Try as she might to hide it, she still loved him, too. And he would do everything in his power to make her realize it. He knew they had some challenges ahead of them, but even those could be worked out. They had to be. Because his life wasn't as meaningful without her in it.

"I know and you're absolutely right. But I intend to make amends, Ashela, for every wrong I've done you. All I ask is to be given a chance to make you happy."

Suddenly, Ashela believed him because she wanted to, needed to. All she knew was that when he'd held her in his arms, she felt free to taste life again.

Free to be trusting and daring again.

And finally, buffeted by the winds of fate, Ashela felt free to love again. Once and for all.

The End

In Loving Memory

Phyllis Hyman
(1949-1995)

Grover Washington, Jr.
(1943-1999)

With the passing of these two all-time greats…
Heaven's become a little sweeter.

Dear Readers:

As previously stated, my hero (Sam Ross) is a real, live person. As such, please allow me to share a letter I received from him while completing the editing for *A Twist of Fate.*

Robyn,

Thank you for remembering me. I have just finished reading your book, *A Twist of Fate.* You have done a wonderful job of writing a story that arouses curiosity and interest, and that appeals to one's own secrets and desires of the heart. So often life and society requires us to wear a facade of respectability designed to convey a favorable impression of who we are as complete individuals. This facade, however, does not accurately reflect our innermost thoughts, feelings, and most assuredly our wild and provocative fantasies.

We are all aware that on the surface these real and deeply-rooted feelings are often in conflict with the spiritual, moral, and ethical values that are acceptable to society. Thus, we learn to conform our behavior in such a way that it serves as a substitute for who we really are. Your books provide a vehicle through which we can safely live out our fantasies of fame, power, money, and sexual desire and gratification. They offer us a placebo given as a harmless substance to humor, flatter, or please the reader in his/her attempt to satisfy an underlying desire of the heart.

It is clear that you have done your homework. Your characters are brought to life with the realization that almost all of your readers are aware of someone who has had a similar experience (if not themselves). Your characters weave a tapestry of life experiences that are truly the "fabric of our lives."

I am very happy for you, and proud of you. I see nothing but a bright and successful future ahead of you. So write on, my sister!

Sincerely,

Sam Ross,
A Strong Black Man

P.S. I loved reading about myself.

Please share your thoughts with me. Email me at robynwilliams@msn.com